JOHN BUCHAN

# THE ADVENTURES OF DICKSON McCUNN

HUNTINGTOWER
CASTLE GAY
THE HOUSE OF THE FOUR WINDS

PENGUIN BOOKS

PENGUIN BOOKS

Published by the Penguin Group
Penguin Books Ltd, 27 Wrights Lane, London W8 5TZ, England
Penguin Books USA Inc., 375 Hudson Street, New York, New York 10014, USA
Penguin Books Australia Ltd, Ringwood, Victoria, Australia
Penguin Books Canada Ltd, 10 Alcorn Avenue, Toronto, Ontario, Canada M4V 3B2
Penguin Books (NZ) Ltd, 182–190 Wairau Road, Auckland 10, New Zealand

Penguin Books Ltd, Registered Offices: Harmondsworth, Middlesex, England

*Huntingtower* first published 1922
Published in Penguin Books 1956

*Castle Gay* first published 1925
Published in Penguin Books 1956

*The House of the Four Winds* first published 1925
Published in Penguin Books 1956

This omnibus edition first published 1994
1 3 5 7 9 10 8 6 4 2

Printed in England by Clays Ltd, St Ives plc

CONTENTS

# HUNTINGTOWER

TO

## *W. P. Ker*

If the Professor of Poetry in the University of Oxford has not forgotten the rock whence he was hewn, this simple story may give an hour of entertainment. I offer it to you because I think you have met my friend Dickson McCunn, and I dare to hope that you may even in your many sojournings in the Westlands have encountered one or other of the Gorbals Die-Hards. If you share my kindly feeling for Dickson, you will be interested in some facts which I have lately ascertained about his ancestry. In his veins there flows a portion of the redoubtable blood of the Nicol Jarvies. When the Bailie, you remember, returned from his journey to Rob Roy beyond the Highland Line, he espoused his housekeeper Mattie, 'an honest man's daughter and a near cousin o' the Laird o' Limmerfield'. The union was blessed with a son, who succeeded to the Bailie's business and in due course begat daughters, one of whom married a certain Ebenezer McCunn, of whom there is record in the archives of the Hammermen of Glasgow. Ebenezer's grandson, Peter by name, was Provost of Kirkintilloch, and his second son was the father of my hero by his marriage with Robina Dickson, eldest daughter of one Robert Dickson, a tenant-farmer in the Lennox. So there are coloured threads in Mr McCunn's pedigree, and, like the Bailie, he can count kin, should he wish, with Rob Roy himself through 'the auld wife ayont the fire at Stuckavrallachan'.

Such as it is, I dedicate to you the story, and ask for no better verdict on it than that of that profound critic of life and literature, Mr Huckleberry Finn, who observed of the *Pilgrim's Progress* that he 'considered the statements interesting, but tough'.

J. B.

## CONTENTS

# PROLOGUE

THE girl came into the room with a darting movement like a swallow, looked round her with the same birdlike quickness, and then ran across the polished floor to where a young man sat on a sofa with one leg laid along it.

'I have saved you this dance, Quentin,' she said, pronouncing the name with a pretty staccato. 'You must be lonely not dancing, so I will sit with you. What shall we talk about?'

The young man did not answer at once, for his gaze was held by her face. He had never dreamed that the gawky and rather plain little girl whom he had romped with long ago in Paris would grow into such a being. The clean delicate lines of her figure, the exquisite pure colouring of hair and skin, the charming young arrogance of the eyes – this was beauty, he reflected, a miracle, a revelation. Her virginal fineness and her dress, which was the tint of pale fire, gave her the air of a creature of ice and flame.

'About yourself, please, Saskia,' he said. 'Are you happy now that you are a grown-up lady?'

'Happy!' Her voice had a thrill in it like music, frosty music. 'The days are far too short. I grudge the hours when I must sleep. They say it is sad for me to make my début in a time of war. But the world is very kind to me, and after all it is a victorious war for our Russia. And listen to me, Quentin. Tomorrow I am to be allowed to begin nursing at the Alexander Hospital. What do you think of that?'

The time was January 1916, and the place a room in the great Nirski Palace. No hint of war, no breath from the snowy streets, entered that curious chamber where Prince Peter Nirski kept some of the chief of his famous treasures. It was notable for its lack of drapery and upholstering – only a sofa or two and a few fine rugs on the cedar floor. The walls were of a green marble veined like malachite, the ceiling was of darker marble inlaid with white intaglios. Scattered everywhere were tables and cabinets laded with celadon china, and carved jade, and ivories, and shimmering Persian and Rhodian vessels. In all the room there was scarcely anything of metal and no touch of gilding or bright colour. The light came from green alabaster censers, and the place swam in a cold green radiance like some cavern below the sea. The air was warm and scented, and though it was very quiet there, a hum of voices and the strains of dance music drifted to it from the pillared corridor in which could be seen the glare of lights from the great ballroom beyond.

The young man had a thin face with lines of suffering round the mouth and eyes. The warm room had given him a high colour, which increased his air of fragility. He felt a little choked by the place, which seemed to him for both body and mind a hot-house, though he knew very well that the Nirski Palace on this gala evening was in no way typical of the land or its masters. Only a week ago he had been eating black bread with its owner in a hut on the Volhynian front.

'You have become amazing, Saskia,' he said. 'I won't pay my old playfellow compliments; besides, you must be tired of them. I wish you happiness all the day long like a fairy-tale Princess. But a crock like me can't do much to help you to it. The service seems to be the wrong way round, for here you are wasting your time talking to me.'

She put her hand on his. 'Poor Quentin! Is the leg very bad?'

He laughed. 'Oh, no. It's mending famously. I'll be able to get about without a stick in another month, and then you've got to teach me all the new dances.'

The jigging music of a two-step floated down the corridor. It made the young man's brow contract, for it brought to him a vision of dead faces in the gloom of a November dusk. He had once had a friend who used to whistle that air, and he had seen him die in the Hollebeke mud. There was something macabre in the tune ... He was surely morbid this evening, for there seemed something macabre about the house, the room, the dancing, all Russia . . . These last days he had suffered from a sense of calamity impending, of a dark curtain drawing down upon a splendid world. They didn't agree with him at the Embassy, but he could not get rid of the notion.

The girl saw his sudden abstraction.

'What are you thinking about?' she asked. It had been her favourite question as a child.

'I was thinking that I rather wished you were still in Paris.'

'But why?'

'Because I think you would be safer.'

'Oh, what nonsense, Quentin dear! Where should I be safe if not in my own Russia, where I have friends – oh, so many, and tribes and tribes of relations? It is France and England that are unsafe with the German guns grumbling at their doors . . . My complaint is that my life is too cosseted and padded. I am too secure, and I do not want to be secure.'

The young man lifted a heavy casket from a table at his elbow. It was of dark green imperial jade, with a wonderfully carved lid. He took off the lid and picked up three small oddments of ivory – a priest with a beard, a tiny soldier, and a draught-ox. Putting the three in a triangle, he balanced the jade box on them.

'Look, Saskia! If you were living inside that box you would think it very secure. You would note the thickness of the walls and the hardness of the stone, and you would dream away in a peaceful green dusk. But all the time it would be held up by trifles – brittle trifles.'

She shook her head. 'You do not understand. You cannot understand. We are a very old and strong people with roots deep, deep in the earth.'

'Please God you are right,' he said. 'But, Saskia, you know that if I can ever serve you, you have only to command me. Now I can do no more for you than the mouse for the lion – at the beginning of the story. But the story had an end, you remember, and some day it may be in my power to help you. Promise to send for me.'

The girl laughed merrily. 'The King of Spain's daughter,' she quoted,

*Came to visit me*
*And all for the love*
*Of my little nut-tree.*

The other laughed also, as a young man in the uniform of the Preobrajenski Guards approached to claim the girl. 'Even a nut-tree may be a shelter in a storm,' he said.

'Of course I promise, Quentin,' she said. '*Au revoir*. Soon I will come and take you to supper, and we will talk of nothing but nut-trees.'

He watched the two leave the room, her gown glowing like a tongue of fire in the shadowy archway. Then he slowly rose to his feet, for he thought that for a little he would watch the dancing. Something moved beside him, and he turned in time to prevent the jade casket from crashing to the floor. Two of the supports had slipped.

He replaced the thing on its proper table and stood silent for a moment.

'The priest and the soldier gone, and only the beast of burden left . . . If I were inclined to be superstitious, I should call that a dashed bad omen.'

CHAPTER ONE

# HOW A RETIRED PROVISION MERCHANT FELT THE IMPULSE OF SPRING



MR DICKSON MCCUNN completed the polishing of his smooth cheeks with the towel, glanced appreciatively at their reflexion in the looking-glass, and then permitted his eyes to stray out of the window. In the little garden lilacs were budding, and there was a gold line of daffodils beside the tiny greenhouse. Beyond the sooty wall a birch flaunted its new tassels, and the jackdaws were circling about the steeple of the Guthrie Memorial Kirk. A blackbird whistled from a thornbush, and Mr McCunn was inspired to follow its example. He began a tolerable version of 'Roy's Wife of Aldivalloch'.

He felt singularly light-hearted, and the immediate cause was his safety razor. A week ago he had bought the thing in a sudden fit of enterprise, and now he shaved in five minutes, where before he had taken twenty, and no longer confronted his fellows, at least one day in three, with a countenance ludicrously mottled by sticking-plaster. Calculation revealed to him the fact that in his fifty-five years, having begun to shave at eighteen, he had wasted three thousand three hundred and seventy hours – or one hundred and forty days – or between four and five months – by his neglect of this admirable invention. Now he felt that he had stolen a march on Time. He had fallen heir, thus late, to a fortune in unpurchasable leisure.

He began to dress himself in the sombre clothes in which he had been accustomed for thirty-five years and more to go down to the shop in Mearns Street. And then a thought came to him which made him discard the grey-striped trousers, sit down on the edge of his bed, and muse.

Since Saturday the shop was a thing of the past. On Saturday at half-past eleven, to the accompaniment of a glass of dubious sherry, he had completed the arrangements by which the provision shop in Mearns Street, which had borne so long the legend of D. McCunn, together with the branches in Crossmyloof and the Shaws, became the property of a company, yclept the United Supply Stores, Limited. He had received in payment cash, debentures, and preference shares, and his lawyers and his own acumen had acclaimed the bargain. But all the week-end he had been a little sad. It was the end of so old a song, and he knew no other tune to sing. He was comfortably off, healthy, free from any particular cares in life, but free too from any particular duties. 'Will I be going to turn into a useless old man?' he asked himself.

But he had woke up this Monday to the sound of the blackbird, and the world, which had seemed rather empty twelve hours before, was now brisk and alluring. His prowess in quick shaving assured him of his youth. 'I'm no' that dead old,' he observed, as he sat on the edge of the bed, to his reflexion in the big looking-glass.

It was not an old face. The sandy hair was a little thin on the top and a little grey at the temples, the figure was perhaps a little too full for youthful elegance, and an athlete would have censured the neck as too fleshy for perfect health. But the cheeks were rosy, the skin clear, and the pale eyes singularly childlike. They were a little weak, those eyes, and had some difficulty in looking for long at the same object, so that Mr McCunn did not stare people in the face, and had, in consequence, at one time in his career acquired a perfectly undeserved reputation for cunning. He shaved clean, and looked uncommonly like a wise, plump schoolboy. As he gazed at his simulacrum he stopped whistling 'Roy's Wife' and let his countenance harden into a noble sternness. Then he laughed, and observed in the language of his youth that there was 'life in the auld dowg yet'. In that moment the soul of Mr McCunn conceived the Great Plan.

The first sign of it was that he swept all his business garments unceremoniously on to the floor. The next that he rootled at the bottom of a deep drawer and extracted a most disreputable tweed suit. It had once been what I believe is called a Lovat mixture, but was now a nondescript sub-fusc, with bright patches of colour like moss on whinstone. He regarded it lovingly, for it had been for twenty years his holiday wear, emerging annually for a hallowed month to be stained with salt and bleached with sun. He put it on, and stood shrouded in an odour of camphor. A pair of thick nailed boots and a flannel shirt and collar completed the equipment of the sportsman. He had another long look at himself in the glass, and then descended whistling to breakfast. This time the tune was 'Macgregors' Gathering', and the sound of it stirred the grimy lips of a man outside who was delivering coals – himself a Macgregor – to follow suit. Mr McCunn was a very fountain of music that morning.

Tibby, the aged maid, had his newspaper and letters waiting by his plate, and a dish of ham and eggs frizzling near the fire. He fell to ravenously but still musingly, and he had reached the stage of scones and jam before he glanced at his correspondence. There was a letter from his wife now holidaying at the Neuk Hydropathic. She reported that her health was improving, and that she had met various people who had known somebody who had known somebody else whom she had once known herself. Mr McCunn read the dutiful pages and smiled. 'Mamma's enjoying herself fine,' he observed to the teapot. He knew that for his wife the earthly paradise was a hydropathic, where she put on her afternoon dress and every jewel she possessed when she rose in the morning, ate large meals of which the novelty atoned for the nastiness, and collected an immense casual acquaintance, with whom she discussed ailments, ministers, sudden deaths, and the intricate genealogies of her class. For his part he rancorously hated hydropathics, having once spent a black week under the roof of one in his wife's company. He detested the food, the Turkish baths (he had a passionate aversion to baring his body before strangers), the inability to find anything to do, and the compulsion to endless small talk. A thought flitted over his mind which he was too loyal to formulate. Once he and his wife had had similar likings, but they had taken different roads since their child died. Janet! He saw again – he was never quite free from the sight – the solemn little white-frocked girl who had died long ago in the spring.

It may have been the thought of the Neuk Hydropathic, or more likely the thin clean scent of the daffodils with which Tibby had decked the table, but long ere breakfast was finished the Great Plan had ceased to be an airy vision and become a sober well-masoned structure. Mr McCunn – I may confess it at the start – was an incurable romantic.

He had had a humdrum life since the day when he had first entered his uncle's shop with the hope of some day succeeding that honest grocer; and his feet had never strayed a yard from his sober rut. But his mind, like the Dying Gladiator's, had been far away. As a boy he had voyaged among books, and they had given him a world where he could shape his career according to his whimsical fancy. Not that Mr McCunn was what is known as a great reader. He read slowly and fastidiously, and sought in literature for one thing alone. Sir Walter Scott had been his first guide, but he read the novels not for their insight into human character or for their historical pageantry, but because they gave him material wherewith to construct fantastic journeys. It was the same with Dickens. A lit tavern, a stage-coach, post-horses, the clack of hoofs on a frosty road, went to his head like wine. He was a Jacobite not because he had any views on Divine Right, but because he had always before his eyes a picture of a knot of adventurers in cloaks, new landed from France among the western heather.

On this select basis he had built up his small library – Defoe, Hakluyt, Hazlitt and the essayists, Boswell, some indifferent romances, and a shelf of spirited poetry. His tastes became known, and he acquired a reputation for a scholarly habit. He was president of the Literary Society of the Guthrie Memorial Kirk, and read to its members a variety of papers full of a gusto which rarely became critical. He had been three times chairman at Burns Anniversary dinners, and had delivered orations in eulogy of the national Bard; not because he greatly admired him – he thought him rather vulgar – but because he took Burns as an emblem of the un-Burns-like literature which he loved. Mr McCunn was no scholar and was sublimely unconscious of background. He grew his flowers in his small garden-plot oblivious of their origin so long as they gave him the colour and scent he sought. Scent, I say, for he appreciated more than the mere picturesque. He had a passion for words and cadences, and would be haunted for weeks by a cunning phrase, savouring it as a connoisseur savours a vintage. Wherefore long ago, when he could ill afford it, he had purchased the Edinburgh *Stevenson.* They were the only large books on his shelves, for he had a liking for small volumes – things he could stuff into his pocket in that sudden journey which he loved to contemplate.

Only he had never taken it. The shop had tied him up for eleven months in the year, and the twelfth had always found him settled decorously with his wife in some seaside villa. He had not fretted, for he was content with dreams. He was always a little tired, too, when the holidays came, and his wife told him he was growing old. He consoled himself with tags from the more philosophic of his authors, but he scarcely needed consolation. For he had large stores of modest contentment.

But now something had happened. A spring morning and a safety razor had convinced him that he was still young. Since yesterday he was a man of a large leisure. Providence had done for him what he would never have done for himself. The rut in which he had travelled so long had given place to open country. He repeated to himself one of the quotations with which he had been wont to stir the literary young men at the Guthrie Memorial Kirk:

*What's a man's age? He must hurry more, that's all;*
*Cram in a day, what his youth took a year to hold:*
*When we mind labour, then only, we're too old –*
*What age had Methusalem when he begat Saul?*

He would go journeying – who but he? – pleasantly.

It sounds a trivial resolve, but it quickened Mr McCunn to the depths of his being. A holiday, and alone! On foot, of course, for he must travel light. He would buckle on a pack after the approved fashion. He had the very thing in a drawer upstairs, which he had bought some years ago at a sale. That and a waterproof and a stick, and his outfit was complete. A book, too, and, as he lit his first pipe, he considered what it should be. Poetry, clearly, for it was the spring, and besides poetry could be got in pleasantly small bulk. He stood before his bookshelves trying to select a volume, rejecting one after another as inapposite. Browning – Keats, Shelley – they seemed more suited for the hearth than for the roadside. He did not want anything Scots, for he was of opinion that spring came more richly in England and that English people had a better notion of it. He was tempted by the Oxford Anthology, but was deterred by its thickness, for he did not possess the thin-paper edition. Finally he selected Izaak Walton. He had never fished in his life, but *The Compleat Angler* seemed to fit his mood. It was old and curious and learned and fragrant with the youth of things. He remembered its falling cadences, its country songs and wise meditations. Decidedly it was the right scrip for his pilgrimage.

Characteristically he thought last of where he was to go. Every bit of the world beyond his front door had its charms to the seeing eye. There seemed nothing common or unclean that fresh morning. Even a walk among coal-pits had its attractions. . . . But since he had the right to choose, he lingered over it like an epicure. Not the Highlands, for spring came late among their sour mosses. Some place where there were fields and woods and inns, somewhere, too, within call of the sea. It must not be too remote, for he had no time to waste on train journeys; nor too near, for he wanted a countryside untainted. Presently he thought of Carrick. A good, green land, as he remembered it, with purposeful white roads and public-houses sacred to the memory of Burns; near the hills but yet lowland, and with a bright sea chafing on its shores. He decided on Carrick, found a map, and planned his journey.

Then he routed out his knapsack, packed it with a modest change of raiment, and sent out Tibby to buy chocolate and tobacco and to cash a cheque at the Strathclyde Bank. Till Tibby returned he occupied himself with delicious dreams . . . He saw himself daily growing browner and leaner, swinging along broad highways or wandering in bypaths. He pictured his seasons of ease, when he unslung his pack and smoked in some clump of lilacs by a burnside – he remembered a phrase of Stevenson's somewhat like that. He would meet and talk with all sorts of folk; an exhilarating prospect, for Mr McCunn loved his kind. There would be the evening hour before he reached his inn, when, pleasantly tired, he would top some ridge and see the welcoming lights of a little town. There would be the lamp-lit after-supper time when he would read and reflect, and the start in the gay morning, when tobacco tastes sweetest and even fifty-five seems young. It would be holiday of the purest, for no business now tugged at his coattails. He was beginning a new life, he told himself, when he could cultivate the seedling interests which had withered beneath the far-reaching shade of the shop. Was ever a man more fortunate or more free?

Tibby was told that he was going off for a week or two. No letters need be forwarded, for he would be constantly moving, but Mrs McCunn at the Neuk Hydropathic would be kept informed of his whereabouts. Presently he stood on his doorstep, a stocky figure in ancient tweeds, with a bulging pack slung on his arm, and a stout hazel stick in his hand. A passer-by would have remarked an elderly shopkeeper bent apparently on a day in the country, a common little man on a prosaic errand. But the passer-by would have been wrong, for he could not see into the heart. The plump citizen was the eternal pilgrim; he was Jason, Ulysses, Eric the Red, Albuquerque, Cortez – starting out to discover new worlds.

Before he left Mr McCunn had given Tibby a letter to post. That morning he had received an epistle from a benevolent acquaintance, one Mackintosh, regarding a group of urchins who called themselves the 'Gorbals Die-Hards'. Behind the premises in Mearns Street lay a tract of slums, full of mischievous boys, with whom his staff waged truceless war. But lately there had started among them a kind of unauthorized and unofficial Boy Scouts, who, without uniform or badge or any kind of paraphernalia, followed the banner of Sir Robert Baden-Powell and subjected themselves to a rude discipline. They were far too poor to join an orthodox troop, but they faithfully copied what they believed to be the practices of more fortunate boys. Mr McCunn had witnessed their pathetic parades, and had even passed the time of day with their leader, a red-haired savage called Dougal. The philanthropic Mackintosh had taken an interest in the gang and now desired subscriptions to send them to camp in the country.

Mr McCunn, in his new exhilaration, felt that he could not deny to others what he proposed for himself. His last act before leaving was to send Mackintosh ten pounds.

CHAPTER TWO

# OF MR JOHN HERITAGE AND THE DIFFERENCE IN POINTS OF VIEW

DICKSON MCCUNN was never to forget the first stage in that pilgrimage. A little after midday he descended from a grimy third-class carriage at a little station whose name I have forgotten. In the village near-by he purchased some new-baked buns and ginger biscuits, to which he was partial, and followed by the shouts of urchins, who admired his pack – 'Look at the auld man gaun to the schule' – he emerged into open country. The late April noon gleamed like a frosty morning, but the air, though tonic, was kind. The road ran over sweeps of moorland where curlews wailed, and into lowland pastures dotted with very white, very vocal lambs. The young grass had the warm fragrance of new milk. As he went he munched his buns, for he had resolved to have no plethoric midday meal, and presently he found the burnside nook of his fancy, and halted to smoke. On a patch of turf close to a grey stone bridge he had out his Walton and read the chapter on 'The Chavender or Chub'. The collocation of words delighted him and inspired him to verse. 'Lavender or Lub' – 'Pavender or Pub' – 'Gravender or Grub' – but the monosyllables proved too vulgar for poetry. Regretfully he desisted.

The rest of the road was as idyllic as the start. He would tramp steadily for a mile or so and then saunter, leaning over bridges to watch the trout in the pools, admiring from a dry-stone dyke the unsteady gambols of new-born lambs, kicking up dust from strips of moor-burn on the heather. Once by a fir-wood he was privileged to surprise three lunatic hares waltzing. His cheeks glowed with the sun; he moved in an atmosphere of pastoral, serene and contented. When the shadows began to lengthen he arrived at the village of Cloncae, where he proposed to lie. The inn looked dirty, but he found a decent widow, above whose door ran the legend in home-made lettering, 'Mrs brockie tea and Coffee', and who was willing to give him quarters. There he supped handsomely off ham and eggs, and dipped into a work called *Covenanting Worthies*, which garnished a table decorated with sea-shells. At half-past nine precisely he retired to bed and unhesitating sleep.

Next morning he awoke to a changed world. The sky was grey and so low that his outlook was bounded by a cabbage garden, while a surly wind prophesied rain. It was chilly, too, and he had his breakfast beside the kitchen fire. Mrs Brockie could not spare a capital letter for her surname on the sign-board, but she exalted it in her talk. He heard of a multitude of Brockies, ascendant, descendant, and collateral, who seemed to be in a fair way to inherit the earth. Dickson listened sympathetically, and lingered by the fire. He felt stiff from yesterday's exercise, and the edge was off his spirit.

The start was not quite what he had pictured. His pack seemed heavier, his boots tighter, and his pipe drew badly. The first miles were all uphill, with a wind tingling his ears, and no colours in the landscape but brown and grey. Suddenly he awoke to the fact that he was dismal, and thrust the notion behind him. He expanded his chest and drew in long draughts of air. He told himself that this sharp weather was better than sunshine. He remembered that all travellers in romances battled with mist and rain. Presently his body recovered comfort and vigour, and his mind worked itself into cheerfulness.

He overtook a party of tramps and fell into talk with them. He had always had a fancy for the class, though he had never known anything nearer it than city beggars. He pictured them as philosophic vagabonds, full of quaint turns of speech, unconscious Borrovians. With these samples his disillusionment was speedy. The party was made up of a ferret-faced man with a red nose, a draggle-tailed woman, and a child in a crazy perambulator. Their conversation was one-sided, for it immediately resolved itself into a whining chronicle of misfortunes and petitions for relief. It cost him half a crown to be rid of them.

The road was alive with tramps that day. The next one did

the accosting. Hailing Mr McCunn as 'Guv'nor', he asked to be told the way to Manchester. The objective seemed so enterprising that Dickson was impelled to ask questions, and heard, in what appeared to be in the accents of the Colonies, the tale of a career of unvarying calamity. There was nothing merry or philosophic about this adventurer. Nay, there was something menacing. He eyed his companion's waterproof covetously, and declared that he had had one like it which had been stolen from him the day before. Had the place been lonely he might have contemplated highway robbery, but they were at the entrance to a village, and the sight of a public-house awoke his thirst. Dickson parted with him at the cost of sixpence for a drink.

He had no more company that morning except an aged stone-breaker whom he convoyed for half a mile. The stone-breaker also was soured with the world. He walked with a limp, which, he said, was due to an accident years before, when he had been run into by 'ane o' thae damned velocipeeds'. The word revived in Dickson memories of his youth, and he was prepared to be friendly. But the ancient would have none of it. He inquired morosely what he was after, and, on being told, remarked that he might have learned more sense. 'It's a daft-like thing for an auld man like you to be traivellin' the roads. Ye maun be ill-off for a job.' Questioned as to himself, he became, as the newspapers say, 'reticent', and having reached his bing of stones, turned rudely to his duties. 'Awa' hame wi' ye,' were his parting words. 'It's idle scoondrels like you that maks wark for honest folk like me.'

The morning was not a success, but the strong air had given Dickson such an appetite that he resolved to break his rule, and, on reaching the little town of Kilchrist, he sought luncheon at the chief hotel. There he found that which revived his spirits. A solitary bagman shared the meal, who revealed the fact that he was in the grocery line. There followed a well-informed and most technical conversation. He was drawn to speak of the United Supply Stores, Limited, of their prospects and of their predecessor, Mr McCunn, whom he knew well by repute but had never met. 'Yon's the clever one,' he observed.

'I've always said there's no longer head in the city of Glasgow than McCunn. An old-fashioned firm, but it has aye managed to keep up with the times. He's just retired, they tell me, and in my opinion it's a big loss to the provision trade. . . .' Dickson's heart glowed within him. Here was Romance; to be praised incognito; to enter a casual inn and find that fame had preceded him. He warmed to the bagman, insisted on giving him a liqueur and a cigar, and finally revealed himself. 'I'm Dickson McCunn,' he said, 'taking a bit holiday. If there's anything I can do for you when I get back, just let me know.' With mutual esteem they parted.

He had need of all his good spirits, for he emerged into an unrelenting drizzle. The environs of Kilchrist are at the best unlovely, and in the wet they were as melancholy as a graveyard. But the encounter with the bagman had worked wonders with Dickson, and he strode lustily into the weather, his waterproof collar buttoned round his chin. The road climbed to a bare moor, where lagoons had formed in the ruts, and the mist showed on each side only a yard or two of soaking heather. Soon he was wet; presently every part of him – boots, body, and pack – was one vast sponge. The waterproof was not water-proof, and the rain penetrated to his most intimate garments. Little he cared. He felt lighter, younger, than on the idyllic previous day. He enjoyed the buffets of the storm, and one wet mile succeeded another to the accompaniment of Dickson's shouts and laughter. There was no one abroad that afternoon, so he could talk aloud to himself and repeat his favourite poems. About five in the evening there presented himself at the Black Bull Inn at Kirkmichael a soaked, disreputable, but most cheerful traveller.

Now the Black Bull at Kirkmichael is one of the few very good inns left in the world. It is an old place and an hospitable, for it has been for generations a haunt of anglers, who above all other men understand comfort. There are always bright fires there, and hot water, and old soft leather arm-chairs, and an aroma of good food and good tobacco, and giant trout in glass cases, and pictures of Captain Barclay of Urie walking to London, and Mr Ramsay of Barnton winning a horse-race, and the three-volume edition of the Waverley Novels with many volumes missing, and indeed all those things which an inn should have. Also there used to be – there may still be – sound vintage claret in the cellars. The Black Bull expects its guests to arrive in every stage of dishevelment, and Dickson was received by a cordial landlord, who offered dry garments as a matter of course. The pack proved to have resisted the elements, and a suit of clothes and slippers were provided by the house. Dickson, after a glass of toddy, wallowed in a hot bath, which washed all the stiffness out of him. He had a fire in his bedroom, beside which he wrote the opening passages of that diary he had vowed to keep, descanting lyrically upon the joys of ill weather. At seven o'clock, warm and satisfied in soul, and with his body clad in raiment several sizes too large for it, he descended to dinner.

At one end of the long table in the dining-room sat a group of anglers. They looked jovial fellows, and Dickson would fain have joined them; but, having been fishing all day in the Loch o' the Threshes, they were talking their own talk, and he feared that his admiration for Izaak Walton did not qualify him to butt into the erudite discussions of fishermen. The landlord seemed to think likewise, for he drew back a chair for him at the other end, where sat a young man absorbed in a book. Dickson gave him good evening, and got an abstracted reply. The young man supped the Black Bull's excellent broth with one hand, and with the other turned the pages of his volume. A glance convinced Dickson that the work was French, a literature which did not interest him. He knew little of the tongue and suspected it of impropriety.

Another guest entered and took the chair opposite the bookish young man. He was also young – not more than thirty-three – and to Dickson's eye was the kind of person he would have liked to resemble. He was tall and free from any superfluous flesh; his face was lean, fine-drawn, and deeply sunburnt, so that the hair above showed oddly pale; the hands were brown and beautifully shaped, but the forearm revealed by the loose cuffs of his shirt was as brawny as a blacksmith's. He had rather pale blue eyes, which seemed to have looked much at the sun, and a small moustache the colour of ripe hay. His voice was low and pleasant, and he pronounced his words precisely, like a foreigner.

He was very ready to talk, but in defiance of Dr Johnson's warning, his talk was all questions. He wanted to know everything about the neighbourhood – who lived in what houses, what were the distances between the towns, what harbours would admit what class of vessel. Smiling agreeably, he put Dickson through a catechism to which he knew none of the answers. The landlord was called in, and proved more helpful. But on one matter he was fairly at a loss. The catechist asked about a house called Darkwater, and was met with a shake of the head. 'I know no sic-like name in this countryside, sir,' and the catechist looked disappointed.

The literary young man said nothing, but ate trout abstractedly, one eye on his book. The fish had been caught by the anglers in the Loch o' the Threshes, and phrases describing their capture floated from the other end of the table. The young man had a second helping, and then refused the excellent hill mutton that followed, contenting himself with cheese. Not so Dickson and the catechist. They ate everything that was set before them, topping up with a glass of port. Then the latter, who had been talking illuminatingly about Spain, rose, bowed, and left the table, leaving Dickson, who liked to linger over his meals, to the society of the ichthyophagous student.

He nodded towards the book. 'Interesting?' he asked.

The young man shook his head and displayed the name on the cover. 'Anatole France. I used to be crazy about him, but now he seems rather a back number.' Then he glanced towards the just-vacated chair. 'Australian,' he said.

'How d'you know?'

'Can't mistake them. There's nothing else so lean and fine produced on the globe to-day. I was next door to them at Pozières and saw them fight. Lord! Such men! Now and then you had a freak, but most looked like Phoebus Apollo.'

Dickson gazed with a new respect at his neighbour, for he had not associated him with battlefields. During the war he had been a fervent patriot, but, though he had never heard a shot himself, so many of his friends' sons and nephews, not to mention cousins of his own, had seen service, that he had come to regard the experience as commonplace. Lions in Africa and bandits in Mexico seemed to him novel and romantic things, but not trenches and aeroplanes which were the whole world's property. But he could scarcely fit his neighbour into even his haziest picture of war. The young man was tall and a little round-shouldered; he had short-sighted, rather prominent brown eyes, untidy black hair, and dark eyebrows which came near to meeting. He wore a knickerbocker suit of bluish-grey tweed, a pale blue shirt, a pale blue collar, and a dark blue tie – a symphony of colour which seemed too elaborately considered to be quite natural. Dickson had set him down as an artist or a newspaper correspondent, objects to him of lively interest. But now the classification must be reconsidered.

'So you were in the war,' he said encouragingly.

'Four blasted years,' was the savage reply. 'And I never want to hear the name of the beastly thing again.'

'You said he was an Australian,' said Dickson, casting back. 'But I thought Australians had a queer accent, like the English.'

'They've all kind of accents, but you can never mistake their voice. It's got the sun in it. Canadians have got grinding ice in theirs, and Virginians have got butter. So have the Irish. In Britain there are no voices, only speaking-tubes. It isn't safe to judge men by their accent only. You yourself I take to be Scotch, but for all I know you may be a senator from Chicago or a Boer General.'

'I'm from Glasgow. My name's Dickson McCunn.' He had a faint hope that the announcement might affect the other as it had affected the bagman at Kilchrist.

'Golly, what a name!' exclaimed the young man rudely.

Dickson was nettled. 'It's very old Highland,' he said. 'It means the son of a dog.'

'Which – Christian name or surname?' Then the young man appeared to think he had gone too far, for he smiled pleasantly. 'And a very good name too. Mine is prosaic by comparison. They call me John Heritage.'

'That,' said Dickson, mollified, 'is like a name out of a book. With that name by rights you should be a poet.'

Gloom settled on the young man's countenance. 'It's a dashed sight too poetic. It's like Edwin Arnold and Alfred Austin and Dante Gabriel Rossetti. Great poets have vulgar monosyllables for names, like Keats. The new Shakespeare when he comes along will probably be called Grubb or Jubber, if he isn't Jones. With a name like yours I might have a chance. *You* should be the poet.'

'I'm very fond of reading,' said Dickson modestly.

A slow smile crumpled Mr Heritage's face. 'There's a fire in the smoking-room,' he observed as he rose. 'We'd better bag the arm-chairs before these fishing louts take them.' Dickson followed obediently. This was the kind of chance acquaintance for whom he had hoped, and he was prepared to make the most of him.

The fire burned bright in the little dusky smoking-room, lighted by one oil-lamp. Mr Heritage flung himself into a chair, stretched his long legs, and lit a pipe.

'You like reading?' he asked. 'What sort? Any use for poetry?'

'Plenty,' said Dickson. 'I've aye been fond of learning it up and repeating it to myself when I had nothing to do. In church and waiting on trains, like. It used to be Tennyson, but now it's more Browning. I can say a lot of Browning.'

The other screwed his face into an expression of disgust. 'I know the stuff. "Damask cheeks and dewy sister eyelids." Or else the Ercles vein – "God's in His Heaven, all's right with the world." No good, Mr McCunn. All back numbers. Poetry's not a thing of pretty round phrases or noisy invocations. It's life itself, with the tang of the raw world in it – not a sweetmeat for middle-class women in parlours.'

'Are you a poet, Mr Heritage?'

'No, Dogson, I'm a paper-maker.'

This was a new view to Mr McCunn. 'I just once knew a paper-maker,' he observed reflectively. 'They called him Tosh. He drank a bit.'

'Well, I don't drink,' said the other. 'I'm a paper-maker,

but that's for my bread and butter. Some day for my own sake I may be a poet.'

'Have you published anything?'

The eager admiration in Dickson's tone gratified Mr Heritage. He drew from his pocket a slim book. 'My firstfruits,' he said, rather shyly.

Dickson received it with reverence. It was a small volume in grey paper boards with a white label on the back, and it was lettered: *Whorls – John Heritage's Book*. He turned the pages and read a little. 'It's a nice wee book,' he observed at length.

'Good God, if you call it nice, I must have failed pretty badly,' was the irritated answer.

Dickson read more deeply and was puzzled. It seemed worse than the worst of Browning to understand. He found one poem about a garden entitled 'Revue'. 'Crimson and resonant clangs the dawn,' said the poet. Then he went on to describe noonday:

*Sunflowers, tall Grenadiers, ogle the roses' short-skirted ballet.*
*The fumes of dark sweet wine hidden in frail petals*
*Madden the drunkard bees.*

This seemed to him an odd way to look at things, and he boggled over a phrase about an 'epicene lily'. Then came evening: 'The painted gauze of the stars flutters in a fold of twilight crape,' sang Mr Heritage; and again, 'The moon's pale leprosy sloughs the fields.'

Dickson turned to other verses which apparently enshrined the writer's memory of the trenches. They were largely compounded of oaths, and rather horrible, lingering lovingly over sights and smells which every one is aware of, but most people contrive to forget. He did not like them. Finally he skimmed a poem about a lady who turned into a bird. The evolution was described with intimate anatomical details which scared the honest reader.

He kept his eyes on the book, for he did not know what to say. The trick seemed to be to describe nature in metaphors mostly drawn from music-halls and haberdashers' shops, and, when at a loss, to fall to cursing. He thought it frankly very bad, and he laboured to find words which would combine politeness and honesty.

'Well?' said the poet.

'There's a lot of fine things here, but – but the lines don't just seem to scan very well.'

Mr Heritage laughed. 'Now I can place you exactly. You like the meek rhyme and the conventional epithet. Well, I don't. The world has passed beyond that prettiness. You want the moon described as a Huntress or a gold disc or a flower – I say it's oftener like a beer barrel or a cheese. You want a wealth of jolly words and real things ruled out as unfit for poetry. I say there's nothing unfit for poetry. Nothing, Dogson! Poetry's everywhere, and the real thing is commoner among drabs and pot-houses and rubbish-heaps than in your Sunday parlours. The poet's business is to distil it out of rottenness, and show that it is all one spirit, the thing that keeps the stars in their place. . . . I wanted to call my book *Drains*, for drains are sheer poetry carrying off the excess and discards of human life to make the fields green and the corn ripen. But the publishers kicked. So I called it *Whorls*, to express my view of the exquisite involution of all things. Poetry is the fourth dimension of the soul. . . . Well, let's hear about your taste in prose.'

Mr McCunn was much bewildered, and a little inclined to be cross. He disliked being called Dogson, which seemed to him an abuse of his etymological confidences. But his habit of politeness held.

He explained rather haltingly his preferences in prose.

Mr Heritage listened with wrinkled brows.

'You're even deeper in the mud than I thought,' he remarked. 'You live in a world of painted laths and shadows. All this passion for the picturesque! Trash, my dear man, like a schoolgirl's novelette heroes. You make up romances about gipsies and sailors, and the blackguards they call pioneers, but you know nothing about them. If you did, you would find they had none of the gilt and gloss you imagine. But the great things they have got in common with all humanity you ignore. It's like – it's like sentimentalizing about a pancake because it looked like a buttercup, and all the while not knowing that it was good to eat.'

At that moment the Australian entered the room to get a light for his pipe. He wore a motor-cyclist's overalls and appeared to be about to take the road. He bade them good night, and it seemed to Dickson that his face, seen in the glow of the fire, was drawn and anxious, unlike that of the agreeable companion at dinner.

'There,' said Mr Heritage, nodding after the departing figure. 'I dare say you have been telling yourself stories about that chap – life in the bush, stock-riding, and the rest of it. But probably he's a bank-clerk from Melbourne. . . . Your romanticism is one vast self-delusion, and it blinds your eye to the real thing. We have got to clear it out, and with it all the damnable humbug of the Kelt.'

Mr McCunn, who spelt the word with a soft 'C', was puzzled. 'I thought a kelt was a kind of a no-weel fish,' he interposed.

But the other, in the flood-tide of his argument, ignored the interruption. 'That's the value of the war,' he went on. 'It has bust up all the old conventions, and we've got to finish the destruction before we can build. It is the same with literature and religion, and society and politics. At them with the axe, say I. I have no use for priests and pedants. I've no use for upper classes and middle classes. There's only one class that matters, the plain man, the workers, who live close to life.'

'The place for you,' said Dickson dryly, 'is in Russia among the Bolsheviks.'

Mr Heritage approved. 'They are doing a great work in their own fashion. We needn't imitate all their methods – they're a trifle crude and have too many Jews among them – but they've got hold of the right end of the stick. They seek truth and reality.'

Mr McCunn was slowly being roused.

'What brings you wandering hereaways?' he asked.

'Exercise,' was the answer. 'I've been kept pretty closely tied up all winter. And I want leisure and quiet to think over things.'

'Well, there's one subject you might turn your attention to. You'll have been educated like a gentleman?'

'Nine wasted years – five at Harrow, four at Cambridge.'

'See here, then. You're daft about the working-class and have no use for any other. But what in the name of goodness do you know about working-men? . . . I come out of them myself, and have lived next door to them all my days. Take them one way and another, they're a decent sort, good and bad like the rest of us. But there's a wheen daft folk that would set them up as models – close to truth and reality, says you. It's sheer ignorance, for you're about as well acquainted with the working-man as with King Solomon. You say I make up fine stories about tinklers and sailor-men because I know nothing about them. That's maybe true. But you're at the same job yourself. You idealize the working-man, you and your kind, because you're ignorant. You say that he's seeking for truth, when he's only looking for a drink and a rise in wages. You tell me he's near reality, but I tell you that his notion of reality is often just a short working day and looking on at a footba'-match on Saturday. . . . And when you run down what you call the middle-classes that do three-quarters of the world's work and keep the machine going and the working-man in a job, then I tell you you're talking havers. Havers!'

Mr McCunn, having delivered his defence of the bourgeoisie, rose abruptly and went to bed. He felt jarred and irritated. His innocent little private domain had been badly trampled by this stray bull of a poet. But as he lay in bed, before blowing out his candle, he had recourse to Walton, and found a passage on which, as on a pillow, he went peacefully to sleep:

*

'As I left this place, and entered into the next field, a second pleasure entertained me; 'twas a handsome milkmaid, that had not yet attained so much age and wisdom as to load her mind with any fears of many things that will never be, as too many men too often do; but she cast away all care, and sang like a nightingale; her voice was good, and the ditty fitted for it; it was the smooth song that was made by *Kit Marlow* now at least fifty years ago. And the milkmaid's mother sung an answer to it, which was made by *Sir Walter Raleigh* in his younger days. They were old-fashioned poetry, but choicely good; I think much better than the strong lines that are now in fashion in this critical age.'

CHAPTER THREE

# HOW CHILDE ROLAND AND ANOTHER CAME TO THE DARK TOWER

DICKSON woke with a vague sense of irritation. As his recollections took form they produced a very unpleasant picture of Mr John Heritage. The poet had loosened all his placid idols, so that they shook and rattled in the niches where they had been erstwhile so secure. Mr McCunn had a mind of a singular candour, and was prepared most honestly at all times to revise his views. But by this iconoclast he had been only irritated and in no way convinced. '*Sich* poetry!' he muttered to himself as he shivered in his bath (a daily cold tub instead of his customary hot one on Saturday night being part of the discipline of his holiday). 'And yon blethers about the working-man!' he ingeminated as he shaved. He breakfasted alone, having outstripped even the fishermen, and as he ate he arrived at conclusions. He had a great respect for youth, but a line must be drawn somewhere. 'The man's a child,' he decided, 'and not like to grow up. The way he's besotted on everything daftlike, if it's only *new*. And he's no rightly young either – speaks like an auld dominie, whiles. And he's rather impident,' he concluded, with memories of 'Dogson' . . . He was very clear that he never wanted to see him again; that was the reason of his early breakfast. Having clarified his mind by definitions, Dickson felt comforted. He paid his bill, took an affectionate farewell of the landlord, and at 7.30 precisely stepped out into the gleaming morning.

It was such a day as only a Scots April can show. The cobbled streets of Kirkmichael still shone with the night's rain, but the storm clouds had fled before a mild south wind, and the whole circumference of the sky was a delicate translucent blue. Homely breakfast smells came from the houses and delighted Mr McCunn's nostrils; a squalling child was a pleasant reminder of an awakening world, the urban counterpart to the morning song of birds; even the sanitary cart seemed a picturesque vehicle. He bought his ration of buns and ginger biscuits at a baker's shop whence various ragamuffin boys were preparing to distribute the householders' bread, and took his way up the Gallows Hill to the Burgh Muir almost with regret at leaving so pleasant a habitation.

A chronicle of ripe vintages must pass lightly over small beer. I will not dwell on his leisurely progress in the bright weather, or on his luncheon in a coppice of young firs, or on his thoughts which had returned to the idyllic. I take up the narrative at about three o'clock in the afternoon, when he is revealed seated on a milestone examining his map. For he had come, all unwitting, to a turning of the ways, and his choice is the cause of this veracious history.

The place was high up on a bare moor, which showed a white lodge among pines, a white cottage in a green nook by a burnside, and no other marks of human dwelling. To his left, which was the east, the heather rose to a low ridge of hill, much scarred with peat-bogs, behind which appeared the blue shoulder of a considerable mountain. Before him the road was lost momentarily in the woods of a shooting-box, but reappeared at a great distance climbing a swell of upland which seemed to be the glacis of a jumble of bold summits. There was a pass there, the map told him, which led into Galloway. It was the road he had meant to follow, but as he sat on the milestone his purpose wavered. For there seemed greater attractions in the country which lay to the westward. Mr McCunn, be it remembered, was not in search of brown heath and shaggy wood; he wanted greenery and the spring.

Westward there ran out a peninsula in the shape of an isosceles triangle, of which his present high-road was the base. At a distance of a mile or so a railway ran parallel to the road, and he could see the smoke of a goods train waiting at a tiny station islanded in acres of bog. Thence the moor swept down to meadows and scattered copses, above which hung a thin haze of smoke which betokened a village. Beyond it were further woodlands, not firs but old shady trees, and as they narrowed to a point the gleam of two tiny estuaries appeared on either side. He could not see the final cape, but he saw the sea beyond it, flawed with catspaws, gold in the afternoon sun, and on it a small herring smack flapping listless sails.

Something in the view caught and held his fancy. He conned his map, and made out the names. The peninsula was called the Cruives – an old name apparently, for it was in antique lettering. He vaguely remembered that 'cruives' had something to do with fishing, doubtless in the two streams which flanked it. One he had already crossed, the Laver, a clear tumbling water springing from green hills; the other, the Garple, descended from the rougher mountains to the south. The hidden village bore the name of Dalquharter, and the uncouth syllables awoke some vague recollection in his mind. The great house in the trees beyond – it must be a great house, for the map showed large policies – was Huntingtower.

The last name fascinated and almost decided him. He pictured an ancient keep by the sea, defended by converging rivers, which some old Comyn lord of Galloway had built to command the shore road, and from which he had sallied to hunt in his wild hills . . . He liked the way the moor dropped down to green meadows, and the mystery of the dark woods beyond. He wanted to explore the twin waters, and see how they entered that strange shimmering sea. The odd names, the odd cul-de-sac of a peninsula, powerfully attracted him. Why should he not spend a night there, for the map showed clearly that Dalquharter had an inn? He must decide promptly, for before him a side-road left the highway, and the signpost bore the legend, 'Dalquharter and Huntingtower'.

Mr McCunn, being a cautious and pious man, took the omens. He tossed a penny – heads go on, tails turn aside. It fell tails.

He knew as soon as he had taken three steps down the side-road that he was doing something momentous, and the exhilaration of enterprise stole into his soul. It occurred to him that this was the kind of landscape that he had always especially hankered after, and had made pictures of when he had a longing for the country on him – a wooded cape between streams, with meadows inland and then a long lift of heather. He had the same feeling of expectancy, of something most interesting and curious on the eve of happening, that he had had long ago when he waited on the curtain rising at his first play. His spirits soared like the lark, and he took to singing. If only the inn at Dalquharter were snug and empty, this was going to be a day in ten thousand. Thus mirthfully he swung down the rough grass-grown road, past the railway, till he came to a point where heath began to merge in pasture, and dry-stone walls split the moor into fields. Suddenly his pace slackened and song died on his lips. For approaching from the right by a tributary path was the Poet.

Mr Heritage saw him afar off and waved a friendly hand. In spite of his chagrin Dickson could not but confess that he had misjudged his critic. Striding with long steps over the heather, his jacket open to the wind, his face aglow, and his capless head like a whin-bush for disorder, he cut a more wholesome and picturesque figure than in the smoking-room the night before. He seemed to be in a companionable mood, for he brandished his stick and shouted greetings.

'Well met!' he cried; 'I was hoping to fall in with you again. You must have thought me a pretty fair cub last night.'

'I did that,' was the dry answer.

'Well, I want to apologize. God knows what made me treat you to a university-extension lecture. I may not agree with you, but every man's entitled to his own views, and it was dashed poor form for me to start jawing you.'

Mr McCunn had no gift of nursing anger, and was very susceptible to apologies.

'That's all right,' he murmured. 'Don't mention it. I'm wondering what brought you down here, for it's off the road.'

'Caprice. Pure caprice. I liked the look of this butt-end of nowhere.'

'Same here. I've aye thought there was something terrible nice about a wee cape with a village at the neck of it and a burn each side.'

'Now that's interesting,' said Mr Heritage. 'You're obsessed by a particular type of landscape. Ever read Freud?'

Dickson shook his head.

'Well, you've got an odd complex somewhere. I wonder where the key lies. Cape – woods – two rivers – moor behind. Ever been in love, Dogson?'

Mr McCunn was startled. 'Love' was a word rarely mentioned in his circle except on death-beds. 'I've been a married man for thirty years,' he said hurriedly.

'That won't do. It should have been a hopeless affair – the last sight of the lady on a spur of coast with water on three sides – that kind of thing, you know. Or it might have happened to an ancestor . . . But you don't look the kind of breed for hopeless attachments. More likely some scoundrelly old Dogson long ago found sanctuary in this sort of place. Do you dream about it?'

'Not exactly.'

'Well, I do. The queer thing is that I've got the same prepossession as you. As soon as I spotted this Cruives place on the map this morning, I saw it was what I was after. When I came in sight of it I almost shouted. I don't very often dream, but when I do that's the place I frequent. Odd, isn't it?'

Mr McCunn was deeply interested at this unexpected revelation of romance. 'Maybe it's being in love,' he daringly observed.

The Poet demurred. 'No. I'm not a connoisseur of obvious sentiment. That explanation might fit your case, but not mine. I'm pretty certain there's something hideous at the back of *my* complex – some grim old business tucked away back in the ages. For though I'm attracted by the place, I'm frightened too!'

There seemed no room for fear in the delicate landscape now opening before them. In front in groves of birch and rowan smoked the first houses of a tiny village. The road had become a green 'loaning', on the ample margin of which cattle grazed. The moorland still showed itself in spits of heather, and some distance off, where a rivulet ran in a hollow, there were signs of a fire and figures near it. These last Mr Heritage regarded with disapproval.

'Some infernal trippers!' he murmured. 'Or Boy Scouts.

They desecrate everything. Why can't the *tunicatus popellus* keep away from a paradise like this!' Dickson, a democrat who felt nothing incongruous in the presence of other holiday-makers, was meditating a sharp rejoinder, when Mr Heritage's tone changed.

'Ye gods! What a village!' he cried, as they turned a corner. There were not more than a dozen whitewashed houses, all set in little gardens of wallflower and daffodil and early fruit blossom. A triangle of green filled the intervening space, and in it stood an ancient wooden pump. There was no schoolhouse or kirk; not even a post-office – only a red box in a cottage side. Beyond rose the high wall and the dark trees of the demesne, and to the right up a by-road which clung to the park edge stood a two-storeyed building which bore the legend 'The Cruives Inn'.

The Poet became lyrical. 'At last!' he cried. 'The village of my dreams! Not a sign of commerce! No church or school or beastly recreation hall! Nothing but these divine little cottages and an ancient pub! Dogson, I warn you, I'm going to have the devil of a tea.' And he declaimed:

*Thou shalt hear a song*
*After a while which Gods may listen to;*
*But place the flask upon the board and wait*
*Until the stranger hath allayed his thirst,*
*For poets, grasshoppers, and nightingales*
*Sing cheerily but when the throat is moist.*

Dickson, too, longed with sensual gusto for tea. But, as they drew nearer, the inn lost its hospitable look. The cobbles of the yard were weedy, as if rarely visited by traffic, a pane in a window was broken, and the blinds hung tattered. The garden was a wilderness, and the doorstep had not been scoured for weeks. But the place had a landlord, for he had seen them approach and was waiting at the door to meet them.

He was a big man in his shirt sleeves, wearing old riding breeches unbuttoned at the knees, and thick ploughman's boots. He had no leggings, and his fleshy calves were imperfectly covered with woollen socks. His face was large and pale, his neck bulged, and he had a gross unshaven jowl. He was a type familiar to students of society; not the innkeeper, which is a thing consistent with good breeding and all the refinements; a type not unknown in the House of Lords, especially among recent creations, common enough in the House of Commons and the City of London, and by no means infrequent in the governing circles of Labour; the type known to the discerning as the Licensed Victualler.

His face was wrinkled in official smiles, and he gave the travellers a hearty good afternoon.

'Can we stop here for the night?' Dickson asked.

The landlord looked sharply at him, and then replied to Mr Heritage. His expression passed from official bonhomie to official contrition.

'Impossible, gentlemen. Quite impossible. . . . Ye couldn't have come at a worse time. I've only been here a fortnight myself, and we haven't got right shaken down yet. Even then I might have made shift to do with ye, but the fact is we've illness in the house, and I'm fair at my wits' end. It breaks my heart to turn gentlemen away and me that keen to get the business started. But there it is!' He spat vigorously as if to emphasize the desperation of his quandary.

The man was clearly Scots, but his native speech was overlaid with something alien, something which might have been acquired in America or in going down to the sea in ships. He hitched his breeches, too, with a nautical air.

'Is there nowhere else we can put up?' Dickson asked.

'Not in this one-horse place. Just a wheen auld wives that packed thegether they haven't room for an extra hen. But it's grand weather, and it's not above seven miles to Auchenlochan. Say the word and I'll yoke the horse and drive ye there.'

'Thank you. We prefer to walk,' said Mr Heritage. Dickson would have tarried to inquire after the illness in the house, but his companion hurried him off. Once he looked back, and saw the landlord still on the doorstep gazing after them.

'That fellow's a swine,' said Mr Heritage sourly. 'I wouldn't trust my neck in his pot-house. Now, Dogson, I'm hanged if

I'm going to leave this place. We'll find a corner in the village somehow. Besides, I'm determined on tea.'

The little street slept in the clear pure light of an early April evening. Blue shadows lay on the white road, and a delicate aroma of cooking tantalized hungry nostrils. The near meadows shone like pale gold against the dark lift of the moor. A light wind had begun to blow from the west and carried the faintest tang of salt. The village at that hour was pure Paradise, and Dickson was of the Poet's opinion. At all costs they must spend the night there.

They selected a cottage whiter and neater than the others, which stood at a corner, where a narrow lane turned southward. Its thatched roof had been lately repaired, and starched curtains of a dazzling whiteness decorated the small, closely-shut windows. Likewise it had a green door and a polished brass knocker.

Tacitly the duty of envoy was entrusted to Mr McCunn. Leaving the other at the gate, he advanced up the little path lined with quartz stones, and politely but firmly dropped the brass knocker. He must have been observed; for ere the noise had ceased the door opened, and an elderly woman stood before him. She had a sharply-cut face, the rudiments of a beard, big spectacles on her nose, and an old-fashioned lace cap on her smooth white hair. A little grim she looked at first sight, because of her thin lips and Roman nose, but her mild curious eyes corrected the impression and gave the envoy confidence.

'Good afternoon, mistress,' he said, broadening his voice to something more rustical than his normal Glasgow speech. 'Me and my friend are paying our first visit here, and we're terrible taken up with the place. We would like to bide the night, but the inn is no' taking folk. Is there any chance, think you, of a bed here?'

'I'll no tell ye a lee,' said the woman. 'There's twae guid beds in the loft. But I dinna tak' lodgers and I dinna want to be bothered wi' ye. I'm an auld wumman and no' as stoot as I was. Ye'd better try doun the street. Eppie Home micht tak' ye.'

Dickson wore his most ingratiating smile. 'But, mistress, Eppie Home's house is no' yours. We've taken a tremendous fancy to this bit. Can you no' manage to put up with us for the one night? We're quiet auld-fashioned folk and we'll no' trouble you much. Just our tea and maybe an egg to it, and a bowl of porridge in the morning.'

The woman seemed to relent. 'Whaur's your freend?' she asked, peering over her spectacles towards the garden gate. The waiting Mr Heritage, seeing her eyes moving in his direction, took off his cap with a brave gesture and advanced. 'Glorious weather, madam,' he declared.

'English,' whispered Dickson to the woman, in explanation.

She examined the Poet's neat clothes and Mr McCunn's homely garments, and apparently found them reassuring. 'Come in,' she said shortly. 'I see ye're wilfu' folk and I'll hae to dae my best for ye.'

A quarter of an hour later the two travellers, having been introduced to two spotless beds in the loft, and having washed luxuriously at the pump in the back yard, were seated in Mrs Morran's kitchen before a meal which fulfilled their wildest dreams. She had been baking that morning, so there were white scones and barley scones, and oaten farles, and russet pancakes. There were three boiled eggs for each of them; there was a segment of an immense currant cake ('a present from my guid brither last Hogmanay'); there was skim-milk cheese; there were several kinds of jam, and there was a pot of dark-gold heather honey. 'Try hinny and aitcake,' said their hostess. 'My man used to say he never fund onything as guid in a' his days.'

Presently they heard her story. Her name was Morran, and she had been a widow these ten years. Of her family her son was in South Africa, one daughter a lady's-maid in London, and the other married to a schoolmaster in Kyle. The son had been in France fighting, and had come safely through. He had spent a month or two with her before his return, and, she feared, had found it dull. 'There's no' a man body in the place. Naething but auld wives.'

That was what the innkeeper had told them. Mr McCunn inquired concerning the inn.

'There's new folk just come. What's this they ca' them? – Robson – Dobson – aye, Dobson. What for wad they no' tak' ye in? Does the man think he's a laird to refuse folk that gait?'

'He said he had illness in the house.'

Mrs Morran meditated. 'Whae in the world can be lyin' there? The man bides his lane. He got a lassie frae Auchenlochan to cook, but she and her box gaed off in the post-cairt yestreen. I doot he tell't ye a lee, though it's no for me to juidge him. I've never spoken a word to ane o' thae new folk.'

Dickson inquired about the 'new folk'.

'They're a' new come in the last three weeks, and there's no' a man o' the auld stock left. John Blackstocks at the Wast Lodge dee'd o' pneumony last back-end, and auld Simon Tappie at the Gairdens flitted to Maybole a year come Mairtinmas. There's naebody at the Gairdens noo, but there's a man come to the Wast Lodge, a blackavised body wi' a face like bendleather. Tam Robison used to bide at the South Lodge, but Tam got killed about Mesopotamy, and his wife took the bairns to her guidsire up at the Garpleheid. I seen the man that's in the South Lodge gaun up the street when I was finishin' my denner – a shilpit body and a lameter, but he hirples as fast as ither folk run. He's no' bonny to look at. I canna think what the factor's ettlin' at to let sic ill-faured chiels come about the toun.'

Their hostess was rapidly rising in Dickson's esteem. She sat very straight in her chair, eating with the careful gentility of a bird, and primming her thin lips after every mouthful of tea.

'Who bides in the Big House?' he asked. 'Huntingtower is the name, isn't it?'

'When I was a lassie they ca'ed it Dalquharter Hoose, and Huntingtower was the auld rickle o' stanes at the sea-end. But naething wad serve the last laird's faither but he maun change the name, for he was clean daft about what they ca' antickities. Ye speir whae bides in the Hoose? Naebody, since the young laird dee'd. It's standin' cauld and lanely and steikit, and it aince the cheeriest dwallin' in a' Carrick.'

Mrs Morran's tone grew tragic. 'It's a queer warld wi'out the auld gentry. My faither and my guidsire and his faither afore him served the Kennedys, and my man Dauvit Morran was gemkeeper to them, and afore I mairried I was ane o' the table-maids. They were kind folk, the Kennedys, and, like a' the rale gentry, maist mindfu' o' them that served them. Sic merry nichts I've seen in the auld Hoose, at Hallowe'en and Hogmanay, and at the servants' balls and the waddin's o' the young leddies! But the laird bode to waste his siller in stane and lime, and hadna that much to leave to his bairns. And now they're a' scattered or deid.'

Her grave face wore the tenderness which comes from affectionate reminiscence.

'There was never sic a laddie as young Maister Quentin. No' a week gaed by but he was in here, cryin', "Phemie Morran, I've come till my tea!" Fine he likit my treacle scones, puir man. There wasna ane in the countryside sae bauld a rider at the hunt, or sic a skeely fisher. And he was clever at his books tae, a graund scholar, they said, and ettlin' at bein' what they ca' a dipplemat. But that's a' bye wi'.'

'Quentin Kennedy – the fellow in the Tins?' Heritage asked. 'I saw him in Rome when he was with the Mission.'

'I dinna ken. He was a brave sodger, but he wasna long fechtin' in France till he got a bullet in his breist. Syne we heard tell o' him in far awa' bits like Russia; and syne cam' the end o' the war and we lookit to see him back, fishin' the waters and ridin' like Jehu as in the auld days. But wae's me! It wasna permitted. The next news we got, the puir laddie was deid o' influenzy and buried somewhere about France. The wanchancy bullet maun have weakened his chest, nae doot. So that's the end o' the guid stock o' Kennedy o' Huntingtower, whae hae been great folk sin' the time o' Robert Bruce. And noo the Hoose is shut up till the lawyers can get somebody sae far left to himsel' as to tak' it on lease, and in thae dear days it's no' just onybody that wants a muckle castle.'

'Who are the lawyers?' Dickson asked.

'Glendonan and Speirs in Embro. But they never look near the place, and Maister Loudon in Auchenlochan does the factorin'. He's let the public an' filled the twae lodges, and he'll be thinkin' nae doot that he's done eneuch.'

Mrs Morran had poured some hot water into the big slop-bowl, and had begun the operation known as 'synding out' the cups. It was a hint that the meal was over, and Dickson and Heritage rose from the table. Followed by an injunction to be back for supper 'on the chap o' nine', they strolled out into the evening. Two hours of some sort of daylight remained, and the travellers had that impulse to activity which comes to all men who, after a day of exercise and emptiness, are stayed with a satisfying tea.

'You should be happy, Dogson,' said the Poet. 'Here we have all the materials for your blessed romance – old mansion, extinct family, village deserted of men, and an innkeeper whom I suspect of being a villain. I feel almost a convert to your nonsense myself. We'll have a look at the House.'

They turned down the road which ran north by the park wall, past the inn, which looked more abandoned than ever, till they came to an entrance which was clearly the West Lodge. It had once been a pretty, modish cottage, with a thatched roof and dormer windows, but now it was badly in need of repair. A window-pane was broken and stuffed with a sack, the posts of the porch were giving inwards, and the thatch was crumbling under the attentions of a colony of starlings. The great iron gates were rusty, and on the coat of arms above them the gilding was patchy and tarnished.

Apparently the gates were locked, and even the side wicket failed to open to Heritage's vigorous shaking. Inside a weedy drive disappeared among ragged rhododendrons.

The noise brought a man to the lodge door. He was a sturdy fellow in a suit of black clothes which had not been made for him. He might have been a butler *en déshabillé*, but for the presence of a pair of field boots into which he had tucked the ends of his trousers. The curious thing about him was his face, which was decorated with features so tiny as to give the impression of a monstrous child. Each in itself was well enough formed, but eyes, nose, mouth, chin were of a smallness curiously out of proportion to the head and body. Such an anomaly might have been redeemed by the expression; good-humour would have invested it with an air of agreeable farce. But there was no friendliness in the man's face. It was set like a judge's in a stony impassiveness.

'May we walk up to the House?' Heritage asked. 'We are here for a night and should like to have a look at it.'

The man advanced a step. He had either a bad cold, or a voice comparable in size to his features.

'There's no entrance here,' he said huskily. 'I have strict orders.'

'Oh, come now,' said Heritage. 'It can do nobody any harm if you let us in for half an hour.'

The man advanced another step.

'You shall not come in. Go away from here. Go away, I tell you. It is private.' The words spoken by the small mouth in the small voice had a kind of childish ferocity.

The travellers turned their back on him and continued their way.

'Sich a curmudgeon!' Dickson commented. His face had flushed, for he was susceptible to rudeness. 'Did you notice? That man's a foreigner.'

'He's a brute,' said Heritage. 'But I'm not going to be done in by that class of lad. There can be no gates on the sea side, so we'll work round that way, for I won't sleep till I've seen the place.'

Presently the trees grew thinner, and the road plunged through thickets of hazel till it came to a sudden stop in a field. There the cover ceased wholly, and below them lay the glen of the Laver. Steep green banks descended to a stream which swept in coils of gold into the eye of the sunset. A little farther down the channel broadened, the slopes fell back a little, and a tongue of glittering sea ran up to meet the hill waters. The Laver is a gentle stream after it leaves its cradle heights, a stream of clear pools and long bright shallows, winding by moorland steadings and upland meadows; but in its last half-mile it goes mad, and imitates its childhood when it tumbled over granite shelves. Down in that green place the crystal water gushed and frolicked as if determined on one hour of rapturous life before joining the sedater sea.

Heritage flung himself on the turf.

'This is a good place! Ye gods, what a good place! Dogson, aren't you glad you came? I think everything's bewitched tonight. That village is bewitched, and that old woman's tea. Good white magic! And that foul innkeeper and that brigand at the gate. Black magic! And now here is the home of all enchantment – "island valley of Avilion" – "waters that listen for lovers" – all the rest of it!'

Dickson observed and marvelled.

'I can't make you out, Mr Heritage. You were saying last night you were a great democrat, and yet you were objecting to yon laddies camping on the moor. And you very near bit the neb off me when I said I liked Tennyson. And now . . .' Mr McCunn's command of language was inadequate to describe the transformation.

'You're a precise, pragmatical Scot,' was the answer. 'Hang it, man, don't remind me that I'm inconsistent. I've a poet's licence to play the fool, and if you don't understand me, I don't in the least understand myself. All I know is that I'm feeling young and jolly, and that it's the spring.'

Mr Heritage was assuredly in a strange mood. He began to whistle with a far-away look in his eye.

'Do you know what that is?' he asked suddenly.

Dickson, who could not detect any tune, said No.

'It's an aria from a Russian opera that came out just before the war. I've forgotten the name of the fellow who wrote it. Jolly thing, isn't it? I always remind myself of it when I'm in this mood, for it is linked with the greatest experience of my life. You said, I think, that you had never been in love?'

Dickson replied in the native fashion. 'Have you?' he asked.

'I have, and I am – been for two years. I was down with my battalion on the Italian front early in 1918, and because I could speak the language they hoicked me out and sent me to Rome on a liaison job. It was Easter time and fine weather, and, being glad to get out of the trenches, I was pretty well pleased with myself and enjoying life . . . In the place where I stayed there was a girl. She was a Russian, a princess of a great family, but a refugee, and of course as poor as sin . . . I remember how badly dressed she was among all the well-to-do Romans. But, my God, what a beauty! There was never anything in the world like her . . . She was little more than a child, and she used to sing that air in the morning as she went down the stairs . . . They sent me back to the front before I had a chance of getting to know her, but she used to give me little timid good mornings, and her voice and eyes were like an angel's . . . I'm over my head in love, but it's hopeless, quite hopeless. I shall never see her again.'

'I'm sure I'm honoured by your confidence,' said Dickson reverently.

The Poet, who seemed to draw exhilaration from the memory of his sorrows, arose and fetched him a clout on the back. 'Don't talk of confidence, as if you were a reporter,' he said. 'What about that House? If we're to see it before the dark comes we'd better hustle.'

The green slopes on their left, as they ran seaward, were clothed towards their summit with a tangle of broom and light scrub. The two forced their way through it, and found to their surprise that on this side there were no defences of the Huntingtower demesne. Along the crest ran a path which had once been gravelled and trimmed. Beyond, through a thicket of laurels and rhododendrons, they came on a long unkempt aisle of grass, which seemed to be one of those side avenues often found in connexion with old Scots dwellings. Keeping along this they reached a grove of beech and holly through which showed a dim shape of masonry. By a common impulse they moved stealthily, crouching in cover, till at the far side of the wood they found a sunk fence and looked over an acre or two of what had once been lawn and flower-beds to the front of the mansion.

The outline of the building was clearly silhouetted against the glowing west, but since they were looking at the east face the detail was all in shadow. But, dim as it was, the sight was enough to give Dickson the surprise of his life. He had expected something old and baronial. But this was new, raw and new, not twenty years built. Some madness had prompted its creator to set up a replica of a Tudor house in a countryside where the thing was unheard of. All the tricks were there – oriel windows, lozenged panes, high twisted chimney stacks; the very stone was red, as if to imitate the mellow brick of some ancient Kentish manor. It was new, but it was also decaying. The creepers had fallen from the walls, the pilasters on the terrace were tumbling down, lichen and moss were on the doorsteps. Shuttered, silent, abandoned, it stood like a harsh *memento mori* of human hopes.

Dickson had never before been affected by an inanimate thing with so strong a sense of disquiet. He had pictured an old stone tower on a bright headland; he found instead this raw thing among trees. The decadence of the brand-new repels as something against nature, and this new thing was decadent. But there was a mysterious life in it, for though not a chimney smoked, it seemed to enshrine a personality and to wear a sinister aura. He felt a lively distaste, which was almost fear. He wanted to get far away from it as fast as possible. The sun, now sinking very low, sent up rays which kindled the crests of a group of firs to the left of the front door. He had the absurd fancy that they were torches flaming before a bier.

It was well that the two had moved quietly and kept in shadow. Footsteps fell on their ears, on the path which threaded the lawn just beyond the sunk-fence. It was the keeper of the West Lodge and he carried something on his back, but both that and his face were indistinct in the half-light.

Other footsteps were heard, coming from the other side of the lawn. A man's shod feet rang on the stone of a flagged path, and from their irregular fall it was plain that he was lame. The two men met near the door, and spoke together. Then they separated, and moved one down each side of the house. To the two watchers they had the air of a patrol, or of warders pacing the corridors of a prison.

"Let's get out of this," said Dickson, and turned to go.

The air had the curious stillness which precedes the moment

of sunset, when the birds of day have stopped their noises and the sounds of night have not begun. But suddenly in the silence fell notes of music. They seemed to come from the house, a voice singing softly but with great beauty and clearness.

Dickson halted in his steps. The tune, whatever it was, was like a fresh wind to blow aside his depression. The house no longer looked sepulchral. He saw that the two men had hurried back from their patrol, had met and exchanged some message, and made off again as if alarmed by the music. Then he noticed his companion . . .

Heritage was on one knee with his face rapt and listening. He got to his feet and appeared to be about to make for the House. Dickson caught him by the arm and dragged him into the bushes, and he followed unresistingly, like a man in a dream. They ploughed through the thicket, recrossed the grass avenue, and scrambled down the hillside to the banks of the stream.

Then for the first time Dickson observed that his companion's face was very white, and that sweat stood on his temples. Heritage lay down and lapped up water like a dog. Then he turned a wild eye on the other.

'I am going back,' he said. 'That is the voice of the girl I saw in Rome, and it is singing her song!'

CHAPTER FOUR

# DOUGAL

'YOU'LL do nothing of the kind,' said Dickson. 'You're coming home to your supper. It was to be on the chap of nine.'

'I'm going back to that place.'

The man was clearly demented and must be humoured. 'Well, you must wait till the morn's morning. It's very near dark now, and those are two ugly customers wandering about yonder. You'd better sleep the night on it.'

Mr Heritage seemed to be persuaded. He suffered himself to be led up the now dusky slopes to the gate where the road from the village ended. He walked listlessly like a man engaged in painful reflexion. Once only he broke the silence.

'You heard the singing?' he asked.

Dickson was a very poor hand at a lie. 'I heard something,' he admitted.

'You heard a girl's voice singing?'

'It sounded like that,' was the admission. 'But I'm thinking it might have been a seagull.'

'You're a fool,' said the Poet rudely.

The return was a melancholy business, compared to the bright speed of the outward journey. Dickson's mind was a chaos of feelings, all of them unpleasant. He had run up against something which he violently, blindly detested, and the trouble was that he could not tell why. It was all perfectly absurd, for why on earth should an ugly house, some overgrown trees, and a couple of ill-favoured servants so malignly affect him? Yet this was the fact; he had strayed out of Arcady into a sphere that filled him with revolt and a nameless fear. Never in his experience had he felt like this, this foolish childish panic which took all the colour and zest out of life. He tried to laugh at himself but failed. Heritage, stumbling along by his side, effectually crushed his effort to discover humour in the situation. Some exhalation from that infernal place had driven the Poet mad. And then that voice singing! A seagull, he had said. More like a nightingale, he reflected – a bird which in the flesh he had never met.

Mrs Morran had the lamp lit and a fire burning in her cheerful kitchen. The sight of it somewhat restored Dickson's equanimity, and to his surprise he found that he had an appetite for supper. There was new milk, thick with cream, and most of the dainties which had appeared at tea, supplemented by a noble dish of shimmering 'potted-head'. The hostess did not share their meal, being engaged in some duties in the little cubbyhole known as the back kitchen.

Heritage drank a glass of milk but would not touch food. 'I called this place Paradise four hours ago,' he said. 'So it is, but I fancy it is next door to Hell. There is something devilish going on inside that park wall, and I mean to get to the bottom of it.'

'Hoots! Nonsense!' Dickson replied with affected cheerfulness. 'To-morrow you and me will take the road for Auchenlochan. We needn't trouble ourselves about an ugly old house and a wheen impident lodge-keepers.'

'To-morrow I'm going to get inside the place. Don't come unless you like, but it's no use arguing with me. My mind is made up.'

Heritage cleared a space on the table and spread out a section of a large-scale ordnance map.

'I must clear my head about the topography, the same as if this were a battle-ground. Look here, Dogson . . . The road past the inn that we went by to-night runs north and south.' He tore a page from a note-book and proceeded to make a rough sketch . . . 'One end we know abuts on the Laver glen, and the other stops at the South Lodge. Inside the wall which follows the road is a long belt of plantation – mostly beeches and ash – then to the west a kind of park, and beyond that the lawns of the house. Strips of plantation with avenues between follow the north and south sides of the park. On the sea side of the House are the stables and what looks like a walled garden, and beyond them what seems to be open ground with an old dovecot marked, and the ruins of Huntingtower keep. Beyond that there is more open ground, till you come to the cliffs of the cape. Have you got that? ... It looks possible from the contouring to get on to the sea cliffs by following the Laver, for all that side is broken up into ravines ... But look at the other side – the Garple glen. It's evidently a deep-cut gully, and at the bottom it opens out into a little harbour. There's deep water there, you observe. Now the House on the south side – the Garple side – is built fairly close to the edge of the cliffs. Is that all clear in your head? We can't reconnoitre unless we've got a working notion of the lie of the land.'

Dickson was about to protest that he had no intention of reconnoitring, when a hubbub arose in the back kitchen. Mrs Morran's voice was heard in shrill protest.

'Ye ill laddie! Eh – ye – ill – laddie! [*crescendo*] Makin' a hash o' my back door wi' your dirty feet! What are ye slinkin' roond here for, when I tell't ye this mornin' that I wad sell ye nae mair scones till ye paid for the last lot? Ye're a wheen thievin' hungry callants, and if there were a polisman in the place I'd gie ye in chairge ... What's that ye say? Ye're no' wantin' meat? Ye want to speak to the gentlemen that's bidin' here? Ye ken the auld ane, says you? I believe it's a muckle lee, but there's the gentlemen to answer ye theirsels.'

Mrs Morran, brandishing a dishclout dramatically, flung open the door, and with a vigorous push propelled into the kitchen a singular figure.

It was a stunted boy, who from his face might have been fifteen years old, but had the stature of a child of twelve. He had a thatch of fiery red hair above a pale freckled countenance. His nose was snub, his eyes a sulky grey-green, and his wide mouth disclosed large and damaged teeth. But remarkable as was his visage, his clothing was still stranger. On his head was the regulation Boy Scout hat, but it was several sizes too big, and was squashed down upon his immense red ears. He wore a very ancient khaki shirt, which had once belonged to a full-grown soldier, and the spacious sleeves were rolled up at the shoulders and tied with string, revealing a pair of skinny arms. Round his middle hung what was meant to be a kilt – a kilt of home manufacture, which may once have been a tablecloth, for its bold pattern suggested no known clan tartan. He had a massive belt, in which was stuck a broken gully-knife, and round his neck was knotted the remnant of what had once been a silk bandanna. His legs and feet were bare, blue, scratched, and very dirty, and his toes had the prehensile look common to monkeys and small boys who summer and winter go bootless. In his hand was a long ash-pole, new cut from some coppice.

The apparition stood glum and lowering on the kitchen floor. As Dickson stared at it he recalled Mearns Street and the band of irregular Boy Scouts who paraded to the roll of tin cans. Before him stood Dougal, Chieftain of the Gorbals Die-Hards. Suddenly he remembered the philanthropic Mackintosh, and his own subscription of ten pounds to the camp fund. It pleased him to find the rascals here, for in the unpleasant affairs on the verge of which he felt himself they were a comforting reminder of the peace of home.

'I'm glad to see you, Dougal,' he said pleasantly. 'How are you all getting on?' And then, with a vague reminiscence of the Scouts' code – 'Have you been minding to perform a good deed every day?'

The Chieftain's brow darkened.

'"*Good deeds!*"' he repeated bitterly. 'I tell ye I'm fair wore out wi' good deeds. Yon man Mackintosh tell't me this was going to be a grand holiday. Holiday! Govey Dick! It's been like a Setterday night in Main Street – a' fechtin', fechtin'.'

No collocation of letters could reproduce Dougal's accent, and I will not attempt it. There was a touch of Irish in it, a spice of music-hall patter, as well as the odd lilt of the Glasgow vernacular. He was strong in vowels, but the consonants, especially the letter 't', were only aspirations.

'Sit down and let's hear about things,' said Dickson.

The boy turned his head to the still open back door, where Mrs Morran could be heard at her labours. He stepped across and shut it. 'I'm no' wantin' that auld wife to hear,' he said. Then he squatted down on the patchwork rug by the hearth, and warmed his blue-black shins. Looking into the glow of the fire, he observed, 'I seen you two up by the Big Hoose the night.'

'The devil you did,' said Heritage, roused to a sudden attention. 'And where were you?'

'Seven feet from your head, up a tree. It's my chief hidy-hole, an Gosh! I need one, for Lean's after me wi' a gun. He had a shot at me two days syne.'

Dickson exclaimed, and Dougal with morose pride showed a rent in his kilt. 'If I had had on breeks, he'd ha' got me.'

'Who's Lean?' Heritage asked.

'The man wi' the black coat. The other – the lame one – they ca' Spittal.'

'How d'you know?'

'I've listened to them crackin' thegither.'

'But what for did the man want to shoot at you?' asked the scandalized Dickson.

'What for? Because they're frightened to death o' onybody going near their auld Hoose. They're a pair of deevils, worse nor any Red Indian, but for a' that they're sweatin' wi' fright. What for? says you. Because they're hidin' a Secret. I knew it as soon as I seen the man Lean's face. I once seen the same kind o' scoondrel at the picters. When he opened his mouth to swear, I kenned he was a foreigner, like the lads down at the Broomielaw. That looked black, but I hadn't got at the worst of it. Then he loosed off at me wi' his gun.'

'Were you not feared?' said Dickson.

'Ay, I was feared. But ye'll no' choke off the Gorbals Die-Hards wi' a gun. We held a meetin' round the camp fire, and we resolved to get to the bottom o' the business. Me bein' their Chief, it was my duty to make what they ca' a reckonis-since, for that was the dangerous job. So a' this day I've been going on my belly about thae policies. I've found out some queer things.'

Heritage had risen and was staring down at the small squatting figure.

'What have you found out? Quick. Tell me at once.' His voice was sharp and excited.

'Bide a wee,' said the unwinking Dougal. 'I'm no' going to let ye into this business till I ken that ye'll help. It's a far bigger job than I thought. There's more in it than Lean and Spittal. There's the big man that keeps the public – Dobson, they ca' him. He's a Namerican, which looks bad. And there's two-three tinklers campin' down in the Garple Dean. They're in it, for Dobson was colloguin' wi' them a' mornin'. When I seen ye, I thought ye were more o' the gang, till I mindit that one o' ye was auld McCunn that has the shop in Mearns Street. I seen that ye didn't like the look o' Lean, and I followed ye here, for I was thinkin' I needit help.'

Heritage plucked Dougal by the shoulder and lifted him to his feet.

'For God's sake, boy,' he cried, 'tell us what you know!'

'Will ye help?'

'Of course, you little fool.'

'Then swear,' said the ritualist. From a grimy wallet he extracted a limp little volume which proved to be a damaged copy of a work entitled *Sacred Songs and Solos*. 'Here! Take that in your right hand and put your left hand on my pole, and say after me, "I swear no' to blab what is telled me in secret, and to be swift and sure in obeyin' orders, s'help me God!" Syne kiss the bookie.'

Dickson at first refused, declaring it was all havers, but Heritage's docility persuaded him to follow suit. The two were sworn.

'Now,' said Heritage.

Dougal squatted again on the hearth-rug, and gathered the eyes of his audience. He was enjoying himself.

'This day,' he said slowly, 'I got inside the Hoose.'

'Stout fellow,' said Heritage; 'and what did you find there?'

'I got inside that Hoose, but it wasn't once or twice I tried. I found a corner where I was out o' sight o' anybody unless they had come there seekin' me, and I sklimmed up a rone pipe, but a' the windies were lockit and I verra near broke my neck. Syne I tried the roof, and a sore sklim I had, but when I got there there were no skylights. At the end I got in by the coal-hole. That's why ye're maybe thinkin' I'm no' very clean.'

Heritage's patience was nearly exhausted.

'I don't want to hear how you got in. What did you find, you little devil?'

'Inside the Hoose,' said Dougal slowly (and there was a melancholy sense of anti-climax in his voice, as of one who had hoped to speak of gold and jewels and armed men) – 'inside that Hoose there's nothing but two women.'

Heritage sat down before him with a stern face.

'Describe them,' he commanded.

'One o' them is dead auld, as auld as the wife here. She didn't look to me very right in the head.'

'And the other?'

'Oh, just a lassie.'

'What was she like?'

Dougal seemed to be searching for adequate words. 'She is ...' he began. Then a popular song gave him inspiration. 'She's pure as the lully in the dell!'

In no way discomposed by Heritage's fierce interrogatory air, he continued: 'She's either foreign or English, for she couldn't understand what I said, and I could make nothing o' her clippit tongue. But I could see she had been greetin'. She looked feared, yet kind o' determined. I speired if I could do anything for her, and when she got my meaning she was terrible anxious to ken if I had seen a man – a big man, she said, wi' a yellow beard. She didn't seem to ken his name, or else she wouldn't tell me. The auld wife was mortal feared, and was aye speakin' in a foreign langwidge. I seen at once that what frightened them was Lean and his friends, and I was just starting to speir about them when there came a sound like a man walkin' along the passage. She was for hidin' me in behind a sofy, but I wasn't going to be trapped like that, so I got out by the other door and down the kitchen stairs and into the coal-hole. Gosh, it was a near thing!'

The boy was on his feet. 'I must be off to the camp to give out the orders for the morn. I'm going back to that Hoose, for it's a fight atween the Gorbals Die-Hards and the scoondrels that are frightenin' thae women. The question is, Are ye comin' with me? Mind, ye've sworn. But if ye're no', I'm going mysel', though I'll no' deny I'd be glad o' company. *You* anyway –' he added, nodding at Heritage. 'Maybe auld McCunn wouldn't get through the coal-hole.'

'You're an impident laddie,' said the outraged Dickson. 'It's no' likely we're coming with you. Breaking into other folks' houses! It's a job for the police!'

'Please yersel',' said the Chieftain, and looked at Heritage.

'I'm on,' said that gentleman.

'Well, just you set out the morn as if ye were for a walk up the Garple glen. I'll be on the road and I'll have orders for ye.'

Without more ado Dougal left by way of the back kitchen. There was a brief denunciation from Mrs Morran, then the outer door banged and he was gone.

The Poet sat still with his head in his hands, while Dickson, acutely uneasy, prowled about the floor. He had forgotten even to light his pipe.

'You'll not be thinking of heeding that ragamuffin boy,' he ventured.

'I'm certainly going to get into the House to-morrow,' Heritage answered, 'and if he can show me a way so much the better. He's a spirited youth. Do you breed many like him in Glasgow?'

'Plenty,' said Dickson sourly. 'See here, Mr Heritage. You can't expect me to be going about burgling houses on the word of a blagyird laddie. I'm a respectable man – aye been. Besides, I'm here for a holiday, and I've no call to be mixing myself up in strangers' affairs.'

'You haven't. Only, you see, I think there's a friend of mine in that place, and anyhow there are women in trouble. If you like, we'll say good-bye after breakfast, and you can continue as if you had never turned aside to this damned peninsula. But I've got to stay.'

Dickson groaned. What had become of his dream of idylls, his gentle bookish romance? Vanished before a reality which smacked horribly of crude melodrama and possibly of sordid crime. His gorge rose at the picture, but a thought troubled him. Perhaps all romance in its hour of happening was rough and ugly like this, and only shone rosy in the retrospect. Was he being false to his deepest faith?

'Let's have Mrs Morran in,' he ventured. 'She's a wise old body and I'd like to hear her opinion of this business. We'll get common sense from her.'

'I don't object,' said Heritage. 'But no amount of common sense will change my mind.'

Their hostess forestalled them by returning at that moment to the kitchen.

'We want your advice, mistress,' Dickson told her, and accordingly, like a barrister with a client, she seated herself carefully in the big easy chair, found and adjusted her spectacles, and waited with hands folded on her lap to hear the business. Dickson narrated their pre-supper doings, and gave a sketch of Dougal's evidence. His exposition was cautious and colourless, and without conviction. He seemed to expect a robust incredulity in his hearer.

Mrs Morran listened with the gravity of one in church. When Dickson finished she seemed to meditate.

'There's no blagyird trick that would surprise me in thae new folk. What's that ye ca' them – Lean and Spittal? Eppie Home threepit to me they were furriners, and these are no furrin names.'

'What I want to hear from you, Mrs Morran,' said Dickson impressively, 'is whether you think there's anything in that boy's story?'

'I think it's maist likely true. He's a terrible impident callant, but he's no' a leear.'

'Then you think that a gang of ruffians have got two lone women shut up in that house for their own purposes?'

'I wadna wonder.'

'But it's ridiculous! This is a Christian and law-abiding country. What would the police say?'

'They never troubled Dalquharter muckle. There's no' a polisman nearer than Knockraw – yin Johnnie Trummle, and he's as useless as a frostit tattie.'

'The wiselike thing, as I think,' said Dickson, 'would be to turn the Procurator-Fiscal on to the job. It's his business, no' ours.'

'Well, I wadna say but ye're richt,' said the lady.

'What would you do if you were us?' Dickson's tone was subtly confidential. 'My friend here wants to get into the House the morn with that red-haired laddie to satisfy himself about the facts. I say no. Let sleeping dogs lie, I say, and if you think the beasts are mad, report to the authorities. What would you do yourself?'

'If I were you,' came the emphatic reply, 'I would tak' the first train hame the morn, and when I got hame I wad bide there. Ye're a dacent body, but ye're no' the kind to be traivellin' the roads.'

'And if you were me?' Heritage asked with his queer crooked smile.

'If I was young and yauld like you I wad gang into the Hoose, and I wadna rest till I had riddled oot the truith and jyled every scoondrel about the place. If ye dinna gang, 'faith I'll kilt my coats and gang mysel'. I havena served the Kennedys for forty year no' to hae the honour o' the Hoose at my hert . . . Ye speired my advice, sirs, and ye've gotten it. Now I maun clear awa' your supper.'

Dickson asked for a candle, and, as on the previous night, went abruptly to bed. The oracle of prudence to which he had appealed had betrayed him and counselled folly. But was it folly? For him, assuredly, for Dickson McCunn, late of Mearns Street, Glasgow, wholesale and retail provision merchant, elder in the Guthrie Memorial Kirk, and fifty-five years of age. Ay, that was the rub. He was getting old. The woman had seen it and had advised him to go home. Yet the plea was curiously irksome, though it gave him the excuse he needed. If you played at being young, you had to take up the obligations of youth, and he thought derisively of his boyish exhilaration of the past days. Derisively, but also sadly. What had become of that innocent joviality he had dreamed of, that happy morning pilgrimage of spring enlivened by tags from the poets? His goddess had played him false. Romance had put upon him too hard a trial.

He lay long awake, torn between common sense and a desire to be loyal to some vague whimsical standard. Heritage a yard distant appeared also to be sleepless, for the bed creaked with his turning. Dickson found himself envying one whose troubles, whatever they might be, were not those of a divided mind.

## CHAPTER FIVE

# OF THE PRINCESS IN THE TOWER

VERY early next morning, while Mrs Morran was still cooking breakfast, Dickson and Heritage might have been observed taking the air in the village street. It was the Poet who had insisted upon this walk, and he had his own purpose. They looked at the spires of smoke piercing the windless air, and studied the daffodils in the cottage gardens. Dickson was glum, but Heritage seemed in high spirits. He varied his garrulity with spells of cheerful whistling.

They strode along the road by the park wall till they reached the inn. There Heritage's music waxed peculiarly loud. Presently from the yard, unshaven and looking as if he had slept in his clothes, came Dobson the innkeeper.

'Good morning,' said the Poet. 'I hope the sickness in your house is on the mend?'

'Thank ye, it's no worse,' was the reply, but in the man's heavy face there was little civility. His small grey eyes searched their faces.

'We're just waiting for breakfast to get on the road again. I'm jolly glad we spent the night here. We found quarters after all, you know.'

'So I see. Whereabouts, may I ask?'

'Mrs Morran's. We could always have got in there, but we didn't want to fuss an old lady, so we thought we'd try the inn first. She's my friend's aunt.'

At this amazing falsehood Dickson started, and the man observed his surprise. The eyes were turned on him like a searchlight. They roused antagonism in his peaceful soul, and with that antagonism came an impulse to back up the Poet. 'Ay,' he said, 'she's my Auntie Phemie, my mother's half-sister.'

The man turned on Heritage.

'Where are ye for the day?'

'Auchenlochan,' said Dickson hastily. He was still determined to shake the dust of Dalquharter from his feet.

The innkeeper sensibly brightened. 'Well, ye'll have a fine walk. I must go in and see about my own breakfast. Good day to ye, gentlemen.'

'That,' said Heritage as they entered the village street again, 'is the first step in camouflage, to put the enemy off his guard.'

'It was an abominable lie,' said Dickson crossly.

'Not at all. It was a necessary and proper *ruse de guerre*. It explained why we spent the night here, and now Dobson and his friends can get about their day's work with an easy mind. Their suspicions are temporarily allayed, and that will make our job easier.'

'I'm not coming with you.'

'I never said you were. By "we" I refer to myself and the red-headed boy.'

'Mistress, you're my auntie,' Dickson informed Mrs Morran as she set the porridge on the table. 'This gentleman has just been telling the man at the inn that you're my Auntie Phemie.'

For a second their hostess looked bewildered. Then the corners of her prim mouth moved upwards in a slow smile.

'I see,' she said. 'Weel, maybe it was weel done. But if ye're my nevoy ye'll hae to keep up my credit, for we're a bauld and siccar lot.'

Half an hour later there was a furious dissension when Dickson attempted to pay for the night's entertainment. Mrs Morran would have none of it. 'Ye're no' awa' yet,' she said tartly, and the matter was complicated by Heritage's refusal to take part in the debate. He stood aside and grinned, till Dickson in despair returned his notecase to his pocket, murmuring darkly that 'he would send it from Glasgow.'

The road to Auchenlochan left the main village street at right angles by the side of Mrs Morran's cottage. It was a better road than that by which they had come yesterday, for by it twice daily the post-cart travelled to the post-town. It ran on the edge of the moor and on the lip of the Garple glen, till it crossed that stream and, keeping near the coast, emerged after five miles into the cultivated flats of the Lochan valley. The morning was fine, the keen air invited to high spirits, plovers piped entrancingly over the bent and linnets sang in the whins, there was a solid breakfast behind him, and the promise of a cheerful road till luncheon. The stage was set for good humour, but Dickson's heart, which should have been ascending with the larks, stuck leadenly in his boots. He was not even relieved at putting Dalquharter behind him. The atmosphere of that unhallowed place lay still on his soul. He hated it, but he hated himself more. Here was one who had hugged himself all his days as an adventurer waiting his chance, running away at the first challenge of adventure; a lover of Romance who fled from the earliest overture of his goddess. He was ashamed and angry, but what else was there to do? Burglary in the company of a queer poet and a queerer urchin? It was unthinkable.

Presently, as they tramped silently on, they came to the bridge beneath which the peaty waters of the Garple ran in porter-coloured pools and tawny cascades. From a clump of elders on the other side Dougal emerged. A barefoot boy, dressed in much the same parody of a Boy Scout's uniform, but with corduroy shorts instead of a kilt, stood before him at rigid attention. Some command was issued, the child saluted, and trotted back past the travellers with never a look at them. Discipline was strong among the Gorbals Die-Hards; no Chief of Staff ever conversed with his General under a stricter etiquette.

Dougal received the travellers with the condescension of a regular towards civilians.

'They're off their gawrd,' he announced. 'Thomas Yownie has been shadowin' them since skreigh o' day, and he reports that Dobson and Lean followed ye till ye were out o' sight o' the houses, and syne Lean got a spy-glass and watched ye till the road turned in among the trees. That satisfied them, and they're both away back to their jobs. Thomas Yownie's the fell yin. Ye'll no fickle Thomas Yownie.'

Dougal extricated from his pouch the fag of a cigarette, lit it, and puffed meditatively. 'I did a reckonissince mysel' this morning. I was up at the Hoose afore it was light, and tried the door o' the coal-hole. I doot they've gotten on our tracks, for it was lockit – aye, and wedged from the inside.'

Dickson brightened. Was the insane venture off?

'For a wee bit I was fair beat. But I mindit that the lassie was allowed to walk in a kind o' a glass hoose on the side farthest away from the Garple. That was where she was singin' yest'reen. So I reckonissinced in that direction, and I fund a queer place.' *Sacred Songs and Solos* was requisitioned, and on a page of it Dougal proceeded to make marks with the stump of a carpenter's pencil. 'See here,' he commanded. 'There's the glass place wi' a door into the Hoose. That door maun be open or the lassie maun hae the key, for she comes there whenever she likes. Now, at each end o' the place the doors are lockit, but the front that looks on the garden is open, wi' muckle posts and flower-pots. The trouble is that that side there's maybe twenty feet o' a wall between the pawrapet and the ground. It's an auld wall wi' cracks and holes in it, and it wouldn't be ill to sklim. That's why they let her gang there when she wants, for a lassie couldn't get away without breakin' her neck.'

'Could we climb it?' Heritage asked.

The boy wrinkled his brows. 'I could manage it mysel' – I think – and maybe you. I doubt if auld McCunn could get up. Ye'd have to be mighty carefu' that nobody saw ye, for your hinder end, as ye were sklimmin', wad be a grand mark for a gun.'

'Lead on,' said Heritage. 'We'll try the veranda.'

They both looked at Dickson, and Dickson, scarlet in the face, looked back at them. He had suddenly found the thought of a solitary march to Auchenlochan intolerable. Once again he was at the parting of the ways, and once more caprice determined his decision. That the coal-hole was out of the question had worked a change in his views. Somehow it seemed to him less burglarious to enter by a veranda. He felt very frightened but – for the moment – quite resolute.

'I'm coming with you,' he said.

'Sportsman,' said Heritage, and held out his hand. 'Well

done, the auld yin,' said the Chieftain of the Gorbals Die-Hards. Dickson's quaking heart experienced a momentary bound as he followed Heritage down the track into the Garple Dean.

The track wound through a thick covert of hazels, now close to the rushing water, now high upon the bank so that clear sky showed through the fringes of the wood. When they had gone a little way Dougal halted them.

'It's a ticklish job,' he whispered. 'There's the tinklers, mind, that's campin' in the Dean. If they're still in their camp we can get by easy enough, but they're maybe wanderin' about the wud after rabbits . . . Then we maun ford the water, for ye'll no' cross it lower down where it's deep . . . Our road is on the Hoose side o' the Dean, and it's awfu' public if there's onybody on the other side, though it's hid well enough from folk up in the policies . . . Ye maun do exactly what I tell ye. When we get near danger I'll scout on ahead, and I daur ye to move a hair o' your heid till I give the word.'

Presently, when they were at the edge of the water, Dougal announced his intention of crossing. Three boulders in the stream made a bridge for an active man, and Heritage hopped lightly over. Not so Dickson, who stuck fast on the second stone, and would certainly have fallen in had not Dougal plunged into the current and steadied him with a grimy hand. The leap was at last successfully taken, and the three scrambled up a rough scaur, all reddened with iron springs, till they struck a slender track running down the Dean on its northern side. Here the undergrowth was very thick, and they had gone the better part of half a mile before the covert thinned sufficiently to show them the stream beneath. Then Dougal halted them with a finger on his lips, and crept forward alone.

He returned in three minutes. 'Coast's clear,' he whispered. 'The tinklers are eatin' their breakfast. They're late at their meat though they're up early seekin' it.'

Progress was now very slow and secret, and mainly on all fours. At one point Dougal nodded downward, and the other two saw on a patch of turf, where the Garple began to widen into its estuary, a group of figures round a small fire. There were four of them, all men, and Dickson thought he had never seen such ruffianly-looking customers. After that they moved high up the slope, in a shallow glade of a tributary burn, till they came out of the trees and found themselves looking seaward.

On one side was the House, a hundred yards or so back from the edge, the roof showing above the precipitous scarp. Half-way down the slope became easier, a jumble of boulders and boiler-plates, till it reached the waters of the small haven, which lay calm as a mill-pond in the windless forenoon. The haven broadened out at its foot and revealed a segment of blue sea. The opposite shore was flatter, and showed what looked like an old wharf and the ruins of buildings, behind which rose a bank clad with scrub and surmounted by some gnarled and wind-crooked firs.

'There's dashed little cover here,' said Heritage.

'There's no muckle,' Dougal assented. 'But they canna see us from the policies, and it's no' like there's anybody watchin' from the Hoose. The danger is somebody on the other side, but we'll have to risk it. Once among thae big stones we're safe. Are ye ready?'

Five minutes later Dickson found himself gasping in the lee of a boulder, while Dougal was making a cast forward. The scout returned with a hopeful report. 'I think we're safe till we get into the policies. There's a road that the auld folk made when ships used to come here. Down there it's deeper than Clyde at the Broomielaw. Has the auld yin got his wind yet? There's no time to waste.'

Up that broken hillside they crawled, well in the cover of the tumbled stones, till they reached a low wall which was the boundary of the garden. The House was now behind them on their right rear, and as they topped the crest they had a glimpse of an ancient dovecot and the ruins of the old Huntingtower on the short thymy turf which ran seaward to the cliffs. Dougal led them along a sunk fence which divided the downs from the lawns behind the house, and, avoiding the stables, brought them by devious ways to a thicket of rhododendrons and broom. On all fours they travelled the length of the place, and came to the edge where some forgotten gardeners had once tended a herbaceous border. The border was now rank and wild, and, lying flat under the shade of an azalea and peering through the young spears of iris, Dickson and Heritage regarded the north-western façade of the house.

The ground before them had been a sunken garden, from which a steep wall, once covered with creepers and rock plants, rose to a long veranda, which was pillared and open on that side; but at each end built up half-way and glazed for the rest. There was a glass roof, and inside untended shrubs sprawled in broken plaster vases.

'Ye maun bide here,' said Dougal, 'and no cheep above your breath. Afore we dare to try that wall, I maun ken where Lean and Spittal and Dobson are. I'm off to spy the policies.' He glided out of sight behind a clump of pampas grass.

For hours, so it seemed, Dickson was left to his own unpleasant reflexions. His body, prone on the moist earth, was fairly comfortable, but his mind was ill at ease. The scramble up the hillside had convinced him that he was growing old, and there was no rebound in his soul to counter the conviction. He felt listless, spiritless – an apathy with fright trembling somewhere at the back of it. He regarded the veranda wall with foreboding. How on earth could he climb that? And if he did there would be his exposed hinder-parts inviting a shot from some malevolent gentleman among the trees. He reflected that he would give a large sum of money to be out of this preposterous adventure.

Heritage's hand was stretched towards him, containing two of Mrs Morran's jellied scones, of which the Poet had been wise enough to bring a supply in his pocket. The food cheered him, for he was growing very hungry, and he began to take an interest in the scene before him instead of his own thoughts. He observed every detail of the veranda. There was a door at one end, he noted, giving on a path which wound down to the sunk garden. As he looked he heard a sound of steps and saw a man ascending this path.

It was the lame man whom Dougal had called Spittal, the dweller in the South Lodge. Seen at closer quarters he was an odd-looking being, lean as a heron, wry-necked, but amazingly quick on his feet. Had not Mrs Morran said that he hobbled as fast as other folk ran? He kept his eyes on the ground and seemed to be talking to himself as he went, but he was alert enough, for the dropping of a twig from a dying magnolia transferred him in an instant into a figure of active vigilance. No risks could be run with that watcher. He took a key from his pocket, opened the garden door, and entered the veranda. For a moment his shuffle sounded on its tiled floor, and then he entered the door admitting from the veranda to the House. It was clearly unlocked, for there came no sound of a turning key.

Dickson had finished the last crumbs of his scones before the man emerged again. He seemed to be in a greater hurry than ever as he locked the garden door behind him and hobbled along the west front of the House till he was lost to sight. After that the time passed slowly. A pair of yellow wagtails arrived and played at hide-and-seek among the stuccoed pillars. The little dry scratch of their claws was heard clearly in the still air. Dickson had almost fallen asleep when a smothered exclamation from Heritage woke him to attention. A girl had appeared in the veranda.

Above the parapet he saw only her body from the waist up. She seemed to be clad in bright colours, for something red was round her shoulders and her hair was bound with an orange scarf. She was tall – that he could tell, tall and slim and very young. Her face was turned seaward, and she stood for a little scanning the broad channel, shading her eyes as if to search for something on the extreme horizon. The air was very quiet and he thought that he could hear her sigh. Then she turned and re-entered the House, while Heritage by his side began to curse under his breath with a shocking fervour.

One of Dickson's troubles had been that he did not really believe Dougal's story, and the sight of the girl removed one doubt. That bright exotic thing did not belong to the Cruives or to Scotland at all, and that she should be in the House removed the place from the conventional dwelling to which the laws against burglary applied.

There was a rustle among the rhododendrons and the fiery face of Dougal appeared. He lay between the other two, his chin on his hands, and grunted out his report.

'After they had their dinner Dobson and Lean yokit a horse and went off to Auchenlochan. I seen them pass the Garple brig, so that's two accounted for. Has Spittal been round here?'

'Half an hour ago,' said Heritage, consulting a wrist watch.

'It was him that keepit me waitin' so long. But he's safe enough now, for five minutes syne he was splittin' firewood at the back door o' his hoose . . . I've found a ladder, an auld yin in ahint yon lot o' bushes. It'll help wi' the wall. There! I've gotten my breath again and we can start.'

The ladder was fetched by Heritage and proved to be ancient and wanting many rungs, but sufficient in length. The three stood silent for a moment, listening like stags, and then ran across the intervening lawn to the foot of the veranda wall. Dougal went up first, then Heritage, and lastly Dickson, stiff and giddy from his long lie under the bushes. Below the parapet the veranda floor was heaped with old garden litter, rotten matting, dead or derelict bulbs, fibre, withies, and strawberry nets. It was Dougal's intention to pull up the ladder and hide it among the rubbish against the hour of departure. But Dickson had barely put his foot on the parapet when there was a sound of steps within the House approaching the veranda door.

The ladder was left alone. Dougal's hand brought Dickson summarily to the floor, where he was fairly well concealed by a mess of matting. Unfortunately his head was in the vicinity of some upturned pot-plants, so that a cactus tickled his brow and a spike of aloe supported painfully the back of his neck. Heritage was prone behind two old water-butts, and Dougal was in a hamper which had once contained seed potatoes. The house door had panels of opaque glass, so the new-comer could not see the doings of the three till it was opened, and by that time all were in cover.

The man – it was Spittal – walked rapidly along the veranda and out of the garden door. He was talking to himself again, and Dickson, who had a glimpse of his face, thought he looked both evil and furious. Then came some anxious moments, for had the man glanced back when he was once outside, he must have seen the tell-tale ladder. But he seemed immersed in his own reflexions, for he hobbled steadily along the house front till he was lost to sight.

'That'll be the end o' them the day,' said Dougal, as he helped Heritage to pull up the ladder and stow it away. 'We've got the place to oursels, now. Forward, men, forward.' He tried the handle of the House door and led the way in.

A narrow paved passage took them into what had once been the garden room, where the lady of the house had arranged her flowers, and the tennis racquets and croquet mallets had been kept. It was very dusty, and on the cobwebbed walls still hung a few soiled garden overalls. A door beyond opened into a huge murky hall, murky, for the windows were shuttered, and the only light came through things like port-holes far up in the wall. Dougal, who seemed to know his way about, halted them. 'Stop here till I scout a bit. The women bide in a wee room through that muckle door.' Bare feet stole across the oak flooring, there was the sound of a door swinging on its hinges, and then silence and darkness. Dickson put out a hand for companionship and clutched Heritage's; to his surprise it was cold and all a-tremble. They listened for voices, and thought they could detect a far-away sob.

It was some minutes before Dougal returned. 'A bonny kettle o' fish,' he whispered. 'They're both greetin'. We're just in time. Come on, the pair o' ye.'

Through a green baize door they entered a passage which led to the kitchen regions, and turned in at the first door on their right. From its situation Dickson calculated that the room lay on the seaward side of the House next to the veranda. The light was bad, for the two windows were partially shuttered, but it had plainly been a smoking-room, for there were pipe-racks by the hearth, and on the walls a number of old school and college photographs, a couple of oars with emblazoned names, and a variety of stags' and roebucks' heads. There was no fire in the grate, but a small oil-stove burned inside the fender. In a stiff-backed chair sat an elderly woman, who seemed to feel the cold, for she was muffled to the neck in a fur coat. Beside her, so that the late afternoon light caught her face and head, stood a girl.

Dickson's first impression was of a tall child. The pose, startled and wild and yet curiously stiff and self-conscious, was that of a child striving to remember a forgotten lesson. One hand clutched a handkerchief, the other was closing and unclosing on a knob of the chair back. She was staring at Dougal, who stood like a gnome in the centre of the floor. 'Here's the gentlemen I was tellin' ye about,' was his introduction, but her eyes did not move.

Then Heritage stepped forward. 'We have met before, Mademoiselle,' he said. 'Do you remember Easter in 1918 – in the house in the Trinità dei Monti?'

The girl looked at him.

'I do not remember,' she said slowly.

'But I was the English officer who had the apartments on the floor below you. I saw you every morning. You spoke to me sometimes.'

'You are a soldier?' she asked, with a new note in her voice.

'I was then – till the war finished.'

'And now? Why have you come here?'

'To offer you help if you need it. If not, to ask your pardon and go away.'

The shrouded figure in the chair burst suddenly into rapid hysterical talk in some foreign tongue which Dickson suspected of being French. Heritage replied in the same language, and the girl joined in with sharp questions. Then the Poet turned to Dickson.

'This is my friend. If you will trust us we will do our best to help you.'

The eyes rested on Dickson's face, and he realized that he was in the presence of something the like of which he had never met in his life before. It was a loveliness greater than he had imagined was permitted by the Almighty to His creatures.

The little face was more square than oval, with a low broad brow and proud exquisite eyebrows. The eyes were of a colour which he could never decide on; afterwards he used to allege obscurely that they were the colour of everything in spring. There was a delicate pallor in the cheeks, and the face bore signs of suffering and care, possibly even of hunger; but for all that there was youth there, eternal and triumphant! Not youth such as he had known it, but youth with all history behind it, youth with centuries of command in its blood and the world's treasures of beauty and pride in its ancestry. Strange, he thought, that a thing so fine should be so masterful. He felt abashed in every inch of him.

As the eyes rested on him their sorrowfulness seemed to be shot with humour. A ghost of a smile lurked there, to which Dickson promptly responded. He grinned and bowed.

'Very pleased to meet you, Mem. I'm Mr McCunn from Glasgow.'

'You don't even know my name,' she said.

'We don't,' said Heritage.

'They call me Saskia. This,' nodding to the chair, 'is my cousin Eugénie . . . We are in very great trouble. But why should I tell you? I do not know you. You cannot help me.'

'We can try,' said Heritage. 'Part of your trouble we know already through that boy. You are imprisoned in this place by scoundrels. We are here to help you to get out. We want to ask no questions – only to do what you bid us.'

'You are not strong enough,' she said sadly. 'A young man – an old man – and a little boy. There are many against us, and any moment there may be more.'

It was Dougal's turn to break in. 'There's Lean and Spittal and Dobson and four tinklers in the Dean – that's seven; but there's us three and five more Gorbals Die-Hards – that's eight.'

There was something in the boy's truculent courage that cheered her.

'I wonder,' she said, and her eyes fell on each in turn.

Dickson felt impelled to intervene.

'I think this is a perfectly simple business. Here's a lady shut up in this house against her will by a wheen blagyirds. This is a free country and the law doesn't permit that. My advice is for one of us to inform the police at Auchenlochan and get Dobson and his friends took up and the lady set free to do what she likes. That is, if these folks are really molesting her, which is not yet quite clear to my mind.'

'Alas! It is not so simple as that,' she said. 'I dare not invoke your English law, for perhaps in the eyes of that law I am a thief.'

'Deary me, that's a bad business,' said the startled Dickson.

The two women talked together in some strange tongue, and the elder appeared to be pleading and the younger objecting. Then Saskia seemed to come to a decision.

'I will tell you all,' and she looked straight at Heritage. 'I do not think you would be cruel or false, for you have honourable faces . . . Listen, then. I am a Russian, and for two years have been an exile. I will not speak of my house, for it is no more, or how I escaped, for it is the common tale of all of us. I have seen things more terrible than any dream and yet lived, but I have paid a price for such experience. First I went to Italy where there were friends, and I wished only to have peace among kindly people. About poverty I do not care, for, to us, who have lost all the great things, the want of bread is a little matter. But peace was forbidden me, for I learned that we Russians had to win back our fatherland again, and that the weakest must work in that cause. So I was set my task, and it was very hard . . . There were jewels which once belonged to my Emperor – they had been stolen by the brigands and must be recovered. There were others still hidden in Russia which must be brought to a safe place. In that work I was ordered to share.'

She spoke in almost perfect English, with a certain foreign precision. Suddenly she changed to French, and talked rapidly to Heritage.

'She has told me about her family,' he said, turning to Dickson. 'It is among the greatest in Russia, the very greatest after the throne.' Dickson could only stare.

'Our enemies soon discovered me,' she went on. 'Oh, but

they are very clever, these enemies, and they have all the criminals of the world to aid them. Here you do not understand what they are. You good people in England think they are well-meaning dreamers who are forced into violence by the persecution of Western Europe. But you are wrong. Some honest fools there are among them, but the power – the true power – lies with madmen and degenerates, and they have for allies the special devil that dwells in each country. That is why they cast their nets as wide as mankind.'

She shivered, and for a second her face wore a look which Dickson never forgot, the look of one who has looked over the edge of life into the outer dark.

'There were certain jewels of great price which were about to be turned into guns and armies for our enemies. These our people recovered, and the charge of them was laid on me. Who would suspect, they said, a foolish girl? But our enemies were very clever, and soon the hunt was cried against me. They tried to rob me of them, but they failed, for I too had become clever. Then they asked the help of the law – first in Italy and then in France. Oh, it was subtly done. Respectable bourgeois, who hated the Bolsheviki but had bought long ago the bonds of my country, desired to be repaid their debts out of the property of the Russian Crown which might be found in the West. But behind them were the Jews, and behind the Jews our unsleeping enemies. Once I was enmeshed in the law I would be safe for them, and presently they would find the hiding-place of the treasure, and while the bourgeois were clamouring in the courts it would be safe in their pockets. So I fled. For months I have been fleeing and hiding. They have tried to kidnap me many times, and once they have tried to kill me, but I, too, have become clever – oh, so clever. And I have learned not to fear.'

This simple recital affected Dickson's honest soul with the liveliest indignation. 'Sich doings!' he exclaimed, and he could not forbear from whispering to Heritage an extract from that gentleman's conversation the first night at Kirkmichael. 'We needn't imitate all their methods, but they've got hold of the right end of the stick. They seek truth and reality.' The reply from the Poet was an angry shrug.

'Why and how did you come here?' he asked.

'I always meant to come to England, for I thought it the sanest place in a mad world. Also it is a good country to hide in, for it is apart from Europe, and your police, as I thought, do not permit evil men to be their own law. But especially I had a friend, a Scottish gentleman, whom I knew in the days when we Russians were still a nation. I saw him again in Italy, and since he was kind and brave I told him some part of my troubles. He was called Quentin Kennedy, and now he is dead. He told me that in Scotland he had a lonely château, where I could hide secretly and safely, and against the day when I might be hard-pressed he gave me a letter to his steward, bidding him welcome me as a guest when I made application. At that time I did not think I would need such sanctuary, but a month ago the need became urgent, for the hunt in France was very close on me. So I sent a message to the steward as Captain Kennedy told me.'

'What is his name?' Heritage asked.

She spelt it, 'Monsieur Loudon – L-O-U-D-O-N in the town of Auchenlochan.'

'The factor,' said Dickson. 'And what then?'

'Some spy must have found me out. I had a letter from this Loudon bidding me come to Auchenlochan. There I found no steward to receive me, but another letter saying that that night a carriage would be in waiting to bring me here. It was midnight when we arrived, and we were brought in by strange ways to this house, with no light but a single candle. Here we were welcomed indeed, but by an enemy.'

'Which?' asked Heritage. 'Dobson or Lean or Spittal?'

'Dobson I do not know. Léon was there. He is no Russian, but a Belgian who was a valet in my father's service till he joined the Bolsheviki. Next day the Lett Spidel came, and I knew that I was in very truth entrapped. For of all our enemies he is, save one, the most subtle and unwearied.'

Her voice had trailed off into flat weariness. Again Dickson was reminded of a child, for her arms hung limp by her side; and her slim figure in its odd clothes was curiously like that of a boy in a school blazer. Another resemblance perplexed him.

She had a hint of Janet – about the mouth – Janet, that solemn little girl those twenty years in her grave.

Heritage was wrinkling his brows. 'I don't think I quite understand. The jewels? You have them with you?'

She nodded.

'These men wanted to rob you. Why didn't they do it between here and Auchenlochan? You had no chance to hide them on the journey. Why did they let you come here where you were in a better position to baffle them?'

She shook her head. 'I cannot explain – except, perhaps, that Spidel had not arrived that night, and Léon may have been waiting instructions.'

The other still looked dissatisfied. 'They are either clumsier villains than I take them to be, or there is something deeper in the business than we understand. These jewels – are they here?'

His tone was so sharp that she looked startled – almost suspicious. Then she saw that in his face which reassured her. 'I have them hidden here. I have grown very skilful in hiding things.'

'Have they searched for them?'

'The first day they demanded them of me. I denied all knowledge. Then they ransacked this house – I think they ransack it daily, but I am too clever for them. I am not allowed to go beyond the veranda, and when at first I disobeyed there was always one of them in wait to force me back with a pistol behind my head. Every morning Léon brings us food for the day – good food, but not enough, so that Cousin Eugénie is always hungry, and each day he and Spidel question and threaten me. This afternoon Spidel has told me that their patience is at an end. He has given me till to-morrow at noon to produce the jewels. If not, he says I will die.'

'Mercy on us!' Dickson exclaimed.

'There will be no mercy for us,' she said solemnly. 'He and his kind think as little of shedding blood as of spilling water. But I do not think he will kill me. I think I will kill him first, but after that I shall surely die. As for Cousin Eugénie, I do not know.'

Her level matter-of-fact tone seemed to Dickson most shocking, for he could not treat it as mere melodrama. It carried a horrid conviction. 'We must get you out of this at once,' he declared.

'I cannot leave. I will tell you why. When I came to this country I appointed one to meet me here. He is a kinsman who knows England well, for he fought in your army. With him by my side I have no fear. It is altogether needful that I wait for him.'

'Then there is something more which you haven't told us?' Heritage asked.

Was there the faintest shadow of a blush on her cheek? 'There is something more,' she said.

She spoke to Heritage in French, and Dickson caught the name 'Alexis' and a word which sounded like 'prance'. The Poet listened eagerly and nodded. 'I have heard of him,' he said.

'But have you not seen him? A tall man with a yellow beard, who bears himself proudly. Being of my mother's race he has eyes like mine.'

'That's the man she was askin' me about yesterday,' said Dougal, who had squatted on the floor.

Heritage shook his head. 'We only came here last night. When did you expect Prince – your friend?'

'I hoped to find him here before me. Oh, it is his not coming that terrifies me. I must wait and hope. But if he does not come in time another may come before him.'

'The ones already here are not all the enemies that threaten you?'

'Indeed, no. The worst has still to come, and till I know he is here I do not greatly fear Spidel or Léon. They receive orders and do not give them.'

Heritage ran a perplexed hand through his hair. The sunset which had been flaming for some time in the unshuttered panes was now passing into the dark. The girl lit a lamp after first shuttering the rest of the windows. As she turned up the wick the odd dusty room and its strange company were revealed more clearly, and Dickson saw with a shock how haggard was the beautiful face. A great pity seized him and almost conquered his timidity.

'It is very difficult to help you,' Heritage was saying. 'You won't leave this place, and you won't claim the protection of the law. You are very independent, Mademoiselle, but it can't go on for ever. The man you fear may arrive at any moment. At any moment, too, your treasure may be discovered.'

'It is that that weighs on me,' she cried. 'The jewels! They are my solemn trust, but they burden me terribly. If I were only rid of them and knew them to be safe I should face the rest with a braver mind.'

'If you'll take my advice,' said Dickson slowly, 'you'll get them deposited in a bank and take a receipt for them. A Scotch bank is no' in a hurry to surrender a deposit without it gets the proper authority.'

Heritage brought his hands together with a smack. 'That's an idea. Will you trust us to take these things and deposit them safely?'

For a little she was silent and her eyes were fixed on each of the trio in turn. 'I will trust you,' she said at last. 'I think you will not betray me.'

'By God, we won't!' said the Poet fervently. 'Dogson, it's up to you. You march off to Glasgow in double quick time and place the stuff in your own name in your own bank. There's not a moment to lose. D'you hear?'

'I will that.' To his own surprise Dickson spoke without hesitation. Partly it was because of his merchant's sense of property, which made him hate the thought that miscreants should acquire that to which they had no title; but mainly it was the appeal in those haggard childish eyes. 'But I'm not going to be tramping the country in the night carrying a fortune and seeking for trains that aren't there. I'll go the first thing in the morning.'

'Where are they?' Heritage asked.

'That I do not tell. But I will fetch them.'

She left the room, and presently returned with three odd little parcels wrapped in leather and tied with thongs of raw hide. She gave them to Heritage, who held them appraisingly in his hand and then passed them to Dickson.

'I do not ask about their contents. We take them from you as they are, and, please God, when the moment comes they will be returned to you as you gave them. You trust us, Mademoiselle?'

'I trust you, for you are a soldier. Oh, and I thank you from my heart, my friends.' She held out a hand to each, which caused Heritage to grow suddenly very red.

'I will remain in the neighbourhood to await developments,' he said. 'We had better leave you now. Dougal, lead on.'

Before going, he took the girl's hand again, and with a sudden movement bent and kissed it. Dickson shook it heartily. 'Cheer up, Mem,' he observed. 'There's a better time coming.' His last recollection of her eyes was a soft mistiness not far from tears. His pouch and pipe had strange company jostling them in his pocket as he followed the others down the ladder into the night.

Dougal insisted that they must return by the road of the morning. 'We daren't go by the Laver, for that would bring us by the public-house. If the worst comes to the worst, and we fall in wi' any of the deevils, they must think ye've changed your mind and come back from Auchenlochan.'

The night smelt fresh and moist as if a break in the weather were imminent. As they scrambled along the Garple Dean a pinprick of light below showed where the tinklers were busy by their fire. Dickson's spirits suffered a sharp fall and he began to marvel at his temerity. What in Heaven's name had he undertaken? To carry very precious things, to which certainly he had no right, through the enemy to distant Glasgow. How could he escape the notice of the watchers? He was already suspect, and the sight of him back again in Dalquharter would double that suspicion. He must brazen it out, but he distrusted his powers with such tell-tale stuff in his pockets. They might murder him anywhere on the moor road or in an empty railway carriage. An unpleasant memory of various novels he had read in which such things happened haunted his mind . . .

There was just one consolation. This job over, he would be quit of the whole business. And honourably quit, too, for he would have played a manly part in a most unpleasant affair. He could retire to the idyllic with the knowledge that he had not been wanting when Romance called. Not a soul should ever hear of it, but he saw himself in the future tramping green roads or sitting by his winter fireside pleasantly retelling himself the tale.

Before they came to the Garple bridge Dougal insisted that they should separate, remarking that 'it would never do if we were seen thegither.' Heritage was despatched by a short cut over fields to the left, which eventually, after one or two plunges into ditches, landed him safely in Mrs Morran's back yard. Dickson and Dougal crossed the bridge and tramped Dalquharter-wards by the highway. There was no sign of human life in that quiet place with owls hooting and rabbits rustling in the undergrowth. Beyond the woods they came in sight of the light in the back kitchen, and both seemed to relax their watchfulness when it was most needed. Dougal sniffed the air and looked seaward.

'It's coming on to rain,' he observed. 'There should be a muckle star there, and when you can't see it it means wet weather wi' this wind.'

'What star?' Dickson asked.

'The one wi' the Irish-lukkin' name. What's that they call it? O'Brien?' And he pointed to where the constellation of the Hunter should have been declining on the western horizon.

There was a bend of the road behind them, and suddenly round it came a dogcart driven rapidly. Dougal slipped like a weasel into a bush, and presently Dickson stood revealed in the glare of a lamp. The horse was pulled up sharply and the driver called out to him. He saw that it was Dobson the innkeeper with Léon beside him.

'Who is it?' cried the voice. 'Oh, you! I thought ye were off the day?'

Dickson rose nobly to the occasion.

'I thought myself I was. But I didn't think much of Auchenlochan, and I took a fancy to come back and spend the last night of my holiday with my Auntie. I'm off to Glasgow first thing the morn's morn.'

'So!' said the voice. 'Queer thing I never saw ye on the Auchenlochan road, where ye can see three mile before ye.'

'I left early and took it easy along the shore.'

'Did ye so? Well, good-night to ye.'

Five minutes later Dickson walked into Mrs Morran's kitchen, where Heritage was busy making up for a day of short provender.

'I'm for Glasgow to-morrow, Auntie Phemie,' he cried. 'I want you to loan me a wee trunk with a key, and steek the door and windows, for I've a lot to tell you.'

CHAPTER SIX

# HOW MR McCUNN DEPARTED WITH RELIEF AND RETURNED WITH RESOLUTION

AT seven o'clock on the following morning the post-cart, summoned by an early message from Mrs Morran, appeared outside the cottage. In it sat the ancient postman, whose real home was Auchenlochan, but who slept alternate nights in Dalquharter, and beside him Dobson the innkeeper. Dickson and his hostess stood at the garden-gate, the former with his pack on his back, and at his feet a small stout wooden box, of the kind in which cheeses are transported, garnished with an immense padlock. Heritage for obvious reasons did not appear; at the moment he was crouched on the floor of the loft watching the departure through a gap in the dimity curtains.

The traveller, after making sure that Dobson was looking, furtively slipped the key of the trunk into his knapsack.

'Well, good-bye, Auntie Phemie,' he said. 'I'm sure you've been awful kind to me, and I don't know how to thank you for all you're sending.'

'Tuts, Dickson, my man, they're hungry folk about Glesca that'll be glad o' my scones and jeelie. Tell Mirren I'm rale pleased wi' her man, and haste ye back soon.'

The trunk was deposited on the floor of the cart, and Dickson clambered into the back seat. He was thankful that he had not to sit next to Dobson, for he had tell-tale stuff on his person. The morning was wet, so he wore his waterproof, which concealed his odd tendency to stoutness about the middle.

Mrs Morran played her part well, with all the becoming gravity of an affectionate aunt, but as soon as the post-cart turned the bend of the road her demeanour changed. She was torn with convulsions of silent laughter. She retreated to the kitchen, sank into a chair, wrapped her face in her apron and rocked. Heritage, descending, found her struggling to regain composure. 'D'ye ken his wife's name?' she gasped. 'I ca'ed her Mirren! And maybe the body's no' mairried! Hech sirs! Hech sirs!'

Meantime Dickson was bumping along the moor-road on the back of the post-cart. He had worked out a plan, just as he had been used aforetime to devise a deal in foodstuffs. He had expected one of the watchers to turn up, and was rather relieved that it should be Dobson, whom he regarded as 'the most natural beast' of the three. Somehow he did not think that he would be molested before he reached the station, since his enemies would still be undecided in their minds. Probably they only wanted to make sure that he had really departed to forget all about him. But if not, he had his plan ready.

'Are you travelling to-day?' he asked the innkeeper.

'Just as far as the station to see about some oil-cake I'm expectin'. What's in your wee kist? Ye came here wi' nothing but the bag on your back.'

'Ay, the kist is no' mine. It's my auntie's. She's a kind body, and nothing would serve but she must pack a box for me to take back. Let me see. There's a baking of scones; three pots of honey and one of rhubarb jam – she was aye famous for her rhubarb jam; a mutton ham, which you can't get for love or money in Glasgow; some home-made black puddings, and a wee skim-milk cheese. I doubt I'll have to take a cab from the station.'

Dobson appeared satisfied, lit a short pipe, and relapsed into meditation. The long uphill road, ever climbing to where far off showed the tiny whitewashed buildings which were the railway station, seemed interminable this morning. The aged postman addressed strange objurgations to his aged horse and muttered reflexions to himself, the innkeeper smoked, and Dickson stared back into the misty hollow where lay Dalquharter. The south-west wind had brought up a screen of rain clouds and washed all the countryside in a soft wet grey. But the eye could still travel a fair distance, and Dickson thought he had a glimpse of a figure on a bicycle leaving the village two miles back. He wondered who it could be. Not Heritage, who had no bicycle. Perhaps some woman who was conspicuously late for the train. Women were the chief cyclists nowadays in country places.

Then he forgot about the bicycle and twisted his neck to watch the station. It was less than a mile off now, and they had no time to spare, for away to the south among the hummocks of the bog he saw the smoke of the train coming from Auchenlochan. The postman also saw it and whipped up his beast into a clumsy canter. Dickson, always nervous about being late for trains, forced his eyes away and regarded again the road behind him. Suddenly the cyclist had become quite plain – a little more than a mile behind – a man, and pedalling furiously in spite of the stiff ascent . . . It could only be one person – Léon. He must have discovered their visit to the House yesterday and be on the way to warn Dobson. If he reached the station before the train, there would be no journey to Glasgow that day for one respectable citizen.

Dickson was in a fever of impatience and fright. He dared not adjure the postman to hurry, lest Dobson should turn his head and descry his colleague. But the ancient man had begun to realize the shortness of time and was urging the cart along at a fair pace, since they were now on the flatter shelf of land which carried the railway. Dickson kept his eyes fixed on the bicycle and his teeth shut tight on his lower lip. Now it was hidden by the last dip of hill; now it emerged into view not a quarter of a mile behind, and its rider gave vent to a shrill call. Luckily the innkeeper did not hear, for at that moment with a jolt the cart pulled up at the station door, accompanied by the roar of the incoming train.

Dickson whipped down from the back seat and seized the solitary porter. 'Label the box for Glasgow and into the van with it. Quick, man, and there'll be a shilling for you.' He had been doing some rapid thinking these last minutes and had made up his mind. If Dobson and he were alone in a carriage he could not have the box there; that must be elsewhere, so that Dobson could not examine it if he were set on violence, somewhere in which it could still be a focus of suspicion and attract attention from his person. He took his ticket, and rushed on to the platform, to find the porter and the box at the door of the guard's van. Dobson was not there. With the vigour of a fussy traveller he shouted directions to the guard to take good care of his luggage, hurled a shilling at the porter, and ran for a carriage. At that moment he became aware of Dobson hurrying through the entrance. He must have met Léon and heard news from him, for his face was red and his ugly brows darkening.

The train was in motion. 'Here, you!' Dobson's voice shouted. 'Stop! I want a word wi' ye.' Dickson plunged at a third-class carriage, for he saw faces behind the misty panes, and above all things then he feared an empty compartment. He clambered on to the step, but the handle would not turn, and with a sharp pang of fear he felt the innkeeper's grip on his arm. Then some Samaritan from within let down the window, opened the door, and pulled him up. He fell on a seat, and a second later Dobson staggered in beside him.

Thank Heaven, the dirty little carriage was nearly full. There were two herds, each with a dog and a long hazel crook, and an elderly woman who looked like a ploughman's wife out for a day's marketing. And there was one other whom Dickson recognized with peculiar joy – the bagman in the provision line of business whom he had met three days before at Kilchrist.

The recognition was mutual. 'Mr McCunn!' the bagman exclaimed. 'My, but that was running it fine! I hope you've had a pleasant holiday, sir?'

'Very pleasant. I've been spending two nights with friends down hereaways. I've been very fortunate in the weather, for it has broke just when I'm leaving.'

Dickson sank back on the hard cushions. It had been a near thing, but so far he had won. He wished his heart did not beat so fast, and he hoped he did not betray his disorder in his face. Very deliberately he hunted for his pipe and filled it slowly. Then he turned to Dobson. 'I didn't know you were travelling the day. What about your oil-cake?'

'I've changed my mind,' was the gruff answer.

'Was that you I heard crying on me when we were running for the train?'

'Ay. I thought ye had forgot about your kist.'

'No fear,' said Dickson. 'I'm no' likely to forget my auntie's scones.'

He laughed pleasantly and then turned to the bagman. Thereafter the compartment hummed with the technicalities of the grocery trade. He exerted himself to draw out his companion, to have him refer to the great firm of D. McCunn, so that the innkeeper might be ashamed of his suspicions. What nonsense to imagine that a noted and wealthy Glasgow merchant – the bagman's tone was almost reverential – would concern himself with the affairs of a forgotten village and a tumbledown house!

Presently the train drew up at Kirkmichael station. The woman descended, and Dobson, after making sure that no one else meant to follow her example, also left the carriage. A porter was shouting: 'Fast train to Glasgow – Glasgow next stop.' Dickson watched the innkeeper shoulder his way through the crowd in the direction of the booking office. 'He's off to send a telegram,' he decided. 'There'll be trouble waiting for me at the other end.'

When the train moved on he found himself disinclined for further talk. He had suddenly become meditative, and curled up in a corner with his head hard against the window pane, watching the wet fields and glistening roads as they slipped past. He had his plans made for his conduct at Glasgow, but, Lord! how he loathed the whole business! Last night he had had a kind of gusto in his desire to circumvent villainy; at Dalquharter station he had enjoyed a momentary sense of triumph; now he felt very small, lonely, and forlorn. Only one thought far at the back of his mind cropped up now and then to give him comfort. He was entering on the last lap. Once get this detestable errand done and he would be a free man, free to go back to the kindly humdrum life from which he should never have strayed. Never again, he vowed, never again. Rather would he spend the rest of his days in hydropathics than come within the pale of such horrible adventure. Romance, forsooth! This was not the mild goddess he had sought, but an awful harpy who battened on the souls of men.

He had some bad minutes as the train passed through the suburbs and along the grimy embankment by which the southern lines enter the city. But as it rumbled over the river bridge and slowed down before the terminus his vitality suddenly revived. He was a business man, and there was now something for him to do.

After a rapid farewell to the bagman, he found a porter and hustled his box out of the van in the direction of the left-luggage office. Spies, summoned by Dobson's telegram, were, he was convinced, watching his every movement, and he meant to see that they missed nothing. He received his ticket for the box, and slowly and ostentatiously stowed it away in his pack. Swinging the said pack on his arm, he sauntered through the entrance hall to the row of waiting taxi-cabs, and selected that one which seemed to him to have the oldest and most doddering driver. He deposited the pack inside on the seat, and then stood still as if struck with a sudden thought.

'I breakfasted terrible early,' he told the driver. 'I think I'll have a bite to eat. Will you wait?'

'Ay,' said the man, who was reading a grubby sheet of newspaper. 'I'll wait as long as ye like, for it's you that pays.'

Dickson left his pack in the cab and, oddly enough for a careful man, he did not shut the door. He re-entered the station, strolled to the bookstall, and bought a *Glasgow Herald*. His steps then tended to the refreshment-room, where he ordered a cup of coffee and two Bath buns, and seated himself at a small table. There he was soon immersed in the financial news, and though he sipped his coffee he left the buns untasted. He took out a penknife and cut various extracts from the *Herald*, bestowing them carefully in his pocket. An observer would have seen an elderly gentleman absorbed in market quotations.

After a quarter of an hour had been spent in this performance he happened to glance at the clock and rose with an exclamation. He bustled out to his taxi and found the driver still intent upon his reading. 'Here I am at last,' he said cheerily, and had a foot on the step, when he stopped suddenly with a cry. It was a cry of alarm, but also of satisfaction.

'What's become of my pack? I left it on the seat, and now it's gone! There's been a thief here.'

The driver, roused from his lethargy, protested in the name of his gods that no one had been near it. 'Ye took it into the station wi' ye,' he urged.

'I did nothing of the kind. Just you wait here till I see the inspector. A bonny watch *you* keep on a gentleman's things.'

But Dickson did not interview the railway authorities. Instead he hurried to the left-luggage office. 'I deposited a small box here a short time ago. I mind the number. Is it there still?'

The attendant glanced at the shelf. 'A wee deal box with iron bands. It was took out ten minutes syne. A man brought the ticket and took it away on his shoulder.'

'Thank you. There's been a mistake, but the blame's mine. My man mistook my orders.'

Then he returned to the now nervous taxi-driver. 'I've taken it up with the station-master and he's putting the police on. You'll likely be wanted, so I gave him your number. It's a fair disgrace that there should be so many thieves about this station. It's not the first time I've lost things. Drive me to West George Street and look sharp.' And he slammed the door with the violence of an angry man.

But his reflexions were not violent, for he smiled to himself. 'That was pretty neat. They'll take some time to get the kist open, for I dropped the key out of the train after we left Kirkmichael. That gives me a fair start. If I hadn't thought of that, they'd have found some way to grip me and ripe me long before I got to the Bank.' He shuddered as he thought of the dangers he had escaped. 'As it is, they're off the track for half an hour at least, while they're rummaging among Auntie Phemie's scones.' At the thought he laughed heartily, and when he brought the taxi-cab to a standstill by rapping on the front window, he left it with a temper apparently restored. Obviously he had no grudge against the driver, who to his immense surprise was rewarded with ten shillings.

Three minutes later Mr McCunn might have been seen entering the head office of the Strathclyde Bank and inquiring for the manager. There was no hesitation about him now, for his foot was on his native heath. The chief cashier received him with deference in spite of his unorthodox garb, for he was not the least honoured of the bank's customers. As it chanced he had been talking about him that very morning to a gentleman from London. 'The strength of this city,' he had said, tapping his eyeglasses on his knuckles, 'does not lie in its dozen very rich men, but in the hundred or two homely folk who make no parade of wealth. Men like Dickson McCunn, for example, who live all their life in a semi-detached villa and die worth half a million.' And the Londoner had cordially assented.

So Dickson was ushered promptly into an inner room, and was warmly greeted by Mr Mackintosh, the patron of the Gorbals Die-Hards.

'I must thank you for your generous donation, McCunn. Those boys will get a little fresh air and quiet after the smoke and din of Glasgow. A little country peace to smooth out the creases in their poor little souls.'

'Maybe,' said Dickson, with a vivid recollection of Dougal as he had last seen him. Somehow he did not think that peace was likely to be the portion of that devoted band. 'But I've not come here to speak about that.'

He took off his waterproof; then his coat and waistcoat; and showed himself a strange figure with sundry bulges about the middle. The manager's eyes grew very round. Presently these excrescences were revealed as linen bags sewn on to his shirt, and fitting into the hollow between ribs and hip. With some difficulty he slit the bags and extracted three hide-bound packages.

'See here, Mackintosh,' he said solemnly. 'I hand you over these parcels, and you're to put them in the innermost corner of your strong room. You needn't open them. Just put them away as they are, and write me a receipt for them. Write it now.'

Mr Mackintosh obediently took pen in hand.

'What'll I call them?' he asked.

'Just the three leather parcels handed to you by Dickson McCunn, Esq., naming the date.'

Mr Mackintosh wrote. He signed his name with his usual flourish and handed the slip to his client.

'Now,' said Dickson, 'you'll put that receipt in the strong box where you keep my securities, and you'll give it up to nobody but me in person and you'll surrender the parcels only on presentation of the receipt. D'you understand?'

'Perfectly. May I ask any questions?'

'You'd better not if you don't want to hear lees.'

'What's in the packages?' Mr Mackintosh weighed them in his hand.

'That's asking,' said Dickson. 'But I'll tell ye this much. It's jools.'

'Your own?'

'No, but I'm their trustee.'

'Valuable?'

'I was hearing they were worth more than a million pounds.'

'God bless my soul,' said the startled manager. 'I don't like this kind of business, McCunn.'

'No more do I. But you'll do it to oblige an old friend and a good customer. If you don't know much about the packages you know all about me. Now, mind, I trust you.'

Mr Mackintosh forced himself to a joke. 'Did you maybe steal them?'

Dickson grinned. 'Just what I did. And that being so, I want you to let me out by the back door.'

When he found himself in the street he felt the huge relief of a boy who had emerged with credit from the dentist's chair. Remembering that there would be no midday dinner for him at home, his first step was to feed heavily at a restaurant. He had, so far as he could see, surmounted all his troubles, his one regret being that he had lost his pack, which contained among other things his Izaak Walton and his safety razor. He bought another razor and a new Walton, and mounted an electric tram-car *en route* for home.

Very contented with himself he felt as the car swung across the Clyde bridge. He had done well – but of that he did not want to think, for the whole beastly thing was over. He was going to bury that memory, to be resurrected perhaps on a later day when the unpleasantness had been forgotten. Heritage had his address, and knew where to come when it was time to claim the jewels. As for the watchers, they must have ceased to suspect him, when they discovered the innocent contents of his knapsack and Mrs Morran's box. Home for him, and a luxurious tea by his own fireside; and then an evening with his books, for Heritage's nonsense had stimulated his literary fervour. He would dip into his old favourites again to confirm his faith. To-morrow he would go for a jaunt somewhere – perhaps down the Clyde, or to the South of England, which he had heard was a pleasant, thickly peopled country. No more lonely inns and deserted villages for him; henceforth he would make certain of comfort and peace.

The rain had stopped, and, as the car moved down the dreary vista of Eglinton Street, the sky opened into fields of blue and the April sun silvered the puddles. It was in such place and under such weather that Dickson suffered an overwhelming experience.

It is beyond my skill, being all unlearned in the game of psycho-analysis, to explain how this thing happened, I concern myself only with facts. Suddenly the pretty veil of self-satisfaction was rent from top to bottom, and Dickson saw a figure of himself within, a smug leaden little figure which simpered and preened itself and was hollow as a rotten nut. And he hated it.

The horrid truth burst on him that Heritage had been right. He only played with life. That imbecile image was a mere spectator, content to applaud, but shrinking from the contact of reality. It had been all right as a provision merchant, but when it fancied itself capable of higher things it had deceived itself. Foolish little image with its brave dreams and its swelling words from Browning! All make-believe of the feeblest. He was a coward, running away at the first threat of danger. It was as if he were watching a tall stranger with a wand pointing to the embarrassed phantom that was himself, and ruthlessly exposing its frailties! And yet the pitiless showman was himself too – himself as he wanted to be, cheerful, brave, resourceful, indomitable.

Dickson suffered a spasm of mortal agony. 'Oh, I'm surely not so bad as all that,' he groaned. But the hurt was not only in his pride. He saw himself being forced to new decisions, and each alternative was of the blackest. He fairly shivered with the horror of it. The car slipped past a suburban station from which passengers were emerging – comfortable black-coated men such as he had once been. He was bitterly angry with Providence for picking him out of the great crowd of sedentary folk for this sore ordeal. 'Why was I tethered to sich a conscience?' was his moan. But there was that stern inquisitor with his pointer exploring his soul. 'You flatter yourself you have done your share,' he was saying. 'You will make pretty stories about it to yourself, and some day you may tell your friends, modestly disclaiming any special credit. But you will be a liar, for you know you are afraid. You are running away when the work is scarcely begun, and leaving it to a few boys and a poet whom you had the impudence the other day to despise. I think you are worse than a coward. I think you are a cad.'

His fellow-passengers on the top of the car saw an absorbed middle-aged gentleman who seemed to have something the matter with his bronchial tubes. They could not guess at the tortured soul. The decision was coming nearer, the alternatives loomed up dark and inevitable. On one side was submission to ignominy, on the other a return to that place which he detested, and yet loathed himself for detesting. 'It seems I'm not likely to have much peace either way,' he reflected dismally.

How the conflict would have ended had it continued on these lines I cannot say. The soul of Mr McCunn was being assailed by moral and metaphysical adversaries with which he had not been trained to deal. But suddenly it leapt from negatives to positives. He saw the face of the girl in the shuttered House, so fair and young and yet so haggard. It seemed to be appealing to him to rescue it from a great loneliness and fear. Yes, he had been right, it had a strange look of his Janet – the wide-open eyes, the solemn mouth. What was to become of that child if he failed her in her need?

Now Dickson was a practical man, and this view of the case brought him into a world which he understood. 'It's fair ridiculous,' he reflected. 'Nobody there to take a grip of things. Just a wheen Gorbals keelies and the lad Heritage. Not a business man among the lot.'

The alternatives, which hove before him like two great banks of cloud, were altering their appearance. One was becoming faint and tenuous; the other, solid as ever, was just a shade less black. He lifted his eyes and saw in the near distance the corner of the road which led to his home. 'I must decide before I reach that corner,' he told himself.

Then his mind became apathetic. He began to whistle dismally through his teeth, watching the corner as it came nearer. The car stopped with a jerk. 'I'll go back,' he said aloud, clambering down the steps. The truth was he had decided five minutes before when he first saw Janet's face.

He walked briskly to his house, entirely refusing to waste any more energy on reflexion. 'This is a business proposition,' he told himself, 'and I'm going to handle it as sich.' Tibby was surprised to see him and offered him tea in vain. 'I'm just back for a few minutes. Let's see the letters.'

There was one from his wife. She proposed to stay another week at the Neuk Hydropathic and suggested that he might join her and bring her home. He sat down and wrote a long affectionate reply, declining, but expressing his delight that she was soon returning. 'That's very likely the last time Mamma will hear from me,' he reflected, but – oddly enough – without any great fluttering of the heart.

Then he proceeded to be furiously busy. He sent out Tibby to buy another knapsack and to order a cab and to cash a considerable cheque. In the knapsack he packed a fresh change of clothing and the new safety razor, but no books, for he was past the need of them. That done, he drove to his solicitors.

'What like a firm are Glendonan and Speirs in Edinburgh?' he asked the senior partner.

'Oh, very respectable. Very respectable indeed. Regular Edinburgh W.S. lot. Do a lot of factoring.'

'I want you to telephone through to them and inquire about a place in Carrick called Huntingtower, near the village of Dalquharter. I understand it's to let, and I'm thinking of taking a lease of it.'

The senior partner after some delay got through to Edinburgh, and was presently engaged in the feverish dialectic which the long-distance telephone involves. 'I want to speak to Mr Glendonan himself . . . Yes, yes, Mr Caw of Paton and Linklater . . . Good afternoon . . . Huntingtower. Yes, in Carrick. Not to let? But I understand it's been in the market for some months. You say you've an idea it has just been let. But my client is positive that you're mistaken, unless the agreement was made this morning . . . You'll inquire? Oh, I see. The actual factoring is done by your local agent, Mr James Loudon, in Auchenlochan. You think my client had better get into touch with him at once. Just wait a minute, please.'

He put his hand over the receiver. 'Usual Edinburgh way of doing business,' he observed caustically. 'What do you want done?'

'I'll run down and see this Loudon. Tell Glendonan and Spiers to advise him to expect me, for I'll go this very day.'

Mr Caw resumed his conversation. 'My client would like a telegram sent at once to Mr Loudon introducing him. He's Mr Dickson McCunn of Mearns Street – the great provision merchant, you know. Oh, yes! Good for any rent. Refer if you like to the Strathclyde Bank, but you can take my word for it. Thank you. Then that's settled. Good-bye.'

Dickson's next visit was to a gunmaker who was a fellow-elder with him in the Guthrie Memorial Kirk.

'I want a pistol and a lot of cartridges,' he announced. 'I'm not caring what kind it is, so long as it is a good one and not too big.'

'For yourself?' the gunmaker asked. 'You must have a licence, I doubt, and there's a lot of new regulations.'

'I can't wait on a licence. It's for a cousin of mine who's off to Mexico at once. You've got to find some way of obliging an old friend, Mr McNair.'

Mr McNair scratched his head. 'I don't see how I can sell you one. But I'll tell you what I'll do – I'll lend you one. It belongs to my nephew, Peter Tait, and has been lying in a drawer ever since he came back from the front. He has no use for it now that he's a placed minister.'

So Dickson bestowed in the pockets of his waterproof a service revolver and fifty cartridges, and bade his cab take him to the shop in Mearns Street. For a moment the sight of the familiar place struck a pang to his breast, but he choked down unavailing regrets. He ordered a great hamper of foodstuffs – the most delicate kind of tinned goods, two perfect hams, tongues, Strassburg pies, chocolate, cakes, biscuits, and, as a last thought, half a dozen bottles of old liqueur brandy. It was to be carefully packed, addressed to Mrs Morran, Dalquharter Station, and delivered in time for him to take down by the 7.33 train. Then he drove to the terminus and dined with something like a desperate peace in his heart.

On this occasion he took a first-class ticket, for he wanted to be alone. As the lights began to be lit in the wayside stations and the clear April dusk darkened into night, his thoughts were sombre yet resigned. He opened the window and let the sharp air of the Renfrewshire uplands fill the carriage. It was fine weather again after the rain, and a bright constellation – perhaps Dougal's friend O'Brien – hung in the western sky. How happy he would have been a week ago had he been starting thus for a country holiday! He could sniff the faint scent of moor-burn and ploughed earth which had always been his first reminder of spring. But he had been pitchforked out of that old happy world and could never enter it again. Alas! for the roadside fire, the cosy inn, the *Compleat Angler*, the Chavender or Chub!

And yet – and yet! He had done the right thing, though the Lord alone knew how it would end. He began to pluck courage from his very melancholy, and hope from his reflexions upon the transitoriness of life. He was austerely following Romance as he conceived it, and if that capricious lady had taken one dream from him she might yet reward him with a better. Tags of poetry came into his head which seemed to favour this philosophy – particularly some lines of Browning on which he used to discourse to his Kirk Literary Society. Uncommon silly, he considered, these homilies of his must have been, mere twitterings of the unfledged. But now he saw more in the lines, a deeper interpretation which he had earned the right to make.

*Oh world, where all things change and nought abides,*
*Oh life, the long mutation – is it so?*
*Is it with life as with the body's change? –*
*Where, e'en tho' better follow, good must pass.*

That was as far as he could get, though he cudgelled his memory to continue. Moralizing thus, he became drowsy, and was almost asleep when the train drew up at the station of Kirkmichael.

CHAPTER SEVEN

# SUNDRY DOINGS IN THE MIRK

FROM Kirkmichael on the train stopped at every station, but no passenger seemed to leave or arrive at the little platforms white in the moon. At Dalquharter the case of provisions was safely transferred to the porter with instructions to take charge of it till it was sent for. During the next ten minutes Dickson's mind began to work upon his problem with a certain briskness. It was all nonsense that the law of Scotland could not be summoned to the defence. The jewels had been safely got rid of, and who was to dispute their possession? Not Dobson and his crew, who had no sort of title, and were out for naked robbery. The girl had spoken of greater dangers from new enemies – kidnapping, perhaps. Well, that was felony, and the police must be brought in. Probably if all were known the three watchers had criminal records, pages long, filed at Scotland Yard. The man to deal with that side of the business was Loudon the factor, and to him he was bound in the first place. He had made a clear picture in his head of this Loudon – a derelict old country writer, formal, pedantic, lazy, anxious only to get an unprofitable business off his hands with the least possible trouble, never going near the place himself, and ably supported in his lethargy by conceited Edinburgh Writers to the Signet. 'Sich notions of business!' he murmured. 'I wonder that there's a single county family in Scotland no' in the bankruptcy court!' It was his mission to wake up Mr James Loudon.

Arrived at Auchenlochan he went first to the Salutation Hotel, a pretentious place sacred to golfers. There he engaged a bedroom for the night and, having certain scruples, paid for it in advance. He also had some sandwiches prepared which he stowed in his pack, and filled his flask with whisky. 'I'm going home to Glasgow by the first train to-morrow,' he told the landlady, 'and now I've got to see a friend. I'll not be back till late.' He was assured that there would be no difficulty about his admittance at any hour, and directed how to find Mr Loudon's dwelling.

It was an old house fronting direct on the street, with a fanlight above the door and a neat brass plate bearing the legend 'Mr James Loudon, Writer'. A lane ran up one side leading apparently to a garden, for the moonlight showed the dusk of trees. In front was the main street of Auchenlochan, now deserted save for a single roisterer, and opposite stood the ancient town house, with arches where the country folk came at the spring and autumn hiring fairs. Dickson rang the antiquated bell, and was presently admitted to a dark hall floored with oilcloth, where a single gas-jet showed that on one side was the business office and on the other the living-rooms. Mr Loudon was at supper, he was told, and he sent in his card. Almost at once the door at the end on the left side was flung open and a large figure appeared flourishing a napkin. 'Come in, sir, come in,' it cried. 'I've just finished a bite of meat. Very glad to see you. Here, Maggie, what d'you mean by keeping the gentleman standing in that outer darkness?'

The room into which Dickson was ushered was small and bright, with a red paper on the walls, a fire burning, and a big oil lamp in the centre of a table. Clearly Mr Loudon had no wife, for it was a bachelor's den in every line of it. A cloth was laid on a corner of the table, in which stood the remnants of a meal. Mr Loudon seemed to have been about to make a brew of punch, for a kettle simmered by the fire, and lemons and sugar flanked a pot-bellied whisky decanter of the type that used to be known as a 'mason's mell'.

The sight of the lawyer was a surprise to Dickson and dissipated his notions of an aged and lethargic incompetent. Mr Loudon was a strongly built man who could not be a year over fifty. He had a ruddy face, clean shaven except for a grizzled moustache; his grizzled hair was thinning round the temples; but his skin was unwrinkled and his eyes had all the vigour of youth. His tweed suit was well cut, and the buff waistcoat with flaps and pockets and the plain leather watchguard hinted at the sportsman, as did the half-dozen racing prints on the wall. A pleasant high-coloured figure he made; his voice had the frank ring due to much use out of doors; and his expression had the singular candour which comes from grey eyes with large pupils and a narrow iris.

'Sit down, Mr McCunn. Take the arm-chair by the fire. I've had a wire from Glendonan and Speirs about you. I was just going to have a glass of toddy – a grand thing for these uncertain April nights. You'll join me? No? Well, you'll smoke anyway. There's cigars at your elbow. Certainly, a pipe if you like. This is Liberty Hall.'

Dickson found some difficulty in the part for which he had cast himself. He had expected to condescend upon an elderly inept and give him sharp instructions; instead he found himself faced with a jovial, virile figure which certainly did not suggest incompetence. It has been mentioned already that he had always great difficulty in looking any one in the face, and this difficulty was intensified when he found himself confronted with bold and candid eyes. He felt abashed and a little nervous.

'I've come to see you about Huntingtower House,' he began.

'I know. So Glendonans informed me. Well, I'm very glad to hear it. The place has been standing empty far too long, and that is worse for a new house than an old house. There's not much money to spend on it either, unless we can make sure of a good tenant. How did you hear about it?'

'I was taking a bit holiday and I spent a night at Dalquharter with an old auntie of mine. You must understand I've just retired from business, and I'm thinking of finding a country place. I used to have the big provision shop in Mearns Street – now the United Supply Stores, Limited. You've maybe heard of it?'

The other bowed and smiled. 'Who hasn't? The name of Dickson McCunn is known far beyond the city of Glasgow.'

Dickson was not insensible of the flattery, and he continued with more freedom. 'I took a walk and got a glisk of the House, and I liked the look of it. You see, I want a quiet bit a good long way from a town, and at the same time a house with all modern conveniences. I suppose Huntingtower has that?'

'When it was built fifteen years ago it was considered a model – six bathrooms, its own electric light plant, steam heating, and independent boiler for hot water, the whole bag of tricks. I won't say but what some of these contrivances will want looking to, for the place has been some time empty, but there can be nothing very far wrong, and I can guarantee that the bones of the house are good.'

'Well, that's all right,' said Dickson. 'I don't mind spending a little money myself if the place suits me. But of that, of course, I'm not yet certain, for I've only had a glimpse of the outside. I wanted to get into the policies, but a man at the lodge wouldn't let me. They're a mighty uncivil lot down there.'

'I'm very sorry to hear that,' said Mr Loudon in a tone of concern.

'Ay, and if I take the place I'll stipulate that you get rid of the lodgekeepers.'

'There won't be the slightest difficulty about that, for they are only weekly tenants. But I'm vexed to hear they were uncivil. I was glad to get any tenant that offered, and they were well recommended to me.'

'They're foreigners.'

'One of them is – a Belgian refugee that Lady Morewood took an interest in. But the other – Spittal, they call him – I thought he was Scotch.'

'He's not that. And I don't like the innkeeper either. I would want him shifted.'

Mr Loudon laughed. 'I dare say Dobson is a rough diamond. There's worse folk in the world all the same, but I don't think he will want to stay. He only went there to pass the time till he heard from his brother in Vancouver. He's a roving spirit, and will be off overseas again.'

'That's all right!' said Dickson, who was beginning to have horrid suspicions that he might be on a wild-goose chase after all. 'Well, the next thing is for me to see over the House.'

'Certainly. I'd like to go with you myself. What day would suit you? Let me see. This is Friday. What about this day week?'

'I was thinking of to-morrow. Since I'm down in these parts I may as well get the job done.'

Mr Loudon looked puzzled. 'I quite see that. But I don't think it's possible. You see, I have to consult the owners and get their consent to a lease. Of course they have the general purpose of letting, but – well, they're queer folk the Kennedys,' and his face wore the half-embarrassed smile of an honest man preparing to make confidences. 'When poor Mr Quentin died, the place went to his two sisters in joint ownership. A very bad arrangement, as you can imagine. It isn't entailed, and I've always been pressing them to sell, but so far they won't hear of it. They both married Englishmen, so it will take a day or two to get in touch with them. One, Mrs Stukely, lives in Devonshire. The other – Miss Katie that was – married Sir Francis Morewood, the general, and I hear that she's expected back in London next Monday from the Riviera. I'll wire and write first thing to-morrow morning. But you must give me a day or two.'

Dickson felt himself waking up. His doubts about his own sanity were dissolving, for, as his mind reasoned, the factor was prepared to do anything he asked – but only after a week had gone. What he was concerned with was the next few days.

'All the same I would like to have a look at the place to-morrow, even if nothing comes of it.'

Mr Loudon looked seriously perplexed. 'You will think me absurdly fussy, Mr McCunn, but I must really beg of you to give up the idea. The Kennedys, as I have said, are – well, not exactly like other people, and I have the strictest orders not to let any one visit the house without their express leave. It sounds a ridiculous rule, but I assure you it's as much as my job is worth to disregard it.'

'D'you mean to say not a soul is allowed inside the House?'

'Not a soul.'

'Well, Mr Loudon, I'm going to tell you a queer thing, which I think you ought to know. When I was taking a walk the other night – your Belgian wouldn't let me into the policies, but I went down the glen – what's that they call it? the Garple Dean – I got round the back where the old ruin stands and I had a good look at the House. I tell you there was somebody in it.'

'It would be Spittal, who acts as caretaker.'

'It was not. It was a woman. I saw her on the veranda.'

The candid grey eyes were looking straight at Dickson, who managed to bring his own shy orbs to meet them. He thought that he detected a shade of hesitation. Then Mr Loudon got up from his chair and stood on the hearthrug looking down at his visitor. He laughed, with some embarrassment, but ever so pleasantly.

'I really don't know what you will think of me, Mr McCunn. Here are you, coming to do us all a kindness, and lease that infernal white elephant, and here have I been steadily hoaxing you for the last five minutes. I humbly ask your pardon. Set it down to the loyalty of an old family lawyer. Now, I am going to tell you the truth and take you into our confidence, for I know we are safe with you. The Kennedys are – always have been – just a wee bit queer. Old inbred stock, you know. They will produce somebody like poor Mr Quentin, who was as sane as you or me, but as a rule in every generation there is one member of the family – or more – who is just a little bit –' and he tapped his forehead. 'Nothing violent, you understand, but just not quite "wise and world-like", as the old folk say. Well, there's a certain old lady, an aunt of Mr Quentin and his sisters, who has always been about tenpence in the shilling. Usually she lives at Bournemouth, but one of her crazes is a passion for Huntingtower, and the Kennedys have always humoured her and had her to stay every spring. When the House was shut up that became impossible, but this year she took such a craving to come back, that Lady Morewood asked me to arrange it. It had to be kept very quiet, but the poor old thing is perfectly harmless, and just sits and knits with her maid and looks out of the seaward windows. Now you see why I can't take you there to-morrow. I have to get rid of the old lady, who in any case was travelling south early next week. Do you understand?'

'Perfectly,' said Dickson with some fervour. He had learned exactly what he wanted. The factor was telling him lies. Now he knew where to place Mr Loudon.

He always looked back upon what followed as a very creditable piece of play-acting for a man who had small experience in that line.

'Is the old lady a wee wizened body, with a black cap and something like a white cashmere shawl round her shoulders?'

'You describe her exactly,' Mr Loudon replied eagerly.

'That would explain the foreigners.'

'Of course. We couldn't have natives who would make the thing the clash of the countryside.'

'Of course not. But it must be a difficult job to keep a business like that quiet. Any wandering policeman might start inquiries. And supposing the lady became violent?'

'Oh, there's no fear of that. Besides, I've a position in this country – Deputy Fiscal and so forth – and a friend of the Chief Constable. I think I may be trusted to do a little private explaining if the need arose.'

'I see,' said Dickson. He saw, indeed, a great deal which would give him food for furious thought. 'Well, I must just possess my soul in patience. Here's my Glasgow address, and I look to you to send me a telegram whenever you're ready for me. I'm at the Salutation to-night, and go home to-morrow with the first train. Wait a minute' – and he pulled out his watch – 'there's a train stops at Auchenlochan at 10.17. I think I'll catch that ... Well, Mr Loudon, I'm very much obliged to you, and I'm glad to think that it'll no' be long till we renew our acquaintance.'

The factor accompanied him to the door, diffusing geniality. 'Very pleased indeed to have met you. A pleasant journey and a quick return.'

The street was still empty. Into a corner of the arches opposite the moon was shining, and Dickson retired thither to consult his map of the neighbourhood. He found what he wanted, and, as he lifted his eyes, caught sight of a man coming down the causeway. Promptly he retired into the shadow and watched the new-comer. There could be no mistake about the figure; the bulk, the walk, the carriage of the head marked it for Dobson. The innkeeper went slowly past the factor's house; then halted and retraced his steps; then, making sure that the street was empty, turned into the side lane which led to the garden.

This was what sailors call a cross-bearing, and strengthened Dickson's conviction. He delayed no longer, but hurried down the side street by which the north road leaves the town.

He had crossed the bridge of Lochan and was climbing the steep ascent which led to the heathy plateau separating the stream from the Garple before he had got his mind quite clear on the case. *First*, Loudon was in the plot, whatever it was; responsible for the details of the girl's imprisonment, but not the main author. That must be the Unknown who was still to come, from whom Spidel took his orders. Dobson was probably Loudon's special henchman, working directly under him. *Secondly*, the immediate object had been the jewels, and they were happily safe in the vaults of the incorruptible Mackintosh. But, *third* – and this only on Saskia's evidence – the worst danger to her began with the arrival of the Unknown. What could that be? Probably, kidnapping. He was prepared to believe anything of people like Bolsheviks. And, *fourth*, this danger was due within the next day or two. Loudon had been quite willing to let him into the house and to sack all the watchers within a week from that date. The natural and right thing was to summon the aid of the law, but, *fifth*, that would be a slow business with Loudon able to put spokes in the wheels and befog the authorities, and the mischief would be done before a single policeman showed his face in Dalquharter. Therefore, *sixth*, he and Heritage must hold the fort in the meantime, and he would send a wire to his lawyer, Mr Caw, to get to work with the constabulary. *Seventh*, he himself was probably free from suspicion in both Loudon's and Dobson's minds as a harmless fool. But that freedom would not survive his reappearance in Dalquharter. He could say, to be sure, that he had come back to see his auntie, but that would not satisfy the watchers, since, so far as they knew, he was the only man outside the gang who was aware that people were dwelling in the House. They would not tolerate his presence in the neighbourhood.

He formulated his conclusions as if it were an ordinary business deal, and rather to his surprise was not conscious of any fear. As he pulled together the belt of his waterproof he felt the reassuring bulges in its pockets which were his pistol and cartridges. He reflected that it must be very difficult to miss with a pistol if you fired it at, say, three yards, and if there was to be shooting that would be his range. Mr McCunn had stumbled on the precious truth that the best way to be rid of quaking knees is to keep a busy mind.

He crossed the ridge of the plateau and looked down on the Garple glen. There were the lights of Dalquharter – or rather a single light, for the inhabitants went early to bed. His intention was to seek quarters with Mrs Morran, when his eye caught a gleam in a hollow of the moor a little to the east. He knew it for the camp-fire around which Dougal's warriors bivouacked. The notion came to him to go there instead, and hear the news of the day before entering the cottage. So he crossed the bridge, skirted a plantation of firs, and scrambled through the broom and heather in what he took to be the right direction.

The moon had gone down, and the quest was not easy. Dickson had come to the conclusion that he was on the wrong road, when he was summoned by a voice which seemed to arise out of the ground.

'Who goes there?'

'What's that you say?'

'Who goes there?' The point of a pole was held firmly against his chest.

'I'm Mr McCunn, a friend of Dougal's.'

'Stand, friend.' The shadow before him whistled and another shadow appeared. 'Report to the Chief that there's a man here, name o' McCunn, seekin' for him.'

Presently the messenger returned with Dougal and a cheap lantern which he flashed in Dickson's face.

'Oh, it's you,' said that leader, who had his jaw bound up as if he had the toothache. 'What are ye doing back here?'

'To tell the truth, Dougal,' was the answer, 'I couldn't stay away. I was fair miserable when I thought of Mr Heritage and you laddies left to yourselves. My conscience simply wouldn't let me stop at home, so here I am.'

Dougal grunted, but clearly he approved, for from that moment he treated Dickson with a new respect. Formerly when he had referred to him at all it had been as 'auld McCunn'. Now it was 'Mister McCunn'. He was given rank as a worthy civilian ally.

The bivouac was a cheerful place in the wet night. A great fire of pine roots and old paling posts hissed in the fine rain, and around it crouched several urchins busy making oatmeal cakes in the embers. On one side a respectable lean-to had been constructed by nailing a plank to two fir-trees, running sloping poles thence to the ground, and thatching the whole with spruce branches and heather. On the other side two small dilapidated home-made tents were pitched. Dougal motioned his companion into the lean-to, where they had some privacy from the rest of the band.

'Well, what's your news?' Dickson asked. He noticed that the Chieftain seemed to have been comprehensively in the wars, for apart from the bandage on his jaw, he had numerous small cuts on his brow, and a great rent in one of his shirt sleeves. Also he appeared to be going lame, and when he spoke a new gap was revealed in his large teeth.

'Things,' said Dougal solemnly, 'has come to a bonny cripus. This very night we've been in a battle.'

He spat fiercely, and the light of war burned in his eyes.

'It was the tinklers from the Garple Dean. They yokit on us about seven o'clock, just at the darkenin'. First they tried to bounce us. We weren't wanted here, they said, so we'd better clear. I telled them that it was them that wasn't wanted. "Awa' to Finnick," said I. "D'ye think we take our orders from dirty ne'er-do-weels like you?" "By God," says they, "we'll cut your lights out," and then the battle started.'

'What happened?' Dickson asked excitedly.

'They were four muckle men against six laddies, and they thought they had an easy job! Little they kenned the Gorbals Die-Hards! I had been expectin' something of the kind, and had made my plans. They first tried to pu' down our tents and burn them. I let them get within five yards, reservin' my fire. The first volley – stones from our hands and our catties – halted them, and before they could recover three of us had got hold o' burnin' sticks frae the fire and were lammin' into them. We kinnled their claes, and they fell back swearin' and stampin' to get the fire out. Then I gave the word and we were on them wi' our poles, usin' the points accordin' to instructions. My orders was to keep a good distance, for if they had grippit one o' us he'd ha' been done for. They were roarin' mad by now, and twae had out their knives, but they couldn't do muckle, for it was gettin' dark, and they didn't ken the ground like us, and were aye trippin' and tumblin'. But they pressed us hard, and one o' them landed me an awful clype on the jaw. They were still aiming at our tents, and I saw that if they got near the fire again it would be the end o' us. So I blew my whistle for Thomas Yownie, who was in command o' the other half of us, with instructions to fall upon their rear. That brought Thomas up, and the tinklers had to face round about and fight a battle on two fronts. We charged them and they broke, and the last seen o' them they were coolin' their burns in the Garple.'

'Well done, man. Had you many casualties?'

'We're a' a wee thing battered, but nothing to hurt. I'm the worst, for one o' them had a grip o' me for about three seconds, and Gosh! he was fierce.'

'They're beaten off for the night, anyway?'

'Ay, for the night. But they'll come back, never fear. That's why I said that things had come to a cripus.'

'What's the news from the House?'

'A quiet day, and no word o' Lean or Dobson.'

Dickson nodded. 'They were hunting me.'

'Mr Heritage has gone to bide in the Hoose. They were watchin' the Garple Dean, so I took him round by the Laver foot and up the rocks. He's a soople yin, yon. We fund a road up the rocks and got in by the verandy. Did ye ken that the lassie had a pistol? Well, she has, and it seems that Mr Heritage is a good shot wi' a pistol, so there's some hope thereaways . . . Are the jools safe?'

'Safe in the bank. But the jools were not the main thing.'

Dougal nodded. 'So I was thinkin'. The lassie wasn't muckle the easier for gettin' rid o' them. I didn't just quite understand what she said to Mr Heritage, for they were aye wanderin' into foreign langwidges, but it seems she's terrible feared o' somebody that may turn up any moment. What's the reason I can't say. She's maybe got a secret, or maybe it's just that she's ower bonny.'

'That's the trouble,' said Dickson, and proceeded to recount his interview with the factor, to which Dougal gave close attention. 'Now the way I read the thing is this. There's a plot to kidnap that lady for some infernal purpose, and it depends on the arrival of some person or persons, and it's due to happen in the next day or two. If we try to work it through the police alone, they'll beat us, for Loudon will manage to hang the business up till it's too late. So we must take on the job ourselves. We must stand a siege, Mr Heritage and me and you laddies, and for that purpose we'd better all keep together. It won't be extra easy to carry her off from all of us, and if they do manage it we'll stick to their heels . . . Man, Dougal, isn't it a queer thing that whiles law-abiding folk have to make their own laws? . . . So my plan is that the lot of us get into the House and form a garrison. If you don't, the tinklers will come back and you'll no' beat them in the daylight.'

'I doubt no',' said Dougal. 'But what about our meat?'

'We must lay in provisions. We'll get what we can from Mrs Morran, and I've left a big box of fancy things at Dalquharter station. Can you laddies manage to get it down here?'

Dougal reflected. 'Ay, we can hire Mrs Sempill's powny, the same that fetched our kit.'

'Well, that's your job to-morrow. See, I'll write you a line to the station-master. And will you undertake to get it some way into the House?'

'There's just the one road open – by the rocks. It'll have to be done. It *can* be done.'

'And I've another job. I'm writing this telegram to a friend in Glasgow who will put a spoke in Mr Loudon's wheel. I want one of you to go to Kirkmichael to send it from the telegraph office there.'

Dougal placed the wire to Mr Caw in his bosom. 'What about yourself? We want somebody outside to keep his eyes open. It's bad strawtegy to cut off your communications.'

Dickson thought for a moment. 'I believe you're right. I believe the best plan for me is to go back to Mrs Morran's as soon as the old body's like to be awake. You can always get at me there, for it's easy to slip into her back kitchen without anybody in the village seeing you . . . Yes, I'll do that, and you'll come and report developments to me. And now I'm for a bite and a pipe. It's hungry work travelling the country in the small hours.'

'I'm going to introjuice ye to the rest o' us,' said Dougal. 'Here, men!' he called, and four figures rose from the side of the fire. As Dickson munched a sandwich he passed in review the whole company of the Gorbals Die-Hards, for the pickets were also brought in, two others taking their places. There was Thomas Yownie, the Chief of Staff, with a wrist wound up in the handkerchief which he had borrowed from his neck. There was a burly lad who wore trousers much too large for him, and who was known as Peer Pairson, a contraction presumably for Peter Paterson. After him came a lean tall boy who answered to the name of Napoleon. There was a midget of a child, desperately sooty in the face either from battle or from fire-tending, who was presented as Wee Jaikie. Last came the picket who had held his pole at Dickson's chest, a sandy-haired warrior with a snub nose and the mouth and jaw of a pug-dog. He was Old Bill, or, in Dougal's parlance, 'Auld Bull'.

The Chieftain viewed his scarred following with a grim content. 'That's a tough lot for ye, Mr McCunn. Used a' their days wi' sleepin' in coalrees and dunnies and dodgin' the polis. Ye'll no beat the Gorbals Die-Hards.'

'You're right, Dougal,' said Dickson. 'There's just the six of you. If there were a dozen, I think this country would be needing some new kind of a government.'

## CHAPTER EIGHT

# HOW A MIDDLE-AGED CRUSADER ACCEPTED A CHALLENGE

THE first cocks had just begun to crow and the clocks had not yet struck five when Dickson presented himself at Mrs Morran's back door. That active woman had already been half an hour out of bed, and was drinking her morning cup of tea in the kitchen. She received him with cordiality, nay, with relief.

'Eh, sir, but I'm glad to see ye back. Guid kens what's gaun on at the Hoose thae days. Mr Heritage left here yestreen, creepin' round by dyke-sides and berry-busses like a wheasel. It's a mercy to get a responsible man in the place. I aye had a notion ye wad come back, for, thinks I, nevoy Dickson is no the yin to desert folk in trouble . . . Whaur's my wee kist? . . . Lost, ye say. That's a peety, for it's been my cheese-box thae thirty year.'

Dickson ascended to the loft, having announced his need of at least three hours' sleep. As he rolled into bed his mind was curiously at ease. He felt equipped for any call that might be made on him. That Mrs Morran should welcome him back as a resource in need gave him a new assurance of manhood.

He woke between nine and ten to the sound of rain lashing against the garret window. As he picked his way out of the mazes of sleep and recovered the skein of his immediate past, he found to his disgust that he had lost his composure. All the flock of fears, that had left him when on the top of the Glasgow tram-car he had made the great decision, had flown back again and settled like black crows on his spirit. He was running a horrible risk and all for a whim. What business had he to be mixing himself up in things he did not understand? It might be a huge mistake, and then he would be a laughing stock; for a moment he repented his telegram to Mr Caw. Then he recanted that suspicion; there could be no mistake, except the fatal one that he had taken on a job too big for him. He sat on the edge of his bed and shivered with his eyes on the grey drift of rain. He would have felt more stout-hearted had the sun been shining.

He shuffled to the window and looked out. There in the village street was Dobson, and Dobson saw him. That was a bad blunder, for his reason told him that he should have kept his presence in Dalquharter hid as long as possible.

There was a knock at the cottage door, and presently Mrs Morran appeared.

'It's the man frae the inn,' she announced. 'He's wantin' a word wi' ye. Speakin' verra ceevil, too.'

'Tell him to come up,' said Dickson. He might as well get the interview over. Dobson had seen Loudon and must know of their conversation. The sight of himself back again when he had pretended to be off to Glasgow would remove him effectually from the class of the unsuspected. He wondered just what line Dobson would take.

The innkeeper obtruded his bulk through the low door. His face was wrinkled into a smile, which nevertheless left the small eyes ungenial. His voice had a loud vulgar cordiality. Suddenly Dickson was conscious of a resemblance, a resemblance to somebody whom he had recently seen. It was Loudon. There was the same thrusting of the chin forward, the same odd cheek-bones, the same unctuous heartiness of speech. The innkeeper, well washed and polished and dressed, would be no bad copy of the factor. They must be near kin, perhaps brothers.

'Good morning to you, Mr McCunn. Man, it's pitifu' weather, and just when the farmers are wanting a dry seed-bed. What brings ye back here? Ye travel the country like a drover.'

'Oh, I'm a free man now and I took a fancy to this place. An idle body has nothing to do but please himself.'

'I hear ye're taking a lease of Huntingtower?'

'Now who told you that?'

'Just the clash of the place. Is it true?'

Dickson looked sly and a little annoyed.

'I maybe had half a thought of it, but I'll thank you not to repeat the story. It's a big house for a plain man like me, and I haven't properly inspected it.'

'Oh, I'll keep mum, never fear. But if ye've that sort of notion, I can understand you not being able to keep away from the place.'

'That may be the fact,' Dickson admitted.

'Well! It's just on that point I want a word with you.' The innkeeper seated himself unbidden on the chair which held Dickson's modest raiment. He leaned forward and with a coarse forefinger tapped Dickson's pyjama-clad knees. 'I can't have ye wandering about the place. I'm very sorry, but I've got my orders from Mr Loudon. So if you think that by bidin' here you can see more of the House and the policies, ye're wrong, Mr McCunn. It can't be allowed, for we're no' ready for ye yet. D'ye understand? That's Mr Loudon's orders ... Now, would it not be a far better plan if ye went back to Glasgow and came back in a week's time? I'm thinking of your own comfort, Mr McCunnn.'

Dickson was cogitating hard. This man was clearly instructed to get rid of him at all costs for the next few days. The neighbourhood had to be cleared for some black business. The tinklers had been deputed to drive out the Gorbals Die-Hards, and as for Heritage they seemed to have lost track of him. He, Dickson, was now the chief object of their care. But what could Dobson do if he refused? He dared not show his true hand. Yet he might, if sufficiently irritated. It became Dickson's immediate object to get the innkeeper to reveal himself by rousing his temper. He did not stop to consider the policy of this course; he imperatively wanted things cleared up and the issue made plain.

'I'm sure I'm much obliged to you for thinking so much about my comfort,' he said in a voice into which he hoped he had insinuated a sneer. 'But I'm bound to say you're awful suspicious folk about here. You needn't be feared for your old policies. There's plenty of nice walks about the roads, and I want to explore the sea-coast.'

The last words seemed to annoy the innkeeper. 'That's no' allowed either,' he said. 'The shore's as private as the policies . . . Well, I wish ye joy tramping the roads in the glaur.'

'It's a queer thing,' said Dickson meditatively, 'that you should keep a hotel and yet be set on discouraging people from visiting this neighbourhood. I tell you what, I believe that hotel of yours is all sham. You've some other business, you and these lodgekeepers, and in my opinion it's not a very creditable one.'

'What d'ye mean?' asked Dobson sharply.

'Just what I say. You must expect a body to be suspicious, if you treat him as you're treating me.' Loudon must have told this man the story with which he had been fobbed off about the half-witted Kennedy relative. Would Dobson refer to that?

The innkeeper had an ugly look on his face, but he controlled his temper with an effort.

'There's no cause for suspicion,' he said. 'As far as I'm concerned it's all honest and above-board.'

'It doesn't look like it. It looks as if you were hiding something up in the House which you don't want me to see.'

Dobson jumped from his chair, his face pale with anger. A man in pyjamas on a raw morning does not feel at his bravest, and Dickson quailed under the expectation of assault. But even in his fright he realized that Loudon could not have told Dobson the tale of the half-witted lady. The last remark had cut clean through all camouflage and reached the quick.

'What the hell d'ye mean?' he cried. 'Ye're a spy, are ye? Ye fat little fool, for two cents I'd wring your neck.'

Now it is an odd trait of certain mild people that a suspicion of threat, a hint of bullying, will rouse some unsuspected obstinacy deep down in their souls. The insolence of the man's speech woke a quiet but efficient little devil in Dickson.

'That's a bonny tone to adopt in addressing a gentleman. If you've nothing to hide what way are you so touchy? I can't be a spy unless there's something to spy on.'

The innkeeper pulled himself together. He was apparently

acting on instructions, and had not yet come to the end of them. He made an attempt at a smile.

'I'm sure I beg your pardon if I spoke too hot. But it nettled me to hear ye say that . . . I'll be quite frank with ye, Mr McCunn, and, believe me, I'm speaking in your best interests. I give ye my word there's nothing wrong up at the House. I'm on the side of the law, and when I tell ye the whole story ye'll admit it. But I can't tell it ye yet . . . This is a wild, lonely bit, and very few folk bide in it. And these are wild times, when a lot of queer things happen that never get into the papers. I tell ye it's for your own good to leave Dalquharter for the present. More I can't say, but I ask ye to look at it as a sensible man. Ye're one that's accustomed to a quiet life and no' meant for rough work. Ye'll do no good if you stay, and, maybe, ye'll land yourself in bad trouble.'

'Mercy on us!' Dickson exclaimed. 'What is it you're expecting? Sinn Fein?'

The innkeeper nodded. 'Something like that.'

'Did you ever hear the like? I never did think much of the Irish.'

'Then ye'll take my advice and go home? Tell ye what, I'll drive ye to the station.'

Dickson got up from the bed, found his new safety-razor and began to strop it. 'No, I think I'll bide. If you're right there'll be more to see than glaury roads.'

'I'm warning ye, fair and honest. Ye . . . can't . . . be . . . allowed . . . to . . . stay . . . here!'

'Well, I never!' said Dickson. 'Is there any law in Scotland, think you, that forbids a man to stop a day or two with his auntie?'

'Ye'll stay?'

'Ay, I'll stay.'

'By God, we'll see about that.'

For a moment Dickson thought that he would be attacked, and he measured the distance that separated him from the peg whence hung his waterproof with the pistol in its pocket. But the man restrained himself and moved to the door. There he stood and cursed him with a violence and a venom which

Dickson had not believed possible. The full hand was on the table now.

'Ye wee pot-bellied, pig-heided Glasgow grocer' (I paraphrase), 'would *you* set up to defy me? I tell ye, I'll make ye rue the day ye were born.' His parting words were a brilliant sketch of the maltreatment in store for the body of the defiant one.

'Impident dog,' said Dickson without heat. He noted with pleasure that the innkeeper hit his head violently against the low lintel, and, missing a step, fell down the loft stairs into the kitchen, where Mrs Morran's tongue could be heard speeding him trenchantly from the premises.

Left to himself, Dickson dressed leisurely, and by and by went down to the kitchen and watched his hostess making broth. The fracas with Dobson had done him all the good in the world, for it had cleared the problem of dubieties and had put an edge on his temper. But he realized that it made his continued stay in the cottage undesirable. He was now the focus of all suspicion, and the innkeeper would be as good as his word and try to drive him out of the place by force. Kidnapping, most likely, and that would be highly unpleasant, besides putting an end to his usefulness. Clearly he must join the others. The soul of Dickson hungered at the moment for human companionship. He felt that his courage would be sufficient for any team-work, but might waver again if he were left to play a lone hand.

He lunched nobly off three plates of Mrs Morran's kail – an early lunch, for that lady, having breakfasted at five, partook of the midday meal about eleven. Then he explored her library, and settled himself by the fire with a volume of Covenanting tales, entitled *Gleanings among the Mountains*. It was a most practical work for one in his position, for it told how various eminent saints of that era escaped the attention of Claverhouse's dragoons. Dickson stored up in his memory several of the incidents in case they should come in handy. He wondered if any of his forbears had been Covenanters; it comforted him to think that some old progenitor might have hunkered behind turf walls and been chased for his life in the heather. 'Just like me,' he reflected. 'But the dragoons weren't foreigners, and there was a kind of decency about Claverhouse too.'

About four o'clock Dougal presented himself in the back kitchen. He was an even wilder figure than usual, for his bare legs were mud to the knees, his kilt and shirt clung sopping to his body, and, having lost his hat, his wet hair was plastered over his eyes. Mrs Morran said, not unkindly, that he looked 'like a wull-cat glowerin' through a whin buss.'

'How are you, Dougal?' Dickson asked genially. 'Is the peace of nature smoothing out the creases in your poor little soul?'

'What's that ye say?'

'Oh, just what I heard a man say in Glasgow. How have you got on?'

'No' so bad. Your telegram was sent this mornin'. Old Bill took it in to Kirkmichael. That's the first thing. Second, Thomas Yownie has took a party to get down the box from the station. He got Mrs Sempill's powny, and he took the box ayont the Laver by the ford at the herd's hoose and got it on to the shore maybe a mile ayont Laverfoot. He managed to get the machine up as far as the water, but he could get no farther, for ye'll no' get a machine over the wee waterfa' just before the Laver ends in the sea. So he sent one o' the men back with it to Mrs. Sempill, and, since the box was ower heavy to carry, he opened it and took the stuff across in bits. It's a' safe in the hole at the foot o' the Huntingtower rocks, and he reports that the rain has done it no harm. Thomas has made a good job of it. Ye'll no' fickle Thomas Yownie.'

'And what about your camp on the moor?'

'It was broke up afore daylight. Some of our things we've got with us, but most is hid near at hand. The tents are in the auld wife's hen-hoose,' and he jerked his disreputable head in the direction of the back door.

'Have the tinklers been back?'

'Aye. They turned up about ten o'clock, no doubt intendin' murder. I left Wee Jaikie to watch developments. They fund him sittin' on a stone, greetin' sore. When he saw them, he up and started to run, and they cried on him to stop, but he wouldn't listen. Then they cried out where were the rest, and he telled them they were feared for their lives and had run away. After that they offered to catch him, but ye'll no' catch Jaikie in a hurry. When he had run round about them till they were wappit, he out wi' his catty and got one o' them on the lug. Syne he made for the Laverfoot and reported.'

'Man, Dougal, you've managed fine. Now I've something to tell you,' and Dickson recounted his interview with the inn-keeper. 'I don't think it's safe for me to bide here, and if I did, I wouldn't be any use, hiding in cellars and such like, and not daring to stir a foot. I'm coming with you to the House. Now tell me how to get there.'

Dougal agreed to this view. 'There's been nothing doing at the Hoose the day, but they're keepin' a close watch on the policies. The cripus may come any moment. There's no doubt, Mr McCunn, that ye're in danger, for they'll serve you as the tinklers tried to serve us. Listen to me. Ye'll walk up the station road, and take the second turn on your left, a wee grass road that'll bring ye to the ford at the herd's hoose. Cross the Laver – there's a plank bridge – and take straight across the moor in the direction of the peakit hill they call Grey Carrick. Ye'll come to a big burn, which ye must follow till ye get to the shore. Then turn south, keepin' the water's edge till ye reach the Laver, where you'll find one o' us to show ye the rest of the road . . . I must be off now, and I advise ye not to be slow of startin', for wi' this rain the water's risin' quick. It's a mercy it's such coarse weather, for it spoils the veesibility.'

'Auntie Phemie,' said Dickson a few minutes later, 'will you oblige me by coming for a short walk?'

'The man's daft,' was the answer.

'I'm not. I'll explain if you'll listen . . . You see,' he concluded, 'the dangerous bit for me is just the mile out of the village. They'll no' be so likely to try violence if there's somebody with me that could be a witness. Besides, they'll maybe suspect less if they just see a decent body out for a breath of air with his auntie.'

Mrs Morran said nothing, but retired, and returned presently equipped for the road. She had indued her feet with goloshes and pinned up her skirts till they looked like some demented Paris mode. An ancient bonnet was tied under her chin with strings, and her equipment was completed by an exceedingly smart tortoise-shell-handled umbrella, which, she explained, had been a Christmas present from her son.

'I'll convoy ye as far as the Laverfoot herd's,' she announced. 'The wife's a freend o' mine and will set me a bit on the road back. Ye needna fash for me. I'm used to a' weathers.'

The rain had declined to a fine drizzle, but a tearing wind from the south-west scoured the land. Beyond the shelter of the trees the moor was a battle-ground of gusts which swept the puddles into spindrift and gave to the stagnant bog-pools the appearance of running water. The wind was behind the travellers, and Mrs Morran, like a full-rigged ship, was hustled before it, so that Dickson who had linked arms with her, was sometimes compelled to trot.

'However will you get home, mistress?' he murmured anxiously.

'Fine. The wind will fa' at the darkenin'. This'll be a sair time for ships at sea.'

Not a soul was about, as they breasted the ascent of the station road and turned down the grassy bypath to the Laverfoot herd's. The herd's wife saw them from afar and was at the door to receive them.

'Megsty! Phemie Morran!' she shrilled. 'Wha wad ettle to see ye on a day like this? John's awa' at Dumfries, buyin' tups. Come in, the baith o' ye. The kettle's on the boil.'

'This is my nevoy Dickson,' said Mrs Morran. 'He's gaun to stretch his legs ayont the burn, and come back by the Ayr road. But I'll be blithe to tak' my tea wi' ye, Elspeth . . . Now, Dickson, I'll expect ye hame on the chap o' seeven.'

He crossed the rising stream on a swaying plank and struck into the moorland, as Dougal had ordered, keeping the bald top of Grey Carrick before him. In that wild place with the tempest battling overhead he had no fear of human enemies. Steadily he covered the ground, till he reached the west-flowing burn, that was to lead him to the shore. He found it an entertaining companion, swirling into black pools, foaming over little falls, and lying in dark canal-like stretches in the flats. Presently it began to descend steeply in a narrow green gully, where the going was bad, and Dickson, weighted with pack and waterproof, had much ado to keep his feet on the sodden slopes. Then, as he rounded a crook of hill, the ground fell away from his feet, the burn swept in a water-slide to the boulders of the shore, and the storm-tossed sea lay before him.

It was now that he began to feel nervous. Being on the coast again seemed to bring him inside his enemies' territory, and had not Dobson specifically forbidden the shore? It was here that they might be looking for him. He felt himself out of condition, very wet and very warm, but he attained a creditable pace, for he struck a road which had been used by manure-carts collecting seaweed. There were faint marks on it, which he took to be the wheels of Dougal's 'machine' carrying the provision-box. Yes. On a patch of gravel there was a double set of tracks, which showed how it had returned to Mrs Sempill. He was exposed to the full force of the wind, and the strenuousness of his bodily exertions kept his fears quiescent, till the cliffs on his left sunk suddenly and the valley of the Laver lay before him.

A small figure rose from the shelter of a boulder, the warrior who bore the name of Old Bill. He saluted gravely.

'Ye're just in time. The water has rose three inches since I've been here. Ye'd better strip.'

Dickson removed his boots and socks. 'Breeks too,' commanded the boy; 'there's deep holes ayont thae stanes.'

Dickson obeyed, feeling very chilly, and rather improper. 'Now follow me,' said the guide. The next moment he was stepping delicately on very sharp pebbles, holding on to the end of the scout's pole, while an icy stream ran to his knees.

The Laver as it reaches the sea broadens out to the width of fifty or sixty yards and tumbles over little shelves of rock to meet the waves. Usually it is shallow, but now it was swollen to an average depth of a foot or more, and there were deeper pockets. Dickson made the passage slowly and miserably, sometimes crying out with pain as his toes struck a sharper flint, once or twice sitting down on a boulder to blow like a whale, once slipping on his knees and wetting the strange excrescence about his middle, which was his tucked-up waterproof. But the crossing was at length achieved, and on a patch of sea-pinks he dried himself perfunctorily and hastily put on his garments. Old Bill, who seemed to be regardless of wind or water, squatted beside him and whistled through his teeth.

Above them hung the sheer cliffs of the Huntingtower cape, so sheer that a man below was completely hidden from any watcher on the top. Dickson's heart fell, for he did not profess to be a cragsman and had indeed a horror of precipitous places. But as the two scrambled along the foot, they passed deep-cut gullies and fissures, most of them unclimbable, but offering something more hopeful than the face. At one of these Old Bill halted, and led the way up and over a chaos of fallen rock and loose sand. The grey weather had brought on the dark prematurely, and in the half-light it seemed that this ravine was blocked by an unscalable nose of rock. Here Old Bill whistled, and there was a reply from above. Round the corner of the nose came Dougal.

'Up here,' he commanded. 'It was Mr Heritage that fund this road.'

Dickson and his guide squeezed themselves between the nose and the cliff up a spout of stones, and found themselves in an upper storey of the gulley, very steep, but practicable even for one who was no cragsman. This in turn ran out against a wall up which there led only a narrow chimney. At the foot of this were two of the Die-Hards, and there were others above, for a rope hung down, by the aid of which a package was even now ascending.

'That's the top,' said Dougal, pointing to the rim of sky, 'and that's the last o' the supplies.' Dickson noticed that he spoke in a whisper, and that all the movements of the Die-Hards were judicious and stealthy. 'Now, it's your turn. Take a good grip o' the rope, and ye'll find plenty holes for your feet. It's no more than ten yards and ye're well held above.'

Dickson made the attempt and found it easier than he expected. The only trouble was his pack and waterproof, which had a tendency to catch on jags of rock. A hand was reached out to him, he was pulled over the edge, and then pushed down on his face.

When he lifted his head Dougal and the others had joined him, and the whole company of the Die-Hards was assembled on a patch of grass which was concealed from the landward view by a thicket of hazels. Another, whom he recognized as Heritage, was coiling up the rope.

'We'd better get all the stuff into the old Tower for the present,' Heritage was saying. 'It's too risky to move it into the House now. We'll need the thickest darkness for that, after the moon is down. Quick, for the beastly thing will be rising soon, and before that we must all be indoors.'

Then he turned to Dickson and gripped his hand. 'You're a high class of sportsman, Dogson. And I think you're just in time.'

'Are they due to-night?' Dickson asked in an excited whisper, faint against the wind.

'I don't know about They. But I've got a notion that some devilish queer things will happen before to-morrow morning.'

CHAPTER NINE

# THE FIRST BATTLE OF THE CRUIVES

THE old keep of Huntingtower stood some three hundred yards from the edge of the cliffs, a gnarled wood of hazels and oaks protecting it from the sea-winds. It was still in fair preservation, having till twenty years before been an adjunct of the house of Dalquharter, and used as kitchen, buttery, and servants' quarters. There had been residential wings attached, dating from the mid-eighteenth century, but these had been pulled down and used for the foundations of the new mansion. Now it stood a lonely shell, its three storeys, each a single great room connected by a spiral stone staircase, being dedicated to lumber and the storage of produce. But it was dry and intact, its massive oak doors defied any weapon short of artillery, its narrow unglazed windows would scarcely have admitted a cat – a place portentously strong, gloomy, but yet habitable.

Dougal opened the main door with a massy key. 'The lassie fund it,' he whispered to Dickson, 'somewhere about the kitchen – and I guessed it was the key o' this castle. I was thinkin' that if things got ower hot it would be a good plan to flit here. Change our base, like.' The Chieftain's occasional studies in war had trained his tongue to a military jargon.

In the ground room lay a fine assortment of oddments, including old bedsteads and servants' furniture, and what looked like ancient discarded deerskin rugs. Dust lay thick over everything, and they heard the scurry of rats. A dismal place, indeed, but Dickson felt only its strangeness. The comfort of being back again among allies had quickened his spirit to an adventurous mood. The old lords of Huntingtower had once quarrelled and revelled and plotted here, and now here he was at the same game. Present and past joined hands over the gulf of years. The saga of Huntingtower was not ended.

The Die-Hards had brought with them their scanty bedding, their lanterns, and camp-kettles. These and the provisions from Mearns Street were stowed away in a corner.

'Now for the Hoose, men,' said Dougal. They stole over the downs to the shrubbery, and Dickson found himself almost in the same place as he had lain in three days before, watching a dusky lawn, while the wet earth soaked through his trouser knees and the drip from the azaleas trickled over his spine. Two of the boys fetched the ladder and placed it against the veranda wall. Heritage first, then Dickson, darted across the lawn and made the ascent. The six scouts followed, and the ladder was pulled up and hidden among the veranda litter. For a second the whole eight stood still and listened. There was no sound except the murmur of the now falling wind and the melancholy hooting of owls. The garrison had entered the Dark Tower.

A council in whispers was held in the garden-room.

'Nobody must show a light,' Heritage observed. 'It mustn't be known that we're here. Only the Princess will have a lamp. Yes' – this in answer to Dickson – 'she knows that we're coming – you too. We'll hunt for quarters later upstairs. You scouts, you must picket every possible entrance. The windows are safe, I think, for they are locked from the inside. So is the main door. But there's the veranda door, of which they have a key, and the back door beside the kitchen, and I'm not at all sure that there's not a way in by the boiler-house. You understand. We're holding this place against all comers. We must barricade the danger points. The headquarters of the garrison will be in the hall, where a scout must be always on duty. You've all got whistles? Well, if there's an attempt on the veranda door the picket will whistle once, if at the back door twice, if anywhere else three times, and it's everybody's duty, except the picket who whistles, to get back to the hall for orders.'

'That's so,' assented Dougal.

'If the enemy forces an entrance we must overpower him. Any means you like. Sticks or fists, and remember if it's a scrap in the dark to make for the man's throat. I expect you little devils have eyes like cats. The scoundrels must be kept away from the ladies at all costs. If the worst comes to the worst, the Princess has a revolver.'

'So have I,' said Dickson. 'I got it in Glasgow.'

'The deuce you have! Can you use it?'

'I don't know.'

'Well, you can hand it over to me, if you like. But it oughtn't to come to shooting, if it's only the three of them. The eight of us should be able to manage three and one of them lame. If the others turn up – well, God help us all! But we've got to make sure of one thing, that no one lays hands on the Princess so long as there's one of us left alive to hit out.'

'Ye needn't be feared for that,' said Dougal. There was no light in the room, but Dickson was certain that the morose face of the Chieftain was lit with unholy joy.

'Then off with you. Mr McCunn and I will explain matters to the ladies.'

When they were alone, Heritage's voice took a different key. 'We're in for it, Dogson, old man. There's no doubt these three scoundrels expect reinforcements at any moment, and with them will be one who is the devil incarnate. He's the only thing on earth that that brave girl fears. It seems he is in love with her and has pestered her for years. She hated the sight of him, but he wouldn't take no, and being a powerful man – rich and well-born and all the rest of it – she had a desperate time. I gather he was pretty high in favour with the old Court. Then when the Bolsheviks started he went over to them, like plenty of other grandees, and now he's one of their chief brains – none of your callow revolutionaries, but a man of the world, a kind of genius, she says, who can hold his own anywhere. She believes him to be in this country, and only waiting the right moment to turn up. Oh, it sounds ridiculous, I know, in Britain in the twentieth century, but I learned in the war that civilization anywhere is a very thin crust. There are a hundred ways by which that kind of fellow could bamboozle all our law and police and spirit her away. That's the kind of crowd we have to face.'

'Did she say what he was like in appearance?'

'A face like an angel – a lost angel, she says.'

Dickson suddenly had an inspiration.

'D'you mind the man you said was an Australian – at Kirkmichael? I thought myself he was a foreigner. Well, he was asking for a place he called Darkwater, and there's no sich place in the countryside. I believe he meant Dalquharter. I believe he's the man she's feared of.'

A gasped 'By Jove!' came from the darkness. 'Dogson, you've hit it. That was five days ago, and he must have got on the right trail by this time. He'll be here to-night. That's why the three have been lying so quiet to-day. Well, we'll go through with it, even if we haven't a dog's chance! Only I'm sorry that you should be mixed up in such a hopeless business.'

'Why me more than you?'

'Because it's all pure pride and joy for me to be here. Good God, I wouldn't be elsewhere for worlds. It's the great hour of my life. I would gladly die for her.'

'Tuts, that's no' the way to talk, man. Time enough to speak about dying when there's no other way out. I'm looking at this thing in a business way. We'd better be seeing the ladies.'

They groped into the pitchy hall, somewhere in which a Die-Hard was on picket, and down the passage to the smoking-room. Dickson blinked in the light of a very feeble lamp and Heritage saw that his hands were cumbered with packages. He deposited them on a sofa and made a ducking bow.

'I've come back, Mem, and glad to be back. Your jools are in safe keeping, and not all the blagyirds in creation could get at them. I've come to tell you to cheer up – a stout heart to a stey brae, as the old folk say. I'm handling this affair as a business proposition, so don't be feared, Mem. If there are enemies seeking you, there's friends on the road too . . . Now, you'll have had your dinner, but you'd maybe like a little dessert.'

He spread before them a huge box of chocolates, the best that Mearns Street could produce, a box of candied fruits, and another of salted almonds. Then from his hideously over-crowded pockets he took another box, which he offered rather shyly. 'That's some powder for your complexion. They tell me that ladies find it useful whiles.'

The girl's strained face watched him at first in mystification, and then broke slowly into a smile. Youth came back to it, the smile changed to a laugh, a low rippling laugh like far-away bells. She took both his hands.

'You are kind,' she said, 'you are kind and brave. You are a de-ar.'

And then she kissed him.

Now, as far as Dickson could remember, no one had ever kissed him except his wife. The light touch of her lips on his forehead was like the pressing of an electric button which explodes some powerful charge and alters the face of a countryside. He blushed scarlet; then he wanted to cry; then he wanted to sing. An immense exhilaration seized him, and I am certain that if at that moment the serried ranks of Bolshevy had appeared in the doorway, Dickson would have hurled himself upon them with a joyful shout.

Cousin Eugénie was earnestly eating chocolates, but Saskia had other business.

'You will hold the house?' she asked.

'Please God, yes,' said Heritage. 'I look at it this way. The time is very near when your three gaolers expect the others, their masters. They have not troubled you in the past two days as they threatened, because it was not worth while. But they won't want to let you out of their sight in the final hours, so they will almost certainly come here to be on the spot. Our object is to keep them out and confuse their plans. Somewhere in this neighbourhood, probably very near, is the man you fear most. If we nonplus the three watchers, they'll have to revise their policy, and that means a delay, and every hour's delay is a gain. Mr McCunn has found out that the factor Loudon is in the plot, and he has purchase enough, it seems, to blanket for a time any appeal to the law. But Mr McCunn has taken steps to circumvent him, and in twenty-four hours we should have help here.'

'I do not want the help of your law,' the girl interrupted. 'It will entangle me.'

'Not a bit of it,' said Dickson cheerfully. 'You see, Mem, they've clean lost track of the jools, and nobody knows where they are but me. I'm a truthful man, but I'll lie like a packman if I'm asked questions. For the rest, it's a question of kidnapping, I understand, and that's a thing that's not to be allowed. My advice is to go to our beds and get a little sleep while there's a chance of it. The Gorbals Die-Hards are grand watch-dogs.'

This view sounded so reasonable that it was at once acted upon. The ladies' chamber was next door to the smoking-room – what had been the old schoolroom. Heritage arranged with Saskia that the lamp was to be kept burning low, and that on no account were they to move unless summoned by him. Then he and Dickson made their way to the hall, where there was a faint glimmer from the moon in the upper unshuttered windows – enough to reveal the figure of Wee Jaikie on duty at the foot of the staircase. They ascended to the second floor, where, in a large room above the hall, Heritage had bestowed his pack. He had managed to open a fold of the shutters, and there was sufficient light to see two big mahogany bedsteads without mattresses or bedclothes, and wardrobes and chests of drawers sheeted in holland. Outside the wind was rising again, but the rain had stopped. Angry watery clouds scurried across the heavens.

Dickson made a pillow of his waterproof, stretched himself on one of the bedsteads, and, so quiet was his conscience and so weary his body from the buffetings of the past days, was almost instantly asleep. It seemed to him that he had scarcely closed his eyes when he was awakened by Dougal's hand pinching his shoulder. He gathered that the moon was setting, for the room was pitchy dark.

'The three o' them is approachin' the kitchen door,' whispered the Chieftain. 'I seen them from a spy-hole I made out o' a ventilator.'

'Is it barricaded?' asked Heritage, who had apparently not been asleep.

'Aye, but I've thought o' a far better plan. Why should we keep them out? They'll be safer inside. Listen! We might manage to get them in one at a time. If they can't get in at the kitchen door, they'll send one o' them round to get in by another door and open to them. That gives us a chance to get them separated, and lock them up. There's walth o' closets and hidy-holes all over the place, each with good doors and good keys to them. Supposin' we get the three o' them shut up – the others, when they come, will have nobody to guide them. Of course some time or other the three will break out, but it may be ower late for them. At present we're besieged and they're roamin' the country. Would it no' be far better if they were the ones lockit up and we were goin' loose?'

'Supposing they don't come in one at a time?' Dickson objected.

'We'll make them,' said Dougal firmly. 'There's no time to waste. Are ye for it?'

'Yes,' said Heritage. 'Who's at the kitchen door?'

'Peter Paterson. I told him no' to whistle, but to wait on me ... Keep your boots off. Ye're better in your stockin' feet. Wait you in the hall and see ye're well hidden, for likely whoever comes in will have a lantern. Just you keep quiet unless I give ye a cry. I've planned it a' out, and we're ready for them.'

Dougal disappeared, and Dickson and Heritage, with their boots tied round their necks by their laces, crept out to the upper landing. The hall was impenetrably dark, but full of voices, for the wind was talking in the ceiling beams, and murmuring through the long passages. The walls creaked and muttered and little bits of plaster fluttered down. The noise was an advantage for the game of hide-and-seek they proposed to play, but it made it hard to detect the enemy's approach. Dickson, in order to get properly wakened, adventured as far as the smoking-room. It was black with night, but below the door of the adjacent room a faint line of light showed where the Princess's lamp was burning. He advanced to the window, and heard distinctly a foot on the gravel path that led to the veranda. This sent him back to the hall in search of Dougal, whom he encountered in the passage. That boy could certainly see in the dark, for he caught Dickson's wrist without hesitation.

'We've got Spittal in the wine-cellar,' he whispered triumphantly. 'The kitchen door was barricaded, and when they tried it, it wouldn't open. "Bide here," says Dobson to Spittal, "and we'll go round by another door and come back and open to ye." So off they went, and by that time Peter Paterson and me had the barricade down. As we expected, Spittal tries the key again and it opens quite easy. He comes in and locks it behind him, and, Dobson having took away the lantern, he gropes his way very carefu' towards the kitchen. There's a point where the wine-cellar door and the scullery door are aside each other. He should have taken the second, but I had it shut so he takes the first. Peter Paterson gave him a wee shove and he fell down the two-three steps into the cellar, and we turned the key on him. Yon cellar has a grand door and no windies.'

'And Dobson and Léon are at the veranda door? With a light?'

'Thomas Yownie's on duty there. Ye can trust him. Ye'll no fickle Thomas Yownie.'

The next minutes were for Dickson a delirium of excitement not unpleasantly shot with flashes of doubt and fear. As a child he had played hide-and-seek, and his memory had always cherished the delights of the game. But how marvellous to play it thus in a great empty house, at dark of night, with the heaven filled with tempest, and with death or wounds as the stakes!

He took refuge in a corner where a tapestry curtain and the side of a Dutch awmry gave him shelter, and from where he stood he could see the garden-room and the beginning of the tiled passage which led to the veranda door. That is to say, he could have seen these things if there had been any light, which there was not. He heard the soft flitting of bare feet, for a delicate sound is often audible in a din when a loud noise is obscured. Then a gale of wind blew towards him, as from an open door, and far away gleamed the flickering light of a lantern.

Suddenly the light disappeared and there was a clatter on the floor and a breaking of glass. Either the wind or Thomas Yownie.

The veranda door was shut, a match spluttered and the lantern was relit. Dobson and Léon came into the hall, both clad in long mackintoshes which glistened from the weather. Dobson halted and listened to the wind howling in the upper spaces. He cursed it bitterly, looked at his watch, and then made an observation which woke the liveliest interest in Dickson lurking beside the awmry and Heritage ensconced in the shadow of a window-seat.

'He's late. He should have been here five minutes syne. It would be a dirty road for his car.'

So the Unknown was coming that night. The news made Dickson the more resolved to get the watchers under lock and key before reinforcements arrived, and so put grit in their wheels. Then his party must escape – flee anywhere so long as it was far from Dalquharter.

'You stop here,' said Dobson, 'I'll go down and let Spidel in. We want another lamp. Get the one that the women use, and for God's sake get a move on.'

The sound of his feet died in the kitchen passage and then rung again on the stone stairs. Dickson's ear of faith heard also the soft patter of naked feet as the Die-Hards preceded and followed him. He was delivering himself blind and bound into their hands.

For a minute or two there was no sound but the wind, which had found a loose chimney cowl on the roof and screwed out of it an odd sound like the drone of a bagpipe. Dickson, unable to remain any longer in one place, moved into the centre of the hall, believing that Léon had gone to the smoking-room. It was a dangerous thing to do, for suddenly a match was lit a yard from him. He had the sense to drop low, and so was out of the main glare of the light. The man with the match apparently had no more, judging by his execrations. Dickson stood stock still, longing for the wind to fall so that he might hear the sound of the fellow's boots on the stone floor. He gathered that they were moving towards the smoking-room.

'Heritage,' he whispered as loud as he dared, but there was no answer.

Then suddenly a moving body collided with him. He jumped a step back and then stood at attention. 'Is that you, Dobson?' a voice asked.

Now behold the occasional advantage of a nickname. Dickson thought he was being addressed as 'Dogson' after the Poet's fashion. Had he dreamed it was Léon he would not have replied, but fluttered off into the shadows, and so missed a piece of vital news.

'Ay, it's me,' he whispered.

His voice and accent were Scotch, like Dobson's, and Léon suspected nothing.

'I do not like this wind,' he grumbled. 'The Captain's letter said at dawn, but there is no chance of the Danish brig making your little harbour in this weather. She must lie off and land the men by boats. That I do not like. It is too public.'

The news – tremendous news, for it told that the newcomers would come by sea, which had never before entered Dickson's head – so interested him that he stood dumb and ruminating. The silence made the Belgian suspect; he put out a hand and felt a waterproofed arm which might have been Dobson's. But the height of the shoulder proved that it was not the burly innkeeper. There was an oath, a quick movement, and Dickson went down with a knee on his chest and two hands at his throat.

'Heritage,' he gasped. 'Help!'

There was a sound of furniture scraped violently on the floor. A gurgle from Dickson served as a guide, and the Poet suddenly cascaded over the combatants. He felt for a head, found Léon's, and gripped the neck so savagely that the owner loosened his hold on Dickson. The last-named found himself being buffeted violently by heavy-shod feet which seemed to be manoeuvring before an unseen enemy. He rolled out of the road and encountered another pair of feet, this time unshod. Then came a sound of a concussion, as if metal or wood had struck some part of a human frame, and then a stumble and fall.

After that a good many things all seemed to happen at once. There was a sudden light, which showed Léon blinking with a short loaded life-preserver in his hand, and Heritage prone in front of him on the floor. It also showed Dickson the figure of Dougal, and more than one Die-Hard in the background. The light went out as suddenly as it had appeared. There was a whistle and a hoarse 'Come on, men,' and then for two seconds there was a desperate silent combat. It ended with Léon's head meeting the floor so violently that its possessor became oblivious of further proceedings. He was dragged into a cubby-hole, which had once been used for coats and rugs, and the door locked on him. Then the light sprang forth again. It revealed Dougal and five Die-Hards, somewhat the worse for wear; it revealed also Dickson squatted with outspread waterproof very like a sitting hen.

'Where's Dobson?' he asked.

'In the boiler-house,' and for once Dougal's gravity had laughter in it. 'Govey Dick! but yon was a fecht! Me and Peter Paterson and Wee Jaikie started it, but it was the whole company afore the end. Are ye better, Jaikie?'

'Ay, I'm better,' said a pallid midget.

'He kickit Jaikie in the stomach and Jaikie was seeck,' Dougal explained. 'That's the three accounted for. Now they're safe for five hours at the least. I think mysel' that Dobson will be the first to get out, but he'll have his work letting out the others. Now, I'm for flittin' to the old Tower. They'll no ken where we are for a long time, and anyway yon place will be far easier to defend. Without they kindle a fire and smoke us out, I don't see how they'll beat us. Our provisions are a' there, and there's a grand well o' water inside. Forbye there's the road down the rocks that'll keep our communications open . . . But what's come to Mr Heritage?'

Dickson to his shame had forgotten all about his friend. The Poet lay very quiet with his head on one side and his legs crooked limply. Blood trickled over his eyes from an ugly scar on his forehead. Dickson felt his heart and pulse and found them faint but regular. The man had got a swinging blow and might have a slight concussion; for the present he was unconscious.

'All the more reason why we should flit,' said Dougal. 'What d'ye say, Mr McCunn?'

'Flit, of course, but further than the old Tower. What's the time?' He lifted Heritage's wrist and saw from his watch that it was half-past three. 'Mercy! It's nearly morning. Afore we put these blagyirds away, they were conversing, at least Léon and Dobson were. They said that they expected somebody every moment, but that the car would be late. We've still got that Somebody to tackle. Then Léon spoke to me in the dark, thinking I was Dobson, and cursed the wind, saying it would keep the Danish brig from getting in at dawn as had been intended. D'you see what that means? The worst of the lot, the ones the ladies are in terror of, are coming by sea. Ay, and they can return by sea. We thought that the attack would be by land, and that even if they succeeded we could hang on to their heels and follow them, till we got them stopped. But that's impossible! If they come in from the water, they can go out by the water, and there'll never be more heard tell of the ladies or of you or me.'

Dougal's face was once again sunk in gloom. 'What's your plan, then?'

'We must get the ladies away from here – away inland, far from the sea. The rest of us must stand a siege in the old Tower, so that the enemy will think we're all there. Please God we'll hold out long enough for help to arrive. But we mustn't hang about here. There's the man Dobson mentioned – he may come any second, and we want to be away first. Get the ladder, Dougal . . . Four of you take Mr Heritage, and two come with me and carry the ladies' things. It's no' raining, but the wind's enough to take the wings off a seagull.'

Dickson roused Saskia and her cousin, bidding them be ready in ten minutes. Then with the help of the Die-Hards he proceeded to transport the necessary supplies – the stove, oil, dishes, clothes, and wraps; more than one journey was needed of small boys, hidden under clouds of baggage. When everything had gone he collected the keys, behind which, in various quarters of the house, three gaolers fumed impotently, and gave them to Wee Jaikie to dispose of in some secret nook. Then he led the two ladies to the veranda, the elder cross and sleepy, the younger alert at the prospect of movement.

'Tell me again,' she said. 'You have locked all the three up, and they are now the imprisoned?'

'Well, it was the boys that, properly speaking, did the locking up.'

'It is a great – how do you say? – a turning of the tables. Ah – what is that?'

At the end of the veranda there was a clattering down of pots which could not be due to the wind, since the place was sheltered. There was as yet only the faintest hint of light, and black night still lurked in the crannies. Followed another fall of pots, as from a clumsy intruder, and then a man appeared, clear against the glass door by which the path descended to the rock garden.

It was the fourth man, whom the three prisoners had awaited. Dickson had no doubt at all about his identity. He was that villain from whom all the others took their orders, the man whom the Princess shuddered at. Before starting he had loaded his pistol. Now he tugged it from his waterproof pocket, pointed it at the other and fired.

The man seemed to be hit, for he spun round and clapped a hand to his left arm. Then he fled through the door, which he left open.

Dickson was after him like a hound. At the door he saw him running and raised his pistol for another shot. Then he dropped it, for he saw something in the crouching, dodging figure which was familiar.

'A mistake,' he explained to Jaikie when he returned. 'But the shot wasn't wasted. I've just had a good try at killing the factor!'

## CHAPTER TEN

# DEALS WITH AN ESCAPE AND A JOURNEY

FIVE scouts' lanterns burned smokily in the ground room of the keep when Dickson ushered his charges through its cavernous door. The lights flickered in the gusts that swept after them and whistled through the slits of windows, so that the place was full of monstrous shadows, and its accustomed odour of mould and disuse was changed to a salty freshness. Upstairs on the first floor Thomas Yownie had deposited the ladies' baggage, and was busy making beds out of derelict iron bedsteads and the wraps brought from their room. On the ground floor on a heap of litter covered by an old scout's blanket lay Heritage, with Dougal in attendance.

The Chieftain had washed the blood from the Poet's brow, and the touch of cold water was bringing back his senses. Saskia with a cry flew to him, and waved off Dickson who had fetched one of the bottles of liqueur brandy. She slipped a hand inside his shirt and felt the beating of his heart. Then her slim fingers ran over his forehead.

'A bad blow,' she muttered, 'but I do not think he is ill. There is no fracture. When I nursed in the Alexander Hospital I learnt much about head wounds. Do not give him cognac if you value his life.'

Heritage was talking now and with strange tongues. Phrases like 'lined digesters' and 'free sulphurous acid' came from his lips. He implored someone to tell him if 'the first cook' was finished, and he upbraided someone else for 'cooling off' too fast.

The girl raised her head. 'But I fear he has become mad,' she said.

'Wheesht, Mem,' said Dickson, who recognized the jargon. 'He's a paper-maker.'

Saskia sat down on the litter and lifted his head so that it rested on her breast. Dougal at her bidding brought a certain case from her baggage, and with swift, capable hands she made a bandage and rubbed the wound with ointment before tying it up. Then her fingers seemed to play about his temples and along his cheeks and neck. She was the professional nurse now, absorbed, sexless. Heritage ceased to babble, his eyes shut and he was asleep.

She remained where she was, so that the Poet, when a few minutes later he woke, found himself lying with his head in her lap. She spoke first, in an imperative tone: 'You are well now. Your head does not ache. You are strong again.'

'No. Yes,' he murmured. Then more clearly: 'Where am I? Oh, I remember, I caught a lick on the head. What's become of the brutes?'

Dickson, who had extracted food from the Mearns Street box and was pressing it on the others, replied through a mouthful of biscuit: 'We're in the old Tower. The three are lockit up in the House. Are you feeling better, Mr Heritage?'

The Poet suddenly realized Saskia's position and the blood came to his pale face. He got to his feet with an effort and held out a hand to the girl. 'I'm all right now, I think. Only a little dicky on my legs. A thousand thanks, Princess. I've given you a lot of trouble.'

She smiled at him tenderly. 'You say that when you have risked your life for me.'

'There's no time to waste,' the relentless Dougal broke in. 'Comin' over here, I heard a shot. What was it?'

'It was me,' said Dickson. 'I was shootin' at the factor.'

'Did ye hit him?'

'I think so, but I'm sorry to say not badly. When I last saw him he was running too quick for a sore hurt man. When I fired I thought it was the other man – the one they were expecting.'

Dickson marvelled at himself, yet his speech was not bravado, but the honest expression of his mind. He was keyed up to a mood in which he feared nothing very much, certainly not the laws of his country. If he fell in with the Unknown, he was entirely resolved, if his Maker permitted him, to do murder as being the simplest and justest solution. And if in the pursuit of this laudable intention he happened to wing lesser game it was no fault of his.

'Well, it's a pity ye didn't get him,' said Dougal, 'him being what we ken him to be . . . I'm for holding a council o' war, and considerin' the whole position. So far we haven't done that badly. We've shifted our base without serious casualties. We've got a far better position to hold, for there's too many ways into yon Hoose, and here there's just one. Besides, we've fickled the enemy. They'll take some time to find out where we've gone. But, mind you, we can't count on their staying long shut up. Dobson's no safe in the boiler-house, for there's a skylight far up and he'll see it when the light comes and maybe before. So we'd better get our plans ready. A word with ye, Mr McCunn,' and he led Dickson aside.

'D'ye ken what these blagyirds were up to?' he whispered fiercely in Dickson's ear. 'They were goin' to pushion the lassie. How do I ken, says you? Because Thomas Yownie heard Dobson say to Lean at the scullery door, "Have ye got the dope?" he says, and Lean says, "Aye." Thomas mindit the word for he had heard about it at the picters.'

Dickson exclaimed in horror.

'What d'ye make o' that? I'll tell ye. They wanted to make sure of her, but they wouldn't have thought o' dope unless the men they expectit were due to arrive any moment. As I see it, we've to face a siege not by the three but by a dozen or more, and it'll no' be long till it starts. Now, isn't it a mercy we're safe in here?'

Dickson returned to the others with a grave face.

'Where d'you think the new folk are coming from?' he asked.

Heritage answered, 'From Auchenlochan, I suppose? Or perhaps down from the hills?'

'You're wrong.' And he told of Léon's mistaken confidences to him in the darkness. 'They are coming from the sea, just like the old pirates.'

'The sea,' Heritage repeated in a dazed voice.

'Ay, the sea. Think what that means. If they had been coming by the roads, we could have kept track of them, even if they beat us, and some of these laddies could have stuck to them and followed them up till help came. It can't be such an easy job to carry a young lady against her will along Scotch roads. But the sea's a different matter. If they've got a fast boat they could be out of the Firth and away beyond the law before we could wake up a single policeman. Ay, and even if the Government took it up and warned all the ports and ships at sea, what's to hinder them to find a hidy-hole about Ireland – or Norway? I tell you, it's a far more desperate business than I thought, and it'll no' do to wait on and trust that the Chief Constable will turn up afore the mischief's done.'

'The moral,' said Heritage, 'is that there can be no surrender. We've got to stick it out in this old place at all costs.'

'No,' said Dickson emphatically. 'The moral is that we must shift the ladies. We've got the chance while Dobson and his friends are locked up. Let's get them as far away as we can from the sea. They're far safer tramping the moors, and it's no' likely the new folk will dare to follow us.'

'But I cannot go.' Saskia, who had been listening intently, shook her head. 'I promised to wait till my friend came. If I leave I shall never find him.'

'If you stay you certainly never will, for you'll be away with the ruffians. Take a sensible view, Mem. You'll be no good to your friend or your friend to you if before night you're rocking in a ship.'

The girl shook her head again, gently but decisively. 'It was our arrangement. I cannot break it. Besides, I am sure that he will come in time, for he has never failed –'

There was a desperate finality about the quiet tones and the weary face with the shadow of a smile on it.

Then Heritage spoke. 'I don't think your plan will quite do, Dogson. Supposing we all break for the hinterland and the Danish brig finds the birds flown, that won't end the trouble. They will get on the Princess's trail, and the whole persecution will start again. I want to see things brought to a head here and now. If we can stick it out here long enough, we may trap the whole push and rid the world of a pretty gang of miscreants. Let them show their hand, and then, if the police are here by that time, we can jug the lot for piracy or something worse.'

'That's all right,' said Dougal, 'but we'd put up a better fight if we had the women off our mind. I've aye read that when a castle was going to be besieged the first thing was to get rid of the civilians.'

'Sensible to the last, Dougal,' said Dickson approvingly. 'That's just what I'm saying. I'm strong for a fight, but put the ladies in a safe bit first, for they're our weak point.'

'Do you think that if you were fighting my enemies I would consent to be absent?' came Saskia's reproachful question.

''Deed no, Mem,' said Dickson heartily. His martial spirit was with Heritage, but his prudence did not sleep, and he suddenly saw a way of placating both. 'Just you listen to what I propose. What do we amount to? Mr Heritage, six laddies, and myself – and I'm no more used to fighting than an old wife. We've seven desperate villains against us, and afore night they may be seventy. We've a fine old castle here, but for defence we want more than stone walls – we want a garrison. I tell you we must get help somewhere. Ay, but how, says you? Well, coming here I noticed a gentleman's house away up ayont the railway and close to the hills. The laird's maybe not at home, but there will be men there of some kind – gamekeepers and woodmen and such like. My plan is to go there at once and ask for help. Now, it's useless me going alone, for nobody would listen to me. They'd tell me to go back to the shop or they'd think me demented. But with you, Mem, it would be a different matter. They wouldn't disbelieve you. So I want you to come with me, and to come at once, for God knows how soon our need will be sore. We'll leave your cousin with Mrs Morran in the village, for bed's the place for her, and then you and me will be off on our business.'

The girl looked at Heritage, who nodded. 'It's the only

way,' he said. 'Get every man jack you can raise, and if it's humanly possible get a gun or two. I believe there's time enough, for I don't see the brig arriving in broad daylight.'

'D'you not?' Dickson asked rudely. 'Have you considered what day this is? It's the Sabbath, the best of days for an ill deed. There's no kirk hereaways, and everybody in the parish will be sitting indoors by the fire.' He looked at his watch. 'In half an hour it'll be light. Haste you, Mem, and get ready. Dougal, what's the weather?'

The Chieftain swung open the door, and sniffed the air. The wind had fallen for the time being, and the surge of the tides below the rocks rose like the clamour of a mob. With the lull, mist and a thin drizzle had cloaked the world again.

To Dickson's surprise Dougal seemed to be in good spirits. He began to sing to a hymn tune a strange ditty.

*Class-conscious we are, and class-conscious wull be*
*Till our fit's on the neck o' the Boorjoyzee.*

'What on earth are you singing?' Dickson inquired.

Dougal grinned. 'Wee Jaikie went to a Socialist Sunday School last winter because he heard they were for fechtin' battles. Ay, and they telled him he was to jine a thing called an International, and Jaikie thought it was a fitba' club. But when he fund out there was no magic lantern or swaree at Christmas he gie'd it the chuck. They learned him a heap o' queer songs. That's one.'

'What does the last word mean?'

'I don't ken. Jaikie thought it was some kind of a draigon.'

'It's a daft-like thing anyway . . . When's high water?'

Dougal answered that to the best of his knowledge it fell between four and five in the afternoon.

'Then that's when we may expect the foreign gentry if they think to bring their boat in to the Garplefoot . . . Dougal, lad, I trust you to keep a most careful and prayerful watch. You had better get the Die-Hards out of the Tower and all round the place afore Dobson and Co get loose, or you'll no' get a chance later. Don't lose your mobility, as the sodgers say.

Mr Heritage can hold the fort, but you laddies should be spread out like a screen.'

'That was my notion,' said Dougal. 'I'll detail two Die-Hards – Thomas Yownie and Wee Jaikie – to keep in touch with ye and watch for ye comin' back. Thomas ye ken already; ye'll no fickle Thomas Yownie. But don't be mistook about Wee Jaikie. He's terrible fond of greetin', but it's no fright with him but excitement. It's just a habit he's gotten. When ye see Jaikie begin to greet, ye may be sure that Jaikie's gettin' dangerous.'

The door shut behind them and Dickson found himself with his two charges in a world dim with fog and rain and the still lingering darkness. The air was raw, and had the sour smell which comes from soaked earth and wet boughs when the leaves are not yet fledged. Both the women were miserably equipped for such an expedition. Cousin Eugénie trailed heavy furs, Saskia's only wrap was a bright-coloured shawl about her shoulders, and both wore thin foreign shoes. Dickson insisted on stripping off his trusty waterproof and forcing it on the Princess, on whose slim body it hung very loose and very short. The elder woman stumbled and whimpered and needed the constant support of his arm, walking like a townswoman from the knees. But Saskia swung from the hips like a free woman, and Dickson had much ado to keep up with her. She seemed to delight in the bitter freshness of the dawn, inhaling deep breaths of it, and humming fragments of a tune.

Guided by Thomas Yownie they took the road which Dickson and Heritage had travelled the first evening, through the shrubberies on the north side of the House and the side avenue beyond which the ground fell to the Laver glen. On their right the House rose like a dark cloud, but Dickson had lost his terror of it. There were three angry men inside it, he remembered: long let them stay there. He marvelled at his mood, and also rejoiced, for his worst fear had always been that he might prove a coward. Now he was puzzled to think how he could ever be frightened again, for his one object was to succeed, and in that absorption fear seemed to him merely a waste of time. 'It all comes of treating the thing as a business proposition,' he told himself.

But there was far more in his heart than this sober resolution. He was intoxicated with the resurgence of youth and felt a rapture of audacity which he never remembered in his decorous boyhood. 'I haven't been doing badly for an old man,' he reflected with glee. What, oh what had become of the pillar of commerce, the man who might have been a Bailie had he sought municipal honours, the elder in the Guthrie Memorial Kirk, the instructor of literary young men? In the past three days he had levanted with jewels which had once been an Emperor's and certainly were not his; he had burglariously entered and made free of a strange house; he had played hide-and-seek at the risk of his neck and had wrestled in the dark with a foreign miscreant; he had shot at an eminent solicitor with intent to kill; and he was now engaged in tramping the world with a fairy-tale Princess. I blush to confess that of each of his doings he was unashamedly proud, and thirsted for many more in the same line. 'Gosh, but I'm seeing life,' was his unregenerate conclusion.

Without sight or sound of a human being, they descended to the Laver, climbed again by the cart track, and passed the deserted West Lodge and inn to the village. It was almost full dawn when the three stood in Mrs Morran's kitchen.

'I've brought you two ladies, Auntie Phemie,' said Dickson.

They made an odd group in that cheerful place, where the new-lit fire was crackling in the big grate – the wet undignified form of Dickson, unshaven of cheek and chin and disreputable in garb; the shrouded figure of Cousin Eugénie, who had sunk into the arm-chair and closed her eyes; the slim girl, into whose face the weather had whipped a glow like blossom; and the hostess, with her petticoats kilted and an ancient mutch on her head.

Mrs Morran looked once at Saskia, and then did a thing which she had not done since her girlhood. She curtseyed.

'I'm proud to see ye here, Mem. Off wi' your things, and I'll get ye dry claes. Losh, ye're fair soppin'. And your shoon! Ye maun change your feet . . . Dickson! Awa' up to the loft, and dinna you stir till I give ye a cry. The leddies will change by the fire. And you, Mem' – this to Cousin Eugénie – 'the place for you's your bed. I'll kinnle a fire ben the hoose in a jiffey. And syne ye'll have breakfast – ye'll hae a cup o' tea wi' me now, for the kettle's just on the boil. Awa' wi' ye, Dickson,' and she stamped her foot.

Dickson departed, and in the loft washed his face, and smoked a pipe on the edge of the bed, watching the mist eddying up the village street. From below rose the sounds of hospitable bustle, and when after some twenty minutes' vigil he descended, he found Saskia toasting stockinged toes by the fire in the great arm-chair, and Mrs Morran setting the table.

'Auntie Phemie, hearken to me. We've taken on too big a job for two men and six laddies, and help we've got to get, and that this very morning. D'you mind the big white house away up near the hills ayont the station and east of the Ayr road? It looked like a gentleman's shooting lodge. I was thinking of trying there. Mercy!'

The exclamation was wrung from him by his eyes settling on Saskia and noting her apparel. Gone were her thin foreign clothes, and in their place she wore a heavy tweed skirt cut very short, and thick homespun stockings, which had been made for someone with larger feet than hers. A pair of the coarse low-heeled shoes which country folk wear in the farm-yard stood warming by the hearth. She still had her russet jumper, but round her neck hung a grey wool scarf, of the kind known as a 'comforter'. Amazingly pretty she looked in Dickson's eyes, but with a different kind of prettiness. The sense of fragility had fled, and he saw how nobly built she was for all her exquisiteness. She looked like a queen, he thought, but a queen to go gipsying through the world with.

'Ay, they're some o' Elspeth's things, rale guid furthy claes,' said Mrs Morran complacently. 'And the shoon are what she used to gang about the byres wi' when she was in the Castlewham dairy. The leddy was tellin' me she was for trampin' the hills, and thae things will keep her dry and warm ... I ken the hoose ye mean. They ca' it the Mains of Garple. And I ken the man that bides in it. He's yin Sir

Erchibald Roylance. English, but his mither was a Dalziel. I'm no weel acquaint wi' his forbears, but I'm weel eneuch acquaint wi' Sir Erchie, and "better a guid coo than a coo o' a guid kind," as my mither used to say. He used to be an awfu' wild callant, a freend o' puir Maister Quentin, and up to ony deevilry. But they tell me he's a quieter lad since the war, and sair lamed by fa'in' oot o' an airyplane.'

'Will he be at the Mains just now?' Dickson asked.

'I wadna wonder. He has a muckle place in England, but he aye used to come here in the back-end for the shootin' and in April for birds. He's clean daft about birds. He'll be out a' day at the Craig watchin' solans, or lyin' a' mornin' i' the moss lookin' at bog-blitters.'

'Will he help, think you?'

'I'll wager he'll help. Onyway it's your best chance, and better a wee bush than nae bield. Now, sit in to your breakfast.'

It was a merry meal. Mrs Morran dispensed tea and gnomic wisdom. Saskia ate heartily, speaking little, but once or twice laying her hand softly on her hostess's gnarled fingers. Dickson was in such spirits that he gobbled shamelessly, being both hungry and hurried, and he spoke of the still unconquered enemy with ease and disrespect, so that Mrs Morran was moved to observe that there was 'naething sae bauld as a blind mear.' But when in a sudden return of modesty he belittled his usefulness and talked sombrely of his mature years he was told that he 'wad never be auld wi' sae muckle honesty.' Indeed it was very clear that Mrs Morran approved of her nephew.

They did not linger over breakfast, for both were impatient to be on the road. Mrs Morran assisted Saskia to put on Elspeth's shoes. '"Even a young fit finds comfort in an auld bauchle," as my mother, honest woman, used to say.' Dickson's waterproof was restored to him, and for Saskia an old raincoat belonging to the son in South Africa was discovered, which fitted her better. 'Siccan weather,' said the hostess, as she opened the door to let in a swirl of wind. 'The deil's aye kind to his ain. Haste ye back, Mem, and be sure I'll tak' guid care o' your leddy cousin.'

The proper way to the Mains of Garple was either by the station and the Ayr road, or by the Auchenlochan highway, branching off half a mile beyond the Garple bridge. But Dickson, who had been studying the map and fancied himself as a pathfinder, chose the direct route across the Long Muir as being at once shorter and more sequestered. With the dawn the wind had risen again, but it had shifted towards the north-west and was many degrees colder. The mist was furling on the hills like sails, the rain had ceased, and out at sea the eye covered a mile or two of wild water. The moor was drenching wet, and the peat bogs were brimming with inky pools, so that soon the travellers were soaked to the knees. Dickson had no fear of pursuit, for he calculated that Dobson and his friends, even if they had got out, would be busy looking for the truants in the vicinity of the House and would presently be engaged with the old Tower. But he realized, too, that speed on his errand was vital, for at any moment the Unknown might arrive from the sea.

So he kept up a good pace, half-running, half-striding, till they had passed the railway, and he found himself gasping with a stitch in his side, and compelled to rest in the lee of what had once been a sheepfold. Saskia amazed him. She moved over the rough heather like a deer, and it was her hand that helped him across the deeper hags. Before such youth and vigour he felt clumsy and old. She stood looking down at him as he recovered his breath, cool, unruffled, alert as Diana. His mind fled to Heritage, and it occurred to him suddenly that the Poet had set his affections very high. Loyalty drove him to speak a word for his friend.

'I've got the easy job,' he said. 'Mr Heritage will have the whole pack on him in that old Tower, and him with such a sore clout on his head. I've left him my pistol. He's a terrible brave man!'

She smiled.

'Ay, and he's a poet too.'

'So?' she said. 'I did not know. He is very young.'

'He's a man of very high ideels.'

She puzzled at the word, and then smiled. 'He is like many

of our young men in Russia, the students – his mind is in a ferment and he does not know what he wants. But he is brave.'

This seemed to Dickson's loyal soul but a chilly tribute.

'I think he is in love with me,' she continued.

He looked up startled, and saw in her face that which gave him a view into a strange new world. He had thought that women blushed when they talked of love, but her eyes were as grave and candid as a boy's. Here was one who had gone through waters so deep that she had lost the foibles of sex. Love to her was only a word of ill omen, a threat on the lips of brutes, an extra battalion of peril in an army of perplexities. He felt like some homely rustic who finds himself swept unwittingly into the moonlight hunt of Artemis and her maidens.

'He is a romantic,' she said. 'I have known so many like him.'

'He's no' that,' said Dickson shortly. 'Why, he used to be aye laughing at me for being romantic. He's one that's looking for truth and reality, he says, and he's terrible down on the kind of poetry I like myself.'

She smiled. 'They all talk so. But you, my friend Dickson' (she pronounced the name in two staccato syllables ever so prettily), 'you are different. Tell me about yourself.'

'I'm just what you see – a middle-aged retired grocer.'

'Grocer?' she queried. 'Ah, yes, *épicier*. But you are a very remarkable *épicier*. Mr Heritage I understand, but you and those little boys – no. I am sure of one thing – you are not a romantic. You are too humorous and – and – I think you are like Ulysses, for it would not be easy to defeat you.'

Her eyes were kind, nay affectionate, and Dickson experienced a preposterous rapture in his soul, followed by a sinking, as he realized how far the job was still from being completed.

'We must be getting on, Mem,' he said hastily, and the two plunged again into the heather.

The Ayr road was crossed, and the fir wood around the Mains became visible, and presently the white gates of the entrance. A wind-blown spire of smoke beyond the trees proclaimed that the house was not untenanted. As they entered the drive the Scots firs were tossing in the gale, which blew fiercely at this altitude, but, the dwelling itself being more in the hollow, the daffodil clumps on the lawn were but mildly fluttered.

The door was opened by a one-armed butler who bore all the marks of the old regular soldier. Dickson produced a card and asked to see his master on urgent business. Sir Archibald was at home, he was told, and had just finished breakfast. The two were led into a large bare chamber which had all the chill and mustiness of a bachelor's drawing-room. The butler returned, and said Sir Archibald would see him. 'I'd better go myself first and prepare the way, Mem,' Dickson whispered, and followed the man across the hall.

He found himself ushered into a fair-sized room where a bright fire was burning. On a table lay the remains of breakfast, and the odour of food mingled pleasantly with the scent of peat. The horns and heads of big game, foxes' masks, the model of a gigantic salmon, and several bookcases adorned the walls, and books and maps were mixed with decanters and cigar-boxes on the long sideboard. After the wild out of doors the place seemed the very shrine of comfort. A young man sat in an arm-chair by the fire with a leg on a stool; he was smoking a pipe, and reading the *Field*, and on another stool at his elbow was a pile of new novels. He was a pleasant brown-faced young man, with remarkably smooth hair and a roving humorous eye.

'Come in, Mr McCunn. Very glad to see you. If, as I take it, you're the grocer, you're a household name in these parts. I get all my supplies from you, and I've just been makin' inroads on one of your divine hams. Now, what can I do for you?'

'I'm very proud to hear what you say, Sir Archibald. But I've not come on business. I've come with the queerest story you ever heard in your life and I've come to ask your help.'

'Go ahead. A good story is just what I want this vile mornin'.'

'I'm not here alone. I've a lady with me.'

'God bless my soul! A lady!'

'Aye, a princess. She's in the next room.'

The young man looked wildly at him and waved the book he had been reading.

'Excuse me, Mr McCunn, but are you quite sober? I beg your pardon. I see you are. But you know, it isn't done. Princesses don't as a rule come here after breakfast to pass the time of day. It's more absurd than this shocker I've been readin'.'

'All the same it's a fact. She'll tell you the story herself, and you'll believe her quick enough. But to prepare your mind I'll just give you a sketch of the events of the last few days.'

Before the sketch was concluded the young man had violently rung the bell. 'Sime,' he shouted to the servant, 'clear away this mess and lay the table again. Order more breakfast, all the breakfast you can get. Open the windows and get the tobacco smoke out of the air. Tidy up the place for there's a lady comin'. Quick, you juggins!'

He was on his feet now, and, with his arm in Dickson's, was heading for the door.

'My sainted aunt! And you topped off with pottin' at the factor. I've seen a few things in my day, but I'm blessed if I ever met a bird like you!'

## CHAPTER ELEVEN

# GRAVITY OUT OF BED

It is probable that Sir Archibald Roylance did not altogether believe Dickson's tale; it may be that he considered him an agreeable romancer, or a little mad, or no more than a relief to the tedium of a wet Sunday morning. But his incredulity did not survive one glance at Saskia as she stood in that bleak drawing-room among Victorian water-colours and faded chintzes. The young man's boyishness deserted him. He stopped short in his tracks, and made a profound and awkward bow. 'I am at your service, Mademoiselle,' he said, amazed at himself. The words seemed to have come out of a confused memory of plays and novels.

She inclined her head – a little on one side, and looked towards Dickson.

'Sir Archibald's going to do his best for us,' said that squire of dames. 'I was telling him that we had had our breakfast.'

'Let's get out of this sepulchre,' said their host, who was recovering himself. 'There's a roasting fire in my den. Of course you'll have something to eat – hot coffee, anyhow – I've trained my cook to make coffee like a Frenchwoman. The housekeeper will take charge of you, if you want to tidy up, and you must excuse our ramshackle ways, please. I don't believe there's ever been a lady in this house before, you know.'

He led her to the smoking-room and ensconced her in the great chair by the fire. Smilingly she refused a series of offers which ranged from a sheepskin mantle which he had got in the Pamirs and which he thought might fit her, to hot whisky and water as a specific against a chill. But she accepted a pair of slippers and deftly kicked off the brogues provided by Mrs Morran. Also, while Dickson started rapaciously on a second breakfast, she allowed him to pour her out a cup of coffee.

'You are a soldier?' she asked.

'Two years infantry – 5th Battalion Lennox Highlanders, and then Flying Corps. Top-hole time I had too till the day before the Armistice, when my luck gave out and I took a nasty toss. Consequently I'm not as fast on my legs now as I'd like to be.'

'You were a friend of Captain Kennedy?'

'His oldest. We were at the same private school, and he was at m' tutor's, and we were never much separated till he went abroad to cram for the Diplomatic and I started east to shoot things.'

'Then I will tell you what I told Captain Kennedy.' Saskia, looking into the heart of the peats, began the story of which we have already heard a version, but she told it differently, for she was telling it to one who more or less belonged to her own world. She mentioned names at which the other nodded. She spoke of a certain Paul Abreskov. 'I heard of him at Bokhara in 1912,' said Sir Archie, and his face grew solemn. Sometimes she lapsed into French, and her hearer's brow wrinkled, but he appeared to follow. When she had finished he drew a long breath.

'My aunt! What a time you've been through! I've seen pluck in my day, but yours! It's not thinkable. D'you mind if I ask a question, Princess? Bolshevism we know all about, and I admit Trotsky and his friends are a pretty effective push; but how on earth have they got a world-wide graft going in the time so that they can stretch their net to an out-of-the-way spot like this? It looks as if they had struck a Napoleon somewhere.'

'You do not understand,' she said. 'I cannot make anyone understand – except a Russian. My country has been broken to pieces, and there is no law in it; therefore it is a nursery of crime. So would England be, or France, if you had suffered the same misfortunes. My people are not wickeder than others, but for the moment they are sick and have no strength. As for the government of the Bolsheviki it matters little, for it will pass. Some parts of it may remain, but it is a government of the sick and fevered, and cannot endure in health. Lenin may be a good man – I do not think so, but I do not know – but if he were an archangel he could not alter things. Russia is mortally sick and therefore all evil is unchained, and the criminals have no one to check them. There is crime everywhere in the world, and the unfettered crime in Russia is so powerful that it stretches its hand to crime throughout the globe and there is a great mobilizing everywhere of wicked men. Once you boasted that law was international and that the police in one land worked with the police of all others. To-day that is true about criminals. After a war evil passions are loosed, and, since Russia is broken, in her they can make their headquarters ... It is not Bolshevism, the theory, you need fear, for that is a weak and dying thing. It is crime, which to-day finds its seat in my country, but is not only Russian. It has no fatherland. It is as old as human nature and as wide as the earth.'

'I see,' said Sir Archie. 'Gad, here have I been vegetatin' and thinkin' that all excitement had gone out of life with the war, and sometimes even regrettin' that the beastly old thing was over, and all the while the world fairly hummin' with interest. And Loudon too!'

'I would like your candid opinion on yon factor, Sir Archibald,' said Dickson.

'I can't say I ever liked him, and I've once or twice had a row with him, for he used to bring his pals to shoot over Dalquharter and he didn't quite play the game by me. But I know dashed little about him, for I've been a lot away. Bit hairy about the heels, of course. A great figure at local race-meetin's, and used to toady old Carforth and the huntin' crowd. He has a pretty big reputation as a sharp lawyer and some of the thick-headed lairds swear by him, but Quentin never could stick him. It's quite likely he's been gettin' into Queer Street, for he was always speculatin' in horseflesh, and I fancy he plunged a bit on the Turf. But I can't think how he got mixed up in this show.'

'I'm positive Dobson's his brother.'

'And put this business in his way. That would explain it all right ... He must be runnin' for pretty big stakes, for that kind of lad don't dabble in crime for six-and-eightpence ...

Now for the layout. You've got three men shut up in Dalquharter House, who by this time have probably escaped. One of you – what's his name? – Heritage? – is in the old Tower, and you think that *they* think the Princess is still there and will sit round the place like terriers. Sometime to-day the Danish brig will arrive with reinforcements, and then there will be a hefty fight. Well, the first thing to be done is to get rid of Loudon's stymie with the authorities. Princess, I'm going to carry you off in my car to the Chief Constable. The second thing is for you after that to stay on here. It's a deadly place on a wet day, but it's safe enough.'

Saskia shook her head and Dickson spoke for her.

'You'll no' get her to stop here. I've done my best, but she's determined to be back at Dalquharter. You see she's expecting a friend, and besides, if there's going to be a battle she'd like to be in it. Is that so, Mem?'

Sir Archie looked helplessly around him, and the sight of the girl's face convinced him that argument would be fruitless. 'Anyhow she must come with me to the Chief Constable. Lethington's a slow bird on the wing, and I don't see myself convincin' him that he must get busy unless I can produce the Princess. Even then it may be a tough job, for it's Sunday, and in these parts people go to sleep till Monday mornin'.'

'That's just what I'm trying to get at,' said Dickson. 'By all means go to the Chief Constable, and tell him it's life or death. My lawyer in Glasgow, Mr Caw, will have been stirring him up yesterday, and you two should complete the job ... But what I'm feared is that he'll not be in time. As you say, it's the Sabbath day, and the police are terrible slow. Now any moment that brig may be here, and the trouble will start. I'm wanting to save the Princess, but I'm wanting too to give these blagyirds the roughest handling they ever got in their lives. Therefore I say there's no time to lose. We're far ower few to put up a fight, and we want every man you've got about this place to hold the fort till the police come.'

Sir Archibald looked upon the earnest flushed face of Dickson with admiration. 'I'm blessed if you're not the most whole-hearted brigand I've ever struck.'

'I'm not. I'm just a business man.'

'Do you realize that you're levying a private war and breaking every law of the land?'

'Hoots!' said Dickson. 'I don't care a docken about the law. I'm for seeing this job through. What force can you produce?'

'Only cripples, I'm afraid. There's Sime, my butler. He was a Fusilier Jock and, as you saw, has lost an arm. Then McGuffog the keeper is a good man, but he's still got a Turkish bullet in his thigh. The chauffeur, Carfrae, was in the Yeomanry, and lost half a foot; and there's myself, as lame as a duck. The herds on the home farm are no good, for one's seventy and the other is in bed with jaundice. The Mains can produce four men, but they're rather a job lot.'

'They'll do fine,' said Dickson heartily. 'All sodgers, and no doubt all good shots. Have you plenty guns?'

Sir Archie burst into uproarious laughter. 'Mr McCunn, you're a man after my own heart. I'm under your orders. If I had a boy I'd put him into the provision trade, for it's the place to see fightin'. Yes, we've no end of guns. I advise shot-guns, for they've more stoppin' power in a rush than a rifle, and I take it it's a rough-and-tumble we're lookin' for.'

'Right,' said Dickson. 'I saw a bicycle in the hall. I want you to lend it me, for I must be getting back. You'll take the Princess and do the best you can with the Chief Constable.'

'And then?'

'Then you'll load up your car with your folk, and come down the hill to Dalquharter. There'll be a laddie, or maybe more than one, waiting for you on this side the village to give you instructions. Take your orders from them. If it's a red-haired ruffian called Dougal you'll be wise to heed what he says, for he has a grand head for battles.'

Five minutes later Dickson was pursuing a quavering course like a snipe down the avenue. He was a miserable performer on a bicycle. Not for twenty years had he bestridden one, and he did not understand such new devices as free-wheels and change of gears. The mounting had been the worst part, and it had only been achieved by the help of a rockery. He had begun by cutting into two flower-beds, and missing a birch tree by inches. But he clung on desperately, well knowing that if he fell off it would be hard to remount, and at length he gained the avenue. When he passed the lodge gates he was riding fairly straight, and when he turned off the Ayr highway to the side road that led to Dalquharter he was more or less master of his machine.

He crossed the Garple by an ancient hunchbacked bridge, observing even in his absorption with the handle-bars that the stream was in roaring spate. He wrestled up the further hill with aching calf-muscles, and got to the top just before his strength gave out. Then as the road turned seaward he had the slope with him, and enjoyed some respite. It was no case for putting up his feet, for the gale was blowing hard on his right cheek, but the downward grade enabled him to keep his course with little exertion. His anxiety to get back to the scene of action was for the moment appeased, since he knew he was making as good speed as the weather allowed, so he had leisure for thought.

But the mind of this preposterous being was not on the business before him. He dallied with irrelevant things – with the problems of youth and love. He was beginning to be very nervous about Heritage, not as the solitary garrison of the old Tower, but as the lover of Saskia. That everybody should be in love with her appeared to him only proper, for he had never met her like, and assumed that it did not exist. The desire of the moth for the star seemed to him a reasonable thing, since hopeless loyalty and unrequited passion were the eternal stock-in-trade of romance. He wished he were twenty-five himself to have the chance of indulging in such sentimentality for such a lady. But Heritage was not like him and would never be content with a romantic folly . . . He had been in love with her for two years – a long time. He spoke about wanting to die for her, which was a flight beyond Dickson himself. 'I doubt it will be what they call a "grand passion",' he reflected with reverence. But it was hopeless; he saw quite clearly that it was hopeless.

Why, he could not have explained, for Dickson's instincts

were subtler than his intelligence. He recognized that the two belonged to different circles of being, which nowhere intersected. That mysterious lady, whose eyes had looked through life to the other side, was no mate for the Poet. His faithful soul was agitated, for he had developed for Heritage a sincere affection. It would break his heart, poor man. There was he holding the fort alone and cheering himself with delightful fancies about one remoter than the moon. Dickson wanted happy endings, and here there was no hope of such. He hated to admit that life could be crooked, but the optimist in him was now fairly dashed.

Sir Archie might be the fortunate man, for of course he would soon be in love with her, if he were not so already. Dickson like all his class had a profound regard for the country gentry. The business Scot does not usually revere wealth, though he may pursue it earnestly, nor does he specially admire rank in the common sense. But for ancient race he has respect in his bones, though it may happen that in public he denies it, and the laird has for him a secular association with good family . . . Sir Archie might do. He was young, good-looking, obviously gallant . . . But no! He was not quite right either. Just a trifle too light in weight, too boyish and callow. The Princess must have youth, but it should be mighty youth, the youth of a Napoleon or a Caesar. He reflected that the Great Montrose, for whom he had a special veneration, might have filled the bill. Or young Harry with his beaver up? Or Claverhouse in the picture with the flush of temper on his cheek?

The meditations of the match-making Dickson came to an abrupt end. He had been riding negligently, his head bent against the wind, and his eyes vaguely fixed on the wet hill-gravel of the road. Of his immediate environs he was pretty well unconscious. Suddenly he was aware of figures on each side of him who advanced menacingly. Stung to activity he attempted to increase his pace, which was already good, for the road at this point descended steeply. Then, before he could prevent it, a stick was thrust into his front wheel, and the next second he was describing a curve through the air. His head took the ground, he felt a spasm of blinding pain, and then a sense of horrible suffocation before his wits left him.

'Are ye sure it's the richt man, Ecky?' said a voice which he did not hear.

'Sure. It's the Glesca body Dobson telled us to look for yesterday. It's a pund note atween us for this job. We'll tie him up in the wud till we've time to attend to him.'

'Is he bad?'

'It doesna maitter,' said the one called Ecky. 'He'll be deid onyway long afore the morn.'

*

Mrs Morran all forenoon was in a state of unSabbatical disquiet. After she had seen Saskia and Dickson start she finished her housewifely duties, took Cousin Eugénie her breakfast, and made preparation for the midday dinner. The invalid in the bed in the parlour was not a repaying subject. Cousin Eugénie belonged to that type of elderly women who, having been spoiled in youth, find the rest of life fall far short of their expectations. Her voice had acquired a perpetual wail, and the corners of what had once been a pretty mouth drooped in an eternal peevishness. She found herself in a morass of misery and shabby discomfort, but had her days continued in an even tenor she would still have lamented. 'A dingy body,' was Mrs Morran's comment, but she laboured in kindness. Unhappily they had no common language, and it was only by signs that the hostess could discover her wants and show her goodwill. She fed her and bathed her face, saw to the fire and left her to sleep. 'I'm boilin' a hen to mak' broth for your denner, Mem. Try and get a bit sleep now.' The purport of the advice was clear, and Cousin Eugénie turned obediently on her pillow.

It was Mrs Morran's custom of a Sunday to spend the morning in devout meditation. Some years before she had given up tramping the five miles to kirk, on the ground that having been a regular attendant for fifty years she had got all the good out of it that was probable. Instead she read slowly aloud to herself the sermon printed in a certain religious weekly which reached her every Saturday, and concluded with a chapter or two of the Bible. But to-day something had gone wrong with her mind. She could not follow the thread of the Reverend Doctor MacMichael's discourse. She could not fix her attention on the wanderings and misdeeds of Israel as recorded in the Book of Exodus. She must always be getting up to look at the pot on the fire, or to open the back door and study the weather. For a little she fought against her unrest, and then she gave up the attempt at concentration. She took the big pot off the fire and allowed it to simmer, and presently she fetched her boots and umbrella, and kilted her petticoats. 'I'll be none the waur o' a breath o' caller air,' she decided.

The wind was blowing great guns but there was only the thinnest sprinkle of rain. Sitting on the hen-house roof and munching a raw turnip was a figure which she recognized as the smallest of the Die-Hards. Between bites he was singing dolefully to the tune of 'Annie Laurie' one of the ditties of his quondam Sunday school:

*The Boorjoys' brays are bonnie,*
*Too-roo-ra-roo-raloo,*
*But the Worrkers o' the Worrld*
*Wull gar them a' look blue,*
*Wull gar them a' look blue,*
*And droon them in the sea,*
*And – for bonnie Annie Laurie*
*I'll lay me down and dee.*

'Losh, laddie,' she cried, 'that's cauld food for the stamach. Come indoors about midday and I'll gie ye a plate o' broth!' The Die-Hard saluted and continued on the turnip.

She took the Auchenlochan road across the Garple bridge, for that was the best road to the Mains, and by it Dickson and the others might be returning. Her equanimity at all seasons was like a Turk's, and she would not have admitted that anything mortal had power to upset or excite her: nevertheless it was a fast-beating heart that she now bore beneath her Sunday jacket. Great events, she felt, were on the eve of happening, and of them she was a part. Dickson's anxiety was hers, to bring things to a business-like conclusion. The honour of Huntingtower was at stake and of the old Kennedys. She was carrying out Mr Quentin's commands, the dead boy who used to clamour for her treacle scones. And there was more than duty in it, for youth was not dead in her old heart, and adventure had still power to quicken it.

Mrs Morran walked well, with the steady long paces of the Scots countrywoman. She left the Auchenlochan road and took the side path along the tableland to the Mains. But for the surge of the gale and the far-borne boom of the furious sea there was little noise; not a bird cried in the uneasy air. With the wind behind her Mrs Morran breasted the ascent till she had on her right the moorland running south to the Lochan valley and on her left Garple chafing in its deep forested gorges. Her eyes were quick and she noted with interest a weasel creeping from a fern-clad cairn. A little way on she passed an old ewe in difficulties and assisted it to rise. 'But for me, my wumman, ye'd hae been braxy ere nicht,' she told it as it departed bleating. Then she realized that she had come a certain distance. 'Losh, I maun be gettin' back or the hen will be spiled,' she cried, and was on the verge of turning.

But something caught her eye a hundred yards farther on the road. It was something which moved with the wind like a wounded bird, fluttering from the roadside to a puddle and then back to the rushes. She advanced to it, missed it, and caught it.

It was an old dingy green felt hat, and she recognized it as Dickson's.

Mrs Morran's brain, after a second of confusion, worked fast and clearly. She examined the road and saw that a little way on the gravel had been violently agitated. She detected several prints of hobnailed boots. There were prints, too, on a patch of peat on the south side behind a tall bank of sods. 'That's where they were hidin',' she concluded. Then she explored on the other side in a thicket of hazels and wild raspberries, and presently her perseverance was rewarded.

The scrub was all crushed and pressed as if several persons had been forcing a passage. In a hollow was a gleam of something white. She moved towards it with a quaking heart, and was relieved to find that it was only a new and expensive bicycle with the front wheel badly buckled.

Mrs Morran delayed no longer. If she had walked well on her out journey, she beat all records on the return. Sometimes she would run till her breath failed; then she would slow down till anxiety once more quickened her pace. To her joy, on the Dalquharter side of the Garple bridge she observed the figure of a Die-Hard. Breathless, flushed, with her bonnet awry and her umbrella held like a scimitar, she seized on the boy.

'Awfu' doin's! They've grippit Maister McCunn up the Mains road just afore the second milestone and forenent the auld bucht. I fund his hat, and a bicycle's lyin' broken in the wud. Haste ye, man, and get the rest and awa' and seek him. It'll be the tinklers frae the Dean. I'd gang mysel', but my legs are ower auld. Oh, laddie, dinna stop to speir questions. They'll hae him murdered or awa' to sea. And maybe the leddy was wi' him and they've got them baith. Wae's me! Wae's me!'

The Die-Hard, who was Wee Jaikie, did not delay. His eyes had filled with tears at her news, which we know to have been his habit. When Mrs Morran, after indulging in a moment of barbaric keening, looked back the road she had come, she saw a small figure trotting up the hill like a terrier who has been left behind. As he trotted he wept bitterly. Jaikie was getting dangerous.

CHAPTER TWELVE

# HOW MR McCUNN COMMITTED AN ASSAULT UPON AN ALLY

DICKSON always maintained that his senses did not leave him for more than a second or two, but he admitted that he did not remember very clearly the events of the next few hours. He was conscious of a bad pain above his eyes, and something wet trickling down his cheek. There was a perpetual sound of water in his ears and of men's voices. He found himself dropped roughly on the ground and forced to walk, and was aware that his legs were inclined to wobble. Somebody had a grip on each arm, so that he could not defend his face from the brambles, and that worried him, for his whole head seemed one aching bruise and he dreaded anything touching it. But all the time he did not open his mouth, for silence was the one duty that his muddled wits enforced. He felt that he was not the master of his mind, and he dreaded what he might disclose if he began to babble.

Presently there came a blank space of which he had no recollection at all. The movement had stopped, and he was allowed to sprawl on the ground. He thought that his head had got another whack from a bough, and that the pain put him into a stupor. When he awoke he was alone.

He discovered that he was strapped very tightly to a young Scotch fir. His arms were bent behind him and his wrists tied together with cords knotted at the back of the tree; his legs were shackled, and further cords fastened them to the bole. Also there was a halter round the trunk and just under his chin, so that while he breathed freely enough, he could not move his head. Before him was a tangle of bracken and scrub, and beyond that the gloom of dense pines; but as he could see only directly in front his prospect was strictly circumscribed.

Very slowly he began to take his bearings. The pain in his head was now dulled and quite bearable, and the flow of blood had stopped, for he felt the encrustation of it beginning on his cheeks. There was a tremendous noise all around him, and he traced this to the swaying of tree-tops in the gale. But there was an undercurrent of deeper sound – water surely, water churning among rocks. It was a stream – the Garple of course – and then he remembered where he was and what had happened.

I do not wish to portray Dickson as a hero, for nothing would annoy him more; but I am bound to say that his first clear thought was not of his own danger. It was intense exasperation at the miscarriage of his plans. Long ago he should have been with Dougal arranging operations, giving him news of Sir Archie, finding out how Heritage was faring, deciding how to use the coming reinforcements. Instead he was trussed up in a wood, a prisoner of the enemy, and utterly useless to his side. He tugged at his bonds, and nearly throttled himself. But they were of good tarry cord and did not give a fraction of an inch. Tears of bitter rage filled his eyes and made furrows on his encrusted cheeks. Idiot that he had been, he had wrecked everything! What would Saskia and Dougal and Sir Archie do without a business man by their side? There would be a muddle, and the little party would walk into a trap. He saw it all very clearly. The men from the sea would overpower them, there would be murder done, and an easy capture of the Princess; and the police would turn up at long last to find an empty headland.

He had also most comprehensively wrecked himself, and at the thought genuine panic seized him. There was no earthly chance of escape, for he was tucked away in this infernal jungle till such time as his enemies had time to deal with him. As to what that dealing would be like he had no doubts, for they knew that he had been their chief opponent. Those desperate ruffians would not scruple to put an end to him. His mind dwelt with horrible fascination upon throat-cutting, no doubt because of the presence of the cord below his chin. He had heard it was not a painful death; at any rate he remembered a clerk he had once had, a feeble, timid creature, who had twice attempted suicide that way. Surely it could not be very bad, and it would soon be over.

But another thought came to him. They would carry him off in the ship and settle with him at their leisure. No swift merciful death for him. He had read dreadful tales of the Bolsheviks' skill in torture, and now they all came back to him – stories of Chinese mercenaries, and men buried alive, and death by agonizing inches. He felt suddenly very cold and sick, and hung in his bonds, for he had no strength in his limbs. Then the pressure on his throat braced him, and also quickened his numb mind. The liveliest terror ran like quicksilver through his veins.

He endured some moments of this anguish, till after many despairing clutches at his wits he managed to attain a measure of self-control. He certainly wasn't going to allow himself to become mad. Death was death whatever form it took, and he had to face death as many better men had done before him. He had often thought about it and wondered how he should behave if the thing came to him. Respectably, he had hoped; heroically, he had sworn in his moments of confidence. But he had never for an instant dreamed of this cold, lonely, dreadful business. Last Sunday, he remembered, he had been basking in the afternoon sun in his little garden and reading about the end of Fergus MacIvor in *Waverley* and thrilling to the romance of it; and Tibby had come out and summoned him in to tea. Then he had rather wanted to be a Jacobite in the '45 and in peril of his neck, and now Providence had taken him most terribly at his word.

A week ago –! He groaned at the remembrance of that sunny garden. In seven days he had found a new world and tried a new life, and had come now to the end of it. He did not want to die, less now than ever with such wide horizons opening before him. But that was the worst of it, he reflected, for to have a great life great hazards must be taken, and there was always the risk of this sudden extinguisher . . . Had he to choose again, far better the smooth sheltered bypath than this accursed romantic highway on to which he had blundered . . .

No, by Heaven, no! Confound it, if he had to choose he would do it all again. Something stiff and indomitable in his soul was bracing him to a manlier humour. There was no one to see the figure strapped to the fir, but had there been a witness he would have noted that at this stage Dickson shut his teeth and that his troubled eyes looked very steadily before him.

His business, he felt, was to keep from thinking, for if he thought at all there would be a flow of memories – of his wife, his home, his books, his friends – to unman him. So he steeled himself to blankness, like a sleepless man imagining white sheep in a gate . . . He noted a robin below the hazels, strutting impudently. And there was a tit on a bracken frond, which made the thing sway like one of the see-saws he used to play with as a boy. There was no wind in that undergrowth, and any movement must be due to bird or beast. The tit flew off, and the oscillations of the bracken slowly died away. Then they began again, but more violently, and Dickson could not see the bird that caused them. It must be something down at the roots of the covert, a rabbit, perhaps, or a fox, or a weasel.

He watched for the first sign of the beast, and thought he caught a glimpse of tawny fur. Yes, there it was – pale dirty yellow, a weasel clearly. Then suddenly the patch grew larger, and to his amazement he looked at a human face – the face of a pallid small boy.

A head disentangled itself, followed by thin shoulders, and then by a pair of very dirty bare legs. The figure raised itself and looked sharply round to make certain that the coast was clear. Then it stood up and saluted, revealing the well-known lineaments of Wee Jaikie.

At the sight Dickson knew that he was safe by that certainty of instinct which is independent of proof, like the man who prays for a sign and has his prayer answered. He observed that the boy was quietly sobbing. Jaikie surveyed the position for an instant with red-rimmed eyes and then unclasped a knife, feeling the edge of the blade on his thumb. He darted behind the fir, and a second later Dickson's wrists were free. Then he sawed at the legs, and cut the shackles which tied them together, and then – most circumspectly – assaulted the cord which bound Dickson's neck to the trunk. There now remained only the two bonds which fastened the legs and the body to the tree.

There was a sound in the wood different from the wind and stream. Jaikie listened like a startled hind.

'They're comin' back,' he gasped. 'Just you bide where ye are and let on ye're still tied up.'

He disappeared in the scrub as inconspicuously as a rat, while two of the tinklers came up the slope from the waterside. Dickson in a fever of impatience cursed Wee Jaikie for not cutting his remaining bonds so that he could at least have made a dash for freedom. And then he realized that the boy had been right. Feeble and cramped as he was, he would have stood no chance in a race.

One of the tinklers was the man called Ecky. He had been running hard, and was mopping his brow.

'Hob's seen the brig,' he said. 'It's droppin' anchor ayont the Dookits whaur there's a bield frae the wund and deep water. They'll be landit in half an 'oor. Awa' you up to the Hoose and tell Dobson, and me and Sim and Hob will meet the boats at the Garplefit.'

The other cast a glance towards Dickson.

'What about him?' he asked.

The two scrutinized their prisoner from a distance of a few paces. Dickson, well aware of his peril, held himself as stiff as if every bond had been in place. The thought flashed on him that if he were too immobile they might think he was dying or dead, and come close to examine him. If they only kept their distance, the dusk of the wood would prevent them detecting Jaikie's handiwork.

'What'll you take to let me go?' he asked plaintively.

'Naething that you could offer, my mannie,' said Ecky.

'I'll give you a five-pound note apiece.'

'Produce the siller,' said the other.

'It's in my pocket.'

'It's no that. We riped your pooches lang syne.'

'I'll take you to Glasgow with me and pay you there. Honour bright.'

Ecky spat. 'D'ye think we're gowks? Man, there's no siller ye could pay wad mak' it worth our while to lowse ye. Bide quiet there and ye'll see some queer things ere nicht. C'way, Davie.'

The two set off at a good pace down the stream, while Dickson's pulsing heart returned to its normal rhythm. As the sound of their feet died away Wee Jaikie crawled out from cover, dry-eyed now and very business-like. He slit the last thongs, and Dickson fell limply on his face.

'Losh, laddie, I'm awful stiff,' he groaned. 'Now, listen. Away all your pith to Dougal, and tell him that the brig's in and the men will be landing inside the hour. Tell him I'm coming as fast as my legs will let me. The Princess will likely be there already and Sir Archibald and his men, but if they're no', tell Dougal they're coming. Haste you, Jaikie. And see here, I'll never forget what you've done for me the day. You're a fine wee laddie!'

The obedient Die-Hard disappeared, and Dickson painfully and laboriously set himself to climb the slope. He decided that his quickest and safest route lay by the highroad, and he had also some hopes of recovering his bicycle. On examining his body he seemed to have sustained no very great damage, except a painful cramping of legs and arms and a certain dizziness in the head. His pockets had been thoroughly rifled, and he reflected with amusement that he, the well-to-do Mr McCunn, did not possess at the moment a single copper.

But his spirits were soaring, for somehow his escape had given him an assurance of ultimate success. Providence had directly interfered on his behalf by the hand of Wee Jaikie, and that surely meant that it would see him through. But his chief emotion was an ardour of impatience to get to the scene of action. He must be at Dalquharter before the men from the sea; he must find Dougal and discover his dispositions. Heritage would be on guard in the Tower, and in a very little the enemy would be round it. It would be just like the Princess to try and enter there, but at all costs that must be hindered. She and Sir Archie must not be cornered in stone walls, but must keep their communications open and fall on the enemy's flank. Oh, if the police would only come in time, what a rounding-up of miscreants that day would see!

As the trees thinned on the brow of the slope and he saw the sky, he realized that the afternoon was far advanced. It must be well on for five o'clock. The wind still blew furiously, and the oaks on the fringes of the wood were whipped like saplings. Ruefully he admitted that the gale would not defeat the enemy. If the brig found a sheltered anchorage on the south side of the headland beyond the Garple, it would be easy enough for boats to make the Garple mouth, though it might be a difficult job to get out again. The thought quickened his steps, and he came out of cover on to the public road without a prior reconnaissance.

Just in front of him stood a motor-bicycle. Something had gone wrong with it for its owner was tinkering at it, on the side farthest from Dickson. A wild hope seized him that this might be the vanguard of the police, and he went boldly towards it. The owner, who was kneeling, raised his face at the sound of footsteps and Dickson looked into his eyes.

He recognized them only too well. They belonged to the man he had seen in the inn at Kirkmichael, the man whom Heritage had decided to be an Australian, but whom they now knew to be their arch-enemy – the man called Paul who had persecuted the Princess for years and whom alone of all beings on earth she feared. He had been expected before, but had arrived now in the nick of time while the brig was casting anchor. Saskia had said that he had a devil's brain, and Dickson, as he stared at him, saw a fiendish cleverness in his straight brows and a remorseless cruelty in his stiff jaw and his pale eyes.

He achieved the bravest act of his life. Shaky and dizzy as he was, with freedom newly opened to him and the mental torments of his captivity still an awful recollection, he did not hesitate. He saw before him the villain of the drama, the one man that stood between the Princess and peace of mind. He regarded no consequences, gave no heed to his own fate, and thought only how to put his enemy out of action. There was a big spanner lying on the ground. He seized it and with all his strength smote at the man's face.

The motor-cyclist, kneeling and working hard at his machine, had raised his head at Dickson's approach and beheld a wild apparition – a short man in ragged tweeds, with a bloody brow and long smears of blood on his cheeks. The next second he observed the threat of attack, and ducked his head so that the spanner only grazed his scalp. The motor-bicycle toppled over, its owner sprang to his feet, and found the short man, very pale and gasping, about to renew the assault. In such a crisis there was no time for inquiry, and the cyclist was well trained in self-defence. He leaped the prostrate bicycle, and before his assailant could get in a blow brought his left fist into violent contact with his chin. Dickson tottered back a step or two and then subsided among the bracken.

He did not lose his senses, but he had no more strength in him. He felt horribly ill, and struggled in vain to get up. The cyclist, a gigantic figure, towered above him. 'Who the devil are you?' he was asking. 'What do you mean by it?'

Dickson had no breath for words, and knew that if he tried to speak he would be very sick. He could only stare up like a dog at the angry eyes. Angry beyond question they were, but surely not malevolent. Indeed, as they looked at the shameful figure on the ground, amusement filled them. The face relaxed into a smile.

'Who on earth are you?' the voice repeated. And then into it came recognition. 'I've seen you before. I believe you're the little man I saw last week at the Black Bull. Be so good as to explain why you want to murder me.'

Explanation was beyond Dickson, but his conviction was being woefully shaken. Saskia had said her enemy was as beautiful as a devil – he remembered the phrase, for he had thought it ridiculous. This man was magnificent, but there was nothing devilish in his lean grave face.

'What's your name?' the voice was asking.

'Tell me yours first,' Dickson essayed to stutter between spasms of nausea.

'My name is Alexander Nicholson,' was the answer.

'Then you're no' the man.' It was a cry of wrath and despair.

'You're a very desperate little chap. For whom had I the honour to be mistaken?'

Dickson had now wriggled into a sitting position and had clasped his hands above his aching head.

'I thought you were a Russian, name of Paul,' he groaned.

'Paul! Paul who?'

'Just Paul. A Bolshevik and an awful bad lot.'

Dickson could not see the change which his words wrought in the other's face. He found himself picked up in strong arms and carried to a bog-pool where his battered face was carefully washed, his throbbing brows laved, and a wet handkerchief bound over them. Then he was given brandy in the socket of a flask, which eased his nausea. The cyclist ran his bicycle to the roadside, and found a seat for Dickson behind the turf-dyke of the old bucht.

'Now you are going to tell me everything,' he said. 'If the Paul who is your enemy is the Paul I think him, then we are allies.'

But Dickson did not need this assurance. His mind had suddenly received a revelation. The Princess had expected an enemy, but also a friend. Might not this be the long-awaited friend, for whose sake she was rooted to Huntingtower with all its terrors?

'Are you sure your name's no' Alexis?' he asked.

'In my own country I was called Alexis Nicolaevitch, for I am a Russian. But for some years I have made my home with your folk, and I call myself Alexander Nicholson, which is the English form. Who told you about Alexis?'

'Give me your hand,' said Dickson shamefacedly. 'Man, she's been looking for you for weeks. You're terribly behind the fair.'

'She!' he cried. 'For God's sake, tell me what you mean.'

'Ay, she – the Princess. But what are we havering here for? I tell you at this moment she's somewhere down about the old Tower, and there's boat-loads of blagyirds landing from the sea. Help me up, man, for I must be off. The story will keep.

Losh, it's very near the darkening. If you're Alexis, you're just about in time for a battle.'

But Dickson on his feet was but a frail creature. He was still deplorably giddy, and his legs showed an unpleasing tendency to crumple. 'I'm fair done,' he moaned. 'You see, I've been tied up all day to a tree and had two sore bashes on my head. Get you on that bicycle and hurry on, and I'll hirple after you the best I can. I'll direct you the road, and if you're lucky you'll find a Die-Hard about the village. Away with you, man, and never mind me.'

'We go together,' said the other quietly. 'You can sit behind me and hang on to my waist. Before you turned up I had pretty well got the thing in order.'

Dickson in a fever of impatience sat by while the Russian put the finishing touches to the machine, and as well as his anxiety allowed put him in possession of the main facts of the story. He told of how he and Heritage had come to Dalquharter, of the first meeting with Saskia, of the trip to Glasgow with the jewels, of the exposure of Loudon the factor, of last night's doings in the House, and of the journey that morning to the Mains of Garple. He sketched the figures on the scene – Heritage and Sir Archie, Dobson and his gang, the Gorbals Die-Hards. He told of the enemy's plans so far as he knew them.

'Looked at from a business point of view,' he said, 'the situation's like this. There's Heritage in the Tower, with Dobson, Léon, and Spidel sitting round him. Somewhere about the place there's the Princess and Sir Archibald and three men with guns from the Mains. Dougal and his five laddies are running loose in the policies. And there's four tinklers and God knows how many foreign ruffians pushing up from the Garplefoot, and a brig lying waiting to carry off the ladies. Likewise there's the police, somewhere on the road, though the dear kens when they'll turn up. It's awful the incompetence of our Government, and the rates and taxes that high! . . . And there's you and me by this roadside, and me no more use than a tattie-bogle . . . That's the situation, and the question is what's our plan to be? We must keep the blagyirds in play till the police come, and at the same time we must keep the Princess out of danger. That's why I'm wanting back, for they've sore need of a business head. Yon Sir Archibald's a fine fellow, but I doubt he'll be a bit rash, and the Princess is no' to hold or bind. Our first job is to find Dougal and get a grip of the facts.'

'I am going to the Princess,' said the Russian.

'Ay, that'll be best. You'll be maybe able to manage her, for you'll be well acquaint.'

'She is my kinswoman. She is also my affianced wife.'

'Keep us!' Dickson exclaimed, with a doleful thought of Heritage. 'What ailed you then no' to look after her better?'

'We have been long separated, because it was her will. She had work to do and disappeared from me, though I searched all Europe for her. Then she sent me word, when the danger became extreme, and summoned me to her aid. But she gave me poor directions, for she did not know her own plans very clearly. She spoke of a place called Darkwater, and I have been hunting half Scotland for it. It was only last night that I heard of Dalquharter and guessed that that might be the name. But I was far down in Galloway, and have ridden fifty miles to-day.'

'It's a queer thing, but I wouldn't take you for a Russian.'

Alexis finished his work and put away his tools. 'For the present,' he said, 'I am an Englishman, till my country comes again to her senses. Ten years ago I left Russia, for I was sick of the foolishness of my class and wanted a free life in a new world. I went to Australia and made good as an engineer. I am a partner in a firm which is pretty well known even in Britain. When war broke out I returned to fight for my people, and when Russia fell out of the war, I joined the Australians in France and fought with them till the Armistice. And now I have only one duty left, to save the Princess and take her with me to my new home till Russia is a nation once more.'

Dickson whistled joyfully. 'So Mr Heritage was right. He aye said you were an Australian ... And you're a business man! That's grand hearing and puts my mind at rest. You must take charge of the party at the House, for Sir Archibald's a daft young lad and Mr Heritage is a poet. I thought I would have to go myself, but I doubt I would just be a hindrance with my dwaibly legs. I'd be better outside, watching for the police ... Are you ready, sir?'

Dickson not without difficulty perched himself astride the luggage carrier, firmly grasping the rider round the middle. The machine started, but it was evidently in a bad way, for it made poor going till the descent towards the main Auchenlochan road. On the slope it warmed up and they crossed the Garple bridge at a fair pace. There was to be no pleasant April twilight, for the stormy sky had already made dusk, and in a very little the dark would fall. So sombre was the evening that Dickson did not notice a figure in the shadow of the roadside pines till it whistled shrilly on its fingers. He cried on Alexis to stop, and, this being accomplished with some suddenness, fell off at Dougal's feet.

'What's the news?' he demanded.

Dougal glanced at Alexis and seemed to approve his looks.

'Napoleon has just reported that three boat-loads, making either twenty-three or twenty-four men – they were gey ill to count – has landed at Garplefit and is makin' their way to the auld Tower. The tinklers warned Dobson and soon it'll be a' bye wi' Heritage.'

'The Princess is not there?' was Dickson's anxious inquiry.

'Na, na. Heritage is there his lone. They were for joinin' him, but I wouldn't let them. She came wi' a man they call Sir Erchibald and three gemkeepers wi' guns. I stoppit their cawr up the road and tell't them the lie o' the land. Yon Sir Erchibald has poor notions o' strawtegy. He was for bangin' into the auld Tower straight away and shootin' Dobson if he tried to stop them. "Havers," say I, "let them break their teeth on the Tower, thinkin' the leddy's inside, and that'll give us time, for Heritage is no' the lad to surrender in a hurry."'

'Where are they now?'

'In the Hoose o' Dalquharter, and a sore job I had gettin' them in. We've shifted our base again, without the enemy suspectin'.'

'Any word of the police?'

'The polis!' and Dougal spat cynically. 'It seems they're a

dour crop to shift. Sir Erchibald was sayin' that him and the lassie had been to the Chief Constable, but the man was terrible auld and slow. They persuadit him, but he threepit that it would take a long time to collect his men and that there was no danger o' the brig landin' afore night. He's wrong there onyway, for they're landit.'

'Dougal,' said Dickson, 'you've heard the Princess speak of a friend she was expecting here called Alexis. This is him. You can address him as Mr Nicholson. Just arrived in the nick of time. You must get him into the House, for he's the best right to be beside the lady . . . Jaikie would tell you that I've been sore mishandled the day, and am no' very fit for a battle. But Mr Nicholson's a business man and he'll do as well. You're keeping the Die-Hards outside, I hope?'

'Ay. Thomas Yownie's in charge, and Jaikie will be in and out with orders. They've instructions to watch for the polis, and keep an eye on the Garplefit. It'a a mortal long front to hold, but there's no other way. I must be in the Hoose mysel'. Thomas Yownie's headquarters is the auld wife's hen-hoose.'

At that moment in a pause of the gale came the far-borne echo of a shot.

'Pistol,' said Alexis.

'Heritage,' said Dougal. 'Trade will be gettin' brisk with him. Start your machine and I'll hang on ahint. We'll try the road by the West Lodge.'

Presently the pair disappeared in the dusk, the noise of the engine was swallowed up in the wild orchestra of the wind, and Dickson hobbled towards the village in a state of excitement which made him oblivious of his wounds. That lonely pistol shot was, he felt, the bell to ring up the curtain on the last act of the play.

CHAPTER THIRTEEN

# THE COMING OF THE DANISH BRIG

MR JOHN HERITAGE, solitary in the old Tower, found much to occupy his mind. His giddiness was passing, though the dregs of a headache remained, and his spirits rose with his responsibilities. At daybreak he breakfasted out of the Mearns Street provision box, and made tea in one of the Die-Hards' camp kettles. Next he gave some attention to his toilet, necessary after the rough-and-tumble of the night. He made shift to bathe in icy water from the Tower well, shaved, tidied up his clothes and found a clean shirt from his pack. He carefully brushed his hair, reminding himself that thus had the Spartans done before Thermopylae. The neat and somewhat pallid young man that emerged from these rites then ascended to the first floor to reconnoitre the landscape from the narrow unglazed windows.

If any one had told him a week ago that he would be in so strange a world he would have quarrelled violently with his informant. A week ago he was a cynical clear-sighted modern, a contemner of illusions, a swallower of formulas, a breaker of shams – one who had seen through the heroical and found it silly. Romance and such-like toys were playthings for fatted middle-age, not for strenuous and cold-eyed youth. But the truth was that now he was altogether spellbound by these toys. To think that he was serving his lady was rapture – ecstasy, that for her he was single-handed venturing all. He rejoiced to be alone with his private fancies. His one fear was that the part he had cast himself for might be needless, that the men from the sea would not come, or that reinforcements would arrive before he should be called upon. He hoped alone to make a stand against thousands. What the upshot might be he did not trouble to inquire. Of course the Princess would be saved, but first he must glut his appetite for the heroic.

He made a diary of events that day, just as he used to do at the front. At twenty minutes past eight he saw the first figure coming from the House. It was Spidel, who limped round the Tower, tried the door, and came to a halt below the window. Heritage stuck out his head and wished him good morning, getting in reply an amazed stare. The man was not disposed to talk, though Heritage made some interesting observations on the weather, but departed quicker than he came, in the direction of the West Lodge.

Just before nine o'clock he returned with Dobson and Léon. They made a very complete reconnaissance of the Tower, and for a moment Heritage thought that they were about to try to force an entrance. They tugged and hammered at the great oak door, which he had further strengthened by erecting behind it a pile of the heaviest lumber he could find in the place. It was imperative that they should not get in, and he got Dickson's pistol ready with the firm intention of shooting them if necessary. But they did nothing, except to hold a conference in the hazel clump a hundred yards to the north, when Dobson seemed to be laying down the law, and Léon spoke rapidly with a great fluttering of hands. They were obviously puzzled by the sight of Heritage, whom they believed to have left the neighbourhood. Then Dobson went off, leaving Léon and Spidel on guard, one at the edge of the shrubberies between the Tower and the House, the other on the side nearest the Laver glen. These were their posts, but they did sentry-go around the building, and passed so close to Heritage's window that he could have tossed a cigarette on their heads.

It occurred to him that he ought to get busy with camouflage. They must be convinced that the Princess was in the place, for he wanted their whole mind to be devoted to the siege. He rummaged among the ladies' baggage, and extracted a skirt and a coloured scarf. The latter he managed to flutter so that it could be seen at the window the next time one of the watchers came within sight. He also fixed up the skirt so that the fringe of it could be seen, and, when Léon appeared below, he was in the shadow talking rapid French in a very fair imitation of the tones of Cousin Eugénie. The ruse had its effect, for Léon promptly went off to tell Spidel, and when Dobson appeared he too was given the news. This seemed to settle their plans, for all three remained on guard, Dobson nearest to the Tower, seated on an outcrop of rock with his mackintosh collar turned up, and his eyes usually on the misty sea.

By this time it was eleven o'clock, and the next three hours passed slowly with Heritage. He fell to picturing the fortunes of his friends. Dickson and the Princess should by this time be far inland, out of danger and in the way of finding succour. He was confident that they would return, but he trusted not too soon, for he hoped for a run for his money as Horatius on the bridge. After that he was a little torn in his mind. He wanted the Princess to come back and to be somewhere near if there was a fight going, so that she might be a witness of his devotion. But she must not herself run any risk, and he became anxious when he remembered her terrible sang-froid. Dickson could no more restrain her than a child could hold a greyhound . . . But of course it would never come to that. The police would turn up long before the brig appeared – Dougal had thought that would not be till high tide, between four and five – and the only danger would be to the pirates. The three watchers would be put in the bag, and the men from the sea would walk into a neat trap. This reflexion seemed to take all the colour out of Heritage's prospect. Peril and heroism were not to be his lot – only boredom.

A little after twelve two of the tinklers appeared with some news which made Dobson laugh and pat them on the shoulder. He seemed to be giving them directions, pointing seaward and southward. He nodded to the Tower, where Heritage took the opportunity of again fluttering Saskia's scarf athwart the window. The tinklers departed at a trot, and Dobson lit his pipe as if well pleased. He had some trouble with it in the wind, which had risen to an uncanny violence. Even the solid Tower rocked with it, and the sea was a waste of spindrift and low scurrying cloud. Heritage discovered a new anxiety – this time about the possibility of the brig landing at all.

He wanted a complete bag, and it would be tragic if they got only the three seedy ruffians now circumambulating his fortress.

About one o'clock he was greatly cheered by the sight of Dougal. At the moment Dobson was lunching off a hunk of bread and cheese directly between the Tower and the House, just short of the crest of the ridge on the other side of which lay the stables and the shrubberies; Léon was on the north side opposite the Tower door, and Spidel was at the south end near the edge of the Garple glen. Heritage, watching the ridge behind Dobson and the upper windows of the House which appeared over it, saw on the very crest something like a tuft of rusty bracken which he had not noticed before. Presently the tuft moved, and a hand shot up from it waving a rag of some sort. Dobson at the moment was engaged with a bottle of porter, and Heritage could safely wave a hand in reply. He could now make out clearly the red head of Dougal.

The Chieftain, having located the three watchers, proceeded to give an exhibition of his prowess for the benefit of the lonely inmate of the Tower. Using as cover a drift of bracken, he wormed his way down till he was not six yards from Dobson, and Heritage had the privilege of seeing his grinning countenance a very little way above the innkeeper's head. Then he crawled back and reached the neighbourhood of Léon, who was sitting on a fallen Scotch fir. At that moment it occurred to the Belgian to visit Dobson. Heritage's breath stopped, but Dougal was ready, and froze into a motionless blur in the shadow of a hazel bush. Then he crawled very fast into the hollow where Léon had been sitting, seized something which looked like a bottle, and scrambled back to the ridge. At the top he waved the object, whatever it was, but Heritage could not reply, for Dobson happened to be looking towards the window. That was the last he saw of the Chieftain, but presently he realized what was the booty he had annexed. It must be Léon's life-preserver, which the night before had broken Heritage's head.

After that cheering episode boredom again set in. He collected some food from the Mearns Street box, and indulged himself with a glass of liqueur brandy. He was beginning to feel miserably cold, so he carried up some broken wood and made a fire on the immense hearth in the upper chamber. Anxiety was clouding his mind again, for it was now two o'clock, and there was no sign of the reinforcements which Dickson and the Princess had gone to find. The minutes passed, and soon it was three o'clock, and from the window he saw only the top of the gaunt shuttered House, now and then hidden by squalls of sleet, and Dobson squatted like an Eskimo, and trees dancing like a witch-wood in the gale. All the vigour of the morning seemed to have gone out of his blood; he felt lonely and apprehensive and puzzled. He wished he had Dickson beside him, for that little man's cheerful voice and complacent triviality would be a comfort . . . Also, he was abominably cold. He put on his waterproof, and turned his attention to the fire. It needed re-kindling, and he hunted in his pockets for paper, finding only the slim volume lettered *Whorls*.

I set it down as the most significant commentary on his state of mind. He regarded the book with intense disfavour, tore it in two, and used a handful of its fine deckle-edged leaves to get the fire going. They burned well, and presently the rest followed. Well for Dickson's peace of soul that he was not a witness of such vandalism.

A little warmer but in no way more cheerful, he resumed his watch near the window. The day was getting darker, and promised an early dusk. His watch told him that it was after four, and still nothing had happened. Where on earth were Dickson and the Princess? Where in the name of all that was holy were the police? Any minute now the brig might arrive and land its men, and he would be left there as a burnt-offering to their wrath. There must have been an infernal muddle somewhere . . . Anyhow the Princess was out of the trouble, but where the Lord alone knew . . . Perhaps the reinforcements were lying in wait for the boats at the Garplefoot. That struck him as a likely explanation, and comforted him. Very soon he might hear the sound of an engagement to the south, and the next thing would be Dobson and his crew in flight. He was determined to be in the show somehow and would be very close on their heels. He felt a peculiar dislike to all three, but especially to Léon. The Belgian's small baby features had for four days set him clenching his fists when he thought of them.

The next thing he saw was one of the tinklers running hard towards the Tower. He cried something to Dobson, which Heritage could not catch, but which woke the latter to activity. The innkeeper shouted to Léon and Spidel, and the tinkler was excitedly questioned. Dobson laughed and slapped his thigh. He gave orders to the others, and himself joined the tinkler and hurried off in the direction of the Garplefoot. Something was happening there, something of ill omen, for the man's face and manner had been triumphant. Were the boats landing?

As Heritage puzzled over this event, another figure appeared on the scene. It was a big man in knickerbockers and mackintosh, who came round the end of the House from the direction of the South Lodge. At first he thought it was the advance-guard from his own side, the help which Dickson had gone to find, and he only restrained himself in time from shouting a welcome. But surely their supports would not advance so confidently in enemy country. The man strode over the slopes as if looking for somebody; then he caught sight of Léon and waved him to come. Léon must have known him, for he hastened to obey.

The two were about thirty yards from Heritage's window. Léon was telling some story volubly, pointing now to the Tower and now towards the sea. The big man nodded as if satisfied. Heritage noted that his right arm was tied up, and that the mackintosh sleeve was empty, and that brought him enlightenment. It was Loudon the factor, whom Dickson had winged the night before. The two of them passed out of view in the direction of Spidel.

The sight awoke Heritage to the supreme unpleasantness of his position. He was utterly alone on the headland, and his allies had vanished into space, while the enemy plans, moving like clockwork, were approaching their consummation. For a second he thought of leaving the Tower and hiding somewhere in the cliffs. He dismissed the notion unwillingly, for he remembered the task that had been set him. He was there to hold the fort to the last – to gain time, though he could not for the life of him see what use time was to be when all the strategy of his own side seemed to have miscarried. Anyhow, the blackguards would be sold, for they would not find the Princess. But he felt a horrid void in the pit of his stomach, and a looseness about his knees.

The moments passed more quickly as he wrestled with his fears. The next he knew the empty space below his window was filling with figures. There was a great crowd of them, rough fellows with seamen's coats, still dripping as if they had had a wet landing. Dobson was with them, but for the rest they were strange figures.

Now that the expected had come at last Heritage's nerves grew calmer. He made out that the newcomers were trying the door, and he waited to hear it fall, for such a mob could soon force it. But instead a voice called from beneath.

'Will you please open to us?' it said.

He stuck his head out and saw a little group with one man at the head of it, a young man clad in oilskins whose face was dim in the murky evening. The voice was that of a gentleman.

'I have orders to open to no one,' Heritage replied.

'Then I fear we must force an entrance,' said the voice.

'You can go to the devil,' said Heritage.

That defiance was the screw which his nerves needed. His temper had risen, he had forgotten all about the Princess, he did not even remember his isolation. His job was to make a fight for it. He ran up the staircase which led to the attics of the Tower, for he recollected that there was a window there which looked over the space before the door. The place was ruinous, the floor filled with holes, and a part of the roof sagged down in a corner. The stones around the window were loose and crumbling, and he managed to pull several out so that the slit was enlarged. He found himself looking down on a crowd of men, who had lifted the fallen tree on which Léon had perched, and were about to use it as a battering ram.

'The first fellow who comes within six yards of the door I shoot,' he shouted.

There was a white wave below as every face was turned to him. He ducked back his head in time as a bullet chipped the side of the window.

But his position was a good one, for he had a hole in the broken wall through which he could see, and could shoot with his hand at the edge of the window while keeping his body in cover. The battering party resumed their task, and as the tree swung nearer, he fired at the foremost of them. He missed, but the shot for a moment suspended operations.

Again they came on, and again he fired. This time he damaged somebody, for the trunk was dropped.

A voice gave orders, a sharp authoritative voice. The battering squad dissolved, and there was a general withdrawal out of the line of fire from the window. Was it possible that he had intimidated them? He could hear the sound of voices, and then a single figure came into sight again, holding something in its hand.

He did not fire for he recognized the futility of his efforts. The baseball swing of the figure below could not be mistaken. There was a roar beneath, and a flash of fire, as the bomb exploded on the door. Then came a rush of men, and the Tower had fallen.

Heritage clambered through a hole in the roof and gained the topmost parapet. He had still a pocketful of cartridges, and there in a coign of the old battlements he would prove an ugly customer to the pursuit. Only one at a time could reach that siege perilous . . . They would not take long to search the lower rooms, and then would be hot on the trail of the man who had fooled them. He had not a scrap of fear left or even of anger – only triumph at the thought of how properly those ruffians had been sold. 'Like schoolboys they who unaware' – instead of two women they had found a man with a gun. And the Princess was miles off and forever beyond their reach. When they had settled with him they would no doubt burn the House down, but that would serve them little. From his airy pinnacle he could see the whole sea-front of

Huntingtower, a blur in the dusk but for the ghostly eyes of its white-shuttered windows.

Something was coming from it, running lightly over the lawns, lost for an instant in the trees, and then appearing clear on the crest of the ridge where some hours earlier Dougal had lain. With horror he saw that it was a girl. She stood with the wind plucking at her skirts and hair, and she cried in a high, clear voice which pierced even the confusion of the gale. What she cried he could not tell, for it was in a strange tongue . . .

But it reached the besiegers. There was a sudden silence in the din below him and then a confusion of shouting. The men seemed to be pouring out of the gap which had been the doorway, and as he peered over the parapet first one and then another entered his area of vision. The girl on the ridge, as soon as she saw that she had attracted attention, turned and ran back, and after her up the slopes went the pursuit bunched like hounds on a good scent.

Mr John Heritage, swearing terribly, started to retrace his steps.

CHAPTER FOURTEEN

# THE SECOND BATTLE OF THE CRUIVES

THE military historian must often make shift to write of battles with slender data, but he can pad out his deficiencies by learned parallels. If his were the talented pen describing this, the latest action fought on British soil against a foreign foe, he would no doubt be crippled by the absence of written orders and war diaries. But how eloquently he would descant on the resemblance between Dougal and Gouraud – how the plan of leaving the enemy to waste his strength upon a deserted position was that which on the 15th of July 1918 the French general had used with decisive effect in Champagne! But Dougal had never heard of Gouraud, and I cannot claim that, like the Happy Warrior, he

*through the heat of conflict kept the law*
*In calmness made, and saw what he foresaw.*

I have had the benefit of discussing the affair with him and his colleagues, but I should offend against historic truth if I represented the main action as anything but a scrimmage – a 'soldiers' battle', the historian would say, a Malplaquet, an Albuera.

Just after half-past three that afternoon the Commander-in-Chief was revealed in a very bad temper. He had intercepted Sir Archie's car, and, since Léon was known to be fully occupied, had brought it in by the West Lodge, and hidden it behind a clump of laurels. There he had held a hoarse council of war. He had cast an appraising eye over Sime the butler, Carfrae the chauffeur, and McGuffog the gamekeeper, and his brows had lightened when he beheld Sir Archie with an armful of guns and two big cartridge-magazines. But they had darkened again at the first words of the leader of the reinforcements.

'Now for the Tower,' Sir Archie had observed cheerfully. 'We should be a match for the three watchers, my lad, and it's time that poor devil What's-his-name was relieved.'

'A bonny-like plan that would be,' said Dougal. 'Man, ye would be walkin' into the very trap they want. In an hour, or maybe two, the rest will turn up from the sea and they'd have ye tight by the neck. Na, na! It's time we're wantin', and the longer they think we're a' in the auld Tower the better for us. What news o' the polis?'

He listened to Sir Archie's report with a gloomy face.

'Not afore the darkenin'? They'll be ower late – the polis are aye ower late. It looks as if we had the job to do oursels. What's *your* notion?'

'God knows,' said the baronet, whose eyes were on Saskia. 'What's yours?'

The deference conciliated Dougal. 'There's just the one plan that's worth a docken. There's five o' us here, and there's plenty weapons. Besides there's five Die-Hards somewhere about, and though they've never tried it afore they can be trusted to loose off a gun. My advice is to hide at the Garplefoot and stop the boats landin'. We'd have the tinklers on our flank, no doubt, but I'm not muckle feared o' them. It wouldn't be easy for the boats to get in wi' this tearing' wind and us firin' volleys from the shore.'

Sir Archie stared at him with admiration. 'You're a hearty young fire-eater. But, Great Scott! we can't go pottin' at strangers before we find out their business. This is a law-abidin' country, and we're not entitled to start shootin' except in self-defence. You can wash that plan out, for it ain't feasible.'

Dougal spat cynically. 'For all that it's the right strawtegy. Man, we might sink the lot, and then turn and settle wi' Dobson, and all afore the first polisman showed his neb. It would be a grand performance. But I was feared ye wouldn't be for it . . . Well, there's just the one other thing to do. We must get inside the Hoose and put it in a state of defence. Heritage has McCunn's pistol, and he'll keep them busy for a bit. When they've finished wi' him and find the place is empty, they'll try the Hoose and we'll give them a warm reception. That should keep us goin' till the polis arrive, unless they're comin' wi' the blind carrier.'

Sir Archie nodded. 'But why put ourselves in their power at all? They're at present barking up the wrong tree. Let them bark up another wrong 'un. Why shouldn't the House remain empty? I take it we're here to protect the Princess. Well, we'll have done that if they go off empty-handed.'

Dougal looked up to the heavens. 'I wish McCunn was here,' he sighed. 'Ay, we've got to protect the Princess, and there's just the one way to do it, and that's to put an end to this crowd o' blagyirds. If they gang empty-handed, they'll come again another day, either here or somewhere else, and it won't be long afore they get the lassie. But if we finish with them now she can sit down wi' an easy mind. That's why we've got to hang on to them till the polis comes. There's no way out o' this business but a battle.'

He found an ally. 'Dougal is right,' said Saskia. 'If I am to have peace, by some way or other the fangs of my enemies must be drawn for ever.'

He swung round and addressed her formally. 'Mem, I'm askin' ye for the last time. Will ye keep out of this business? Will ye gang back and sit doun aside Mrs Morran's fire and have your tea and wait till we come for ye. Ye can do no good, and ye're puttin' yourself terrible in the enemy's power. If we're beat and ye're no' there, they get very little satisfaction, but if they get *you* they get what they've come seekin'. I tell ye straight – ye're an encumbrance.'

She laughed mischievously. 'I can shoot better than you,' she said.

He ignored the taunt. 'Will ye listen to sense and fall to the rear?'

'I will not,' she said.

'Then gang your own gait. I'm ower wise to argy-bargy wi' women. The Hoose be it!'

It was a journey which sorely tried Dougal's temper. The only way in was by the veranda, but the door at the west end had been locked, and the ladder had disappeared. Now, of his party three were lame, one lacked an arm, and one was a girl; besides, there were the guns and cartridges to transport. Moreover, at more than one point before the veranda was reached the route was commanded by a point on the ridge near the old Tower, and that had been Spidel's position when Dougal made his last reconnaissance. It behoved to pass these points swiftly and unobtrusively, and his company was neither swift nor unobtrusive. McGuffog had a genius for tripping over obstacles, and Sir Archie was for ever proffering his aid to Saskia, who was in a position to give rather than to receive, being far the most active of the party. Once Dougal had to take the gamekeeper's head and force it down, a performance which would have led to an immediate assault but for Sir Archie's presence. Nor did the latter escape. 'Will ye stop heedin' the lassie, and attend to your own job,' the Chieftain growled. 'Ye're makin' as much noise as a road-roller.'

Arrived at the foot of the veranda wall there remained the problem of the escalade. Dougal clambered up like a squirrel by the help of cracks in the stones, and he could be heard trying the handle of the door into the House. He was absent for about five minutes, and then his head peeped over the edge accompanied by the hooks of an iron ladder. 'From the boiler-house,' he informed them as they stood clear for the thing to drop. It proved to be little more than half the height of the wall.

Saskia ascended first, and had no difficulty in pulling herself over the parapet. Then came the guns and ammunition, and then the one-armed Sime, who turned out to be an athlete. But it was no easy matter getting up the last three. Sir Archie anathematized his frailties. 'Nice old crock to go tiger-shootin' with,' he told the Princess. 'But set me to something where my confounded leg don't get in the way, and I'm still pretty useful!' Dougal, mopping his brow with the rag he called his handkerchief, observed sourly that he objected to going scouting with a herd of elephants.

Once indoors his spirits rose. The party from the Mains had brought several electric torches, and the one lamp was presently found and lit. 'We can't count on the polis,' Dougal announced, 'and when the foreigners is finished wi' the Tower they'll come on here. If no', we must make them. What is it the sodgers call it? Forcin' a battle? Now see here! There's the two roads into this place, the back door and the verandy, leavin' out the front door which is chained and lockit. They'll try those two roads first, and we must get them well barricaded in time. But mind, if there's a good few o' them, it'll be an easy job to batter in the front door or the windies, so we maun be ready for that.'

He told off a fatigue party – the Princess, Sir Archie, and McGuffog – to help in moving furniture to the several doors. Sime and Carfrae attended to the kitchen entrance, while he himself made a tour of the ground-floor windows. For half an hour the empty house was loud with strange sounds. McGuffog, who was a giant in strength, filled the passage at the veranda end with an assortment of furniture ranging from a grand piano to a vast mahogany sofa, while Saskia and Sir Archie pillaged the bedrooms and packed up the interstices with mattresses in lieu of sandbags. Dougal on his turn saw fit to approve their work.

'That'll fickle the blagyirds. Down at the kitchen door we've got a mangle, five wash-tubs, and the best part of a ton o' coal. It's the windies I'm anxious about, for they're ower big to fill up. But I've gotten tubs o' water below them and a lot o' wire-nettin' I fund in the cellar.'

Sir Archie morosely wiped his brow. 'I can't say I ever hated a job more,' he told Saskia. 'It seems pretty cool to march into somebody else's house and make free with his furniture. I hope to goodness our friends from the sea do turn up, or we'll look pretty foolish. Loudon will have a score against me he won't forget.'

'Ye're no' weakenin'?' asked Dougal fiercely.

'Not a bit. Only hopin' somebody hasn't made a mighty big mistake.'

'Ye needn't be feared for that. Now you listen to your instructions. We're terrible few for such a big place, but we maun make up for shortness o' numbers by extra mobility.

The gemkeeper will keep the windy that looks on the verandy, and fell any man that gets through. You'll hold the verandy door, and the ither lame man – is't Carfrae ye call him? – will keep the back door. I've telled the one-armed man, who has some kind of a head on him, that he maun keep on the move, watchin' to see if they try the front door or any o' the other windies. If they do, he takes his station there. D'ye follow?'

Sir Archie nodded gloomily.

'What is my post?' Saskia asked.

'I've appointed ye my Chief of Staff,' was the answer. 'Ye see we've no reserves. If this door's the dangerous bit, it maun be reinforced from elsewhere; and that'll want savage thinkin'. Ye'll have to be aye on the move, Mem, and keep me informed. If they break in at two bits, we're beat, and there'll be nothing for it but to retire to our last position. Ye ken the room ayont the hall where they keep the coats. That's our last trench, and at the worst we fall back there and stick it out. It has a strong door and a wee windy, so they'll no' be able to get in on our rear. We should be able to put up a good defence there, unless they fire the place over our heads ... Now, we'd better give out the guns.'

'We don't want any shootin' if we can avoid it,' said Sir Archie, who found his distaste for Dougal growing, though he was under the spell of the one being there who knew precisely his own mind.

'Just what I was goin' to say. My instructions is, reserve your fire, and don't loose off till you have a man up against the end o' your barrel.'

'Good Lord, we'll get into a horrible row. The whole thing may be a mistake, and we'll be had up for wholesale homicide. No man shall fire unless I give the word.'

The Commander-in-Chief looked at him darkly. Some bitter retort was on his tongue, but he restrained himself.

'It appears,' he said, 'that ye think I'm doin' all this for fun. I'll no' argy wi' ye. There can be just the one general in a battle, but I'll give ye permission to say the word when to fire ... Macgreegor!' he muttered, a strange expletive only used in moments of deep emotion. 'I'll wager ye'll be for sayin' the word afore I'd say it mysel'.'

He turned to the Princess. 'I hand over to you, till I am back, for I maun be off and see to the Die-Hards. I wish I could bring them in here, but I daren't lose my communications. I'll likely get in by the boiler-house skylight when I come back, but it might be as well to keep a road open here unless ye're actually attacked.'

Dougal clambered over the mattresses and the grand piano; a flicker of waning daylight appeared for a second as he squeezed through the door, and Sir Archie was left staring at the wrathful countenance of McGuffog. He laughed ruefully.

'I've been in about forty battles, and here's that little devil rather worried about my pluck and talkin' to me like a corps commander to a newly joined second-lieutenant. All the same he's a remarkable child, and we'd better behave as if we were in for a real shindy. What do you think, Princess?'

'I think we are in for what you call a shindy. I am in command, remember. I order you to serve out the guns.'

This was done, a shot-gun and a hundred cartridges to each, while McGuffog, who was a marksman, was also given a sporting Mannlicher, and two other rifles, a .303 and a small-bore Holland, were kept in reserve in the hall. Sir Archie, free from Dougal's compelling presence, gave the gamekeeper peremptory orders not to shoot till he was bidden, and Carfrae at the kitchen door was warned to the same effect. The shuttered house, where the only light apart from the garden-room was the feeble spark of the electric torches, had the most disastrous effect upon his spirits. The gale which roared in the chimney and eddied among the rafters of the hall seemed an infernal commotion in a tomb.

'Let's go upstairs,' he told Saskia; 'there must be a view from the upper windows.'

'You can see the top of the old Tower, and part of the sea,' she said. 'I know it well, for it was my only amusement to look at it. On clear days, too, one could see high mountains far in the west.' His depression seemed to have affected her, for she spoke listlessly, unlike the vivid creature who had led the way in.

In a gaunt west-looking bedroom, the one in which Heritage and Dickson had camped the night before, they opened a fold of the shutters and looked out into a world of grey wrack and driving rain. The Tower roof showed mistily beyond the ridge of down, but its environs were not in their prospect. The lower regions of the House had been gloomy enough, but this bleak place with its drab outlook struck a chill to Sir Archie's soul. He dolefully lit a cigarette.

'This is a pretty rotten show for you,' he told her. 'It strikes me as a rather unpleasant brand of nightmare.'

'I have been living with nightmares for three years,' she said wearily.

He cast his eyes round the room. 'I think the Kennedys were mad to build this confounded barrack. I've always disliked it, and old Quentin hadn't any use for it either. Cold, cheerless, raw monstrosity! It hasn't been a very giddy place for you, Princess.'

'It has been my prison, when I hoped it would be a sanctuary. But it may yet be my salvation.'

'I'm sure I hope so. I say, you must be jolly hungry. I don't suppose there's any chance of tea for you.'

She shook her head. She was looking fixedly at the Tower, as if she expected something to appear there, and he followed her eyes.

'Rum old shell, that. Quentin used to keep all kinds of live stock there, and when we were boys it was our castle where we played at bein' robber chiefs. It'll be dashed queer if the real thing should turn up this time. I suppose McCunn's Poet is roostin' there all by his lone. Can't say I envy him his job.'

Suddenly she caught his arm. 'I see a man,' she whispered. 'There! He is behind those far bushes. There is his head again!'

It was clearly a man, but he presently disappeared, for he had come round by the south end of the House, past the stables, and had now gone over the ridge.

'The cut of his jib is uncommonly like Loudon, the factor. I thought McCunn had stretched him on a bed of pain. Lord, if this thing should turn out a farce, I simply can't face Loudon . . . I say, Princess, you don't suppose by any chance that McCunn's a little bit wrong in the head?'

She turned her candid eyes on him. 'You are in a very doubting mood.'

'My feet are cold and I don't mind admittin' it. Hanged if I know what it is, but I don't feel this show a bit real. If it isn't, we're in a fair way to make howlin' idiots of ourselves, and get pretty well embroiled with the law. It's all right for the red-haired boy, for he can take everything seriously, even play. I could do the same thing myself when I was a kid. I don't mind runnin' some kinds of risk – I've had a few in my time – but this is so infernally outlandish, and I – I don't quite believe in it. That is to say, I believe in it right enough when I look at you or listen to McCunn, but as soon as my eyes are off you I begin to doubt again. I'm gettin' old and I've a stake in the country, and I dare say I'm gettin' a bit of a prig – anyway I don't want to make a jackass of myself. Besides, there's this foul weather and this beastly house to ice my feet.'

He broke off with an exclamation, for on the grey cloud-bounded stage in which the roof of the Tower was the central feature, actors had appeared. Dim hurrying shapes showed through the mist, dipping over the ridge, as if coming from the Garplefoot.

She seized his arm and he saw that her listlessness was gone. Her eyes were shining.

'It is they,' she cried. 'The nightmare is real at last. Do you doubt now?'

He could only stare, for these shapes arriving and vanishing like wisps of fog still seemed to him phantasmal. The girl held his arm tightly clutched, and craned towards the window space. He tried to open the frame, and succeeded in smashing the glass. A swirl of wind drove inwards and blew a loose lock of Saskia's hair across his brow.

'I wish Dougal were back,' he muttered, and then came the crack of a shot.

The pressure on his arm slackened, and a pale face was turned to him. 'He is alone – Mr Heritage. He has no chance. They will kill him like a dog.'

'They'll never get in,' he assured her. 'Dougal said the place could hold out for hours.'

Another shot followed and presently a third. She twined her hands and her eyes were wild.

'We can't leave him to be killed,' she gasped.

'It's the only game. We're playin' for time, remember. Besides, he won't be killed. Great Scott!'

As he spoke, a sudden explosion cleft the drone of the wind and a patch of gloom flashed into yellow light.

'Bomb!' he cried. 'Lord, I might have thought of that.'

The girl had sprung back from the window. 'I cannot bear it. I will not see him murdered in sight of his friends. I am going to show myself, and when they see me they will leave him . . . No, you must stay here. Presently they will be round this house. Don't be afraid for me – I am very quick of foot.'

'For God's sake, don't! Here, Princess, stop,' and he clutched at her skirt. 'Look here, I'll go.'

'You can't. You have been wounded. I am in command, you know. Keep the door open till I come back.'

He hobbled after her, but she easily eluded him. She was smiling now, and blew a kiss to him. 'La, la, la,' she trilled, as she ran down the stairs. He heard her voice below, admonishing McGuffog. Then he pulled himself together and went back to the window. He had brought the little Holland with him, and he poked its barrel through the hole in the glass.

'Curse my game leg,' he said, almost cheerfully, for the situation was now becoming one with which he could cope. 'I ought to be able to hold up the pursuit a bit. My aunt! What a girl!'

With the rifle cuddled to his shoulder he watched a slim figure come into sight on the lawn, running towards the ridge. He reflected that she must have dropped from the high veranda wall. That reminded him that something must be done to make the wall climbable for her return, so he went down to McGuffog, and the two squeezed through the barricaded door to the veranda. The boilerhouse ladder was still in position, but it did not reach half the height, so McGuffog was adjured to stand by to help, and in the meantime to wait on duty by the wall. Then he hurried upstairs to his watch-tower.

The girl was in sight, almost on the crest of the high ground. There she stood for a moment, one hand clutching at her errant hair, the other shielding her eyes from the sting of the rain. He heard her cry, as Heritage had heard her, but since the wind was blowing towards him the sound came louder and fuller. Again she cried, and then stood motionless with her hands above her head. It was only for an instant, for the next he saw she had turned and was racing down the slope, jumping the little scrogs of hazel like a deer. On the ridge appeared faces, and then over it swept a mob of men.

She had a start of some fifty yards, and laboured to increase it, having doubtless the veranda wall in mind. Sir Archie, sick with anxiety, nevertheless spared time to admire her prowess. 'Gad! she's a miler,' he ejaculated. 'She'll do it. I'm hanged if she don't do it.'

Against men in seamen's boots and heavy clothing she had a clear advantage. But two shook themselves loose from the pack and began to gain on her. At the main shrubbery they were not thirty yards behind, and in her passage through it her skirts must have delayed her, for when she emerged the pursuit had halved the distance. He got the sights of the rifle on the first man, but the lawns sloped up towards the house, and to his consternation he found that the girl was in the line of fire. Madly he ran to the other window of the room, tore back the shutters, shivered the glass, and flung his rifle to his shoulder. The fellow was within three yards of her, but, thank God! he had now a clear field. He fired low and just ahead of him, and had the satisfaction to see him drop like a rabbit, shot in the leg. His companion stumbled over him, and for a moment the girl was safe.

But her speed was failing. She passed out of sight on the veranda side of the house, and the rest of the pack had gained ominously over the easier ground of the lawn. He thought for a moment of trying to stop them by his fire, but realized that if every shot told there would still be enough of them left to make sure of her capture. The only chance was at the veranda, and he went downstairs at a pace undreamed of since the days when he had two whole legs.

McGuffog, Mannlicher in hand, was poking his neck over the wall. The pursuit had turned the corner and were about twenty yards off; the girl was at the foot of the ladder, breathless, drooping with fatigue. She tried to climb, limply and feebly, and very slowly, as if she were too giddy to see clear. Above were two cripples, and at her back the van of the now triumphant pack.

Sir Archie, game leg or no, was on the parapet preparing to drop down and hold off the pursuit were it only for seconds. But at that moment he was aware that the situation had changed.

At the foot of the ladder a tall man seemed to have sprung out of the ground. He caught the girl in his arms, climbed the ladder, and McGuffog's great hands reached down and seized her and swung her into safety. Up the wall, by means of cracks and tufts, was shinning a small boy.

The stranger coolly faced the pursuers, and at the sight of him they checked, those behind stumbling against those in front. He was speaking to them in a foreign tongue, and to Sir Archie's ear the words were like the crack of a lash. The hesitation was only for a moment, for a voice among them cried out, and the whole pack gave tongue shrilly and surged on again. But that instant of check had given the stranger his chance. He was up the ladder, and, gripping the parapet, found rest for his feet in a fissure. Then he bent down, drew up the ladder, handed it to McGuffog, and with a mighty heave pulled himself over the top.

He seemed to hope to defend the veranda, but the door at the west end was being assailed by a contingent of the enemy, and he saw that its thin woodwork was yielding.

'Into the House,' he cried, as he picked up the ladder and tossed it over the wall on the pack surging below. He was only just in time, for the west door yielded. In two steps he had followed McGuffog through the chink into the passage, and the concussion of the grand piano pushed hard against the veranda door from within coincided with the first battering on the said door from without.

In the garden-room the feeble lamp showed a strange grouping. Saskia had sunk into a chair to get her breath, and seemed too dazed to be aware of her surroundings. Dougal was manfully striving to appear at his ease, but his lip was quivering.

'A near thing that time,' he observed. 'It was the blame of that man's auld motor-bicycle.'

The stranger cast sharp eyes around the place and company.

'An awkward corner, gentlemen,' he said. 'How many are there of you? Four men and a boy? And you have placed guards at all the entrances?'

'They have bombs,' Sir Archie reminded him.

'No doubt. But I do not think they will use them here – or their guns, unless there is no other way. Their purpose is kidnapping, and they hope to do it secretly and slip off without leaving a trace. If they slaughter us, as they easily can, the cry will be out against them, and their vessel will be unpleasantly hunted. Half their purpose is already spoiled, for it is no longer secret ... They may break us by sheer weight, and I fancy the first shooting will be done by us. It's the windows I'm afraid of.'

Some tone in his quiet voice reached the girl in the wicker chair. She looked up wildly, saw him, and with a cry of 'Alesha' ran to his arms. There she hung, while his hand fondled her hair, like a mother with a scared child. Sir Archie, watching the whole thing in some stupefaction, thought he had never in his days seen more nobly matched human creatures.

'It is my friend,' she cried triumphantly, 'the friend whom I appointed to meet me here. Oh, I did well to trust him. Now we need not fear anything.'

As if in ironical answer came a great crashing at the veranda door, and the twanging of chords cruelly mishandled.

The grand piano was suffering internally from the assaults of the boiler-house ladder.

'Wull I gie them a shot?' was McGuffog's hoarse inquiry.

'Action stations,' Alexis ordered, for the command seemed to have shifted to him from Dougal. 'The windows are the danger. The boy will patrol the ground floor, and give us warning, and I and this man,' pointing to Sime, 'will be ready at the threatened point. And, for God's sake, no shooting, unless I give the word. If we take them on at that game we haven't a chance.'

He said something to Saskia in Russian and she smiled assent and went to Sir Archie's side. 'You and I must keep this door,' she said.

Sir Archie was never very clear afterwards about the events of the next hour. The Princess was in the maddest spirits, as if the burden of three years had slipped from her and she was back in her first girlhood. She sang as she carried more lumber to the pile – perhaps the song which had once entranced Heritage, but Sir Archie had no ear for music. She mocked at the furious blows which rained at the other end, for the door had gone now, and in the windy gap could be seen a blur of dark faces. Oddly enough, he found his own spirits mounting to meet hers. It was real business at last, the qualms of the civilian had been forgotten, and there was rising in him that joy in a scrap which had once made him one of the most daring airmen on the Western Front. The only thing that worried him now was the coyness about shooting. What on earth were his rifles and shot-guns for unless to be used? He had seen the enemy from the veranda wall, and a more ruffianly crew he had never dreamed of. They meant the uttermost business, and against such it was surely the duty of good citizens to wage whole-hearted war.

The Princess was humming to herself a nursery rhyme. '*The King of Spain's daughter*,' she crooned, '*came to visit me, and all for the sake* – Oh, that poor piano!' In her clear voice she cried something in Russian, and the wind carried a laugh from the veranda. At the sound of it she stopped. 'I had forgotten,' she said. 'Paul is there. I had forgotten.' After that she was very quiet, but she redoubled her labours at the barricade.

To the man it seemed that the pressure from without was slackening. He called to McGuffog to ask about the garden-room window, and the reply was reassuring. The gamekeeper was gloomily contemplating Dougal's tubs of water and wire-netting, as he might have contemplated a vermin trap.

Sir Archie was growing acutely anxious – the anxiety of the defender of a straggling fortress which is vulnerable at a dozen points. It seemed to him that strange noises were coming from the rooms beyond the hall. Did the back door lie that way? And was not there a smell of smoke in the air? If they tried fire in such a gale the place would burn like matchwood.

He left his post and in the hall found Dougal.

'All quiet,' the Chieftain reported. 'Far ower quiet. I don't like it. The enemy's no' puttin' out his strength yet. The Russian says a' the west windies are terrible dangerous. Him and the chauffeur's doin' their best, but ye can't block thae muckle glass panes.'

He returned to the Princess, and found that the attack had indeed languished on that particular barricade. The withers of the grand piano were left unwrung, and only a faint scuffling informed him that the veranda was not empty. 'They're gathering for an attack elsewhere,' he told himself. But what if that attack were a feint? He and McGuffog must stick to their post, for in his belief the veranda door and the garden-room window were the easiest places where an entry in mass could be forced.

Suddenly Dougal's whistle blew, and with it came a most almighty crash somewhere towards the west side. With a shout of 'Hold tight, McGuffog,' Sir Archie bolted into the hall, and, led by the sound, reached what had once been the ladies' bedroom. A strange sight met his eyes, for the whole framework of one window seemed to have been thrust inward, and in the gap Alexis was swinging a fender. Three of the enemy were in the room – one senseless on the floor, one in the grip of Sime, whose single hand was tightly clenched on his throat, and one engaged with Dougal in a corner. The Die-Hard leader was sore pressed, and to his help Sir Archie went. The fresh assault made the seaman duck his head, and Dougal seized the occasion to smite him hard with something which caused him to roll over. It was Léon's life-preserver which he had annexed that afternoon.

Alexis at the window seemed to have for a moment daunted the attack. 'Bring that table,' he cried, and the thing was jammed into the gap. 'Now you' – this to Sime – 'get the man from the back door to hold this place with his gun. There's no attack there. It's about time for shooting now, or we'll have them in our rear. What in heaven is that?'

It was McGuffog whose great bellow resounded down the corridor. Sir Archie turned and shuffled back, to be met by a distressing spectacle. The lamp, burning as peacefully as it might have burned on an old lady's tea-table, revealed the window of the garden-room driven bodily inward, shutters and all, and now forming an inclined bridge over Dougal's ineffectual tubs. In front of it stood McGuffog, swinging his gun by the barrel and yelling curses, which, being mainly couched in the vernacular, were happily meaningless to Saskia. She herself stood at the hall door, plucking at something hidden in her breast. He saw that it was a little ivory-handled pistol.

The enemy's feint had succeeded, for even as Sir Archie looked three men leaped into the room. On the neck of one the butt of McGuffog's gun crashed, but two scrambled to their feet and made for the girl. Sir Archie met the first with his fist, a clean drive on the jaw, followed by a damaging hook with his left that put him out of action. The other hesitated for an instant and was lost, for McGuffog caught him by the waist from behind and sent him through the broken frame to join his comrades without.

'Up the stairs,' Dougal was shouting, for the little room beyond the hall was clearly impossible. 'Our flank's turned. They're pourin' through the other windy.' Out of a corner of his eye Sir Archie caught sight of Alexis, with Sime and

Carfrae in support, being slowly forced towards them along the corridor. 'Upstairs,' he shouted. 'Come on, McGuffog. Lead on, Princess.' He dashed out the lamp, and the place was in darkness.

With this retreat from the forward trench line ended the opening phase of the battle. It was achieved in good order, and position was taken up on the first floor landing, dominating the main staircase and the passage that led to the back stairs. At their back was a short corridor ending in a window which gave on the north side of the House above the veranda, and from which an active man might descend to the veranda roof. It had been carefully reconnoitred beforehand by Dougal, and his were the dispositions.

The odd thing was that the retreating force were in good heart. The three men from the Mains were warming to their work, and McGuffog wore an air of genial ferocity. 'Dashed fine position I call this,' said Sir Archie. Only Alexis was silent and preoccupied. 'We are still at their mercy,' he said. 'Pray God your police come soon.' He forbade shooting yet awhile. 'The lady is our strong card,' he said. 'They won't use their guns while she is with us, but if it ever comes to shooting they can wipe us out in a couple of minutes. One of you watch that window, for Paul Abreskov is no fool.'

Their exhilaration was short-lived. Below in the hall it was black darkness save for a greyness at the entrance of the veranda passage; but the defence was soon aware that the place was thick with men. Presently there came a scuffling from Carfrae's post towards the back stairs, and a cry as of someone choking. And at the same moment a flare was lit below which brought the whole hall from floor to rafters into blinding light.

It revealed a crowd of figures, some still in the hall and some half-way up the stairs, and it revealed, too, more figures at the end of the upper landing where Carfrae had been stationed. The shapes were motionless like mannequins in a shop window.

'They've got us treed all right,' Sir Archie groaned. 'What the devil are they waiting for?'

'They wait for their leader,' said Alexis.

No one of the party will ever forget the ensuing minutes. After the hubbub of the barricades the ominous silence was like icy water, chilling and petrifying with an indefinable fear. There was no sound but the wind, but presently mingled with it came odd wild voices.

'Hear to the whaups,' McGuffog whispered.

Sir Archie, who found the tension unbearable, sought relief in contradiction. 'You're an unscientific brute, McGuffog,' he told his henchman. 'It's a disgrace that a gamekeeper should be such a rotten naturalist. What would whaups be doin' on the shore at this time of year?'

'A' the same, I could swear it's whaups, Sir Erchibald.'

Then Dougal broke in and his voice was excited. 'It's no whaups. That's our patrol signal. Man, there's hope for us yet. I believe it's the polis.'

His words were unheeded, for the figures below drew apart and a young man came through them. His beautifully-shaped dark head was bare, and as he moved he unbuttoned his oilskins and showed the trim dark-blue garb of the yachtsman. He walked confidently up the stairs, an odd elegant figure among his heavy companions.

'Good afternoon, Alexis,' he said in English. 'I think we may now regard this interesting episode as closed. I take it that you surrender. Saskia, dear, you are coming with me on a little journey. Will you tell my men where to find your baggage?'

The reply was in Russian. Alexis' voice was as cool as the other's, and it seemed to wake him to anger. He replied in a rapid torrent of words, and appealed to the men below, who shouted back. The flare was dying down, and shadows again hid most of the hall.

Dougal crept up behind Sir Archie. 'Here, I think it's the polis. They're whistlin' outbye, and I hear folk cryin' to each other – no' the foreigners.'

Again Alexis spoke, and then Saskia joined in. What she said rang sharp with contempt, and her fingers played with her little pistol.

Suddenly, before the young man could answer, Dobson bustled towards him. The innkeeper was labouring under some strong emotion, for he seemed to be pleading and pointing urgently towards the door.

'I tell ye it's the polis,' whispered Dougal. 'They're nickit.'

There was a swaying in the crowd and anxious faces. Men surged in, whispered, and went out, and a clamour arose which the leader stilled with a fierce gesture.

'You there,' he cried, looking up, 'you English. We mean you no ill, but I require you to hand over to me the lady and the Russian who is with her. I give you a minute by my watch to decide. If you refuse, my men are behind you and around you, and you go with me to be punished at my leisure.'

'I warn you,' cried Sir Archie. 'We are armed, and will shoot down anyone who dares to lay a hand on us.'

'You fool,' came the answer. 'I can send you all to eternity before you touch a trigger.'

Léon was by his side now – Léon and Spidel, imploring him to do something which he angrily refused. Outside there was a new clamour, faces showing at the door and then vanishing, and an anxious hum filled the hall . . . Dobson appeared again and this time he was a figure of fury.

'Are ye daft, man?' he cried. 'I tell ye the polis are closin' round us, and there's no' a moment to lose if we would get back to the boats. If ye'll no' think o' your own neck, I'm thinkin' o' mine. The whole thing's a bloody misfire. Come on, lads, if ye're no besotted on destruction.'

Léon laid a hand on the leader's arm and was roughly shaken off. Spidel fared no better, and the little group on the upper landing saw the two shrug their shoulders and make for the door. The hall was emptying fast and the watchers had gone from the back stairs. The young man's voice rose to a scream; he commanded, threatened, cursed; but panic was in the air and he had lost his mastery.

'Quick,' croaked Dougal, 'now's the time for the counter-attack.'

But the figure on the stairs held them motionless. They could not see his face, but by instinct they knew that it was distraught with fury and defeat. The flare blazed up again as the flame caught a knot of fresh powder, and once more the place was bright with the uncanny light ... The hall was empty save for the pale man who was in the act of turning.

He looked back. 'If I go now, I will return. The world is not wide enough to hide you from me, Saskia.'

'You will never get her,' said Alexis.

A sudden devil flamed into his eyes, the devil of some ancestral savagery, which would destroy what is desired but unattainable. He swung round, his hand went to his pocket, something clicked, and his arm shot out like a baseball pitcher's.

So intent was the gaze of the others on him, that they did not see a second figure ascending the stairs. Just as Alexis flung himself before the Princess, the new-comer caught the young man's outstretched arm and wrenched something from his hand. The next second he had hurled it into a far corner where stood the great fireplace. There was a blinding sheet of flame, a dull roar, and then billow upon billow of acrid smoke. As it cleared they saw that the fine Italian chimneypiece, the pride of the builder of the House, was a mass of splinters, and that a great hole had been blown through the wall into what had been the dining-room ... A figure was sitting on the bottom step feeling its bruises. The last enemy had gone.

When Mr John Heritage raised his eyes he saw the Princess with a very pale face in the arms of a tall man whom he had never seen before. If he was surprised at the sight, he did not show it. 'Nasty little bomb that. I remember we struck the brand first in July '18.'

'Are they rounded up?' Sir Archie asked.

'They've bolted. Whether they'll get away is another matter. I left half the mounted police a minute ago at the top of the West Lodge avenue. The other lot went to the Garple-foot to cut off the boats.'

'Good Lord, man,' Sir Archie cried, 'the police have been here for the last ten minutes.'

'You're wrong. They came with me.'

'Then what on earth –' began the astonished baronet. He

stopped short, for he suddenly got his answer. Into the hall from the veranda limped a boy. Never was there seen so ruinous a child. He was dripping wet, his shirt was all but torn off his back, his bleeding nose was poorly staunched by a wisp of handkerchief, his breeches were in ribbons, and his poor bare legs looked as if they had been comprehensively kicked and scratched. Limpingly he entered, yet with a kind of pride, like some small cock-sparrow who has lost most of his plumage but has vanquished his adversary.

With a yell Dougal went down the stairs. The boy saluted him, and they gravely shook hands. It was the meeting of Wellington and Blücher.

The Chieftain's voice shrilled in triumph, but there was a break in it. The glory was almost too great to be borne.

'I kenned it,' he cried. 'It was the Gorbals Die-Hards. There stands the man that done it . . . Ye'll no' fickle Thomas Yownie.'

## CHAPTER FIFTEEN

# THE GORBALS DIE-HARDS GO INTO ACTION

WE left Mr McCunn, full of aches but desperately resolute in spirit, hobbling by the Auchenlochan road into the village of Dalquharter. His goal was Mrs Morran's hen-house, which was Thomas Yownie's *poste de commandement*. The rain had come on again, and, though in other weather there would have been a slow twilight, already the shadow of night had the world in its grip. The sea even from the high ground was invisible, and all to westward and windward was a ragged screen of dark cloud. It was foul weather for foul deeds.

Thomas Yownie was not in the hen-house, but in Mrs Morran's kitchen, and with him were the pug-faced boy known as Old Bill, and the sturdy figure of Peter Paterson. But the floor was held by the hostess. She still wore her big boots, her petticoats were still kilted, and round her venerable head in lieu of a bonnet was drawn a tartan shawl.

'Eh, Dickson, but I'm blithe to see ye. And, puir man, ye've been sair mishandled. This is the awfu'est Sabbath day that ever you and me pit in. I hope it'll be forgiven us . . . Whaur's the young leddy?'

'Dougal was saying she was in the House with Sir Archibald and the men from the Mains.'

'Wae's me!' Mrs Morran keened. 'And what kind o' place is yon for her? Thae laddies tell me there's boatfu's o' scoondrels landit at the Garplefit. They'll try the auld Tower, but they'll no' wait there when they find it toom, and they'll be inside the Hoose in a jiffy and awa' wi' the puir lassie. Sirs, it maunna be. Ye're lippenin' to the polis, but in a' my days I never kenned the polis in time. We maun be up and daein' oorsels. Oh, if I could get a haud o' that red-heided Dougal . . .'

As she spoke there came on the wind the dull reverberation of an explosion.

'Keep us, what's that?' she cried.

'It's dinnymite,' said Peter Paterson.

'That's the end o' the auld Tower,' observed Thomas Yownie in his quiet, even voice. 'And it's likely the end o' the man Heritage.'

'Lord peety us!' the old woman wailed. 'And us standin' here like stookies and no' liftin' a hand. Awa' wi ye, laddies, and dae something. Awa' you too, Dickson, or I'll tak' the road mysel'.'

'I've got orders,' said the Chief of Staff, 'no' to move till the sityation's clear. Napoleon's up at the Tower and Jaikie's in the policies. I maun wait on their reports.'

For a moment Mrs Morran's attention was distracted by Dickson, who suddenly felt very faint and sat down heavily on a kitchen chair. 'Man, ye're as white as a dish-clout,' she exclaimed with compunction. 'Ye're fair wore out, and ye'll have had nae meat sin' your breakfast. See, and I'll get ye a cup o' tea.'

She proved to be in the right, for as soon as Dickson had swallowed some mouthfuls of her strong scalding brew the colour came back to his cheeks, and he announced that he felt better. 'Ye'll fortify it wi' a dram,' she told him, and produced a black bottle from her cupboard. 'My father aye said that guid whisky and het tea keepit the doctor's gig oot o' the close.'

The back door opened and Napoleon entered, his thin shanks blue with cold. He saluted and made his report in a voice shrill with excitement.

'The Tower has fallen. They've blown in the big door, and the feck o' them's inside.'

'And Mr Heritage?' was Dickson's anxious inquiry.

'When I last saw him he was up at a windy, shootin'. I think he's gotten on to the roof. I wouldna wonder but the place is on fire.'

'Here, this is awful,' Dickson groaned. 'We can't let Mr Heritage be killed that way. What strength is the enemy?'

'I counted twenty-seven, and there's stragglers comin' up from the boats.'

'And there's me and you five laddies here, and Dougal and the others shut up in the House.' He stopped in sheer despair. It was a fix from which the most enlightened business mind showed no escape. Prudence, inventiveness, were no longer in question; only some desperate course of violence.

'We must create a diversion,' he said. 'I'm for the Tower, and you laddies must come with me. We'll maybe see a chance. Oh, but I wish I had my wee pistol.'

'If ye're gaun there, Dickson, I'm comin' wi' ye,' Mrs Morran announced.

Her words revealed to Dickson the preposterousness of the whole situation, and for all his anxiety he laughed. 'Five laddies, a middle-aged man, and an auld wife,' he cried. 'Dod, it's pretty hopeless. It's like the thing in the Bible about the weak things of the world trying to confound the strong.'

'The Bible's whiles richt,' Mrs Morran answered drily. 'Come on, for there's no time to loss.'

The door opened again to admit the figure of Wee Jaikie. There were no tears in his eyes, and his face was very white.

'They're a' round the Hoose,' he croaked. 'I was up a tree forenent the verandy and seen them. The lassie ran oot and cried on them from the top o' the brae, and they a' turned and hunted her back. Gosh, but it was a near thing. I seen the Captain sklimmin' the wall, and a muckle man took the lassie and flung her up the ladder. They got inside just in time and steekit the door, and now the whole pack is roarin' round the Hoose seekin' a road in. They'll no' be long over the job, neither.'

'What about Mr Heritage?'

'They're no' heedin' about him any more. The auld Tower's bleezin'.'

'Worse and worse,' said Dickson. 'If the police don't come in the next ten minutes, they'll be away with the Princess. They've beaten all Dougal's plans, and it's a straight fight with odds of six to one. It's not possible.'

Mrs Morran for the first time seemed to lose hope. 'Eh, the

puir lassie!' she wailed, and sinking on a chair covered her face with her shawl.

'Laddies, can you no' think of a plan?' asked Dickson, his voice flat with despair.

Then Thomas Yownie spoke. So far he had been silent, but under his tangled thatch of hair his mind had been busy. Jaikie's report seemed to bring him to a decision.

'It's gey dark,' he said, 'and it's gettin' darker.'

There was that in his voice which promised something, and Dickson listened.

'The enemy's mostly foreigners, but Dobson's there and I think he's a kind of guide to them. Dobson's feared of the polis, and if we can terrify Dobson he'll terrify the rest.'

'Ay, but where are the police?'

'They're no' here yet, but they're comin'. The fear o' them is aye in Dobson's mind. If he thinks the polis has arrived, he'll put the wind up the lot ... *We* maun be the polis.'

Dickson could only stare while the Chief of Staff unfolded his scheme. I do not know to whom the Muse of History will give the credit of the tactics of 'infiltration', whether to Ludendorff or von Hutier or some other proud captain of Germany, or to Foch, who revised and perfected them. But I know that the same notion was at this moment of crisis conceived by Thomas Yownie, whom no parents acknowledged, who slept usually in a coal cellar, and who had picked up his education among Gorbals closes and along the wharves of Clyde.

'It's gettin' dark,' he said, 'and the enemy are that busy tryin' to break into the Hoose that they'll no' be thinkin' o' their rear. The five o' us Die-Hards is grand at dodgin' and keepin' out of sight, and what hinders us to get in among them, so that they'll hear us but never see us. We're used to the ways o' the polis, and can imitate them fine. Forbye we've all got our whistles, which are the same as a bobbie's birl, and Old Bill and Peter are grand at copyin' a man's voice. Since the Captain is shut up in the Hoose, the command falls to me, and that's my plan.'

With a piece of chalk he drew on the kitchen floor a rough

sketch of the environs of Huntingtower. Peter Paterson was to move from the shrubberies beyond the veranda, Napoleon from the stables, Old Bill from the Tower, while Wee Jaikie and Thomas himself were to advance as if from the Garple-foot, so that the enemy might fear for his communications. 'As soon as one o' ye gets into position he's to gie the patrol cry, and when each o' ye has heard five cries, he's to advance. Begin birlin' and roarin' afore ye get among them, and keep it up till ye're at the Hoose wall. If they've gotten inside, in ye go after them. I trust each Die-Hard to use his judgement, and above all to keep out o' sight and no let himsel' be grippit.'

The plan, like all great tactics, was simple, and no sooner was it expounded than it was put into action. The Die-Hards faded out of the kitchen like fog-wreaths, and Dickson and Mrs Morran were left looking at each other. They did not look long. The bare feet of Wee Jaikie had not crossed the threshold fifty seconds, before they were followed by Mrs Morran's out-of-doors boots and Dickson's tackets. Arm in arm the two hobbled down the back path behind the village which led to the South Lodge. The gate was unlocked, for the warder was busy elsewhere, and they hastened up the avenue. Far off Dickson thought he saw shapes fleeting across the park, which he took to be the shock-troops of his own side, and he seemed to hear snatches of song. Jaikie was giving tongue, and this was what he sang:

*Proley Tarians, arise!*
*Wave the Red Flag to the skies,*
*Heed nae mair the Fat Man's lees,*
*Stap them doun his throat!*
*Nocht to loss except our chains –*

But he tripped over a rabbit wire and thereafter conserved his breath.

The wind was so loud that no sound reached them from the House, which, blank and immense, now loomed before them. Dickson's ears were alert for the noise of shots or the dull crash of bombs; hearing nothing, he feared the worst, and hurried Mrs Morran at a pace which endangered her life.

He had no fear for himself, arguing that his foes were seeking higher game, and judging, too, that the main battle must be round the veranda at the other end. The two passed the shrubbery where the road forked, one path running to the back door and one to the stables. They took the latter and presently came out on the downs, with the ravine of the Garple on their left, the stables in front, and on the right the hollow of a formal garden running along the west side of the House.

The gale was so fierce, now that they had no wind-break between them and the ocean, that Mrs Morran could wrestle with it no longer, and found shelter in the lee of a clump of rhododendrons. Darkness had all but fallen, and the House was a black shadow against the dusky sky, while a confused greyness marked the sea. The old Tower showed a tooth of masonry; there was no glow from it, so the fire, which Jaikie had reported, must have died down. A whaup cried loudly, and very eerily: then another.

The birds stirred up Mrs Morran. 'That's the laddies' patrol,' she gasped. 'Count the cries, Dickson.'

Another bird wailed, this time very near. Then there was perhaps three minutes' silence till a fainter wheeple came from the direction of the Tower. 'Four,' said Dickson, but he waited in vain on the fifth. He had not the acute hearing of the boys, and could not catch the faint echo of Peter Paterson's signal beyond the veranda. The next he heard was a shrill whistle cutting into the wind, and then others in rapid succession from different quarters, and something which might have been the hoarse shouting of angry men.

The Gorbals Die-Hards had gone into action.

Dull prose is no medium to tell of that wild adventure. The sober sequence of the military historian is out of place in recording deeds that knew not sequence or sobriety. Were I a bard, I would cast this tale in excited verse, with a lilt which would catch the speed of the reality. I would sing of Napoleon, not unworthy of his great namesake, who penetrated to the very window of the ladies' bedroom, where the framework had been driven in and men were pouring through; of how there he made such pandemonium with his whistle that men tumbled back and ran about blindly seeking for guidance; of how in the long run his pugnacity mastered him, so that he engaged in combat with an unknown figure and the two rolled into what had once been a fountain. I would hymn Peter Paterson, who across tracts of darkness engaged Old Bill in a conversation which would have done no discredit to a Gallowgate policeman. He pretended to be making reports and seeking orders. 'We've gotten three o' the deevils, sir. What'll we dae wi' them?' he shouted; and back would come the reply in a slightly more genteel voice: 'Fall them to the rear. Tamson has charge of the prisoners.' Or it would be: 'They've gotten pistols, sir. What's the orders?' and the answer would be: 'Stick to your batons. The guns are posted on the knowe, so we needn't hurry.' And over all the din there would be a perpetual whistling and a yelling of 'Hands up!'

I would sing, too, of Wee Jaikie, who was having the red-letter hour of his life. His fragile form moved like a lizard in places where no mortal could be expected, and he varied his duties with impish assaults upon the persons of such as came in his way. His whistle blew in a man's ear one second and the next yards away. Sometimes he was moved to song, and unearthly fragments of 'Class-conscious we are' or 'Proley Tarians, arise!' mingled with the din, like the cry of seagulls in a storm. He saw a bright light flare up within the House which warned him not to enter, but he got as far as the garden-room, in whose dark corners he made havoc. Indeed he was almost too successful, for he created panic where he went, and one or two fired blindly at the quarter where he had last been heard. These shots were followed by frenzied prohibitions from Spidel and were not repeated. Presently he felt that aimless surge of men that is the prelude to flight, and heard Dobson's great voice roaring in the hall. Convinced that the crisis had come, he made his way outside, prepared to harass the rear of any retirement. Tears now flowed down his face, and he could not have spoken for sobs, but he had never been so happy.

But chiefly would I celebrate Thomas Yownie, for it was he who brought fear into the heart of Dobson. He had a voice of singular compass, and from the veranda he made it echo round the House. The efforts of Old Bill and Peter Paterson had been skilful indeed, but those of Thomas Yownie were deadly. To some leader beyond he shouted news: 'Robison's just about finished wi' his lot, and then he'll get the boats.' A furious charge upset him, and for a moment he thought he had been discovered. But it was only Dobson rushing to Léon, who was leading the men in the doorway. Thomas fled to the far end of the veranda, and again lifted up his voice. 'All foreigners,' he shouted, 'except the man Dobson. Ay. Ay. Ye've got Loudon? Well done!'

It must have been this last performance which broke Dobson's nerve and convinced him that the one hope lay in a rapid retreat to the Garplefoot. There was a tumbling of men in the doorway, a muttering of strange tongues, and the vision of the innkeeper shouting to Léon and Spidel. For a second he was seen in the faint reflexion that the light in the hall cast as far as the veranda, a wild figure urging the retreat with a pistol clapped to the head of those who were too confused by the hurricane of events to grasp the situation. Some of them dropped over the wall, but most huddled like sheep through the door on the west side, a jumble of struggling, blasphemous mortality. Thomas Yownie, staggered at the success of his tactics, yet kept his head and did his utmost to confuse the retreat, and the triumphant shouts and whistles of the other Die-Hards showed that they were not unmindful of this final duty . . .

The veranda was empty, and he was just about to enter the House, when through the west door came a figure, breathing hard and bent apparently on the same errand. Thomas prepared for battle, determined that no straggler of the enemy should now wrest from him victory, but, as the figure came into the faint glow at the doorway, he recognized it as Heritage. And at the same moment he heard something which made his tense nerves relax. Away on the right came sounds, a thud of galloping horses on grass and the jingle of bridle reins and the voices of men. It was the real thing at last. It is a sad commentary on his career, but now for the first time in his brief existence Thomas Yownie felt charitably disposed towards the police.

*

The Poet, since we left him blaspheming on the roof of the Tower, had been having a crowded hour of most inglorious life. He had started to descend at a furious pace, and his first misadventure was that he stumbled and dropped Dickson's pistol over the parapet. He tried to mark where it might have fallen in the gloom below, and this lost him precious minutes. When he slithered through the trap into the attic room, where he had tried to hold up the attack, he discovered that it was full of smoke which sought in vain to escape by the narrow window. Volumes of it were pouring up the stairs, and when he attempted to descend, he found himself choked and blinded. He rushed gasping to the window, filled his lungs with fresh air, and tried again, but he got no farther than the first turn, from which he could see through the cloud red tongues of flame in the ground room. This was solemn indeed, so he sought another way out. He got on the roof, for he remembered a chimney-stack, cloaked with ivy, which was built straight from the ground, and he thought he might climb down it.

He found the chimney and began the descent confidently, for he had once borne a good reputation at the Montervers and Cortina. At first all went well, for stones stuck out at decent intervals like the rungs of a ladder, and roots of ivy supplemented their deficiencies. But presently he came to a place where the masonry had crumbled into a cave, and left a gap some twenty feet high. Below it he could dimly see a thick mass of ivy which would enable him to cover the further forty feet to the ground, but at that cave he stuck most finally. All around the lime and stone had lapsed into débris, and he could find no safe foothold. Worse still, the block on which he relied proved loose, and only by a dangerous traverse did he avert disaster.

There he hung for a minute or two, with a cold void in his

stomach. He had always distrusted the handiwork of man as a place to scramble on, and now he was planted in the dark on a decomposing wall, with an excellent chance of breaking his neck, and with the most urgent need for haste. He could see the windows of the House, and, since he was sheltered from the gale, he could hear the faint sound of blows on woodwork. There was clearly the devil to pay there, and yet here he was helplessly stuck . . . Setting his teeth, he started to ascend again. Better the fire than this cold breakneck emptiness.

It took him the better part of half an hour to get back, and he passed through many moments of acute fear. Footholds which had seemed secure enough in the descent now proved impossible, and more than once he had his heart in his mouth when a rotten ivy stump or a wedge of stone gave in his hands, and dropped dully into the pit of night, leaving him crazily spread-eagled. When at last he reached the top he rolled on his back and felt very sick. Then, as he realized his safety, his impatience revived. At all costs he would force his way out though he should be grilled like a herring.

The smoke was less thick in the attic, and with his handkerchief wet with the rain and bound across his mouth he made a dash for the ground room. It was as hot as a furnace, for everything inflammable in it seemed to have caught fire, and the lumber glowed in piles of hot ashes. But the floor and walls were stone, and only the blazing jambs of the door stood between him and the outer air. He had burned himself considerably as he stumbled downwards, and the pain drove him to a wild leap through the broken arch, where he miscalculated the distance, charred his shins, and brought down a red-hot fragment of the lintel on his head. But the thing was done, and a minute later he was rolling like a dog in the wet bracken to cool his burns and put out various smouldering patches on his raiment.

Then he started running for the House, but, confused by the darkness, he bore too much to the north, and came out in the side avenue from which he and Dickson had reconnoitred on the first evening. He saw on the right a glow in the veranda which, as we know, was the reflexion of the flare in the hall, and he heard a babble of voices. But he heard something more, for away on his left was the sound which Thomas Yownie was soon to hear – the trampling of horses. It was the police at last, and his task was to guide them at once to the critical point of action . . . Three minutes later a figure like a scarecrow was admonishing a bewildered sergeant, while his hands plucked feverishly at a horse's bridle.

*

It is time to return to Dickson in his clump of rhododendrons. Tragically aware of his impotence he listened to the tumult of the Die-Hards, hopeful when it was loud, despairing when there came a moment's lull, while Mrs Morran like a Greek chorus drew loudly upon her store of proverbial philosophy and her memory of Scripture texts. Twice he tried to reconnoitre towards the scene of battle, but only blundered into sunken plots and pits in the Dutch garden. Finally he squatted beside Mrs Morran, lit his pipe, and took a firm hold on his patience.

It was not tested for long. Presently he was aware that a change had come over the scene – that the Die-Hards' whistles and shouts were being drowned in another sound, the cries of panicky men. Dobson's bellow was wafted to him. 'Auntie Phemie,' he shouted, 'the innkeeper's getting rattled. Dod, I believe they're running.' For at that moment twenty paces on his left the van of the retreat crashed through the creepers on the garden's edge and leaped the wall that separated it from the cliffs of the Garplefoot.

The old woman was on her feet.

'God be thankit, is't the polis?'

'Maybe. Maybe no'. But they're running.'

Another bunch of men raced past, and he heard Dobson's voice.

'I tell you, they're broke. Listen, it's horses. Ay, it's the police, but it was the Die-Hards that did the job . . . Here! They mustn't escape. Have the police had the sense to send men to the Garplefoot?'

Mrs Morran, a figure like an ancient prophetess, with her tartan shawl lashing in the gale, clutched him by the shoulder.

'Doun to the waterside and stop them. Ye'll no' be beat by wee laddies! On wi' ye and I'll follow! There's gaun to be a juidgment on evil-doers this nicht.'

Dickson needed no urging. His heart was hot within him, and the weariness and stiffness had gone from his limbs. He, too, tumbled over the wall, and made for what he thought was the route by which he had originally ascended from the stream. As he ran he made ridiculous efforts to cry like a whaup in the hope of summoning the Die-Hards. One, indeed, he found – Napoleon, who had suffered a grievous pounding in the fountain, and had only escaped by an eel-like agility which had aforetime served him in good stead with the law of his native city. Lucky for Dickson was the meeting, for he had forgotten the road and would certainly have broken his neck. Led by the Die-Hard he slid forty feet over screes and boiler-plates, with the gale plucking at him, found a path, lost it, and then tumbled down a raw bank of earth to the flat ground beside the harbour. During all this performance, he has told me, he had no thought of fear, nor any clear notion what he meant to do. He just wanted to be in at the finish of the job.

Through the narrow entrance the gale blew as through a funnel, and the usually placid waters of the harbour were a froth of angry waves. Two boats had been launched and were plunging furiously, and on one of them a lantern dipped and fell. By its light he could see men holding a further boat by the shore. There was no sign of the police; he reflected that probably they had become tangled in the Garple Dean. The third boat was waiting for some one.

Dickson – a new Ajax by the ships – divined who this some one must be and realized his duty. It was the leader, the arch-enemy, the man whose escape must at all costs be stopped. Perhaps he had the Princess with him, thus snatching victory from apparent defeat. In any case he must be tackled, and a fierce anxiety gripped his heart. 'Aye finish a job,' he told himself, and peered up into the darkness of the cliffs, wondering just how he should set about it, for except in the last few days he had never engaged in combat with a fellow-creature.

'When he comes, you grip his legs,' he told Napoleon, 'and get him down. He'll have a pistol, and we're done if he's on his feet.'

There was a cry from the boats, a shout of guidance, and the light on the water was waved madly. 'They must have good eyesight,' thought Dickson, for he could see nothing. And then suddenly he was aware of steps in front of him, and a shape like a man rising out of the void at his left hand.

In the darkness Napoleon missed his tackle, and the full shock came on Dickson. He aimed at what he thought was the enemy's throat, found only an arm, and was shaken off as a mastiff might shake off a toy terrier. He made another clutch, fell, and in falling caught his opponent's leg so that he brought him down. The man was immensely agile, for he was up in a second and something hot and bright blew into Dickson's face. The pistol bullet had passed through the collar of his faithful waterproof, slightly singeing his neck. But it served its purpose, for Dickson paused, gasping, to consider where he had been hit, and before he could resume the chase the last boat had pushed off into deep water.

To be shot at from close quarters is always irritating, and the novelty of the experience increased Dickson's natural wrath. He fumed on the shore like a deerhound when the stag has taken to the sea. So hot was his blood that he would have cheerfully assaulted the whole crew had they been within his reach. Napoleon, who had been incapacitated for speed by having his stomach and bare shanks savagely trampled upon, joined him, and together they watched the bobbing black specks as they crawled out of the estuary into the grey spindrift which marked the harbour mouth.

But as he looked the wrath died out of Dickson's soul. For he saw that the boats had indeed sailed on a desperate venture, and that a pursuer was on their track more potent than his breathless middle-age. The tide was on the ebb, and the gale was driving the Atlantic breakers shoreward, and in the jaws of the entrance the two waters met in an unearthly turmoil.

Above the noise of the wind came the roar of the flooded Garple and the fret of the harbour, and far beyond all the crashing thunder of the conflict at the harbour mouth. Even in the darkness, against the still faintly grey western sky, the spume could be seen rising like waterspouts. But it was the ear rather than the eye which made certain presage of disaster. No boat could face the challenge of that loud portal.

As Dickson struggled against the wind and stared, his heart melted and a great awe fell upon him. He may have wept; it is certain that he prayed. 'Poor souls, poor souls!' he repeated. 'I doubt the last hour or two has been a poor preparation for eternity.'

*

The tide next day brought the dead ashore. Among them was a young man, different in dress and appearance from the rest – a young man with a noble head and a finely-cut classic face, which was not marred like the others from pounding among the Garple rocks. His dark hair was washed back from his brow, and the mouth, which had been hard in life, was now relaxed in the strange innocence of death.

Dickson gazed at the body and observed that there was a slight deformation between the shoulders.

'Poor fellow,' he said. 'That explains a lot . . . As my father used to say, cripples have a right to be cankered.'

## CHAPTER SIXTEEN

# IN WHICH A PRINCESS LEAVES A DARK TOWER AND A PROVISION MERCHANT RETURNS TO HIS FAMILY

THE three days of storm ended in the night, and with the wild weather there departed from the Cruives something which had weighed on Dickson's spirits since he first saw the place. Monday – only a week from the morning when he had conceived his plan of holiday – saw the return of the sun and the bland airs of spring. Beyond the blue of the yet restless waters rose dim mountains tipped with snow, like some Mediterranean seascape. Nesting birds were busy on the Laver banks and in the Huntingtower thickets; the village smoked peacefully to the clear skies; even the House looked cheerful if dishevelled. The Garple Dean was a garden of swaying larches, linnets, and wild anemones. Assuredly, thought Dickson, there had come a mighty change in the countryside, and he meditated a future discourse to the Literary Society of the Guthrie Memorial Kirk on 'Natural Beauty in Relation to the Mind of Man.'

It remains for the chronicler to gather up the loose ends of his tale. There was no newspaper story with bold headlines of this the most recent assault on the shores of Britain. Alexis Nicolaevitch, once a Prince of Muscovy and now Mr Alexander Nicholson of the rising firm of Sprot and Nicholson of Melbourne, had interest enough to prevent it. For it was clear that if Saskia was to be saved from persecution, her enemies must disappear without trace from the world, and no story be told of the wild venture which was their undoing. The constabulary of Carrick and Scotland Yard were indisposed to ask questions, under a hint from their superiors, the more so as no serious damage had been done to the persons of His Majesty's lieges, and no lives had been lost except by the violence of Nature. The Procurator-Fiscal investigated the case of the drowned men, and reported that so many foreign sailors, names and origins unknown, had perished in attempting to return to their ship at the Garplefoot. The Danish brig had vanished into the mist of the northern seas. But one signal calamity the Procurator-Fiscal had to record. The body of Loudon the factor was found on the Monday morning below the cliffs, his neck broken by a fall. In the darkness and confusion he must have tried to escape in that direction, and he had chosen an impracticable road or had slipped on the edge. It was returned as 'death by misadventure', and the *Carrick Herald* and the *Auchenlochan Advertiser* excelled themselves in eulogy. Mr Loudon, they said, had been widely known in the south-west of Scotland as an able and trusted lawyer, an assiduous public servant, and not least as a good sportsman. It was the last trait which had led to his death, for, in his enthusiasm for wild nature, he had been studying bird life on the cliffs of the Cruives during the storm, and had made that fatal slip which had deprived the shire of a wise counsellor and the best of good fellows.

The tinklers of the Garplefoot took themselves off, and where they may now be pursuing their devious courses is unknown to the chronicler. Dobson, too, disappeared, for he was not among the dead from the boats. He knew the neighbourhood, and probably made his way to some port from which he took passage to one or other of those foreign lands which had formerly been honoured by his patronage. Nor did all the Russians perish. Three were found skulking next morning in the woods, starving and ignorant of any tongue but their own, and five more came ashore much battered but alive. Alexis took charge of the eight survivors, and arranged to pay their passage to one of the British Dominions and to give them a start in a new life. They were broken creatures, with the dazed look of lost animals, and four of them had been peasants on Saskia's estates. Alexis spoke to them in their own language. 'In my grandfather's time,' he said, 'you were serfs. Then there came a change, and for some time you were free men. Now you have slipped back into being slaves again – the worst of slaveries, for you have been the serfs of fools and scoundrels and the black passion of your own hearts. I give you a chance of becoming free men once more. You have the task before you of working out your own salvation. Go, and God be with you.'

*

Before we take leave of these companions of a single week I would present them to you again as they appeared on a certain sunny afternoon when the episode of Huntingtower was on the eve of closing. First we see Saskia and Alexis walking on the thymy sward of the cliff-top, looking out to the fretted blue of the sea. It is a fitting place for lovers – above all for lovers who have turned the page on a dark preface, and have before them still the long bright volume of life. The girl has her arm linked in the man's, but as they walk she breaks often away from him, to dart into copses, to gather flowers, or to peer over the brink where the gulls wheel and oyster-catchers pipe among the shingle. She is no more the tragic muse of the past week, but a laughing child again, full of snatches of song, her eyes bright with expectation. They talk of the new world which lies before them, and her voice is happy. Then her brows contract, and, as she flings herself down on a patch of young heather, her air is thoughtful.

'I have been back among fairy tales,' she says. 'I do not quite understand, Alesha. Those gallant little boys! They are youth, and youth is always full of strangeness. Mr Heritage! He is youth, too, and poetry, perhaps, and a soldier's tradition. I think I know him . . . But what about Dickson? He is the *petit bourgeois*, the *épicier*, the class which the world ridicules. He is unbelievable. The others with good fortune I might find elsewhere – in Russia perhaps. But not Dickson.'

'No,' is the answer. 'You will not find him in Russia. He is what they call the middle-class, which we who were foolish used to laugh at. But he is the stuff which above all others makes a great people. He will endure when aristocracies crack and proletariats crumble. In our own land we have never known him, but till we create him our land will not be a nation.'

*

Half a mile away on the edge of the Laver glen Dickson and Heritage are together, Dickson placidly smoking on a tree-stump and Heritage walking excitedly about and cutting with his stick at the bracken. Sundry bandages and strips of sticking plaster still adorn the Poet, but his clothes have been tidied up by Mrs Morran, and he has recovered something of his old precision of garb. The eyes of both are fixed on the two figures on the cliff-top. Dickson feels acutely uneasy. It is the first time that he has been alone with Heritage since the arrival of Alexis shivered the Poet's dream. He looks to see a tragic grief; to his amazement he beholds something very like exultation.

'The trouble about you, Dogson,' says Heritage, 'is that you're a bit of an anarchist. All you false romantics are. You don't see the extraordinary beauty of the conventions which time has consecrated. You always want novelty, you know, and the novel is usually the ugly and rarely the true. I am for romance, but upon the old, noble classic lines.'

Dickson is scarcely listening. His eyes are on the distant lovers, and he longs to say something which will gently and graciously express his sympathy with his friend.

'I'm afraid,' he begins hesitatingly, 'I'm afraid you've had a bad blow, Mr Heritage. You're taking it awful well, and I honour you for it.'

The Poet flings back his head. 'I am reconciled,' he says. 'After all " 'tis better to have loved and lost," you know. It has been a great experience and has shown me my own heart. I love her, I shall always love her, but I realize that she was never meant for me. Thank God I've been able to serve her – that is all a moth can ask of a star. I'm a better man for it, Dogson. She will be a glorious memory, and Lord! what poetry I shall write! I give her up joyfully, for she has found her mate. "Let us not to the marriage of true minds admit impediments!" The thing's too perfect to grieve about . . . Look! There is romance incarnate.'

He points to the figures now silhouetted against the farther sea. 'How does it do, Dogson?' he cries. '"And on her lover's arm she leant" – what next? You know the thing.'

Dickson assists and Heritage declaims:

*And on her lover's arm she leant*
*And round her waist she felt it fold,*
*And far across the hills they went*
*In that new world which is the old:*
*Across the hills and far away*
*Beyond their utmost purple rim,*
*And deep into the dying day*
*The happy princess followed him.*

He repeats the last two lines twice and draws a deep breath. 'How right!' he cries. 'How absolutely right! Lord! It's astonishing how that old bird Tennyson got the goods!'

*

After that Dickson leaves him and wanders among the thickets on the edge of the Huntingtower policies above the Laver glen. He feels childishly happy, wonderfully young, and at the same time supernaturally wise. Sometimes he thinks the past week has been a dream, till he touches the sticking-plaster on his brow, and finds that his left thigh is still a mass of bruises and that his right leg is woefully stiff. With that the past becomes very real again, and he sees the Garple Dean in that stormy afternoon, he wrestles again at midnight in the dark House, he stands with quaking heart by the boats to cut off the retreat. He sees it all, but without terror in the recollection, rather with gusto and a modest pride. 'I've surely had a remarkable time,' he tells himself, and then Romance, the goddess whom he has worshipped so long, marries that furious week with the idyllic. He is supremely content, for he knows that in his humble way he has not been found wanting. Once more for him the Chavender or Chub, and long dreams among summer hills. His mind flies to the days ahead of him, when he will go wandering with his pack in many green places. Happy days they will be, the prospect with which he has always charmed his mind. Yes, but they will be different from what he had fancied, for he is another man than the complacent little fellow who set out a week ago on his travels. He has now assurance of himself, assurance of his faith. Romance, he sees, is one and indivisible . . .

Below him by the edge of the stream he sees the encampment of the Gorbals Die-Hards. He calls and waves a hand, and his signal is answered. It seems to be washing day, for some scanty and tattered raiment is drying on the sward. The band is evidently in session, for it is sitting in a circle, deep in talk.

As he looks at the ancient tents, the humble equipment, the ring of small shockheads, a great tenderness comes over him. The Die-Hards are so tiny, so poor, so pitifully handicapped, and yet so bold in their meagreness. Not one of them has had anything that might be called a chance. Their few years have been spent in kennels and closes, always hungry and hunted, with none to care for them; their childish ears have been habituated to every coarseness, their small minds filled with the desperate shifts of living . . . And yet, what a heavenly spark was in them! He had always thought nobly of the soul; now he wants to get on his knees before the queer greatness of humanity.

A figure disengages itself from the group, and Dougal makes his way up the hill towards him. The Chieftain is not more reputable in garb than when we first saw him, nor is he more cheerful of countenance. He has one arm in a sling made out of his neckerchief, and his scraggy little throat rises bare from his voluminous shirt. All that can be said for him is that he is appreciably cleaner. He comes to a standstill and salutes with a special formality.

'Dougal,' says Dickson, 'I've been thinking. You're the grandest lot of wee laddies I ever heard tell of, and, forbye, you've saved my life. Now, I'm getting on in years, though you'll admit that I'm not that dead old, and I'm not a poor man, and I haven't chick or child to look after. None of you has ever had a proper chance or been right fed or educated or taken care of. I've just the one thing to say to you. From now on you're *my* bairns, every one of you. You're fine laddies, and I'm going to see that you turn into fine men. There's the stuff in you to make Generals and Provosts – ay, and Prime Ministers, and Dod! it'll not be my blame if it doesn't get out.'

Dougal listens gravely and again salutes.

'I've brought ye a message,' he says. 'We've just had a meetin' and I've to report that ye've been unanimously eleckit Chief Die-Hard. We're a' hopin' ye'll accept.'

'I accept,' Dickson replies. 'Proudly and gratefully I accept.'

*

The last scene is some days later, in a certain southern suburb of Glasgow. Ulysses has come back to Ithaca, and is sitting by his fireside, waiting for the return of Penelope from the Neuk Hydropathic. There is a chill in the air, so a fire is burning in the grate, but the laden tea-table is bright with the first blooms of lilac. Dickson, in a new suit with a flower in his buttonhole, looks none the worse for his travels, save that there is still sticking-plaster on his deeply sunburnt brow. He waits impatiently with his eye on the black marble timepiece, and he fingers something in his pocket.

Presently the sound of wheels is heard, and the pea-hen voice of Tibby announces the arrival of Penelope. Dickson rushes to the door, and at the threshold welcomes his wife with a resounding kiss. He leads her into the parlour and settles her in her own chair.

'My! but it's nice to be home again!' she says. 'And everything that comfortable. I've had a fine time, but there's no place like your own fireside. You're looking awful well, Dickson. But losh! What have you been doing to your head?'

'Just a small tumble. It's very near mended already. Ay, I've had a grand walking tour, but the weather was a wee bit thrawn. It's nice to see you back again, Mamma. Now that I'm an idle man you and me must take a lot of jaunts together.'

She beams on him as she stays herself with Tibby's scones, and when the meal is ended, Dickson draws from his pocket a slim case. The jewels have been restored to Saskia, but this is one of her own which she has bestowed upon Dickson as a parting memento. He opens the case and reveals a necklet of emeralds, any one of which is worth half the street.

'This is a present for you,' he says bashfully.

Mrs McCunn's eyes open wide. 'You're far too kind,' she gasps. 'It must have cost an awful lot of money.'

'It didn't cost me that much,' is the truthful answer.

She fingers the trinket and then clasps it round her neck, where the green depths of the stones glow against the black satin of her bodice. Her eyes are moist as she looks at him. 'You've been a kind man to me,' she says, and she kisses him as she has not done since Janet's death.

She stands up and admires the necklet in the mirror. Romance once more, thinks Dickson. That which has graced the slim throats of princesses in far-away courts now adorns an elderly matron in a semi-detached villa; the jewels of the wild Nausicaa have fallen to the housewife Penelope.

Mrs McCunn preens herself before the glass. 'I call it very genteel,' she says. 'Real stylish. It might be worn by a queen.'

'I wouldn't say but it has,' says Dickson.

# CASTLE GAY

TO

SIR ALEXANDER GRANT, Bart.

OF LOGIE AND RELUGAS

*this comedy is inscribed with*
*gratitude and affection*

## CONTENTS

## CHAPTER ONE

# TELLS OF A RUGBY THREE-QUARTER

MR DICKSON MCCUNN laid down the newspaper, took his spectacles from his nose, and polished them with a blue-and-white spotted handkerchief.

'It will be a great match,' he observed to his wife. 'I wish I was there to see. These Kangaroos must be a fearsome lot.' Then he smiled reflectively. 'Our laddies are not turning out so bad, Mamma. Here's Jaikie, and him not yet twenty, and he has his name blazing in the papers as if he was a Cabinet Minister.'

Mrs McCunn, a placid lady of a comfortable figure, knitted steadily. She did not share her husband's enthusiasms.

'I know fine,' she said, 'that Jaikie will be coming back with a bandaged head and his arm in a sling. Rugby in my opinion is not a game for Christians. It's fair savagery.'

'Hoots, toots! It's a grand ploy for young folk. You must pay a price for fame, you know. Besides, Jaikie hasn't got hurt this long time back. He's learning caution as he grows older, or maybe he's getting better at the job. You mind when he was at the school we used to have the doctor to him every second Saturday night. ... He was always a terrible bold laddie, and when he was getting dangerous his eyes used to run with tears. He's quit of that habit now, but they tell me that when he's real excited he turns as white as paper. Well, well! we've all got our queer ways. Here's a biography of him and the other players. What's this it says?'

Mr McCunn resumed his spectacles.

'Here it is. "J. Galt, born in Glasgow. Educated at the Western Academy and St Mark's College, Cambridge ... played last year against Oxford in the victorious Cambridge fifteen, when he scored three tries. ... This is his first International ... equally distinguished in defence and attack. ... Perhaps the most unpredictable of wing three-quarters now playing. ...' Oh, and here's another bit of "Gossip about the Teams".' He removed his spectacles and laughed heartily. 'That's good. It calls him a "scholar and a gentleman". That's what they always say about University players. Well, I'll warrant he's as good a gentleman as any, though he comes out of a back street in the Gorbals. I'm not so sure about the scholar. But he can always do anything he sets his mind to, and he's a worse glutton for books than me. No man can tell what may happen to Jaikie yet. ... We can take credit for these laddies of ours, for they're all in the way of doing well for themselves, but there's just the two of them that I feel are like our own bairns. Just Jaikie and Dougal – and goodness knows what will be the end of that red-headed Dougal. Jaikie's a douce body, but there's a determined daftness about Dougal. I wish he wasn't so taken up with his misguided politics.'

'I hope they'll not miss their train,' said the lady. 'Supper's at eight, and they should be here by seven-thirty, unless Jaikie's in the hospital.'

'No fear,' was the cheerful answer. 'More likely some of the Kangaroos will be there. We should get a telegram about the match by six o'clock.'

So after tea, while his wife departed on some domestic task, Mr McCunn took his ease with a pipe in a wicker chair on the little terrace which looked seaward. He had found the hermitage for which he had long sought, and was well content with it. The six years which had passed since he forsook the city of Glasgow and became a countryman had done little to alter his appearance. The hair had indeed gone completely from the top of his head, and what was left was greying, but there were few lines on his smooth, ruddy face, and the pale eyes had still the innocence and ardour of youth. His figure had improved, for country exercise and a sparer diet had checked the movement towards rotundity. When not engaged in some active enterprise, it was his habit to wear a tailed coat and trousers of tweed, a garb which from his boyish recollection he thought proper for a country laird, but which to the ordinary observer suggested a bookmaker. Gradually, a little self-consciously, he had acquired what he considered to be the habits of the class. He walked in his garden with a spud, his capacious pockets containing a pruning knife and twine; he could talk quite learnedly of crops and stock, and, though he never shouldered a gun, of the prospects of game; and a fat spaniel was rarely absent from his heels.

This home he had chosen was on the spur of a Carrick moor, with the sea to the west, and to the south and east a distant prospect of the blue Galloway hills. After much thought he had rejected the various country houses which were open to his purchase; he felt it necessary to erect his own sanctuary, conformable to his modest but peculiar tastes. A farm of some five hundred acres had been bought, most of it pasture-fields fenced by dry-stone dykes, but with a considerable stretch of broom and heather, and one big plantation of larch. Much of this he let off, but he retained a hundred acres where he and his grieve could make disastrous essays in agriculture. The old farm-house had been a whitewashed edifice of eight rooms, with ample outbuildings, and this he had converted into a commodious dwelling, with half a dozen spare bedrooms, and a large chamber which was at once library, smoking-room and business-room. I do not defend Mr McCunn's taste, for he had a memory stored with bad precedents. He hankered after little pepper-box turrets, which he thought the badge of ancientry, and in internal decoration he had an unhallowed longing for mahogany panelling, like a ship's saloon. Also he doted on his vast sweep of gravel. Yet he had on the whole made a pleasing thing of Blaweary (it was the name which had first taken his fancy), for he stuck to harled and whitewashed walls, and he had a passion for green turf, so that, beyond the odious gravel, the lawns swept to the meadows unbroken by formal flowerbeds. These lawns were his special hobby. 'There's not a yard of turf about the place,' he would say, 'that's not as well kept as a putting-green.'

The owner from his wicker-chair looked over the said lawns to a rough pasture to where his cows were at graze, and then beyond a patch of yellowing bracken to the tops of a fir plantation. After that the ground fell more steeply, so that the tree-tops were silhouetted against the distant blue of the sea.

It was mid-October, but the air was as balmy as June, and only the earlier dusk told of the declining year. Mr McCunn was under strict domestic orders not to sit out of doors after sunset, but he had dropped asleep and the twilight was falling when he was roused by a maid with a telegram.

In his excitement he could not find his spectacles. He tore open the envelope and thrust the pink form into the maid's face. 'Read it, lassie – read it,' he cried, forgetting the decorum of the master of a household.

'Coming seven-thirty,' the girl read primly. 'Match won by a single point.' Mr McCunn upset his chair, and ran, whooping, in search of his wife.

The historian must return upon his tracks in order to tell of the great event thus baldly announced. That year the Antipodes had despatched to Britain such a constellation of Rugby stars that the hearts of the home enthusiasts became as water and their joints were loosened. For years they had known and suffered from the quality of those tall young men from the South, whom the sun had toughened and tautened – their superb physique, their resourcefulness, their uncanny combination. Hitherto, while the fame of one or two players had reached these shores, the teams had been in the main a batch of dark horses, and there had been no exact knowledge to set a bar to hope. But now Australia had gathered herself together for a mighty effort, and had sent to the field a fifteen most of whose members were known only too well. She had collected her sons wherever they were to be found. Four had already played for British Universities; three had won a formidable repute in international matches in which their country of ultimate origin had entitled them to play.

What club, county, or nation could resist so well equipped an enemy? And, as luck decided, it fell to Scotland, which had been having a series of disastrous seasons, to take the first shock.

That ancient land seemed for the moment to have forgotten her prowess. She could produce a strong, hard-working and effective pack, but her great three-quarter line had gone, and she had lost the scrum-half who the year before had been her chief support. Most of her fifteen were new to an international game, and had never played together. The danger lay in the enemy halves and three-quarters. The Kangaroos had two halves possessed of miraculous hands and a perfect knowledge of the game. They might be trusted to get the ball to their three-quarters, who were reputed to be the most formidable combination that ever played on turf. On the left wing was the mighty Charvill, an Oxford Blue and an English International; on the right Martineau, who had won fame on the cinder-track as well as on the football field. The centres were two cunning brothers, Clauson by name, who played in unison like Siamese twins. Against such a four Scotland could scrape up only a quartet of possibles, men of promise but not yet of performance. The hosts of Tuscany seemed strong out of all proportion to the puny defenders of Rome. And as the Scottish right-wing three-quarter, to frustrate the terrible Charvill, stood the tiny figure of J. Galt, Cambridge University, five foot six inches in height and slim as a wagtail.

To the crowd of sixty thousand and more that waited for the teams to enter the field was vouchsafed one slender comfort. The weather, which at Blaweary was clear and sunny, was abominable in the Scottish midlands. It had rained all the preceding night, and it was hoped that the ground might be soft, inclining to mud – mud dear to the heart of our islanders but hateful to men accustomed to the firm soil of the South.

The game began in a slight drizzle, and for Scotland it began disastrously. The first scrimmage was in the centre of the ground, and the ball came out to the Kangaroo scrum-half, who sent it to his stand-off. From him it went to Clauson, and then to Martineau, who ran round his opposing wing, dodged the Scottish full-back, and scored a try, which was converted. After five minutes the Kangaroos led by five points.

After that the Scottish forwards woke up, and there was a spell of stubborn defence. The Scottish full-back had a long shot at goal from a free kick, and missed, but for the rest most of the play was in the Scottish twenty-five. The Scottish pack strove their hardest, but they did no more than hold their opponents. Then once more there came a quick heel out, which went to one of the Clausons, a smart cut-through, a try secured between the posts and easily converted. The score was now ten points to nil.

Depression settled upon the crowd as deep as the weather, which had stopped raining but had developed into a sour *haar*. Followed a period of constant kicking into touch, a dull game which the Kangaroos were supposed to eschew. Just before half-time there was a thin ray of comfort. The Scottish left-wing three-quarter, one Smail, a Borderer, intercepted a Kangaroo pass and reached the enemy twenty-five before he was brought down from behind by Martineau's marvellous sprinting. He had been within sight of success, and half-time came with a faint hope that there was still a chance of averting a runaway defeat.

The second half began with three points to Scotland, secured from a penalty kick. Also the Scottish forwards seemed to have got a new lease of life. They carried the game well into the enemy territory, dribbling irresistibly in their loose rushes, and hooking and heeling in the grand manner from the scrums. The white uniforms of the Kangaroos were now plentifully soiled, and the dark blue of the Scots made them look the less bedraggled side. All but J. Galt. His duty had been that of desperate defence conducted with a resolute ferocity, and he had suffered in it. His jersey was half torn off his back, and his shorts were in ribbons: he limped heavily, and his small face looked as if it had been ground into the mud of his native land. He felt dull and stupid, as if he had been slightly concussed. His gift had hitherto been for invisibility; his fame had been made as a will-o'-the-wisp; now he seemed to be cast for the part of that Arnold von Winkelreid who drew spears to his bosom.

The ball was now coming out to the Scottish halves, but they mishandled it. It seemed impossible to get their three-quarters going. The ball either went loose, or was intercepted, or the holder was promptly tackled, and whenever there seemed a chance of a run there was always either a forward pass or a knock-on. At this period of the game the Scottish forwards were carrying everything on their shoulders, and their backs seemed hopeless. Any moment, too, might see the deadly echelon of the Kangaroo three-quarters ripple down the field.

And then came one of those sudden gifts of fortune which make Rugby an image of life. The ball came out from a heel in a scrum not far from the Kangaroo twenty-five, and went to the Kangaroo stand-off half. He dropped it, and, before he could recover, it was gathered by the Scottish stand-off. He sent it to Smail, who passed back to the Scottish left-centre, one Morrison, an Academical from Oxford who had hitherto been pretty much of a passenger. Morrison had the good luck to have a clear avenue before him, and he had a gift of pace. Dodging the Kangaroo full-back with a neat swerve, he scored in the corner of the goal-line amid a pandemonium of cheers. The try was miraculously converted, and the score stood at ten points to eight, with fifteen minutes to play.

Now began an epic struggle, not the least dramatic in the history of the game since a century ago the Rugby schoolboy William Webb Ellis first 'took the ball in his arms and ran with it.' The Kangaroos had no mind to let victory slip from their grasp, and, working like one man, they set themselves to assure it. For a little their magnificent three-quarter line seemed to have dropped out of the picture, but now most theatrically it returned to it. From a scrimmage in the Kangaroo half of the field, the ball went to their stand-off and from him to Martineau. At the moment the Scottish players were badly placed, for their three-quarters were standing wide in order to overlap the faster enemy line. It was a perfect occasion for one of Martineau's deadly runs. He was, however, well tackled by Morrison and passed back to his scrum half, who kicked ahead towards the left wing to Charvill. The latter gathered the ball at top-speed, and went racing down the touch-line with nothing before him but the Scottish right-wing three-quarter. It seemed a certain score, and there fell on the spectators a sudden hush. That small figure, not hitherto renowned for pace, could never match the Australian's long, loping, deadly stride.

Had Jaikie had six more inches of height he would have failed. But a resolute small man who tackles low is the hardest defence to get round. Jaikie hurled himself at Charvill, and was handed off by a mighty palm. But he staggered back in the direction of his own goal, and there was just one fraction of a second for him to make another attempt. This time he succeeded. Charvill's great figure seemed to dive forward on the top of his tiny assailant, and the ball rolled into touch. For a minute, while the heavens echoed with the shouting, Jaikie lay on the ground bruised and winded. Then he got up, shook himself, like a heroic, bedraggled sparrow, and hobbled back to his place.

There were still five minutes before the whistle, and these minutes were that electric testing time, when one side is intent to consolidate a victory and the other resolute to avert too crushing a defeat. Scotland had never hoped to win; she had already done far better than her expectations, and she gathered herself together for a mighty effort to hold what she had gained. Her hopes lay still in her forwards. Her backs had far surpassed their form, but they were now almost at their last gasp.

But in one of them there was a touch of that genius which can triumph over fatigue. Jaikie had never in his life played so gruelling a game. He was accustomed to being maltreated, but now he seemed to have been pounded and smothered and kicked and flung about till he doubted whether he had a single bone undamaged. His whole body was one huge ache. Only the brain under his thatch of hair was still working well. . . . The Kangaroo pack had gone down field with a mighty rush, and there was a scrum close to one of the Clausons, but it was now very greasy, and the light was bad, and he missed his catch. More, he stumbled after it and fell, for he had had a punishing game. Jaikie on the wing suddenly saw his chance. He darted in and gathered the ball, dodging Clauson's weary tackle. There was no other man of his side at hand to take a pass, but there seemed just a slender chance for a cut-through. He himself of course would be downed by Charvill, but there was a fraction of a hope, if he could gain a dozen yards, that he might be able to pass to Smail, who was not so closely marked.

His first obstacle was the Kangaroo scrum-half, who had come across the field. To him he adroitly sold the dummy, and ran towards the right touch-line, since there was no sign of Smail. He had little hope of success, for it must be only a question of seconds before he was brought down. He did not hear the roar from the spectators as he appeared in the open, for he was thinking of Charvill waiting for his revenge, and he was conscious that his heart was behaving violently quite outside its proper place. But he was also conscious that in some mysterious way he had got a second wind, and that his body seemed a trifle less leaden.

He was now past the half-way line, a little distance ahead of one of the Clausons, with no colleague near him, and with Charvill racing to intercept him. For one of Jaikie's inches there could be no hand-off, but he had learned in his extreme youth certain arts not commonly familiar to Rugby players. He was a most cunning dodger. To the yelling crowd he appeared to be aiming at a direct collision with the Kangaroo left-wing. But just as it looked as if a two-seater must meet a Rolls-Royce head-on at full speed, the two-seater swerved and Jaikie wriggled somehow below Charvill's arm. The sixty thousand people stood on their seats waving caps and umbrellas and shouting like lunatics, for Charvill was prone on the ground, and Jaikie was stolidly cantering on.

He was now at the twenty-five line, and the Kangaroo full-back awaited him. This was a small man, very little taller than Jaikie, but immensely broad and solid, and a superlative place-kick. A different physique would have easily stopped the runner, now at the very limits of his strength, but the Kangaroo was too slow in his tackle to meet Jaikie's swerve. He retained indeed in his massive fist a considerable part of Jaikie's jersey, but the half-naked wearer managed to stumble on just ahead of him, and secured a try in the extreme corner. There he lay with his nose in the mud, utterly breathless, but obscurely happy. He was still dazed and panting when a minute later the whistle blew, and a noise like the Last Trump told him that by a single point he had won the match for his country.

There was a long table below the Grand Stand, a table reserved for the Press. On it might have been observed a wild figure with red hair dancing a war dance of triumph. Presently the table collapsed under him, and the rending of timber and the recriminations of journalists were added to the apocalyptic din.

At eight o'clock sharp a party of four sat down to supper at Blaweary. The McCunns did not dine in the evening, for Dickson declared that dinner was a stiff, unfriendly repast, associated in his mind with the genteel in cities. He clung to the fashions of his youth – ate a large meal at one o'clock, and a heavy tea about half-past four, and had supper at eight from October to May, and in the long summer days whenever he chose to come indoors. Mrs McCunn had grumbled at first, having dim social aspirations, but it was useless to resist her husband's stout conservatism. For the evening meal she was in the habit of arraying herself in black silk and many ornaments, and Dickson on occasions of ceremony was persuaded to put on a dinner jacket; but to-night he had declined to change, on the ground that the guests were only Dougal and Jaikie.

There were candles on the table in the pleasant dining-room, and one large lamp on the sideboard. Dickson had been stubborn about electric light, holding that a faint odour of paraffin was part of the amenities of a country house. A bright fire crackled on the hearth for the October evenings at Blaweary were chilly.

The host was in the best of humours. 'Here's the kind of food for hungry folk. Ham and eggs – and a bit of the salmon I catched yesterday! Did you hear that I fell in, and Adam had to gaff me before he gaffed the fish? Everything except the loaf is our own providing – the eggs are our hens', the ham's my own rearing and curing, the salmon is my catching, and the scones are Mamma's baking. There's a bottle of champagne to drink Jaikie's health. Man, Jaikie, it's an extraordinary thing you've taken so little hurt. We were expecting to see you a complete lameter, with your head in bandages.'

Jaikie laughed. 'I was in more danger from the crowd at the end than from the Kangaroos. It's Dougal that's lame. He fell through the reporters' table.'

He spoke with the slight sing-song which is ineradicable in one born in the West of Scotland, but otherwise he spoke pure English for he had an imitative ear and unconsciously acquired the speech of a new environment. One did not think of Jaikie as short, but as slight, for he was admirably proportioned and balanced. His hair was soft and light and unruly. And the small wedge of face beneath the thatch had an air of curious refinement and delicacy, almost of wistfulness. This was partly due to a neat pointed chin and a cherubic mouth, but chiefly to large grey eyes which were as appealing as a spaniel's. He was the incarnation of gentleness, with a hint of pathos so that old ladies longed to mother him, and fools occasionally despised him – to their undoing. He had the look of one continually surprised at life, and a little lost in it. Tonight his face from much contact with mother earth had something of the blue battered appearance of a pugilist's, so that he seemed to be a cherub, but a damaged cherub, who had been violently ejected from his celestial home.

The fourth at the table, Dougal Crombie, made a strong contrast to Jaikie's elegance. The aforetime chieftain of the Gorbals Diehards had grown into a powerful young man, about five feet ten inches in height, with massive shoulders and a fist like a blacksmith's. Adolescence had revised the disproportions of boyhood. His head no longer appeared to be too big for his body; it was massive, not monstrous. The fiery red of his hair had toned down to a deeper shade. The art of the dentist had repaired the irregularities of his teeth. His features were rugged but not unpleasing. But the eyes remained the same, grey-green, deep-set, sullen, smouldering with a fierce vitality. To a stranger there was something about him which held the fancy, as if a door had been opened into the past. Even so must have looked some Pictish warrior, who brewed heather-ale, and was beaten back from Hadrian's Wall;

even so some Highland cateran who fired the barns of the Lennox; even so many a saturnine judge of Session and heavy-handed Border laird. Dougal in appearance was what our grandfathers called a 'Gothic survival'. His manner to the world was apt to be assertive and cynical; he seemed to be everlastingly in a hurry, and apt to jostle others off the foot-path. It was unpleasant, many found, to argue with him, for his eye expressed a surly contempt; but they were wrong – it was only interest. Dougal was absorbed in life, and since his absorption was fiercer than other people's, it was misunderstood. Therefore he had few friends; but to those few – the McCunns, Jaikie, and perhaps two others – he was attached with a dog-like fidelity. With them he was at his ease and no longer *farouche*; he talked less, and would smile happily to himself, as if their presence made him content. They gave him the only home life he had ever known.

Mr McCunn spoke of those who had years before acknowledged Dougal's sway.

'You'll want to have the last news,' he said. 'Bill's getting on grand in Australia. He's on his own wee farm in what they call a group settlement, and his last letter says that he's gotten all the roots grubbed up and is starting his first ploughing, and that he's doing fine with his hens and his dairy cows. That's the kind of job for Bill – there was always more muscle than brains in him, but there's a heap of commonsense ... Napoleon's in a bank in Montreal – went there from the London office last July. He'll rise in the world no doubt, for he has a great head for figures. Peter Paterson is just coming out for a doctor, and he has lifted a tremendous bursary – I don't mind the name of it, but it will see him through his last year in the hospitals. Who would have said that Peter would turn out scientific, and him such a through-other laddie? – But Thomas Yownie is the big surprise. Thomas you mind, was all for being a pirate. Well, he'll soon be a minister. He had aye a grand voice, and they tell me his sermons would wile the birds from the trees. ... That's the lot, except for you and Jaikie. Man, as Chief Diehard, I'm proud of my command.'

Dickson beamed on them affectionately, and they listened with a show of interest, but they did not share his paternal pride. Youth at twenty is full of hard patches. Already to the two young men the world of six years ago and its denizens had become hazy. They were remotely interested in the fates of their old comrades, but no more. The day would come when they would dwell sentimentally on the past: now they thought chiefly of the present, of the future, and of themselves.

'And how are you getting on yourself, Dougal?' Dickson asked.

'We read your things in the paper, and we whiles read about you. I see you're running for Parliament.'

'I'm running, but I won't get in. Not yet.'

'Man, I wish you were on a better side. You've got an ill nest. I was reading this very morning a speech by yon Tombs – he's one of your big men, isn't he? – blazing away about the sins of the boorjoysee. That's just Mamma and me.'

'It's not you. And Tombs, anyway, is a trumpery body. I have no use for the intellectual on the make, for there's nothing in him but vanity. But see here, Mr McCunn. The common people of this land are coming to their own nowadays. I know what they need and I know what they're thinking, for I come out of them myself. They want interpreting and they want guiding. Is it not right that a man like me should take a hand in it?'

Dickson looked wise. 'Yes, if you keep your head. But you know fine, Dougal, that those who set out to lead the mob are apt to end by following. You're in a kittle trade, my man. And how do you reconcile your views with your profession? You've got a good job with the Craw papers. You'll be aspiring some day to edit one of them. But what does Mr Craw say to your politics?'

The speaker's eye had a twinkle in it, but Dougal's face, hitherto as urbane as his rugged features permitted, suddenly became grim.

'Craw,' he cried. 'Yon's the worst fatted calf of them all. Yon's the old wife. There's no bigger humbug walking on God's earth to-day than Thomas Carlyle Craw. I take his wages, because I give good value for them. I can make up a paper with any man, and I've a knack of descriptive writing. But thank God! I've nothing to do with his shoddy politics. I put nothing of myself into his rotten papers. I keep that for the *Outward* every second Saturday.'

'You do,' said Dickson dryly. 'I've been reading some queer things there. What ails you at what you call "modern Scotland"? By your way of it we've sold our souls to the English and the Irish.'

'So we have.' Dougal had relapsed again into comparative meekness. It was as if he had felt that what he had to say was not in keeping with a firelit room and a bountiful table. He had the air of being a repository of dark things which were not yet ready for the light.

'Anyway, Scotland did fine the day. It's time to drink Jaikie's health.'

This ceremony over, Dickson remained with his glass uplifted.

'We'll drink to your health, Dougal, and pray Heaven, as the Bible says, to keep your feet from falling. It would be a sad day for your friends if you were to end in jyle. . . . And now I want to hear what you two are proposing to do with yourselves. You say you have a week's holiday, and it's a fortnight before Jaikie goes back to Cambridge.'

'We're going into the Canonry,' said Jaikie.

'Well, it's a fine countryside, the Canonry. Many a grand day I've had on its hill burns. But it's too late for the fishing. . . . I see from the papers that there's a by-election on now. Is Dougal going to sow tares by the roadside?'

'He would like to,' said Jaikie, 'but he won't be allowed. We'll keep to the hills, and our headquarters will be the Back House of the Garroch. It's an old haunt of ours.'

'Fine I know it. Many a time when I've been fishing Loch Garroch I've gone in there for my tea. What's the wife's name now? Catterick? Aye, it was Catterick, and her man came from Sanquhar way. We'll get out a map after supper and you'll show me your road. The next best thing to tramping the hills yourself is to plan out another man's travels. There's grand hills round the Garroch – the Muneraw and the Yirnie and the Calmarton and the Caldron. ... Stop a minute. Doesn't Mr Craw bide somewhere in the Canonry? Are you going to give him a call, Dougal?'

'That's a long way down Glen Callowa,' said Jaikie. 'We mean to keep to the high tops. If the weather holds, there's nothing to beat a Canonry October.'

'You're a pair of desperate characters,' said Dickson jocosely. 'You're going to a place which is thrang with a by-election, and for ordinary you'll not keep Dougal away from politics any more than a tyke from an ash-bucket. But you say you're not heeding the election. It's the high hills for you – but it's past the time for fishing, and young legs like yours will cover every top in a couple of days. I wish you mayna get into mischief. I'm afraid of Dougal with his daftness. He'll be for starting a new Jacobite rebellion "Kenmure's on and awa', Willie".'

Mr McCunn whistled a stave of the song. His spirits were soaring.

'Well, I'll be at hand to bail you out. ... And remember that I'm old, but not dead-old. If you set up the Standard on Garroch side, send me word and I'll on with my boots and join you.'

CHAPTER TWO

# INTRODUCES A GREAT MAN IN ADVERSITY

FIFTY-EIGHT years before the date of this tale a child was born in the school-house of the landward parish of Kilmaclavers in the Kingdom of Fife. The schoolmaster was one Campbell Craw, who at the age of forty-five had espoused the widow of the provost of the adjacent seaport of Partankirk, a lady his junior by a single summer. Mr Craw was a Scots dominie of the old style, capable of sending boys direct to the middle class of Humanity at St Andrew's, one who esteemed his profession, and wore in the presence of his fellows an almost episcopal dignity. He was recognized in the parish and far beyond it as a 'deep student', and, when questions of debate were referred to his arbitrament, he would give his verdict with a weight of polysyllables which at once awed and convinced his hearers. The natural suspicion which might have attached to such profundity was countered by the fact that Mr Craw was an elder of the Free Kirk and in politics a sound Gladstonian. His wife was a kindred spirit, but, in her, religion of a kind took the place of philosophy. She was a noted connoisseur of sermons, who would travel miles to hear some select preacher, and her voice had acquired something of the pulpit monotone. Her world was the Church, in which she hoped that her solitary child would some day be a polished pillar.

The infant was baptized by the name of Thomas Carlyle, after the sage whom his father chiefly venerated; Mrs Craw had graciously resigned her own preference, which was Robert Rainy, after the leader of her communion. Never was a son the object of higher expectations or more deeply pondered plans. He had come to them unexpectedly; the late Provost of Partankirk had left no offspring; he was at once the child of their old age, and the sole hope of their house. Both parents agreed that he must be a minister, and he spent his early years in an atmosphere of dedication. Some day he would be a great man, and the episodes of his youth must be such as would impress the readers of his ultimate biography. Every letter he wrote was treasured by a fond mother. Each New Year's Day his father presented him with a lengthy epistle, in the style of an evangelical Lord Chesterfield, which put on record the schoolmaster's more recent reflections on life: a copy was carefully filed for the future biographer. His studies were minutely regulated. At five, although he was still shaky in English grammar, he had mastered the Greek alphabet. At eight he had begun Hebrew. At nine he had read *Paradise Lost*, Young's *Night Thoughts*, and most of Mr Robert Pollok's *Course of Time*. At eleven he had himself, to his parents' delight, begun the first canto of an epic on the subject of Eternity.

It was the way to produce a complete prig, but somehow Thomas Carlyle was not the ordinary prig. For one thing, he was clearly not born for high scholastic attainments. There was a chronic inaccuracy in him which vexed his father's soul. He was made to dabble in many branches of learning, but he seemed incapable of exact proficiency in any. When he had finished with the school of Kilmaclavers, he attended for two years the famous academy of Partankirk, which had many times won the first place in the college bursaries. But he was never head boy, or near it, and the bursary which he ultimately won (at Edinburgh) was only a small one, fitted to his place of twenty-seventh in the list. But he was noted for his mental activity. He read everything he could lay his hand on, and remembered a good deal of it. He was highly susceptible to new ideas, which he frequently misunderstood. At first he was unpopular among his contemporaries, because of his incapacity for any game and his disinclination to use his fists, but in each circle he entered he won his way eventually to tolerance if not to popularity. For he was fruitful of notions; he could tell his illiterate comrades wonderful things which he had picked up from his voracious reading; he could suggest magnificent schemes, though in carrying them out he was at the best a camp-follower.

At the age of twenty we find Thomas Carlyle Craw in the last year of his Edinburgh arts course, designing to migrate presently to a theological college. His career has not been distinguished, though he won a fifth prize in the English Literature class and a medal for an essay on his namesake. But he has been active in undergraduate journalism, and has contributed many pieces to the evening papers. Also he has continued his miscellaneous reading, and is widely if inaccurately informed on every current topic. His chief regret is that he is a miserable public speaker, his few efforts having been attended by instant failure, and this is making him lukewarm about a ministerial career. His true weapon, he feels, is the pen, not the tongue. Otherwise he is happy, for he is never bored – and pleasantly discontented, for he is devouringly ambitious. In two things his upbringing has left an abiding mark. The aura of dedication hangs over him; he regards himself as predestined to be a great man, though he is still doubtful about the kind of greatness to be attained. Also father and mother have combined to give him a serious view of life. He does not belie his name, for the sage of Ecclefechan has bequeathed him some rags of his mantle. He must always be generalizing, seeking for principles, philosophizing; he loves a formula rather than a fact: he is heavily weighted with unction; rhetoric is in every fibre. He has a mission to teach the world, and, as he walks the pavements, his head is full of profound aphorisms or moving perorations – not the least being the obituary which some day men will write of him. One phrase in it will be, 'He was the Moses who led the people across the desert to the Promised Land'; but what the Promised Land was to be like he would have been puzzled to say.

That winter he suffered his first calamity. For Campbell Craw fell ill of pneumonia and died, and a month later Euphemia, his wife, followed him to Kilmaclavers churchyard. Thomas Carlyle was left alone in the world, for his nearest relative was a cousin in Manitoba whom he had never seen. He was an affectionate soul and mourned his parents sincerely; when his grief had dulled a little he wrote a short biography of them, 'A Father and a Mother in Israel,' which appeared in the *Partankirk Advertiser* and was justly admired. He was left now to his own resources, to shape his life without the tender admonitions of the school-house. Long and solemnly he perpended the question of the ministry. It had been his parents' choice for him, he had been 'dedicated' to it, he could not lightly forsake it. But his manifest lack of preaching endowments – he had a weak, high-pitched voice and an extreme nervousness – convinced him that common sense must prevail over filial piety. He discussed the matter with the Minister of Kilmaclavers, who approved. 'There's more ways of preaching than in a pulpit,' was that sage's verdict.

So Thomas decided upon letters. His parents had bequeathed him nearly three thousand pounds, he had no debts, he was accustomed to live sparingly; on such a foundation it seemed to him that he could safely build the first storey of what should one day be a towering edifice. After taking an undistinguished degree, he migrated to London, according to the secular fashion of ambitious Scottish youth.

His first enterprises were failures. The serious monthlies would have none of his portentous treatises on the conduct of life, and *The Times* brusquely refused a set of articles on current politics, in the writing of which he had almost wept at his own eloquence. But he found a niche in a popular religious weekly, where, under the signature of 'Simon the Tanner', he commented upon books and movements and personalities.

Soon that niche became a roomy pulpit, from which every week he fulminated, argued, and sentimentalized with immense acceptation. His columns became the most popular feature of that popular journal. He knew nothing accurately about any subject in the world, but he could clothe his ignorance in pontifical vestments and give his confusion the accents of authority. He had a remarkable flair for discerning and elaborating the tiny quantum of popular knowledge on any matter. Above all, he was interesting and aggressively practical. He took the hand of the half-educated and made them believe that he was leading them to the inner courts of wisdom. Every flicker of public emotion was fanned by him into a respectable little flame. He could be fiercely sarcastic in the manner of his namesake, he could wallow in the last banalities of sentiment, he could even be jocose and kittenish, but he knew his audience and never for a moment lost touch with it. 'Helpful' was the epithet most commonly applied to him. He was there to encourage and assist, and his answers to correspondents began to fill a large space in his chosen journal.

So at the age of twenty-four Thomas was making a good income, and was beginning to be much in request by uplift societies. He resolutely refused to appear in public: he was too wise to let his halting utterance weaken the impression of his facile pen. But a noble discontent was his, and he marshalled his forces for another advance. Generations on his mother's side of small traders in Partankirk had given him considerable business acumen, and he realized that the way to fortune did not lie in writing for other men. He must own the paper which had its vogue from his talents, and draw to himself the whole profits of exploiting the public taste. Looking about him, he decided that there was room for a weekly journal at a popular price, which would make its appeal to the huge class of the aspiring half-baked, then being turned out by free education. They were not ardent politicians; they were not scholars; they were homely, simple folk, who wanted a little politics, a little science, a little religion, set to a domestic tune. So he broke with his employers, and, greatly daring, started his own penny weekly. He had considerably added to his little fortune, for he had no extravagant tastes, and he had made many friends in the circles of prosperous nonconformity. There was a spice of the gambler in Thomas, for every penny he possessed or could borrow he put into the new venture.

The *Centre-Forward* was a success from the first. The name was a stroke of genius; being drawn from the popular sport of football, it was intelligible to everyone, and it sounded a new slogan. The paper would be in the van of progressive thought, but also in the centre of the road, contemptuous alike of right-hand action and left-hand revolution. It appeared at that happy time in the nineties when the world was comfortable, mildly progressive, and very willing to be amused by toys.

And Thomas was an adroit editor. He invented ingenious competitions and offered prizes of a magnitude hitherto unknown in British journalism. He discovered three new poets – poetry was for the moment in fashion – and two new and now completely forgotten humorists, and he made each reader share in the discovery and feel that he too was playing the part of a modest Maecenas. He exposed abuses with a trenchant pen, when his lawyers had convinced him that he was on safe legal ground. Weekly he addressed the world, under his own signature, on every conceivable topic and with an air of lofty brotherhood, so that the humblest subscriber felt that the editor was his friend. The name of Thomas Carlyle Craw might be lightly regarded by superfine critics, but by some hundreds of thousands of plain Britons it was extolled and venerated.

Thomas was an acute man of business. The *Centre-Forward* was never allowed to languish for the lack of novelties; it grew in size, improved in paper and type, carried a great weight of advertisements, and presently became a pioneer in cheap pictures. Every detail of its manufacture and distribution, in which it struck out many new lines, he personally supervised. Also it became the parent of several offspring. It was the time when the gardening craze was beginning in England, and *The Country-Dweller* was founded, a sumptuously produced monthly which made a feature of its illustrations. This did no more than pay its way, but a children's halfpenny made a big hit, and an unctuous and snobbish penny weekly for the home made a bigger. He acquired also several trade journals, and put them on a paying basis.

When the South African war broke out Thomas was a wealthy man, piling up revenue yearly, for he still lived in two rooms in Marylebone and spent nothing on himself. The war more than doubled his profits. In the *Centre-Forward* he had long been a moderate exponent of the new imperialism, and his own series of articles 'The Romance of Empire' had had a large sale when issued as a book. Now he became a fervent patriot. He exposed abuses in the conduct of the campaign – always on the best legal advice, he had much to say about inefficient generals, he appeared before the world as the soldiers' friend. The result was a new paper, *Mother England*, price one penny, which was the *Centre-Forward* adapted to a lower strata of democracy – a little slangy and vulgar, deliberately sensational, but eminently sound at heart. Once a month Thomas Carlyle Craw compelled the motley array of its subscribers to view the world from his own lofty watch-tower.

Fortune treated him kindly. After the war came the Liberal revival, and he saw his chance. His politics now acquired a party character, and he became the chief Free Trade trumpet in the generally Protectionist orchestra of the Press. Once again he took a bold step, for he started a new halfpenny daily. For the better part of a year it hovered on the brink of failure, and the profits on Thomas's other publications went into its devouring maw. Then, suddenly, it turned the corner, and raced up the slope to the pinnacle of public favour. The *View* fed an appetite the existence of which Thomas alone had divined. It was bright and fresh and admirably put together; large sums were spent on special correspondence; its picture pages were the best of their kind; every brand of notable, at high fees, enlivened its pages. But above all it was a paper for the home and the home-maker, and the female sex became its faithful votaries. Much of this success was due to Thomas himself. He made himself the centre of the paper and the exponent of its policy. Once a week, in the *View*, as in the *Centre-Forward*, he summarized the problems of immediate interest and delivered his weighty judgements.

He was compelled to change his simple habits of life. He was compelled, indeed, elaborately to seek seclusion. There was no other alternative for one who had no gift of utterance and had hitherto gone little into society. With hundreds daily clamouring for interviews, demanding his help in cash or influence, urging policies and persons upon his notice, he must needs flee to sanctuary. In the palatial offices which he built in the neighbourhood of Fleet Street he had a modest flat, where he occasionally passed a night behind a barbed-wire entanglement of secretaries. But for the rest he had no known abode, though here I am privileged to say that he kept suites at several hotels, English and foreign, in the name of his principal aide-de-camp.

He escaped the publicity given to most press magnates by the Great War, for he used the staffs of his many papers as a bodyguard for his anonymity. The Prime Minister might summon him to urgent conferences, but Thomas did not attend – he sent an editor. New Year and Birthday honours were offered and curtly declined. Yet Thomas was only physically in retreat; spiritually he held the forefront of the stage. His signed articles had a prodigious vogue. Again, as fifteen years before, he was the friend of the men in the trenches; his criticisms of generals and politicians were taken seriously, for they were in accord with the suspicions and fears of the ordinary man. On the whole the Craw Press played a useful part in the great struggle. Its ultimatums were at any rate free from the charge of having any personal motive, and it preserved a reasonable standard of decency and good sense. Above all it was sturdily optimistic even in the darkest days.

The end of the war found Thomas with fifteen successful papers under his control, including a somewhat highbrow Sunday publication, an immense fortune rapidly increasing by judicious investment, and a commanding if ill-defined position in the public eye. He permitted himself one concession to his admirers. His portrait now appeared regularly in his own prints. It showed a middle-aged baldish man, with a round head and a countenance of bland benevolence. His eyes were obscured by large tortoise-shell spectacles, but they had a kindly gleam, and redeemed for suavity the high cheekbones and the firmly compressed lips. A suspicion of a retreating chin helped to produce the effect of friendliness, while the high forehead augured wisdom. It was the face which the public had somehow always imagined, and it did much to define Thomas's personality in his readers' eyes.

The step had its importance, for he had now become a figure of almost international note. Weekly he emerged from the shadows where he lived to give counsel and encouragement to humanity. He was Optimism incarnate, Hope embodied not in a slim nymph but in a purposeful and masculine Colossus. His articles were printed in all his papers and syndicated in the American and Continental press. *Sursum Corda* was his motto. A Browning in journalese, his aim was to see the bright side of everything, to expound partial evil as universal good. Was there a slump in the basic industries? It was only the prelude to an industrial revival, in which Britain would lead the world in new export trades. Was there unrest among the workers? It was a proof of life, that 'loyal unrest' inseparable from Freedom. High-speed motoring, jazz music, and the odd habits of the young were signs of a new Elizabethan uplift of spirit. Were the churches sparsely attended? It only meant that mankind was reaching after a wider revelation. For every difficulty Thomas Carlyle Craw had his happy solution. The Veiled Prophet was also the Smiling Philosopher. Cheerfulness in his hands was not a penny whistle but a trumpet.

He had of course his critics. Rude persons declared that his optimism was a blend of Martin Tupper and the worst kind of transatlantic uplift-merchant. Superfine people commented upon the meagreness of his thought and the turgidity of his style. Reformers in a hurry considered his soothing syrup a deadly opiate. The caustic asked who had made this tripe-merchant a judge in Israel. Experts complained that whenever he condescended to details he talked nonsense. But these were the captious few; the many had only admiration and gratitude. In innumerable simple homes, in schoolrooms, in village clubs, in ministers' studies, the face of Thomas Carlyle Craw beamed benevolently from the walls. He had fulfilled the ambition both of his parents and himself; he spoke from his pulpit *urbi et orbi*; he was a Moses to guide his people to the Promised Land.

The politics of the Craw Press were now generally Conservative, but Thomas kept himself aloof from party warfare. He supported, and mildly criticized, whatever Government was in power. In foreign affairs alone he allowed himself a certain latitude. His personal knowledge of other lands was confined to visits to familiar Riviera resorts, when he felt that he needed a little rest and sunshine. But he developed an acute interest in Continental politics, and was in the habit of sending out bright young men to act as private intelligence-officers. While mildly supporting the League of Nations, he was highly critical of the settlement made at Versailles, and took under his wing various countries which he considered to have a grievance. On such matters he permitted himself to write with assurance, almost truculence. He was furiously against any recognition of Russia, but he demanded that judgement of the Fascist régime in Italy should be held in abeyance, and that the world should wait respectfully on the results of that bold experiment.

But it was in the hard case of Evallonia that he specially interested himself. It will be remembered that a republic had been established there in 1919, apparently with the consent of its people. But rifts had since appeared within the lute. There was a strong monarchist party among the Evallonians, who wished to reinstate their former dynasty, at present represented by an attractive young Prince, and at the same time insisted on the revision of Evallonian boundaries. To this party Thomas gave eloquent support. He believed in democracy, he told his millions of readers, and a kingdom (*teste* Britain) was as democratic a thing as a republic: if the Evallonians wanted a monarch they should be allowed to have one: certain lost territories, too, must be restored, unless they wished to see Evallonia Irredenta a permanent plague-spot. His advocacy made a profound impression in the south and east of Europe, and to Evallonian monarchists the name of Craw became what that of Palmerston was once to Italy and Gladstone to Bulgaria. The mildness of his published portraits did not damp them; they remembered that the great Cavour had looked like Mr Pickwick. A cigar, a begonia, a new scent, and a fashionable hotel in the Evallonian capital were named in his honour.

Such at the date of this tale was the position of Thomas Carlyle Craw in the world of affairs. He was an illustrious figure, and a self-satisfied, though scarcely a happy, man. For he suffered from a curious dread which the scientific call *agoraphobia*. A master of publicity, he shrank from it in person. This was partly policy. He had the acumen to see that retirement was his chief asset; he was the prophet, speaking from within the shrine, a voice which would lose its awfulness if it were associated too closely with human lineaments. But there was also timidity, a shrinking of the flesh. He had accustomed himself for thirty years to live in a shell, and he had a molluscan dread of venturing outside it. A lion on paper, he suspected that he would be a rabbit in personal intercourse. He realized that his vanity would receive cruel wounds, that rough hands would paw his prophetic mantle. How could he meet a rampant socialist or a republican Evallonian face to face? The thought sent a shiver down his spine. . . .

So his sensitiveness became a disease, and he guarded his seclusion with a vestal jealousy. He had accumulated a personal staff of highly paid watch-dogs, whose business was not only the direction of the gigantic Craw Press but the guardianship of the shrine consecrated to its master. There was his principal secretary, Freddy Barbon, the son of a bankrupt Irish peer, who combined the duties of grand vizier and major-domo. There was his general manager, Archibald Bamff, who had been with him since the early days of the *Centre-Forward*. There was Sigismund Allins, an elegant young man who went much into society, and acted, unknown to the world, as his chief's main intelligence-officer. There was Bannister, half valet, half butler, and Miss Elena Cazenove, a spinster of forty-five and the most efficient of stenographers. With the exception of Bamff, this entourage attended his steps – but never together, lest people should talk. Like the police in a Royal procession, they preceded or followed his actual movements and made straight the path for him. Among them he ruled as a mild tyrant, arbitrary but not unkindly. If the world of men had to be kept at a distance lest it should upset his poise and wound his vanity, he had created a little world which could be, so to speak, his own personality writ large.

It is the foible of a Scot that he can never cut the bonds which bind him to his own country. Thomas had happy recollections of his childhood on the bleak shores of Fife, and a large stock of national piety. He knew in his inmost heart that he would rather win the approval of Kilmaclavers and Partankirk than the plaudits of Europe. The affection had taken practical form. He had decided that his principal hermitage must be north of the Tweed. Fife and the East coast were too much of a home country for his purpose, the Highlands were too remote from London, so he settled upon the south-west corner, the district known as the Canonry, as at once secluded and accessible. He had no wish to cumber himself with land, for Thomas desired material possessions as little as he desired titles; so he leased from Lord Rhynns (whose wife's health and declining fortune compelled him to spend most of the year abroad) the ancient demesne of Castle Gay. The place, it will be remembered, lies in the loveliest part of the glen of the Callowa, in the parish of Knockraw, adjoining the village of Starr, and some five miles from the town of Portaway, which is on the main line to London. A high wall surrounds a wild park of a thousand acres, in the heart of which stands a grey stone castle, for whose keep Bruces and Comyns and Macdowalls contended seven centuries ago. In its cincture of blue mountains it has the air of a place at once fortified and forgotten, and here Thomas found that secure retirement so needful for one who had taken upon himself the direction of the major problems of the globe. The road up the glen led nowhere, the fishing was his own and no tourist disturbed the shining reaches of the Callowa, the hamlet of Starr had less than fifty inhabitants, and the folk of the Canonry are not the type to pry into the affairs of eminence in retreat. To the countryside he was only the Castle tenant – 'yin Craw, a newspaper body frae England.' They did not read his weekly pronouncements, preferring older and stronger fare.

But at the date of this tale a thorn had fixed itself in Thomas's pillow. Politics had broken in upon his moorland peace. There was a by-election in the Canonry, an important by-election, for it was regarded as a test of the popularity of the Government's new agricultural policy. The Canonry in its seaward fringe is highly farmed, and its uplands are famous pasture;

its people, traditionally Liberal, have always been looked upon as possessing the toughest core of northern common sense. How would such a region regard a scheme which was a violent departure from the historic attitude of Britain towards the British farmer? The matter was hotly canvassed, and, since a General Election was not far distant, this contest became the cynosure of political eyes. Every paper sent a special correspondent, and the candidates found their halting utterances lavishly reported. The Canonry woke up one morning to find itself 'news'.

Thomas did not like it. He resented this publicity at his doorstep. His own press was instructed to deal with the subject in obscure paragraphs, but he could not control his rivals. He was in terror lest he should somehow be brought into the limelight – a bogus interview, perhaps – such things had happened – there were endless chances of impairing his carefully constructed dignity. He decided that it would be wiser if he left the place until after the declaration of the poll. The necessity gave him acute annoyance, for he loved the soft bright October weather at Castle Gay better than any other season of the year. The thought of his suite at Aix – taken in the name of Mr Frederick Barbon – offered him no consolation.

But first he must visit Glasgow to arrange with his builders for some reforms in the water supply, which, with the assent of Lord Rhynns, he proposed to have installed in his absence. Therefore, on the evening of the Kangaroo match already described, his discreet and potent figure might have been seen on the platform of Kirkmichael as he returned from the western metropolis. It was his habit to be met there by car, so as to avoid the tedium of changing trains and the publicity of Portaway station.

Now, as it chanced, there was another election in process. The students of the western capital were engaged in choosing their Lord Rector. On this occasion there was a straight contest; no freak candidates, nationalist, sectarian, or intellectual, obscured the issue. The Conservative nominee was a prominent member of the Cabinet, the Liberal the leader of the Old

Guard of that faith. Enthusiasm waxed high, and violence was not absent – the violence without bitterness which is the happy mark of Scottish rectorial contests. Already there had been many fantastic doings. The Conservative headquarters were decorated by night with Liberal red paint, prints which set the law of libel at naught were sold in the streets, songs of a surprising ribaldry were composed to the discredit of the opposing candidates. No undergraduate protagonist had a single physical, mental, or moral oddity which went unadvertised. One distinguished triumph the Liberals had won. A lanky Conservative leader had been kidnapped, dressed in child's shorts, blouse, socks, and beribboned sailor hat, and attached by padlocked chains to the college railings, where, like a culprit in the stocks, for a solid hour he had made sport for the populace. Such an indignity could not go unavenged, and the Conservatives were out for blood.

The foremost of the Liberal leaders was a man, older than the majority of students, who, having forsaken the law, was now pursuing a belated medical course. It is sufficient to say that his name was Linklater, for he does not come into this story. The important thing about him for us is his appearance. He looked older than his thirty-two years, and was of a comfortable figure, almost wholly bald, with a round face, tightly compressed lips, high cheek-bones and large tortoise-shell spectacles. It was his habit to wear a soft black hat of the kind which is fashionable among statesmen, anarchists, and young careerists. In all these respects he was the image of Thomas Carlyle Craw. His parental abode was Kirkmichael, where his father was a Baptist minister.

On the evening in question Thomas strode to the door of the Kirkmichael booking-office, and to his surprise found that his car was not there. It was a drizzling evening, the same weather that the day before had graced the Kangaroo match. The weather had been fine when he left Castle Gay in the morning, but he had brought a light raincoat with which he now invested his comfortable person. There were no porters about, and in the dingy station yard there was no vehicle except an antique Ford.

His eye was on the entrance to the yard, where he expected to see any moment the headlights of his car in the wet dusk, when he suddenly found his arms seized. At the same moment a scarf was thrown over his head which stopped all utterance. ... About what happened next he was never quite clear, but he felt himself swung by strong arms into the ancient Ford. Through the folds of the scarf he heard its protesting start. He tried to scream, he tried to struggle, but voice and movement were forbidden him. ...

He became a prey to the most devastating fear. Who were his assailants, Bolshevists, anarchists, Evallonian Republicans, the minions of a rival press? Or was it an American group which had offered him two days ago by cable ten millions for his properties? ... Whither was he bound? A motor launch on the coast, some den in a city slum? ...

After an hour's self-torture he found the scarf switched from his head. He was in a car with five large young men in waterproofs, each with a muffler covering the lower part of his face. The rain had ceased, and they seemed to be climbing high up on to the starlit moors. He had a whiff of wet bracken and heather.

He found his voice, and with what resolution he could muster he demanded to know the reason of the outrage and the goal of his journey.

'It's all right, Linklater,' said one of them. 'You'll know soon enough.'

They called him Linklater! The whole thing was a blunder. His incognito was preserved. The habit of a lifetime held, and he protested no more.

## CHAPTER THREE

# THE BACK HOUSE OF THE GARROCH

THE road to the springs of the Garroch water, a stream which never descends to the lowlands but runs its whole course in the heart of the mossy hills, is for the motorist a matter of wide and devious circuits. It approaches its goal circumspectly, with an air of cautious reconnaissance. But the foot-traveller has an easier access. He can take the cart-road which runs through the heather of the Clachlands glen and across the intervening hills by the Nick of the Threshes. Beyond that he will look into the amphitheatre of the Garroch, with the loch of that name dark under the shadow of the Caldron, and the stream twining in silver links through the moss, and the white ribbon of highway, on which wheeled vehicles may move, ending in the yard of a moorland cottage.

The Blaweary car had carried Jaikie and Dougal swiftly over the first fifteen miles of their journey. At about three o'clock of the October afternoon they had reached the last green cup where the Clachlands had its source, and were leisurely climbing the hill towards the Nick. Both had ancient knapsacks on their shoulders, but it was their only point of resemblance. Dougal was clad in a new suit of rough tweed knickerbockers which did not fit him well; he had become very hot and carried his jacket on his arm, and he had no hat. Jaikie was in old flannels, for he abominated heavy raiment, and, being always more or less in training, his slender figure looked pleasantly cool and trim. Sometimes they sauntered, sometimes they strode, and now and then they halted, when Dougal had something to say. For Dougal was in the first stage of holiday, when to his closest friend he had to unburden himself of six months' store of conversation. It was as inevitable as the heat and discomfort which must attend the first day's walk, before his body rid itself of its sedentary heaviness. Jaikie spoke little; his fate in life was to be a listener.

It is unfair to eavesdrop on the babble of youth when its flow has been long pent up. Dougal's ran like Ariel over land and sea, with excursions into the upper air. He had recovered his only confidant, and did not mean to spare him. Sometimes he touched upon his daily task – its languors and difficulties, the harassments of the trivial, the profound stupidity of the middle-aged. He defended hotly his politics, and drew so many fine distinctions between his creed and those of all other men, that it appeared that his party was in the loyal, compact, and portable form of his single self. Then ensued torrential confessions of faith and audacious ambition. He was not splashing – he was swimming with a clean stroke to a clear goal. With his pen and voice he was making his power felt, and in time the world would listen to him. His message? There followed a statement of ideals which was nobly eclectic. Dougal was at once nationalist and internationalist, humanitarian and man of iron, realist and poet.

They were now in the Nick of the Threshes, where, in a pad of green lawn between two heathery steeps, a well bubbled among mosses. The thirsty idealist flung himself on the ground and drank deep. He rose with his forelock dripping.

'I sometimes think you are slipping away from me, Jaikie,' he said. 'You've changed a lot in the last two years. ... You live in a different kind of world from me, and every year you're getting less and less of a Scotsman. ... And I've a notion, when I pour out my news to you and haver about myself, that you're criticizing me all the time in your own mind. Am I not right? You're terribly polite, and you never say much, but I can feel you're laughing at me. Kindly, maybe, but laughing all the same. You're saying to yourself, "Dougal gets dafter every day. He's no better than a savage." '

Jaikie regarded the flushed and bedewed countenance of his friend, and the smile that broadened over his small face was not critical.

'I often think you're daft, Dougal. But then I like daftness.'

'Anyway, you've none of it yourself. You're the wisest man I ever met. That's where you and I differ. I'm always burning or freezing, and you keep a nice, average, normal temperature.

I take desperate likes and dislikes. You've something good to say about the worst scallywag, and, if you haven't, you hold your tongue. I'm all for flinging my cap over the moon, while you keep yours snug on your head. No. No' – he quelled an anticipated protest. 'It's the same in your football. It was like that yesterday afternoon. You never run your head against a stone wall. You wait till you see your chance, and then you're on to it like forked lightning, but you're determined not to waste one atom of your strength.'

'That's surely Scotch enough,' laughed Jaikie. 'I'm economical.'

'No, it's not Scotch. We're not an economical race. I don't know what half-wit invented that libel. We spend ourselves – we've always spent ourselves – on unprofitable causes. What's the phrase – *perfervidium ingenium*? There's not much of the perfervid about you, Jaikie.'

'No?' said the other, politely, interrogatory.

'No. You've all the pluck in creation, but its the considering kind. You remember how Alan Breck defined his own courage – "Just great penetration and knowledge of affairs." That's yours. ... Not that you haven't got the other kind too. David Balfour's kind – "auld, cauld, dour, deidly courage".'

'I've no courage,' said Jaikie. 'I'm nearly always in a funk.'

'Aye, that's how you would put it. You've picked up the English trick of understatement – what they call *meiosis* in the grammar books. I doubt you and me are very unlike. You'll not catch me understanding. I want to shout both my vices and my virtues on the house-tops. ... If I dislike a man I want to hit him on the head, while you'd be wondering if the fault wasn't in yourself. ... If I want a thing changed I must drive at it like a young bull. If I think there's dirty work going on I'm for starting a revolution. ... You don't seem to care very much about anything, and you're too fond of playing the devil's advocate. There was a time ...'

'I don't think I've changed,' said Jaikie. 'I'm a slow fellow, and I'm so desperately interested in things that I feel my way cautiously. You see, I like so much that I haven't a great deal of time for hating. I'm not a crusader like you, Dougal.'

'I'm a poor sort of crusader,' said Dougal ruefully. 'I get into a tearing passion about something I know very little about, and when I learn more my passion ebbs away. But still I've a good hearty stock of dislikes and they keep me from boredom. That's the difference between us. I'm for breaking a man's head, and I probably end by shaking hands. You begin by shaking hands. . . . All the same, God help the man or woman or creed or party that you make up your slow mind to dislike. . . . I'm going to make a stir in the world, but I know that I'll never be formidable. I'm not so sure about you.'

'I don't want to be formidable.'

'And that's maybe just the reason why you will be – some day. But I'm serious, Jaikie. It's a sad business if two ancient friends like you and me are starting to walk on different sides of the road. Our tracks are beginning to diverge, and, though we're still side by side, in ten years we may be miles apart. . . . You're not the good Scotsman you used to be. Here am I driving myself mad with the sight of my native land running down the brae – the cities filling up with Irish, the countryside losing its folk, our law and our letters and our language as decrepit as an old wife. Damn it, man, in another half century there will be nothing left, and we'll be a mere disconsidered province of England. . . . But you never bother your head about it. Indeed, I think you've gone over to the English. What was it I heard you saying to Mr McCunn last night? – that the English had the most polite genius of any people because they had the most humour?'

'Well, it's true,' Jaikie answered. 'But every day I spend out of Scotland I like it better. When I've nothing else to do I run over in my mind the places I love best – mostly in the Canonry – and when I get a sniff of wood smoke it makes me sick with longing for peat-reek. Do you think I could forget that?'

Jaikie pointed to the scene which was now spread before them, for they had emerged from the Nick of the Threshes and were beginning the long descent to the Garroch. The October afternoon was warm and windless, and not a wisp of cloud broke the level blue of the sky. Such weather in July would have meant that the distances were dim, but on this autumn day, which had begun with frost, there was a crystalline sharpness of outline in the remotest hills. The mountains huddled around the amphitheatre, the round bald forehead of the Yirnie, the twin peaks of the Caldron which hid a tarn in their corrie, the steel-grey fortress of the Calmarton, the vast menacing bulk of the Muneraw. On the far horizon the blue of the sky seemed to fade into white, and a hill shoulder which rose in one of the gaps had an air of infinite distance. The bog in the valley was a mosaic of colours like an Eastern carpet, and the Garroch water twined through it like some fantastic pictured stream in a missal. A glimpse could be had of Loch Garroch, dark as ink in the shadow of the Caldron. There were many sounds, the tinkle of falling burns far below, a faint calling of sheep, an occasional note of a bird. Yet the place had an overmastering silence, a quiet distilled of the blue heavens and the primeval desert. In that loneliness lay the tale of ages since the world's birth, the song of life and death as uttered by wild living things since the rocks first had form.

The two did not speak for a little. They had seen that which touched in both some deep elemental spring of desire.

Down on the level of the moss, where the green track wound among the haggs, Dougal found his tongue.

'I would like your advice, Jaikie,' he said, 'about a point of conduct. It's not precisely a moral question, but it's a matter of good taste. I'm drawing a big salary from the Craw firm, and I believe I give good value for it. But all the time I'm despising my job, and despising the paper I help to make up, and despising myself. Thank God, I've nothing to do with the policy, but I ask myself if I'm justified in taking money from a thing which turns my stomach.'

'But you're no more responsible for the paper than the head of the case-room that sets the type. You're a technical expert.'

'That's the answer I've been giving myself, but I'm not sure that it's sound. It's quite true that my leaving Craw's would make no difference – they'd get as good a man next day at a lower wage – maybe at the same wage, for I will say that for them, they're not skinflints. But it's a bad thing to work at something you can't respect. I'm condescending on my job, and that's ruin for a man's soul.'

'I see very little harm in the Craw papers,' said Jaikie. 'They're silly, but they're decent enough.'

'Decent!' Dougal cried. 'That's just what they are not. They're the most indecent publications on God's earth. They're not vicious, if that's what you mean. They would be more decent if they had a touch of blackguardism. They pander to everything that's shoddy and slushy and third-rate in human nature. Their politics are an opiate to prevent folk thinking. Their endless stunts, their competitions and insurances and country-holiday schemes – that's the ordinary dodge to get up their circulation, so as to raise their advertisement prices. I don't mind that for it's just common business. It's their uplift, their infernal uplift that makes my spine cold. Oh, Lord! There's not a vulgar instinct, not a half-baked silliness, in the whole nation that they don't dig out and print in leaded type. And above all, there's the man Craw.'

'Did you ever meet him?' Jaikie asked.

'Never. Who has? They tell me he has a house somewhere in the Canonry, when he gets tired of his apartments in foreign hotels. But I study Craw. I'm a specialist in Craw. I've four big press-cutting books at home full of Craw. Here's some of the latest.'

Dougal dived into a pocket and produced a batch of newspaper cuttings.

'They're mostly about Evallonia. I don't worry about that. If Craw wants to be a kingmaker he must fight it out with his Evallonians. ... But listen to some of the other titles. 'Mr Craw's Advice to Youth!' 'Mr Craw on the Modern Drama.' – He must have sat in the darkness at the back of a box, for he'd never show up in the stalls. – 'Mr Craw on Modern Marriage.' – A fine lot he knows about it! – 'Mr Craw warns the Trade Unions' – The devil he does! – 'Mr Craw on the Greatness of England.' 'Mr Craw's Open Letter to the President of the U.S.A.' Will nobody give the body a flea in his ear? ... I could write a book about Craw. He's perpetually denouncing, but always with a hopeful smirk. I've discovered his formula. 'This is the best of all possible worlds, and everything in it is a necessary evil.' He wants to be half tonic and half sedative, but for me he's just a plain emetic.'

Dougal waved the cuttings like a flag.

'The man is impregnable, for he never reads any paper but his own, and he has himself guarded like a gun-factory. But I've a notion that some day I'll get him face to face. Some day I'll have the chance of telling him just what I think of him, and what every honest man –'

Jaikie by a dexterous twitch got possession of the cuttings, crumpled them into a ball, dropped it into a patch of peat, and ground it down with his heel.

'What's that you've done?' Dougal cried angrily. 'You've spoiled my Craw collection.'

'Better than spoiling our holiday. Look here, Dougal, my lad. For a week you've got to put Craw and all his works out of your head. We are back in an older and pleasanter world, and I won't have it wrecked by your filthy journalism. . . .'

For the better part of five minutes there was a rough-and-tumble on the green motor-road, from which Jaikie ultimately escaped and fled. When peace was made the two found themselves at a gate in a dry-stone dyke.

'Thank God,' said Dougal. 'Here is the Back House at last. I want my tea.'

Their track led them into a little yard behind the cottage, and they made their way to the front, where the slender highway which ascended the valley of the Garroch came to an end in a space of hill gravel before the door. The house was something more than a cottage, for fifty years ago it had been the residence of a prosperous sheep-farmer, before the fashion of 'led' farms had spread over the upland glens. It was of two storeys and had a little wing at right angles, the corner between being filled with a huge bush of white roses. The roof was slated, the granite walls had been newly white-washed and were painted with the last glories of a tropaeolum. A grove of scarlet-berried rowans flanked one end, beyond which lay the walled garden of potatoes and gooseberry bushes, varied with golden-rod and late-flowering phloxes. At the other end were the thatched outhouses and the walls of a sheepfold, where the apparatus for boiling tar rose like a miniature gallows above the dipping-trough. The place slept in a sunny peace. There was a hum of bees from the garden, a slow contented clucking of hens, the echo of a plashing stream descending the steeps of the Caldron, but the undertones made by these sounds were engulfed in the dominant silence. The scent of the moorlands, compounded of miles of stone and heather and winds sharp and pure as the sea, made a masterful background from which it was possible to pick out homelier odours – peat-reek, sheep, the smell of cooking food.

To ear, eye, and nostril, the place sent a message of intimate and delicate comfort.

The noise of their feet on the gravel brought someone in haste to the door. It was a woman of between forty and fifty, built like a heroine of the Sagas, deep-bosomed, massive, straight as a grenadier. Her broad comely face was brown like a berry, and the dark eyes and hair told of gypsy blood in her ancestry. Her arms were bare, for she had been making butter, and her skirts were kilted, revealing a bright-coloured petticoat, so that she had the air of a Highland warrior.

But in place of the boisterous welcome which Jaikie had expected, her greeting was laughter. She stood in the doorway and shook. Then she held up her hand to enjoin silence, and marched the two travellers to the garden gate out of earshot of the house.

'Did you get my postcard, Mrs Catterick?' Jaikie asked, when they had come to a standstill under a rowan tree.

'Aye, I got your postcaird, and I'm blithe to see ye baith. But ye come at an unco time. I've gotten anither visitor.'

'We don't want to inconvenience you,' Jaikie began. 'We can easily go down the water to the Mains of Garroch. The herd there will take us in.'

'Ye'll dae nae siccan thing. It will never be said that Tibby Catterick turned twae auld freends frae her door, and there's beds to spare for ye baith. ... But ye come at an unco time and ye find me at an unco job. I'm a jyler.'

'A what?'

'A jyler. I've a man inbye, and I'm under bond no to let him stir a fit frae the Back House till the morn's morn. . . . I'll tell ye the gospel truth. My guid-brither's son – him that's comin' out for a minister – is at the college, and the morn the students are electin' what they ca' a Rector. Weel, Erchie's a stirrin' lad and takes muckle ado wi' their politics. It seems that there was a man on the ither side that they wanted to get oot o' the road – it was fair eneugh, for he had pitten some terrible affronts on Erchie. So what maun the daft laddie dae but kidnap him? How it was done I canna tell, but he brocht him late last night in a cawr, and pit me on my aith no to let him leave the place for thirty 'oors. . . . So you see I'm turned jyler.' Mrs Catterick again shook with silent merriment.

'Have you got him indoors now?'

'He's ben the hoose in the best room. I kinnled a fire for him, for he's a cauldrife body. What's he like? Oh, a fosy wee man wi' a bald heid and terrible braw claithes. Ye wad say he was ower auld to be a student, but Erchie says it takes a lang time to get through as a doctor. Linklater, they ca' him.'

'Has he given you any trouble?' Dougal asked anxiously. He seemed to long to assist in the task of gaoler.

'No him. My man's awa wi' the crocks to Gledmouth, and as ye ken, we hae nae weans, but I could manage twa o' him my lane. But he never offered to resist. Just ate his supper as if he was in his ain hoose, and spak nae word except to say that he likit my scones. I lent him yin o' John's sarks for a nicht-gown and this mornin' he shaved himsel' wi' John's razor. He's a quiet, saft-spoken wee body, but there's nae crack in him. He speaks wi' a kind o' English tongue and he ca's me Madam. I doot that deil Erchie maun be in the wrang o' it, but kin's kin and I maun tak the wyte o' his cantrips.'

Again Jaikie became apologetic and proposed withdrawal, and again his proposal was rejected.

'Ye kin bide here fine,' said Mrs Catterick, 'now that ye ken the truth. I couldna tell it ye at the door-cheek, for ye were just forenent his windy. . . . Ye'll hae your meat wi' me in the kitchen, and ye can hae the twa beds in the loft. . . . Ye'd better no gang near Linklater, for he maybe wadna like folk to ken o' this performance – nor Erchie neither. He has never stirred frae his room this day, and he's spak no word except to speir what place he was in and how far it was frae Glen Callowa. . . . Now I think o't, that was a queer thing to speir, for Erchie said he brocht him frae Kirkmichael. . . . Oh, and he was wantin' to send a telegram, but I tell't him there was nae office within saxteen miles and the post wadna be up the water till the morn. . . . I'm just wonderin' how he'll get off the morn, for he hasna the buits for walkin'. Ye never saw sic snod, wee, pappymashy things on a man's feet. But there's two bicycles, yin o' John's and yin that belongs to the young herd at the west hirsel. Wi' yin o' them he'll maybe manage down the road. . . . But there's nae sense in crossin' brigs till ye come to them. I've been thrang wi' the kirnin', but the butter's come, and the kettle's on the boil. Your tea will be ready as sune as ye've gotten your faces washed.'

Half an hour later Jaikie and Dougal sat in the kitchen, staying a hearty hunger with farles of oatcake and newly-baked scones, and a healthier thirst with immense cups of strong-brewed tea. Their hostess, now garbed somewhat more decorously, presided at the table. She apologized for the delay.

'I had to gie Linklater his tea. He's gettin' terrible restless, puir man. He's been tryin' to read books in the best room, but he canna fix his mind, and he's aye writin' telegrams. He kens ye're here, and spiered whae ye were, and I telled him twa young lads that were trampin' the country. I could see that he was feared o' ye, and nae wonder. It would be sair on a decent body if folk heard that he had been kidnapped by a deil like Erchie. I tried to set his mind at rest about the morn, and telled him about John's bicycle.'

But the meal was not the jovial affair which Jaikie remembered of old. Mrs Catterick was preoccupied, and did not expand, as was her custom, in hilarious gossip. This new task of gaoler lay heavy on her shoulders. She seemed always to be listening for sounds from the farther part of the house. Twice she left the table and tiptoed along the passage to listen at the door.

'He's awfu' restless,' she reported. 'He's walkin' aboot the floor like a hen on a het girdle. I wish he mayna lose his reason. Dod, I'll warm Erchie's lugs for this ploy when I get hauld o' him. Sic a job to saddle on a decent wumman!'

Then for a little there was peace, for a question of Jaikie's led their hostess to an account of the great April storm of that year.

'Thirty and three o' the hill lambs deid in ae nicht. ... John was oot in the snaw for nineteen 'oors and I never looked to see him mair. Puir man, when he cam in at last he couldna eat – just a dram o' whisky in het milk – and he sleepit around the clock. ... John was fires in ilka room and lambs afore them in a' the blankets I possessed. ... Aye, and it waur when the snaw went and the floods cam. The moss was like a sea, and the Caldron was streikit wi' roarin' burns. We never saw the post for a week, and every brig atween here and Portaway gaed doun to the Solway. ... Wheesht!'

She broke off and listened. A faint cry of 'Madam' came from the other end of the house.

'It's him. It's Linklater. "Madam" he ca's me. Keep us a'!'

She hurried from the kitchen, shutting the door carefully behind her.

When she returned it was with a solemn face.

'He's wonderin' if ane o' you lads wad take a telegram for him to the office. He's terrible set on't. "Madam," he says wi' his Englishy voice, "I assure you it's a matter of the utmost importance." '

'Nonsense,' said Dougal. 'Sixteen miles after a long day's tramp! He can easily wait till the morning. Besides, the office would be closed before we got there.'

'Aye, but hearken.' Mrs Catterick's voice was hushed in awe. 'He offers twenty punds to the man that will dae his will. He's gotten the notes in his pooch.'

'Now where on earth,' said Dougal, 'did a medical student get twenty pounds?'

'He's no like a student. The mair I look at him the better I see that he's nane o' the rough clan that Erchie rins wi'. He's yin that's been used wi' his comforts. And he's aulder than I thocht – an aulder man than John. I wadna say but that blagyird Erchie has kidnapped a Lord Provost, and whaur will we a' be then?'

'We had better interview him,' said Dougal. 'It's a shame to let him fret himself.'

'Ane at a time,' advised Mrs Catterick, 'for he's as skeery as a cowt. You gang, Dougal. Ye ken the ways o' the college lads.'

Dougal departed and the two left behind fell silent. Mrs Catterick's instinct for the dramatic had been roused, and she kept her eye on the door, through which the envoy would return, as if it had been the curtain of a stage play. Even Jaikie's placidity was stirred.

'This is a funny business, Mrs Catterick,' he said. 'Dougal and I come here for peace, and we find the Back House of the Garroch turned into a robbers' den. The Canonry is becoming a stirring place. You've an election on, too.'

'So I was hearin', and the post brings us papers about it. John maun try and vote, if he can get an orra day atween the sales. He votit last time, honest man, but we never heard richt whae got in. We're ower far up the glens for poalitics. Wheesht! Is that Dougal?'

It was not. He did not return for nearly half an hour, and when he came it was to put his head inside the door and violently beckon Jaikie. He led him out of doors to the corner of the garden, and then turned on him a face so excited and portentous that the appropriate utterance should have been a shout. He did not shout: he whispered hoarsely.

'Do you mind our talk coming up the road? . . . Providence has taken me at my word. . . . Who do you think is sitting ben the house? It's the man Craw!'

CHAPTER FOUR

# THE RECONNAISSANCE OF CASTLE GAY

THE westering sun was lighting up the homely furniture of Mrs Catterick's best room – the sheepskins on the floor, the framed photographs decorated with strings of curlews' eggs on the walls – when Dougal and Jaikie entered the presence of the great man. Mr Craw was not at the moment an impressive figure. The schoolmaster's son of Kilmaclavers had been so long habituated to the attentions of an assiduous valet that he had found some difficulty in making his own toilet. His scanty hair was in disorder, and his spruce blue suit had attracted a good deal of whitewash from the walls of his narrow bedroom. Also he had lost what novelists call his poise. He sat in a horsehair-covered armchair drawn up at a table, and strove to look as if he had command of the situation, but his eye was uncertain and his fingers drummed nervously.

'This is Mr Galt, sir,' said Dougal, adding, 'of St Mark's College, Cambridge.'

Mr Craw nodded.

'Your friend is to be trusted?' and his wavering eyes sought Jaikie. What he saw cannot have greatly reassured him for Jaikie was struggling with a strong inclination to laugh.

'I have need to be careful,' he said, fixing his gaze upon a photograph of the late Queen Victoria and picking his words. 'I find myself, through no fault of my own, in a very delicate position. I have been the subject of an outrage on the part of – of some young men of whom I know nothing. I do not blame them. I have been myself a student of a Scottish University. ... But it is unfortunate – most unfortunate. It was apparently a case of mistaken identity. Happily I was not recognized. ... I am a figure of some note in the world. You will understand that I do not wish to have my name associated with an undergraduate – "rag", I think, is the word.'

His two hearers nodded gravely. They were bound to respect such patent unhappiness.

'Mr – I beg your pardon – Crombie? – has told me that he is employed on one of my papers. Therefore I have a right to call upon his assistance. He informs me that I can also count on your goodwill and discretion, sir,' and he inclined his head towards Jaikie. 'It is imperative that this foolish affair should never be known to the public. I have been successful in life, and therefore I have rivals. I have taken a strong stand in public affairs, and therefore I have enemies. My position, as you are no doubt aware, is one of authority, and I do not wish my usefulness to be impaired by becoming the centre of a ridiculous tale.'

Mr Craw was losing his nervousness and growing fluent. He felt that these two young men were of his own household, and he spoke to them as he would have addressed Freddy Barbon, or Sigismund Allins, or Archibald Bamff, or Bannister, his butler, or that efficient spinster, Miss Elena Cazenove.

'I don't think you need be afraid, sir,' said Dougal. 'The students who kidnapped you will have discovered their mistake as soon as they saw the real Linklater going about this morning. They won't have a notion who was kidnapped, and they won't want to inquire. You may be sure that they will lie very low about the whole business. What is to hinder you sending a wire to Castle Gay to have a car up here to-morrow, and go back to your own house as if nothing had happened? Mrs Catterick doesn't know you from Adam, and you may trust Jaikie and me to hold our tongues.'

'Unfortunately the situation is not so simple.' Mr Craw blinked his eyes, as if to shut out an unpleasing picture, and his hands began to flutter again. 'At this moment there is a by-election in the Canonry – a spectacular by-election. ... The place is full of journalists – special correspondents – from the London papers. They were anxious to drag me into the election, but I have consistently refused. I cannot embroil myself in local politics. Indeed, I intended to go abroad, for this inroad upon my rural peace is in the highest degree distasteful. ... You may be very certain that these journalists are at this moment nosing about Castle Gay. Now, my household must have been alarmed when I did not return last night. I have a discreet staff, but they were bound to set inquiries on foot. They must have telephoned to Glasgow, and they may even have consulted the police. Some rumours must have got abroad, and the approaches to my house will be watched. If one of these journalists learns that I am here – the telegraph office in these country parts is a centre of gossip – he will follow up the trail. He will interview the woman of this cottage, he will wire to Glasgow, and presently the whole ridiculous business will be disclosed, and there will be inch headlines in every paper except my own.'

'There's something in that,' said Dougal. 'I know the ways of those London journalists, and they're a dour crop to shift. What's your plan, sir?'

'I have written a letter.' He produced one of Mrs Catterick's disgraceful sheets of notepaper on which her disgraceful pen had done violence to Mr Craw's neat commercial hand. 'I want this put into the hand of my private secretary, Mr Barbon, at once. Every hour's delay increases the danger.'

'Would it not be best,' Dougal suggested, 'if you got on to one of the bicycles – there are two in the outhouse, Mrs Catterick says – and I escorted you to Castle Gay this very night? It's only about twenty miles.'

'I have never ridden a bicycle in my life,' said Mr Craw coldly. 'My plan is the only one, I fear. I am entitled to call upon you to help me.'

It was Jaikie who answered. The first day's walk in the hills was always an intoxication to him, and Mrs Catterick's tea had banished every trace of fatigue.

'It's a grand night, Dougal,' he said, 'and there's a moon. I'll be home before midnight. There's nothing I would like better than a ride down Garroch to the Callowa. I know the road as well as my own name.'

'We'll go together,' said Dougal firmly. 'I'm feeling fresher than when I started. . . . What are your instructions, sir?'

'You will deliver this letter direct into Mr Barbon's hands. I have asked him to send a car in this direction to-morrow before midday, and I will walk down the glen to meet it. It will wait for me a mile or so from this house. ... You need not say how I came here. I am not in the habit of explaining my doings to my staff.'

Mr Craw enclosed his letter in a shameful envelope and addressed it. His movements were brisker now and he had recovered his self-possession. 'I shall not forget this, Mr Crombie,' he said benignly. 'You are fortunate in being able to do me a service.'

Dougal and Jaikie betook themselves to the outhouse to examine the bicycles of John Catterick and the herd of the west hirsel.

'I eat the man's bread,' said the former, 'so I am bound to help him, but God forbid I should ever want to accept his favours. It's unbelievable that we should spend the first night of our holiday trying to save the face of Craw. ... Did you ever see such an image? He's more preposterous even than I thought. But there's decency in all things, and if Craw's bones are to be picked it will be me that has the picking of them, and not those London corbies.'

But this truculence did not represent Dougal's true mind, which presently became apparent to his companion as they bumped their way among the heather bushes and flood-gravel which composed the upper part of the Garroch road. He was undeniably excited. He was a subaltern officer in a great army, and now he had been brought face to face with the general-in-chief. However ill he might think of that general, there was romance in the sudden juxtaposition, something to set the heart beating and to fire the fancy. Dougal regarded Mr Craw much as a stalwart republican might look on a legitimate but ineffectual monarch; yet the stoutest republican is not proof against an innocent snobbery and will hurry to a street corner to see the monarch pass. Moreover, this general-in-chief was in difficulties; his immediate comfort depended upon the humble subaltern. So Dougal was in an excited mood and inclined to babble. He was determined to do his best for his chief, but he tried to salve his self-respect by a critical aloofness.

'What do you think of the great Craw?' he asked Jaikie.

'He seems a pleasant fellow,' was the answer.

'Oh, he's soft-spoken enough. He had the good manners of one accustomed to having his own way. But, man, to hear him talk was just like hearing a grandfather clock ticking. He's one mass of artifice.'

Dougal proceeded to a dissection of Mr Craw's mind which caused him considerable satisfaction. He proved beyond question that the great man had no brains of his own, but was only an echo, a repository for other men's ideas. 'A cistern, not a spring,' was his conclusion. But he was a little dashed by Jaikie, who listened patiently to the analysis, and then remarked that he was talking rubbish.

'If a man does as much in the world as Craw, and makes himself as important, it's nonsense to say he has no brains. He must have plenty, though they may not be the kind you like. You know very well, Dougal, that you're mighty pleased to have the chance of doing the great man a favour. And maybe rather flattered.'

The other did not reply for a moment. 'Perhaps I am,' he said at length. 'We're all snobs in a way – all but you. You're the only democrat I know. What's the phrase – "Fellow to a beggar and brother to a king, if he be found worthy"? It's no credit to you – it's just the way you're made.'

After that it was impossible to get a word out of Jaikie, and even Dougal drifted by way of monosyllables into silence, for the place and the hour had their overmastering enchantments. There was no evening mist, and in the twilight every hill stood out clean-cut in a purple monochrome. Soon the road skirted the shores of the Lower Loch Garroch, twining among small thickets of birch and hazel, with the dark water on its right lapping ghostly shingle. Presently the glen narrowed and the Garroch grumbled to itself in deep linns, appearing now and then on some rockshelf in a broad pool which caught the last amethyst light of day. There had been no lamps attached to the bicycles of John Catterick and the herd of the west hirsel, so the travellers must needs move circumspectly.

And then the hills fell back, the glen became a valley,

and the Garroch ran free in wild meadows of rush and bracken.

The road continued downstream to the junction with the Callowa not far from the town of Portaway. But to reach Castle Gay it was necessary to break off and take the hill-road on the left, which crossed the containing ridge and debouched in the upper part of Glen Callowa. The two riders dismounted, and walked the road which wound from one grassy howe to another till they reached the low saddle called the Pad o' the Slack, and looked down upon a broader vale. Not that they had any prospect from it – for it was now very dark, the deep autumn darkness which precedes moonrise; but they had an instinct that there was freer space before them. They remounted their bicycles, and cautiously descended a road with many awkward angles and hairpin bends, till they found themselves among trees, and suddenly came on to a metalled highway.

'Keep to the right,' Jaikie directed. 'We're not more than two miles from the Castle gates.'

The place had the unmistakable character of a demesne. Even in the gloom it had an air of being well cared for, and the moon, which now began to send a shiver of light through the darkness, revealed a high wall on the left – no drystone dyke but a masoned wall with a coping. The woods, too, were not the scrub of the hills, but well-grown timber trees and plantations of fir. Then the wall fell back, there were two big patches of greensward protected by chains and white stones, and between them a sweep of gravel, a castellated lodge, and vast gates like a portcullis. The Lord Rhynns of three generations ago had been unhappily affected by the Gothic Revival.

'Here's the place,' said Dougal. 'It's a mighty shell for such a wee body as Craw.'

The gates were locked. There was a huge bell pendant from one of the pillars and this Jaikie rang. It echoed voluminously in the stillness, but there was no sign of life in the lodge. He rang again and yet again, making the night hideous, while Dougal hammered at the massive ironwork of the gate.

'They're all dead or drunk,' the latter said. 'I'm positive

there's folk in the lodge. I saw a bit of a light in the upper window. What for will they not open?'

Jaikie had abandoned the bell and was peering through the ironwork.

'Dougal,' he whispered excitedly, 'look here. This gate is not meant to open. Look what's behind it. It's a barricade. There's two big logs jammed between the posts. The thing would keep a Tank out. Whoever is in there is terrified of something.'

'There's somebody in the lodge watching us. I'm certain of that. What do they mean by behaving as if they were besieged? I don't like it, Jaikie. There's something here we don't understand – and Craw doesn't understand. How can they expect to defend as big a space as a park? Any active man could get over the wall.'

'Maybe they want to keep out motors. . . . Well, we needn't waste time here. That letter has got to be delivered, and there's more roads than the main road.'

'Is there another entrance?'

'Yes. This is the main one, but there's a second lodge a mile beyond Starr – that's the village – on the Knockraw road. But we needn't worry about that. We can leave our bicycles, and get into the park by the Callowa bridge.'

They remounted and resumed their course along the highway. One or two cottages were passed, which showed no sign of life, since the folk in these parts rise early and go early to bed. But in an open space a light was visible from a larger house on the slope to the right. Then came a descent and the noise of a rapid stream.

The bicycles were shoved under a hawthorn bush, and Jaikie clambered on to the extreme edge of the bridge parapet.

'We can do it,' he reported. 'A hand traverse for a yard or two and then a ten-foot drop. There's bracken below, so it will be soft falling.'

Five minutes later the two were emerging from a bracken covert on to the lawn-like turf which fringed the Callowa. The moon was now well up in the sky, and they could see before them the famous wild park of Castle Gay. The guidebooks relate that in it are both red deer and fallow deer, and in one part a few of the ancient Caledonian wild cattle. But these denizens must have fallen asleep, for as Jaikie and Dougal followed the river they saw nothing but an occasional rabbit and a belated heron. They kept to the stream side, for Jaikie had once studied the ordnance map and remembered that the Castle was close to the water.

The place was so magical that one of the two forgot his errand. It was a cup among high hills, but, seen in that light, the hills were dwarfed, and Jaikie with a start realized that the comb of mountain, which seemed little more than an adjacent hillock, must be a ridge of the great Muneraw, twenty miles distant. The patches of wood were black as ink against the pale mystery of the moonlit sward. The river was dark too, except where a shallow reflected the moon. The silence was broken only by the small noises of wild animals, the ripple of the stream, and an occasional splash of a running salmon.

Then, as they topped a slope, the house lay before them. It stood on its own little plateau with the ground falling from it towards the park and the stream, and behind it the fir-clad Castle Hill. The moon turned it into ivory, so that it had the air of some precious Chinese carving on a jade stand. In such a setting it looked tiny, and one had to measure it with the neighbouring landscape to realize that it was a considerable pile. But if it did not awe by its size, it ravished the eyes with its perfection. Whatever may have been crude and ugly in it, the jerry-building of our ancestors, the demented reconstruction of our forefathers, was mellowed by night into a classic grace. Jaikie began to whistle softly with pure delight, for he had seen a vision.

The practical Dougal had his mind on business. 'It's past eleven o'clock, and it looks as if they were all in their beds. I don't see a light. There'll be gardens to get through before we reach the door. We'd better look out for dogs too. The folk here seem a bit jumpy in their nerves.'

But it was no dog that obstructed them. Since they had come in sight of their goal they had moved with circumspection, and, being trained of old to the game, were as noiseless as ferrets. They had left the wilder part of the park, had crossed a piece of meadowland from which an aftermath of hay had lately been taken, and could already see beyond a ha-ha the terraces of a formal garden. But while they guarded against sound, their eyes were too much on their destination to be wary about the foreground.

So it befell that they crossed the ha-ha at the very point where a gentleman was taking his ease. Dougal fell over him, and the two travellers found themselves looking at the startled face of a small man in knickerbockers.

His pipe had dropped from his mouth. Jaikie picked it up and presented it to him. 'I beg your pardon, sir,' he said, 'I hope you're not hurt.' In the depths of the ha-ha there was shadow, and Jaikie took the victim of Dougal's haste for someone on the Castle staff.

'What are you doing here?' The man's air was at once apologetic and defiant. There was that in his tone which implied that he might in turn be asked his business, that he had no prescriptive right to be sitting in that ha-ha at midnight.

So Jaikie answered: 'Just the same as you. Taking the air and admiring the view.'

The little man was recovering himself.

'You gave me quite a start when you jumped on the top of me. I thought it was one of the gamekeepers after a poacher.' He began to fill his pipe. 'More by token, who are you?'

'Oh, we're a couple of undergraduates seeing the world. We wanted a look at the Castle, and there's not much you can see from the high-road, so we got in at the bridge and came up the stream. ... We're strangers here. There's an inn at Starr, isn't there? What sort of place is it?'

'Nothing to write home about,' was the answer. 'You'd better go on to Portaway. ... So you're undergraduates? I thought that maybe you were of my own profession, and I was going to be a bit jealous. I'm on the staff of the *Live Wire*.'

Dougal's hand surreptitiously found Jaikie's wrist and held it tight.

'I suppose you're up here to cover the by-election,' he

observed, in a voice which he strove to keep flat and uninterested.

'By-election be hanged! That was my original job, but I'm on to far bigger business. Do you know who lives in that house?'

Two heads were mendaciously shaken.

'The great Craw! Thomas Carlyle Craw! The man that owns all the uplift papers. If you've never heard of Craw, Oxford's more of a mausoleum than I thought.'

'We're Cambridge,' said Jaikie, 'and of course we've heard of Craw. What about him?'

'Simply that he's the mystery man of journalism. You hear of him but you never see him. He's a kind of Delphic oracle that never shows his face. The *Wire* doesn't care a hoot for by-elections, but it cares a whole lot about Craw. He's our big rival, and we love him as much as a cat loves water. He's a go-getter is Craw. There's a deep commercial purpose behind all his sanctimonious bilge, and he knows how to rake in the shekels. His circulation figures are steadily beating ours by at least ten per cent. He has made himself the idol of his public, and, till we pull off the prophet's mantle and knock out some of the sawdust, he has us licked all the time. But it's the deuce and all to get at him, for the blighter is as shy as a wood-nymph. So, when this election started my chief says to me: "Here's our chance at last," he says. "Off you go, Tibbets, and draw the badger. Get him into the limelight somehow. Show him up for the almighty fool he is. Publicity about Craw," he says, "any kind of publicity that will take the gilt off the image. It's the chance of your life!" '

'Any luck?' Dougal asked casually.

Mr Tibbets voice became solemn. 'I believe,' he said, 'that I am on the edge of the world's biggest scoop. I discovered in half a day that we could never get Craw to mix himself up in an election. He knows too much. He isn't going to have the *Wire* and a dozen other papers printing his halting utterances *verbatim* in leaded type, and making nice, friendly comments. . . . No, that cock won't fight. But I've found a better. D'you know what will be the main headline in to-morrow's *Wire*?

It will be "*Mysterious Disappearance of Mr Craw – Household Distracted.*" – And by God, it will be true – every word of it. The man's lost.'

'How do you mean?'

'Just lost. He never came backl ast night.'

'Why should he? He has probably offed it abroad – to give the election a miss.'

'Not a bit of it. He meant to go abroad to-morrow, and all the arrangements were made – I found out all that from standing a drink to his second chauffeur. But he was expected back last night, and his car was meeting him at Kirkmichael. He never appeared. He has a staff like Buckingham Palace, and they were on the telephone all evening to Glasgow. It seems he left Glasgow right enough. ... I got that from the chauffeur fellow, who's new and not so damned secretive as the rest. So I went to Kirkmichael this morning on a motor-bike, and the ticket collector remembered Craw coming off the Glasgow train. He disappeared into the void somewhere between here and Kirkmichael at some time after 7.15 last night. Take my word for it, a judgement has fallen upon Craw.'

'Aren't you presuming too much?' Jaikie asked. 'He may have changed his mind and be coming back to-morrow – or be back now – or he's wiring his servants to meet him somewhere. Then you and the *Wire* will look rather foolish.'

'It's a risk, no doubt, but it's worth taking. And if you had seen his secretary's face you wouldn't think it much of a risk. I never saw a chap so scared as that secretary man. He started off this afternoon in a sports-model at eighty miles an hour and was back an hour later as if he had seen his father's ghost. ... What's more, this place is in a state of siege. They wouldn't let me in at the lodge gates. I made a long detour and got in by the back premises, and blessed if I hadn't to run for my life! ... Don't tell me. The people in that house are terrified of something, and Craw isn't there, and they don't know why Craw isn't there. ... That's the mystery I'm out to solve, and I'll get to the bottom of it or my name isn't Albert Tibbets.'

'I don't quite see the point,' said Jaikie. 'If you got him on a platform you might make capital out of his foolishness. But if some accident has happened to him, you can't make capital out of a man's misfortunes.'

'We can out of Craw's. Don't you see we can crack the shell of mystery? We can make him *news* – like any shop-girl who runs away from home or city gent that loses his memory. We can upset his blasted dignity.'

Dougal got up. 'We'll leave you to your midnight reveries, Mr Tibbets. We're for bed. Where are your headquarters?'

'Portaway is my base. But my post at present is in and around this park. I'm accustomed to roughing it.'

'Well, good night and good luck to you.'

The two retraced their steps down the stream.

'This letter will have to wait till the morn's morn,' said Dougal. 'Craw was right. It hasn't taken long for the opposition Press to get after him. It's our business, Jaikie, my man, to make the *Wire* the laughing-stock of British journalism. . . . Not that Tibbets isn't a dangerous fellow. Pray Heaven he doesn't get on the track of the students' rag, for that's just the kind of yarn he wants. . . . They say that dog doesn't eat dog, but I swear before I've done with him to chew yon tyke's ear. . . . I'm beginning to think very kindly of Craw.'

CHAPTER FIVE

# INTRODUCES A LADY

JAIKIE was roused next morning in his little room in the Westwater Arms by Dougal sitting down heavily on his toes. He was a sound sleeper, and was apt to return but slowly to a waking world. Yet even to his confused perceptions the state of the light seemed to mark an hour considerably later than that of seven a.m. which had been the appointed time. He reached for his watch and saw that it was nearly nine o'clock.

'You never called me,' he explained apologetically.

'I did not, but I've been up since six myself. I've been thinking hard. Jaikie, there's more in this business than meets the eye. I've lain awake half the night considering it. But first I had to act. We can't let the *Wire*'s stuff go uncontradicted. So I bicycled into Portaway and called up the office on the telephone. I caught Tavish just as he was going out to his breakfast. I had to take risks, so I said I was speaking from Castle Gay on Mr Craw's behalf. . . . Tavish must have wondered what I was doing there. . . . I said that Mr Craw had left for the Continent yesterday and would be away some weeks, and that an announcement to that effect was to appear in all the Craw papers.'

'Did he raise any objection?'

'I thought he would, for this is the first time that Craw has advertised his movements, and I was prepared with the most circumstantial lies. But I didn't need to lie, for he took it like a lamb. Indeed, it was piper's news I was giving him, for he had had the same instructions already. What do you think of that?'

'He got them from Barbon the secretary?'

'Not a bit of it. He had no word from Castle Gay. He got them yesterday afternoon from London. Now, who sent them?'

'The London office.'

'I don't believe it. Bamff, the General Manager, is away in Canada over the new paper contracts. Don't tell me that Craw instructed London to make the announcement before he was bagged by the students. It isn't his way. ... There's somebody else at work on this job, somebody that wants to have it believed that Craw is out of the country.'

Jaikie shook a sceptical head.

'You were always too ingenious, Dougal. You've got Craw on the brain, and are determined to find melodrama. ... Order my breakfast like a good chap. I'll be down in twenty minutes.'

Jaikie bathed in the ancient contrivance of wood and tin, which was all that the inn provided, and was busy shaving when Dougal returned. The latter sat himself resolutely on the bed.

'The sooner we are at the Castle the better,' he observed, as if the remark were the result of a chain of profound reasoning. 'The more I think of this affair the less I like it. I'm not exactly in love with Craw, but he's my chief, and I'm for him every time against his trade rivals. Compared to the *Wire* crowd, Craw is respectable. What I want to get at is the state of mind of the folk in the Castle. They're afraid of the journalists, and they've cause. A fellow like Tibbets is as dangerous as nitro-glycerine. They've lost Craw, and they want to keep it quiet till they find him again. So far it's plain sailing. But what in Heaven's name did they mean by barricading the gate at the big lodge?'

'To prevent themselves being taken by surprise by journalists in motor-cars or on motor-bicycles,' said Jaikie, who was now trying to flatten out his rebellious hair.

'But that's not sense. To barricade the gate was just to give the journalists the kind of news they wanted. "Mr Craw's House in a State of Siege." "Amazing Precautions at Castle Gay" – think of the headlines! Barbon and the rest know everything about newspaper tricks, and we must assume that they haven't suddenly become congenital idiots. ... No, Jaikie my lad, they're afraid – blind afraid – of something more than the journalists, and the sooner we find out what it is the better for you and me and Craw. ... I'll give you twenty minutes to eat your breakfast, and then we take the road. It'll be by the bridge and the water-side, the same as last night.'

It was a still hazy autumn morning with the promise of a warm midday. The woods through which the two sped were loud with pheasants, the shooting of which would be at the best perfunctory, for the tenant at the Castle never handled a gun. No one was on the road, except an aged stonebreaker in a retired nook. They hid their bicycles with some care in a mossy covert, for they might be for some time separated from them, and, after a careful reconnaissance to see that they were unobserved, entered the park by way of the bridge parapet, the traverse and the ten-foot drop. This time they had not the friendly night to shield them, and they did not venture on the lawn-like turf by the stream side. Instead they followed a devious route among brackeny hollows, where they could not be seen from any higher ground. The prospect from the highway was, they knew, shut out by the boundary wall.

Dougal moved fast with a sense of purpose like a dog on a scent. He had lost his holiday discursiveness, and had no inclination to linger in bypaths earthly or spiritual. But Jaikie had his familiar air of detachment. He did not appear to take his errand with any seriousness or to be much concerned with the mysteries which filled Dougal's thoughts. He was revelling in the sounds and scents of October in that paradise which possessed the charm of both lowland and highland. The film of morning was still silver-grey on rush and grass and heather, and the pools of the Callowa smoked delicately. The day revealed some of the park's features which night had obscured. In particular there was a tiny lochan, thronged with wildfowl, which was connected by a reedy burn with the Callowa. A herd of dappled fallow-deer broke out of thicket, and somewhere near a stag was belling.

The house came suddenly into sight at a slightly different angle from that of the night before. They were on higher ground, and had a full view of the terrace, where even now two gardeners were trimming the grass edges of the plots. That seemed normal enough, and so did the spires of smoke ascending straight from the chimneys into the windless air.

They stood behind a gnarled, low-spreading oak, which must have been there as a seedling when steel-bonneted reivers rode that way and the castle was a keep. Dougal's hand shaded his eyes, and he scanned warily every detail of the scene.

'We must push forward,' he said. 'If anyone tries to stop us we can say we've a letter to Mr Barbon from Mr Craw. Knowing Barbon's name will be a sort of passport. Keep your eyes skinned for Tibbets, for he mustn't see us. I daresay he'll be at his breakfast in Portaway – he'll be needing it if he has been hunkering here all night. We haven't ...'

He broke off, for at that instant two animals precipitated themselves against his calves, thereby nearly unbalancing him. They were obviously dogs, but of a breed with which Dougal was unfamiliar. They had large sagacious heads, gentle and profoundly tragic eyes, and legs over which they seemed to have no sort of control. Over Dougal they sprawled and slobbered, while he strove to evade their caresses.

Then came a second surprise, for a voice spoke out of the tree above them. The voice was peremptory and it was young. It said, 'Down, Tactful! Down, Pensive!' And then it added in a slightly milder tone: 'What are *you* doing here?'

These last words were so plainly addressed to the two travellers that they looked up into the covert, half green, half russet, above their heads. There, seated in a crutch made by two branches, they beheld to their amazement a girl.

Her face was visible between the branches, but the rest of her was hidden, except one slim pendant brown leg ending in a somewhat battered shoe. The face regarded them solemnly, reprovingly, suspiciously. It was a pretty face, a little sunburnt, not innocent of freckles, and it was surmounted by a mop of tawny gold hair. The eyes were blue and stern. The beagle pups, having finished their overtures to Dougal, were now making ineffective leaps at her shoe.

'How did you get up that tree?' The question was wrung from Jaikie, a specialist in such matters, as he regarded the branchless bole and the considerable elevation of the bough on which she sat.

'Quite easily,' was the answer. 'I have climbed much harder

trees than this. But that is not the question. What are you two doing here?'

'What are you?'

'I have permission to go anywhere in the Castle grounds. I have a key for the gates. But you are trespassers, and there'll be an awful row if Mackillop catches you.'

'We're not,' said Dougal. 'We're carrying a letter from Mr Craw to Mr Barbon. I have it in my pocket.'

'Is that true?' The eyes were sceptical, but also startled.

For answer Dougal drew the missive from his inner pocket. 'There it is: "The Honourable Frederick Barbon". Look for yourself!'

The girl peered down at the superscription. The degraded envelope of Mrs Catterick's did not perhaps carry conviction, but something in the two faces below persuaded her of their honesty. With a swift movement she wriggled out of the crutch, caught a bough with both hands, and dropped lightly to the ground. With two deft kicks she repelled the attentions of Tactful and Pensive, and stood before the travellers, smoothing down her short skirt. She was about Jaikie's height, very slim and straight, and her interrogation was that of a general to his staff.

'You come from Mr Craw?'

'Yes.'

'When did you leave him?'

'Last night.'

'Glory be! Let's sit down. There's no hurry, and we must move very carefully. For I may as well let you know that the Devil has got into this place. Yes. The Devil. I don't quite know what form he has taken, but he's rampant in Castle Gay. I came here this morning to prospect, for I feel in a way responsible. You see it belongs to my father, and Mr Craw's our tenant. My name is Alison Westwater.'

'Same name as the pub in Starr?' asked Dougal, who liked to connect his knowledge organically.

She nodded. 'The Westwater Arms. Yes, that's my family. I live at the Mains with my aunt, while Papa and Mama are on the Continent. I wouldn't go. I said, "You can't expect me after a filthy summer in London to go tramping about France wearing tidy clothes and meeting the same idiotic people." I had a year at school in Paris and that gave me all the France I want in this life. I said, "Castle Gay's my home, though you've chosen to let it to a funny little man, and I'm not going to miss my whack of Scotland." So I hopped it here at the end of July, and I've been having a pretty peaceful time ever since. You see, all the outdoor people are *our* people, and Mr Craw has been very nice about it, and lets me fish in the Callowa and all the lochs and treat the place as if he wasn't there.'

'Do you know Mr Craw well?' Dougal asked.

'I have seen him three times and talked to him once – when Aunt Harriet took me to tea with him. I thought him rather a dear, but quite helpless. Talks just like a book, and doesn't appear to understand much of what you say to him. I suppose he is very clever, but he seems to want a lot of looking after. You never saw such a staff. There's a solemn butler called Bannister. I believe Bannister washes Mr Craw's face and tucks him into bed. . . . There's a typewriting woman by the name of Cazenove with a sharp nose and horn spectacles, who never takes her eyes off him, and is always presenting him with papers to read. It's slavery of some kind, but whether she's his slave or he's her slave I don't know. I had to break a plate at tea, just to remind myself that there was such a thing as liberty. . . . Then there is Mr Allins, a very glossy young man. You've probably come across him, for he goes about a lot. Mr Allins fancies himself the perfect man of the world and a great charmer. I think if you met him you would say he wasn't quite a gentleman.' She smiled confidentially at the two, as if she assumed that their standards must coincide with hers.

'Mr Barbon?' Dougal asked.

'And of course there's Freddy. There's nothing wrong with Freddy in that way. He's some sort of a cousin of ours. Freddy is the chief of staff and has everything on his shoulders. He is very kind and anxious, poor dear, and now the crash has come! Not to put too fine a point on it, for the last twenty-four hours Freddy has gone clean off his head. . . .'

She stopped at an exclamation from Jaikie. He had one of those small field-glasses which are adapted for a single eye, with which he had been examining the approaches to the castle.

'Tibbets can't have had much of a breakfast,' he announced. 'I see him sitting in that trench place.'

'Who is Tibbets?' she demanded.

'He's a journalist, on the *Live Wire*, one of Mr Craw's rivals. We ran into him late last night, and that's why we couldn't deliver the letter.'

'Little beast! That's the first of Freddy's anxieties. This place has been besieged by journalists for a week, all trying to get at Mr Craw. ... Then the night before last Mr Craw did not come home. *You* know where he is, but Freddy doesn't, so that's the second of his troubles. Somehow the fact of Mr Craw's disappearance has leaked out, and the journalists have got hold of it, and yesterday it almost came to keeping them off with a gun. ... And out of the sky dropped the last straw.'

She paused dramatically.

'I don't know the truth about it, for I haven't seen Freddy since yesterday morning. I think he must have had a letter, for he rushed to the Mains and left a message for Aunt Harriet that she was on no account to let any stranger into the house or speak to anybody or give any information. He can't have meant the journalists only, for we knew all about them. ... After that, just after luncheon, while I was out for a walk, I saw a big car arrive with three men in it. It tried to get in at the West Lodge, but Jamieson – that's the lodge-keeper – wouldn't open the gate. I thought that odd, but when I went riding in the evening I couldn't get in at the West Lodge either. They had jammed trunks of trees across. That means that Freddy is rattled out of his senses. He thinks he is besieged. Is there any word for that but lunacy? I can understand his being worried about the journalists and Mr Craw not coming home. But this! Isn't it what they call persecution-mania? I'm sorry about it, for I like Freddy.'

'The man's black afraid of something,' said Dougal, 'but maybe he has cause. Maybe it's something new – something we know nothing about.'

The girl nodded. 'It looks like it. Meantime, where is Mr Craw? It's your turn to take up the tale.'

'He's at the Back House of the Garroch, waiting for Barbon to send a car to fetch him.'

Miss Westwater whistled. 'Now how on earth did he get there? I know the place. It's on our land. I remember the shepherd's wife. A big, handsome, gypsy-looking woman, isn't she?'

Dougal briefly but dramatically told the story of the rape of Mr Craw. The girl listened with open eyes and an astonishment which left no room for laughter.

'Marvellous!' was her comment. 'Simply marvellous! That it should happen to Mr Craw of all people! I love those students. . . . What by the way are you? You haven't told me.'

'Jaikie here is an undergraduate – Cambridge.'

'Beastly place! I'm sorry, but my sympathies are all with Oxford.'

'And I'm a journalist by trade. I'm on one of the Craw papers. I've no sort of admiration for Craw, but of course I'm on his side in this row. The question is –'

Jaikie, who had been busy with his glass, suddenly clutched the speaker by the hair and forced him down. He had no need to perform the same office for Miss Westwater, for at his first movement she had flung herself on her face. The three were on a small eminence of turf with thick bracken before and behind them, and in this they lay crouched.

'What is it?' Dougal whispered.

'There's a man in the hollow,' said Jaikie. 'He's up to no good, for he's keeping well in cover. Wait here, and I'll stalk him.'

He wriggled into the fern, and it was a quarter of an hour before he returned. 'It's a man, and he's wearing a queer kind of knicker bocker suit. He hasn't the look of a journalist. He has some notion of keeping cover, for I could get no more than a glimpse of him. He's trying to get to the house, so we'll hope he'll tumble over Tibbets in the ditch, as Dougal and I did last night.'

'The plot thickens!' The girl's eyes were bright with excitement. 'He's probably one of the strangers who came in the car. ... The question is, what is to be done next? Mr Craw is at the Back House of the Garroch, twenty miles away, and no one knows it but us three. We have to get him home without the unfriendly journalists knowing about it.'

'We have also to get him out of the country,' said Dougal. 'There was some nonsense in the *Wire* this morning about his being lost, but all the Craw papers will announce that he has left for the Continent. ... But the first thing is to get him home. We'd better be thinking about delivering that letter, Jaikie.'

'Wait a moment,' said the girl. 'How are you going to deliver the letter? Freddy won't let you near him, even though you say you come from Mr Craw. He'll consider it a *ruse de guerre*, and small blame to him. I don't know what journalists look like as a class, but I suppose you bear the mark of your profession.'

'True. But maybe he wouldn't suspect Jaikie.'

'He'll suspect anyone. He has journalists on the brain just now.'

'But he'd recognize the handwriting.'

'Perhaps, if the letter got to him. But it won't. ... Besides, the man in the ha-ha – what do you call him – Tibbets? – will see you. And the other man who is crawling down there. All the approaches to the house on this side are as bare as a billiard table. At present you two are dark horses. The enemy doesn't connect you with Mr Craw, and that's very important, for you are the clue to Mr Craw's whereabouts. We mustn't give that card away. We don't want Tibbets on your track, for it leads direct to the Back House of the Garroch.'

'That's common sense,' said Dougal with conviction. 'What's your plan, then?'

The girl sat hunched in the fern, with her chin on one hand, and her eyes on the house and its terraces, where the gardeners were busy with the plots as if nothing could mar its modish tranquillity.

'It's all very exciting and difficult. We three are the only people in the world who can do anything to help. Somehow we must get hold of Freddy Barbon and pool our knowledge. I'm beginning to think that he may not be really off his head – only legitimately rattled. What about getting him to come to the Mains? I could send a message by Middlemas – that's our butler – he wouldn't suspect him. Also we could get Aunt Harriet's advice. She can be very wise when she wants to. And –'

She broke off.

'Mother of Moses!' she cried, invoking a saint not known to the Calendar. 'I quite forgot. There's an Australian cousin coming to stay. He's arriving in time for luncheon. He should be a tower of strength. His name is Charvill – Robin Charvill. He's at Oxford and a famous football player. He played in the international match two days ago.'

'I saw him,' said Jaikie.

'He's marvellous, isn't he?'

'Marvellous.'

'Well, we can count him in. That makes four of us – five if we include Aunt Harriet. A pretty useful support for the distraught Freddy! The next thing to do is to get you inconspicuously to the Mains. I'll show you the best way.'

Dougal, who had been knitting his brows, suddenly gave a shout.

'What like was the man you stalked down there?' he demanded of Jaikie.

'I didn't see much of him. He was wearing queer clothes – tight breeches and a belt round his waist.'

'Foreign looking?'

'Perhaps.'

He turned to the girl.

'And the men you saw yesterday in the car? Were they foreigners?'

She considered. 'They didn't look quite English. One had a short black beard. I remember that one had a long pale face.'

'I've got it,' Dougal cried. 'No wonder Barbon's scared. It's the Evallonian Republicans! They're after Craw!'

## CHAPTER SIX

# THE TROUBLES OF A PRIVATE SECRETARY

THE pleasant dwelling, known as the Mains of Starr, or more commonly the Mains, stands on a shelf of hillside above the highway, with a fine prospect over the park of Castle Gay to the rolling healthy uplands which form the grousemoor of Knockraw. From it indeed had shone that light which Jaikie and Dougal had observed the previous night after they left the barricaded lodge. It is low and whitewashed; it has a rounded front like the poop of a three-decker; its gables are crow-stepped; its air is resolutely of the past.

As such it was a fitting house for its present occupant. In every family there are members who act as guardians of its records and repositories of its traditions. Their sole distinction is their family connexion, and they take good care that the world shall not forget it. In Scotland they are usually high-nosed maiden ladies, and such a spinsterhood might well have seemed to be the destiny of Harriet Westwater. But on a visit to Egypt one winter, she had met and espoused a colonel of Sappers, called Brisbane-Brown, and for a happy decade had followed the drum in his company. He rose to be a major-general before he died of pneumonia (the result of a bitter day in an Irish snipe-bog), and left her a well-dowered widow.

The marriage had been a success, but the change of name had been meaningless, for the lady did not cease to be a Westwater. It used to be the fashion in Scotland for a married woman to retain her maiden name even on her tombstone, and this custom she had always followed in spirit. The Brisbane-Browns gave her no genealogical satisfaction. They were Browns from nowhere, who for five generations had served in the military forces of the Crown and had spent most of their lives abroad. The 'Brisbane' was not a link with the ancient Scottish house of that ilk; the General's father had been born in the capital of Queensland, and the word had been retained in the family's nomenclature to distinguish it from innumerable other Browns. As wife and widow she remained a Westwater, and the centre of her world was Castle Gay.

Her brother, Lord Rhynns, did not share her creed, for increasing financial embarrassments had made him a harsh realist; but though acutely aware of his imperfections, she felt for him, as head of the family, the reverence with which the devout regard a Prince of the Church. Her pretty invalidish sister-in-law – a type which she would normally have regarded with contempt – shared in the same glamour. But it was for their only child, Alison, that her family loyalty burned most fiercely. That summer, at immense discomfort to herself, she had chaperoned the girl in her first London season. Her house was Alison's home, and she strove to bring her up in conformity with the fashions of her own childhood. She signally failed, but she did not repine, for behind her tartness lay a large, tolerant humour, which gave her an odd kinship with youth. The girl's slanginess and tom-boyishness were proofs of spirit – a Westwater characteristic; her youthful intolerance was not unpleasing to a laudator of the past; her passionate love of Castle Gay was a variant of her own clannishness. After the experience of a modern season she thanked her Maker that her niece was not one of the lisping mannequins who flutter between London night-clubs and the sands of Deauville or the Lido.

To the tenant of the Castle she was well disposed. She knew nothing of him except that he was a newspaper magnate and very rich, but he paid her brother a large rent, and did not, like too many tenants nowadays, fill the house with noisy underbred parties, or outrage the sense of decency of the estate servants. She respected Mr Craw for his rigid seclusion. On the occasion of her solitary visit to him she had been a little shocked by the luxury of his establishment, till she reflected that a millionaire must spend his money on something, and that three footmen and a horde of secretaries were on the whole innocent extravagances. But indeed Mr Craw and the world for which he stood scarcely came within the orbit of her thoughts. She was no more interested in him than in the family affairs of the Portaway grocer who supplied her with provisions.

Politics she cared nothing for, except in so far as they affected the families which she had known all her life. When there was a chance of Cousin Georgie Whitehaven's second boy being given a post in the Ministry, she was much excited, but she would have been puzzled to name two other members of that Ministry, and of its policy she knew nothing at all. She read and re-read the books which she had loved from of old, and very occasionally a new work, generally a biography, which was well spoken of by her friends. She had never heard of Marcel Proust, but she could have passed a stiff examination in Shakespeare, Jane Austen, and Walter Scott. Morris and Burne-Jones had once enchained her youthful fancy; she could repeat a good deal of the more decorous parts of Swinburne; she found little merit in recent painting, except in one or two of Sargent's portraits. Her only musician was Beethoven, but she was a learned connoisseur of Scottish airs.

In her small way she was a notable administrator. The Edinburgh firm of Writers to the Signet who managed her affairs had cause to respect her acumen. Her banker knew her as a shrewd judge of investments. The household at the Mains ran with a clockwork precision, and all the servants, from the butler, Middlemas, to the kitchenmaid, were conscious of her guiding hand. Out of doors an ancient gardener and a boy from the village wrought under her supervision, for she was a keen horticulturist, and won prizes at all the local flower-shows for her sweet-peas and cauliflowers. She had given up her carriage, and refused to have a motor-car; but she drove two fat lazy ponies in a phaeton, and occasionally a well-bred grey gelding in a high dog-cart. The older folk in the countryside liked to see her pass. She was their one link with a vanished world which they now and then recalled with regret.

Mrs Brisbane-Brown was a relic, but only the unthinking would have called her a snob. For snobbishness implies some sense of insecurity, and she was perfectly secure. She was a specialist, a specialist in kindred. Much has been made in history and fiction of the younger son, but we are apt to forget the younger daughters – the inconspicuous gentlewomen who cling loyally to the skirts of their families, since their birth is their chief title to consideration, and labour to preserve many ancient trifling things which the world to-day holds in small esteem. Mrs Brisbane-Brown loved all that had continuance, and strove to rivet the weakening links. She kept in touch with the remotest members of her own house, and, being an indefatigable letter writer, she constituted herself a *trait d'union* for a whole chain of allied families. She was a benevolent aunt to a motley of nephews and nieces who were not nephews and nieces by any recognized table of affinity, and a cousin to many whose cousinship was remote even by Scottish standards. This passion for kinship she carried beyond her own class. She knew every ascendant and descendant and collateral among the farmers and cottagers of the countryside. Newcomers she regarded with suspicion, unless they could link themselves on to some of the Hislops and Blairs and Macmichaels whom she knew to be as long descended as the Westwaters themselves. Her aristocracy was wholly of race; it had nothing to do with position or wealth; it was a creed belated, no doubt, and reactionary, but it was not vulgar.

Jaikie and Dougal made a stealthy exit from the park by the gate in the wall which Alison had unlocked for them. Then with a promise to appear at the Mains for luncheon at one o'clock, they sought the inn at Starr, where they had left their knapsacks, recovering on the road their bicycles from the hazel covert. They said little to each other for both their minds were full of a new and surprising experience. Dougal was profoundly occupied with the Craw problem, and his own interpretation of its latest developments. Now and then he would mutter to himself, 'It's the Evallonians all right. Poor old Craw has pulled the string of the shower-bath this time.' Jaikie it must be confessed, was thinking chiefly of Alison. He wished he was like Charvill, and could call her cousin.

As they made their way to the Mains they encountered

Tibbets on his motor-bicycle, a dishevelled figure, rather gummy about the eyes. He dismounted to greet them.

'Any luck?' Dougal asked.

He shook his head. 'Not yet. I'll have to try other tactics. I'm off to Portaway to get to-day's *Wire*. And you?'

'We're continuing our travels. The *Wire* will keep us informed about your doings, no doubt. Good-bye.'

Tibbets was off with a trail of dust and petrol fumes. Dougal watched him disappear round a corner.

'Lucky he doesn't know yet what a chance he has. God help Craw if Tibbets once gets on to the Evallonians!'

With this pious thought they entered the gate of the Mains, and pushed their bicycles up the steep avenue of sycamores and horse-chestnuts. The leaves were yellowing with the morning frosts, and the fallen nuts crackled under the wheels, but, when they reached the lawn, plots and borders had still a summer glory of flowers. Great banks of Michaelmas daisies made a glow like an autumn sunset, and multi-coloured dahlias stood stiffly like grenadiers on parade. The two followed Middlemas through the shadowy hall with a certain nervousness. It seemed odd to be going to luncheon in a strange house at the invitation of a girl whom they had seen that morning for the first time.

They were five minutes late owing to Tibbets, and the mistress of the house was a precisian in punctuality. Consequently they were ushered into the dining-room, where the meal had already begun. It was a shy business, for Alison did not know their names. She waved a friendly hand. 'These are my friends, Aunt Hatty,' she began, when she was interrupted by a tall young man who made a third at the table.

'Great Scot!' he cried, after one stare at Jaikie. 'It's Galt! Whoever thought of seeing you here!' And he seized Jaikie's hand in a massive fist. 'You're entertaining a first-rate celebrity, Aunt Harriet. This is the famous John Galt, the greatest Rugby three-quarter playing to-day. I'm bound to say that in self-defence, for he did me in most nobly on Wednesday.'

The lady at the head of the table extended a gracious hand. 'I am very glad to see you, Mr Galt. You bear a name which is famous for other things than football. Was it a kinsman who gave us the *Annals of the Parish*?'

Jaikie, a little confused, said no, and presented Dougal, who was met with a similar genealogical probing. 'I used to know Crombies in Kincardine. One commanded a battalion of the Gordons when I was in India. You remind me of him in your colouring.'

These startling recognitions had the effect of putting Dougal more at his ease. He felt that he and Jaikie were being pleasantly absorbed into an unfamiliar atmosphere. Jaikie on the contrary was made slightly unhappy, the more so as the girl beside whom he sat turned on him reproachful eyes.

'You ought to have told me you played in the match,' she said, 'when I spoke about Cousin Robin. I might have made an awful *gaffe*.'

'We were talking about more solemn things than football,' he replied; adding, 'I thought Mr Barbon would be here.'

'He is coming at three. Such a time we had getting hold of him! They wouldn't let Middlemas in – he only managed it through one of our maids who's engaged to the second footman. ... But we mustn't talk about it now. My aunt forbids disagreeable topics at lunch, just as she won't let Tactful and Pensive into the dining-room.'

Mrs Brisbane-Brown had strong views about the kind of talk which aids digestion. It must not be argumentative, and it must not be agitating. It was best, she thought, when it was mildly reminiscent. But her reminiscences were not mildly phrased; as a rule they pointed with some acerbity the contrast between a dignified past and an unworthy present. She had been brought up in the school of straight backs, and sat as erect as a life-guardsman. A stiff net collar held her head high, a head neat and poised like that of a superior bird of prey. She had the same small high-bridged nose as her niece, and that, combined with a slight droop at the corners of her mouth, gave her an air of severity which was redeemed by her bright humorous brown eyes. Her voice was high and toneless, and, when she was displeased, of a peculiar detached, insulting flatness, but this again was atoned for by a very pleasant, ready, girlish laugh. Mrs Brisbane-Brown was a good example of the art of ageing gracefully. Her complexion, always a little high coloured from being much out of doors, would have done credit to a woman of twenty-five; her figure had the trimness of youth; but the fine wrinkles about her eyes and the streak of grey in her hair told of the passage of time. She looked her fifty-seven years; but she looked what fifty-seven should be at its happiest.

The dining-room was of a piece with its mistress. It was full of pictures, most of them copies of the Rhynns family portraits, done by herself, and one fine Canaletto which she had inherited from her mother. There was a Rhynns with long love-locks and armour, a Rhynns in periwig and lace, a Rhynns in a high-collared coat and cravat, and the original Sir Andrew Westwater, who had acquired Castle Gay by marriage with the Macdowall heiress, and who looked every inch the ruffian he was. There were prints, too, those mellow mezzotints which are the usual overflow of a great house. The room was sombre and yet cosy, a place that commemorated the past and yet was apt for the present. The arrogant sheen of the mahogany table, which mirrored the old silver and the great bowl of sunflowers (the Westwater crest), seemed to Dougal to typify all that he publicly protested against and secretly respected.

The hostess was cross-examining Mr Charvill about his knowledge of Scotland, which, it appeared, was confined to one visit to a Highland shooting lodge.

'Then you know nothing about us at all,' she declared firmly. 'Scotland is the Lowlands. Here we have a civilization of our own, just as good as England, but quite different. The Highlands are a sad, depopulated place, full of midges and kilted haberdashers. I know your Highland lodges – my husband had an unfortunate craze for stalking – gehennas of pitch-pine and deer's hair – not a bed fit to sleep in, and nothing for the unfortunate women to do but stump in hobnails between the showers along boggy roads!'

Charvill laughed. 'I admit I was wet most of the time, but

it was glorious fun. I never in my life had so much hard exercise.'

'You can walk?'

'A bit. I was brought up pretty well on horseback, but since I came to England I have learned to use my legs.'

'Then you are a fortunate young man. I cannot think what is to become of the youth of to-day. I was staying at Glenavelin last year, and the young men when they went to fish motored the half-mile to the river. My cousin had a wire from a friend who had taken Machray forest, begging him to find somebody over fifty to kill his stags, since his house was full of boys who could not get up the hills. You two,' her eyes passed from Dougal to Jaikie, 'are on a walking tour. I'm very glad to hear it. That is a rational kind of holiday.'

She embarked on stories of the great walkers of a century ago – Barclay of Urie, Horatio Ross, Lord John Kenedy. 'My father in his youth once walked from Edinburgh to Castle Gay. He took two days, and he had to carry the little spaniel that accompanied him for the last twenty miles. We don't breed such young men to-day. I daresay they are more discreet and less of an anxiety to their parents, and I know that they don't drink so much. But they are a feeble folk, like the conies. They never want to fling their caps over the moon. There is a lamentable scarcity of wild oats of the right kind.'

'Aunt Harriet,' said the girl, 'is thinking of the young men she saw at balls this summer.'

Mrs Brisbane-Brown raised her hands. 'Did you ever know such a kindergarten? Pallid infants with vacant faces. It was cruel to ask a girl to waste her time over them.'

'You asked *me*, you know, in spite of my protests.'

'And rightly, my dear. It is a thing every girl must go through – her form of public-school education. But I sincerely pitied you, my poor child. When I was young and went to balls I danced with interesting people – soldiers, and diplomats, and young politicians. They may have been at the balls this season, but I never saw them. What I did see were hordes upon hordes of children – a sort of *crèche* – vapid boys who were probably still at school or only just beginning the University. What has become of the sound English doctrine that the upbringing of our male youth should be monastic till at least twenty-one? We are getting as bad as the Americans with their ghastly co-education.'

Jaikie was glad when they rose from the table. He had wanted to look at Alison, who sat next him, but that meant turning his head deliberately, and he had been too shy. He wished that, like Dougal, he had sat opposite her. Yet he had been cheered by Mrs Brisbane-Brown's diatribes. Her condemnation of modern youth excluded by implication the three who lunched with her. She approved of Charvill of course. Who wouldn't? Charvill with his frank kindliness, his height, his orthodox good looks, was the kind of person Jaikie would have envied, had it been his nature to envy. But it would appear that she also approved of Dougal and himself, and Jaikie experienced a sudden lift of the heart.

Now he was free to look at Alison, as she stood very slim and golden in the big sunlit drawing-room. It was the most beautiful Jaikie had ever beheld. The chairs and sofas were covered with a bright, large-patterned chintz, all roses, parrots, and hollyhocks; the carpet was a faded Aubusson, rescued from a bedroom in Castle Gay; above the mantelpiece, in a gilt case, hung a sword of honour presented to the late General Brisbane-Brown, and on the polished parts of the floor, which the Aubusson did not reach, lay various trophies of his marksmanship. There was a huge white fleecy rug, and between that and the fire a huge brass fender. There were vitrines full of coins and medals and Roman lamps and flint arrows and enamelled snuff-boxes, and cabinets displaying Worcester china and Leeds earthenware. On the white walls were cases of miniatures, and samplers, and two exquisite framed fans, and a multitude of water-colours, all the work of Mrs Brisbane-Brown. There were views from the terraces of Florentine villas, and sunsets on the Nile, and dawns over Indian deserts, and glimpses of a dozen strange lands. The series was her travel diary, the trophy of her wanderings, just as a man will mount heads on the walls of his smoking-room. But the best picture was that presented by the two windows, which showed the wild woods and hollows of the Castle park below, bright in the October afternoon, running to the dim purple of the Knockraw heather.

In this cheerful and gracious room, before Middlemas had finished serving coffee, before Jaikie had made up his mind whether he preferred Alison in her present tidiness or in the gipsydom of the morning, there appeared a figure which effectually banished its complacent tranquillity.

Mr Frederick Barbon entered by an open window, and his clothes and shoes bore the marks of a rough journey. Yet neither clothes nor figure seemed adapted for such adventures. Mr Barbon's appearance was what old-fashioned people would have called 'distinguished'. He was very slim and elegant, and he had that useful colouring which does not change between the ages of thirty and fifty; that is to say, he had prematurely grizzled locks and a young complexion. His features were classic in their regularity. Sometimes he looked like a successful actor; sometimes, when in attendance on his master, like a very superior footman in mufti who had not got the powder out of his hair; but there were moments when he was taken for an eminent statesman. It was his nervous blue eyes which betrayed him, for Mr Barbon was an anxious soul. He liked his little comforts, he liked to feel important and privileged, and he knew only too well what it was to be a poor gentleman tossed from dilemma to dilemma by the unsympathetic horns of destiny. Since the war – when he had held a commission in the Foot Guards – he had been successively, but not successfully, a land-agent (the property was soon sold), a dealer in motor-cars (the business went speedily bankrupt), a stockbroker on half-commission, the manager of a tourist agency, an advertisement tout, and a highly incompetent society journalist. From his father, the aged and penniless Clonkilty, he could expect nothing. Then in the service of Mr Craw he had found an undreamed of haven; and he was as determined as King Charles the Second that he would never go wandering again. Consequently he was always anxious. He was an admirable private secretary, but he was fussy. The dread that haunted his dreams was of being hurled once more into the cold world of economic strife.

He sank wearily into a chair and accepted a cup of coffee.

'I had to make a detour of nearly three miles,' he explained, 'and come down on this place from the hill. I daren't stop long either. Where is Mr Craw's letter?'

Dougal presented the missive, which Mr Barbon tore open and devoured. A heavy sigh escaped him.

'Lucky I didn't get this sooner and act upon it,' he said. 'Mr Craw wants to come back. But the one place he mustn't come near is Castle Gay.'

Dougal, though very hungry and usually a stout trencherman, had not enjoyed his luncheon. Indeed he had done less than justice to the excellent food provided. He was acutely aware of being in an unfamiliar environment, to which he should have been hostile, but which as a matter of plain fact he enjoyed with trepidation. Unlike Jaikie he bristled with class-consciousness. Mrs Brisbane-Brown's kindly arrogance, the long-descended air of her possessions, the atmosphere of privilege so secure that it need not conceal itself – he was aware of it with a half-guilty joy. The consequence was that he was adrift from his moorings, and not well at ease. He had not spoken at table except in answer to questions, and he now stood in the drawing-room like a colt in a flower-garden, not very certain what to do with his legs.

The sight of the embarrassed Barbon revived him. Here was something he could understand, a problem in his own world. Craw might be a fool, but he belonged to his own totem, and this Barbon man (of his hostess's world) was clearly unfit to deal with the web in which his employer had entangled himself. He found his voice. He gave the company a succinct account of how Mr Craw had come to be in the Back House of the Garroch.

'That's all I have to tell. Now you take up the story. I want to hear everything that happened since Wednesday night, when Mr Craw did not come home.'

The voice was peremptory, and Mr Barbon raised his distinguished eyebrows. Even in his perplexity he felt bound to resent this tone.

'I'm afraid . . . I . . . I don't quite understand your position, Mr –'

'My name's Crombie. I'm on one of the Craw papers. My interest in straightening things out is the same as yours. So let's pool our knowledge and be quick about it. You began to get anxious about Mr Craw at half-past eight on Wednesday, and very anxious by ten. What did you do?'

'We communicated with Glasgow – with Mr Craw's architect. He had accompanied him to the station and seen him leave by the six-five train. We communicated with Kirkmichael station and learned that he arrived there. Then I informed the police – very confidentially of course.'

'The journalists got wind of that. They were bound to, since they sit like jackdaws on the steps of the telegraph office. So much for Wednesday. What about yesterday?'

'I had a very anxious day,' said Mr Barbon, passing a weary hand over his forehead and stroking back his thick grizzled hair. 'I hadn't a notion what to think or do. Mr Craw, you must understand, intended to go abroad. He was to have left this morning, catching the London express at Gledmouth. Miss Cazenove and I were to have accompanied him, and all arrangements had been made. It seemed to me that he might have chosen to expedite his departure, though such a thing was very unlike his usual custom. So I got the London office to make inquiries, and ascertained that he had not travelled south. You are aware of Mr Craw's dislike of publicity. I found myself in a very serious quandary. I had to find out what had become of him. Anything might have happened – an accident, an outrage. And I had to do this without giving any clue to those infernal reporters.'

'Practically impossible,' said Dougal. 'No wonder you were in a bit of a stew. I suppose they were round the house like bees yesterday.'

'Like wasps,' said Mr Barbon tragically. 'We kept them at arm's length, but they have defeated us.' He produced from his pocket and unfolded a copy of a journal. 'We have special arrangements at the Castle for an early delivery of newspapers, and this is to-day's *Live Wire*. Observe the headings.'

'I know all about that,' said Dougal. 'We ran across the *Wire* man – Tibbets they call him – and he was fair busting with his news. But this will only make the *Wire* crowd look foolish if they can't follow it up. That's what we've got to prevent. I took the liberty this morning of speaking to Tavish in Glasgow on the telephone, and authorizing him – I pretended I was speaking for Mr Craw – to announce that Mr Craw had left for the Continent. That will give us cover to work behind.'

'You might have spared yourself the trouble,' said Mr Barbon, unfolding another news-sheet. 'This is to-day's issue of the *View*. It contains that announcement. It was inserted by the London office. Now who authorized it?'

'I heard of that from Tavish. Could it have been Mr Craw?'

'It was not Mr Craw. That I can vouch for, unless he sent the authorization after half-past seven on Wednesday evening, which on your story is impossible. It was sent by some person or persons who contrived to impress the London office with their authority, and who wished to have it believed that Mr Craw was out of the country. For their own purpose. Now, what purpose?'

'I think I can make a guess,' said Dougal eagerly.

'There is no need of guess-work. It is a matter of certain and damning knowledge. Mr Craw left for Glasgow on Wednesday before his mail arrived. In that mail was a registered letter. It was marked "most confidential" and elaborately sealed. I deal with Mr Craw's correspondence, but letters marked in such a way I occasionally leave for him to open, so I did not touch that letter. Then, yesterday morning, at the height of my anxieties, I had a telephone message.'

Mr Barbon paused dramatically. 'It was not from London. It was from Knockraw House, a place some five miles from here. I knew that Knockraw had been let for the late autumn, but I had not heard the name of the tenant. It is the best grouse-moor in the neighbourhood. The speaker referred to a confidential letter which he said Mr Craw had received on the previous day, and he added that he and his friends proposed to call upon Mr Craw that afternoon at three o'clock. I said that Mr Craw was not at home, but the speaker assured me that Mr Craw would be at home to him. I did not dare say any more, but I asked for the name. It was given me as Casimir – only the one word. Then I think the speaker rang off.'

'I considered it my duty,' Mr Barbon continued, 'to open the confidential letter. When I read it, I realized that instead of being in the frying-pan we were in the middle of the fire. For that letter was written in the name of the inner circle of the –'

'Evallonian Republicans,' interjected Dougal, seeking a cheap triumph.

'It was not. It was the Evallonian Monarchists.'

'Good God!' Dougal was genuinely startled, for he saw suddenly a problem with the most dismal implications.

'They said that their plans were approaching maturity, and that they had come to consult with their chief well-wisher. There was an immense amount of high-flown compliment in it after the Evallonian fashion, but there was one thing clear. These people are in deadly earnest. They have taken Knockraw for the purpose, and they have had the assurance to announce to the world Mr Craw's absence abroad so that they may have him to themselves without interruption. They must have had private information about his movements, and his intention of leaving Scotland. I don't know much about Evallonian politics – they were a personal hobby of Mr Craw's – but I know enough to realize that the party who wish to upset the republic are pretty desperate fellows. It was not only the certain notoriety of the thing which alarmed me, though that was bad enough. Imagine the play that our rivals would make with the story of Mr Craw plotting with foreign adventurers to upset a Government with which Britain is in friendly relations! It was the effect upon Mr Craw himself. He hates anything to do with the rough-and-tumble of political life. He is quite unfit to deal with such people. He is a thinker and an inspirer – a seer in a watchtower, and such men lose their power if they go down into the arena.'

This was so manifestly an extract from the table-talk of Mr Craw that Dougal could not repress a grin.

'You laugh,' said Mr Barbon gloomily, 'but there is nothing to laugh at. The fortunes of a great man and a great Press are at this moment on a razor-edge.'

'Jaikie,' said Dougal in a whisper, 'Mr McCunn was a true prophet. He said we were maybe going to set up the Jacobite standard on Garroch side. There's a risk of another kind of Jacobite standard being set up on Callowa side. It's a colossal joke on the part of Providence.'

Mr Barbon continued his tale.

'I felt utterly helpless. I did not know where Mr Craw was. I had the threatening hordes of journalists to consider. I had those foreign desperadoes at the gates. They must not be allowed to approach Castle Gay. I had no fear that Casimir and his friends would take the journalists into their confidence, but I was terribly afraid that the journalists would get on to the trail of Casimir. An Eastern European house-party at Knockraw is a pretty obvious mark. . . . I gave orders that no one was to be admitted at either lodge. I went further and had the gates barricaded, in case there was an attempt to force them.'

'You lost your head there,' said Dougal. 'You were making the journalists a gift.'

'Perhaps I did. But when one thinks of Eastern Europe one thinks of violence. Look at this letter I received this morning. Note that it is addressed to me by my full name.'

The writer with great simplicity and in perfect English informed the Honourable Frederick Barbon, M.C., that it was quite futile to attempt to deny his friends entrance to Castle Gay, but that they had no wish to embarrass him. To-morrow at 11 a.m. they would wait upon Mr Craw, and if they were again refused they would take other means of securing an audience.

Dougal whistled. 'The writer of this knows all about the journalists. And he knows that Mr Craw is not at the Castle, but believes that you are hiding him somewhere. They've a pretty useful intelligence department.'

Mrs Brisbane-Brown, who had listened to Mr Barbon's recital with composure, now entered the conversation.

'You mustn't let your nerves get the upper hand of you, Freddy. Try to take things more calmly. I'm afraid that poor Mr Craw has himself to thank for his predicament. Why will newspaper owners meddle with things they don't understand? Politics should be left to those who make a profession of them. But we must do our best to help him. Mr Crombie,' she turned to Dougal, whose grim face was heavy with thought, 'you look capable. What do you propose?'

The fire of battle had kindled in Dougal's eyes, and Jaikie saw something which he remembered from the old days.

'I think,' he said, 'that we're in for a stiff campaign, and that it must be conducted on two fronts. We must find some way of heading off those Evallonians, and it won't be easy. When a foreigner gets a notion into his head he's apt to turn into a demented crusader. They're all the same – Socialists, Communists, Fascists, Republicans, Monarchists – I daresay Monarchists are the worst, for they've less inside their heads to begin with. . . . And we must do it without giving the journalists a hint of what is happening. We must suppress Tibbets by force, if necessary.'

'Perhaps the Evallonians will do that for you,' suggested Alison.

'Very likely they will. . . . The second front is wherever Mr Craw may be. At all costs he must be kept away from here. Now, he can't stay at the Back House of Garroch. The journalists will very soon be on to the Glasgow students, and they'll hear about the kidnapping, and they'll track him to the Back House. I needn't tell you that it's all up with us if any reporter gets sight of Mr Craw. I think he had better be smuggled out of the country as quickly as possible.'

Mr Barbon shook his head.

'Impossible!' he murmured. 'I've already thought of that plan and rejected it. The Evallonians will discover it and follow him, and they will find him in a foreign land without friends. I wonder if you understand that Mr Craw will be terrified at the thought of meeting them. Terrified! That is his nature. I think he would prefer to risk everything and come back here rather than fall into their hands in another country than his own. He has always been a little suspicious of foreigners.'

'Very well. He can't come back here, but he needn't go abroad. He must disappear. Now, how is that to be managed?'

'Jaikie,' he said, after a moment's reflection, 'this is your job. You'll have to take charge of the Craw front.'

Jaikie opened his eyes. He had not been attending very carefully, for the preoccupations of the others had allowed him to stare at Alison, and he had been wondering whether her hair should be called red or golden. For certain it had no connexion with Dougal's. ... Also, why a jumper and short tweed skirt made a girl look so much more feminine than flowing draperies.

'I don't quite understand,' he said.

'It's simple enough. We're going to have some difficult work on the home front, and the problem is hopeless if it's complicated by the presence of Mr Craw. One of us has to be in constant attendance on him, and keep him buried. ...'

'But where?'

'Anywhere you like, as long as you get him away from the Back House of the Garroch. He'll not object. He's not looking for any Evallonians. You've the whole of Scotland, and England too, to choose from. Pick your own hidy-hole. He'll not be difficult to hide, for few people know him by sight and he looks a commonplace little body. It's you or me – and better you than me, for you're easy tempered, and I doubt Mr Craw and I would quarrel the first day.'

Jaikie caught Alison's eyes and saw in them so keen a zest for a new, exciting adventure that his own interest kindled. He would have immensely preferred to be engaged on the home front, but he saw the force of Dougal's argument. He had a sudden vision of himself, tramping muddy roads in October rain, putting up at third-rate inns, eating bread and cheese in the heather – and by his side, a badly scared millionaire, a fugitive leader of the people. Jaikie rarely laughed aloud, but at the vision his face broke into a slow smile.

'I'll need a pair of boots,' he said, 'not for myself – for Mr Craw. The things he is wearing would be knocked to pieces in half a day.'

Mr Barbon, whose dejection had brightened at the sound of Dougal's crisp mandates, declared that the boots would be furnished. He suggested other necessaries, which Jaikie ultimately reduced to a toothbrush, a razor, spare shirts, and pyjamas. A servant from the Castle would deliver them a mile up the road.

'You'd better be off,' Dougal advised. 'He'll have been ranging round the Back House these four hours like a hyena, and if you don't hurry we'll have him arriving here on his two legs. . . . You'll have to give us an address for letters, for we must have some means of communication.'

'Let it be Post Office, Portaway,' said Jaikie; and added, in reply to the astonished stare of the other, 'Unless there's a reflector above, the best hiding-place is under the light.'

CHAPTER SEVEN

# BEGINNING OF A GREAT MAN'S EXILE



JAIKIE had not a pleasant journey that autumn afternoon over the ridge that separates Callowa from Garroch and up the latter stream to the dark hills of its source. To begin with, he was wheeling the bicycle which Dougal had ridden, for that compromising object must be restored as soon as possible to its owner; and, since this was no easy business on indifferent roads, he had to walk most of the way. Also, in addition to the pack on his back, he had Dougal's which contained the parcel duly handed over to him a mile up the road by a Castle Gay servant. ... But his chief discomfort was spiritual.

From his tenderest years he had been something of a philosopher. It was his quaint and placid reasonableness which had induced Dickson McCunn, when he took in hand the destinies of the Gorbals Diehards, to receive him into his own household. He had virtually adopted Jaikie, because he seemed more broken to domesticity than any of the others. The boy had speedily become at home in his new environment, and with effortless ease had accepted and adapted himself to the successive new worlds which opened to him. He had the gift of living for the moment where troubles were concerned and not anticipating them, but in pleasant things of letting his fancy fly happily ahead. So he accepted docilely his present task, since he was convinced of the reason for it; Dougal was right – he was the better person of the two to deal with Craw. ... But the other, imaginative side of him, was in revolt. That morning he had received an illumination. He had met the most delightful human being he had ever encountered. And now he was banished from her presence.

He was not greatly interested in Craw. Dougal was different; to Dougal Craw was a figure of mystery and power; there was romance in the midge controlling the fate of the elephant. To Jaikie he was only a dull, sententious, elderly gentleman, probably with a bad temper, and he was chained to him for an indefinite number of days. It sounded a bleak kind of holiday. . . . But at Castle Gay there were the Evallonians, and Mrs Brisbane-Brown, and an immense old house now in a state of siege, and Alison's bright eyes, and a stage set for preposterous adventures. The lucky Dougal was there in the front of it, while he was condemned to wander lonely in the wings.

But, as the increasing badness of the road made riding impossible, and walking gave him a better chance for reflection, the prospect slowly brightened. It had been a fortunate inspiration of his, the decision to keep Craw hidden in the near neighbourhood. It had been good sense, too, for the best place for concealment was the unexpected. He would not be too far from the main scene of conflict, and he might even have a chance of a share in it. . . . Gradually his interest began to wake in the task itself. After all he had the vital role. If a man-hunt was on foot, he had charge of the quarry. It was going to be a difficult business, and it might be exciting. He remembered the glow in Alison's eyes, and the way she had twined and untwined her fingers. They were playing in the same game, and if he succeeded it was her approval he would win. Craw was of no more interest to him than the ball in a Rugby match, but he was determined to score a try with him between the posts.

In this more cheerful mood he arrived at the Back House about the hour of seven, when the dark had fallen. Mrs Catterick met him with an anxious face and the high lilt of the voice which in her type is the consequence of anxiety.

'Ye're back? Blithe I am to see ye. And ye're your lane? Dougal's awa on anither job, says you? Eh, man, ye've been sair looked for. The body ben the hoose has been neither to haud nor to bind. He was a mile doun the road this mornin' in his pappymashy buits. He didna' tak' a bite o' dinner, and sin' syne he's been sittin' glunchin' or lookin' out o' the windy.' Then, in a lowered voice, 'For guid sake, Jaikie, do something, or he'll lose his reason.'

'It's all right, Mrs Catterick. I've come back to look after him. Can you put up with us for another night? We'll be off to-morrow morning.'

'Fine that. John'll no be hame or Monday. Ye'll hae your supper thegither? It's an ill job a jyler's. Erchie will whistle lang ere he sees me at it again.'

Jaikie did not at once seek Mr Craw's presence. He spread his map of the Canonry on the kitchen table and brooded over it. It was only when he knew from the clatter of dishes that the meal was ready in the best room that he sought that chamber.

He found the great man regarding distastefully a large dish of bacon and eggs and a monstrous brown teapot enveloped in a knitted cosy of purple and green. He had found John Catterick's razor too much for him, for he had not shaved that morning, his suit had acquired further whitewash from the walls of his bedroom, and his scanty hair was innocent of the brush. He had the air of one who had not slept well and had much on his mind.

The eyes which he turned on Jaikie had the petulance of a sulky child.

'So you've come at last,' he grumbled. 'Where is Mr Crombie? Have you brought a car?'

'I came on a bicycle. Dougal – Mr Crombie – is staying at Castle Gay.'

'What on earth do you mean? Did you deliver my letter to Mr Barbon?'

Jaikie nodded. He felt suddenly rather dashed in spirits. Mr Craw, untidy and unshaven and as cross as a bear, was not an attractive figure, least of all as a companion for an indefinite future.

'I had better tell you exactly what happened,' he said, and he recounted the incidents of the previous evening up to the meeting with Tibbets. 'So we decided that it would be wiser not to try to deliver the letter last night.'

Mr Craw's face showed extreme irritation, not unmingled with alarm.

'The insolence of it!' he declared. 'You say the *Wire* man has got the story of my disappearance, and has published it in to-day's issue? He knows nothing of the cause which brought me here?'

'Nothing. And he need never know, unless he tracks you to this place. The *Wire* stands a good chance of making a public goat of itself. Dougal telephoned your Glasgow office and your own papers published to-day the announcement that you had gone abroad.'

Mr Craw looked relieved. 'That was well done. As a matter of fact I had planned to go abroad to-day, though I did not intend to announce it. It has never been my habit to placard my movements like a court circular. . . . So far so good, Mr Galt. I shall travel south to-morrow night. But what possessed Barbon not to send the car at once? I must go back to Castle Gay before I leave, and the sooner the better. My reappearance will spike the guns of my journalistic enemies.'

'It would,' Jaikie assented. 'But there's another difficulty, Mr Craw. The announcement of your going abroad to-day was not sent to your papers first by Dougal. It was sent by very different people. The day before yesterday, when you were in Glasgow, these same people sent you a letter. Yesterday they telephoned to Mr Barbon, wanting to see you, and then he opened the letter. Here it is.' He presented the missive whose heavy seals Mr Barbon had already broken.

Mr Craw looked at the first page, and then subsided heavily into a chair. He fumbled feverishly for his glasses, and his shaking hand had much ado to fix them on his nose. As he read, his naturally ruddy complexion changed to a clayey white. He finished his reading, and sat staring before him with unseeing eyes, his fingers picking nervously at the sheets of notepaper. Jaikie, convinced that he was about to have a fit, and very much alarmed, poured him out a scalding cup of tea. He drank a mouthful, and spilled some over his waistcoat.

It was a full minute before he recovered a degree of self-possession, but self-possession only made him look more ghastly, for it revealed the perturbation of his mind.

'You have read this?' he stammered.

'No. But Mr Barbon told us the contents of it.'

'Us?' he almost screamed.

'Yes. We had a kind of conference on the situation this afternoon. At the Mains. There was Mr Barbon, and Miss

Westwater, and her aunt, and Dougal and myself. We made a sort of plan, and that's why I'm here.'

Mr Craw clutched at his dignity, but he could not grasp it. The voice which came from his lips was small, and plaintive, and childish, and, as Jaikie noted, it had lost its precise intonation and had returned to the broad vowels of Kilmaclavers.

'This is a dreadful business. ... You can't realize how dreadful. ... I can't meet these people. I can't be implicated in this affair. It would mean absolute ruin to my reputation. ... Even the fact of their being in this countryside is terribly compromising. Suppose my enemies got word of it! They would put the worst construction on it, and they would make the public believe it. ... As you are aware, I have taken a strong line about Evallonian politics – an honest line. I cannot recant my views without looking a fool. But if I do not recant my views, the presence of those infernal fools will make the world believe that I am actually dabbling in their conspiracies. I, who have kept myself aloof from the remotest semblance of political intrigue! Oh, it is too monstrous!'

'I don't think the *Wire* people will get hold of it very easily,' was Jaikie's attempt at comfort.

'Why not?' he snapped.

'Because the Evallonians will prevent it. They seem determined people, determined to have you to themselves. Otherwise they wouldn't have got your papers to announce that you had gone abroad.'

This was poor comfort to Mr Craw. He ejaculated 'Good God!' and fell into a painful meditation. It was not only his repute he was thinking of, but his personal safety. These men had come to coerce him, and their coercion would not stop at trifles. I do not know what picture presented itself to his vision, but it was probably something highly melodramatic (for he knew nothing at first hand of foreign peoples) – dark sinister men, incredibly cunning, with merciless faces and lethal weapons in every pocket. He groaned aloud. Then a thought struck him.

'You say they telephoned to Castle Gay,' he asked wildly. 'Where are they?'

'They are at Knockraw. They have taken the place for the autumn. Mr Barbon, as I told you, refused to let them in. They seemed to know about your absence from the Castle, but they believe that he can put his hand on you if he wants. So they are going there at eleven o'clock to-morrow morning, and they say they will take no denial.'

'At Knockraw!' It was the cry of a fugitive who learns that the avenger of blood is in the next room.

'Yes,' said Jaikie. 'We've got the Recording Angel established in our back garden on a strictly legal tenure. We must face that fact.'

Mr Craw seemed disinclined to face it. He sunk his face in his hands and miserably hunched his shoulders. Jaikie observed that the bacon and eggs were growing cold, but the natural annoyance of a hungry man was lost in pity for the dejected figure before him. Here was one who must have remarkable talents – business talents, at any rate, even if he were not much of a thinker or teacher. He was accustomed to make men do what he wanted. He had the gift of impressing millions of people with his strength and wisdom. He must often have taken decisions which required nerve and courage. He had inordinate riches, and to Jaikie, who had not a penny, the acquisition of great wealth seemed proof of a rare and mysterious power. Yet here was this great man, unshaven and unkempt, sunk in childish despair, because of a situation which to the spectator himself seemed simple and rather amusing.

Jaikie had a considerable stock of natural piety. He hated to see human nature, in which he profoundly believed, making a discreditable exhibition of itself. Above all he hated to see an old man – Mr Craw seemed to him very old, far older than Dickson McCunn – behaving badly. He could not bring himself to admit that age, which brought success, did not also bring wisdom. Moreover he was by nature kindly, and did not like to see a fellow-being in pain. So he applied himself to the duties of comforter.

'Cheer up, Mr Craw,' he said. 'This thing is not so bad as all that. There's at least three ways out of it.'

There was no answer, save for a slight straightening of the shoulders, so Jaikie continued:

'First, you can carry things with a high hand. Go back to Castle Gay and tell every spying journalist to go to blazes. Sit down in your own house and be master there. Your position won't suffer. If the *Wire* gets hold of the story of the students' rag, what does it matter? It will be forgotten in two days, when the next murder or divorce comes along. Besides, you behaved well in it. You kept your temper. It's not a thing to be ashamed of. The folk who'll look foolish will be Tibbets with his bogus mysteries, and the editor who printed his stuff. If I were you I'd put the whole story of your adventure in your own papers and make a good yarn of it. Then you'll have people laughing with you, not at you.'

Mr Craw was listening. Jaikie understood him to murmur something about Evallonians.

'As for the Evallonians,' he continued, 'I'd meet them. Ask the whole bally lot to luncheon or dinner. Tell them that Evallonia is not your native land, and that you'll take no part in her politics. Surely a man can have his views about a foreign country without being asked to get a gun and fight for it. If they turn nasty, tell them also to go to the devil. This is a free country, and a law-abiding country. There's the police in the last resort. And you could raise a defence force from Castle Gay itself that would make yon foreign bandits look silly. Never mind if the thing gets into the papers. You'll have behaved well, and you'll have reason to be proud of it.'

Jaikie spoke in a tone of extreme gentleness and moderation. He was most anxious to convince his hearer of the desirability of this course, for it would remove all his own troubles. He and Dougal would be able with a clear conscience to continue their walking tour, and every minute his distaste was increasing for the prospect of taking the road in Mr Craw's company.

But that moderation was an error in tactics. Had he spoken harshly, violently, presenting any other course as naked cowardice, it is possible that he might have struck an answering spark from Mr Craw's temper, and forced him to a declaration from which he could not have retreated. His equable reasonableness was his undoing. The man sitting hunched up in the chair considered the proposal, and his terrors, since they were not over-ridden by anger, presented it in repulsive colours to his reason.

'No,' he said, 'I can't do that. It is not possible. ... You do not understand. ... I am not an ordinary man. My position is unique. I have won an influence, which I hold in trust for great public causes. I dare not impair it by being mixed up in a farce or brawling.'

Jaikie recognized the decision as final. He also inferred from the characteristic stateliness of the words and the recovered refinement of the accent, that Mr Craw was beginning to be himself again.

'Very well,' he said briskly. 'The second way is that you go abroad as if nothing had happened. We can get a car to take you to Gledmouth, and Mr Barbon will bring on your baggage. Go anywhere you like abroad, and leave the Evallonians to beat on the door of an empty house. If their mission becomes known, it won't do you any harm, for you'll be able to prove an alibi.'

Mr Craw's consideration of this project was brief, and his rejection was passionate. Mr Barbon had been right in his forecast.

'No, no,' he cried, 'that is utterly and eternally impossible. On the Continent of Europe I should be at their mercy. They are organized in every capital. Their intelligence service would discover me – you admit yourself that they know a good deal about my affairs even in this country. I should have no protection, for I do not believe in the Continental police.'

'What are you afraid of?' Jaikie asked with a touch of irritation. 'Kidnapping?'

Mr Craw assented darkly. 'Some kind of violence,' he said.

'But,' Jaikie argued in a voice which he tried to keep pleasant, 'how would that serve their purpose? They don't need you as a hostage. They certainly don't want you as a leader of an armed revolution. They want the support of your papers, and the influence which they think you possess with the British Government. You're no use to them except functioning in London.'

It was a second mistake in tactics, for Jaikie's words implied some disparagement of Craw the man as contrasted with Craw the newspaper proprietor. There was indignation as well as fear in the reply.

'No. I will not go abroad at such a time. It would be insanity. It would be suicide. You must permit me to judge what is politic in such circumstances. I assure you I do not speak without reflection.'

'Very well,' said Jaikie, whose spirits had descended to his boots. 'You can't go back to Castle Gay. You won't go abroad. You must stay in this country and lie low till the Evallonians clear out.'

Mr Craw said nothing, but by his silence he signified an unwilling assent to this alternative.

'But when?' he asked drearily after a pause. 'When will the Evallonians give up their mission? Have we any security for their going within a reasonable time? You say that they have taken Knockraw for the season. They may stay till Christmas.'

'We've left a pretty effective gang behind us to speed their departure.'

'Who?'

'Well, there's Mrs Brisbane-Brown. I wouldn't like to be opposed to yon woman.'

'The tenant of the Mains. I scarcely know her.'

'No, she said that when she met you you looked at her as if she were Lady Godiva. Then there's her niece, Miss Westwater.'

'The child I have seen riding in the park? What can she do?'

Jaikie smiled. 'She might do a lot. And there's your staff at the Castle, Mr Barbon and the rest. And most important of all, there's Dougal.'

Mr Craw brightened perceptibly at the last name. Dougal was his own henchman, an active member of the great Craw brotherhood. From him he could look for loyal and presumably competent service. Jaikie saw the change in expression, and improved the occasion.

'You don't know Dougal as I know him. He's the most determined fellow on earth. He'll stick at nothing. I'll wager he'll shift the Evallonians, if he has to take smoke bombs and poison gas. ... Isn't it about time that we had supper? I'm famished with hunger.'

The bacon and eggs had to be sent back to be heated up, and Mrs Catterick had to make a fresh brew of tea. Under the cheering influence of the thought of Dougal Mr Craw made quite a respectable meal. A cigar would have assisted his comfort, but he had long ago emptied his case, and he was compelled to accept one of Jaikie's cheap Virginian cigarettes. His face remained a little clouded, and he frequently corrugated his brows in thought, but the black despair of half an hour ago had left him.

When the remains of the supper had been cleared away he asked to see Jaikie's map, which for some time he studied intently.

'I must reach the railway as soon as possible,' he said. 'On the other side from Castle Gay, of course. I must try to walk to some place where I can hire a conveyance.'

'Where did you think of going?' Jaikie asked.

'London,' was the reply. 'I can find privacy in the suite in my office.'

'Have you considered that that will be watched? These Evallonians, as we know, are careful people who mean business, and they seem to have a pretty useful intelligence system. You will be besieged in your office just as badly as if you were at Castle Gay. And with far more publicity.'

Mr Craw pondered ruefully. 'You think so? Perhaps you are right. What about a quiet hotel?'

Jaikie shook his head. 'No good. They will find you out. And if you go to Glasgow or Edinburgh or Manchester or Bournemouth it will be the same. It doesn't do to underrate the cleverness of the enemy. If Mr Craw goes anywhere in these islands as Mr Craw some hint of it will get out, and they'll be on to it like a knife.'

Despair was creeping back into the other's face. 'Have you any other course to suggest?' he faltered.

'I propose that you and I go where you're not expected, and that's just in the Canonry. The Evallonians will look for you in Castle Gay and everywhere else except in its immediate neighbourhood. It's darkest under the light, you see. Nobody knows you by sight, and you and I can take a quiet saunter through the Canonry without anybody being the wiser, while Dougal finishes the job at the Castle.'

Mr Craw's face was a blank, and Jaikie hastened to complete his sketch.

'We'll be on a walking tour, the same as Dougal and I proposed, but we'll get out of the hills. An empty countryside like this is too conspicuous. ... I know the place, and I'll guarantee to keep you well hidden. I've brought Dougal's pack for you. In it there's a suit of pyjamas and a razor and some shirts and things which I got from Mr Barbon ...'

Mr Craw cried out like one in pain.

'... and a pair of strong boots,' Jaikie concluded soothingly. 'I'm glad I remembered that. The boots you have on would be in ribbons the first day on these stony roads.'

It was Jaikie's third error in tactics. Mr Craw had experienced various emotions, including terror, that evening, and now he was filled with horrified disgust. He had created himself a padded and cosseted life; he had scaled an eminence of high importance; he had made his daily existence a ritual every item of which satisfied his self-esteem. And now this outrageous young man proposed that he should scrap it all and descend to the pit out of which thirty years ago he had climbed. Even for safety the price was far too high. Better the perils of high politics, where at least he would remain a figure of consequence. He actually shivered with revulsion, and his anger gave him a momentary air of dignity and power.

'I never,' he said slowly, 'never in my life listened to anything so preposterous. You suggest that I – *I* – should join you in wandering like a tramp through muddy Scottish parishes and sleeping in mean inns! ... To-morrow I shall go to London. And meantime I am going to bed.'

## CHAPTER EIGHT

# CASIMIR

MISS ALISON WESTWATER rose early on the following morning, and made her way on foot through the now unbarricaded lodge-gates to the Castle. The fateful meeting with the Evallonians, to which she had not been bidden, was at eleven, and before that hour she had much to do.

She was admitted by Bannister. 'I don't want to see Mr Barbon,' she said. 'I want to talk to you.' Bannister, in his morning undress, bowed gravely, and led her into the little room on the left side of the hall where her father used to keep his boots and fishing-rods.

Bannister was not the conventional butler. He was not portly, or sleek or pompous, or soft-voiced, though he was certainly soft-footed. He was tall and lean, with a stoop which, so far from being servile, was almost condescending. He spoke the most correct English, and was wont to spend his holidays at a good hotel in this or that watering-place, where his well-cut clothes, his quiet air, his wide knowledge of the world, and his somewhat elaborate manners caused him to be taken in the smoking-room for a member of the Diplomatic Service. He had begun life in a famous training-stable at Newmarket, but had been compelled to relinquish the career of a jockey at the age of eighteen owing to the rate at which he grew. Thereafter he had passed through various domestic posts, always in the best houses, till the age of forty-seven found him butler to that respected but ineffective statesman, the Marquis of Oronsay. At the lamented death of his patron he had passed to Mr Craw, who believed that a man who had managed four different houses for an irascible master with signal success would suit his own more modest requirements. He was right in his judgement. Bannister was a born organizer, and would have made an excellent Quartermaster-General. The household at Castle Gay moved on oiled castors, and Mr Craw's comfort and dignity and his jealous retirement suffered no jar in Bannister's hands. Mr Barbon might direct the strategy, but it was the butler who saw to the tactics.

The part suited him exactly, for Bannister was accustomed to generous establishments – *ubi multa supersunt* – and he loved mystery. It was meat and drink to him to be the guardian of a secret, and a master who had to be zealously shielded from the public eye was the master he loved to serve. He had acquired the taste originally from much reading of sensational fiction, and it had been fostered by the circumstances of his life. He had been an entranced repository of many secrets. He knew why the Duke of Mull had not received the Garter; why the engagement between Sir John Rampole and the Chicago heiress was broken off – a tale for which many an American paper would have gladly paid ten thousand dollars; almost alone he could have given a full account of the scandals of the Braddisdale marriage; he could have explained the true reason for the retirement from the service of the State of one distinguished Ambassador, and the inexplicable breakdown in Parliament of a rising Under-Secretary. His recollections, if divulged, might have made him the humble Greville of his age. But they were never divulged – and never would be. Bannister was confidential, because he enjoyed keeping a secret more than other men enjoy telling one. It gave him a sense of mystery and power.

There was only one thing wanting to his satisfaction. He had a profound – and, as he would have readily admitted, an illogical – liking for the aristocracy. He wished that his master had accepted a peerage, like other Press magnates; in his eyes a new title was better than none at all. For ancient families with chequered pasts he had a romantic reverence. He had studied in the county histories the story of the house of Rhynns, and it fulfilled his most exacting demands. It pleased him to dwell in a mansion consecrated by so many misdeeds. He wished that he could meet Lord Rhynns in the flesh. He respected the household at the Mains as the one link between himself and the older nobility. Mrs Brisbane-Brown was his notion of what a middle-aged gentlewoman should be; and he had admired from afar Alison galloping in the park. She was like the Ladies Ermyntrude and Gwendolen of whom he had read long ago, and whom he still cherished as an ideal, in spite of a lifetime of disillusionment. There was a fount of poetry welling somewhere in Bannister's breast.

'I've come to talk to you, Bannister,' the girl began, 'about the mess we're in. It concerns us all, for as long as Mr Craw lives in Castle Gay we're bound to help him. As you are aware, he has disappeared. But, as you may have heard, we have a rough notion of where he is. Well, we've got to straighten out things here while he is absent. Hold the fort, you know.'

The butler bowed gravely.

'First, there's the foreigners, who are coming here at eleven.'

'If I might hazard a suggestion,' Bannister interrupted. 'Are you certain, Miss, that these foreigners are what they claim to be?'

'What do you mean?'

'Is it not possible that they are a gang of international crooks who call themselves Evallonians, knowing Mr Craw's interest in that country, and wish to effect an entry into the castle for sinister purposes?'

'But they have taken Knockraw shooting.'

'It might be a blind.'

The girl considered. 'No,' she said emphatically. 'That is impossible. You've been reading too many detective stories, Bannister. It would be imbecility for a gang of crooks to take the line they have. It would be giving themselves away hopelessly. ... These people are all right. They represent the Evallonian Monarchist party, which may be silly but is quite respectable. Mr Barbon knows all about them. One is Count Casimir Muresco. Another is Prince Odalisque, or some name like that. And there's a Professor Something or other, who Mr Crombie says has a European reputation for something. No doubt about it. They're tremendous swells, and we've got to treat them as such. That's one of the things I came to speak to you about. We're not going to produce Mr Craw, which is what they want, but, till we see our way clear, we must snow them under with hospitality. If they are sportsmen, as they pretend to be, they must have the run of the Callowa and if Knockraw is not enough for them we must put the Castle moors at their disposal. Oh, and the Blae Moss. They're sure to want to shoot snipe. The grouse is only found in Britain, but there must be plenty of snipe in Evallonia. You know that they're all coming to dine here to-night?'

'So Mr Barbon informed me.'

'Well, it must be a Belshazzar. That's a family word of ours for a regular banquet. You must get the chef to put his best foot forward. Tell him he's feeding Princes and Ministers and he'll produce something surprising. I don't suppose he knows any special Evallonian dishes, so the menu had better have a touch of Scotland. They'll appreciate local colour. We ought to have a haggis as one of the entrées, and grouse, of course, and Mackillop must dig a salmon out of the Callowa. I saw a great brute jumping in the Dirt Pot. ... Plenty of flowers, too. I don't know what your cellar is like?'

'I can vouch for it, Miss. Shall the footmen wear their gala liveries? Mr Craw made a point of their possessing them.'

'Certainly. ... We have to make an impression, you see. We can't produce Mr Craw, but we must impress them with our importance, so that they will take what we tell them as if it came from Mr Craw. Do you see what I mean? We want them to go away as soon as possible, but to go away satisfied and comfortable, so that they won't come back again.'

'What will be the party at dinner?'

'The three Evallonians – the Count, and the Prince, and the Herr Professor. You can get the names right from Mr Barbon. Mr Barbon and Mr Crombie, of course, who are staying in the house. My aunt and Mr Charvill and myself. It's overweighted with men, but we can't help that.'

'May I ask one question, Miss? Mr Crombie, now. He is not quite what I have been accustomed to. He is a very peremptory gentleman. He has taken it upon himself to give me orders.'

'Obey them, Bannister, obey them on your life. Mr Crombie is one of Mr Craw's trusted lieutenants. You may consider him the leader of our side. ... That brings me to the second thing I wanted to say to you. What about the journalists?'

'We have had a visit from three already this morning.' There was the flicker of a smile on the butler's face. 'I made a point of interviewing them myself.' He draw three cards from a waistcoat pocket, and exhibited them. They bore the names of three celebrated newspapers, but the *Wire* was not among them. 'They asked to see Mr Craw, and according to my instructions I informed them that Mr Craw had gone abroad. They appeared to accept my statement, but showed a desire to engage me in conversation. All three exhibited money, which I presume they intended as a bribe. That, of course, led to their summary dismissal.'

'That's all right,' the girl declared, 'that's plain sailing. But I don't like Tibbets keeping away. Mr Crombie says that he's by far the most dangerous. Look here, Bannister, this is your very particular job. You must see that none of these reporters gets into the Castle and that nobody from the Castle gossips with them. If they once get on the trail of the Evallonians we're done. The lodge-keeper has orders not to admit anybody who looks like a journalist. I'll get hold of Mackillop and tell him to clear out anybody found in the policies. He can pretend they're poachers. I wonder what on earth Tibbets is up to at this moment?'

Dougal could have provided part of the answer to that question. The night before, when it was settled that he should take up his quarters in the Castle, he had wired to his Glasgow lodgings to have his dress clothes sent on by train. That morning he had been to Portaway station to collect them, in a car hired from the Westwater Arms, and in a Portaway street he had run across Tibbets. The journalist's face did not show, as he had hoped, embarrassment and disappointment. On the contrary the light of victorious battle was in his eye.

'I thought you were off for good,' was his greeting, to which Dougal replied with a story of the breakdown of his bicycle and his compulsory severance from his friend. 'I doubt I'll have to give up this exhibition,' Dougal said. 'How are you getting on yourself? I read your thing in the *Wire* last night.'

'Did you see the Craw papers? They announced that Craw had gone abroad. It was heaven's own luck that they only got that out the same day as my story, and now it's bloody war between us, for our credit is at stake. I wired to my chief, and I've just got his reply. What do you think it is? Craw never left the country. Places were booked for him in the boat train yesterday in the name of his man Barbon, but he never used them. Our information is certain. That means that Craw's papers are lying. Lying to cover something, and what that something is I'm going to find out before I'm a day older. I'm waiting here for another telegram, and then I'll go up the Callowa to comfort Barbon.'

Dougal made an inconspicuous exit from the station, after satisfying himself that Tibbets was not about. He left his suit-case at the Starr Inn, with word that it would be sent for later, for he did not wish to publish his connexion with the Castle any sooner than was needful. He entered the park by the gate in the wall which he opened with Alison's key, and had immediately to present his credentials – a chit signed by Barbon – to a minion of Mackillop's, the head keeper, who was lurking in a covert. He was admitted to the house by Bannister at ten minutes to eleven, five minutes after Alison had left on her quest of Mackillop and a Callowa salmon.

The party from Knockraw was punctual. Mr Barbon and Dougal received them in the library, a vast apartment on the first floor, lit by six narrow windows and commanding a view of the terrace and the windings of the river. The seventh Lord Rhynns had been a collector, and from the latticed shelves looked down an imposing array of eighteenth-century quartos and folios. Various pieces of classical sculpture occupied black marble pedestals, and a small, richly carved sarcophagus, of a stone which looked like old ivory, had a place of honour under the great Flemish tapestry, which adorned the only wall free of books. The gilt baroque clock on the mantelpiece had not finished chiming when Bannister ushered in the visitors.

They bowed from their hips at the door, and they bowed again when they were within a yard of Barbon. One of the three spoke. He was a tall thin man with a white face, deep-set brown eyes, and short curly brown hair. Except for his nose he would have been theatrically handsome, but his nose was a pronounced snub. Yet this imperfection gave to his face a vigour and an attractiveness which more regular features might have lacked. He looked amazingly competent and vital. His companions were a slim, older man with greying hair, and a burly fellow with spectacles and a black beard. All three were ceremoniously garbed in morning coats and white linen and dark ties. Dougal wondered if they had motored from Knockraw in top hats.

'Permit me to make the necessary introductions,' said the spokesman. 'I am your correspondent, Count Casimir Muresco. This is Prince Odalchini, and this is Herr Doctor Jagon of the University of Melina. We are the chosen and accredited representatives of the Nationalist Party of Evallonia.'

Barbon had dressed himself carefully for the occasion, and his flawless grey suit made a painful contrast to Dougal's ill-fitting knickerbockers. He looked more than ever like an actor who had just taken his cue in a romantic Victorian comedy.

'My name is Barbon,' he said, 'Frederick Barbon. As you are no doubt aware, I am Mr Craw's principal confidential secretary.'

'You are the second son of Lord Clonkilty, is it not so?' said the Prince. 'You I have seen once before – at Monte Carlo.'

Barbon bowed. 'I am honoured by your recollection. This is Mr Crombie, one of Mr Craw's chief assistants in the management of his newspapers.'

The three strangers bowed, and Dougal managed to incline his stiff neck.

'You wish to see Mr Craw. Mr Craw unfortunately is not at home. But in his absence my colleague and I are here to do what we can for you.'

'You do not know where Mr Craw is?' inquired Count Casimir sharply.

'Not at this moment,' replied Barbon truthfully. 'Mr Craw is in the habit of going off occasionally on private business.'

'That is a misfortune, but it is temporary. Mr Craw will no doubt return soon. We are in no hurry, for we are at present residents in your beautiful country. You are in Mr Craw's confidence, and therefore we will speak to you as we would speak to him.'

Barbon motioned them to a table, where were five chairs, and ink, pens, and blotting paper set out as for a board meeting. He and Dougal took their seats on one side, and the three Evallonians on the other.

'I will be brief,' said Count Casimir. 'The movement for the restoration of our country to its ancient rights approaches fruition. I have here the details, which I freely offer to you for your study. The day is not yet fixed, but when the word is given the people of Evallonia as one man will rise on behalf of their Prince. The present misgovernors of our land have no popular following, and no credit except among international Jews.'

Mr Barbon averted his eyes from the maps and papers which the other pushed towards him.

'That is what they call a Putsch, isn't it?' he said. 'They haven't been very successful, you know.'

'It is no foolish thing like a Putsch,' Count Casimir replied emphatically. 'You may call it a *coup d'état*, a bloodless *coup d'état*. We have waited till our cause is so strong in Evallonia that there need be no violence. The hated republic will tumble down at a touch like a rotten branch. We shall take the strictest precautions against regrettable incidents. It will be the sudden uprising of a nation, a thing as irresistible as the tides of the sea.'

'You may be right,' said Barbon. 'Obviously we cannot argue the point with you. But what we want to know is why you come to us. Mr Craw has nothing to do with Evallonia's domestic affairs.'

'Alas!' said Prince Odalchini, 'our affairs are no longer domestic. The republic is the creation of the Powers, the circumscription of our territories is the work of the Powers, the detested League of Nations watches us like an elderly and spectacled governess. We shall succeed in our revolution, but we cannot maintain our success unless we can assure ourselves of the neutrality of Europe. That is why we come to Britain. We ask her – how do you say it? – to keep the ring.'

'To Britain, perhaps,' said Barbon. 'But why to Mr Craw?'

Count Casimir laughed. 'You are too modest, my friend. It is the English habit, we know, to reverence historic forms even when the power has gone elsewhere. But we have studied your politics very carefully. The Herr Professor has studied them profoundly. We know that in these days with your universal suffrage the fount of authority is not in King or Cabinet, or even in your Parliament. It lies with the whole mass of your people, and who are their leaders? Not your statesmen, for you have lost your taste for oratory, and no longer attend meetings. It is your newspapers that rule you. What your man in the street reads in his newspaper he believes, What he believes he will make your Parliament believe, and what your Parliament orders your Cabinet must do. Is it not so?'

Mr Barbon smiled wearily at this startling version of constitutional practice.

'I think you rather exaggerate the power of the printed word,' he said.

Count Casimir waved the objection aside.

'We come to Mr Craw,' he went on. 'We say, "You love Evallonia. You have said it often. You have ten – twenty millions of readers who follow you blindly. You will say to them that Evallonia must be free to choose her own form of government, for that is democracy. You will say that this follows from your British principles of policy and from that Puritan religion in which Britain believes. You will preach it to them like a good priest, and you will tell them that it will be a very great sin if they do not permit to others the freedom which they themselves enjoy. The Prime Minister will wake up one morning and find that he has what you call a popular mandate, which if he does not obey he will cease to be Prime Minister. Then, when the day comes for Evallonia to declare herself, he will speak kind words about Evallonia to France and Italy, and he will tell the League of Nations to go to the devil." '

'That's all very well,' Barbon protested. 'But I don't see how putting Prince John on the throne will help you to get back your lost territories.'

'It will be the first step. When we have once again a beloved King, Europe will say, "Beyond doubt Evallonia is a great and happy nation. She is too good and happy a nation to be so small." '

'We speak in the name of democracy,' said the Professor in a booming voice. He spoke at some length, and developed an intricate argument to show the true meaning of the word 'self-determination'. He dealt largely with history; he had much to say of unity of culture as opposed to uniformity of race; he touched upon Fascism, Bolshevism, and what he called 'Americanism'; he made many subtle distinctions, and he concluded with a definition of modern democracy, of which he said the finest flower would be an Evallonia reconstituted according to the ideas of himself and his friends.

Dougal had so far maintained silence, and had studied the faces of the visitors. All three were patently honest. Casimir was the practical man, the schemer, the Cavour of the party. The Prince might be the prophet, the Mazzini – there was a mild and immovable fanaticism in his pale eyes. The Professor was the scholar, who supplied the ammunition of theory. The man had written a famous book on the British Constitution and had a European reputation; but this was Dougal's pet subject, and he suddenly hurled himself into the fray.

It would have been well if he had refrained. For half an hour three bored and mystified auditors were treated to a harangue on the fundamentals of politics, in which Dougal's dialectical zeal led him into so many overstatements that to the scandalized Barbon he seemed to be talking sheer anarchism. Happily to the other two, and possibly to the Professor, he was not very intelligible. For just as in the excitement of debate the Professor lost hold of his careful English and relapsed into Evallonian idioms, so Dougal returned to his ancestral language of Glasgow.

The striking of a single note by the baroque clock gave Count Casimir a chance of breaking off the interview. He gathered up his papers.

'We have opened our case,' he said graciously. 'We will come again to expand it, and meantime you will meditate. . . .

We dine with you to-night at eight o'clock. There will be ladies present? So?'

'One word, Count,' said Barbon. 'We're infernally plagued with journalists. There's a by-election going on now in the neighbourhood, and they all want to get hold of Mr Craw. I needn't tell you that it would be fatal to your case if they got on to your trail – and very annoying to us.'

'Have no fear,' was the answer. 'The official tenant of Knockraw is Mr Williams, a Liverpool merchant. To the world we are three of Mr Williams's business associates who are enjoying his hospitality. All day we shoot at the grouse like sportsmen. In the evening our own servants wait upon us, so there are no eavesdroppers.'

Mr Craw had entertained but little in Castle Gay, but that night his representatives made up for his remissness. The party from the Mains arrived to find the hall blazing with lights, Bannister with the manner of a Court Chamberlain, and the footmen in the sober splendour of their gala liveries. In the great drawing-room, which had scarcely been used in Alison's recollection, Barbon and Dougal were holding in play three voluble gentlemen with velvet collars to their dress-coats and odd bits of ribbon in their buttonholes. Their presentation to the ladies reminded Alison of the Oath of the Tennis Court or some other high and disposed piece of history, and she with difficulty preserved her gravity. Presently in the dining-room, which was a remnant of the old keep and vaulted like a dungeon, they sat down to a meal which the chef was ever afterwards to refer to as his masterpiece.

The scene was so bright with flowers and silver, so benignly backgrounded by the mellow Westwater portraits, that it cast a spell over the company and made everyone content – except Dougal. The Evallonians did not once refer to their mission. They might have been a party of county neighbours, except that their talk was of topics not commonly discussed by Canonry sportsmen. The Prince spoke to Mrs Brisbane-Brown of her own relations, for he had been a secretary of legation in London and had hunted several seasons with the Cottesmore. The Professor oraculated on letters, with an elephantine deference to his hearers' opinions, withdrawing graciously his first judgement that Shakespeare was conspicuously inferior to Mr Bernard Shaw when he saw Mrs Brisbane-Brown's scandalized face. Count Casimir endeavoured to propitiate Dougal, and learned from him many things about the Scottish race which are not printed in the books. All three, even the Professor, understood the art of social intercourse, and the critical Alison had to admit to herself that they did it well. It appeared that the Prince was a keen fisherman, and Count Casimir an ardent snipe shot, and the offer of the Callowa and the Blae Moss was enthusiastically received.

Dougal alone found the evening a failure. He felt that they were wasting time. Again and again he tried to lead the talk to the position of the Press in Britain, in the hope that Mrs Brisbane-Brown, with whom the strangers were obviously impressed, would enlighten them as to its fundamental unimportance. But Mrs Brisbane-Brown refused his lead. Indeed she did the very opposite, for he heard her say to the Professor: 'We have new masters in Britain to-day. Britain still tolerates her aristocracy as a harmless and rather ornamental pet, but if it tried to scratch it would be sent to the stables. Our new masters don't do it badly either. When my brother lived here this was a shabby old country house, but Mr Craw has made it a palace.'

'It is the old passion for romance,' the Professor replied. 'The sense of power is generally accompanied by a taste for grandeur. *Ubi magnitudo ibi splendor*. That, I believe, is St Augustine.'

Late that night, in the smoking-room at Knockraw, there was a consultation. 'Things go well,' said Casimir. 'We have prepared the way, and the Craw *entourage* will not be hostile. I do not like the red-haired youth. He is of the fanatic student type, and his talk is flatulence. Him I regard as an enemy. But Barbon is too colourless and timid to oppose us, and we have won favour, I think, with the high-nosed old woman and the pretty girl. They, as representatives of an ancient house, have doubtless much weight with Craw, who is of the lesser bourgeoisie. With them in view, I think it may be well to play our trump card now. His Royal Highness arrives to-day in London, and is graciously holding himself at our disposal.'

'That thought was in my own mind,' said Prince Odalchini, and the Professor concurred.

At the same hour Dougal at Castle Gay was holding forth to Barbon. 'Things couldn't be worse,' he said. 'The dinner was a big mistake. All that magnificence only increases their belief in Craw's power. We've got to disillusion them. I can't do it, for I can see fine that they think me a Bolshevik. You can't do it, for they believe that you would do anything for a quiet life, and they discount your evidence accordingly. What we want is some real, representative, practical man who would come down like a sledge hammer on their notions – somebody they would be compelled to believe – somebody that they could not help admitting as typical of the British nation.'

'I agree. But where are we going to find him without giving Mr Craw away?'

'There's one man,' said Dougal slowly. 'His name's McCunn – Dickson McCunn – and he lives about fifty miles from here. He was a big businessman in Glasgow – but he's retired now. I never met his equal for whinstone common sense. You've only to look at him to see that what he thinks about forty million others think also. He is the incarnate British spirit. He's a fine man, too, and you could trust him with any secret.'

'How old?' Barbon asked.

'A few years older than Craw. Not unlike him in appearance. The morn's Sunday and there's no train where he lives. What about sending a car with a letter from me and bringing him back, if he'll come? I believe he'd do the trick.'

Barbon, who was ready to seek any port in a storm, and was already in the grip of Dougal's fierce vitality, wearily agreed. The pleasantness of the dinner had for a little banished his anxieties, but these had now returned and he foresaw a sleepless night. His thoughts turned naturally to his errant master.

'I wonder where Mr Craw is at this moment?' he said.

'I wonder, too. But if he's with Jaikie I bet he's seeing life.'

CHAPTER NINE

# THE FIRST DAY OF THE HEJIRA – THE INN AT WATERMEETING

THE October dawn filled the cup of the Garroch with a pale pure light. There had been no frost in the night, but the heather of the bogs, the hill turf, and the gravel of the road had lost their colour under a drench of dew. The mountains were capped with mist, and the air smelt raw and chilly. Jaikie, who, foreseeing a difficult day, had prepared for it by a swim in the loch and a solid breakfast, found it only tonic. Not so Mr Craw, who, as he stood before the cottage, shivered, and buttoned up the collar of his raincoat.

Mrs Catterick scornfully refused payment. 'Is it likely?' she cried. 'Ye didna come here o' your ain wull. A body doesna tak siller for bein' a jyler.'

'I will see that you are compensated in some other way,' Mr Craw said pompously.

He had insisted on wearing his neat boots, which his hostess had described as 'pappymashy', and refused those which Jaikie had brought from Castle Gay. Also he made no offer to assume Dougal's pack, with the consequence that Jaikie added it to his own, and presented the appearance of Christian at the Wicket-gate in some old woodcut from the *Pilgrim's Progress*. Mr Craw even endued his hands with a pair of bright wash-leather gloves, and with his smart Homburg hat and silver-knobbed malacca looked exactly like a modish elderly gentleman about to take a morning stroll at a fashionable health-resort. So incongruous a figure did he present in that wild trough of the hills, that Mrs Catterick cut short her farewells and politely hid her laughter indoors.

Thus fantastically began the great Hejira.

Mr Craw was in a bad temper, and such a mood was new to him, for in his life small berufflements had been so rare that his ordinary manner was a composed geniality. Therefore, besides being cross, he was puzzled, and a little ashamed. He told himself that he was being scandalously treated by Fate, and for the first half-mile hugged his miseries like a sulky child. ... Then he remembered that officially he had never admitted the existence of Fate. In how many eloquent articles had he told his readers that man was the maker of his own fortunes, the captain of his soul? He had preached an optimism secure against the bludgeonings of Chance! This would never do. He cast about to find an attitude which he could justify.

He found it in his intention to go straight to London. There was vigour and decision in that act. He was taking up arms against his sea of troubles. As resolutely as he could he shut out the thought of what might happen when he got to London – further Evallonian solicitations with a horrid chance of publicity. London was at any rate familiar ground, unlike this bleak, sodden wilderness. He had never hated anything so much as that moorland cottage where for two days and three nights he had kept weary vigil. Still more did he loathe the present prospect of sour bent, gaping haggs, and mist low on the naked hills.

'How far is it to the nearest railway station?' he asked the burdened figure at his side.

'It's about twelve miles to Glendonan,' Jaikie answered.

'Do you know anything about the trains?'

'It's a branch line, but there's sure to be an afternoon train to Gledmouth. The night mail stops there about eleven, I think.'

Twelve miles! Mr Craw felt some sinking of the heart, which was succeeded by a sudden consciousness of manhood. He was doing a bold thing, the kind of thing he had always admired. He had not walked twelve miles since he was a boy, but he would force himself to finish the course, however painful it might be. The sight of the laden Jaikie woke a momentary compunction, but he dared not cumber himself with the second pack. After all he was an elderly man and must husband his strength. He would find some way of making it up to Jaikie.

The road, after leaving the Back House of the Garroch, crossed a low pass between the Caldorn and a spur of the great Muneraw, and then, after threading a patch of bog, began to descend to the upper glen of a burn which joined a tributary of the distant Gled. Mr Craw's modish boots had been tolerable on the fine sand and gravel of the first mile. They had become very wet in the tract of the bog, where the heather grew thick in the middle of the road, and long pools of inky water filled the ruts. But as the path began its descent they became an abomination. The surface was cut by frequent rivulets which had brought down in spate large shoals of gravel. Sometimes it was deep, fine scree, sometimes a rockery of sharp-pointed stones. The soles of his boots, thin at the best and now as sodden as a sponge, were no protection against the unyielding granite. His feet were as painful as if he were going barefoot, and his ankles ached with constant slips and twists.

He was getting warm, too. The morning chill had gone out of the air, and, though the sky was still cloudy, there was a faint glow from the hidden sun. Mr Craw began by taking off his gloves. Then he removed his raincoat and carried it on his arm. It kept slipping and he trod on its tail, the while he minced delicately to avoid the sharper stones.

The glen opened and revealed a wide shallow valley down which flowed one of the main affluents of the Gled. The distances were hazy, but there was a glimpse of stubble fields and fir plantations, proof that they were within view of the edge of the moorlands. Mr Craw, who for some time had been walking slowly and in evident pain, sat down on the parapet of a little bridge and lifted his feet from the tormenting ground.

'How many miles more?' he asked, and when told 'Seven', he groaned.

Jaikie unbuckled his packs.

'It's nonsense your wearing these idiotic things,' he said firmly. 'In another hour you'll have lamed yourself for a week.' From Dougal's pack he extracted a pair of stout country boots and from his own a pair of woollen socks. 'If you don't put these on, I'll have to carry you to Glendonan.'

Mr Craw accepted the articles with relief. He bathed his inflamed and aching feet in the burn, and encased them in Jaikie's homespun. When he stood up he regarded his new accoutrements with disfavour. Shooting boots did not harmonize with his neat blue trousers, and he had a pride in a natty appearance. 'I can change back at the station,' he observed, and for the first time that day he stepped out with a certain freedom.

His increased comfort made him magnanimous.

'You had better give me the second pack,' he volunteered.

'I can manage all right,' was Jaikie's answer. 'It's still a long road to Glendonan.'

Presently, as the track dipped to the levels by the stream side, the surface improved, and Mr Craw, relieved of his painful bodily preoccupation and no longer compelled to hop from stone to stone, returned to forecasting the future. To-morrow morning he would be in London. He would go straight to the office, and, the day being Sunday, would have a little time to think things out. Bamff, his manager, was in America. He could not summon Barbon, who had his hands full at Castle Gay. Allins – Allins was on holiday – believed to be in Spain – he might conceivably get hold of Allins. There were others, too, who could assist him – his solicitor, Mr Merkins, of Merkins, Thrawn & Merkins – he had no secrets from him. And Lord Wassall, whom he had recently brought on to the board of the *View* – Wassall was a resourceful fellow, and deeply in his debt.

He was slipping into a better humour. It had been a preposterous adventure – something to laugh over in the future – *meminisse juvabit* – how did the tag go? – he had used it only the other day in one of his articles. . . . He felt rather hungry – no doubt the moorland air. He ought to be able to get a decent dinner in Gledmouth. What about his berth on the sleeping-car? It was the time of the year when a good many people were returning from Scotland. Perhaps he had better wire about it from Glendonan. . . . And then a thought struck him, which brought him to a halt and set him feeling for his pocket-book.

It was Mr Craw's provident habit always to carry in his pocket-book a sum of one hundred pounds in twenty-pound notes as an assurance against accidents. He opened the pocket-book with anxiety, and the notes were not there.

He remembered only too well what had happened. The morning he had gone to Glasgow he had emptied the contents of his pocket-book on his dressing-table in order to find the card with his architect's address. He had not restored the notes, because they made the book too bulky, and he had proposed to get instead two fifty-pound notes from Barbon, who kept the household's petty cash. He had forgotten to do this, and now he had nothing on his person but the loose change left from his Glasgow journey. It lay in his hand, and amounted to twelve shillings, a sixpence, two threepenny bits, and four pennies.

To a man who for the better part of a lifetime has taken money for granted and has never had to give a thought to its importance in the conduct of life, a sudden shortage comes as a horrid surprise. He finds it an outrage alike against decency and dignity. He is flung neck and crop into a world which he does not comprehend, and his dismay is hysterical.

'I have no money,' he stammered, ignoring the petty coins in his palm.

Jaikie slid the packs to the ground.

'But you offered Dougal and me twenty pounds to go to Castle Gay,' he protested.

Mr Craw explained his misadventure. Jaikie extracted from an inner pocket a skimpy leather purse, while the other watched his movements with the eyes of a hungry dog who believes that there is provender going. He assessed its contents.

'I have two pounds, thirteen and ninepence,' he announced. 'I didn't bring much, for you don't spend money in the hills, and I knew that Dougal had plenty.'

'That's no earthly use to me,' Mr Craw wailed.

'I don't know. It will buy you a third-class ticket to London and leave something over for our meals to-day. You're welcome to it.'

'But what will you do?'

'I'll go back to Mrs Catterick, and then I'll find Dougal. I can wire for some more. I'm pretty hard up just now, but there's a few pounds left in my allowance. You see, *you* can't get any more till you get to London.'

Mr Craw's breast was a maelstrom of confused emotions. He was not without the quality which in Scotland is called 'mense', and he was reluctant to take advantage of Jaikie's offer and leave that unfortunate penniless. Moreover, the thought of travelling third-class by night roused his liveliest disgust. Fear, too – for he would be mixed up in the crowd, without protection against the enemies who now beset his path. He shrank like a timid spinster from rough contacts. Almost to be preferred was this howling wilderness to the chances of such sordid travel.

'There's another way,' said the helpful Jaikie. He wanted to get rid of his companion, but he was aware that it was his duty, if possible, to detain that companion at his side, and to detain him in the Canonry. The conclave at the Mains had instructed him to keep Mr Craw hidden, and he had no belief in London as a place of concealment. So, 'against interest', as the lawyers say, he propounded an alternative.

'We could stay hereabouts for a couple of days, and I could borrow a bicycle and slip over to Castle Gay and get some money.'

Mr Craw's face cleared a little. He was certain now that the moors of the Canonry were better than a third-class in the London train. He brooded a little and then announced that he favoured the plan.

'Good,' said Jaikie. 'Well, we needn't go near Glendonan. We'd better strike south and sleep the night at Watermeeting. It's a lonely place, but there's quite a decent little inn, and it's on the road to Gledmouth. To-morrow I'll try to raise a bicycle and get over to Castle Gay, and with luck you may be in London on Monday morning. We needn't hurry, for it's not above ten miles to Watermeeting, and it doesn't matter when we turn up.'

'I insist on carrying one of the packs,' said Mr Craw, and,

his future having cleared a little, and being conscious of better behaviour, he stepped out with a certain alacrity and ease.

Presently they left the road, which descended into the Gled valley, and took a right-hand turning which zigzagged up the containing ridge and came out on a wide benty moor, once the best black-game country in Scotland, which formed the glacis of the chief range of the hills. A little after midday they lunched beside a spring, and Mr Craw was moved to commend Mrs Catterick's scones, which at breakfast he had despised. He accepted one of Jaikie's cigarettes. There was even a little conversation. Jaikie pointed out the main summits among a multitude which had now become ominously blue and clear, and Mr Craw was pleased to show a certain interest in the prospect of the Muneraw, the other side of which, he said, could be seen from the upper windows of Castle Gay. He became almost confidential. Landscape, he said, he loved, but with a temperate affection; his major interest was reserved for humanity. 'In these hills there must be some remarkable people. The shepherds for instance –'

'There's some queer folk in the hills,' said Jaikie. 'And I doubt there's going to be some queer weather before this day is out. The wind's gone to the south-west, and I don't like the way the mist is coming down on the Black Dod.'

He was right in his forecast. About two o'clock there came a sudden sharpness into the air, the hills were blotted out in vapour, and a fine rain descended. The wind rose; the drizzle became a blast, and then a deluge, the slanting, drenching downfall of October. Jaikie's tattered burberry and Mr Craw's smart raincoat were soon black with rain, which soaked the legs of their trousers and trickled behind their upturned collars. To the one this was a common experience, but to the other it was a revelation, for he had not been exposed to weather for many a year. He thought darkly of rheumatism, and twinges he had suffered from two years ago and had gone to Aix to cure. He might get pneumonia – it was a common complaint nowadays – several of his acquaintances had fluffed out like a candle with it – healthy people, too, as healthy as himself. He shivered, and thought he felt a tightness in his chest. 'Can we not shelter?' he asked, casting a woeful eye round the wet periphery of moor.

'It'll last the day,' said Jaikie. 'We'd better step out, and get under cover as soon as we can. There's no house till Watermeeting.'

The thought of Watermeeting did not console Mr Craw. A wetting was bad enough, but at the end of it there was no comforting hot bath and warm dry clothes, and the choice between bed and a deep armchair by a fire. They would have to pig it in a moorland inn, where the food would certainly be execrable, and the bed probably damp, and he had no change of raiment. Once again Mr Craw's mind became almost hysterical. He saw sickness, possibly death, in the near future. His teeth were chattering, and, yes – he was certain he had a pain in his side.

Something loomed up in the haze, and he saw that it was a man with, in front of him, a bedraggled flock of sheep. He was a loutish fellow, much bent in the shoulders, with leggings, which lacked most of the buttons, over his disreputable breeks. By his side padded a big ruffianly collie, and he led by a string a miserable-looking terrier, at which the collie now and then snapped viciously.

The man did not turn as they came abreast. He had a bag slung on his shoulders by a string, from which protruded the nose of a bottle and the sodden end of a newspaper. The peak of his cap hid the upper part of his face; the lower part was composed of an unshaven chin, a gap-toothed mouth, and a ferrety nose.

'Ill weather,' said Jaikie.

'Hellish,' was the answer. A sharp eye stole a sidelong glance and took in Mr Craw's prosperous but water-logged garments. The terrier sniffed wistfully at Jaikie's leg. Jaikie looked like the kind of person who might do something for him.

'Hae ye a smoke?' the drover asked. Jaikie reluctantly parted with a cigarette, which the other lit by making a shelter of his cap against the wind. The terrier, in order to avoid the collie, wove its string round his legs and received a savage kick.

'Where are you bound for?' Jaikie asked.

'Near by. I've brocht thae sheep frae Cumnock way.' Then, as an overflow of water from the creases of his cap reached his unwashed neck, he broke into profanity about the weather, concluding with a malediction on the unhappy terrier, who showed signs of again entangling his lead. The dog seemed to be a cross between wire-haired and Sealyham, a wretched little fellow with a coat as thick as a sheep's, a thin piebald face, whiskers streaked backwards by the wet, and a scared eye. The drover brought his stick down hard on its hind quarters, and as it jumped howling away from him the collie snapped at its head. It was a bad day for the terrier.

'That's a nice little beast,' said Jaikie.

'No bad. Pure-bred Solomon. He's yours if ye'll pay my price.'

'I've no use for a dog. Where did you get him?'

'A freend bred him. I'm askin' a couple o' quid. I brocht him along wi' me to sell. What about the other yin o' ye? He'd be the better o' a dug.'

Mr Craw did not look as if such an acquisition would ease his discomfort. He was glancing nervously at the collie which had turned on him an old-fashioned eye. Jaikie quickened his pace, and began to circumvent the sheep.

'Haud on,' said the drover. 'I turn up the next road. Gie's your crack till the turn.'

But Jaikie had had enough of him, and the last they heard was the whining of the terrier, who had again been maltreated.

'Is that one of the hill shepherds?' Mr Craw asked.

'Hill shepherd! He's some auction-ring tout from Glasgow. Didn't you recognize the tongue? I'm sorry for that little dog. He stole it, of course. I hope he sells it before he kills it.'

The high crown of the moorland now began to fall away into a valley which seemed to be a tributary to the Gled. The two were conscious that they were descending, but they had no prospect beyond a yard or two of dripping roadside heather. Already the burns were rising, and tawny rivulets threaded the road, all moving in the direction they were going. Jaikie set a round pace, for he wanted to save his companion from a chill, and Mr Craw did his best to keep up with it. Sometimes he stopped, put his hand to his side, and gasped – he was looking for the pain which was the precursor of pneumonia. Soon he grew warm, and his breath came short, and there had to be frequent halts to relieve his distress. In this condition of physical wretchedness and the blackest mental gloom Mr Craw became aware of a roaring of flooded waters and a bridge which spanned a porter-coloured torrent. The sight of that wintry stream combined with the driving rain and the enveloping mist to send a chill almost of terror to Mr Craw's heart. He was terribly sundered from the warm kindly world which he knew. Even so, from an icy shore, might some lost Arctic explorer have regarded the approach of the Polar night.

'That's the Gryne burn,' said Jaikie reverentially. 'It's coming down heavy. It joins the Water of Stark out there in the haugh. The inn's not a hundred yards on.'

Presently they reached a low building, a little withdrawn from the road, on which a half-obliterated sign announced that one Thomas Johnston was licensed to sell ale and tobacco. Jaikie's memory was of a sunny place visited once in a hot August noon, when he had drunk ginger beer on the settle by the door, and amid the sleepy clucking of hens and the bleating of sheep had watched the waters of Gryne and Stark beginning their allied journeys to the lowlands. Now, as it came into view through the veils of rain, it looked a shabby place, the roughcast of the walls blotched and peeling, the unthatched stacks of bog-hay sagging drunkenly, and a disconsolate up-ended cart with a broken shaft blocking one of the windows. But at any rate here was shelter, and the smell of peat reek promised a fire.

In the stone-flagged kitchen a woman was sitting beside a table engaged in darning socks – a thin-faced woman with spectacles. The kitchen was warm and comfortable, and since she had been baking earlier in the day, there was an agreeable odour of food. On the big old-fashioned hearth a bank of peats glowed dully, and sent out fine blue spirals.

The woman looked them over very carefully in response to Jaikie's question.

'Bide the nicht? I'm sure I dinna ken. My man's lyin' – he rickit his back bringin' hame the peats, and the doctor winna let him up afore the morn. It's a sair business lookin' after him, and the lassie's awa' hame for her sister's marriage. Ye'll no be wantin' muckle?'

'That's a bad job for you,' said Jaikie sympathetically. 'We won't be much trouble. We'd like to get dry, and we want some food, and a bed to sleep in. We're on a walking tour and we'll take the road again first thing in the morning.'

'I could maybe manage that. There's just the one room, for the ceilings doun in the ither, and we canna get the masons out from Gledmouth to set it right. But there's twa beds in it. . . .'

Then spoke Mr Craw, who had stripped off his raiment and flung it from him, and had edged his way to the warmth of the peats.

'We must have a private room, madam. I presume you have a private sitting-room. Have a fire lit in it as soon as possible.'

'Ye're unco partic'lar,' was the answer. 'What hinders ye to sit in the kitchen? There's the best room, of course, but there hasna been a fire in the grate since last New Year's Day, and I doot the stirlins have been biggin' in the lum.'

'The first thing,' said Jaikie firmly, 'is to get dry. It's too early to go to bed. If you'll show us our room we'll get these wet things off. I can manage fine in pyjamas, but my friend here is not so young as me, and he would be the better of something warmer. You couldn't lend him a pair of breeks, mistress? And maybe an old coat?'

Jaikie, when he chose to wheedle, was hard to resist, and the woman regarded him with favour. She also regarded Mr Craw appraisingly. 'He's just about the size o' my man. I daresay I could find him some old things o' Tam's. . . . Ye'd better tak off your buits here and I'll show ye your bedroom.'

In their wet stocking-soles the travellers followed their hostess up an uncarpeted staircase to a long low room, where were two beds and two wash-stands and little else. The rain drummed on the roof, and the place smelt as damp as a sea-cave. She brought a pail of hot water from the kitchen kettle, and two large rough towels. 'I'll be gettin' your tea ready,' she said. 'Bring doun your wet claithes, and I'll hang them in the kitchen.'

Jaikie stripped to the skin and towelled himself violently, but Mr Craw hung back. He was not accustomed to baring his body before strangers. Slowly and warily he divested himself of what had once been a trim blue suit, the shirt which was now a limp rag, the elegant silk underclothing. Then he stood irresolute and shamefaced, while Jaikie rummaged in the packs and announced gleefully that their contents were quite dry. Jaikie turned to find his companion shivering in the blast from the small window which he had opened.

'Tuts, man, this will never do,' he cried. 'You'll get your death of cold. Rub yourself with the towel. Hard, man! You want to get back your circulation.'

But Mr Craw's efforts were so feeble that Jaikie took the matter in hand. He pummelled and slapped and scrubbed the somewhat obese nudity of his companion, as if he had been grooming a horse. He poured out a share of the hot water from the pail, and made him plunge his head into it.

In the midst of these operations the door was half opened and a bundle of clothes was flung into the room. 'That's the best I can dae for ye,' said the voice of the hostess.

Jaikie invested Mr Craw with a wonderful suit of pale blue silk pyjamas, and over them a pair of Mr Johnston's trousers of well-polished pepper-and-salt homespun, and an ancient black tailed coat which may once have been its owner's garb for Sabbaths and funerals. A strange figure the great man presented as he stumbled down the stairs, for on his feet were silk socks and a pair of soft Russia leather slippers – provided from Castle Gay – while the rest of him was like an elderly tradesman who has relinquished collar and tie in the seclusion of the home. But at any rate he was warm again, and he felt no more premonitions of pneumonia.

Mrs Johnston met them at the foot of the stairs and indicated a door. 'That's the best room. I've kinnled a fire, but I doot it's no drawin' weel wi' thae stirlins.'

They found themselves in a small room in which for a

moment they could see nothing because of the volume of smoke pouring from the newly-lit fire of sticks and peat. The starlings had been malignly active in the chimney. Presently through the haze might be discerned walls yellow with damp, on which hung a number of framed photographs, a mantelpiece adorned with china mugs and a clock out of action, several horsehair-covered chairs, a small, very hard sofa, and a round table decorated with two photograph albums, a book of views of Gledmouth, a workbox, and a blue-glass paraffin lamp.

Jaikie laboured with the poker at the chimney, but the obstruction was beyond him. Blear-eyed and coughing, he turned to find Mr Craw struggling with a hermetically-sealed window.

'We can't stay here,' he spluttered. 'This room's uninhabitable till the chimney's swept. Let's get back to the kitchen. Tea should be ready by now.'

Mrs Johnston had spread a clean cloth on the kitchen table, and ham and eggs were sizzling on the fire. She smiled grimly when she saw them.

'I thocht ye would be smoored in the best room,' she said. 'Thae stirlins are a perfect torment. ... Ay, ye can bide here and welcome. I aye think the kitchen's the nicest bit in the hoose. ... There's a feck of folk on the road the day, for there's bin anither man here wantin' lodgings! I telled him we were fou' up, and that he could mak a bed on the hay in the stable. I didna like the look o' him, but a keeper o' a public daurna refuse a body a meal. He'll hae to get his tea wi' you.'

Presently she planted a vast brown teapot on the table, and dished up the ham and eggs. Then, announcing that she must see her husband, she left the kitchen.

Jaikie fell like a famished man on the viands, and Mr Craw, to his own amazement, followed suit. He had always been a small and fastidious eater, liking only very special kinds of food, and his chef had often a difficult task in tempting his capricious appetite. It was years since he had felt really hungry, and he never looked forward to the hour of dinner with the gusto of less fortunate mortals. But the hard walking in the rain, and the rough towelling in the bedroom, had awakened some forgotten instinct. How unlike the crisp shavings of bacon and the snowy puff-balls of eggs to which he was accustomed was this dish swimming in grease! Yet it tasted far better than anything he had eaten for ages. So did the thick oatcakes and the new scones and the butter and the skim-milk cheese, and the strong tea sent a glow through his body. He had thought that he could tolerate nothing but the best China tea and little of that, and here he was drinking the coarsest Indian brew. ... He felt a sense of physical well-being to which he had long been a stranger. This was almost comfort.

The door opened and there entered the man they had met driving sheep. He had taken off his leggings, and his wet trouser ends flapped over his grimy boots. Otherwise he had made no toilet, except to remove his cap from his head and the bag from his shoulder. His lank black hair straggled over his eyes, and the eyes themselves were unpleasant. There must have been something left in the bottle whose nose had protruded from the bag.

He dropped into a chair and dragged it screamingly after him along the kitchen floor till he was within a yard of the table. Then he recognized the others.

'Ye're here,' he observed. 'Whit was a' your hurry? Gie's a cup o' tea. I'm no wantin' nae meat.'

He was obviously rather drunk. Jaikie handed him a cup of tea, which, having dropped in four lumps of sugar, he drank noisily from the saucer. It steadied him, and he spread a scone thick with butter and jelly and began to wolf it. Mr Craw regarded him with extreme distaste and a little nervousness.

'Whit about the Solomon terrier?' he asked. 'For twa quid he's yours.'

The question was addressed to Mr Craw, who answered coldly that he was not buying dogs.

'Ay, but ye'll buy this dug.'

'Where is it?' Jaikie asked.

'In the stable wi' the ither yin. Toff doesna like the wee dug, so I've tied them up in separate stalls, or he'd hae it chowed up.'

The rest of the meal was given up to efforts on the part of the drover to effect a sale. His price came down to fifteen shillings and a glass of whisky. Questioned by Jaikie as to its pedigree, he embarked on a rambling tale, patently a lie, of a friend who bred Solomons and had presented him with this specimen in payment of a bet. Talk made the drover thirsty. He refused a second cup of tea and shouted for the hostess, and when Mrs Johnston appeared he ordered a bottle of Bass.

Jaikie, remembering the plans for the morrow, asked if there was such as a thing as a bicycle about the place, and was told that her man possessed one. She saw no objection to his borrowing it for half a day. Jaikie had found favour in her eyes.

The drover drank his beer morosely and called for another bottle. Mrs Johnston glanced anxiously at Jaikie as she fulfilled the order, but Jaikie gave no sign. Now beer on the top of whisky is bad for the constitution, especially if little food has accompanied it, and soon the drover began to show that his case was no exception. His silence gave place to a violent garrulity. Thrusting his face close to the scandalized Mr Craw, he announced that that gentleman was gorily well going to buy the Solomon – that he had accepted the offer and that he would be sanguinarily glad to see the immediate colour of his money.

Mr Craw withdrew his chair, and the other lurched to his feet and came after him. The profanity of the drover, delivered in a hoarse roar, brought Mrs Johnston back in alarm. The seller's case was far from clear, but it seemed to be his argument that Mr Craw had taken delivery of a pup and was refusing payment. He was working himself into a fury at what he declared to be a case of strongly qualified bilk.

'Can ye dae naething wi' him?' the hostess wailed to Jaikie.

'I think we've had enough of him,' was the answer. Then he lifted up his voice. 'Hold on, man. Let's see the dog. We've never had a proper look at it.'

But the drover was past caring about the details of the bargain. He was pursuing Mr Craw, who, he alleged, was in possession of monies rightly due to him, and Mr Craw was retreating from the fire to the vacant part of the floor where Jaikie stood.

Then suddenly came violent happenings. 'Open the door, mistress,' cried Jaikie. The drover turned furiously towards the voice, and found himself grabbed from behind and his arms forced back. He was a biggish fellow and managed to shake himself free. There was a vicious look in his eye, and he clutched the bread-knife from the table. Now, Mrs Johnston's rolling-pin lay on the dresser, and with this Jaikie hit him smartly on the wrist, causing the knife to clatter to the floor. The next second Jaikie's head had butted his antagonist in the wind, and, as he stumbled forward gasping, Jaikie twisted his right arm behind his back and held it in a cruel lock. The man had still an arm loose with which he tried to clutch Jaikie's hair, and, to his own amazement, Mr Craw found himself gripping this arm, and endeavouring to imitate Jaikie's tactics, the while he hammered with his knee at the drover's hind-quarters. The propulsion of the two had its effect. The drover shot out of the kitchen into the rain, and the door was locked by Mrs Johnston behind him.

'He'll come back,' Mr Craw quavered, repenting of his temerity.

'Not him,' said Jaikie, as he tried to smooth his hair. 'I know the breed. I know the very Glasgow close he comes out of. There's no fight in that scum. But I'm anxious about the little dog.'

The kitchen was tidied up, and the two sat for a while by the peats. Then Mr Craw professed a desire for bed. Exercise and the recent excitement had made him weary; also he was still nervous about the drover and had a longing for sanctuary. By retiring to bed he would be retiring into the keep of the fortress.

Jaikie escorted him upstairs, helped him to get out of Mr Johnston's trousers, borrowed an extra blanket from the hostess, and an earthenware hot bottle which she called a 'pig', and saw him tucked up comfortably. Then Jaikie disappeared with the lamp, leaving him in solitude and darkness.

Mr Craw for a little experienced the first glimmerings of peace which he had known since that fateful hour at Kirkmichael when his Hejira began. He felt restful and secure, and as his body grew warm and relaxed he had even a moment of complacence. ... He had, unsolicited, helped to eject a ruffian from the inn kitchen. He had laid violent hands upon an enemy. The thing was so novel in his experience that the memory of it sent a curious, pleasant little shiver through his frame. He had shown himself ready in a crisis, instant in action. The thinker had proved himself also the doer. He dwelt happily with the thought. ... Strange waters surrounded him, but so far his head was above the waves. Might there not be a purpose in it all, a high purpose? All great teachers of mankind had had to endure some sojourn in the wilderness. He thought of Mahomet and Buddha, Galileo in prison, Spinoza grinding spectacles. Sometimes he had wondered if his life were not too placid for a man with a mission. These mishaps – temporary, of course – might prove a stepping-stone from which to rise to yet higher things.

Then he remembered the face of the drover as he had last seen him, distorted and malevolent. He had incurred the enmity of a desperate man. Would not his violence be terribly repaid? Even now, as the drunkenness died in him, his enemy would be planning his revenge. To-morrow – what of to-morrow? Mr Craw shuddered, and, as the bedroom door opened and a ray of candle-light ran across the ceiling, he almost cried aloud.

It was only Jaikie, who carried in his arms a small dog. Its thick fleece, once white, was matted in dry mud, and the finer hair of its face and legs, streaked down with wet, gave these parts of it so preposterous an air of leanness, that it looked like a dilapidated toy dog which had lost its wheels. But it appeared to be content. It curled itself at the foot of Jaikie's bed, and, before beginning its own toilet, licked his hand.

'I've bought that fellow's dog,' Jaikie announced. 'It must have been stolen, but it has come through a lot of hands. I beat him down to four shillings.'

'Were you not afraid?' gasped Mr Craw.

'He's practically sober now,' Jaikie went on. 'You see, he barged into the cart beside the door and got a crack on the head that steadied him. There was nothing to be afraid of except his brute of a collie.'

As Jaikie wriggled into bed he leaned forward and patted the head of his purchase. 'I'm going to call him Woolworth,' he said, 'for he's as woolly as a sheep, and he didn't cost much.'

CHAPTER TEN

# THE SECOND DAY OF THE HEJIRA – THE FORD CAR

THE storm blew itself out in the night, and the travellers awoke to a morning of soft lights and clear, rain-washed distances. They awoke also to the peahen call of their hostess at the foot of the stairs.

'Megsty me!' ran the plaint. 'D'ye ken what has happened? The body in the stable is off or I was up, and he's never paid for his supper. ... Waur nor that!' (the voice rose to a keen). 'He's ta'en yae pair o' the breeks that was dryin' afore the fire. The best pair! The blue yins!'

These last words drew Mr Craw precipitately from his bed. He thrust a scared head out of the bedroom door.

'What do you say, woman? My trousers!'

'Aye. Your trousers! Sorrow and disgrace yon blagyird has brocht on this hoose! Whae wad keep a public? But we'll set the pollis on him. As soon as my man's up, he'll yoke the gig an' get the pollis.'

Jaikie added his voice to the clamour.

'I'll be down in a jiffy, mistress, and I'll go after him on your man's bicycle.'

'Ye daurna. He'll kill ye. He's a desperate blagyird.'

'Give me my flannel bags,' said Jaikie, 'and I'll be on the road in ten minutes. He can't be many miles ahead.'

But when the two descended to the kitchen – Mr Craw chastely habited in the trousers of Mr Johnston – they were met by a wild-eyed hostess and an apple-cheeked servant girl.

'Waur and waur!' wailed the former. 'The scoundrel has stole Tam's bicycle, and he didna tak the Glendonan road, but the road to Gledmouth, and that's maistly doun hill. This lassie was bicyclin' back frae her mither's, and at the foot o' the Kirklaw brae she seen something by the roadside. She seen it was a bicycle, and it was a' bashed to bits. The body maun hae run into the brig.'

'How far off?' Jaikie asked.

'The better pairt o' fower miles. Na, ye'll no make up on him. Yon's a soupple blagyird, and he'll be hidin' in a Gledmouth close long or ye gat near him. Wae's me for Tam's guid new bicycle that cost ten pund last Martinmas.'

'Is it much damaged?' Jaikie asked the girl.

'Dung a' to smithers,' was the answer. 'The front wheel's the shape o' a peesweep's egg, and the handle-bars are like a coo's horn.'

'Heard ye ever the like?' Mrs Johnston lamented. 'And the pollis will never get him, and if he did he wad gang to jyle, but he couldna pay the price o' the bicycle. It's an unco blow, for Tam has nae siller to spare.'

It is to Mr Craw's credit that he did not think only of the bearing of this disaster on his own affairs.

'I am very sorry for the misfortune,' he told his hostess. 'At the moment I am travelling light and have little money. But I am not without means, and I will see that you receive the sum of ten pounds within a week.'

He was met by a solemn stare. Certainly with his borrowed trousers, much stained collar, and draggled tie (for Jaikie had forgotten to bring from Castle Gay these minor adornments), he did not look like a moneyed man. 'Thenk ye, kindly,' she said, but it was obvious that she put no trust in his promise.

Breakfast was an uncomfortable meal, hurriedly served, for Mrs Johnston was busy upstairs, preparing for the emergence of her husband from his sick room. Beside Jaikie sat Woolworth, his new purchase, very hungry, but not yet certain how far he dared to presume. He pirouetted about on his lengthy hind legs, and then slapped Jaikie's arm with an urgent paw. Jaikie prepared for him a substantial meal of scraps, which was devoured in a twinkling. 'I wonder when the beast last saw food,' he observed.

Then he borrowed an old dishcloth and a piece of soap, and retired with Woolworth to the pump. When Mr Craw joined them the terrier, shivering violently, and with a face of woe, had been thoroughly scrubbed, and now was having his thick fleece combed with a gap-toothed instrument which Jaikie had discovered in the stable. Followed a drastic dressing down with a broken brush, while Jaikie made the same hissing sounds that had accompanied his towelling of Mr Craw the previous evening. Jaikie said no word of plans at breakfast. He seemed to be waiting for his companion to make the first comment on a shattering miscarriage.

'I cannot go to London in these clothes,' said Mr Craw, looking down at the well-worn grey breeks.

Jaikie's eyes left Woolworth and regarded him critically. He was certainly a different figure from the spruce gentleman who, twenty-four hours ago, had left the Back House of the Garroch. He was not aggressively disreputable, but the combination of trousers, blue jacket, and dirty collar made him look like a jobbing carpenter, or a motor mechanic from some provincial garage. The discordant element in the picture was his face, which belied his garb, for it was the face of a man accustomed to deference, mildly arrogant, complacent for all the trouble in his eyes. Such a face never belonged to a mechanic. Jaikie, puzzled to find a name for the apparition, decided that Mr Craw had become like the man who spoke on Sunday in Hyde Park, a politician from the pavement. He remembered a Communist orator in Glasgow who had something of the same air.

'I can't get to Castle Gay without a bicycle, and be back in time,' was all he said.

'That means postponing still further my journey to London,' said Mr Craw. The curious thing was that he did not say it dolefully. Something had changed him this morning. His tone was resigned, almost philosophic. A sound sleep after a day of hard exercise had given him a novel sense of physical well-being. He had just eaten, with a heavy appetite, a very plain breakfast, at which his chef would have shuddered. The tonic air of the upland morning put vigour into his blood. He was accustomed to start his day with a hot bath, and to emerge from warm rooms with his senses a little dulled. This morning he had had no bath of any kind, yet he felt cleaner than usual, and his eyes and nostrils and ears seemed to be uncommonly awake. He had good long-distance sight, so he discarded his spectacles, which, for the moment were useless, and observed with interest the links of the two flooded streams with some stray cocks of moorland hay bobbing on their current. ... There were golden plover whistling on the hill behind the inn; he heard them with a certain delight in the fitness of their wild call to that desert. ... He sniffed the odour of wet heather and flood water and peat reek – and something else, homely and pleasant, which recalled very distant memories. That was, of course, the smell of cows; he had forgotten that cows smelt so agreeably.

'Have you anything to propose?' he asked in a tone which was quite amiable.

Jaikie looked up sharply, and saw that in his companion's face which he had not seen before, and scarcely expected.

'I doubt there's nothing for it but to make our way round the butt-end of the hills towards Portaway. That will bring us near Castle Gay, and I'll find a chance to see Dougal and Barbon and get some money. ... It's at least twenty-seven miles to Portaway, but we needn't get there to-night. I know most of the herds, and we can easily find a place to stop at when we get tired. It's a grand day for the hills.'

'Very well,' said Mr Craw, and his tone was rather of contentment than of resignation.

They paid their modest bill, and put a luncheon of scones and cheese in their packs, one of which Mr Craw insisted on shouldering. He reiterated his promise to pay for the bicycle, and Mrs Johnston, assured of his good will if not of his means, shook his hand. The voice of the convalescent husband cut short their leave-takings, and their last recollection of the place was a confused noise within caused by that husband, with many appeals to his Maker, beginning a cautious descent of the stairs.

Almost at once they left the Gledmouth highway and turned up a green loaning, an old drove-road which zigzagged along the face of a heather hill. Woolworth at first trotted docilely at Jaikie's heels, but soon, lured by various luscious scents, he took to investigating the environs. There was not a cloud in the sky, and the firmament was the palest blue, infinitely clear, with a quality of light which made the lowlands to the south and east seem like some background in an Italian primitive. There was little sound but the scrunch of their boots on the patches of scree, and a great crying of birds, but from very far away came an echo of bells, ringing to kirk in some distant clachan. Except for an occasional summons to Woolworth Jaikie spoke no word, for he was not much given to speech.

Mr Craw, too, was silent. He was thinking his own thoughts. He was thinking about Death, an odd subject for a shining morning. At the back of his mind he had a great fear of death, against which the consolations were void of that robust philosophy which he had preached in public. His fear took a curious shape. He had made for himself a rich environment of money and houses and servants and prestige. So long as he lived he was on a pinnacle above the crowd, secure from all common ills. But when he died he would be no more than a tramp in a ditch. He would be carried out naked from his cosy shelter to lie in the cold earth, and his soul – he believed in the soul – would go shivering into the infinite spaces. Mr Craw had often rebuked himself for thinking in such materialistic terms of the ultimate mystery, but whatever his reason might say his fancy kept painting the same picture. Stripped cold and bare! The terror of it haunted him, and sometimes he would lay awake at night and grapple with it. . . . He felt that men who led a hard life, the poor man with famine at his threshold, the sailor on the sea, the soldier in the trench, must think of death with more complacency. They had less to lose, there was less to strip from them before the chilly journeying. . . . Sometimes he had wished that he could be like them. If he could only endure discomfort and want for a little – only feel that the gap was narrower between his cosseted life and the cold clay and the outer winds! . . . Now he had a feeling that he was bridging the gap. He was exposed to weather like any tinker, he was enduring fatigue and cold and occasional hunger, and he was almost enjoying it. To this indoor man the outdoor world was revealing itself as something strange and wild and yet with an odd kindness at the heart of it. Dimly there was a revelation at work, not only of Nature but of his own soul.

Jaikie's voice woke him out of his dreams. He had halted, and was pointing to a bird high up in the sky.

'There's a buzzard,' he cried. 'Listen. You're a great writer, Mr Craw, but I think that most writers go wrong about birds. How would you describe that sound?'

'Mewing,' was the answer.

'Right. People talk about a buzzard screaming, but it mews like a sick cat. ... I've heard a kestrel scream, but not a buzzard. Listen to that, too. That's a raven.'

A bird was coasting along the hill-side, with its mate higher up on a bank of shingle.

'They say a raven croaks. It's sharper than that. It's a bark. ... Words are good things, if you get them right.'

Mr Craw was interested. Words were his stock-in-trade, out of which he had won fortune. Was there not capital to be made out of these novel experiences? He saw himself writing with a new realism. He never read criticisms, but he was aware that he had his critics. Here was a chance to confound them.

'I thought that you might want to write,' Jaikie went on, 'so I brought something in my pack. Barbon said you had a special kind of envelope in which you sent your articles, and that these envelopes were opened first in the mail at your office. I got a batch of them from him, and some paper and pencils. He said you always wrote with a pencil.'

Mr Craw was touched. He had not expected such consideration from this taciturn young man. He was also flattered. This youth realized that his was an acquisitive and forward-looking mind, which could turn a harsh experience into a message of comfort for the world. His brain began to work happily at the delightful task of composition. He thought of vivid phrases about weather, homely idioms heard in the inn, word-pictures of landscapes, tough shreds of philosophy, and all coloured with a fine, manly out-of-doors emotion. There was a new manner waiting for him. When they sat down to lunch by a well-head very near the top of the Callowa water-shed, he felt the cheerfulness of one on the brink of successful creation.

Munching his scones and cheese, he became talkative.

'You are a young man,' he said. 'I can remember when I also was twenty. It was a happy time, full of dreams. It has been my good fortune to carry those dreams with me throughout my life. Yes, I think I was not yet twenty when I acquired my philosophy. The revelation came to me after reading Thomas Carlyle's "Characteristics". Do you know the essay?'

Jaikie shook his head. He was an omnivorous reader, but he had found Carlyle heavy going.

'Ah, well! That great man is too little read to-day, but his turn will come again. I learned from him not to put too high a value upon the mere intellect. He taught me that the healthy life is the unconscious life, and that it is in man's dim illogical instincts that truth often lies. We are suffering to-day, Mr Galt, from a surfeit of clever logicians. But it is the biologist rather than the logician or the mathematician to whom we should look for guidance. The infinite power and value of the unreasoned has always been one of my master principles.'

'I know,' said Jaikie. He remembered various articles above Mr Craw's signature which had appealed to what he called 'the abiding instincts of the people', and he had wondered at the time how any man could be so dogmatic about the imponderable.

'From that principle,' the other went on, 'I deduce my optimism. If we live by reason only we must often take a dark view of the world and lose hope. But the irrational instinct is always hopeful, for it is the instinct to live. You must have observed the astonishing cheerfulness of the plain man when the intellectual despairs. It was so in the War. Optimism is not a pre-condition of thought, but it is a pre-condition of life. Thus mankind, which has the will to continue, "never turns its back, but marches breast-forward".' He filled his chest and delivered the full quotation from Browning.

Jaikie, to whom Browning had always seemed like a slightly intoxicated parson, shifted uncomfortably.

'I hope you do not affect pessimism,' said Mr Craw. 'I believe it is often a foolish pose of youth. Dishonest, too.'

'I don't know,' was the answer. 'No. I'm not a pessimist. But I haven't been through bad enough times to justify me in being an optimist. You want to have been pretty badly tried before you have any right to say that the world is good.'

'I do not follow.'

'I mean that to declare oneself an optimist, without having been down into the pit and come out on the other side, looks rather like bragging.'

'I differ profoundly. Personal experience is not the decisive factor. You have the testimony of the ages to support your faith.'

'Did you ever read *Candide*?' Jaikie asked.

'No,' said Mr Craw. 'Why?'

But Jaikie felt that it would take too long to explain, so he did not answer.

The drove-road meandered up and down glens and across hill-shoulders till it found itself descending to the valley of one of the Callowa's principal tributaries, in which ran a road from Gledmouth to Portaway. The travellers late in the afternoon came to the edge of that road, which on their left might be seen winding down from the low moorish tableland by which it had circumvented the barrier of the high mountains. On their right, a quarter of a mile away, it forked, one branch continuing down the stream to Portaway, twelve miles distant, while the other kept west around a wooded spur of hill.

Mr Craw squatted luxuriously on a dry bank of heather. He had not a notion where he had got to, but spiritually he was at ease for he felt once again master of himself. He had stopped forecasting the immediate future, and had his eye on the articles which he was going to write, the fresh accent he would bring to his messages. He sat in a bush like a broody hen, the now shapeless Homburg hat squashed over his head, the image of a ruminating tramp.

Jaikie had gone down to the road fifty yards away, where a stream fell in pools. He was thirsty, since, unlike his companion, he had not drunk copiously of wayside fountains. As he knelt to drink, the noise of an approaching car made him raise his head, and he watched an ancient Ford pass him and take the fork on the left, which was the road to Portaway. It was clearly a hired car, presumably from Gledmouth. In it sat the kind of driver one would expect, a youth with a cap on one side of his brow and an untidy mackintosh. The other occupant was a young man wearing a light grey overcoat and a bowler hat, a young man with a high-coloured face, and a small yellow moustache. It was a lonely place and an unfrequented road, but to his surprise he knew the traveller.

He watched the car swing down the valley towards Portaway, and was busy piecing together certain recollections, when he was recalled to attention by the shouts of Mr Craw from the hill-side. Mr Craw was in a state of excitement. He ran the fifty yards towards Jaikie with surprising agility.

'Did you see that?' he puffed. 'The man in the car. It's my secretary, Sigismund Allins. I tried to stop him, but I was too late. He was on holiday in Spain, and was not expected back for another fortnight. I can only assume that Barbon has recalled him by wire. What a pity we missed him, for he could have provided us with the money we need. At any rate he could have arranged for sending it and my clothes from Castle Gay without troubling you to go there. . . . I am relieved to think that Allins is back. He is a very resourceful man in an emergency.'

'You are sure it was he?'

'Absolutely certain. I had a good look at him as the car passed, but I found my voice too late. I may be trusted to recognize the inmates of my own household.'

Jaikie too had recognized the man, though he did not know his name. His memory went back to an evening in Cambridge a year before, when he had dined in what for him was strange company – the Grey Goose Club, a fraternity of rich young men who affected the Turf. It had been the day before the Cambridgeshire, and the talk had been chiefly of Newmarket. Among the guests had been a brisk gentleman who was not an undergraduate and who had been pointed out to him as a heroic and successful plunger. 'He's got the *View* in his pocket,' his host had told him, 'and that, of course, means that he gets the best tips.' He remembered that he had not liked the guest whose talk sounded to him boastful and indecent. He had set him down as a *faux bonhomme*, noting the cold shiftiness of his light eyes. What was it that Alison had said of Mr Allins? 'If you met him you would say that he wasn't quite a gentleman.' He would certainly go thus far.

The last stage of the day's walk in the purple October dusk was for Mr Craw a pleasant experience. He was agreeably tired. He was very hungry and had Jaikie's promise of a not too distant meal, and his mind – this was always a factor in his comfort – was working busily. The sight of his secretary had assured him that his proper world could be readily recaptured when he wished, but he was content to dwell a little longer in the new world to which he had been so violently introduced. About six o'clock they reached the shepherd's house of the Black Swire, some eight miles from Portaway, the eastern hirsel on the Knockraw estate. There Jaikie was given an effusive welcome by his old friends, the shepherd and his wife, and, since the house was new and commodious, they had a bedroom far superior to Mrs Catterick's or that of the Watermeeting inn. Mr Craw faced without blenching a gigantic supper of the inevitable ham and eggs, and drank three cups of tea. At the meal he condescended affably, and discoursed with the shepherd, who was a stout Radical, on the prospects of the Canonry election. Jaikie had introduced him as a friend from London, and it pleased him to cultivate his anonymity, when by a word he might have set the shepherd staring.

The host and hostess went early to bed, after the fashion of countryfolk, and the two travellers were left alone by the fire. Mr Craw felt wakeful, so he had out the foolscap from Jaikie's pack, and composed an article which, when it appeared two days later, gave pleasure to several million readers. Its subject was the value of the simple human instincts, too often overlaid by the civilized, the essential wisdom of the plain man. Just as a prophet must sojourn occasionally in the wilderness, so it was right for culture now and then to rub shoulders with simplicity, as Antaeus drew his strength from contact with his mother, the Earth.

Jaikie sat by the peats, Woolworth's head against his knee,

and brooded. What he had seen that evening had altered his whole outlook. . . . Allins was not bound for Castle Gay. He had not mentioned it to his companion. But the road to Castle Gay was the right fork, and the car had taken the left. It was less than eight miles to Castle Gay by the straight road at the point where they had seen the car, but it was seventeen by Portaway. . . . Why should Allins go to Portaway when he was supposed to be on holiday? He did not believe for one moment that he had been recalled by Barbon, who had spoken of him coldly. He was Mr Craw's *protégé*, not Barbon's. . . . He must have come from Gledmouth, probably arriving there by the 6.30 train from the south. Why had he chosen that route to Portaway? It was longer than by the coast, and a most indifferent road. But it was lonely, and his only reason must have been that he wanted to be unobserved. . . . Jaikie had a very clear picture of Allins that night at the Grey Goose Club. Was that the sort of fox to be safely domesticated by an innocent like Craw?

The innocent in question was busy at his article, sometimes sucking the end of his pencil, sometimes scribbling with a happy smirk, sometimes staring into the fire. Jaikie, as his eyes dwelt on him, had a sudden conviction about two things. One was that he liked him. The other was that this business was far more complicated than even Dougal realized. It was more than protecting the privacy of a newspaper proprietor and saving his face. There were darker things to be looked for than rival pressmen and persistent Evallonians.

As this conviction became firm in his mind, Jaikie felt an immense access of cheerfulness. There was going to be some fun in the business after all.

CHAPTER ELEVEN

# THE TROUBLES OF A JOURNALIST

Mr Albert Tibbets, after his meeting with Dougal in Portaway, spent an unprofitable day. He duly received the second wire from his chief, confirming him in his view of the Craw mystery, and urging an instant and unrelenting quest. Fired with these admonitions, he proceeded to Castle Gay to carry out his intention of 'comforting Barbon'. But he found many difficulties in his path. He was refused admission, as he expected, at both the lodge gates. When, after a good deal of trouble and considerable loss of skin, he twice made his way into the park, he was set upon by the satellites of Mackillop and rudely ejected. The second time, indeed, he received so rough a handling that his hardy spirit was daunted. He retired to the inn at Starr to write out his notes and perpend the situation.

He was convinced that Mr Craw had been lost, and that he had not travelled south. But it was possible that by this time he was back at the Castle. In that case it was his business to find out the reason why the Castle itself had been so gravely perturbed. There was a mystery somewhere, and it behoved him, for the credit of his paper, to unriddle it. If he could come on the secret, he might use it to compel an interview with Mr Craw, which would be a triumph of a high order. But nothing could be done by daylight with those watchful myrmidons. Mr Tibbets, like other conspirators, waited for the darkness.

He had no particular plan, when, fortified by a good dinner, he set out on his motor-bicycle at the hour of half-past seven. Rather aimlessly he made his way to the principal lodge near the Mains, and set himself down opposite it to smoke a pipe and consider his tactics. Almost immediately he was rewarded by a remarkable sight. A big closed car slid up the road and stopped at the lodge. Apparently it was expected, for the gates were at once opened. It passed through, and the bars fell behind it, but not before Mr Tibbets had had a glimpse of its occupants. He saw that they were men, and one at least was in evening dress, for he caught a glimpse of a white shirt-front.

This was news with a vengeance. This party had come to dine at the Castle – not to stay, for there was no luggage on the car. In time they would return, and it was his business to wait for them and follow them.

For more than three hours he kept his chilly vigil. Nothing passed him on the road except a dog-cart going up the valley, and two farm lads on bicycles. He remembered the other lodge, and had a moment's fear that the visitors might leave by that. Finally, about twenty minutes past eleven, he saw the glow of headlights rising beyond the park walls, the gates opened and the car swung into the highway. Mr Tibbets, with very stiff limbs but an eager heart, mounted his machine and followed it.

It was an easy task, for the car travelled slowly, as if driven by a man not accustomed to the twisting Canonry roads. It turned to the left before Starr village and passed the other lodge. Then it climbed through a mile of firwoods to an open moor, where Mr Tibbets prudently fell some distance behind. Once again he found himself in tortuous roads among pasture-fields, and, coming too quickly round a corner, all but ran into the car, which had halted at another lodge. He subsided quietly into a ditch, and watched the car disappear into a dark avenue of beeches. He noticed that, as at Castle Gay, the lodge-keeper locked the gates behind it.

Mr Tibbet's investigations had given him a fair general idea of the neighbourhood. He recognized the place as Knockraw, which he understood had been let to shooting tenants. His ardour for the quest rose like a rocket. If Craw was still lost, these people must be mixed up in the business for the anxious Barbon would not ask them to dine as a matter of ordinary hospitality. If Craw had returned, what did he want with the strangers – Craw, who notoriously never dined out and led a cloistered life? Who were they? Craw was no sportsman, and could have no interest in sporting neighbours. . . . Mr Tibbets had a stout heart and he determined not to lose the scent. He decided that he had better prospect the immediate neighbourhood of Knockraw. He had a vision of a smoking-room window, perhaps open a little, where he might view the party at close quarters and haply overhear their talk.

He carefully disposed of his bicycle behind a clump of broom and entered the modest demesne of Knockraw. This was easy enough, for only a wire fence separated it from the road. The moon was up by now, the Hunter's Moon shining in a clear sky, and it guided him through the beechwood and a plantation of young spruces to the corner of a walled kitchen garden. Beyond it he saw the rambling whitewashed house, and the square of gravel by the front door. He had run fast and by the shortest road, and as he came in sight of the door the car had only just turned and was making its way to the garage. The household was still awake, for there were half-a-dozen lit windows.

Mr Tibbets, still possessed by the idea of the smoking-room window, began a careful circuit of the dwelling. Keeping strictly in cover, he traversed a lawn with flower-beds, an untidy little rose garden, and a kind of maze composed of ill-clipped yews. The windows on this side were all dark. Then, rounding a corner of the house, he found himself on another rough lawn, cut by two gravelled paths and ending in a shrubbery and some outhouses. There was light here, but it was clearly the kitchen and servants' quarters, so he turned on his tracks, and went back to the front door. He was convinced that the living-rooms, if the party had not gone to bed, must be on the other side of the house, where it abutted on the heathery slopes of Knockraw Hill. This meant a scramble to avoid a dense thicket of rhododendrons, but presently he had passed the corner, and looked down on what was the oldest part of the dwelling. Sure enough there was a lit window – open, too, for the night was mild. He saw an arm draw the curtain, and it was the arm of a man in evening dress.

The sleuth in Mr Tibbets was now fully roused. There was a ledge to the window which would give him cover, and he crawled down the slope towards it. There was a gap in the curtains, and he was able to peep into the room. He saw the back of one man, and noticed that his dress-coat had a velvet collar; the bearded profile of another; and the hand of a third which held a tumbler. They were talking, but in some foreign tongue which Mr Tibbets did not understand. Try as he might he could get no better view. He had raised himself and was peering through the gap, when a movement towards him made him drop flat. A hand shut the windows and fastened the catch. Then he heard a general movement within. The light was put out and the door was closed. The three men had gone to bed.

Bitterly disappointed, Mr Tibbets got to his feet and decided that there was nothing more to be done for the moment. All he had found out was that the three diners at Castle Gay were foreigners, and that one had a black beard. He had studied the bearded profile so carefully that he thought he should know its owner if he met him again. He remounted the slope, intending to pass the rhododendron clump on its upper side. With a dormant household behind him, as he believed, it is possible that he may have gone carelessly. For as he rounded the rhododendrons he was suddenly challenged by a voice from above.

He yielded to the primeval instinct and ran. But he did not run far. He was making for the high road and his motor-bicycle, but he travelled barely fifty yards. For something of an incredible swiftness was at his heels, and he found himself caught by the knees so that he pitched head foremost down the slope towards the front door. Dazed and winded, he found the something sitting on his stomach and holding his throat with unpleasing strictness. His attempts to struggle only tightened the constriction, so he gave up the contest.

After that he scarcely knew what happened to him. His captor seemed to have multiplied himself by two or three, and he felt himself being bundled on to men's shoulders. Then he was borne into darkness, into light, into darkness, and again into bright light. When he returned to full possession of his wits, he was in what seemed to be a cellar, with his wrists and ankles tightly corded and nothing to recline on but a cold stone floor.

Count Casimir Muresco, while completing a leisurely Sunday-morning toilet, was interrupted by Jasper, the butler, a man who in the service of Prince Odalchini had acquired a profound knowledge of many lands and most human conundrums. Jasper reported that the previous night the two footmen, who were also from the Prince's Evallonian estates, having been out late in pursuance of some private business, had caught a poacher in the garden, and, according to the best Evallonian traditions, had trussed him up and deposited him for the night in a cellar, which was the nearest equivalent they could find to the princely dungeons.

Casimir was perturbed by the news, for he was aware that the Evallonian methods were not the British, and he had no desire to antagonize the countryside. He announced that at eleven o'clock he would himself interview the prisoner, and that in the meantime he should be given breakfast.

The interview, when it took place, effectually broke up the peace of mind of the Knockraw establishment. For instead of a local poacher, whom Casimir had intended to dismiss with an admonition and a tip, the prisoner proved to be a journalist in a furious temper. Mr Tibbets had passed a miserable night. The discomfort of his bonds had prevented him from sleeping, and in any case he had only the hard floor for a couch. The consequence was that he had spent the night watches in nursing his wrath, and, having originally been rather scared, had ended by becoming very angry. Patriotism added fuel to his fires. He had been grossly maltreated by foreigners, and he was determined to make his wrongs a second case of Jenkins' Ear, and, in the words of that perjured mariner, to 'commend his soul to God and his cause to his country.' He was convinced that he had fallen into a den of miscreants, who were somehow leagued with Craw, and professional rivalry combined with national prejudices and personal grievances to create a mood of righteous wrath. He had told Jasper what he thought of him when the butler had removed his bonds that morning, and he had in no way been mollified by a breakfast of hot rolls and excellent coffee. Consequently when Casimir appeared at eleven o'clock, he found himself confronted with the British Lion.

Casimir had the wit to see the gravity of the blunder. This was one of the journalists whom at all costs he must avoid – Barbon and Dougal had dinned that into him. He was apparently the most dangerous, for, being a student of the British Press, Casimir had a lively respect for the power of the *Wire*. The fellow had been gravely affronted, and was in the most truculent temper.

Casimir was a man of action. He lapsed into broken English. He apologized profusely – he even wept. The ways of his own land (he did not, of course, mention Evallonia) were different from Scotland, and his servants had been betrayed unwittingly into a grievous fault. Not for the gold of Croesus would he have been a party to an insult to the so-great British Press. But let Mr Tibbets picture the scene – the darkness, the late hour, servants accustomed to predatory and revolutionary peasants, servants knowing nothing of the free and equal British traditions. There was room for an innocent mistake, but he cast ashes on his head that it should have happened to Mr Tibbets. Then Casimir's English began to fail him. He could not explain. He could not make atonement. Let the resources of the establishment be placed at his guest's disposal. A hot bath? Then a car would await him, while his bicycle would be retained and sent on to Portaway.

Casimir overflowed with obscure apologies. He conducted Mr Tibbets himself to a bedroom and prepared his bath. A bed was ready, with pyjamas laid out, and a pleasant fire burning. The journalist began to thaw, for he was very sleepy. He would do as Casimir suggested; afterwards, he told himself, he would pump these penitent foreigners on the subject of Mr Craw. He bathed and retired to rest, and, though he did not know it, the bedroom door was locked and the key in Casimir's pocket.

After a consultation with his colleagues Casimir rang up Castle Gay and poured his difficulties into the sympathetic ear of Barbon. There was now no defect in his English. 'The man will go away full of suspicion,' he said. 'I distrust him. He has not forgiven us, and will make journalistic capital out of his adventures. ... No. He does not know who we are.

but he will make inquiries, and he may find out. . . . You say he is the chief journalistic enemy of Mr Craw. I have a suggestion. He has been trying to enter Castle Gay, and has failed. Let me send him to you. I will say that we cannot express adequately our apologies, but that my good friend Barbon will do that for us. By entering Castle Gay he will be placated. . . . There is no difficulty for Mr Craw is not there. You will receive him as an English friend of mine who desires to add his apologies to ours.'

Mr Barbon's response was not encouraging, but Casimir continued to press his case, and at last prevailed. 'I don't want to be mixed up in this business,' Barbon said, 'but Mr Crombie might manage it. He could talk to him as one journalist to another.' Barbon's voice gradually became more cordial. He was beginning to think that such a visit might help with his own problem. If Tibbets came to Castle Gay, and was well received, and saw for himself that the master of the house was absent, he might be choked off his present dangerous course. There was no reason why he should not write a story for his paper about Castle Gay. It would all tend to show that they had nothing to conceal.

Tibbets slept till half-past three. Then he arose, to find shaving things laid out for him and all the necessaries of the toilet. At the first sign of movement Jasper had been instructed to unlock the bedroom door. Presently came a modest tap, and Casimir appeared, with ungrammatical hopes that his guest had slept well. Tibbets was conducted downstairs where he ate an excellent luncheon, while Casimir entertained him with accounts of the Knockraw sport and questions revealing an abysmal ignorance of British politics. 'My car is waiting for you,' he said; 'to take you wherever you wish to go. But I should be glad if you would permit it to take you first to Castle Gay. I have not been able to express to you our full contrition, but I have asked my friend Mr Barbon, through whose kind offices I took this place, to speak for me and say how little I desire to wound the heart of so eminent an Englishman. I and my friends are, so to say, guests in your country, and we would die sooner than be guilty of a breach of hospitality.'

'That's all right, Count,' said Tibbets. (His host had introduced himself as Count Anton Muratsky and had hinted at a Styrian domicile.) 'We'll say no more about last night. I can see that it was a servant's blunder, and, anyway, I had no business to be wandering about so late close to your house. I lost my road trying to take a short cut. I'll be very glad to look in at Castle Gay. I don't know Mr Barbon, but I'd be pleased to meet him.'

Privately, he exulted. The Fates had done well by him, and had opened the gates of the Dark Tower. He would not be worth much if he couldn't get a good story out of Barbon, whom he had seen from afar and written down as a nincompoop.

He reached Castle Gay in the Knockraw car just about five o'clock. He was obviously expected, for Bannister greeted him with a smiling face – 'From Knockraw, sir?' – and led him upstairs and along a corridor to the library where the day before the Evallonian delegates had been received in conference. Mr Tibbets stared with interest at the vast apartment, with the latticed book-laden shelves lining three walls, the classic sculptures, and the great Flemish tapestry. The room was already dusky with twilight, but there were lights before the main fireplace, and a small table set out for tea. There sat a short elderly gentleman in brown tweeds, who rose at his approach and held out a welcoming hand.

'Come away, Mr Tibbets,' he said, 'and have your tea. I'm fair famished for mine.'

The journalist had the surprise of a not uneventful life. He had entered the palace for an appointment with a major-domo and instead had been ushered into the Presence. He had never seen Mr Craw in the flesh but his features were well known to the world, since weekly his portrait surmounted his articles. Before him beyond doubt was the face that had launched a thousand ships of journalism – the round baldish head, the bland benevolent chin, the high cheek-bones, and shrewdly pursed lips. The familiar horn spectacles were wanting, but they lay beside him on the floor, marking a place in a book. Now that he had Mr Craw not a yard away from him, he began hurriedly to revise certain opinions he had entertained about that gentleman. This man was not any kind of fool. The blue eyes which met his were very wide awake, and there was decision and humour in every line of that Pickwickian countenance.

His breath stopped short at the thought of his good fortune. To be sure the Craw mystery had proved to be nonsense, and he had been barking loudly up the wrong tree. But that stunt could easily be dropped. What mattered was that he was interviewing Craw – the first man in the history of journalism who had ever done it. He would refuse to be bound over to silence. He had got his chance, and nothing could prevent him taking it. . . . But he must walk very warily.

Dickson McCunn had been to church in the morning, and on returning had found Dougal's letter awaiting him, brought by a Castle Gay car. He decided at once to accept the call. The salmon fishing in his own stream was nearly over, the weather was fine, and he felt stirring in him a desire for movement, for enterprise, for new sights and new faces. This longing always attacked him in the spring, but it usually came also in the autumn, just before he snuggled down into the warm domesticity of winter. So he had packed a bag, and had been landed at Castle Gay a little after four o'clock, when Barbon had concluded his telephone conversation with Knockraw.

At once a task had been set him. Dougal declared that he was the man to pacify Tibbets. 'I don't want to appear in the thing, nor Barbon either, for the chap is an enemy. He won't make anything of you – just that you're a friend of the family – and you can pitch him a yarn about the innocent foreigners at Knockraw and how they haven't enough English to explain their penitence. If he asks you about yourself you can explain you have just arrived on a visit, and if he starts on Craw you can say you know nothing about him – that he's away on holiday, and that you're a friend of Barbon's – your niece married his cousin – any lie you like. You've got just the kind of manner to soothe Tibbets, and make him laugh at his troubles and feel rather ashamed of having made so much fuss.'

Dickson lost no time in fulfilling his mission.

'Those poor folk at Knockraw,' he said. 'They've made an awful mess of it, but a man like you can see for yourself that they meant no harm. The Count's a friend of Mr Barbon's and a great sportsman, and it seems they haven't any grouse in their own country – I'm not just sure what it is, but it's somewhere near Austria – so they were determined to take a Scotch moor. The mistake was in bringing a lot of wild heathen servants, when they could have got plenty of decent folk here to do their business. The Count was lamenting on the telephone, thinking you'd set the police and the Procurator-fiscal on him or make a rumpus in the newspapers. But I knew you were not that kind of man, and I told him so.' Dickson beamed pleasantly on his companion.

But Tibbets scarcely appeared to be listening. 'Oh, that business!' he said. 'Of course, it was all a mistake, and I'll never say another word about it.'

'That's fine!' said Dickson heartily. 'I knew you would take it like a sensible fellow. I needn't tell you I've a great admiration for you journalists, and I daresay I often read you in the papers!'

'You read the *Wire*?' asked the startled Tibbets. Mr Craw was generally supposed to look at no papers but his own.

'Not regularly. But I often pick it up. I like a turn at the *Wire*. You've grand pictures, and a brisk way of putting things. I always say there's not a livelier paper in this land than the *Wire*. It keeps a body from languor.'

A small note-book and pencil had emerged from Tibbets' pocket. Dickson observed them unperturbed. The man was a journalist and must be always taking notes.

'Your praise of the *Wire* will give enormous satisfaction,' said Tibbets, and there was almost a quaver in his voice. He neglected the cup of tea which had been poured out for him, and sat gazing at his companion as a hopeful legatee might gaze at a lawyer engaged in reading a will.

'You only arrived to-day, sir?' he asked.

'Just an hour ago. I've been in Carrick. A fine country, Carrick, none better, but the fishing in my waters there is just about over. The Callowa here goes on for another fortnight.

You're not an angler, Mr Tibbets? A pity that, for I might have got Mr Barbon to arrange a day on the Callowa for you.'

Tibbets wrote. Mr Craw as a fisherman was a new conception, for he was commonly believed to be apathetic about field sports.

'Would you care to say anything about the Canonry election, sir?' he asked deferentially.

Dickson laughed and poured himself out a third cup of tea. 'To tell you the truth,' he said, 'I know nothing about it. I'm a poor hand at politics. I suppose I'm what you call a Tory, but I often get very thrawn with the Tories. I don't trust the Socialists, but whiles I think they've a good deal to say for themselves. The fact is, I'm just a plain Scotsman and a plain business man. I'm terrible fond of my native country, but in these days it's no much a man like me can do for her. I'm as one born out of due season, Mr Tibbets. I would have been more use when the job was to hunt the English back over the Cheviots or fight the French. I like straight issues.'

'You believe in a business Government, sir?' Tibbets asked, for this was the *Wire*'s special slogan.

'I believe in the business spirit – giving plain answers to plain questions and finding what's the right job to do and taking off your coat to it. We're all smothered nowadays with fine talk. There's hardly a man in public life with a proper edge to his mind. They keep blazing away about ideals and principles, when all they're seeking is just to win seats at the next election, and meantime folk stand hoasting at the street-corners with no chance of a job. This country, Mr Tibbets, is suffering from nobility of language and ignobility of practice. There's too much damned uplift abroad, and far too little common sense. In the old days, when folk stuck closer to the Bible, there was the fear of hell-fire to remind them that faith without works was dead.'

Dickson said much more, for it was one of his favourite topics. He expanded on the modern lack of reverence for the things that mattered and the abject veneration for trash. He declared that the public mind had been over-lubricated, that discipline and logic were out of fashion, and that the prophets as a fraternity had taken to prophesying smooth things. He just checked himself in time, remembering where he was, for he almost instanced Mr Craw as a chief sinner.

Tibbets scribbled busily, gulped down his cup of now luke-warm tea, and rose to go. He had got an interview which was the chief professional triumph of his career. The Knockraw car was still at his disposal. He could be in Portaway in time to write out his story and send it by the mail which reached London at 4.30 a.m. and so catch the later editions of his paper. Meantime he would telephone to his chief and prepare him for the thunderbolt.

He bowed over Dickson's hand. 'I am honoured to have met you, sir. I can only hope that it is a privilege which may be repeated.'

Dickson sought out Dougal and Barbon in the smoking-room. 'Yon's a pleasant-spoken fellow,' he said. 'I made it all right about Knockraw, and sent him away as crouse as a piper. We had a fine crack, and he wrote down what I said in a wee book. I suppose I've been interviewed, and that's the first time in my life.'

A sudden suspicion awoke in Dougal's eye.

'What kind of thing did you give him?' he asked.

Dickson sketched the main line of his conversation, and Dougal's questions became more peremptory till he had extracted all of Tibbet's interrogatories and Dickson's answers. Then he lay back in his chair and laughed.

'He left in a hurry, you say. No wonder. He has a story that will keep the *Wire* busy for a fortnight. . . . no no, you're not to blame. It's my fault that I never guessed what might happen. Tibbets is a proud man to-night. He took you for Craw, and he's got in his pocket the first interview that Craw ever gave to mortal man. . . . We're in the soup this time, right enough, for you've made the body blaspheme every idol he worships.'

CHAPTER TWELVE

# PORTAWAY – THE GREEN TREE

THE eight miles to Portaway were taken by the travellers at a leisurely pace, so that it was noon before they came in sight of the Canonry's capital. There had been some frost in the night, and, when they started, rime had lain on the stiffened ruts of the road and the wayside grasses. Presently the sun burned it up, and the shorn meadows and berry-laden hedges drowsed under a sky like June. The way, after they had left the Knockraw moors, was mostly through lowlands – fat farms with full stackyards, and woods loud with the salutes of pheasants. Now and then at a high place they stopped to look back to the blue huddle of the great uplands.

'Castle Gay lies yonder.' Jaikie directed his companion's eyes. 'Yon's the Castle Hill.'

Mr Craw viewed the prospect with interest. His home had hitherto been for him a place without environment, like a walled suburban paradise where a city man seeks his repose. He had enjoyed its parks and gardens, but he had no thought of their setting. Now he was realizing that it was only a little piece of a vast and delectable countryside. He had come down from bleak hills into meadows, and by contrast the meadows seemed a blessed arcady. . . . His mind was filled with pleasant and fruitful thoughts. The essence of living lay in its contrasts. The garden redoubled its charm if it marched with heather; the wilderness could be a delight if it came as a relief from a world too fatted and supine. . . . Did not the secret of happiness lie in the true consciousness of environment? Castle Gay was nothing if the thought of it was confined to its park walls. The mind must cultivate a wide orbit, an exact orientation, for the relief from trouble lay in the realization of that trouble's narrow limits. Optimism, a manly optimism, depended only upon the radius of the encircling soul. He had a recollection of Browning: '*Somewhere in the distance Heaven is blue above Mountains where sleep the unsunn'd tarns.'* ... On this theme he saw some eloquent articles ahead of him.

He was also feeling very well. Autumn scents had never come to his nostrils with such aromatic sharpness. The gold and sulphur and russet of the woods had never seemed so marvellous a pageant. He understood that his walks had hitherto, for so many years, been taken with muffled senses – the consequence of little indoor duties. To-day he was feeling the joys of a discoverer. Or was it rediscovery? By the time they had come to the beginnings of Portaway he was growing hungry, and in the narrow street of the Eastgate, as it dropped to the Callowa bridge, they passed a baker's shop. He stared at the window and sniffed the odour from the doorway with an acuteness of recollection which was almost painful. In the window was a heap of newly-baked biscuits, the kind called 'butter biscuits', which are still made in old-fashioned shops in old-fashioned Scots towns. He remembered them in his childhood – how he would flatten his nose of a Saturday against a baker's window in Partankirk, when he had spent his weekly penny, and his soul hungered for these biscuits' delicate crumbly richness. ... He must find a way to return to this shop, and for auld lang syne taste a butter biscuit again.

Jaikie's mind on that morning walk had been differently engaged. He was trying to find a clue through the fog of suspicions which the sight of Sigismund Allins had aroused in him. Allins was a confidential secretary of Mr Craw. He was also a gambler, and a man who bragged of his power with the Craw Press. Allins was, therefore, in all likelihood a dweller in the vicinity of Queer Street. If he had money troubles – and what more likely? – he would try to use his purchase with Craw to help him through. But how? Jaikie had a notion that Mr Craw would not be very tolerant towards Allins's kind of troubles.

Allins had gone off on holiday before the present crisis began, and was not expected back for another fortnight. He had obviously nothing to do with the persecution of Craw by the journalists – there was no profit for him that way. But what about the Evallonians? They had known enough of Craw's ways and had had sufficient power to get his papers to print the announcement of his going abroad. Barbon had assumed that they had an efficient intelligence service. Was it not more likely that they had bought Allins? Why should Allins not be – for a consideration – on their side?

But in that case why had he returned prematurely from his holiday? The wise course, having got his fee, was to stay away till the Evallonians had done their business, in order that he might be free from any charge of complicity. But he had returned secretly by a roundabout road. He could have gone direct to Portaway, for the train which had deposited him at Gledmouth stopped also at that station. He had wanted to be in the neighbourhood, unsuspected, to watch developments. It was a bold course and a dangerous. There must be some compelling motive behind it.

Jaikie questioned Mr Craw about Allins, and got vague answers, for his companion's thoughts were on higher things. Allins had been recommended to him by some business friends; his people were well known in the city; he had been private secretary to Lord Wassell; he was a valuable man, because he went a great deal into society, unlike Barbon, and could always find out what people were talking about. He had been with him two years. Yes, most useful and diplomatic and an excellent linguist. He had often accompanied him abroad, where he seemed to know everybody. Did Barbon like him? Certainly. They were a happy family, with no jealousies, for each had his appointed business. Well off? Apparently. He had a substantial salary, but must spend a good deal beyond it. Undoubtedly he had private means. No, Allins had nothing to do with the management of the papers. He was not seriously interested in politics or literature. His study was mankind. Womenkind, too, perhaps. It was necessary for one like himself, who had heavy intellectual preoccupations, to provide himself with eyes and ears. 'Allins is what you call a man of the world,' said Mr Craw. 'Not the highest type of man, perhaps, but for me indispensable.'

'I don't think he has gone to Castle Gay,' said Jaikie. 'I'm certain he is in Portaway. It is very important that he should not see you.'

Mr Craw asked why.

'Because the game would be up if you were recognized in Portaway, and it would be too dangerous for you to be seen speaking to one of your own secretaries. As you are just now, it wouldn't be easy for anyone to spot you – principally because no one is expecting you, and there isn't the right atmosphere for recognition. But if you and Allins were seen together that might give the clue.'

Mr Craw accepted the reasoning. 'But I must have money – and clothes,' he added.

'I'm going to write to Dougal as soon as we get to Portaway.'

'And I must post the article I wrote last night.'

'There's something else,' said Jaikie. 'You'll have to be in Portaway for at least twenty-four hours, and your rig won't quite do. It's all right except the jacket, which gives you away. We must get you a ready-made jacket to match Johnston's breeks.'

So at a small draper's, almost next door to the baker's shop, a jacket of rough tweed was purchased – what is known to the trade as a 'sports' line, suitable for the honest man who plays bowls or golf after his day's work. Mr Craw was apparently stock-size for this class of jacket, for one was found which fitted him remarkably well. Also two soft collars were purchased for him. Jaikie looked with satisfaction on his handiwork. The raincoat and the hat were now battered by weather out of their former glossiness. Clad in well-worn grey trousers and a jacket of cheap tweed, Mr Craw was the image of the small tradesman on holiday. Having no reading to do, he had discarded his spectacles, and the sun and wind had given him a healthy colouring. Moreover, he had relapsed a little from his careful speech to the early idiom of Kilmaclavers. He would be a clever man, thought Jaikie, who could identify this homeliness with the awful dignity of him who had sat in Mrs Catterick's best room.

The town of Portaway lies on both banks of the Callowa, which there leaves its mountain vale and begins its seven miles of winding through salty pastures to the Solway. The old town is mostly on the left shore; on the right has grown up a suburb of villas and gardens, with one flaring Hydropathic, and a large new Station Hotel, which is the resort of golfers and anglers. The capital of the Canonry is half country market town, half industrial centre, for in the hills to the south-east lie the famous quarries, which employ a large and transient population. Hence the political activities of the constituency centre in the place. The countryside is Tory or Liberal; among the quarrymen is a big Socialist majority, which its mislikers call Communist. As Jaikie and Mr Craw descended the East-gate the posters of all three candidates flaunted in shop windows and on hoardings, and a scarlet rash on a building announced the Labour committee rooms.

In a back street stood the ancient hostelry of the Green Tree, once the fashionable county inn where in autumn the Canonry Club had its dinners, but now the resort only of farmers and the humbler bagman. Jaikie had often slept there on his tramps, and had struck up a friendship with Mrs Fairweather, its buxom proprietress. To his surprise he found that the election had not congested it, for the politicians preferred the more modern hotels across the bridge. He found rooms without trouble, in one of which was a writing-table, for the itch of composition was upon Mr Craw. They lunched satisfactorily in an empty coffee-room, and there at a corner table he proceeded to compose a letter. He wrote not to Dougal but to Alison. Dougal might be suspect, and unable to leave the Castle, while Alison was free as the winds. He asked for money and a parcel of Mr Craw's clothing, but he asked especially for an interview at the Green Tree, fixing for it the hour of 11 a.m. the next day. There were various questions he desired to ask which could only be answered by someone familiar with the Castle *ménage*. It thrilled him to be writing to the girl. He began, 'Dear Miss Westwater,' and then changed it to 'Dear Miss Alison.' There had been something friendly and confidential about her eyes which justified the change. His handwriting was vile, and he regarded the address on the envelope with disfavour. It looked like 'The Horrible Alison Westwater'. He tried to amend it but only made it worse.

Mr Craw proposed to remain indoors and write. This intention was so clear that Jaikie thought it unnecessary to bind him down with instructions. So, depositing the deeply offended Woolworth in his bedroom, Jaikie left the inn and posted his letter to Alison and arranged for the despatch of Mr Craw's precious article by the afternoon train. Then he crossed the Callowa bridge to the new part of the town. He proposed to make a few private inquiries.

He thought it unlikely that Allins would be at the Station Hotel. It was too public a place, and he might be recognized. But he had stayed there once himself, and, according to his fashion had been on good terms with the head porter, so, to make assurance sure, he made it his first port of call. It was as he expected. There was no Sigismund Allins in the register, and no one remotely resembling him staying in the house. The most likely place was the Hydropathic, which had famous electric baths and was visited by an odd assortment of humanity. Thither Jaikie next directed his steps.

The entrance was imposing. He passed a garage full of cars, and the gigantic porch seemed to be crowded with guests drinking their after-luncheon coffee. He had a vision of a hall heaped with golf clubs and expensive baggage. The porter was a vast functionary in blue and gold, with a severe eye. Jaikie rather nervously entered the hall, conscious that his clothes were not in keeping with its grandeur, and asked a stately lady in the bureau if a Mr Allins was living in the house. The lady cast a casual eye at a large volume and told him 'No'.

It was the answer he expected, but he saw that further inquiries were going to be difficult. The porter was too busy and too proud – no chance of establishing confidential relations there. Jaikie emerged from the portals, and finding the Gods unfriendly, decided to appeal to Acheron. He made his way round to the back regions, which had once been stables and coach-houses, and housed now the electric plant and repairing shop for cars. There was a kind of courtyard, with petrol pumps and water pumps, and at the corner to mark the fairway several white stones which in old days had been the seat of relaxing ostlers. On two of these sat two men, both in mechanic's overalls, hotly disputing.

A kind fate had led him that way, for as he sauntered past them he heard the word 'Kangaroos' several times repeated. He heard the names of Morrison and Smail and Charvill – he heard his own, joined by a blasphemous epithet which seemed to be meant as commendation. He sidled towards the speakers.

'What I say,' said one, speaking slowly and with great emphasis, 'is that them that selected oor team should be drooned like kittens in a bucket. It wasna representative. If it had been, we micht hae dung yon Kangaroos a' to hell.'

'Ye're awfu' clever, Wulkie. How wad ye hae seleckit it?'

'I wad hae left Morrison oot, and I wad hae played' – here followed sundry names of no interest to the reader. 'And I wad hae played Galt at stand-off half. It was fair manslaughter pittin' him at wing three-quarter. He hasna the pace nor the wecht.'

'He's a damn fine wee felly,' said the other. 'Ye ken weel he won the match.'

'But he'd have won it better at stand-off. Yon Sneddon was nae mair use than a tattie-bogle. Ye canna pit Galt higher than I pit him, but the richt use wasna made o' him. That's why I wad droon the selectors.'

'I think I would let them live a little longer,' Jaikie interposed. 'After all, we won against odds. Sneddon was better than you think.'

'Did ye see the match?' the man called Wilkie demanded fiercely.

'Yes,' said Jaikie. 'And I still feel it in my bones. You see, I was playing in it.'

The two regarded him wildly, and then a light of recollection awoke in Wilkie's eye. 'By God, it's Galt,' he cried. 'It's J. Galt.' He extended a dirty palm. 'Pit it there. I'm prood to shake hands wi' ye. Man, the wee laddies in Glesca the day are worshippin' bits o' your jersey.'

'It's an occasion to celebrate wi' a drink,' said the other man solemnly. 'But we're baith busy, and there's nae drink to be had in this dam teetotal shop. Will ye no meet us in the Briar

Bush the nicht? There's mony a man in this toun wad be blithe to see J. Galt.'

The ice was now broken, and for five minutes there was a well-informed discussion on the subtler aspects of Rugby football. Then Jaikie gently insinuated his own purpose. He wanted to find out who was living in the Hydropathic, and he did not want to trouble the higher functionaries.

'Nae wonder,' said Wilkie. 'There's a pentit Jezebel in yon bewry that wad bite a body's heid off.'

Was there no one, Jaikie asked, no friend of his friends inside the building with whom he could have a friendly talk?

'There's Tam Grierson, the heid-porter,' he was told. 'He's a decent body, though he looks like a bubbly-jock. He'll be comin' off duty for his tea in ten minutes. He bides at the lodge ayont the big garage. I'll tak ye doun and introduce ye. Tam will be set up to see ye, for he's terribly keen on fitba.'

So presently Jaikie found himself drinking tea with the resplendent personage, who had removed his braided frock-coat for comfort in his own dwelling. Mr Grierson off duty was the soul of friendliness. They spoke of the match, they spoke of Rugby heroes of old days. They spoke of Scotland's chances against England. Then Jaikie introduced the subject of his quest. 'There's a man whose name I'm not very sure about,' he said, 'something like Collins or Allen. My friend, with whom I'm on a walking tour, is anxious to know if he's staying here.' He described in great detail the appearance of Mr Allins, his high colour, his pale eyes, his small yellow moustache.

'Ho!' said the head-porter. 'I ken him fine! He arrived last night. I don't just mind his name. He's a foreigner, anyway, though he speaks English. I heard him jabberin' a foreign langwidge wi' the others.'

'What others?'

'The other foreigners. There's generally a lot o' queer folk bidin' in the Hydro, and a lot o' them's foreigners. But the ones I mean came by the London mail last night, and your freend arrived about dinner-time. He seemed to be very thick wi' them. There's seven o' them a'thegither. Four has never stirred outbye the day. One gaed off in a cawr after lunch, and your freend and the other are down in Portaway. Ye can come back wi' me and see if you can get a glisk o' them.'

Presently the head-porter resumed his braided frock-coat, and, accompanied by Jaikie, returned to the scene of his labours, and incidentally to the grand manner. Jaikie was directed to an inconspicuous seat at the back of the porch, while the head-porter directed the activities of boots and waiters. At first there was a lull. The tea-drinkers had finished their meal and for the most part gone indoors, and on the broad sweep of gravel the dusk descended. The head-porter spared an occasional moment for conversation, but for the most part Jaikie was left to himself to smoke cigarettes and watch the lights spring out in the valley below.

About half-past five the bustle began. The Hydropathic omnibuses began to roll up and discharge new guests, and they were followed by several taxi-cabs and one ancient four-wheeler. 'It's the train frae the south,' he was informed by Grierson, who was at once swept into a whirl of busyness. His barrack-room voice – he had once been a sergeant in the K.O.S.B. – echoed in porch and hall, and he had more than one distinguished passage of arms with a taxi-driver. Jaikie thought he had forgotten him, till suddenly he heard his hoarse whisper in his ear, 'There's your gentry,' and looked up to see two men entering the hotel.

One was beyond doubt Sigismund Allins, the man whom Mr Craw had recognized yesterday in the Gledmouth motor, the man whom he himself had dined opposite at the Grey Goose Club. He was dressed in a golfing suit of *crotal* tweeds, and made an elegant symphony in brown. Jaikie's eye passed to his companion, who was the more conspicuous figure. He was short and square and had a heavy shaven face and small penetrating eyes which were not concealed by his large glasses. He wore an ulster of a type rarely seen on these shores, and a small green hat pushed back from a broad forehead. As the light of the porch fell on him Jaikie had a sudden impression of an enormously vigorous being, who made Allins by his side seem like a wisp of straw.

He had another impression. The two men were talking eagerly in a foreign tongue, and both seemed to be in a state of high excitement. Allins showed it by his twitching lips and nervous hands, the other by his quick purposeful stride and the way he stuck his chin forward. Within the last half-hour they had seen something which had strongly moved them.

This was also the opinion of Grierson, delivered confidentially, as he superintended the moving of some baggage. 'They maun hae been doun meetin' the train,' he whispered, 'and they've gotten either guid news or ill news.'

There was no reason why he should stay longer, so Jaikie took his departure, after asking his friend the head-porter to keep an eye on the foreigners. 'I've my reasons,' he said, 'which I'll tell you later. I'll be up some time to-morrow to have another crack with you.'

At the lodge-gates he encountered the man called Wilkie returning from the town. 'How did ye get on wi' Grierson? Fine? I thocht ye would. Tam's a rale auld-fashioned character, and can be desperate thrawn if ye get the wrang side o' him, but when he's in gude fettle ye'll no find a nicer man. . . . I've been doun at the station. I wanted a word wi' the Knockraw shover.'

'Knockraw?'

'Aye. The folk in Knockraw have hired twae cars from us for the month, but they brocht their ain shover wi' them. A Frenchie. Weel, there was something wrong wi' the clutch o' ane o' them, and they wrote in about it. I saw the cawr in the town, so I went to the station to speak to the man. He was meetin' the express.'

'Was he meeting anyone?'

'Aye, a young lad cam off the train, a lang lad in a blue topcoat. The shover was in a michty hurry to get on the road and he wadna stop to speak to me – said he could come back the morn. I think he said that, but his English is ill to follow.'

'Did the new arrival speak to anyone at the station?'

'No a word. He just banged into the cawr and off.'

Jaikie having a good deal to think about, walked slowly back to the Green Tree. Another Evallonian had arrived to join the Knockraw party. Allins and his friend had been at the station and must have seen him, but they had not accosted him. Was he wrong in his suspicions, and had Allins nothing to do with the Evallonians? . . . Yet the sight of something had put him and his companion into a state of profound excitement. The mystery was getting deeper.

He purchased at the station copies of that day's *View* and *Wire* as an offering for Mr Craw. He also ascertained from a porter, whom he had known of old, that a guest had arrived for Knockraw. 'I should have carried his bag, but yon foreign shover was waitin' for him, and the twae were out o' the station and into the cawr afore ye could bla your nose. Ugh, man! since this damned election sterted Portaway's been a fair penny waddin'. Half the folk that come here the noo should be in a menawgerie.'

Mr Craw was seated by his bedroom fire, writing with great contentment. He announced that he had also been for a walk. Rather shamefacedly he confessed that he had wanted to taste a butter biscuit again, and had made his way to the baker's shop. 'They are quite as good as I thought,' he said. 'I have kept two for you.'

He had an adventure in a small way, for he had seen Mr Allins. Alone, and wearing the russet clothes which Jaikie had observed at the Hydropathic. He had seen him coming up the Eastgate, and, remembering Jaikie's caution, had retired down an alley, whence he had had a good view of him. There was no doubt on the matter; it was Sigismund Allins, the member of his secretariat.

Jaikie presented him with the two papers and sat down to reflect. Suddenly he was startled by the sound which a small animal might make in heavy pain. Mr Craw was reading something in the *Wire* which made him whimper. He finished it, passed a hand over his brow, and let the paper fall to the ground.

On the front page, with inch headlines, was the triumph of Tibbets. 'Mr Craw Speaks to the World!' was the main heading, and there were a number of juicy subsidiaries. The prophet was unveiled with a vengeance. He preached a mercantile and militant patriotism, a downright, heavy-handed, man-of-the-world, damn-your-eyes, matter-of-fact philosophy. Tibbets had done his work well. Everything that the *Wire* had urged was now fathered on the *Wire*'s chief rival. The thing was brilliantly staged – the dim library at Castle Gay, and the robust and bright-eyed sage scintillating among its ancient shadows. Tibbets had behaved well, too. There was not a hint of irony in his style; he wrote as convert and admirer; he suggested that the nation had been long in travail, and had at last produced a Man. The quondam sentimentalist and peace-maker stood revealed as the natural leader of the red-bloods and the diehards.

'What will they think of me?' the small voice wailed. 'Those who have trusted me?'

What indeed! thought Jaikie. The field-marshal who flings his baton into the ash-bin and announces that the enemy have all the virtues, the prophet who tells his impassioned votaries that he has been pulling their leg, the priest who parodies his faith's mysteries – of such was Mr Craw. Jaikie was himself so blankly astonished that he did not trouble to think how, during the last feverish days, that interview could have been given.

He was roused by the injured man getting to his feet. Mr Craw was no longer plaintive – he was determined and he was angry.

'There has been infamous treachery somewhere,' he announced in a full voice. 'Have the goodness to order a car. I start at once for Castle Gay, and there I am going to – to – to wring somebody's neck.'

CHAPTER THIRTEEN

# PORTAWAY – RED DAVIE

JAIKIE lifted his head in astonishment. This was a Craw whom he had not met before – a man of purpose, with his hackles up. He was proposing to take the bold course which Jaikie himself had urged at the Back House of the Garroch, to loose the entangling knot by cutting it. But strangely enough, Jaikie was now averse to that proposal, for he had come to suspect that business was afoot which made it desirable that Mr Craw should keep at a distance from Castle Gay.

'That's a pretty good score for *you*,' he said.

'What do you mean? It's an outrage. It must be at once repudiated.'

'The *Wire* has been hoaxed. You've got them in your hand. They'll have to eat humble pie. But I'm blessed if I know how it happened. Tibbets is no fool, and he would not have printed the stuff unless he believed it to be genuine. Who has been pulling his leg? It can't have been Dougal – he must have known that it was too dangerous.'

'I shall find out at Castle Gay.'

'There's no need to go there – at least there's no hurry. Telegraph to the *View* telling them to announce that the interview in the *Wire* is bogus. I'll take it round to the office before it closes.'

Mr Craw was in the mood for action. He at once drafted a telegram, signing it with the code-word which he employed in emergencies and which would secure the instant attention of his editor. Jaikie took it and departed. 'Remember to order a car,' Mr Craw called after him, but got no reply.

But when he reached the Post Office Jaikie did not send the telegram as originally drafted. It was borne in on him that this bogus interview was a disguised blessing. If it went uncontradicted it would keep Tibbets quiet; it had changed that menacing creature from an enemy to an ally. So on his own responsibility he altered the telegram to 'Do not repudiate *Wire* interview for the moment,' and signed it with Mr Craw's code-word. That would prevent any premature disavowal from Castle Gay.

Jaikie despatched the wire and walked slowly back. His mind was busy with a problem which each hour seemed to develop new ramifications.

There was first the question of Sigismund Allins. Jaikie was firmly resolved that Allins was a rogue, and his chief evidence was his own instinct. There was something fishy about the man's behaviour – his premature and secret return from holiday, his presence at the Hydropathic under another name, his association with the strange foreigners. But above all he remembered Allins's face and manner of speech which had inspired him with profound mistrust. A hard and a varied life had made Jaikie a good impressionist judge of character. He remembered few occasions when he had been wrong.

That morning he had reached a conclusion. Mr Allins – for a consideration – had brought the Evallonians to Knockraw, and had arranged for the announcement of Mr Craw's journey abroad. He was a gambler, and probably hard up. Mr Craw's disappearance, if he was aware of it, must have upset his calculations, but that, after all, was the Evallonians' concern, Allins's task had probably only been to get them into Craw's vicinity. There might be a contingent payment due to him if the Evallonians succeeded in their mission, and in that case it was to his interest to further their efforts. But he could scarcely do that at Castle Gay, for his connivance might leak out. No. It was quite clear that Allins had every reason to be absent during their visit.

Why, then, had he returned? To advise the Evallonians and earn his contingent payment at a safe distance? That was intelligible enough, though dangerous. There must be people in Portaway who knew him by sight, and a rumour of his arrival might reach Castle Gay. He had not disguised himself, except by posing as a foreigner, and he was walking about brazenly in the streets. . . . The more Jaikie thought about it, the less reason he could find for Allins's return. It was a risk which no discreet blackguard would take, and be believed Allins to be discreet. No, there must be some overmastering motive which he could not guess at.

His mind turned to the foreigners at the Hydropathic. Were they Evallonians, a reserve summoned to wait in the background? Jaikie regretted that his ignorance of foreign tongues had prevented his identifying their speech. He could think of no reason for their presence. The business was very secret and did not require numbers. The three plenipotentiaries at Knockraw were abundantly adequate. . . . They had behaved oddly, too. Allins and another had visited the station and witnessed the arrival of a visitor for Knockraw. They had not spoken to him or to the Knockraw chauffeur, and the visitor had left in a mighty hurry, as if anxious to be unobserved. But the sight of him had put Allins and his friend into a state of considerable excitement. He remembered their eager talk at the Hydropathic door.

His reflections came to a sudden halt, for an idea had struck him, an idea so startling that for the moment he could not compass it. He needed more information. The last part of his return was almost a canter.

He found Mr Craw still fuming over the *Wire*.

'I didn't send your telegram,' he said. 'As long as the interview goes unrepudiated it will keep Tibbets quiet, so I think we'd better let it alone for a day or two.'

Mr Craw disregarded this act of indiscipline.

'Have you ordered a car?' he asked crossly.

Jaikie pulled a chair up to the small fire which had been lit by his order, and regarded his companion seriously.

'I don't think you should go back to Castle Gay to-night,' he said. 'You'll only fall into the thick of that Evallonian mess. Perhaps Barbon and Dougal have got it settled, and it would be a pity to spoil their game. By eleven o'clock to-morrow morning we'll know the position, and I think that you should wait at least till then. There's no need to hurry. You've got the *Wire* in a cleft stick.'

Mr Craw's ire was slightly ebbing.

'I shall not rest,' he answered, 'till I have run the author to ground and exposed the whole shameful affair. It is the most scandalous breach of the comity of journalism that I have ever heard of.'

'I agree. But it won't do you any harm. It will only make the *Wire* look foolish. You don't mean to give them any chance to get back on you through the Evallonian business. Up to now you've won all along the line, for they've had to confess their mistake in their mystery stunt about your disappearance, and soon they'll have to climb down about the interview. Don't spoil your success by being in a hurry.'

As I have said, Mr Craw's first fine rapture of wrath was cooling. He saw the good sense of Jaikie's argument. Truth to tell, he had no desire to face the Evallonians, and he was beginning to see that fortune had indeed delivered his rivals into his hands. He did not answer, but he crumpled the *Wire* and tossed it to Jaikie's side of the fireplace. It was a token of his reluctant submission.

'I want to ask you something,' Jaikie continued. 'It's about Evallonia.'

'I prefer not to discuss that hateful subject.'

'I quite understand. But this is really rather important. It's about the Evallonian Republic. What sort of fellows run it?'

'Men utterly out of tune with the national spirit. Adventurers who owe their place to the injudicious patronage of the Great Powers!'

'But what kind of adventurers? Are they the ordinary sort of middle-class republicans that you have, for example, in Germany?'

'By no means. Very much the contrary. My information is that the present Evallonian Government is honeycombed with Communism. I have evidence that certain of its members have the most sinister relations with Moscow. No doubt they speak fair to foreign Powers, but there is reason to believe that they are only waiting to consolidate their position before setting up an imitation of the Soviet régime. One of their number, Mastrovin, is an avowed Communist, who might turn out a second Bela Kun. That is one of the reasons why

Royalism is so living a force in the country. The people realize that it is their only protection against an ultimate anarchy.'

'I see.' Jaikie tapped his teeth with the nail of his right forefinger, a sure proof that he had got something to think about.

'Have you met any of those fellows? Mastrovin, for example?'

'I am glad to say that I have not.'

'You know some of the Royalists?'

'Not personally. I have always in a matter like this avoided personal contacts. They warp the judgement.'

'Who is their leader? I mean, who would sit on the throne if a Royalist revolution succeeded?'

'Prince John, of course.'

'What's he like?'

'I never met him. My reports describe him as an exemplary young man, with great personal charm and a high sense of public duty.'

'How old?'

'Quite young. Twenty-six or twenty-seven. I have seen his portraits, and they reminded me of our own Prince Charles Edward. He is very fair, for his mother was a Scandinavian Princess.'

'I see.' Jaikie asked no more questions, for he had got as much information as for the moment he could digest. He picked up the despised *Wire*, straightened it out, and read the famous interview, which before he had only skimmed.

He read it with a solemn face, for he was aware that Mr Craw's eye was upon him, but he wanted badly to laugh. The thing was magnificent in its way, the idiomatic revelation of a mind at once jovial and cynical. Tibbets could not have invented it all. Where on earth had he got his material?

One passage especially caught his notice.

'*I asked him a little timidly, if he did not think it rash to run counter to the spirit of the age.*

'*In reply Mr Craw relapsed smilingly into the homely idiom of the countryside. "The Spirit of the Age!" he cried. "That's a thing I wouldn't give a docken for."*'

Jaikie was a little startled. He knew someone who was in the habit of refusing to give dockens for things he despised. But that someone had never heard of Tibbets or Castle Gay, and was far away in his modest home of Blaweary.

That day the two travellers escaped from the tyranny of ham and eggs. They ate an excellent plain dinner, cooked especially for them by Mrs Fairweather. Then came the question of how to spend the rest of the evening. Mr Craw was obviously unsettled, and apparently had no desire to cover foolscap in his bedroom, while the mystery afoot in Portaway made Jaikie anxious to make further explorations in the town. The polling was only a few days off, and there was that ferment in the air which accompanies an election. Jaikie proposed a brief inquisition into the politics of the place, and Mr Craw consented.

A country town after dark has a more vivid life than a great city, because that life is more concentrated. There is no business quarter to become a sepulchre after business hours, since the domestic and the commercial are intermingled. A shopkeeper puts up his shutters, has his supper upstairs, and presently descends to join a group on the pavement or in a neighbouring bar parlour. The children do not seem to retire early to bed, but continue their games around the lamp-posts. There are still country carts by the kerbs, stray sheep and cattle are still moving countrywards from the market, and long-striding shepherds butt their way through the crowd. There is a pleasant smell of cooking about, and a hum of compact and contented life. Add the excitement of an election, and you have that busy burghal hive which is the basis of all human society – a snug little commune intent on its own affairs, a world which for the moment owes allegiance to no other.

It was a fine evening, setting to a mild frost, when Jaikie and Mr Craw descended the Eastgate to the cobbled market place where stood the Town Hall. There it appeared from gigantic blue posters that the Conservative candidate, one Sir John Cowden, was holding forth, assisted by a minor member of the Government. The respectable burghers now entering the door did not promise much amusement, so the two turned up the Callowa into the oldest part of the old town, which in other days had been a nest of Radical weavers. Here their ears were greeted by the bray of a loud-speaker to which the wives by their house-doors were listening, and, having traced it to its lair, they found a beaky young man announcing the great Liberal Rally to be held in the new Drill Hall and to be addressed by the candidate, Mr Orlando Greenstone, assisted by no less a personage than his leader, the celebrated Mr Foss Jones.

'Let's go there,' said Jaikie. 'I have never seen Foss Jones. Have you?'

'No,' was the answer, 'but he tried several times to make me a peer.'

They had to retrace their steps, cross the Callowa bridge, and enter a region of villas, gardens, and ugly new kirks. There could be no doubt about the attraction of Mr Foss Jones. The road was thronged with others on the same errand as theirs, and when they reached the Drill Hall they found that it was already crowded to its extreme capacity. An excited gentleman, wearing a yellow rosette, was advising the excluded to go to the hall of a neighbouring church. There an overflow meeting would be held, to which Mr Foss Jones's speech would be relayed, and the great man himself would visit it and say a word.

Jaikie found at his elbow the mechanic from the Hydropathic called Wilkie.

'I'm no gaun to sit like a deaf man listenin' to an ear trumpet,' he was announcing. 'Hullo, Mr Galt! Weel met! I was sayin' that it's a puir way to spend your time sittin' in a cauld kirk to the rumblin' o' a tin trumpet. What about a drink? Or if it's poalitics ye're seekin', let's hear what the Socialists has to say. Their man the nicht is in the Masons' Hall. They say he's no much o' a speaker, but he'll hae a lively crowd aboot him. What d'ye say? ... Fine, man. We'll a' gang thegither. ... Pleased to meet ye, Mr Carlyle. ... Ony relation o' Jock Carlyle, the horse-doctor?'

'Not that I am aware of,' said Mr Craw sourly. He was

annoyed at the liberty taken by Jaikie with his surname, though he realized the reason for it.

To reach the Masons' Hall they had to recross the Callowa and penetrate a mesh of narrow streets east of the market square. The Labour party in Portaway made up for their lack of front-bench oratory by their enthusiasm for their local leaders. Jaikie found himself wedged into a back seat in a hall, which was meant perhaps to hold five hundred and at the moment contained not less than eight. On the platform, seen through a mist of tobacco smoke, sat a number of men in their Sunday clothes and wearing red favours, with a large, square, solemn man, one of the foremen at the Quarries, in the chair. On his right was the Labour candidate, a pleasant-faced youth with curly fair hair, who by the path of an enthusiasm for boys' clubs in the slums had drifted from Conservative pastures into the Socialist fold. He was at present engaged in listening with an appreciative grin to the oratorical efforts of various members of his platform, for that evening's meeting seemed to have been arranged on the anthology principle – a number of short speeches, testifying from different angles to the faith.

'We'll now hear Comrade Erchie Robinson,' the chairman announced. Comrade Robinson rose nervously to his feet, to be received with shouts of 'Come awa, Erchie! Oot w'it, man. Rub their noses in't.' But there was no violence in Comrade Erchie who gave them a dull ten minutes, composed mainly of figures which he read from a penny exercise book. He was followed by Comrade Jimmy Macleish, who was likewise received with favour by the audience and exhorted to 'pu' up his breeks and gie them hell.' But Jimmy, too, was a wet blanket, confining himself to a dirge-like enunciation of Tory misdeeds in various foreign places, the pronunciation of which gave him pain. 'Whaur did ye say that happened?' said a voice. 'Tchemshooershoo,' said Jimmy. 'Man, there couldna be sic a place. Ye've got a cauld in your heid, Jimmy,' was the verdict. The only exception to this dismal decorum was a woman, who had a real gift of scolding rhetoric. Her theme was 'huz puir folk,' and she announced that she came from a 'Glesca stair-heid'. She was vigorous and abusive, but she had a voice like a saw, and five minutes of her were a torment to the ear.

Then the candidate rose. He was elegant, he was wholesome, and he was young; he had not made the mistake of dressing down to his part; in that audience of grim faces, worn with toil and weather, he looked as out of place as a flamingo among crows. His speech, which he delivered with the fluency born of frequent repetition, was an emotional appeal for the under-dog. He deprecated bitterness, he repudiated any intent of violence; such arguments as he gave were a plea rather for a change of heart than a change of the social fabric. He was earnest, he was eloquent, he was transparently honest, and there was something in his youthful candour which attracted his hearers, for his periods were punctuated with loud applause. But from the man on Jaikie's right they evoked only heartbroken groans.

Jaikie looked at his neighbour and recognized him. He was a middle-aged man, with a good deal of hair and beard plentifully streaked with grey. His features were regular and delicate, and his whole air was of breeding and cultivation – all but his eyes, which were like live coals under his shaggy brows. His name was David Antrobus, a name once famous in Latin scholarship, till the War suddenly switched his attention violently on to public affairs. He had been a militant pacifist, and had twice gone to gaol for preaching treason. In 1920 he had visited Russia and had returned a devout votary of Lenin, whose mission it was to put alcohol into the skim milk of British Socialism. In Glasgow he was known as Red Davie, and Jaikie had met him there in Dougal's company, when he had been acutely interested to hear a creed of naked nihilism expounded in accents of the most scholarly precision. He had met him in Cambridge, too, the preceding term. Mr Antrobus had been invited to lecture to a group of young iconoclasts, and Jaikie, in company with certain Rugby notables, had attended. There had been a considerable row and Jaikie, disliking the manner of Mr Antrobus's opponents, had, along with his friends, entered joyfully into the strife, and had helped to conduct the speaker safely to his hotel and next morning to the station.

The man returned Jaikie's glance, and there was recognition in his eyes. 'Mr Galt, isn't it?' he asked. 'I am very glad to see you again. Have you come to spy out the nakedness of the land?'

'I came to be amused,' was the answer. 'I have no politics.'

'Amused!' said Mr Antrobus. 'That is the right word. This man calls himself a Socialist candidate, but his stuff is the merest bleating of the scared bourgeois sheep. Evils, for which the only remedy is blood and steel and the extreme rigour of thought, he would cure with a penny bun.'

'Are you here to help him?'

'I am here to break him,' was the grim answer. 'My business is to hunt down that type of humbug and keep it out of Parliament. Answer me. Would it not terrify you to think that such a thing as that was fighting *beside you* in the day of battle? His place is among our enemies, to be food for our powder.'

Mr Antrobus would have said more, but his attention was distracted by the neighbour on his other side, who asked him a question. He bent his head deferentially to listen, and over the back of it Jaikie saw the strong profile and heavy jaw of the man whom a few hours before he had observed with Allins at the Hydropathic door.

There was a short colloquy between the two, and then Mr Antrobus inclined again towards Jaikie. The man was courtesy incarnate, and he seemed to think that the debt he owed Jaikie for his escape at Cambridge must be paid by a full confession of faith. He enlarged on the folly of British Socialism, the ineptitude and dishonesty of official Labour. 'Toryism,' he said, 'is our enemy – a formidable enemy. We respect it and some day will slay it. Liberalism is an antique which we contemptuously kick out of the road. But Labour is treason, treason to our own cause, and its leaders will have the reward of traitors.'

Jaikie put his mouth close to his ear: 'Who is the man on your right?' he asked. 'I fancy I have seen him before.'

'Abroad?'

'Abroad,' Jaikie mendaciously agreed.

'It must have been abroad for this is his first visit to Britain. It would not do to advertise his name for he is travelling incognito. But to you I can tell it, for I can trust you. He is a very great man, one of the greatest living. Some day soon all the world will ring with his deeds. To me he is an old friend, whom I visit several times each year for counsel and inspiration. He is the great Anton Mastrovin. You have heard of him?'

'Yes. And I must have seen him – perhaps in Vienna. One does not easily forget that face.'

'It is the face of a maker of revolutions,' said Mr Antrobus reverentially.

But at that moment the great man rose, having no doubt had enough, and Mr Antrobus docilely followed him. Jaikie sat tight through the rest of the candidate's speech, and did not squeeze out till the proposing of the resolutions began. But it may be assumed that he did not pay very strict attention to the candidate's ingenious attempt to identify the latest Labour programme with the Sermon on the Mount. He had something more urgent to think about.

## CHAPTER FOURTEEN

# PORTAWAY – ALISON

JAIKIE rose next morning with the light of a stern purpose in his eye. He had thought a good deal about his troubles before he fell asleep, and had come to certain conclusions. . . . But he must go cannily with Mr Craw. That gentleman was in an uncomfortable humour and at breakfast showed every sign of being in a bad temper. The publication of Tibbets's interview had roused a very natural wrath, and, though he had apparently acquiesced in Jaikie's refusal to send his telegram or transport him to Castle Gay, his aspect had been rebellious. At breakfast he refused to talk of the Labour meeting the night before, except to remark that such folly made him sick. Jaikie forbore to disclose his main suspicion. The news of other Evallonians in the field, Evallonians of a darker hue than those at Knockraw, would only scare him and Jaikie preferred an indignant Craw to a panicky one.

Yet it was very necessary to smooth him down, so after breakfast Jaikie and Woolworth went out into the street. At a newsagent's he bought a copy of that morning's *View*, and to his relief observed that Mr Craw's article was on the leader page. There it was, with half-inch headlines, *The Abiding Human Instincts*. That would keep him quiet for a little. He also visited a chemist and purchased two small bottles.

Mr Craw seized avidly on the paper, and a glimmer of satisfaction returned to his face. Jaikie took advantage of it.

'Mr Craw,' he said with some nervousness, 'I found out some queer things yesterday, which I'll tell you when I'm a little more certain about them. But one thing I can tell you now. Your man Allins is a crook.'

Mr Craw raised his head from toothing his own eloquence. 'Stuff and nonsense! What evidence have you?'

'A great deal. Allins has come back mysteriously when he wasn't expected: he has not gone near Castle Gay: he is at the

Hydropathic here under an assumed name, passing as a foreigner: and he is spending his time with the very foreigners who are giving you trouble. Isn't that enough?'

Mr Craw looked perturbed. At the moment he had a healthy dislike of Jaikie, but he believed him to be honest.

'Are you sure of that?'

'Absolutely sure. I suspect a great deal more, but what I'm giving you is rock-bottom fact. ... Now, it's desperately important that Allins shouldn't recognize you. You can see for yourself how that would put the lid on it. So I don't want you to go much about in the daytime. You can stay here and write another of your grand articles. I hope to get money and clothes for you to-day, and then you can carry out your original plan. ... Would you mind if, just for extra security, I touched up your face a little? You see, in these clothes even Allins wouldn't recognize you, especially with the fine complexion the weather has given you. But when you get your proper clothes from Castle Gay it will be different, and we can't afford to run risks.'

It took a good deal of coaxing for Jaikie to accomplish his purpose, but the reading of his own article, and near prospect of getting his own garments, had mollified Mr Craw, and in the end he submitted.

Jaikie, who as a member of the Cambridge A.D.C. knew something about make-up, did not overdo it. He slightly deepened Mr Craw's complexion, turning it from a weather-beaten red to something like a gipsy brown, and he took special pains with the wrists and hands and the tracts behind the ears. He darkened his greying eyebrows and the fringe of hair which enclosed his baldness. But especially he made the lines deeper from the nose to the corner of the mouth, and at the extremity of the eyes. The result was that he did away with the air of Pickwickian benevolence. Mr Craw, when he looked at himself in the mirror, saw a man not more than forty, a hard man who might have been a horse-coper or cattle-dealer, with a good deal of cynicism in his soul and his temper very ready to his hand – which was exactly how he felt. Short of a tropical deluge to wash off the stain, it would not be easy to recognize the bland lineaments which at that moment were confronting the world from the centre of his article in the *View*.

This done, Jaikie proceeded to reconnoitre. He was convinced that Alison would answer his summons and come at eleven o'clock to the Green Tree. He was equally convinced that she would not ask for him, so it was his duty to be ready for her arrival. He found that from the staircase window he had a view of the stable yard and the back door of the inn, and there he set himself to watch for her.

At two minutes before eleven a girl on a pony rode into the yard. He saw her fling her bridle to the solitary stable-boy, and be welcomed by Mrs Fairweather like a long-lost child. She talked to the hostess for a minute or two, while her eyes ran over the adjacent windows. Then she turned, and with a wave of her hand walked towards the street.

Jaikie snatched his hat and followed. He saw her moving towards the Eastgate – a trim figure, booted and spurred, wearing a loose grey coat and a grey felt hat with a kestrel's feather. She never looked behind her, but walked with a purposeful air, crossed the Eastgate, and took a left-hand turning towards the Callowa. Then at last she turned her head, saw Jaikie, and waited for him. There was a frank welcome in her eyes. Jaikie, who for the last few days had been trying to picture them in his mind, realized that he had got them all wrong; they were not bright and stern, but of the profound blue that one generally finds in water which reflects a spring sky.

'I've brought the money,' she said. 'Fifty pounds. I got it from Freddy.' And she handed over a wad of notes.

'And the clothes?'

'Mother of Moses, I forgot the clothes! They can't really matter. What does Mr Craw want with more clothes?'

'He is wearing some pretty queer ones at present. And he wants to go to London.'

'But he mustn't be allowed to go to London. You said yourself that he was safest under the light – here or hereabouts. London would be horribly dangerous.'

'Of course it would. I don't want him to go to London. I'm glad you forgot the clothes.'

'Where is he?'

'Sitting in his room at the Green Tree reading an article he's written in the *View*. He's getting rather difficult to manage.'

'You must keep him there – lock him up, if necessary – for I can tell you things at Castle Gay are in a pretty mess.'

She paused to laugh merrily.

'I don't know where to begin. Well, first of all, Dougal – Mr Crombie – imported a friend of his on Sunday from somewhere in Carrick. His name is Dickson McCunn, and he's the world's darling, but what use Dougal thought he was going to be is beyond me. There was rather a mishap at Knockraw – your friend Tibbets got locked up as a poacher – and Count Casimir was in an awful stew, and sent him over to us to be pacified. Mr McCunn received him, and Tibbets took him for Mr Craw, and wrote down what he said, and published it in an interview in yesterday's *Wire*. Dougal says that the things he said pretty well knock the bottom out of Mr Craw's public form.'

'So that was it,' said Jaikie. 'I very nearly guessed that it was Dickson. Mr Craw didn't like it, but I persuaded him not to get his papers to repudiate it. You see, it rather wipes off Tibbets from our list of enemies.'

'Just what I said,' replied the girl. 'Freddie wanted to wire at once about it, but I stopped him. We can disavow it later when we're out of this mess. . . . Now for the second snag. Count Casimir has also imported an ally, and who do you think it is? Prince John of Evallonia.'

No exclamation could have done justice to Jaikie's emotion. In a flash he saw the explanation of what he had been fumbling after. But all he said was, 'Whatever for?'

'Heaven knows! To impress Mr Craw when they find him. To impress us all. Perhaps to make me fall in love with him. They seem to think I'm rather an important person.'

'Have you seen him?'

'Yes. We all dined at Knockraw last night. The Prince is an agreeable young man, as tall as Robin Charvill, but much slimmer.'

'Handsome?' Jaikie asked with a pang at his heart.

'Extremely. Like an elegant Viking, says Freddy, who doesn't know anything about Vikings. Like the Young Pretender, says Aunt Hatty.'

'Have you fallen in love with him?' The words had not passed his lips before Jaikie repented his audacity.

But the girl only laughed. 'Not a bit of it. I'm not attracted by film stars. He's terribly good-looking, but he's dull as an owl. I can see that he is going to add considerably to our troubles, for he seems quite content to settle down at Knockraw till he can bring his charms to bear on Mr Craw.'

'We must get him shifted out of that,' said Jaikie grimly. 'Now you must hear my story. First of all, that man Allins is a blackguard.'

He recounted briefly the incidents of the past days, dwelling lightly on their travels in the hills, but more fully on the events since their coming to Portaway. The girl listened with widening eyes.

'You see how it is,' he concluded. 'Allins has double-crossed the people at Knockraw. He arranged for their coming here to see Mr Craw, and no doubt got paid for it. That in itself was pretty fair disloyalty to his chief. But he has arranged with the Republicans to catch the Royalists at work, and with their Prince there, too. He must have suspected that they would play the Prince as their trump card. No wonder he was excited when he saw who arrived at the station last night. It'll be jam for the Republicans to find their enemies in the act of plotting with a magnate of the British Press. The Royalists will be blown out of the water – and Mr Craw too. I can tell you the Republicans at the Hydropathic are not innocents, such as you describe the people of Knockraw. They're real hard citizens and they mean business. They've got a man among them who is the toughest Communist in Europe.'

The girl twined her hands. 'Jaikie,' she said, 'things are getting deliciously exciting. What shall we do next?'

He thrilled at the Christian name.

'There's only you and I that can do anything. The first thing is to get Casimir and his friends away from Knockraw.'

'That won't be easy. They're feeling too comfortable. You

see, they've made a devout ally of Mr McCunn. Dougal brought him to Castle Gay because he thought he would talk sense to them – he said he was a typical Briton and would soon convince them that Britain wasn't interested in their plans. Instead of that he has fallen completely under the spell of the Prince. He would talk about nothing else last night coming home – said it was a sin and a shame that such a fine lad should be kept from his rights by a wheen blue-spectacled dominies.' She gave a very good imitation of Dickson's robust accents.

'Just what he'd do. He was always desperately romantic. I think Dougal must have taken leave of his senses. What does Dougal say about things?'

'Chiefly oaths,' said the girl. 'He argues with Casimir and the Professor and makes no more impression than a toothpick on a brick wall. You might say that the situation at Castle Gay was out of hand. The question is, what are you and I going to do?'

The assumption of alliance warmed Jaikie's heart.

'I must get somehow to Knockraw,' he said. 'It had better be to-morrow morning early. There are six of the Republicans here, and this election has brought some queer characters into the town. You may be certain that they're keeping a pretty good watch up the water. The first thing to make sure of is that the Prince does not stir out of doors. You must get Casimir on the telephone and put the fear of God into him about that. Pitch it high enough to scare him. . . . Then you must meet me at Knockraw to-morrow morning. Say eight o'clock. I can tell them all I know, and there's a lot they can tell me that I don't know. But they won't believe me unless you're there to back me up.'

He looked down to find a small dog standing on its hind legs with its paws on his arm.

'What's that?' Alison asked.

'That's Woolworth – the terrier I bought from the drover. I told you about him.'

The girl bent to fondle the dog's head, upon which Woolworth laid muddy paws on the skirts of her coat. 'He must be introduced to Tactful and Pensive,' she said. 'He seems to belong to the same school of thought. . . . I had better get back at once and alarm Knockraw. . . . It's all right. I usually leave my pony at the Green Tree, so there's nothing unusual in my going there. But we'd better not arrive together.'

Jaikie, unwilling to leave her side, accompanied her as far as the Eastgate. But just before they reached it, he stopped short and whistled on Woolworth. He had seen Allins advancing towards them, and Allins had seen the girl. Apparently the latter desired to avoid a meeting, for he turned sharply and dived up a side street.

'What is it?' said Alison, who had been interrupted in the middle of a sentence.

'It's Allins. He saw us both. That's a pity. He and I are bound to have a meeting sooner or later, and I didn't want him to connect me with Castle Gay.'

It was significant of Jaikie's state of mind that, though he allowed five minutes to elapse between Alison's entering the stable yard and his own approach to the inn, the first thing he did when he was inside the door was to rush to the staircase window, where he was rewarded by the sight of a slim figure on a black pony leaving the gate, pursued by Mrs Fairweather's farewells.

As luck would have it the rain began after luncheon, and there was no temptation for Mr Craw to go out of doors. A fire was again lit in his bedroom, and Jaikie sought a bookseller's and purchased him a selection of cheap reprints of the English classics, a gift which was received without gratitude.

'I have got fifty pounds for you,' he told him. 'I saw Miss Westwater this morning.'

Mr Craw showed little interest. The mild satisfaction due to reading and re-reading his own article had ebbed, and he was clearly in a difficult temper.

'But she forgot to bring the clothes. I'm so sorry, Mr Craw, but I'm afraid you can't go to London to-night.'

'I have no intention of going to London to-night,' was the cold answer.

Jaikie regarded him curiously. He thought he realized the reason for this change of purpose. The interview had awakened some long-dormant spirit in Mr Craw. He felt that he was being taken advantage of, that his household gods and his inner personality were being outraged, and he was determined to fight for them. That would have been all to the good four days ago, but now it was the very deuce. Jaikie did not dare tell him the true story of the interview: the thought of Dickson, innocently masquerading as his august self, would only infuriate him. What he wanted was to get back to Castle Gay, and that at all costs must be prevented. So Jaikie imparted a little judicious information.

'I heard from Miss Westwater that Prince John of Evallonia had arrived at Knockraw last night. They all went to dinner there to meet him.'

'Good God!' exclaimed Mr Craw. He was startled at last out of his dumps. 'That is a terrible blunder – a terrible calamity. They won't be able to keep his visit a secret. I shall be credited –' His eyes told the kind of unpleasant thing with which he would be credited.

'Cheer up, sir,' said Jaikie. 'We'll find a way out. But you see how impossible it is for you to go to Castle Gay. . . . And how important it is nobody should recognize you here. . . . If all goes well, you can disavow the interview, and the world will think you have been all the time out of the country.'

Mr Craw said nothing. He had started morosely upon the Essays of Addison, and the big glasses adorning his weather-beaten face gave him the air of a pious bookmaker.

Jaikie went out into the rain and made a few calls. He visited the lounge of the Station Hotel in the hope of finding a thirsty Evallonian comforting himself after the drought of the Hydropathic. But he found nobody there except a stray bagman and one or two rainbound golfers. Then he proceeded to the Hydropathic, where he had a few words with the head-porter. The foreigners were all abroad; they had departed after breakfast in two cars; whither the deponent did not know. Their habits? Well, there were always one or two of them on the road. The young man seemed to spend a lot of time in the town, and Wilkie had reported that he had seen him with some queer-looking folk. 'He's maybe a poalitician,' he added. 'There's a heap o' that trash in Portaway the noo.'

Jaikie penetrated to the back parts of the establishment, and found Wilkie in the boiler house, too much occupied to talk.

'Yon was a dreich show last night, Mr Galt,' was all he found time to say. 'I've tried a' three pairties and there's no ane to mend the ither. My father used to say that in the auld days an election in Portaway was one lang, bluidy battalion. This time I don't believe there'll be a single broken heid. Folks nowadays hae lost a' spunk and pith. There's twa-three Communists in the town, and there's plenty of them among the lads at the Quarries. Maybe they'll brichten up things afore the polling-day.'

'When is that?' Jaikie asked, and was told 'Friday'. 'It'll be a big day in Portaway,' Wilkie added, 'for, forby being the nicht o' the poll, it's the Callowa Club Ball. Fancy dress, nae less. It used to be in the auld Assembly Rooms, but that's a furniture depository noo, so they haud it in the big room at the Station Hotel. I've seen fifty carriages and pairs in Portaway that nicht, but noo it's a' motors.'

Jaikie returned about tea-time, to find that Mr Craw had fallen asleep over Addison. Mercifully he slept for several hours, and awoke in a better temper, and, having had no tea, with a considerable appetite for dinner. He must be given air and exercise, so, after that meal, the rain having ceased, Jaikie proposed a saunter in the town. Mr Craw consented. 'But I will go to no more political meetings,' he said. 'I am not interested in this local dog-fight.'

It was a fresh night, with a south-west wind drifting cloud galleons up from the Solway. They walked down the Callowa side, along the miniature quays, till they were almost outside the town limits, and could see dimly, beyond the last houses, the wide *machars* which stretched to the salt water and Portaway its famous golf course. Presently one of the causes of Mr Craw's oppression became evident. He had caught a cold. He sneezed repeatedly, and admitted, in reply to Jaikie's anxious inquiries, that he had a rawness in the back of his throat and a congested feeling in his head.

'This won't do,' said Jaikie. 'I'm going to take you straight home and put you to bed. But first we'll stop at a chemist's and get you a dose of ammoniated quinine. That generally cures my colds, if I take it at the start.'

They returned to the foot of the Eastgate, just where it joined the market square, and at the corner found a chemist's shop. The owner was about to put up his shutters, but the place still had the dazzling brightness which is associated with the sale of drugs. Mr Craw was accommodated with a small beaker of the bitter compound prescribed by Jaikie, and, as he swallowed it with many grimaces, Jaikie saw a face at the street door looking in on him. It was the face of Allins.

Mr Craw saw it, too, in the middle of his gasping, and, being taken unawares, it is probable that an involuntary recognition entered his eyes before Jaikie could distract his attention. At any rate Jaikie saw on Allins's face, before it disappeared, an unpleasing smile.

He paid for the mixture and hustled Mr Craw out of the shop. Allins did not appear to be in the immediate neighbourhood. 'You saw that?' he whispered. 'I believe he recognized you. We've got to give him the slip. Very likely he's watching us.'

Mr Craw, nervous and flustered, found himself hurried up the Eastgate, to the right, to the left, to the left again; it was like the erratic course of a bolted rabbit. Twice Jaikie stopped, darted into the middle of the street, and looked behind. The third time he did this he took his companion's arm and dragged him into a run. 'The man's following us,' he said.

At all costs the pursuit must be baffled, for till they had thrown it off it was impossible to return to their inn. Once again Jaikie stopped to reconnoitre, and once again his report was bad. 'I see his grey hat. He's not above twenty yards behind.'

Suddenly they found that the people were thicker on the pavement. There was some kind of movement towards a close on their left, as if it led to a meeting. Jaikie resolved to take the chance. Allins would never think they would go indoors he argued, for that would be to enter a trap. He would follow on past the close mouth, and lose their trail.

He drove Mr Craw before him into a narrow passage, which was pretty well crowded. Then they entered a door, and started to climb a long stair. The meeting, whatever it was, was at the top of it. It took them some minutes to get up, and at the top, at the door of the hall, Jaikie looked back. ... To his disgust he saw the hat of Allins among the throng at the bottom.

It was Jaikie's rule, when cornered at football or anything else, to play the boldest game, on the theory that it was what his opponent would least expect. The hall was not large, and it was very full, but at the far end was a platform which still held some vacant seats. In the chair was Red Davie, now engaged in making introductory remarks. In an instant Jaikie had come to a decision. It was impossible to prevent Allins in that narrow hall seeing Mr Craw at close quarters. But he must not have speech with him, and he must see him under circumstances utterly foreign to his past life. This latter was the essence of true bluff. So he marched him boldly up the centre passage and ascended the platform, where he saw two empty seats behind the chairman. He interrupted Red Davie to shake hands effusively, and to introduce Mr Craw. 'My friend, Mr Carlyle,' he said. 'He's one of you. Red hot.'

Red Davie, in his gentle earnest voice and his precise scholarly accents, was delivering a reasoned denunciation of civilized society. He was the chairman, but he was obviously not the principal speaker. Jaikie asked in a whisper of a man behind him who was expected and was told Alec Stubber, a name to conjure with. 'But his train's late and he'll no be here for twenty minutes. They'll be gey sick o' Antrobus by then.'

Jaikie looked down on the upturned faces. He saw Allins standing at the back of the hall near the door, with his eyes fixed on the platform and a half-smile on his face. Was that smile one of recognition or bewilderment? Happily Mr Craw was well hidden by the chairman. ... He saw row upon row of faces, shaven and bearded, young and old, but mostly middle-aged. These were the Communists of the Canonry, and very respectable folk they looked. The Scottish Communist is a much misunderstood person. When he is a true Caledonian, and not a Pole or an Irishman, he is simply the lineal descendant of the old Radical. The Scottish Radical was a man who held a set of inviolable principles on which he was entirely unable to compromise. It did not matter what the principles were; the point was that they were like the laws of Sinai, which could not be added to or subtracted from. When the Liberal party began to compromise, he joined Labour; when Labour began to compromise by a natural transition he became a Communist. Temperamentally he has not changed. He is simply the stuff which in the seventeenth century made the unyielding Covenantor, and in the eighteenth the inflexible Jacobite. He is honesty incarnate, but his mind lacks flexibility.

It was an audience which respected Red Davie, but could not make much of him, and Red Davie felt it himself. The crowd had come to hear Alec Stubber, and was growing a little restless. The chairman looked repeatedly at his watch, and his remarks became more and more staccato. . . . Allins had moved so that he now had a full view of Mr Craw, and his eyes never left him.

Then Jaikie had an inspiration. He whispered fiercely to his neighbour: 'Allins is watching you. There's only one way to put him off the scent. You've got to speak. . . . Denounce the Labour party, as you've often done in the papers. Point out that their principles lead logically to Communism. . . . And, for God's sake, speak as broad as you can. You must. It's the only way.'

Mr Craw would certainly have refused, but he was given no time. Jaikie plucked the chairman's elbow. 'My friend here,' he whispered, 'could carry on for a little. He'd be glad of the chance. He's from Aberdeen, and a great worker in the cause.'

Red Davie caught at the straw. 'Before Comrade Stubber arrives,' he said, 'and that must be in a very few minutes, you will have the privilege of hearing a few words from Comrade

Carroll, who brings to us the fraternal greetings of our Aberdeen comrades. No man in recent years has worked more assiduously for the triumph of the proletariat in that uncompromising quarter of Scotland. I call on Comrade Carroll.'

He turned round, beamed on Mr Craw, and sat down.

It was perhaps the most difficult moment of that great man's life. Crisis had come upon him red-handed. He knew himself for one of the worst speakers in the world, and he – he who had always had a bodyguard to shield him from rough things – who was the most famous living defender of the *status quo* – was called upon to urge its abolition, to address as an anarchist a convention of anarchists. His heart fluttered like a bird, he had a dreadful void in the pit of his stomach, his legs seemed to be made of cotton-wool.

Yet Mr Craw got to his feet. Mr Craw opened his mouth and sounds came forth. The audience listened.

More – Mr Craw said the right things. His first sentences were confused and stuttering, and then he picked up some kind of argument. He had often in the *View* proved with unassailable logic that the principles of Socialism were only half-hearted Communism. He proved it now, but with a difference. For by some strange inspiration he remembered in what company he was, and, whereas in the *View* he had made it his complaint against Labour that it was on the logical road to an abyss called Communism, his charge now was that Labour had not the courage of its principles to advance the further stage to the Communist paradise. ... It was not a good speech, for it was delivered in a strange abstracted voice, as if the speaker were drawing up thoughts from a very deep well. But it was not ill received. Indeed, some of its apophthegms were mildly applauded.

Moreover, it was delivered in the right accent. Jaikie's injunction to 'speak broad' was unconsciously followed. For Mr Craw had not lifted up his voice in public for more than thirty years, not since those student days at Edinburgh, when he had been destined for the ministry and had striven to acquire the arts of oratory. Some chord of memory awoke. He spoke broadly, because in public he had never spoken in any other way. Gone were the refinements of his later days, the clipped vowels, the slurred consonants. The voice which was speaking at Jaikie's ear had the aboriginal plaint of the Kingdom of Fife.

Jaikie, amazed, relieved, delighted, watched Allins and saw the smile fade from his face. This being who stammered a crude Communism in the vernacular was not the man he had suspected. He shrugged his shoulders and jostled his way out of the hall.

As he left, another arrived. Jaikie saw a short square man in a bowler hat and a mackintosh enter and push his way up the middle passage. An exclamation from the chairman, and the applause of the meeting, told him that the great Stubber had appeared at last. Mr Craw, in deference to a tug from Jaikie, sat down, attended by an ovation which was not meant for his efforts.

The two sat out that meeting to its end, and heard many remarkable things from Comrade Stubber, but Jaikie hurried Mr Craw away before he could be questioned as to the progress of Communism in Aberdeen. He raced him back to the Green Tree, and procured from Mrs Fairweather a tumbler of hot whisky and water, which he forced him to drink. Then he paid his tribute.

'Mr Craw,' he said, 'you did one of the bravest things tonight that I ever heard of. It was our only chance, but there's not one man in a million could have taken it. You're a great man. I offer you my humble congratulations.'

Mr Craw blushed like a boy. 'It was rather a dreadful experience,' he said, 'but it seems to have cured my cold.'

CHAPTER FIFTEEN

# DISAPPEARANCE OF MR CRAW

NEXT morning Jaikie arose at six, and, having begged of an early-rising maid a piece of oatcake and two lumps of sugar (a confection to which he was partial), set out on foot for Knockraw. He proposed to make part of his route across country, for he had an idea that the roads in that vicinity, even thus early in the morning, might be under observation.

Mr Craw descended at half-past eight to find a pencilled message from Jaikie saying that he would be absent till luncheon and begging him to keep indoors. Mr Craw scarcely regarded it. He had slept like a top, he ate a hearty breakfast, and all the time he kept talking to himself. For he was being keyed up to a great resolution.

A change had come over him in these last days, and he was slowly becoming conscious of its magnitude. At the Back House of the Garroch he had been perplexed and scared, and had felt himself the undeserving sport of Fortune. His one idea had been to hide himself from Fortune's notice till such time as she changed her mind. His temper had been that of the peevish hare.

But the interview in the *Wire* had kindled his wrath – a new experience for one who for so long had been sheltered from small annoyances. And with that kindling had come unrest, a feeling that he himself must act, else all that he had built might crumble away. He felt a sinking of the foundations under him which made passivity mere folly. Even his personality seemed threatened. Till that accursed interview was disowned, the carefully constructed figure which he had hitherto presented to the world was distorted and awry. ... And at the very moment when he had it in his power to magnify it! Never, he told himself, had his mind been more fruitful than during the recent days. That article in yesterday's *View* was the best he had written for years.

Following upon this restlessness had come a sudden self-confidence. Last night he had attempted an incredibly difficult thing and brought it off. He marvelled at his own courage. Jaikie (whom at the moment he heartily detested) had admitted that he had been very brave. ... Not the only occasion, either. He had endured discomfort uncomplainingly – he had assisted to eject a great hulking bully from a public house. He realized that if anyone had prophesied the least of these doings a week ago he would have laughed incredulously. ... There were unexpected deeps in him. He was a greater man than he had dreamt, and the time had come to show it. Fragments of Jaikie's talk at the Back House of the Garroch returning to his mind as if they had been his own inspiration. 'You can carry things with a high hand.' ... 'Sit down in your own house and be master there.' ... 'If they turn nasty, tell them to go to the devil.' That was precisely what he must do – send his various enemies with a stout heart to the devil.

He particularly wanted to send Allins there. Allins was the second thing that broke his temper. That a man whom he had petted and favoured and trusted should go back on him was more than he could endure. He now believed wholeheartedly in Jaikie's suspicions. Mr Craw had a strong sense of decency, and Allins's behaviour had outraged it to its core. He had an unregenerate longing to buffet his former secretary about the face.

His mind was made up. He would leave Portaway forthwith and hurl himself into the strife. ... The day of panic was over and that of action had dawned! ... But where exactly should he join the battle front? ... Knockraw was out of the question. ... Castle Gay? That was his ultimate destination, but should it be the first? Jaikie had said truly that Barbon and Dougal might have got things well in train, and, if so, it would be a pity to spoil their plans. Besides, Castle Gay would be the objective of his new enemies, that other brand of Evallonian at which Jaikie had hinted. Better to avoid Castle Gay till he had learned the exact lie of the land .... The place for him was the Mains. Mrs Brisbane-Brown, whom he had always respected, lived there; she knew all about his difficulties; so did her niece, who was one of Jaikie's allies. The high-nosed gentility of the Mains seemed in itself a protection. He felt that none of the troubles of a vulgar modern world could penetrate its antique open country.

So with some dregs of timidity still in his heart, but on the whole with a brisk resolution, he left the inn. The wet south-west wind, now grown to half a gale, was blowing up the street. Mr Craw turned up the collar of his thin raincoat, and, having discarded long ago his malacca cane, bought a hazel stick for a shilling in a tobacconist's shop. This purchase revealed the fact that the total wealth now borne in his purse was five shillings and threepence. He was not certain of his road, but he knew that if he kept up the right bank of the Callowa he would reach in time the village of Starr. So he crossed the bridge, and by way of villas and gas-works came into open country.

Knockraw is seven miles from Portaway as the crow flies and after the first two miles Jaikie took the route of the crow. It led him by the skirts of great woods on to a high moorish ridge, which had one supreme advantage in that it commanded at a distance large tracts of the highway. But that highway was deserted except for a solitary Ford van. Jaikie had reached the edge of the Knockraw policies, and the hour was a quarter to eight, before he saw what he expected.

This was a car drawn up in the shelter of a fir wood – an aged car with a disreputable hood, which no doubt belonged to some humble Portaway garage. What was it doing there so early in the morning? It stood in a narrow side-road in which there could be little traffic, but it stood also at a view-point. . . . Jaikie skirted the little park till he reached the slope of Knockraw Hill, and came down on the back of the house much as the luckless Tibbets had done on the previous Saturday night. He observed another strange thing. There was a wood-cutter's road up the hill among the stumps of larches felled in the War, the kind of road where the ruts are deep and the middle green grass. It was not a place where a sane man would take a car except for urgent reasons. Yet Jaikie saw a car moving up that road, not a decayed shandrydan like the other, but a new and powerful car. It stopped at a point which commanded the front door and the main entrance to the house. It could watch unperceived, for it was not in view from below, it was far from any of the roads to the grouse moor, and there were no woodmen at work.

Jaikie made an unconspicuous entrance, dropping into the sunk area behind the kitchen, and entering by the back door. To an Evallonian footman, who in his morning garb looked like an Irish setter, he explained that he was there by appointment; and Jasper, the butler, who came up at that moment, apparently expected him. He was led up a stone stair, divested of a sopping waterproof, and ushered into the low-ceilinged, white panelled dining-room.

In that raw morning hour it was a very cheerful place. Alison sat on the arm of a chair by the fire, with her wet riding-boots stretched out to the blaze. Opposite her stood a young man in knickerbockers, a tall young man, clean-shaven, with a small head, a large nose, and smooth fair hair. Prince Odalchini was making coffee at the table, and the Professor was studying a barograph. Casimir, who was attired remarkably in very loud tweeds and white gaiters, came forward to greet him.

Alison jumped to her feet. 'This is Mr Galt, sir, that I told you about,' she informed the young man. Jaikie was presented to him, and made the kind of bow which he thought might be suitable for royalty. He shook hands with the others, and then his eyes strayed involuntarily to Alison. The fire had flushed her cheeks, and he had the dismal feeling that it would be starkly impossible for anything under the age of ninety to avoid falling in love with her.

They sat down to breakfast, Alison on Prince John's right hand, while Jaikie sat between Casimir and the Professor. Jaikie was very hungry, and his anxieties did not prevent him making an excellent meal, which Casimir thoughtfully did not interrupt with questions. One only he asked: 'I understand that Mr Craw is with you? You have just left him?'

Jaikie was a little startled. Alison must have given this fact away. A moment's reflection assured him that it did not matter. With the Knockraw party the time had come to put all their cards on the table.

'I left him in bed,' he said. 'He had a difficult time last night. We fell in with Allins, and he thought he recognized Mr Craw. We took refuge in a Communist meeting, and Allins followed us. I knew the chairman, and there was nothing for it but to get him to ask Mr Craw to speak. And speak he did. You never heard anything like it. He belted the Labour party for not being logical and taking the next step to Communism, and he did it in the accents of a Fife baillie. That was enough to make Allins realize he was on the wrong scent.'

'How splendid!' Alison cried. 'I never thought ...'

'No more did he. His nearest friends wouldn't recognize him now. He scarcely recognizes himself.'

Jaikie spoke only once again during the meal.

'Do you know this place is watched, sir?' he asked Casimir.

'Watched?' three voices exclaimed as one.

'I came on foot across country,' said Jaikie, 'for I expected something of the kind. There's an old Portaway car in the by-road at the south-west corner of the park, and there's a brand-new car on the wood-road up on the hill. Good stands both, for you'd never notice them, and if you asked questions they'd be ready with a plausible answer. We're up against some cleverish people. Has Miss Westwater told you anything?'

'Only that Mr Sigismund Allins is a rascal,' said Casimir. 'And that is grave news for he knows too much.'

Jaikie looked at the four men, the kindly fanatical eyes of Prince Odalchini, the Professor's heavy honesty, Casimir's alert, clever face, Prince John's youthful elegance, and decided that these at any rate were honest people. Foolish, perhaps, but high-minded. He was a good judge of the other thing, having in his short life met much of it.

The table was pushed back, the company made a circle round the fire, and Jaikie was given a cigarette out of Prince John's case. The others preferred cigars.

'We are ready to listen, Mr Galt,' said Casimir.

Jaikie began with a question. 'It was Allins who arranged your visit here?'

Casimir nodded. 'He has been in touch with us for some time. We regarded him as Mr Craw's plenipotentiary. He assured us that very little was needed to secure Mr Craw's active support.'

'You paid him for his help?'

'We did not call it payment. There was a gift – no great amount – simply to cover expenses and atone for a relinquished holiday.'

'Well, the first thing I have to tell you is that somebody else has paid him more – to put a spoke in your wheel.'

'The present Government in Evallonia!'

'I suppose so. I will tell you all I know, and you can draw your own conclusions.'

Jaikie related the facts of which we are already aware, beginning with his first sight of Allins in the car from Gledmouth on the Sunday evening. When he came to the party of foreigners at the Hydropathic he could only describe them according to the account of the head-porter, for he had not yet seen them. But such as it was his description roused the liveliest interest in his audience.

'A tall man with a red-pointed beard!' Casimir cried. 'That can only be Dedekind.'

'Or Jovian?' Prince Odalchini interjected.

'No. I know for certain that Jovian is sick and has gone to Marienbad. It must be Dedekind. They have used him before for their dirty work. ... And the other – the squat one – that is beyond doubt the Jew Rosenbaum. I thought he was in America. The round-faced, spectacled man I do not know – he might be any one of a dozen. But the youngish man like a horse-breaker – he is assuredly Ricci. Your Royal Highness will remember him – he married the rich American wife. The fifth I take to be one of Calaman's sons. I heard that one was well thought of in the secret service.'

'There's a sixth,' said Jaikie, 'whom I have seen myself. I saw him in Allins's company, and I saw him at a Labour meeting. He's a short, very powerful fellow with big glasses and an underhung jaw that sticks forward. I know his name, too. He's called Mastrovin.'

It was a bombshell of the largest size. 'Mastrovin!' each of them exclaimed. It was as if a flood of dark memories and fears had been unloosed, and every eye was troubled. 'Gracious God!' Casimir murmured. 'And Ricci and Dedekind in conjunction! Crime and fanaticism have indeed joined hands.' He leaned over to Prince John. 'I fear that we have brought your Royal Highness very near to your most deadly enemies.'

Then he bowed to Jaikie. 'You have given us news of extreme importance, and we are most deeply your debtors. If you are to help us – and I think you desire to – it is necessary that you should understand the situation. . . . The present Government in Evallonia is Republican. We believe that it is not loved by the people and but ill suited to the national genius. But it is loved by the powers of Europe, especially by Britain. They see in it a sober, stable bourgeois government such as those enjoyed by France and Germany, and in their own interest the present rulers of Evallonia play up to them. They are always ready with the shibboleths of democracy, and at Geneva they speak wonderful things about peace and loving-kindness. But we, Mr Galt, we who are in close touch with the poor people of Evallonia, know better. We know that the Government is a camarilla of selfish adventurers. Already in many secret ways they are oppressing the poor. They think, most of them, not of Evallonia, but of their own power and their own pockets. And some think of darker things. There are among them men who would lead Evallonia into the black ways of Russia. There is above all this Mastrovin. He holds no portfolio – he has refused many – but he is the power in the background. He is the most subtle and dangerous mind in Europe to-day, and he is a fanatic who cannot be intimidated or persuaded or purchased. Why is he here? Why are Dedekind and Ricci and Calaman and Rosenbaum here? They cannot harm us with the Evallonian people – that they know well, for every day among the Evallonian masses disquiet with their regime is growing and enthusiasm for our Prince as their deliverer. . . . They are desperate men, and they must mean desperate things.'

'I daresay they're all that,' said Jaikie. 'But what kind of desperate act would profit them? That's what puzzles me.'

'They could kidnap his Royal Highness,' Prince Odalchini put in. 'Here – on a foreign shore – far from his friends.'

'I don't think so,' said Jaikie. 'Britain is a bad place for that kind of game – our police are too good. Besides, what would they do with him if they got him? Kidnapping would be far easier on the Continent, and if they wanted that they must have had plenty of chances. ... Suppose they meant to do him bodily harm? Could they choose a worse place than this, where a foreigner is uncommon and conspicuous, and would half-a-dozen of their chief people turn up to do the job? It would be insanity, and they don't strike me as insane.'

'What then is your explanation?' the professor asked sombrely.

'They want to discredit his Royal Highness and his party. You say they can't do that with the Evallonians. But they can do it with the Powers. They can do it with Britain. Suppose they publish to the world details of His Royal Highness and yourselves plotting a revolution on British soil with Mr Craw. We're a queer people, and one thing we can't stand is having our country used for foreign intrigues. The news of it would put up the back of Tory and Socialist alike. And the notion that Mr Craw was in it – well, it would be the end of Mr Craw and the Craw Press.'

'Of course it would,' said Alison, who had followed Jaikie's exposition with appreciative nods.

'I'm certain I'm right. They want to compromise you. They and Allins believe that Mr Craw is at Castle Gay. They know that you are at Knockraw, and they know what they hoped for has happened, and that His Royal Highness is here. They are waiting to find just the kind of compromising situation they want. And they're desperate men, so they won't stick at much to bring it about. I have no doubt at all that Mastrovin has ways and means of mobilizing some pretty tough elements in Portaway. Remember, too, that the election is on Friday, and the Canonry will be upside down that day.'

'By God, I believe the boy is right,' said Casimir, and the professor acquiesced with a solemn nod.

'I've got it,' Jaikie cried. 'I believe Friday – the day after to-morrow – is the day they've chosen to act. The countryside as I say, will be upside down, the police will all be at the polling stations, and there will be a good chance for high-handed proceedings. I can't just guess what these will be, but you may take it that they will be adequate.'

'But they won't find Mr Craw,' put in Alison.

'I don't think that will matter. If they can get you somehow connected with Castle Gay, we'll never be able to persuade people that Mr Craw was not there, or at any rate was not privy to the meeting. Not after that interview in the *Wire*,' and he looked across at Alison. 'The world knows his opinions, and will assume Barbon to have his authority. No, Allins has been lucky, and things up to now have turned out rather well for him.'

'What do you advise?' It was Prince John who spoke. He looked at Jaikie as at another young man who might be more useful than middle-age.

'Well, sir, if we know what they intend – and I think my guess is right – we start with one big advantage. Besides, I might find out a great deal in the next two days. But there's one thing to be done at once. We must shorten our front of defence, and get rid of Knockraw.'

'Will you please explain?' said Casimir.

'You must give up your mission. You must see that it's impossible. You can't do anything with Mr Craw. Even if he were hot on your side, and not scared to death at the very mention of you, you can do nothing with him now. Your business is to prevent this mission of yours becoming a deadly blow to your cause and setting Britain violently against you. You see that?'

The silence proved that they did see it.

'May I ask, Mr Galt,' Casimir spoke, 'what exactly is your position in this affair? Are you one of Mr Craw's journalists, like Mr Crombie?'

'No thank Heaven. I've nothing to do with journalism. My position is the same as Miss Westwater's. We like Mr Craw and we don't like Allins, and we're going to do our best to protect the one and down the other. Our attitude to you is one of benevolent neutrality, but we're for you against the other blighters.'

Prince John laughed. 'That is candid and fair. Go on, sir. What is your plan?'

'You must leave Knockraw, and the sooner the better. It's a rotten place to defend. It's as open as a cricket-field. You and your household must clear out. You've no local people indoors, so you should be able to do that unostentatiously. But you mustn't take his Royal Highness with you. You must depart exactly the same party as you arrived. We must take no chances. Nobody knows that he is with you except Allins and his friends, and nobody else must ever know. He can join you in London, where nothing matters.'

'And meantime what is to become of him?'

'You must entrust him to us. Miss Westwater and I will undertake to get him somehow quietly into England – alone. What do you say, sir?'

'I will gladly entrust myself to Miss Westwater,' said Prince John with a bow.

'Then you must be the first to leave, sir,' said Jaikie. 'Every hour you spend in this house and in this company increases the danger. I think Castle Gay is the right place for you, for it's not very easy for anybody to get near it. But we'll have to move cautiously. I think that the best place to go first will be the Mains.'

Casimir brightened. 'I have a high regard for Mrs Brisbane-Brown,' he announced. 'She might be of the utmost service.'

'I'll back Aunt Harriet to put anything through,' said the loyal Alison.

Jaikie was aware that four pairs of eyes were scrutinizing him closely, and small wonder. He had wandered in out of the rain an hour ago, a complete stranger, and here he was asking four men of ripe experience and high position to put their fortunes in his hands. He faced the scrutiny with his serious, gentle eyes, very little perturbed, for he had a purpose now, and as was his custom was wholly absorbed in it. They saw his small wedge-shaped countenance, his extreme youthfulness, his untidy hair, his shabby clothes, but, being men of penetration, they saw something else – that sudden shadow which seemed to run over his face, tightening it into a mask of resolution. Every line of Jaikie spoke of a brisk purpose. He looked extraordinarily dependable.

Prince John spoke first.

'I was never in love with this venture, my dear Casimir, and now I have only one wish – to be well out of it. We shall be well advised if we are guided by Mr Galt. You and I must clearly separate and not reunite till London. I am the compromising article, but I shall be much less conspicuous alone.'

'We go – when?' said Casimir, looking at Jaikie.

'I should advise to-night – a moonlight flitting, as we say. You can send the keys to the laywers – say you were called home suddenly – anything. It's a foul day, so you'd better stop indoors, or if you go out leave word with your servants to keep a good watch and let nobody in. You have two cars, I think, and they're both hired from Portaway. Leave them in a Gledmouth garage and catch the night train to London. I'll arrange with the Portaway people to send for them – they're friends of mine.'

'And his Royal Highness?'

'I want him out of this house now. This dirty weather will help us. Miss Westwater can arrange for a groom from the Castle to fetch his kit – he'd better come in a dogcart, as if he were on an errand to the servants. Our first job is to get the Prince out of Knockraw and safe in the Mains without any mortal eye seeing him. . . . I'm ready, if you are, sir.'

Jaikie stood up stiffly, for the armchair had been very deep and his legs were rather cramped, and the others rose with him. He asked one more question: 'Was the Prince out of doors yesterday?' and was told that he had been on the moor for some rough shooting. He had worn a different suit from that which he was now wearing, and a white mackintosh. 'Good,' said Jaikie. 'I want him now to put on the oldest and dingiest waterproof you can raise. But you must be sure to have that white mackintosh sent to Castle Gay.' A plan was vaguely building itself up in his head.

Jaikie arranged the departure with an eye to the observation-points on the hill and in the by-road. The mere exit from Knockraw was not a difficult problem; the real trouble would come when they were beyond the policies and in the rough pastures which stretched to the eastern wall of Castle Gay park. Once at that wall they were safe for a time, for there was a gate of which Alison had the key, and inside the park there were Mackillop and his myrmidons to ward off strangers.

Alison had her pony brought round, and set off at a canter down the avenue. Her arrival had been observed, and her going must be not less conspicuous. She rode fast through the drizzle till she reached the steading of Kirnshaw, which is one of the Castle farms. There she left her pony, and returned on foot to a clump of birches at the edge of a broomy common, where she was to meet the others. Her local knowledge could not be dispensed with.

The first part was easy. Jaikie and Prince John emerged from a scullery window and by way of a thicket of laurels reached a fir planting which led to the park boundary. The rain now descended in sheets, and soon they were both comprehensively wet, but it was the right weather for their task. There must be but poor visibility for the watcher on the hill, and the car in the by-road controlled only the direction of Portaway. ... It was easy, too, to cross the road by which Tibbets had pursued the Knockraw car. It was full of twists and turns and at this hour as empty of humanity as the moor. After that came half an hour of slinking through patches of furze and down hedgerow ditches, till the clump of birches was reached, where Alison awaited them. So far the Prince had behaved well, and had obeyed Jaikie as a docile novice in a deer forest obeys a masterful stalker.

But with Alison in the party complications began. They had still three-quarters of a mile to cover before they reached the Castle park wall, and, since they were descending a slope, they were more or less in view of the road from Portaway which followed the left bank of the Callowa. Jaikie, who had a sense for landscape like a wild animal's, had this road always in mind, and sometimes he made them crawl flat for yards, sometimes run hard in cover, sometimes lie on damp earth till some alarm had ceased. The trouble was Prince John, who became suddenly a squire of dames. He wanted to help Alison over every difficulty. He would rise to his full height in crossing a brook that he might give her a hand, he did the same thing in parting the bramble coverts, and he thought it his duty to make polite conversation in spite of Jaikie's warning growl.

The girl, as active as a squirrel, needed no assistance, and was much embarrassed by these attentions. Already Jaikie had forced the Prince's head down into the heather several times when he had raised it to address Alison, and he was just beginning to wonder how his companion was to be sternly reprimanded without *lèse-majesté*, when Alison anticipated him.

'Prince,' she said in her clear high voice, 'do you mind if I mention that for the present the Age of Chivalry has gone?'

They crossed the high-road when, after a reconnaissance by Jaikie, the coast was pronounced clear, and with some difficulty induced the gate in the park wall to open. Now for a space they were safe, so they restored their circulation by running down a glade of bracken to where the Callowa lay in its hollow. The river was rising, but it could be forded at a shallow, and the three splashed through, Alison going first to escape Prince John's obvious intention of carrying her across. After that they went more warily, for there were points in the neighbourhood from which this section of the park could be commanded. Indeed their route was very much that taken by Jaikie and Dougal on their first visit, and they passed under the very tree in which Alison had been perched. Just before noon they reached the gate in the further wall.

Jaikie, with the help of the bough of an adjoining tree, shinned up, raised his head above the top, and cautiously prospected the highway. Opposite was a low fence, and then a slope of hazels and rhododendrons which was part of the Mains demesne. Once inside that pale they were safe. The road was empty. He gave the word, and Alison and the Prince darted across and in a moment were out of sight.

An instant later a man appeared round the bend of the road. He was a fisherman, for he carried a great salmon-rod and he wore brogues and waders. As he came nearer Jaikie recognized him and tumbled off the wall. It was Mr McCunn, who proposed to fish the bridge pool of the river and was taking the quickest way to it.

Jaikie cut short his greeting, for a car was coming down the road. 'Not a word,' he whispered. 'Let me speak. ...' Then, raising his voice, 'It's a grand day for a salmon. ... What's your fancy for flies? ... The water is three feet up already. ...I saw a big one in the Bridge pool, thirty pounds if he was an ounce, but pretty black. ...'

So he chattered as the car passed. It was a two-seater, and in it was one man, Allins. He slowed down, and Jaikie's babble must have come clearly to his ear.

'Have you taken leave of your senses, Jaikie?' the mystified Dickson asked.

'Yes. I'm as daft as a yett in a high wind. D'you know what I've been doing all morning? Dragging a prince through burns and bogs by the hair of his head. ... I'm going to watch you fishing for ten minutes and you've got to answer me some questions.'

When Alison and Prince John halted in a recess of the hazel thicket, whence ran a rustic path to the upper garden, they found another occupant of that hermitage. This was a small man, very wet and muddy, in a ruinous waterproof, rather weary, and apparently in some alarm. It was a full minute before Alison recognized in the scarecrow the celebrated Mr Craw.

CHAPTER SIXTEEN

# ENEMY'S COUNTRY

JAIKIE, being very wet, trotted most of the way back to Portaway. The rudiments of a plan were growing in his mind, and he had a great deal to think about and a great deal to do. ... The enemy was keeping a close watch, and must have got together a pretty considerable posse to help him. It was a bold thing for Allins himself to be in the neighbourhood of Castle Gay. But then, he reflected, Allins's visits there had not been frequent – he generally took his holiday abroad in the autumn – and, when there, he probably never stirred much outside the park gates. Besides, he would not be easy to identify with the collar of his ulster turned up and a cap pulled over his brows. Only one who, like Jaikie himself, was on the look-out for him, would be likely to recognize him. No, Allins was safe enough.

He reached the Green Tree to find no Mr Craw or any message from him, and learned from a maid that he had sallied forth about half-past nine. ... Jaikie sat down and considered, while he ate a luncheon of bread and cheese. Mr Craw could not be wandering about Portaway – he knew the risk he ran in the town. He must have gone up the water. But where? Had he taken the bit between his teeth and returned to Castle Gay? It seemed the only explanation. Mr Craw, puffed up with last night's achievement, had discovered a new self-reliance, and proposed to steer his own course.

It was an unforeseen complication, but there was no help for it. He must trust to luck, and go on with his own preparations. After all, for the moment Mr Craw was not the chief piece on the chess-board.

Jaikie dried the legs of his trousers at Mrs Fairweather's kitchen fire. Then he took some pains with his toilet. His old flannel suit was shabby but well-cut, and, being a tidy mortal, he wore a neat, if slightly bedraggled, soft collar and tie. This would scarcely do, so, at a neighbouring draper's he purchased a rather high, hard, white collar and a very vulgar striped tie. At a pawnshop he invested in an imitation silver watch-chain with a football shield appended, and discarded his own leather guard. His hair was a little too long, and when he had reduced it to further disorder by brushing it straight up, he regarded himself in a mirror and was satisfied. He looked the very image of the third-rate reporter or press-photographer, and he could guarantee an accent to correspond. His get-up was important, since he proposed to make himself ground-bait to attract the enemy.

His business was to find Allins, and he believed that the best covert to draw was the lounge of the Station Hotel. So, accompanied by the neglected Woolworth, he made his way to that hostelry. The hour was half-past two, and he argued that a gentleman who had lunched droughtily in the Hydropathic might be inclined for a mild stimulant. He sought the retreat of his friend, the head-porter, which had the advantage of possessing a glass window which commanded about three-quarters of the lounge.

To his relief he saw Allins sitting by a small table, and beside him Tibbets. They appeared to be deep in talk, Tibbets especially expounding and gesticulating.

That eminent journalist, after his Sunday's triumph, had made a tour of the Canonry to get material for a general article on the prospects of the election. He had returned to Portaway with a longing for better food than that furnished by country inns, and had lunched heavily in the Station Hotel. While in the enjoyment of coffee and a liqueur, he had found himself next to Allins, and according to his wont had entered into conversation. Tibbets was a communicative soul, and in a little time had told his neighbour all about the *Wire* interview, and, since that neighbour showed a flattering interest, had faithfully recounted every detail of his visit to Castle Gay. He had not mentioned his adventure at Knockraw, for he was an honest man, and regarded complete secrecy on that point as part of the price of the Craw interview.

Jaikie observed the two, and rightly deduced what they

were talking about. That was all to the good. It would convince Allins that Mr Craw was at Castle Gay, and lull any suspicion he might have entertained on the subject. He wished he knew himself where Mr Craw was. ... He was reminded of a duty. There was no public telephone in Portaway, and nothing of the kind in the Green Tree, but the head-porter had one in his cubby-hole, and gave him permission to use it. He rang up Castle Gay and asked to speak to Dougal.

When he heard the gruff hullo of his friend, he informed him of Mr Craw's disappearance. Had he arrived at the Castle?

'Good God!' came the answer. 'He's not here. What on earth are we to do? Isn't he somewhere in Portaway?'

'I don't think so. I believe he's on his way to you. I wish ...'

At that moment Jaikie was compelled to ring off, for Tibbets was leaving the lounge, and if he remained at the telephone Tibbets would see him. He particularly did not want to see Tibbets, so he subsided on to the floor. When he rose, Tibbets had left the hotel, but Allins was still in the lounge. He might leave at any moment, so there was no time to be lost.

Followed by Woolworth, whom the rain had made to look like a damp white sponge set on four spindly legs, he sauntered into the lounge and set himself on a couch a yard or two from Allins, the dog squatting docilely beside him. He spoke to Woolworth in a way which was bound to attract the attention of his neighbour. While he looked round, as if for a waiter, he observed that Allins's eye was fixed on him. He hoped that, in spite of his strange collar and tie, Allins would recognize him. He had been seen in company with Alison, he had been seen that very morning outside Castle Gay park: surely these were compromising circumstances which Allins must wish to investigate.

He was right. Allins smiled at him, came over, and sat down beside him on the couch.

'I saw you at the meeting the other night,' he said pleasantly. 'What do you think of the local Communists?'

Jaikie was something of an actor. His manner was slightly defensive, and he looked at the speaker with narrowed eyes.

'Very middling.' His voice was the sing-song of the Glasgow slums. 'My friend wasn't bad. Ye heard him – I saw ye at the back of the hall. But yon Stubber!' He spat neatly into the adjacent fire. 'He was just a flash in the pan. Fine words and no guts. I know the breed!'

'I didn't hear Stubber – I had to leave early. Your friend, now. He seemed to know a good deal, but he wasn't much of an orator.'

'Carroll's his name. Jimmy's red hot. But ye're right. He's no much of a speaker.'

Jaikie extracted from a waistcoat pocket a damaged Virginian cigarette, which he lit by striking a match on the seat of his trousers.

'Have a drink,' said Allins.

'I don't mind if I do.'

'What will you have?'

'A dry Martini. If you had sampled as much bad whisky as me in these country pubs, you would never want to taste it again.'

Two cocktails were brought. 'Here's luck,' said Allins, and Jaikie swallowed his in two gulps as the best way to have done with it. One of his peculiarities was a dislike of alcohol in every form except beer, a dislike increased by various experiments at Cambridge. Another was that alcohol had curiously little effect on him. It made him sick or sleepy, but not drunk.

'Are you a Communist?' Allins asked.

Jaikie looked sly. 'That's asking. ... No, by God, I'm no afraid to confess it. I'm as red as hell. ... That's my private opinion, but I've to earn my living and I keep it dark.'

'What's your profession, if I may ask?'

'I'm a journalist. And with what d'ye think? The Craw Press. I'm on their Glasgow paper. I'm here to cover the election, but our folk don't want much about it, so I've a lot of spare time on my hands.'

'That's an odd place for a man of your opinions to be.'

'Ye may say so. But a chap must live. I'm just biding my time till I can change to something more congenial. But meanwhile I get plenty of fun studying the man Craw.'

'Do you know him?'

'Never clapped eyes on him. None of us have. But he lives in this neighbourhood, and I've been picking up a lot of information about him these last few days.'

Jaikie had the art of watching faces without his scrutiny being observed, for his own eyes appeared to be gentle and abstracted. He respected Allins's address. Allins's manner was at once detached and ingratiating, and he spoke with a suspicion of a foreign accent. His eyes were small, sharp, and observant. He had the high gloss which good living and regular exercise give, but there were anxious lines about the corners of his eyes, and something brutal about the full compressed lips. The man was formidable, for he was desperately anxious; he was in a hole and would stick at little to get out of it.

Jaikie's last words seemed to rouse him to a livelier interest.

'Have another drink,' he said.

'I don't mind if I do. Same as before.'

Allins ordered a single cocktail. Jaikie sipped it, and then took the glass in his right hand. As he spoke he lowered it, and gradually bestowed its contents on the thick damp fleece of the couchant Woolworth, who was so wet already that he took no notice.

'Mr Craw lives here?' said Allins. 'Of course. I remember now. His is the big house some miles up the river.'

'You passed it this morning,' said Jaikie, greatly daring. 'Yon was you wasn't it, that I saw in the two-seater? I was having a yarn with an old fisherman body who had got a day's fishing in the Callowa. I thought that, seeing he was allowed to fish the water, he could tell me something about Craw.'

'And did he?'

'Not him. He was only a Glasgow grocer that had got leave from the factor.'

'Then what have you found out about Mr Craw?'

'The queer thing is that I've found out so little. The man's fair immured, and they won't let people inside the place. I'm grand at getting on with plain folk, and I've made friends with a good few of the people on the estate. It's a daft-like business. They keep the lodge gates locked like prisons, but there's a dozen places you can get into the park. I've been all round the gardens and not a soul to object. I could have got in at any one of twenty windows if I had wanted. Oh, I can tell ye, I've had some fun up there. Craw would fire me the morn if he knew what I had been up to.'

It was Jaikie's cue to appear a little excited, as if the second cocktail had been too much for him.

'Have another drink?' said Allins.

'I don't mind if I do. The same . . . No, wait a jiffey. I'll have a lickyure brandy.'

As the waitress brought the drink, the head-porter also appeared.

'They're ringin' up frae Castle Gay, Mr Galt,' he said. 'Wantin' to know if ye're still in the hotel?'

'Tell them I've just gone,' said Jaikie, and he winked at Allins.

He sipped the brandy and looked mysteriously at his neighbour.

'There's a girl living up thereaways. I don't know her name. But she wants this dog of mine. She saw him in Portaway the other day, and was mad to buy him. It seems that he's like a wee beast she had herself that died. She offered me four pounds for him, but I wasn't for selling. . . . That was her ringing up just now. She's a determined besom. . . . I wonder who she can be. Craw is believed to be a bachelor, but maybe he has had a wife all the time on the sly.'

As Jaikie spoke he decanted the brandy on the back of the sleeping Woolworth. This time he was not so successful. Some of the liqueur got into the little dog's ear, who awoke and violently scratched the place with a paw.

'That beast's got fleas,' said Jaikie with tipsy solemnity.

'What you say about Castle Gay is very strange,' said Allins. 'Why should a great man, a publicist of European reputation, live in such retirement? He can have nothing to conceal.'

Jaikie assumed an air of awful secrecy.

'I'm not so sure. I'm not – so sure – about that.' He thrust his face closer to the other's. 'The man is not doing it because he likes it. There must be a reason. ... I'm going to find out what that reason is. ... I've maybe found it.'

He spoke thickly, but coherently enough. He did not want Allins to think that he was drunk – only excited and voluble.

'Have another drink?'

'Don't mind if I do. Another b-brandy. It must be the last, all the same, or I'll never get out of this hotel. ... What was I saying? Oh ay! About Craw. Well, isn't it ridiculous that he should behave like an old ostrich? Ay, an ostrich. He locks his lodge gates and lets nobody inside his house, but half the population of the Canonry might get in by the park. ... What's Friday? I mean the day after the morn. It's the polling day. The folk up there will all be down at Portaway voting, and they'll make a day of it – ay, and a night of it. ... Man, it would be a grand joke to explore Castle Gay that night. Ye could hold up Craw in his lair – no harm meant, if ye understand, but just to frighten him, and see how he likes publicity. It's what he's made his millions by, but he's queer and feared of a dose of it himself.'

'Why don't you try?' said Allins.

'Because I must think of my job. There might be a regrettable incident, ye see, and I'm not wanting to be fired. Not yet. ... Besides ...'

'Yes?'

'Besides, that kind of ploy wouldn't get me much forward. I want to find out what Craw's feared of, for he's damned feared of something. And the key to it is not in Castle Gay.'

Allins was listening intently, and did not notice the small moan which came from the sleeping Woolworth as something cold splashed in the vicinity of his tail.

'Where?' he asked.

Jaikie leaned towards him and spoke in a thick whisper.

'Did you ever hear of a place called Knockraw?'

'No,' said Allins.

'Well, it's next door to Castle Gay. And there's some funny folk there. Foreigners. ... I've nothing against foreigners. Ye're maybe one yourself. Ye speak a wee thing like it. ... But the Knockraw foreigners are a special kind, and they've got some hold on Craw. I don't yet know what it is, but I'll find out. Never fear, I'll find out. I've been hanging about Knockraw these last few days, and if I liked I could tell ye some queer tales.'

Jaikie suddenly raised his eyes to the clock on the wall and gave a violent start.

'Govey Dick! It's close on four! Here! I must go. I can't sit havering any longer, for I've some stuff to get off with the post. . . . I'm much obliged to ye. It's been very enjoyable. Ye'll keep your mouth shut about what I've told ye, for I'm not wanting to get into Craw's black books.'

He rose slowly to his feet and steadied himself by the table. Allins rose also and held out his hand.

'This has been a very pleasant meeting, Mr Galt,' he said. He had got the name from the head-porter's message. 'I wonder if I could persuade you to repeat it quite soon. This very evening, in fact. I am staying with some friends at the Hydropathic. Could you drop in for a light supper about ten o'clock? We are strangers in Scotland, and should like to hear more from you about local politics – and journalism – and Mr Craw.'

'I don't mind if I do. But the Hydropathic's black teetotal.'

Allins smiled. 'We have means of getting over that difficulty. Ten o'clock sharp. Will you ask for Mr Louvain? That will be splendid. *Au revoir*.'

Jaikie made his way delicately through the lounge as if he were carrying egg-shell china, followed by Woolworth, who paused occasionally to shake himself and who smelt strongly of spirits.

Jaikie dined at the Green Tree, but first he wrote and despatched a letter to Dougal by the country post. He had still no word of the missing Craw. The letter said little, for he did not believe in committing himself on paper, but it asked that Dougal and Barbon and Dickson McCunn should be at the Mains on the following afternoon about three o'clock, and that the Mains party should also muster in full strength. 'We must consult,' Jaikie wrote, 'for I'm anxious about Friday.'

After dinner he put in an hour at a Unionist meeting, which was poorly attended, but which convinced him that the candidate of that party would win, since – so he argued – the non-political voters who did not go to meetings and made up the bulk of the electorate were probably on his side. Then he went for a walk along the Callowa banks. For the first time in this enterprise he was feeling a little nervous. He was about to meet a type of man of whom he knew nothing, and so much hung on the meeting. At five minutes to ten he turned up the hill towards the Hydropathic. He asked Grierson, the head-porter, for Mr Louvain. 'I'll send up and see if they're expecting ye,' was the answer. 'They're queer folk, foreigners, and I daurna take ony liberties.' The message came down that Mr Louvain was awaiting Mr Galt, and Jaikie ascended to the second floor and was shown into a large sitting-room.

A table was laid with a cold supper, and on another stood a little grove of champagne bottles. There were seven men in the room, and they were talking volubly in a foreign tongue when Jaikie entered. All wore dinner jackets, so that Jaikie's shabbiness was accentuated. Allins came forward with outstretched hand. 'This is very good of you, Mr Galt. Let me present you to my friends.'

Names were named, at each of which Jaikie bobbed his head and said, 'Pleased to meet ye,' but they were not the names which Casimir had spoken at Knockraw. Still he could identify them, for the description of the head-porter had been accurate. There was Dedekind, and Ricci, who looked like a groom, and Calaman, and the Jew Rosenbaum, and the nameless nondescript, at the back was the smiling and formidable face of Mastrovin.

This last spoke. 'I have seen Mr Galt before – at a Socialist meeting in this town. He is, I think, a friend of my friend Antrobus.'

'Red Davie,' said Jaikie. 'Ay, I know him a little. Is he still in Portaway?'

'Unfortunately he had to leave this morning. He had a conference to attend in Holland.'

Jaikie was relieved to hear it. Red Davie knew things about

him – Cambridge and such like – which were inconsistent with his present character.

They sat down to supper, and Jaikie toyed with a plate of cold chicken and ham. The others drank champagne, but Jaikie chose beer. He wanted a long drink, for his nervousness had made him thirsty.

The interrogations began at once. There was no pretence of a general interest in British journalism or the politics of the Canonry. These men had urgent business on hand, and had little time to waste. But Mastrovin thought it right to offer a short explanation.

'We do not know Mr Craw,' he said, 'except by repute. But we are a little anxious about him, for we know something about the present tenants of the place you call Knocknaw – Knockraw – or whatever it is. It is fortunate, perhaps, that we should be travelling in Scotland at this time. I understand that you take an interest in Knockraw and have been making certain inquiries. Will you describe the present occupants of the house?'

'Here! Play fair!' said Jaikie. 'I'm a journalist and I'm following my own stunt. I don't see why I should give away my results to anybody.'

His manner was that of a man who realizes that in the past he has been a little drunk and a little too communicative, and who is now resolved to be discreet.

Mastrovin's heavy brows descended. He said something to Allins and Allins whispered a reply, which Jaikie caught. Now Jaikie was no great linguist, but between school and college he had been sent by Dickson McCunn to Montpelier for six months, and had picked up a fair working knowledge of French. Allins's whisper was in French and his words were, 'We'll persuade the little rat to talk. If not, we'll force him.'

Those words made all the difference to Jaikie's comfort. He was called a 'little rat' – he was being threatened; and threats had always one effect on him. They roused his slow temper, and they caused him to turn very pale, just as six years earlier they would have made him weep. Allins saw his whitening face, and thought it was the consequence of Mastrovin's glower and the formidable silence of the company. He saw only a rag of a journalist, who had been drunk in the afternoon, and was now feeling the effects. He did not see the little shiver which ran across Jaikie's face, leaving it grey and pinched, and, even if he had, he would not have known how to interpret it.

'I think you will tell me,' said Mastrovin with a menacing smoothness. 'We will make it worth your while. If you don't, we can make it unpleasant for you.'

Jaikie's acting was admirable. He let a wild eye rove among the faces and apparently find no comfort. Then he seemed to surrender.

'All right. Keep your hair on. ... Well, first there's a man they call the Count – that's all I could get from the Knockraw beaters.'

He described in accurate detail the appearance and garb of Casimir, of the Professor, of Prince Odalchini. He in no way drew upon his imagination, for he was speaking to men to whom the three had for years been familiar.

'Is there not a fourth?' Mastrovin asked.

Jaikie appeared to consider. 'Oh, yes. There's a young one. He came the night before last, and was out shooting yesterday.' He described elaborately the appearance of Prince John. 'He wears a white mackintosh,' he added.

Mastrovin nodded.

'Now, will you tell us why you think these people have some hold on Mr Craw?'

Jaikie appeared to hesitate. 'Well – ye see – I don't just quite like. Ye see, Craw's my employer. ... If he heard I had been mooching round his house and spying – well, I'd be in the soup, wouldn't I?'

The alcoholic bravado of the afternoon had evaporated. Jaikie was now the treacherous journalist, nervous about his job.

'You are afraid of offending Mr Craw,' said Mastrovin. 'Mr Galt, I assure you that you have much more reason to be afraid of offending us. ... Also we will make it worth your while.'

Threats again. Jaikie's face grew a shade paler, and his heart began to thump. He appeared to consider anew.

'Well, I'll tell ye. ... Craw never entertains anybody. His servants tell me that he never has any guests from the neighbourhood inside the door. But the people at Knockraw dined at Castle Gay last Saturday night, and the Castle Gay party dined at Knockraw on Monday night. That looks queer to begin with.'

The others exchanged glances. They apparently had had news of these incidents and Jaikie confirmed it. Their previous knowledge also established Jaikie's accuracy.

'Anything more?'

'Plenty. The people at Knockraw have brought their own servants with them. Everybody inside the house is a foreigner. That looks as if they had something they wanted to keep quiet. ... It would have been far cheaper to get servants in the Canonry, like other tenants.'

Again Mastrovin nodded.

'Anything more?'

'This,' said Jaikie, allowing a smile to wrinkle his pallor. 'These Knockraw foreign servants are never away from Castle Gay. They spend half their time crawling about the place. I've seen one of them right up at the edge of the terrace. I daresay they're all poachers at home, for they're grand hands at keeping cover. Now, what does that mean?' Jaikie seemed to be gaining confidence and warming to his task. 'It means that they're not friends of Craw. They've got something coming for him. They're spying on him. ... I believe they're up to no good.'

Mastrovin bent his brows again.

'That is very interesting and very odd. Can you tell us more, Mr Galt?'

'I can't give ye more facts,' said Jaikie briskly, 'but I can give ye my guesses. ... These Knockraw folk want something out of Craw. And they're going to get it. And they're going to get it soon. I'll tell ye why I think that. The polling's on Friday, and on that day there's a holiday at Castle Gay. Craw's very keen – so they tell me – on his people exercising what he calls their rights as citizens. All the outdoor servants and most of the indoor will be in Portaway, and, if I'm any judge, they'll no be back till morning. Maybe you don't know what a Scotch election is like, especially in the Canonry. There'll be as many drunks in Portaway as on a Saturday night in the Cowcaddens. The Knockraw foreigners will have Craw to themselves, for yon man Barbon, the secretary, is of no mortal use.'

Jaikie observed with delight that his views roused every member of the company to the keenest interest, and he could not but believe that he had somehow given his support to a plan which they had already matured. It was with an air of covering his satisfaction that Mastrovin asked, in a voice which he tried to make uninterested:

'Then you think that the Knockraw people will visit Castle Gay on Friday night?'

'They won't need to visit it; they'll be there already,' said Jaikie.

'What do you mean?'

'I mean that by this time they've all shifted their quarters, bag and baggage, to the Castle.'

'How the devil do you know that?' It was Allins who spoke, and his voice was as sharp as a dog's bark.

'I found it out from one of the Castle maids. I can tell ye it's all arranged. The servants have left, but the gentry are shifting over to the Castle. . . . I was at Knockraw this morning, and I saw them packing the guns in their cases. They're done with shooting for the year, unless,' he added with a grin, 'there's some shooting of a different kind at Castle Gay.'

This news produced an impression as great as the most sensitive narrator could have desired. The seven men talked excitedly among themselves – not, to Jaikie's regret, in French.

'It looks as if ye didn't believe me,' he said, with irritation in his tone. 'Well, all I can say is, send out somebody to Knockraw the morn's morning, and if the place is not all shuttered up and not a chimney smoking, ye can call me the worst kind of liar.'

'We accept what you say, Mr Galt,' said Mastrovin, 'and we will test it. ... Now, on another matter. You say that you have explored the park of the Castle very thoroughly, and have seen the Knockraw servants engaged in the same work. ... We have here a map. As a proof of your good faith perhaps you will show us the route by which these servants approached the gardens unobserved.'

He produced a sheet of the largest-scale Ordnance Survey.

'Fine I can do that,' said Jaikie. 'In my young days I was a Boy Scout. But I'm awful dry with so much talking. I'll thank you for some more beer.'

His glass was filled, and he drained it at a draught, for he was indeed very thirsty. A space was cleared on the table, and with a pencil he showed how the park could be entered at the Callowa bridge and elsewhere, and what sheltered hollows led right up to the edge of the terrace. He even expounded the plan of the house itself. 'There's the front door. ... A man could get in at any of these lower windows. They're never shuttered. ... No, the gardeners' houses are all down by the kitchen garden on the east bank of the Callowa. The chauffeurs and mechanics live on the other side just under the Castle Hill. ... The keepers? Mackillop is miles away at the Blae Moss; one of the under-keepers lodges in Starr, and one lives at the South Lodge. Craw has a very poor notion of guarding his privacy, for all he's so keen on it.'

Jaikie yawned heavily – partly in earnest, for he was very weary. He consulted the cheap watch at the end of his recently purchased chain. He was searching for the right note on which to leave, and presently he found it. It was no occasion for ceremony.

'I wasn't much in my bed last night, and it's time I was there now or I'll be dropping under this table.'

He got to his feet and made an embarrassed survey of the company.

'I'm much obliged to you gentlemen for your hospitality. We've had a great crack, but for God's sake keep it to yourselves. ... I've maybe said more than I should have, but it's your blame for leading me on. ... I want ye to promise that ye'll never mention my name. If it came out that I had been spending my time nosing into his private affairs, Craw would fire me like a shot. ... And he doesn't pay badly.'

'You need not worry, Mr Galt,' said Mastrovin. 'We are not loquacious people. Let me recommend you to be equally silent – especially in your cups.'

'Never fear. I'll take care of that.' Jaikie gave an imbecile giggle, bobbed his head to the company, and took his leave. Allins did not offer his hand or trouble to open the door. They had had all that they wanted from this bibulous, babbling, little reporter.

At the door of the Hydropathic Jaikie remembered suddenly that they had promised to remunerate him for his confidences. He wished he had collected his fee, for he believed in taking every opportunity of spoiling the Egyptians. But he could do nothing now. He was as one who had escaped from the cave of Polyphemus, and it would be folly to go back for his hat.

At the Green Tree he found a note which had been brought by a boy on a bicycle. '*Dear Jaikie,*' he read, '*set your mind at ease. Mr Craw is here at the Mains, being lectured by Aunt Harriet. You have made him twice the man he was. Love from Alison.*'

He read this missive at least eight times. Then he put it carefully into his pocket-book and laid the pocket-book under his pillow. Last night, though that pocket-book contained fifty pounds in Treasury notes, it had lain casually on his dressing-table.

CHAPTER SEVENTEEN

# JAIKIE OPENS HIS COMMUNICATIONS

JAIKIE slept like a log and awoke next morning in high spirits. These were mainly attributable to Alison's letter, which he re-read many times while he dressed. She had called him 'Jaikie' on paper; she had sent him her love: the whole enterprise was a venture of his and Alison's – the others were only lay figures. At breakfast he had some slight uneasiness as to whether he had not been a little too clever. Had he not given too much rein to his ingenuity? . . . He had prevented Prince John joining the others in their midnight flitting. No doubt it was in a general way desirable to scatter in a flight, but he could not conceal from himself that the Prince might now be safe in the English midlands, whereas he was still in the very heart of danger. Well, he had had a reason for that, which he thought Alison would appreciate. . . . And he had gone out of his way to invite an assault on Castle Gay. He had his reason for that, too, many reasons, but the chief, as he confessed to himself, was the desire for revenge. He had been threatened, and to Jaikie a threat was a challenge.

He had spent half an hour in cleansing Woolworth, whose alcoholic flavour the passage of hours had not diminished. His bedroom had smelt like a public house. First he borrowed big scissors from Mrs Fairweather, and clipped the little dog's shaggy fleece and his superabundant beard and whiskers. Then he washed him, protesting bitterly, with soap and hot water, and dried him before the kitchen fire. He made a few alterations in his own get-up. The stiff collar and flamboyant tie of yesterday were discarded, and for neckwear he used a very faded blue scarf, which he tied in the kind of knot affected by loafers who have no pride in their appearance. He might meet Allins or one of the Evallonians in the street, and he had no desire to be recognized. He looked now, he flattered himself, like a young artisan in his working clothes, and to complete the part he invested in an unfashionably shaped cap.

Attended by the shorn and purified Woolworth, he made for the railway station. Portaway, as has been explained, is an important main-line station, but it is also the junction for a tiny single-line railway which runs down the side of the Callowa estuary to the decayed burgh of Fallatown. Once Fallatown was a flourishing port, with a large trade to the Cumberland shore and the Isle of Man, a noted smuggling centre, and the spot from which great men had taken ship in great crises. Now the ancient royal burgh is little more than a hamlet, with a slender fishing industry, a little boat-building, and one small distillery. Jaikie did not propose to go as far as Fallatown, but to stop at the intermediate station of Rinks, where he had some business with a friend.

He crossed the bridge and reached the station without mischance. The rain of the preceding day had gone, and had left one of those tonic October mornings which are among the delicacies of Scottish weather. There was no frost, the air was bracing and yet mild, the sky was an even blue, the distances as sharp as April. From the bridge Jaikie saw the top of the great Muneraw twenty-five miles distant, with every wrinkle clear on its bald face. The weather gave an edge to his good spirits. He bought a third-class return ticket for Rinks, and walked to the far end of the station, to the small siding where the Fallatown train lay, as if he had not a care in the world.

There he got a bad fright. For among the few people on the little platform was Allins, smoking a cigar outside a first-class carriage.

Jaikie hastily retreated. Why on earth was Allins travelling to Fallatown? More important, how on earth was he to escape his notice at such close quarters? At all costs Allins must not know of his visit to Rinks.

He retreated to the booking-office, and at an adjoining bookstall bought a paper with the notion that he might open it to cover his face. In the booking-office was a large comely woman of about thirty, much encumbered with a family. She carried an infant in one arm, and a gigantic basket in the other, and four children of ages from four to ten clung to her skirts. Apparently she desired to buy a ticket and found it difficult to get at her purse because of the encumbrance in her arms. 'I want three return tickets to Fallatown,' she was telling the clerk, while she summoned the oldest child to her aid. 'Hector Alexander, see if you can get Mither's purse oot o' Mither's pooch. Na, na, ye gomeril, that's no whaur it bides. Pity me that I suld hae sic feckless weans. ... Mind the basket, then. ... Canny, it's eggs. ... Gudesakes, ye'll hae them a' broke.'

Hector Alexander showed signs of tears, and one of the toddlers set up a wail. The mother cast an agonized look round and caught sight of Jaikie.

'Can I help ye, mistress?' he said in his friendly voice. 'I'm for Rinks, mysel'. It's a sore job traivellin' wi' a family. Gie me the wean and the basket. Ye havena muckle time, for the train starts in three minutes.'

The flustered woman took one look at his face, and handed over the baby. 'Thank ye kindly. Will ye tak the bairns to the train and I'll get the tickets? Hector Alexander and Jean and Bessie and Tommy, you follow the gentleman. I'm sure I'm awful obliged.'

So it fell out that Jaikie, with an infant beginning to squall held resolutely before his face, a basket in his right hand, and four children attached to different parts of his jacket, made his way to the Fallatown train, passing within ten feet of his enemy. The third-class coach was just behind the engine. Allins did not spare even a glance for the much encumbered youth. Jaikie found a compartment with only one old woman in it, and carefully deposited the basket on the floor and the four children on the seats, the while he made strange noises to soothe the infant. The guard was banging the doors when the hustled mother arrived and sat down heavily in a corner. She cuffed Hector Alexander for blowing his nose in a primitive way, and then snatched the now obstreperous babe from Jaikie's arms. 'Wheesht, daurlin'! Mither's got ye noo. ... Feel in my pooch, Bessie. There's some jujubes there for you and Jean and wee Tommy.'

The old woman surveyed the scene over the top of her spectacles. Then she looked at Jaikie.

'Ye're a young chiel to be the faither o' sae mony weans.'

The mother laughed hilariously. 'He's no their faither. He's just a kind freend. . . . Their faither is in the Gledmouth hospital wi' a broken leg. He works in the Quarries, ye ken, and a month yestreen he got a muckle stane on his leg that brak it like a pipe stapple. . . . Thank ye, he's getting on fine. He'll be out next week. I'm takin' the weans to see their grannie at the Port.'

The infant was quieted, and the two women embarked on a technical discussion of human ailments, while the four children found an absorbing interest in Woolworth. The little dog was deeply offended with his master and showed it by frequent artificial sneezes, but he was not proof against the respectful blandishments of the children. Consequently when he left the carriage at Rinks, he had two of their jujubes sticking in his damp fleece.

Jaikie, with the dog in his arms, sheltered behind a shed till the train had left the platform. He had a glimpse of Allins's unconscious profile as he was borne past. Then he went out to the roadside clachan which was Rinks, and turned his steps over the salty pastures to the riverside.

The *machars*, yellowing with autumn, stretched for miles before him till in the south they ended in a blue line of sea. The Callowa, forgetting its high mountain cradle, had become a sinuous trench with steep mud banks, at the bottom of which – for the tide was out – lay an almost stagnant stream. Above the grasses could be seen here and there the mast of a small vessel, waiting in the trough for the tide. The place was alive with birds – curlew and plover and redshank and sandpiper – and as he jumped the little brackish ditches Jaikie put up skeins of wild duck. It was a world in which it was good to be alive, for in the air there was both the freedom of the hills and the sting of the sea.

Presently he reached a little colony of huts beside the water. Down in the ditch which was the Callowa lay three small luggers; there was an antiquated slip and a yard full of timber.

One of the huts was a dwelling-house, and before its door, sitting on a log was a man in sea-boots and jersey, busy mending a sail. He looked up as Jaikie appeared, dropped his task, took the pipe from his mouth, and grinned broadly. 'Whae would hae thocht to see *you* here?' was his greeting. 'Is Mr McCunn wi' ye?'

'Not this time,' said Jaikie, finding a place on the log. 'But he's in this countryside. How's the world treating you, Mr Maclellan?'

Jaikie had come here several times with Dickson, when the latter, growing weary of hill waters, desired to fill his lungs with sea air, and appease his appetite for slaughter by catching the easy salt-water fish. In Mr Maclellan's boat they had fished the length of the Solway, and beyond it far down the English coast and round the Mull. Once even in a fine April they had crossed to the Isle of Man and made the return journey by night.

'No sae bad,' Maclellan answered Jaikie's question. 'Ye'll see the *Rosabelle*'s new pentit. It's been a fair season for us folk, and the weather has been mercifu'! ... It's ower lown the noo, but it'll no be long or it changes. The auld folk was sayin' that this month will gang oot in snaw. When are you and Mr McCunn comin' to hae a shot at the jukes? The first nip o' frost and there'll be a walth o' birds on the tideway.'

'Mr McCunn's not much of a shot,' said Jaikie, 'and just now he has other things to think about. ... What's that?' he asked suddenly, pointing towards the sea. On the right of what seemed to be the Callowa mouth rose the top-gear of a small ship, a schooner with auxiliary steam.

'That,' said Maclellan, turning his deep-set long-sighted eyes in the direction of Jaikie's finger. 'That's a yatt – a bonny wee yatt. She's lyin' off Fallatown. What she's doin' there I canna tell, unless she belongs to some shooting tenant.'

'Has she been there long?'

'Since the day afore yesterday. I was thinkin' o' takin' the dinghy and gaun down to hae a look at her.'

Jaikie pondered. A yacht at Fallatown at this season of the year was a portent. Now he understood the reason of Allins's journey. ... He understood something more. The people at the Hydropathic would not stick at trifles. Kidnapping? No, there could be no reason for that. They did not want to put themselves in the wrong. But it might be that they would desire to leave quietly and speedily, when their business was done, and a little ship at Fallatown gave them the means. ... Jaikie smiled. It was a pleasure to deal with people who really meant business. He no longer felt that he had been too ingenious.

'Is the *Rosabelle* in good trim?' he said.

'Never better. As ye see, she's new pentit.'

'Well, Mr McCunn wants you to do a job for him. He's staying up the water at Starr, and he has a friend with him who wants to get over to Cumberland to-morrow night. It's a quicker way than going round by Gledmouth and Carlisle. Could you put him over to Markhaven – that's where he wants to go – some time before midnight to-morrow?'

Maclellan considered. 'High tide's about 9.15. I could slip down wi' the ebb. ... There's no muckle wind, but what there is is frae the north. ... Ay, I could set your freend over if he cam here round about eleven – maybe, a wee thing later.'

'That's splendid. Mr McCunn will bring him down. He wants to see you again. ... There's just one small thing. Keep the business entirely to yourself. You see, Mr McCunn's friend has a reason for wanting to get away quietly. ... I'm not quite sure what it is, but there's some tiresome engagement he wants to cut, and it wouldn't do if the story got about that he had made a moonlight flitting to avoid it. He's rather a big man in his way, I believe. A politician, I think.'

Maclellan nodded with profound comprehension. 'There's walth o' poaliticians in the Canonry the noo,' he observed. 'It's a dawg's trade. I don't blame ane o' the poor deevils for takin' the jee. Tell Mr McCunn I'll never breathe a word o't. ... Peety there's nae smugglin' nowadays. I wad be a fine hand at it, bidin' here wi' nae wife and nae neebors.'

Jaikie spent a pleasant morning. He boarded the *Rosabelle* and renewed his memory of her tiny cabin; he enjoyed a rat hunt in Woolworth's company; he helped Maclellan to paint the dinghy: he dined with him at noon on Irish stew. Then he borrowed his bicycle. There was a train to Portaway at 1.30, but it was possible that Allins might travel by it, and Jaikie was taking no needless risks. 'Send back the thing when ye're through wi't,' Maclellan told him. 'I've nae need o't the noo. I thought o' bicycling in to vote the morn, but I'm inclined to bide at hame. I'm sick o' poalitics.'

Going very slow, so that Woolworth might keep up with him, Jaikie managed to avoid Portaway altogether, and joined the Callowa valley three miles above the town. After that he went warily, reconnoitring every turn of the road, till he was inside the Mains avenue. He arrived a few minutes after the hour he had named to Dougal.

At the edge of the lawn Alison was waiting for him.

'Oh, Jaikie,' she cried, 'isn't this a stupendous lark? Such a party in the drawing-room! A real live Pretender to a Throne – and very nice-looking! Freddy as anxious as a hen, and Dougal as cross as thunder – I've discovered that that's Dougal's way of showing nervousness! and Mr Craw! What have you done with Mr Craw? He's as bold as brass, and nobody can manage him except Aunt Hatty. ... Jaikie, you're very disreputable. I don't like your clothes a bit. Where did you get that horrible scarf?'

'I was worse yesterday,' was all that Jaikie would say. 'What I want to know is – have you kept John indoors? And what about the servants? They mustn't talk.'

'He has never put his head outside since he arrived yesterday – except for an hour after dark last night when I took him for a walk on the hill. The servants have nothing to talk about. We call him John, and pretend he is another Australian cousin like Robin. Freddy sent a groom to Knockraw to pick up his kit.'

'How did that go off?'

'All right. The groom went to the back door. There was a good deal of luggage – enough to fill the dogcart. He said he met a lot of people – a man in the avenue and several on the road. I suppose these were the spies?'

'The groom went straight to Castle Gay?'

'Yes. Middlemas arranged for getting the things over here after dark.'

'That was lucky. The sight of the luggage going to the Castle will have helped my reputation for speaking the truth, when the story gets to the Hydropathic this morning. You realize that all this neighbourhood is being watched?'

'Of course I do. It's a delicious feeling. There's been some very odd people in cars and on bicycles up the road, and Mackillop has hunted several out of the park.'

'Mackillop had better stop that,' said Jaikie. 'For the next twenty-four hours it would be as well if the park were open to the public.'

'Are you serious?' Alison looked puzzled. 'Come in at once and explain things. I've had a lot of trouble keeping our own lot quiet. Mr Craw has been rather above himself. That beloved Mr McCunn is my great ally. He said, "I'll take no responsibility about anything till Jaikie comes. It's Jaikie that's got the sow by the lug." '

Mrs Brisbane-Brown's drawing-room was as bright and gracious in the October sun as when Jaikie had visited it a week ago. But then he had entered it with curiosity and trepidation; now it seemed too familiar to give a thought to; it was merely a background for various human beings with whom he had urgent business. The coffee cups were still in the room, and the men were smoking. Prince John wore the clothes he had worn the day before, and in the clear afternoon light looked more elegant than ever. He was talking to Charvill, who was much about his height, and looking up at them was Dickson McCunn in an ancient suit of knickerbockers, listening reverently. The hostess sat in her accustomed chair, busy at her usual needlework, and beside her was the anxious face of Mr Barbon. Dougal was deep in that day's issue of the *View*. But the centre of the company was Mr Craw. He stood with his back to the fire, his legs a little apart, and his eyes on Mrs Brisbane-Brown. He seemed to have recovered his balance, for there was no apology or diffidence in his air. Rather it spoke of renewed authority. He had also recovered his familiar nattiness of attire. Gone were the deplorable garments provided by the Watermeeting innkeeper and the Portaway draper. He wore a neat grey suit with a white line in it, a grey tie with a pearl pin, and the smartest of tan shoes. His garb was almost festive.

'I am very glad to see you, Mr Galt,' said Mrs Brisbane-Brown. 'You look a little the worse for wear. Have you had luncheon? ... Well, you have been giving us all a good deal to think about. It looks as if the situation has rather got out of hand. Perhaps you can clear things up.'

Jaikie's mild eyes scanned the party. He saw Dougal hungry for enlightenment, Mr Barbon fearful lest some new horror should be sprung upon him, Charvill prepared to be amused, Prince John smilingly careless as being used to odd adventures, Dickson puzzled but trustful, Mr Craw profoundly suspicious. He met their eyes in turn, and then he met Alison's, and the lashes of one of hers drooped over her cheek in a conspirator's wink.

'A week ago,' he said slowly, 'I was given my instructions. I was told to find Mr Craw at the Back House of the Garroch and keep him hidden till the Evallonians left Knockraw. I have fulfilled them to the letter. There's not a soul except ourselves knows where Mr Craw has been. Nobody has recognized him. The world believes that he's living quietly at Castle Gay. ... And the Knockraw people by this time must be in London. ...'

Mrs Brisbane-Brown laughed. 'A very good account of your stewardship. ... On the other side the situation can hardly be said to have cleared. We have his Royal Highness here in close hiding, and a number of men in Portaway who mean every kind of mischief to him and to Mr Craw. The question is, what are we to do about it? This state of affairs cannot go on indefinitely.'

'It can't,' said Jaikie. 'It must be cleared up to-morrow night.'

'Will you please explain?'

'It all begins,' said Jaikie, 'with the man Allins.'

'He is shockingly underbred,' said Mrs Brisbane-Brown. 'I never understood why Mr Craw employed him. Poor Freddy can't have been happy with him. ... You think he is something worse?'

'I can prove that he is a rogue,' said Jaikie calmly, and embarked on his tale.

He dealt first with Allins, recounting his meetings with him, from the Cambridge Club to the episode of the previous day. He told the story well, and he purposely made Mr Craw the hero of it – Mr Craw's encounter with Allins in the street, Mr Craw at the Socialist meeting, Mr Craw as a Communist orator. The hero was made a little self-conscious by the narrative, but he was also flattered. He became slightly pink and shifted his feet.

'What astonishing presence of mind!' said Mrs Brisbane-Brown. 'I warmly congratulate you.'

'I must not be understood to have made a speech in favour of Communism,' said Mr Craw. 'It was a speech condemnatory of official Socialism showing its logical culmination.'

'Anyway, it did the trick,' said Jaikie. 'Allins dropped his suspicions. Mr Craw's disguise was pretty good in any case. You saw him yourself yesterday.'

'I did,' said Mrs Brisbane-Brown. 'I thought he was the piano-tuner from Gledmouth, who is a little given to drink.'

Mr Craw frowned. 'Will you continue, Mr Galt? Detail the suspicions you entertain about Mr Allins.'

'He brought the Evallonians to Knockraw, and was paid for it. We have it on their own testimony. He brought the other Evallonians to Portaway and is being paid for it. And the man is in a sweat of fear in case the plot fails. The price must be pretty big.'

'The plot! What is it? What evidence have you?'

'The evidence of my own eyes and ears. I spent part of yesterday afternoon with Allins, and two hours last night with him and his friends.'

Jaikie had an audience which hung on his lips while he told of how he had made himself groundbait for the predatory fish. There was a good deal of the actor in him, and he did full justice to his alcoholic babblings of the afternoon, and the grim inquisition of the evening. He even allowed part of his motive to appear. 'They called me a little rat,' he said meditatively.

'You led them to believe that Count Casimir and his friends were now at Castle Gay. May I ask why?' Mr Craw's voice was harsh with offence.

'Because I wanted the Knockraw people to have plenty of time to get clear.'

'For which purpose I am to be sacrificed?'

'Your interests and theirs are the same. You must see that. What they want is to find the Evallonian Monarchists and Prince John and you yourself in some close relation, and to publish the fact to the world. That would give them a big advantage. It would kill your power to help Casimir and it would put Britain definitely against him. Our people would never stand the notion that you and the Evallonians were conspiring on British soil, and the presence of Prince John would put the lid on it. You see that, don't you?'

'I see that it was desirable to get rid of the Knockraw tenants. ... But I do not see why I should be exposed to a visit from those Republican miscreants.'

'It was the only way to make Casimir's escape certain. ... What will happen, Mr Craw? The Republicans think that Casimir and the Prince are safe at Castle Gay. They won't trouble very much about them till to-morrow night, when they are coming to see you, hoping to catch the lot of you in the very act of conspiracy. They chose Friday because it is the day of the poll, and the countryside will be in a stir, and they think that your outdoor and indoor servants will be mostly in Portaway. Well, all you've got to do is to be there to meet them, and tell them you never heard of any such nonsense, and send them all to blazes. Then it will be they who will look the fools, and you won't be troubled any more from that quarter. We must settle this business once and for all, and give you some security for a quiet life.'

'It will be a very unpleasant experience for me,' said Mr Craw. But there was no panic in his voice, only irritation. The listeners received the impression that there would be a certain asperity in Mr Craw's reception of the Evallonian delegates.

'Of course,' Jaikie added, 'it will all have to be stage-managed a little. You can trust me for that.'

'What I don't understand,' said Mrs Brisbane-Brown, 'is why his Royal Highness did not accompany the Knockraw party. ... It sounds shockingly inhospitable, sir, and I need not tell you how deeply honoured I am to have you in my house. But I am thinking of your own interests. You are the most important personage in this business, and it is imperative to get you out of danger at once. Yet you are still here, in hiding, only five miles from your bitterest enemies.'

Jaikie looked a little embarrassed. 'Perhaps I was wrong, but it seemed to me that the best chance of the Prince's safety was to keep him apart from the others. You see, those people at Portaway are not to be trifled with. They have got lines down everywhere, and for all I know they may have discovered the flight of Casimir and his friends and followed them. But Casimir doesn't greatly matter as long as the Prince is not with them. There's nothing wrong in three Evallonian gentlemen visiting Scotland; the trouble begins when they get into Mr Craw's neighbourhood, and when they have the Prince in their company. I thought it safer to break up the covey.'

'But how is the Prince to get away?'

'I have arranged all that. There's a man, Maclellan, down at Rinks – he's a friend of Mr McCunn. He has a boat, and he'll put the Prince across to Markhaven and never breathe a word about it. My suggestion is that Mr McCunn and the Prince drive to Rinks to-morrow night, getting there about eleven. There's a train leaves Markhaven at 8.15 next morning which gets to London at 4.30. Once in London he is for all practical purposes safe. ... The difficulty will lie in getting him away from here. There's a man in Portaway will bring a car – a friend of mine; but I may as well tell you that every corner of this place will be pretty well watched. I told the Evallonians that the Prince was now at Castle Gay. We must do something to keep up that pretence.'

'To-morrow night is the Callowa Club Ball,' said Mrs Brisbane-Brown, but no one was listening.

'I think Mr Charvill should transfer himself to the Castle as soon as possible,' said Jaikie. 'He's about the Prince's height.'

'I have three tickets for the Ball,' went on the hostess. 'I usually take tickets, but I have not been for years. This year I proposed to take Alison and Robin.'

'Mr Charvill must wear the Prince's white waterproof – whatever the weather – and show himself on the terrace. There will be people to see him, and it will divert attention from the Mains.'

Mrs Brisbane-Brown obtained an audience at last, for she raised her voice to a high pitch of authority.

'I have a plan,' she said. 'His Royal Highness will come with me to the ball. It is fancy dress, and he can go as Prince Charles Edward – I have the clothes, wig and all. They belonged to my husband, who was something of the Prince's height and figure. . . . There will be no need for special precautions. A car from Portaway will take my niece, my cousin, and myself to the Station Hotel. At a certain hour in the evening the Prince will leave us and motor to Rinks, where Mr McCunn will see him safely on board. It is all perfectly simple.'

'That's a good idea,' said Jaikie fervently. He saw the one snag in his plan neatly removed. 'I'll arrange about the car. His Royal Highness must lie very close here till to-morrow evening. It might be a good thing if he went to bed. And Mr Charvill had better get to the Castle and inside that waterproof.'

Mr Craw made one last protest.

'You have cast me for a very unpleasant part.' He looked with disfavour at Jaikie, whom he had come to fear, and with an air of appeal at Dougal, whom he regarded more particularly as his henchman. It was the henchman who replied:

'You'll have nothing to do, Mr Craw. Simply to sit in your own library and watch those foreigners making idiots of themselves. Then you can say what is in your mind, and I hope the Almighty will put some winged words into your mouth.'

An hour later Jaikie stood with Dougal on the terrace of the Mains in the fast-gathering twilight. To them appeared Alison, bearing in her arms a reluctant Woolworth.

'Such a thing has never happened before,' she declared.

'This evil dog of yours has seduced Tactful and Pensive into raiding the chicken run. They have killed three cockerels. ... Jaikie, you've introduced a touch of crime into this quiet countryside.'

'And that's true, Miss Westwater,' said Dougal. 'I don't know if you realize it, but we're up against something rather bigger than we pretend indoors.'

'I want Jaikie to tell me one thing,' said the girl. 'Why didn't he let Prince John go with the others? I wondered at the time. Oh, I know the reason he gave, but it wasn't convincing.'

Jaikie grinned. 'Haven't you guessed? I wanted to please Dickson McCunn. Dougal and I owe everything to him, and it's not much we can do in return. He's a great romantic character, and you can see how he's taken up with Prince John. He was telling me that he has been looking up books at the Castle and finds that the Prince is partly descended from Elizabeth of Bohemia and from the Sobieskis. Prince Charlie's mother was a Sobieski. It will be meat and drink to him to be helping the Prince to escape in the middle of the night in a boat on the Solway shore.'

The girl laughed softly. 'There couldn't be a better reason,' she said. ... 'Then about to-morrow night? Why have you taken such pains to arrange a visit to Castle Gay – telling the enemy that everybody would be there – encouraging them, you might say?'

'It was the common-sense plan. I had other reasons, too, and I'll tell you them. I want to see those blighters made to look foolish. I want to see it with my own eyes. You know, they called me a rat, and tried to threaten me. ... Also, I was thinking of Mr Craw. This last week has made him a new man.'

'That is certainly true. He is losing all his shyness. And Aunt Hatty is so good for him. I believe that, if this crisis goes on much longer, he'll propose to her.'

'To-morrow night,' said Jaikie, 'will put the finishing touch to Mr Craw. If he confronts the Evallonians in his own house and packs them off with a cursing, he'll have henceforth the heart of an African lion.'

'He'll need it,' said Dougal solemnly. 'I tell you we're up

against something pretty big. ... I have the advantage of knowing a little about the gentry down at Portaway. My politics have taken me into some queer places, and I've picked up news that never gets into the Press. ... First of all, Craw is right to some extent about the Evallonian Republic. It's not what the newspapers make out. There's a queer gang behind the scenes – a good deal of graft, a fair amount of crime, and a lump of Communism of rather a dirty colour. ... And these people at the Hydropathic are some of the worst of them. They gave you false names last night, but Casimir, so Miss Westwater tells me, recognized them from your description, and he gave them their right names. I know something about Rosenbaum and Dedekind and Ricci, and I know that their power is on a razor edge, so they won't stick at trifles. ... You may be right. They may only want to find the Monarchists in a thoroughly compromising position and publish it to the world. ... On the other hand, they may have a darker purpose. Or perhaps they have two purposes, and if one fails they will try the other. It would suit their book to make Casimir and Craw the laughing stock of Europe, but it would suit their book even better to have done with Casimir and Co. altogether – and especially with Prince John. ... To remove them quietly somewhere where they would be out of action. ... For I haven't a doubt that Casimir is right, and that any moment Evallonia may kick the Republicans over the border.'

'I thought of that,' said Jaikie. 'They have a yacht waiting at Fallatown.'

Dougal listened with wide eyes to this fresh piece of news.

'To-morrow night,' he said solemnly, 'there's going to be some sort of a battle. And we must prepare every detail as carefully as if it were a real battle. Man, Jaikie,' and he beat his companion's back, 'isn't this like old times?'

'How marvellous!' Alison cried, and the dusk did not conceal the glow in her eyes. 'I'm going to be in it. Do you think I am going to that silly ball? Not I!'

'You will certainly be in it,' Jaikie told her. 'You and I are going to have the busiest evening of our lives.'

## CHAPTER EIGHTEEN

# SOLWAY SANDS

THIS simple tale, which has been compelled to linger in too many sordid by-paths, is to have at least one hour of the idyllic. But an idyll demands a discerning mind, a mind which can savour that quality which we call idyllic, which can realize that Heaven has for a moment brought spirit and matter into exquisite unison. 'We receive but what we give,' says the poet, 'and in our life alone doth Nature live.' Such a mind was Mr McCunn's, such a maker of idylls was the laird of Blaweary. He alone of men perceived the romance into which he had stumbled, and by perceiving created it. *Cogitavit, ergo fuit.*

Prince John did not go to bed on Thursday afternoon as Jaikie advised. On the contrary he played bridge after dinner till close on midnight, and was with difficulty restrained from convoying Robin Charvill on his road to Castle Gay. But next morning he stayed in bed. It was a mild bright day of late autumn; the pheasants were shouting in the woods; the roads were alive with voters hastening to Portaway; Charvill was to be observed, by those who were meant to observe him, sitting on a seat on the Castle terrace in the royal white waterproof: and in the midst of that pleasant bustle of life Prince John was kept firmly between the sheets at the Mains, smoking many cigarettes and reading a detective novel provided by Alison. The cause of his docility was Dickson, who came over after breakfast and took up position in the sitting-room adjoining the royal bed-chamber. It was his duty to see the Prince out of the country, and he was undertaking it in a business spirit.

Jaikie, his headquarters the Green Tree, spent a busy morning over transport. Wilkie, the mechanic at the Hydropathic, was his chief instrument, and he was also his intelligence officer. He brought news of the Evallonians. Allins had been having a good many conferences in the town, he reported, chiefly in a low class of public house. He had also hired two cars for the evening – the cars only, for his party preferred to find the drivers. 'He's got the Station Hotel Daimler,' said Wilkie, 'and young Macvittie's Bentley. They'll be for a long run, nae doot. Maybe they're leaving the place, for Tam Grierson tells me they've got a' their bags packed and have settled their bills. . . . I've got our Rolls for you. Ay, and I've got my orders clear in my mind. I bring the Mains folk down to the Ball, and syne I'm at the hotel at ten-thirty to take the young gentleman doun to Rinks, and back again to take the leddies home. . . . 'Deed, yes, I'll haud my tongue, and yer can see for yersel' I'm speirin' nae questions. For this day and this nicht I'm J. Galt's man and naebody else's.' He laid a confidential and reassuring finger against his nose.

The one incident of note on that day was Jaikie's meeting with Tibbets. He ran against him in the Eastgate, and, on a sudden inspiration, invited him to the Green Tree and stood him luncheon – Mrs Fairweather's plain cooking, far better than the pretentious fare of the Station Hotel.

'Mr Tibbets,' he said solemnly, when his guest had stayed his hunger, 'you're proud of your profession, aren't you?'

'You may say so,' was the answer.

'And you're jealous of its honour? I mean that, while you are always trying to get the better of other papers, yet if any attack is made on the Press as a whole, you all stand together like a stone wall.'

'That's so. We're very proud of our solidarity. You get a Government proposing a dirty deal, and we'd smash them in twenty-four hours.'

'I thought so. You're the most powerful trade union on earth.'

'Just about it.'

'Then listen to me. I'm going to confess something. That walking-tour we told you about was all moonshine. Dougal – he's my friend – he's a journalist on one of the Craw papers, and he's been at Castle Gay for the last week. I'm not a journalist, but there was rather a mix-up and I had to lend a hand. . . . You scored heavily over your interview with Craw.'

'My biggest scoop so far,' said Tibbets modestly.

'Well, it was all bogus, you know. You never saw Craw. You saw another man, a friend of mine, who happened to be staying at the Castle. He didn't know he was being interviewed, so he talked freely. . . . You had a big success, because your readers thought Mr Craw was recanting his opinions, and you emphasized it very respectfully in no less than three leaders. . . . Naturally, Craw's pretty sore.'

Tibbets' jaw had fallen and consternation looked out of his eyes.

'He can't repudiate it,' he stammered.

'Oh yes, he can. He wasn't in the house at the moment. He's there now, but he wasn't last Sunday.'

'Where was he?'

'He was with me,' said Jaikie. 'Don't make any mistake. He has a perfectly watertight alibi. He's only got to publish the facts in his own papers to make the *Wire* look particularly foolish.'

'And me,' said Tibbets in a hollow voice. 'They've just raised my screw. Now they'll fire me.'

'Probably,' said Jaikie coolly. 'It will be the hoax of the year, and the *Wire* is sensitive about hoaxes. It has been had lots of times. . . . But you may ask why the thing hasn't been disavowed already? This is Friday, and your interview appeared last Monday. A telegram to the *View* signed with Craw's private code-word would have done the trick. That telegram was written out, but it wasn't sent. Can you guess why?'

Tibbets, sunk in gloom, looked far from guessing.

'I stopped it. And the reason was because we want your help. What's more, that telegram need never be sent. The interview can remain unrepudiated and your own reputation untarnished. It has done a good deal of harm to Craw, but he'll say no more about it if –'

'If?' came Tibbets' sharp question.

'If you give us a hand in an altogether different matter. Craw is being bullied by a gang of foreigners – Evallonians – Evallonian Republicans. That would be grand stuff for the *Wire*, wouldn't it? Yes, but not a word must appear about it unless it is absolutely necessary, for, you see, this is a case for your famous solidarity. A portion of the British Press is being threatened, and in defence the rest of it must stand shoulder to shoulder. You're the only representative on the spot; and I want you to come with me to-night to Castle Gay to see what happens. There may be no need for your help – in which case you must swear that you'll never breathe a word about the business. On the other hand, you may be badly wanted. In Craw's interest it may be necessary to show up a foreign plot to intimidate a British newspaper proprietor, and between the *Wire* and the *View* we should make a pretty good effort. What do you say?'

Tibbets looked at Jaikie with eyes in which relief was mingled with disappointment.

'Of course I agree,' he said. 'I promise that, unless you give me the word, I will wipe anything I may see or hear clean out of my memory. I promise that, if you give me the word, I will put my back into making the highest and holiest row in the history of the British Press. ... But, Mr Galt, I wish you hadn't brought in that interview as the price of my help. I needn't tell you I'll be thankful if it is allowed to stand. It means a lot to me. But, supposing Craw disowned it straight away, I'd still be glad to come in on to-night's show. I've got my professional standards like other people, and I'm honest about them. If Craw's independence is threatened by somebody outside our trade, then I'm out to defend him, though he were doing his damnedest to break me. Have you got that?'

'I've got it,' said Jaikie, 'and I apologise. You see I'm not a journalist myself.'

Dickson McCunn spent the day, as he would have phrased it, 'in waiting'. He was both courtier and business man. Middlemas was left to see to the packing of the Prince's kit. Dickson's was no menial task; it was for him to act for one day as Chief of Staff to a great man in extremity. He occupied his leisure in investigating Mrs Brisbane-Brown's reference library, where he conned the history of the royal house of Evallonia. There could be no doubt of it; the blood of Stuart and Sobieski ran in the veins of the young gentleman now engaged in bed with a detective novel and a box of cigarettes.

He lunched alone with Mrs Brisbane-Brown. Alison, it appeared, was at the Castle, to which late the night before Mr Craw had also been secretly conveyed. In the afternoon Dickson fell asleep, and later was given a solitary tea by Middlemas. At the darkening Alison returned, the Prince was got out of bed, and there was a great mustering of the late General's Highland accoutrements. Presently Dickson had the felicity of watching a young man in the costume of Prince Charles Edward (and, if the miniature in the drawing-room was to be trusted, favouring the original in most respects) being instructed by Alison, with the assistance of her gramophone, in the movements of the foursome and the eightsome reels. Dickson sat through the performance in a happy trance. The faded Stuart tartan of the kilt and plaid, the old worn velvet of the doublet, the bright silver of dirk and sword-hilt, the dim blue of the Garter riband, were part of something which he had always dreamed. The wig was impossible, for the head of the late General had been larger than the Prince's, but Dickson applauded its absence. He had always thought of Prince Charlie as wearing his own hair, and that hair not too long.

Mrs Brisbane-Brown appeared at dinner '*en grande tenue*', as she expressed it, with a magnificent comb of diamonds surmounting her head. But Alison was in her ordinary outdoor clothes. The ball was not for her, she said, for she had far too much to do. Jaikie was due at the Castle at half-past eight, and she must be there when he arrived. 'That woman Cazenove,' she observed, 'is no manner of use. She has been fluttering around Mr Craw like a scared hen, and undermining his self-confidence. She is undoing all the good you did him, Aunt Hatty. I have told Bannister to carry her to her bedroom and lock her in if she gets hysterical.'

She left before the meal was over, and her adieu to the Prince scandalized Dickson by its informality. 'See that you tie up the collar of your ulster, sir, and tie a muffler round your chin. There are several people near the gate who have no business to be there. I shall have some fun dodging them myself.'

The car, driven by Wilkie, duly arrived at the stroke of nine, and Mrs Brisbane-Brown attended by her nephew, who was muffled, as one would expect in an Australian, against the chills of a Scots October, was packed into it by Middlemas and her maid. Dickson did not show himself. His time was not yet, and he was fortifying himself against it by a pipe and a little hot toddy.

The story of the Ball may be read in the *Canonry Standard and Portaway Advertiser*, where the party from the Mains was incorrectly given as the Honourable Mrs Brisbane-Brown, the Honourable Alison Westwater, and Mr John Charvill. The Australian cousin was a huge success, and to this day many a Canonry maiden retains a tender memory of the tall young Chevalier, who danced beautifully – except in the reels, where he needed much guidance – and whose charm of manner and wide knowledge of the world upset all their preconceived notions of the inhabitants of the Antipodes. His aunt introduced him also to several of the neighbouring lairds, who found him not less agreeable than their womenkind. It was a misfortune that he left so early and so mysteriously. His name was on many virginal programmes for dances after midnight. Lord Fosterton wanted to continue his conversation with him about a new method of rearing partridges, which Mr Charvill had found in Czecho-Slovakia, and young Mr Kennedy of Kenmair, who was in the Diplomatic Service, and whose memory was haunted by a resemblance which he could not define, was anxious to exchange gossip with him about certain circles in Vienna with which he appeared to be familiar. As it was, Mr Charvill departed like Cinderella, but long before Cinderella's hour.

At half-past ten Wilkie returned to the Mains and Dickson's hour had come. He wore a heavy motoring ulster and a soft black hat which belonged to Barbon. It seemed to him the nearest approach he could find to the proper headwear. From Bannister he had borrowed a small revolver, for which he had only four cartridges. He felt it incongruous – it should have been a long sword.

At a quarter to eleven he stood on the pavement outside the Station Hotel, which was empty now, for the crowd which had watched his guests' arrival had departed. A tall figure in a greatcoat came swiftly out. Dickson held the door open while he entered the car, and then got in beside him. His great hour had begun.

I wish that for Dickson's sake I could tell of a hazardous journey, of hostile eyes and sinister faces, of a harsh challenge, a brush with the enemy, an escape achieved in the teeth of odds by the subtlety and valour of the Prince's companion. For such things Dickson longed, and for such he was prepared. But truth compels me to admit that nothing of the sort happened. The idyllic is not the epic. The idyll indeed is an Alexandrian invention, born in the days when the epic spirit had passed out of life. But Dickson, whose soul thirsted for epic, achieved beyond doubt the idyllic.

Prince John was in a cheerful, conversational mood. He was thankful to be out of what promised to be a very tiresome entanglement. He wanted to be back in France, where he was due at a partridge shoot. He had enjoyed the ball, and purposed to take lessons in reel-dancing. 'You have pretty girls in Scotland,' he said, 'but none to touch Miss Westwater. In another year I back her to lead the field. There's a good hotel, you say, at Markhaven, where I can get a few hours' sleep. . . . My friends by this time are in London, but we do not propose to meet till Paris. . . . Happily the wind is slight. I am not the best of sailors.'

He conversed pleasantly, but Dickson's answers, if respectful, were short. He was too busy savouring the situation to talk. He addressed his companion, not as 'Sir', but as 'Sire'.

The car stopped a little beyond the hamlet of Rinks, and 'Wait here,' Dickson told Wilkie; 'I'll be back in less than half an hour.' He humped the heavier of the Prince's two cases (which was all the baggage the Prince proposed to take with him) and led him by a road he knew well over the benty links and by way of many plank bridges across the brackish runnels which drained the marshlands. The moon was high in the heavens and the whole cup of the estuary brimmed with light. The trench of the Callowa was full, a silver snake in a setting of palest gold, and above it, like a magical bird, brooded the *Rosabelle*. Only the rare calls of sea-fowl broke into the low chuckle and whisper of the ebbing tide.

Maclellan was waiting for them, Maclellan in sea-boots and an ancient greatcoat of frieze.

'Man, I'm glad to see ye, Mr McCunn,' was his greeting. 'I'm vexed we're to hae sae little o' ye, but I'm proud to be able to oblige your friend. . . . What did you say his name was? Mr Charles? It's a grand nicht for our job, Mr Charles. The wind's at our back – what there is o't. It's no muckle the noo, but there'll be mair oot on the Solway. We'll be in Markhaven by ane o' the mornin'.'

Dickson's ear caught Maclellan's misapprehension of Charvill. He did not correct it, for the name Maclellan gave the Prince was the name he had long given him in his heart.

Far down the estuary he saw the lights of a ship, and from its funnel a thin fluff of smoke showed against the pale sky.

'That's the yatt that's lyin' off Fallatown,' Maclellan said. 'She's gettin' up steam. She'll be off early in the mornin'.'

It was the last touch that was needed to complete the picture. There lay the enemy ship, the English frigate, to prevent escape. Under its jaws the Prince must slip through to the sanctuary of France. The place was no longer an inlet on a lowland firth. It was Loch Nanuamah under the dark hills of Moidart – it was some Hebridean bay, with outside the vast shadowy plain of the Atlantic.

They were on the deck of the *Rosabelle* now, and, as the Prince unbuttoned his ulster to get at his cigarettes, Dickson saw the flutter of tartan, the gleam of silver, the corner of a blue riband. In that moment his spirit was enlarged. At last – at long last – his dream had come true. He was not pondering romance, he was living it. . . . He was no more the prosperous trader, the cautious business man, the laird of a few humdrum acres, the plump elder whose seat was the chimney-corner. He was young again, and his place was the open road and the seashore and the uncharted world. He was Lochiel, with a price on his head and no home but the heather. . . . He was Montrose in his lonely loyalty. . . . He was Roland in the red twilight of Roncesvalles. . . .

The Prince was saying good-bye.

'I'm very much obliged to you, Mr McCunn. Some day I

hope we may meet again and renew our friendship. Meanwhile, will you wear this as a memento of our pleasant adventure?'

He took a ring from his finger, a plain gold ring set with an engraved cornelian. Dickson received it blindly. He was to remember later the words which accompanied it, but at the moment he scarcely heard them. He took the Prince's hand, bent low and kissed it. Happily Maclellan was not looking.

'God bless your Royal Highness,' he stammered, 'and bring you safe to port. And if you ever have need of me, a word will bring me across the world.'

He was on the bank now, the mooring rope had been loosened, and the *Rosabelle* was slipping gently down the current. Maclellan had begun to hoist the sail. The Prince stood in the stern and waved his hand, but Dickson did not respond. His thoughts were too insurgent for action. His whole soul was drawn to that patch of dark which was the boat, momentarily growing smaller, speeding down a pathway of silver into a golden haze.

'I meant it,' he said firmly to himself. 'By God, I meant it. ... I'm sixty-one years of age on the 15th of next month, but a man's just as old as his heart, and mine's young. I've got the ring. ... And maybe some day I'll get the word!'

He took his seat beside Wilkie and amazed him by his high spirits. All the road to Portaway he sang what seemed to be Jacobite songs. '*I'll to Lochiel and Appin and kneel to them*,' he crooned. When they picked up Mrs Brisbane-Brown at the hotel, she travelled alone inside the car for Dickson resumed the outside seat and his melodies. '*Follow thee, follow thee, wha wadna follow thee!*' he shouted.

'Ye havena got the tune richt,' said the distracted Wilkie.

'Who cares about the tune?' Dickson cried. 'It's the words that matter. And the words are great.'

The car halted in the street of Starr village. Presently Dickson joined Mrs Brisbane-Brown inside, and the place beside the driver was taken by a bulky stranger.

'A friend of mine,' he told the lady. 'He'll maybe come in useful at the Castle.'

CHAPTER NINETEEN

# MR CRAW IS MASTER IN HIS OWN HOUSE

A LITTLE after ten o'clock the front-door bell of Castle Gay was violently rung. The summons was answered by Bannister, unattended by the customary footmen. He opened upon a strange spectacle. A conventicle stood upon the doorstep, no less than six men, and behind them on the gravel were two large cars, in which other figures could be discerned. It was a fine night with a moon, and the astonished butler was left in no doubt as to the strength of the visitors.

An authoritative voice demanded Mr Craw. Bannister, jostled out of all his traditions, admitted that his master was at home.

'We will speak with him,' said the voice.

The butler stammered something about an appointment.

'He will see us,' said the voice firmly. 'You need announce no names. Take us to him at once.' By this time the six were well inside the doorway, and Bannister had retreated nervously into the hall. It was one of the six, not the butler, that shut the door behind them.

Then Bannister seemed to recover himself. He offered to help the leader in removing his coat, for all six wore travelling ulsters. But he was roughly waved aside. 'You will stay here, Hannus,' the leader said to one of the party, 'and if anyone attempts to leave blow your whistle. Our friends outside will watch the other doors. Now, you,' he turned to Bannister, 'take us instantly to Mr Craw.'

The butler was certainly recovering. 'Mr Craw is in the library,' he said, in a tone which was wonderfully composed considering the circumstances. 'One moment, sir, and I will light the staircase.'

He slipped into the cloakroom on the left side of the hall, and in a moment the great staircase was flooded with light. But in his three seconds of absence Bannister had done something more. He had switched on the light in a minute chamber at the base of the tower, which was one of the remnants of the old shell of the castle. This chamber had the advantage of looking directly upon the park, and a light in it shone like a signal beacon down the Callowa vale.

'Will you follow me, sir?' he said, and five of the visitors, with eyes as wary as colts', ascended the broad carpeted stairs, while the sixth remained on duty below, standing rigid in the centre of the Hall as if to avoid an ambush. It was odd behaviour, but not more odd than that shown by the ascending five. Bannister found himself poked in the back by the barrel of a pistol, and, when he looked round, the pistol's owner grinned and nodded, to point his warning that he was not to be trifled with.

Bannister took no notice. He had recovered the impassiveness of a well-trained servant. He behaved as if such visitors and such manners were in no way abnormal, and led them along the upper gallery and flung open the door of the library.

'Gentlemen to see you, sir,' he announced, and when the five had crowded in he shut the door behind them. He seemed to be amused and to have urgent business on hand, for he darted down a side staircase towards the lower regions of the house, and as he went he chuckled.

The library was half in dusk. There was a glow from the big fire on the hearth, and one lamp was lit in the central chandelier. The long lines of vellum and morocco on the walls made a dim pattern in the shadows, and the great Flemish tapestry was only a blur. But there was a reading-lamp on the big table, which partly illumined the blue velvet curtains of the six tall narrow windows.

At the table in his accustomed chair sat Mr Craw, spectacles on nose, and a paper in his hand, and opposite him was the discreet figure of Miss Elena Cazenove, her pencil poised above her notebook. At the end of the table stood Mr Barbon, with an air of a secretary waiting to supplement or endorse some ukase of his chief. Both men wore dinner jackets. It was a pleasant picture of busy domesticity.

Mr Craw raised his eyes from the paper at the interruption. He had nerved himself to a great effort and his heart was beating uncomfortably. But he managed to preserve an air of self-possession. The features of the marble Augustus on the pedestal behind him were not more composed.

'What does this mean?' he said sharply, in a voice to which nervousness gave the proper irritability. 'Bannister!' He raised his voice. But the butler had gone, and the five men in ulsters had approached the table.

He took off his spectacles, but he did not rise. 'Who on earth are you?' he demanded. The words came out like pistol shots. The voice was a little startled, which in the circumstances was right.

'Our names do not matter.' Mastrovin bent his heavy brows upon the comfortable figure in the chair. This was not quite what he had expected. He had hoped to come upon a full conclave, Royalty and Royalists and Craw in the act of conspiring. He had hoped for a dramatic entry, an embarrassed recognition, a profound discomfiture, and he found only an elderly gentleman dictating letters. Instead of a den of foxes he had stumbled upon a kennel of spaniels. He was conscious that he and his companions struck a discordant note in this firelit room. He must make the most of the discord.

'I offer the conventional apologies for our intrusion, Mr Craw,' he said. 'But, as you know well, those who play a certain game cannot always preserve the politenesses. We have come to have a few words with you and your guests.'

'I shall not require you for the present, Miss Cazenove,' said Mr Craw, and the lady clutched her note-book and with a wavering snipe-like motion left the room.

'Well?' said Mr Craw, when the door had closed behind her. He had sat back in his chair and Barbon had moved to his side.

'The guests to whom I refer,' Mastrovin continued, 'are four Evallonian gentlemen in whom we are interested.

'Evallonian gentlemen!' exclaimed Mr Craw. 'Barbon, this man must be mad.'

'Let me give you their names,' said Mastrovin gently. 'They

are Count Casimir Muresco, of whom all the world has heard; Prince Odalchini, and Professor Jagon. Last, but by no means least, there is Prince John, the claimant to the Evallonian throne.'

Mr Craw had pulled himself together and had entered on the line of conduct which had already been anxiously rehearsed.

'I have heard of all four,' he said. 'But what makes you think they are here? I do not keep foreign notables on the ice in my cellar.'

'We have evidence that at this moment they are under your roof. Be well advised, Mr Craw. You cannot deceive us. We are perfectly informed of all that has been happening here. At this moment every exit from your house is watched. You had better surrender at discretion.'

'Barbon,' said Mr Craw in a pained voice, 'what in Heaven's name is he talking about?'

Mr Barbon was fussy and anxious in the ordinary relations of life, but not for nothing did the blood of a Cromwellian Barebones run in his veins. His war record had proved that he could be cool enough in certain emergencies. Now he was rather enjoying himself.

'I'm sure I don't know, sir,' he said. 'The first three men are, or were, the shooting tenants in Knockraw. I knew Count Casimir slightly, and they came to dinner last Saturday night, and we dined with them on Monday. I heard that they had now gone home. I know nothing about Prince John. There was nobody of that name with the Knockraw people when they dined here.'

'I see,' said Mr Craw. He turned to Mastrovin. 'Is that information any use to you? Apparently you must look for your friends at Knockraw. I myself have been away from home and only returned last night. I know nothing whatever about your Evallonians. I never saw them in my life.'

'I am sorry to be obliged to give you the lie,' said Mastrovin. 'We have evidence that three of them came here two days ago. We know that Prince John is here – he was seen here this very day. I warn you, Mr Craw, that we are difficult people to trifle with.'

'I have no desire to trifle with you.' Mr Craw's manner was stately. 'You come here uninvited and cross-examine me in my own library. I have told you the literal truth. You, sir, have the air and speech of a gentleman. I shall be obliged if you will now withdraw.'

For answer the five men came a little nearer, and Barbon sat himself on the arm of his chief's chair. He was beginning to measure the physical prowess of the visitors. The difficulty lay in what they might have in their ulster pockets.

Over the fireplace there was a huge coat of arms in stone, the complete achievement of the house of Westwater, and above this was a tiny balcony. It was flush with the wall and scarcely discernible from below – it was reached by a turret stair from the old keep, and may once have been a hiding place, the Canonry equivalent of a 'priest's hole'. At this moment it held Alison and Jaikie. They had a full view of Mr Craw's face and of the Evallonian profiles.

'Will you inform us who are the present inmates of this house?' Mastrovin asked.

'Let me see,' said Mr Craw. 'Apart from Mr Barbon, whom you see here, there is Miss Cazenove, who has just gone, and Mr Crombie, who is one of my Press assistants. Then there is a young Australian friend called Charvill. There is also a country neighbour, Mr McCunn, but he is out this evening and will not be home till late. That is all, I think, Barbon, besides the domestic staff?'

'Will you kindly have them assembled here?'

The tone nettled Mr Craw, in spite of the restraint he had put upon himself.

'You are insolent, sir,' he rapped out. 'You would be justly served if I summoned my servants and had you kicked out-of-doors. Who are you to issue commands?'

'We happen to be in command,' said Mastrovin with a thrust forward of his heavy chin. 'Your household staff is depleted. Your outdoor staff is in Portaway and will not return until evening. They were seen to leave your park gates. We have our own people inside and outside this house. You will be wise to obey us.'

Mr Craw, having remembered his part, shrugged his shoulders. He touched a button on the table, and Bannister appeared with a suddenness that suggested that he had been lurking outside the door.

'Have the goodness to ask Mr Charvill and Mr Crombie to come here,' he said. 'You will find them, I believe, in the billiard-room.'

The billiard-room was at the other end of the house, but the rapidity with which the two presented themselves argued a less distant lair. Dougal had his pipe, and Robin Charvill had his finger in a novel to mark his place. Mastrovin cast an eye over their physical proportions, which were not contemptible. Craw was, of course, useless, but there were three able-bodied opponents, if trouble came. But he was accustomed to similar situations, and had no doubt about his power to control them.

'You say this is all your household. Very well. We will soon test your truthfulness. We are going to search your house. You four will remain here till I return, and two of my friends will keep you company. You' – he turned to Bannister, who stood discreetly in the background – 'will accompany me.'

Up in the gallery Jaikie chuckled. 'Just what I hoped,' he whispered to Alison. 'Bannister knows what to do. You and I must show them a little sport.' The two slipped out of the turret staircase.

Rosenbaum and Dedekind were the two left behind to guard the prisoners in the library. They had done the same sort of thing before and knew their job for they took up positions to cover the two doors. Each had his right hand in the pocket of his ulster. The face of the Jew Rosenbaum was heavy and solemn, expressionless as a ship's figurehead, but Dedekind was more human. He shifted his feet, undid the top button of his ulster, for the night was not cold and the fire was good, and looked as if he would like to talk. But the party of four seemed to be oblivious of their gaolers. Mr Craw resumed his papers, and Barbon was busy making entries in a note-book, Dougal had picked up a weekly journal, and

Charvill had returned to his novel. They gave a fine example of British phlegm, and disregarded the intruders as completely as if they had been men come to wind up the clocks.

Meantime Bannister, with the injured air of an abbot who is compelled to reveal to some raiding Goths the treasures of his abbey, conducted Mastrovin, Ricci, and Calaman over the castle. They descended into the hall where they found the sixth Evallonian at his lonely post: he reported that he had seen and heard no one. They investigated the big apartments on the ground-floor, including the nest of small rooms beyond the dining-hall. Then they made an elaborate survey of the main bedroom floors, both in the ancient central keep and the more modern wings. They found everything in order. They penetrated to Mr Craw's luxurious chamber, to which he proposed, as we know, to add a private bathroom. They raided the rooms which housed Barbon and Dougal, Charvill and Dickson McCunn, and they satisfied themselves by an inspection of the belongings that the inmates were those whom Bannister named. They entered various bedrooms which were clearly unoccupied. And then they extended their researches to the upper floors.

It was here that their tour became less satisfying. The upper floors of Castle Gay are like a rabbit-warren – clusters of small rooms, tortuous passages on different levels, unexpected staircases, unlooked-for *culs-de-sac*. It was hard for any stranger to preserve his sense of direction, and to keep tally of all that he saw. The business was complicated by the hidden presence of Alison and Jaikie, and of Tibbets, who had been summoned from his own lair. Also of the beagle pups, Tactful and Pensive.

Alison, who knew every cranny of the house, took command, and Jaikie and Tibbets in their stocking-soles followed. ... The Evallonians would hear sudden loud voices at a corridor's end, and on arriving there find no one. Lights would be turned on and as suddenly turned off. There would be a skirl of idiotic laughter as they came into a passage, cold and blue in the light of the moon. ... Also there were dogs, dogs innumerable. A hound would suddenly burst into their midst and disappear. Ricci fell heavily on one of the stairways, because of a dog which swept him off his legs.

The searchers, puffing and bewildered, lost their tempers. Bannister found a pistol clapped to his chest, and turned on Mastrovin a pallid, terror-stricken face.

'What infernal maze is this you have brought us to?' the voice behind the pistol demanded. 'Answer, you fool. There are people here, many people. Who are they?'

The butler was a figure of panic. 'I don't know,' he stammered. 'You have seen the rooms of the staff. Up here no one sleeps. It is the old part of the house. They say it is haunted.'

'Haunted be damned!' Mastrovin turned suddenly and peered into a long, low attic, empty except for some ancient bedsteads. There was a sound without, and as he moved his head he saw the butt-end of a human form disappearing apparently into the ground. It was Tibbets, who was a little behind the others. The sight quickened Mastrovin's paces. For a little he preceded Bannister, darting with surprising rapidity in the direction of any noise. But all that happened was that he hit his head hard on a beam, and, opening a door hastily, all but cascaded down a steep flight of steps. And his movements were enlivened by echoes of ghostly merriment above, below, before, and behind him. . . .

In a secluded corner Alison, Jaikie, and Tibbets were recovering their breath. The girl shook with laughter. 'Was there ever such a game of hide-and-seek?' she panted.

But Jaikie looked grave.

'We mustn't rattle them too much,' he said. 'They're a queer lot, and if we wake the savage in them they may forget their manners. We don't want anything ugly to happen. They'll give up in a little if we let them alone, and go back to the library.'

But it was a full half-hour before Mastrovin left those upper floors, and, with each minute of failure to find what he sought, his fury and suspicion increased. Alison and her two squires followed the party at a discreet distance, till they saw them enter the library corridor. Jaikie took a glance into the hall below, and observed that the Evallonian sentry was no longer there. He knew that he was now lying gagged and trussed in a corner of the cloak-room. The time had come for Mackillop and his friends to act.

The three squeezed into their little gallery above the fireplace, just as the Evallonians entered the library. Mr Craw was still writing in apparent unconcern. As a matter of fact he had written his name six hundred and seventy times on sheets of foolscap by way of steadying his nerves. Dougal was smoking and reading the *New Statesman*. Barbon was apparently asleep, and Charvill still deep in his novel. As they entered, Rosenbaum and Dedekind moved towards them, and there were some rapid questions and answers.

Something which the leader said woke all five into a sudden vigilance. The slouch and embarrassment disappeared, and their bodies seemed to quicken with a new purpose. The five took a step towards the table, and their movements were soft and lithe as panthers. They were no longer clumsy greatcoated foreigners, but beasts of prey.

The sweat stood on Mastrovin's brow, for he was of a heavy habit of body and had had a wearing time upstairs. But his voice had an edge like ice.

'I have seen your house,' he said. 'I am not satisfied. There are people hiding in it. You will bring them to me here at once or . . .'

He paused. There was no need to put his threat into words; it was in every line of his grim face: it was in the sinister bulge of his hand in his ulster pocket.

Mr Craw showed his manhood by acting according to plan. He was desperately afraid, for he had never in his life looked into such furious eyes. But the challenge had come, and he repeated the speech with which he had intended to meet that challenge.

'This is pure brigandage,' he said. 'You have not given me your names, but I know very well who you are. You must be aware, Mr Mastrovin, that you will not further your cause by threatening a British subject in his own house.'

The risk in preparing speeches beforehand is that the conditions of their delivery may be far other than the conditions forecast in their preparation. Mr Craw had assumed that the Evallonians were politicians out to secure a political triumph, and that, when this triumph tarried they would realize that their audacity had defeated its purpose and left them at his mercy. He had forgotten that he might have to deal with men of primeval impulses, whose fury would deaden their ears to common sense.

At the sound of his name Mastrovin seemed to stiffen, as a runner stiffens before the start. Then he laughed, and it was not a pleasant sound. He turned to his followers. 'He knows me,' he cried. 'He is not as innocent as he pretends. He knows of us from our enemies. They are here. We are close to them. Now there will be no mercy.'

In a voice that made Mr Craw jump in his chair he thundered: 'One minute! I will give you one minute!'

He had his pistol out, and little blue barrels gleamed in the hands of the four, covering Barbon, Dougal, and Charvill. Mr Craw sat stupefied and his spectacles in the tense hush made a clatter as they dropped on the table. The gilt baroque clock on the mantelpiece struck the quarter to midnight.

In the little gallery the estate mechanician had that morning arranged a contrivance of bells. There was a button at Jaikie's elbow, and if he pressed it bells would ring in the corridor outside and in the ante-room. There by this time Mackillop and his men were waiting, in two parties of five, all of them old soldiers, armed with rifles and shot guns. At the sound of the bells they would file in and overawe the enemy – ten weapons in ten pairs of resolute hands.

Jaikie's finger was on the button, but he did not press it.

For the first time in his life he had to make a momentous decision. Dougal and he had planned out every detail of that evening's visit, and he believed that they had foreseen every contingency. But they had forgotten one. ... They had forgotten how different these five foreigners below were from themselves. These were men who all their lives had played darkly for dark stakes – who had hunted and been hunted like beasts – to whom murder was an incident in policy – whose natural habitat was the cave and the jungle. He was aware that the atmosphere in the library had changed to something savage and primordial – that human lives hung on a slender hair. A devil had been awakened, a devil who was not politic. ... If Mackillop and his men appeared in the doorway, if the glint of weapons answered those now in the hands of the five, it would be the spark to fire the mine. These men would fight like cornered weasels, oblivious of consequences – as they had often in other lands fought before. No doubt they would be overpowered, but in the meantime – in that warm and gracious room the Den had been re-created, and in that Den there were only blind passions and blind fears.

He did not press the button, for he knew what it would be to waken Hell.

As it was, Hell was evident enough. His companions felt it. Alison's hand tightened convulsively on his arm, and as for Tibbets behind him – he heard Tibbets's teeth chatter. Down below the four men, covered by the five pistols, knew it. Mr Craw's face was the colour of clay, and his eyes stared at Mastrovin as if he were mesmerized. Barbon and Charvill also whitened, and sat like images, and Dougal seemed to be seeking self-command by sucking in his lips against his clenched teeth. In a second anything might happen. The jungle had burst into the flower-garden, and with it the brutes of the jungle. ... A small hopeless sound came from Jaikie's lips which may have been meant for a prayer.

Suddenly he was aware that Mastrovin's eyes had turned to the door which led into the ante-room. Had Mackillop shown himself?

'Stand!' Mastrovin cried. 'Not another step on your life!'

A voice answered the Evallonian's bark, a rich, bland, assured voice.

'Tut, tut, what's all this fuss about?' the voice said. 'Put away that pistol, man, or it'll maybe go off. *Sich* behaviour in a decent man's house!'

Jaikie was looking down upon the bald head of Dickson McCunn – Dickson in his best suit of knickerbockers, his eyes still bright with the memory of his great adventure on the Solway sands, his face ruddy with the night air and as unperturbed as if he were selling tea over the counter. There was even a smile at the corner of his mouth. To Jaikie sick with fear, it seemed as if the wholesome human world had suddenly broken into the Den.

But it was the voice that cracked the spell – that pleasantly, homely, wheedling voice which brought with it daylight and common sense. Each of the five felt its influence. Mastrovin's rigour seemed to relax. He lowered his pistol.

'Who the devil are you?' he grunted.

'My name's McCunn,' came the brisk answer. 'Dickson McCunn. I'm stopping in this house, and I come back to find a scene like a demented movie. It looks as if I'm just in time to prevent you gentlemen making fools of yourselves. I heard that there was a lot of queer folk here, so I took the precaution of bringing Johnnie Doig the policeman with me. It was just as well, for Johnnie and me overheard some awful language. Come in, Johnnie. . . . You're wanted.'

A remarkable figure entered from the ante-room. It was the Starr policeman, a large man with his tunic imperfectly buttoned, and his boots half-laced for he had been roused out of his early slumbers and had dressed in a hurry. He carried his helmet in his hand, and his face wore an air of judicial solemnity.

'Johnnie and me,' said Mr McCunn, 'heard you using language which constitutes an assault in law. Worse than that, you've been guilty of the crime of *hamesucken*. You're foreigners, and maybe no very well acquaint with the law of Scotland, but I can tell you that *hamesucken* is just about the worst offence you can commit, short of taking life. It has been defined as the crime of assaulting a person within his own house. That's what you're busy at now, and many a man has got two years hard for less. Amn't I right, Johnnie?'

'Ye're right, sir,' said the policeman. 'I've made notes o' the langwidge I heard, and I hae got you gentlemen as witnesses. It's *hamesucken* beyond a doubt.' The strange syllables boomed ominously, and their echoes hung in the air like a thunderstorm. 'Gie me the word, sir' – this to Mr Craw – 'and I'll chairge them.' Then to the five: 'Ye'd better hand ower thae pistols, or it'll be the waur for ye.'

For the fraction of a second there was that in Mastrovin's face which augured resistance. Dickson saw it, and grinned.

'Listen to reason, man,' he cried genially, and there was a humorous contempt in his voice which was perhaps its strongest argument. 'I know fine who you are. You're politicians, and you've made a bad mistake. You're looking for folk that never were here. You needn't make things worse. If you try violence, what will happen? You'll be defying the law of Scotland and deforcing the peace, and even if you get away from this countryside – which is not likely – there's not a corner of the globe that could hide you. You'd be brought to justice, and where would your politics be then? I'm speaking as a businessman to folk that I assume to be in possession of their wits. You're in Mr Craw's hands, and there's just the one thing you can do – to throw yourselves on his mercy. If he takes my advice he'll let you go, provided you leave your pistols behind you. They're no the things for folk like you to be trusted with in this quiet countryside.'

Jaikie in the gallery gave a happy sigh. The danger was past. Over the Den had descended the thick, comfortable blanket of convention and law. Melodrama had gone out of the air. Mastrovin and his friends were no longer dangerous, for they had become comic. He prodded Tibbets. 'Down you get. It's time for you to be on the floor of the house.' Things could now proceed according to plan.

Then Mr Craw rose to the height of a great argument. He rescued his spectacles, rested his elbows on the table, and joined his still tremulous finger-tips. Wisdom and authority radiated from him.

'I am inclined,' he said, 'to follow Mr McCunn's advice and let you go. I do not propose to charge you. But, as Mr McCunn has said, in common decency you must be disarmed. Mr Barbon, will you kindly collect these gentlemen's weapons.'

The five were no longer wolves from the wilds: they were

embarrassed political intriguers. Sullenly they dropped their pistols into the waste-paper basket which Barbon presented to them.

Mr Craw continued:

'I would repeat that what I have told you is the literal truth. Your countrymen were at Knockraw and dined here with Mr Barbon, but I did not meet them, for I only returned yesterday. As for Prince John, I do not know what you are talking about. Nobody like him has ever been in Castle Gay. You say that he was seen here this very morning. I suggest that your spies may have seen my friend Mr Charvill, who is spending a few days with me. ... But I am really not concerned to explain the cause of your blunders. The principal is that you have allowed yourself to be misled by an ex-servant of mine. I hope you have made his rascality worth his while, for it looks as if he might be out of employment for some little time.'

Mr Craw was enjoying himself. His voice grew round and soothing. He almost purred his sentences, for every word he spoke made him feel that he had captured at last an authority of which hitherto he had never been quite certain.

'I am perfectly well informed as to who you are,' he went on. 'You, sir,' addressing Mastrovin, 'I have already named, and I congratulate you on your colleagues, Messieurs Dedekind, Rosenbaum, Calaman, and Ricci. They are names not unknown in the political – and criminal – annals of contemporary Europe. ... You have put yourself in a most compromising position. You have come here, at a time when you believe that my staff is depleted with a following of your own, selected from the riff-raff of Portaway. You were mistaken, of course. My staff was not depleted, but increased. At this moment there are ten of my servants, all of whom served in the War, waiting outside this door, and they are armed. Any attempt at violence by you would have been summarily avenged. As for your ragamuffin following, you may be interested to learn that during the last hour or two they have been collected by my keepers and ducked in the Callowa. By now they will have returned to Portaway wiser and wetter men. ...

'As for yourselves, you have committed a grave technical offence. I could charge you, and you would be put at once under arrest. Would it be convenient for the Republican Party of Evallonia to have some of its most active members in a British dock and presently in a British gaol? . . . You are even more completely in my power than you imagine. You have attempted to coerce an important section of the British Press. That, if published, would seal the doom of your party with British public opinion. I have not only my own people here to report the incident in the various newspapers I control, but Mr Tibbets of the *Wire* is present on behalf of my chief competitors, and at my request has put himself in a position also to furnish a full account.'

'But,' said Mr Craw, moving his chair back from the table and folding his arms, 'I do not propose to exact any such revenge. You are free to go as you came. I will neither charge you, nor publish one word of this incident. But a complete record will be prepared of this evening's doings, and I warn you that, if I am ever troubled again in any way by you or your emissaries, that record will be published throughout the world's Press, and you will be made the laughing-stock of Europe.'

Mr Craw ceased, pressed his lips and looked for approbation to Dougal, who nodded friendlily. Mastrovin seemed about to reply, but the nature of his reply will never be known. For Dickson broke in with: 'You'd better hurry, gentlemen. You should be at Fallatown within the next three-quarters of an hour, if your yacht is to catch the tide.'

This final revelation of knowledge shut Mastrovin's lips. He bowed, and without a word led his friends from the room, after which, through the lines of Mackillop's deeply disappointed minions, they descended to the front door and their cars. Dickson chose to accompany and speed the parting guests.

With their departure Mrs Brisbane-Brown entered the library from the ante-room where she had waited under Mr McCunn's strict orders. Jaikie and Alison, whose heads were very close together in the little balcony, observed her arrival with interest.

'Aunt Hatty has been really anxious,' said the girl. 'I know that look on her face. I wonder if she's in love with Mr Craw. I rather think so. ... Jaikie, that was a horrid strain. I feel all slack and run down. Any moment I expected to see those devils shoot. I wouldn't go through that again for a million pounds.'

'No more would Mr Craw. But it will have made a man of him. He's been under fire, so to speak, and now he'll be as bold as brass.'

'He owes it all to you.'

'Not to me,' Jaikie smiled. 'To me he very nearly owed a bullet in his head. To Dickson McCunn. Wasn't he great?'

The girl nodded. 'Mr McCunn goes off in a fury of romance to see a rather dull princeling depart in a boat, because he reminds him of Prince Charlie. And he comes back to step into the most effective kind of realism. He'll never give another thought to what he has just done, though he has saved several lives, but he'll cherish all his days the memory of the parting with Prince John. Was there ever such an extraordinary mixture?'

'We're all like that,' was the answer.

'Not you. You've the realism, but not the sentiment.'

'I wonder,' said Jaikie.

Ten minutes later Mr McCunn was refreshing himself in the library with a whisky-and-soda and sandwiches, for the excitements of the night had quickened his appetite.

'I got the idea,' he explained to Dougal, 'by remembering what Bismarck said during the Schleswig-Holstein affair – when he was asked in Parliament what he would do if the British Army landed on German soil. He said he would send for the police. ... I've always thought that a very good remark. ... If you're faced with folk that are accustomed to shoot it's no good playing the same game, unless you're anxious to get hurt. You want to paralyse them by lapping them in the atmosphere of law and order. Talk business to them. It's whiles a very useful thing to live in a civilized country, and you should take advantage of it.'

'Ay,' he continued, 'I accompanied yon gentry to the door. I thought it my duty to offer them a drink. They refused, though their tongues were hanging out of their mouths. That refusal makes me inclined to think that it will not be very long before Prince John sits on the throne of Evallonia. For it shows that they have no sense of humour, and without humour you cannot run a sweetie-shop, let alone a nation.'

CHAPTER TWENTY

# VALEDICTORY

NEXT evening the sun, as it declined over the Carrick hills, illumined a small figure plodding up the road which led to Loch Garroch. Very small the figure appeared in that spacious twilight solitude, and behind it, around it, in front of it, scampered and sniffed something still smaller. Jaikie and Woolworth were setting out again on their travels, for there was still a week before the University of Cambridge claimed them.

Jaikie had left Castle Gay in a sober and meditative mood. 'So that's that,' had been his not very profound reflection. Things did happen sometimes, he reminded himself, unexpected things, decisive things, momentous incidents clotted together in a little space of time. Who dare say that the world was dull? He and Dougal, setting out on an errand as prosaic as Saul's quest of his father's asses, had been suddenly caught up into a breathless crisis which had stopped only on the near side of tragedy. He had been privileged to witness the discovery by an elderly gentleman of something that might almost be called his soul.

There could be no doubt about Mr Craw. Surprising developments might be looked for in that hitherto shy prophet. He had always been assured enough in his mind, but he had been only a voice booming from the sanctuary. He had been afraid of the actual world. Now that fear had gone, for there is no stiffer confidence than that which is won by a man, otherwise secure, who discovers that the one thing which he has dreaded need only be faced to be overcome. ... Much depended upon Mrs Brisbane-Brown. Jaikie was fairly certain that there would be a marriage between the two, and he approved. They were complementary spirits. The lady's clear, hard, good sense would keep the prophet's feet in safe paths. He would never be timid any more. She would be an antiseptic to his sentimentality. She might make a formidable being out of the phrasing journalist.

Much depended, too, upon Dougal. It was plain that Dougal was now high in the great man's favour. A queer business, thought Jaikie, and yet natural enough. ... Jaikie had no illusions about how he himself was regarded by Mr Craw. Hatred was too strong a word, but beyond doubt there was dislike. He had seen the great man's weakness, whereas Dougal had only been the witness of his strength. ... And Craw and Dougal were alike, too. Both were dogmatists. They might profess different creeds, but they looked on life with the same eyes. Heaven alone knew what the results of the combination would be, but a combination was clearly decreed. Dougal was no more the provincial journalist; he would soon have the chief say in the direction of the Craw Press.

At the thought Jaikie had a momentary pang. He felt very remote not only from the companion of his week's wanderings but from his ancient friend.

Mr Craw had behaved handsomely by him. He had summoned him that morning into his presence and thanked him with a very fair appearance of cordiality. He had had the decency, too, not to attempt to impose on him an obligation of silence as to their joint adventures, thereby showing that he understood at least part of Jaikie's character.

'Mr Galt,' he had said, 'I have been much impressed by your remarkable abilities. I am not clear what is the best avenue for their exercise. But I am deeply in your debt, and I shall be glad to give you any assistance in my power.'

Jaikie had thanked him, and replied that he had not made up his mind.

'You have no basis, no strong impulse?'

Jaikie had shaken his head.

'You are still very young,' Mr Craw had said, 'but you must not postpone your choice too late. You must find a philosophy of life. I had found mine before I was out of my teens. There is no hope for the drifter.'

They had parted amicably, and, as he breasted the hill which led from the Callowa to the Garroch, Jaikie had found himself reflecting on this interview. He realized how oddly detached he was. He was hungry for life, as hungry as Dickson McCunn. He enjoyed every moment, but he knew that his enjoyment came largely from standing a little apart. He was not a cynic, for there was no sourness in him. He had a kindliness towards most things, and a large charity. But he did not take sides. He had not accepted any mood, or creed, or groove of his own. *Vix ea nostra voco* was his motto. He was only a seeker. Dougal wanted to make converts; he himself was still occupied in finding out what was in his soul.

For the first time in his life he had a sense of loneliness. ... There was no help for it. He must be honest with himself. He must go on seeking.

At the top of the hill he halted to look down upon the Garroch glen, with the end of the Lower Loch Garroch a pool of gold in the late October sun. There was a sound behind him, and he turned to see a girl coming over the crest of the hill. It was Alison, and she was in a hurry, for she was hatless, and her cob was in a lather.

She swung herself to the ground with the reins looped round an arm.

'Oh, Jaikie!' she cried. 'Why did you leave without saying good-bye? I only heard by accident that you had gone, and I've had such a hustle to catch you up. Why did you do it?'

'I don't know,' said Jaikie. 'It seemed difficult to say good-bye to you, so I shirked it.' He spoke penitently, but there was no penitence in his face. The plain little wedge of countenance was so lit up that it was almost beautiful.

They sat down on the bank of withered heather and looked over the Garroch to the western hills.

'What fun we have had!' Alison sighed. 'I hate to think that it is over. I hate your going away.'

Jaikie did not answer. It was difficult for one so sparing of speech to find words equal to that sudden glow in his eyes.

'When are we going to meet again?' she asked.

'I don't know,' he said at last. 'But we are going to meet again ... often ... always.'

He turned, and saw in her face that comprehension which needs no words.

They sat for a little, and then she rose. 'I must go back,' she said, 'or Aunt Hatty will be dragging the ponds for me.'

They shook hands, quite prosaically. He watched her mount and turn her horse's head to the Callowa, while he turned his own resolutely to the Garroch. He took a few steps and then looked back. The girl had not moved.

'*Dear Jaikie,*' she said, and the intervening space did not weaken the tenderness of the words. Then she put her horse into a canter, and the last he saw was a golden head disappearing over the brow of the hill.

He quickened his pace, and strode down into the Garroch valley with his mind in a happy confusion. Years later, when the two monosyllables of his name were famous in other circles than those of Rugby football, he was to remember that evening hour as a crisis in his life. For, as he walked, his thoughts moved towards a new clarity and a profound concentration. ... He was no longer alone. The seeker had found something infinitely precious. He had a spur now to endeavour, such endeavour as would make the common bustle of life seem stagnant. A force of high velocity had been unloosed on the world.

These were not Jaikie's explicit thoughts; he only knew that he was happy, and that he was glad to have no companion but Woolworth. He passed the shores of Lower Loch Garroch, and his singing scared the mullards out of the reeds. He came into the wide cup of the Garroch moss, shadowed by its sentinel hills, with the light of the Back House to guide him through the thickening darkness. But he was not conscious of the scene, for he was listening to the songs which youth was crooning in his heart.

Mrs Catterick knew his step on the gravel, and met him at the door.

'Bide the nicht?' she cried. ''Deed ye may, and blithe to see ye! Ye've gotten rid o' the auld man? Whae was he?'

'A gentleman from London. He's safely home now.'

'Keep us a'. Just what I jaloused. That's a stick for me to

haud ower Erchie's heid. Erchie was here twae days syne, speirin' what had come o' the man he had sae sair mishandled. D'ye ken what I said? I said he was deid and buried among the tatties in the yaird. No anither word could Erchie get oot o' me, and he gae'd off wi' an anxious hert. I'll keep him anxious. He'll be expectin' the pollis ony day.'

Five minutes later Jaikie sat in the best room, while his hostess lit the peat fire.

'Ye've been doun by Castle Gay?' she gossiped. 'It's a braw bit, and it's a peety the family canna afford to bide in it. It's let to somebody – I canna mind his name. We're on his lordship's land here, ye ken. There's a picture o' Miss Alison. She used to come often here, and a hellicat lassie she was, but rale frank and innerly. I aye said they wad hae a sair job makin' a young leddy o' her.'

Mrs Catterick pointed to where above the mantelpiece hung a framed photograph of a girl, whose face was bordered by two solemn plaits of hair.

'It's a bonny bit face,' she said reflectively. 'There's daftness in it, but there's something wise and kind in her een. 'Deed, Jaikie, when I come to look at them, they're no unlike your ain.'

# THE HOUSE OF THE FOUR WINDS

# CONTENTS

# PROLOGUE

GREAT events, says the philosophic historian, spring only from great causes, though the immediate occasion may be small; but I think his law must have exceptions. Of the not inconsiderable events which I am about to chronicle, the occasion was trivial, and I find it hard to detect the majestic agency behind them. What world force, for example, ordained that Mr Dickson McCunn should slip into the Tod's Hole in his little salmon river on a bleak night in April; and, without changing his clothes, should thereafter make a tour of inspection of his young lambs? His action was the proximate cause of this tale, but I can see no profounder explanation of it than the inherent perversity of man.

The performance had immediate consequences for Mr McCunn. He awoke next morning with a stiff neck, an aching left shoulder, and a pain in the small of his back – he who never in his life before had had a touch of rheumatism. A vigorous rubbing with embrocation failed to relieve him, and, since he was accustomed to robust health, he found it intolerable to hobble about with a thing like a toothache in several parts of his body. Dr Murdoch was sent for from Auchenlochan, and for a fortnight Mr McCunn had to endure mustard plasters and mustard baths, to swallow various medicines, and to submit to a rigorous diet. The pains declined, but he found himself to his disgust in a low state of general health, easily tired, liable to sudden cramps, and with a poor appetite for his meals. After three weeks of this condition he lost his temper. Summer was beginning, and he reflected that, being now sixty-three years of age, he had only a limited number of summers left to him. His gorge rose at the thought of dragging his wing through the coming delectable months – long-lighted June, the hot July noons with the corncrakes busy in the hay, the days on August hills, red with heather and musical with bees. He curbed his distaste for medical science, and departed to Edinburgh to consult a specialist.

That specialist gave him a purifying time. He tested his blood and his blood pressure, kneaded every part of his frame, and for the better part of a week kept him under observation. At the end he professed himself clear in the general but perplexed in the particular.

'You've never been ill in your life?' he said. 'Well, that is just your trouble. You're an uncommonly strong man – heart, lungs, circulation, digestion, all in first-class order. But it stands to reason that you must have secreted poisons in your body, and you have never got them out. The best prescription for a fit old age is a bad illness in middle life, or, better still, a major operation. It drains off some of the middle-age humours. Well, you haven't had that luck, so you've been a powder magazine with some nasty explosives waiting for the spark. Your tom-fool escapade in the Stinchar provided the spark, and here you are – a healthy man mysteriously gone sick. You've got to be pretty careful, Mr McCunn. It depends on how you behave in the next few months whether you will be able to fish for salmon on your eightieth birthday, or be doddering round with two sticks and a shawl on your seventieth.'

Mr McCunn was scared, penitent, and utterly docile. He professed himself ready for the extremist measures, including the drawing of every tooth in his head.

The specialist smiled. 'I don't recommend anything so drastic. What you want first of all is an exact diagnosis. I can assess your general condition, but I can't put my finger on the precise mischief. That needs a technique which we haven't developed sufficiently in this country. Next, you must have treatment, but treatment is a comparatively simple affair if you first get the right diagnosis. So I am going to send you to Germany.'

Mr McCunn wailed. Banishment from his beloved Blaweary was a bitter pill.

'Yes, to Germany. To quite a pretty place called Rosensee, in Saxon Switzerland. There's a *kurhaus* there run by a man called Christoph. You never heard his name, of course – few people have – but he is a therapeutic genius of the first order. You can take my word for that. I've known him again and again pull people out of their graves. His main subject is nerves, but he is good for everything that is difficult and mysterious, for in my opinion he is the greatest diagnoser in the world. ... By the way, you live in Carrick? Well, I sent one of your neighbours to Rosensee last year – Sir Archibald Roylance – he was having trouble with a damaged leg – and now he walks nearly as well as you and me. It seems there was a misplaced sinew which everybody else had overlooked. ... Dr Christoph will see you three times a day, stare at you like an owl, ask you a thousand questions, and make no comment for at least a fortnight. Then he will deliver judgement, and you make take it that it will be right. After that the treatment is a simple matter. In a week or two you will be got up in green shorts and a Tyrolese hat and an alpenstock and a rope round your middle, climbing the little rocks of those parts. ... Yes, I think I can promise you that you'll be fit and ready for the autumn salmon.'

Mr McCunn, trained to know a competent man when he saw him, accepted the consultant's prescription, and rooms were taken for him at the Rosensee *kurhaus*. His wife did not accompany him for three reasons: first, she had a profound distaste for foreign countries and regarded Germany as still a hostile State; second, she could not believe that rheumatism, which was an hereditary ailment in her own family, need be taken seriously, so she felt no real anxiety about his health; third, he forbade her. She proposed to stay at Blaweary till the end of June, and then to await her husband's return at a Rothesay hydropathic. So, early in the month, Mr McCunn a little disconsolately left these shores. He took with him as body-servant and companion one Peter Wappit, who at Blaweary was gamekeeper, forester, and general handy-man. Peter, having fought in France with the Scots Fusiliers, and having been two years a prisoner in Germany, was believed by his master to be an adept at foreign tongues.

Nor was there any profound reason in the nature of things why Lord Rhynns, a well-preserved gentleman of sixty-seven, should have tumbled into a ditch that spring at Vallescure and broken his left leg. He was an active man and a careful, but his mind had been busy with the Newmarket entries, so that he missed a step, rolled some yards down a steep slope of rock and bracken, and came to rest with a leg doubled unpleasantly under him. The limb was well set, but neuritis followed, with disastrous consequences to the Rhynns *ménage*. For his wife, whose profession was a gentle invalidism, found herself compelled to see to household affairs, and as a result was on the verge of a nervous breakdown. The family moved from watering-place to watering-place, seeking a cure for his lordship's affliction, till at the mountain village of Unnutz Lady Rhynns could bear it no longer. A telegram was dispatched to their only child requiring her instant attendance upon distressed parents.

This was a serious blow to Miss Alison Westwater, who had been making very different plans for the summer. She was then in London, living with her Aunt Harriet, who two years before had espoused Mr Thomas Carlyle Craw, the newspaper magnate. It was the Craws' purpose to go north after Ascot to the Westwater house, Castle Gay, in the Canonry, of which Mr Craw had a long lease, and Alison, for whom a little of London sufficed, had exulted in the prospect. Now she saw before her some dismal weeks – or months – in an alien land, in the company of a valetudinarian mother and a presumably irascible father. Her dreams of Scotland, to which she was passionately attached, of salmon in the Callowa and trout in the hill lochs and bright days among the heather, had to be replaced by a dreary vista of baking foreign roads, garish foreign hotels, tarnished pine woods, tidy clothes, and all the things which her soul abominated.

There was perhaps more of a cosmic motive in the determination that summer of the doings of Mr Dougal Crombie and Sir Archibald Roylance, for in their cases we touch the fringe of high politics. Dougal was now a force, almost *the* force, in the Craw Press. The general manager, Mr Archibald Bamff, was growing old, he had taken to himself a wife, and his fancy toyed pleasantly with retirement to some country hermitage. So in the past year Dougal had been gradually taking over his work, and, since he had the complete confidence of Mr Craw, and the esteem of Mr Craw's masterful wife, he found himself in his early twenties charged with much weighty and troublesome business. He was a power behind the throne, and the more potent because few suspected his presence. Only one or two people – a Cabinet minister, an occasional financial magnate, a few highly placed Government officials – realized the authority that was wielded by this sombre and downright young man. Early in June he set out on an extensive Continental trip, the avowed purpose of which was to look into certain paper-making concerns which Mr Craw had acquired after the war. But his main object was not disclosed, for it was deeply secret. Mr Craw had long interested himself in the republic of Evallonia, his sympathies being with those who sought to restore the ancient monarchy. Now it appeared that the affairs of that country were approaching a crisis, and it was Dougal's mission to spy out the land.

As for Sir Archibald Roylance, he had been saddled with an honourable but distasteful duty. He had been the better part of two years in the House of Commons, and had already made a modest mark. He spoke infrequently and always on matters which he knew something about – the air, agriculture, foreign affairs – and his concise and well-informed speeches were welcomed amid the common verbiage of debate. He had become parliamentary private secretary to the Under-Secretary for Foreign Affairs, who had been at school with him. That summer the usual Disarmament Conference was dragging its slow length along; it became necessary for Mr Despenser, the Under-Secretary, to go to Geneva, and Sir Archie was ordered to accompany him. He received the mandate with little pleasure. The session that summer would end early, and he wanted to get to Crask, for he had been defrauded of his Easter holiday in the Highlands. Geneva he believed might last for months, and he detested the place, which, as Lord Lamancha had once said, was full of the ghosts of mouldy old jurisconsults, and the living presence of cosmopolitan bores. But his spirits had improved when he discovered that he might take Janet with him.

'We'll find a chance of slipping away,' he told his wife. 'One merit of these beastly conferences is that they are always adjourning. We'll hop it into eastern Europe or some other fruity place. Hang it all, now that I've got the use of both legs, I don't see why we shouldn't climb a mountain or two. Dick Hannay's yarns have made me rather keen to try that game.'

Certain of these transmigrations played havoc with the plans of Mr John Galt, of St Mark's College, Cambridge, who, having just attained a second class in his Tripos and having so concluded his university career, felt himself entitled to an adequate holiday. He had intended to make his headquarters at Blaweary, which was the only home he had ever known, and thence to invade the Canonry, fishing its lochs and sleeping in its heather. But Blaweary would presently be shut up in Mr McCunn's absence, and if Alison Westwater was not at Castle Gay, the Canonry lost all its charm. Still, he must have some air and exercise. The summer term had been busy and stuffy, and to a Rugby player there were few attractions in punts among lilied backwaters. He would probably have to go alone to the Canonry, but his fancy had begun to toy with another scheme – a walking tour in south-eastern France or among the Jura foothills, where new sights and smells and sounds would relieve his loneliness. It was characteristic of him that he never thought of finding a male companion; for the last two years Alison had been for him the only companion in the world.

On the 13th of June he was still undecided, but that night his thoughts were narrowed to a happy orbit. For Alison was dining with him before her journey abroad, and together they were going on to a party which the Lamanchas were giving to the delegates to an international conference then in session in London. For one evening at least the world was about to give him all he desired.

It was a warm night, but the great room at Maurice's was cool with fans and sun-blinds, though every table was occupied. From their corner, at the foot of the shallow staircase which is the main entrance, they had an excellent view of the company. There seemed to be a great many uniforms about, and a dazzling array of orders, no doubt in view of the Lamancha function. It was easy to talk, for at Maurice's there is no band till supper-time.

'You shouldn't have brought me here, Jaikie,' said Alison. 'It's too extravagant. And you're giving me far too good a dinner.'

'It's a celebration,' was the answer. 'I've done with Cambridge.'

'Are you sorry?'

'No. I liked it, for I like most things, but I don't want to linger over them.'

The girl laughed merrily, and a smile slowly crept into Jaikie's face.

'You're quite right,' he said. 'That was a priggish thing to say, but it's true, all the same.'

'I know. I never met anyone who wasted so little time in regrets. I wish I were like you, for I want anything I like to go on for ever. Cambridge must have slipped off you like water off a duck's back. What did you get out of it?'

'Peace to grow up. I've very nearly grown up now. I have discovered most of the things I can do and the things I can't. I know the things I like and the things I don't.'

Alison knitted her brows. 'That's not much good. So do I. The thing to find out is, what you can do *best* and what you like *most*. You told me a year ago that that was what you were after. Have you decided?'

'No,' was the glum answer. 'I think I have collected the material, so to speak, but I haven't sorted it out. I was looking to you to help me this summer in the Canonry, and now you're bolting to Italy or somewhere.'

'Not Italy, my dear. A spot called Unnutz in the Tirol. You're not very good at geography.'

'Mayn't I come too?'

'No, you mayn't. You'd simply loathe it. A landscape like a picture postcard. Tennis and bumble-puppy golf and promenades, all in smart clothes. Infinite boring evenings when I have to play picquet with Papa or talk hotel French to Mamma's friends. Besides, my family wouldn't understand you. You haven't been properly presented to them, and Unnutz is not the place for that. You wouldn't be at your best there.'

Two people passed on the way to their table, a tall young man with a lean ruddy face, and a pretty young woman, whose hair was nearly as bright a thing as Alison's. The young woman stopped.

'My dear Allie,' she cried, 'I haven't seen you for ages. Archie, it's Cousin Allie. They tell me you're being dragged abroad, the same as us. What's your penitentiary? Ours is Geneva.'

'Mine's a place in the Tirol. Any chance of our meeting?'

'There might be. Archie has a notion of dashing about, for apparently an international conference is mostly adjournments. He's so spry on his legs since Dr Christoph took him in hand that he rather fancies himself as a mountaineer. What's your address?'

The lady scribbled it down in a notebook which she took from her bag, nodded gaily, and followed her husband and a waiter to their own table. Alison looked after them.

'That's the nicest couple on earth. She was Janet Raden, a sort of cousin of mine. Her husband, Archie Roylance ...'

Jaikie interrupted.

'Great Scot! Is that Sir Archibald Roylance? I once knew him pretty well – for one day. I've told you about the Gorbals Die-hards and Huntingtower. He was the ally we enlisted – lived at a place called the Mains of Garple. Ask Mr McCunn about him. I've often wondered when I should see him again, for I felt pretty certain I would – some day. He hasn't changed much.'

'He can't change. Sir Archie is the most imperishable thing God ever created. He'll be a wild boy till he's ninety. Even with Janet to steady him I consider him dangerous, especially now that he has no longer a game leg. ... Hallo, Jaikie. We're digging into the past tonight. Look who's over there.'

She nodded towards a very brilliant table where some twenty people were dining, most of them in uniform. Among them was a fair young man in ordinary evening dress, without any decorations. He suddenly turned his face, recognized Alison, and, with a word of apology to the others, left his seat and came towards her. When she rose and curtsied, Jaikie had a sudden recollection.

'It is Miss Westwater, is it not?' said the young man, bowing over her hand. 'My adorable preserver! I have not forgotten Prince Charlie and the Solway Sands.'

He turned to Jaikie.

'And the Moltke of the campaign, too! What is the name? Wait a minute. I have it – Jaikie. What fun to see you again! Are you two by any happy chance espoused?'

'Not yet,' said Alison. 'What are you doing in England, sir?'

'Holidaying. I cannot think why all the world does not holiday in England. It is the only really peaceful and pleasant place.'

'How true, sir! I have to go abroad tomorrow, and I feel like an exile.'

'Then why do you go?'

'I am summoned by neglected parents. To Unnutz, in the Tirol.'

The young man's pleasant face grew suddenly grave.

'Unnutz. Above the Waldersee, in the Firnthal?'

'The same. Do you know it, sir?'

'I know it. I do not think it is a very good place for a holiday – not this summer. But if it becomes unpleasant you can return home, for you English are always free to travel. But I should be careful in Unnutz, my dear Miss Westwater, and I should take Mr Jaikie with you as a protector.'

He shook hands and departed smiling, but he left on the two the impression of an unexpected solemnity.

'What do you suppose is worrying Prince John?' Alison asked.

'The affairs of Evallonia. You remember at Castle Gay we thought the Republic would blow up any moment and that a month or two would see Prince John on the throne. That's two years ago and nothing has happened. Dougal is out there now looking into the situation. He may ginger them up.'

'What makes him so solemn about Unnutz? By all accounts it's the ordinary gimcrack little foreign watering-place. He talked of it as if it were a sort of Chicago slum.'

'He is a wise man, for he said you should take me with you.'

They had reached the stage of coffee and cigarettes, and were now more free to watch their neighbours. It was a decorous assembly, in accordance with the traditions of Maurice's, and the only gaiety seemed to be among the womenkind of Prince John's party. The Prince's own face was very clear in the light of an overhanging lamp, and both Alison and Jaikie found themselves watching it – its slight heaviness in repose, its quick vivacity when interested, the smile which drew half its charm from a most attractive wrinkling around the eyes.

'It is the face of a prince,' said Alison, 'but not of a king – at any rate, not the kind of king that wins a throne. There's no dynamite in it.'

'What sort of face do you give makers of revolutions?' Jaikie asked.

The girl swung round and regarded him steadily.

'Your sort,' she said. 'You look so meek and good that everybody loves you. And wise, wise like an old terrier. And yet, in the two years I have known you, you have filled up your time with the craziest things. First' – she counted on her fingers – 'you went off to Baffin Island to trade old rifles for walrus ivory.'

Jaikie grinned. 'I made seventy-three pounds clear: I call that a success.'

'Then you walked from Cambridge to Oxford within a day and a night.'

'That was a failure. I was lame for a fortnight and couldn't play in the Welsh match.'

'You went twice as a deck hand on a Grimsby trawler – first to Bear Island and then to the Whale's Back. I don't know where these places are, but they sound beastly.'

'They are. I was sick most of the time.'

'Last and worst, it was only your exams and my prayers that kept you from trying to circumnavigate Britain in a sailing canoe, when you would certainly have been drowned. What do you mean by it, Jaikie? It looks as if you were as neurotic as a Bloomsbury intellectual, though in a different way. Why this restlessness?'

'I wasn't restless. I did it all quite calmly, on purpose.' Into Jaikie's small face there had come an innocent seriousness.

'You see,' he went on, 'when I was a small boy I was rather a hardy citizen. I've told you about that. Then Mr McCunn civilized me, which I badly needed. But I didn't want it to soften me. We are living in a roughish world today, and it is going to get rougher, and I don't want to think that there is any experience to which I can't face up. I've been trying to keep myself tough. You see what I mean, Alison?'

'I see. It's rather like painting the lily, you know. I wish I were going to the Canonry, for there's a lot of things I want to have out with you. Promise to keep quiet till I come back.'

The Lamanchas' party was so large and crowded that Alison and Jaikie found it easy to compass solitude. Once out of the current that sucked through the drawing-rooms towards the supper-room there were quiet nooks to be discovered in the big house. One such they found in an alcove, where the upper staircase ascended from the first floor, and where, at a safe distance, they could watch the procession of guests. Alison pointed out various celebrities to the interested Jaikie, and a number of relations with whom she had no desire to have closer contact. But on one of the latter she condescended to details. He was a very tall man, whose clothes, even in that well-dressed assembly, were conspicuous for their elegance. He had a neatly trimmed blond beard, and hair worn a little longer than the fashion and as wavy as a smart woman's coiffure. They only saw his profile as he ascended the stairs, and his back as he disappeared into the main drawing-room.

'There's another cousin of mine,' said the girl, 'the queerest in all our queer clan. His name is Randal Glynde, and he has been everything in his time from cow-puncher to film star, not to mention diplomat, and various sorts of soldier, and somebody's private secretary. The family doesn't approve of him, for they never know what he'll do next, but he was very nice to me when I was a little girl, and I used to have a tremendous *culte* for him.'

Jaikie was not listening, for he felt very depressed. This was his last hour with Alison for months, and the light had suddenly gone out of his landscape. He had never been lonely in his life before he met her, having at the worst found good company in himself; but now he longed for a companion, and out of the many millions of the world's inhabitants there was only one that he wanted.

'I can't go to Scotland,' he said. 'Blaweary is impossible, and if I went into the Canonry with you not there I'd howl.'

'Poor Jaikie!' Alison laid a hand upon his. 'But it's only another bit of the toughening you're so fond of. I promise to write to you a great deal, and it won't be long till the autumn. You won't be half as lonely as I.'

'I wish I thought that,' said Jaikie, brightening a little. 'I like being alone, but I don't like being lonely. I think I'll go abroad too.'

'Why don't you join Mr McCunn?'

'He won't let me. He's doing a cure and is forbidden company.'

'Or Dougal?'

'He wouldn't have me either. He thinks he's on some silly kind of secret service, and he's as mysterious about it as a sick owl. But I might go for a tramp somewhere. My finances will just run to it.'

'Hallo, here's Ran,' said Alison. The tall man with the fair beard had drifted towards them, and was now looking down on the girl. On a closer view he appeared to be nearer forty than thirty. Jaikie noticed that he had Alison's piercing blue eyes, with the same dancing light in them. There and then, being accustomed to rapid judgements, he felt well disposed towards the tall stranger.

'Alison dear.' Mr Glynde put his hand on the girl's head. 'I hear that your father has at last achieved gout.'

'No. It's neuritis, which makes him much angrier. He would accept gout as a family legacy, but he dislikes unexpected visitations. I go out to him tomorrow.'

'Unnutz, isn't it? A dreary little place. I fear you won't enjoy it, my dear.'

'Where have you come from, Ran? We last heard of you in Russia.'

'I have been in many places since Russia.' Mr Glynde's voice had an odd quality in it, as if he were gently communing with himself. 'After a time in deep water I come up to breathe, and then go down again.'

'You've chosen very smart clothes to breathe in.'

'I always try to suit my clothes to my company. It is the only way to be inconspicuous.'

'Have you been writing any more poetry?'

'Not a word in English, but I have written some rather charming things in medieval Latin. I'll send you them. It is the best tongue for a vagabond.'

Alison introduced Jaikie.

'Here's another of your totem, Cousin Ran. You can't corrupt him, for he is quite as mad as you.'

Mr Glynde smiled pleasantly as he shook hands, and Jaikie had an impression that his eyes were the most intelligent that he had ever seen, eyes which took in everything, and saw very deep, and had a mind behind them that did not forget. He felt too that something in his own face pleased the other, for there was friendliness behind the inquisition.

'He has just finished Cambridge, and finds himself at a loose end. He is hesitating between Scotland and a tramp on the Continent. What do you advise?'

'When you are young these decisions may be fateful things. I have always trusted to the spin of a coin. I carry with me a Greek stater which has made most of my decisions for me. What about tossing for it?'

He took from the pocket of his white waistcoat a small gold coin and handed it to Jaikie.

'It's a lucky coin,' he said. 'At least it has brought me infinite amusement. Try it.'

Jaikie had a sudden queer feeling that the occasion had become rather solemn, almost sacramental. 'Heads, Scotland, tails abroad,' he said and tossed. It fell tails.

'Behold,' said Mr Glynde, 'your mind is made up for you. You will wander along in the white dust and drink country wine and doze in the woods, knowing that the unseen Powers are with you. Where, by the way, did you think of going? You have no preference? You have been very little abroad? How fortunate to have all Europe spread out for your choice. But I should not go too far east, Mr Galt. Keep to the comfortable west if you want peace. If you go too far east this summer, you may find that the spin of my little stater has been rather too fateful.'

As Jaikie put Alison into a taxi, he observed Mr Glynde leaving the house on foot with a companion. He had a glimpse of that companion's face, and saw that it was Prince John of Evallonia.

CHAPTER ONE

# THE MAN WITH THE ELEPHANT

THE inn at Kremisch, the Stag with the Two Heads, has an upper room so bowed with age that it leans drunkenly over the village street. It is a bare place, which must be chilly in winter, for the old casement has many chinks in it, and the china stove does not look efficient, and the rough beechen table, marked by many beer mugs, and the seats of beechwood and hide are scarcely luxurious. But on this summer night to one who had been tramping all day on roads deep in white dust under a merciless sun, it seemed a haven of ease. Jaikie had eaten an admirable supper on a corner of the table, a supper of cold ham, an omelet, hot toasted rye-cakes and a seductive cheese. He had drunk wine tapped from a barrel and cold as water from a mountain spring, and had concluded with coffee and cream in a blue cup as large as a basin. Now he could light his pipe and watch the green dusk deepen behind the onion spire of the village church.

The milestones in his journey had been the wines. Jaikie was no connoisseur, and indeed as a rule preferred beer, but the vintage of a place seemed to give him the place's flavour and wines made a diary of his pilgrimage. His legs bore him from valley to valley, but he drank himself from atmosphere to atmosphere. He had begun among strong burgundies which needed water to make a thirst-quenching drink, and continued through the thin wines of the hills to the coarse red stuff of south Germany and a dozen forgotten little local products. In one upland place he had found a drink like the grey wine of Anjou, in another a sweet thing like Madeira, and in another a fiery sherry. Each night at the end of his tramp he concocted a long drink, and he stuck manfully to the juice of the grape; so, having a delicate palate and a good memory, he had now behind him a map of his track picked out in honest liquors.

Each was associated with some vision of sun-drenched landscape. He had been a month on the tramp, but he seemed to have walked through continents. As he half dozed at the open window, it was pleasant to let his fancy run back along the road. It had led him through vineyards grey at the fringes with dust, through baking beet-fields and drowsy cornlands and solemn forests; up into wooded hills and flowery meadows, and once or twice almost into the jaws of the great mountains; through every kind of human settlement, from hamlets which were only larger farms to brisk burghs clustered round opulent town houses or castles as old as Charlemagne; by every kind of stream – unfordable great rivers, and milky mountain torrents, and reedy lowland waters, and clear brooks slipping through mint and water-cress. He had walked and walked, seeking to travel and not to arrive, and making no plans except that his face was always to the sunrise. He was very dimly aware at any moment of his whereabouts, for his sole map was a sketchy thing out of a Continental Bradshaw.

But he had walked himself into contentment. At the start he had been restless and lonely. He wished that he could have brought Woolworth, now languishing at Blaweary, but he could not condemn that long-suffering terrier to months of quarantine. He wrote disconsolate letters to Alison in his vile handwriting, and received from her at various *postes-restantes* replies which revealed the dullness of her own life at Unnutz. She had nothing to write about, and it was never her habit to spoil good paper with trivial reflections. There was a time at the start when Jaikie's mind had been filled with exasperating little cares, so that he turned a blank face to the world he was traversing. His future – what was he to do now that he was done with Cambridge? Alison – his need of her grew more desperate every day, but what could he offer her worthy of her acceptance? Only his small dingy self, he concluded, with nothing to his credit except a second-class degree, some repute in Rugby football, and the slenderest of bank balances. It seemed the most preposterous affair of a moth and a star.

But youth and the sun and wide spaces played their old healing part. He began to rise whistling from his bed in a pine wood or in a cheap country inn, with a sense that the earth was very spacious and curious. The strong aromatic sunlight drugged him into cheerfulness. The humours of the road were spread before him. He had learned to talk French fairly well, but his German was scanty; nevertheless, he had the British soldier's gift of establishing friendship on a meagre linguistic basis, and he slipped inside the life of sundry little communities. His passion for new landscapes made every day's march a romance, and, having a love of the human comedy, he found each night's lodging an entertainment. He understood that he was looking at things in a new perspective. What had seemed a dull track between high walls was now expanding into open country.

Especially he thought happily about Alison. He did not think of her as a bored young woman with peevish parents in a dull health resort, but as he knew her in the Canonry, an audacious ally in any venture, staunch as the hills, kind as a west wind. So far as she was concerned, prudential thoughts about the future were an insult. She was there waiting for him as soon as he could climb to her high level. He encountered no delicacy of scene or weather but he longed to have her beside him to enjoy it. He treasured up scraps of wayside humour for her amusement, and even some shy meditations which some day he would confide to her. They did not go into his letters, which became daily scrappier – but these letters now concluded with what for Jaikie were almost the messages of a lover.

He was in a calmer mood, too, about himself. Had he been more worldly-wise he might have reflected that some day he must be a rich man. Dickson McCunn had no chick nor child nor near relation, and he and Dougal were virtually his adopted sons. Dougal was already on the road to wealth and fame, and Dickson would see that Jaikie was well provided for. But characteristically he never thought of that probability. He had his own way to make with no man's aid, and he was only waiting to discover the proper starting-point. But a pleasing lethargy possessed him. This delectable summer world was not the place for making plans. So far he was content with what he had done. Dickson had drawn him out of the depths into the normal light of day, and it had been his business to accustom his eyes to it. He was aware that, without Cambridge, he would have always been a little shy and suspicious of the life of a class into which he had not been born; now he knew it for what it was worth, and could look at it without prejudice but also without glamour. 'Brother to a beggar, and fellow to a king' – what was Dougal's phrase? Jaikie was no theorist, but he had a working philosophy, with the notion at the back of his head that human nature was much the same everywhere, and that one might dig out of the unlikeliest places surprising virtues. He considered that he had been lucky enough to have the right kind of education for the practice of this creed.

But it was no philosopher who sat with his knees hunched on the window-seat, but a drowsy and rather excited boy. His travels had given him more than content, for in these last days a faint but delicious excitement had been creeping into his mind. He was not very certain of his exact whereabouts on the map, but he knew that he had crossed the border of the humdrum world and was in a land of enchantments. There was nothing in the ritual of his days to justify this; his legs like compasses were measuring out the same number of miles; the environment was the same, the slow kindly peasants, the wheel of country life, the same bright mornings and cool evenings, the same plain meals voraciously eaten, and hard beds in which he fell instantly asleep. He could speak little of the language, and he did not know one soul within a hundred miles. He was the humblest of pilgrims, and the lowness of his funds would presently compel his return. Nevertheless, he was ridiculously expectant. He laughed at himself, but he could not banish the mood. He was awaiting something – or something was awaiting him.

The apple-green twilight deepened into emerald, and then into a velvet darkness, for the moon would rise late, and a haze obscured the stars. Long ago the last child had been hunted from the street into bed. Long ago the last villagers had left the seat under the vine trellis where they had been having their evening sederunt. Long ago the oxen had been brought into the byres and the goats driven in from the hillside. A wood wagon had broken down by the bridge, and the blacksmith had been hammering at its axle, but his job was finished, and a spark of a lamp beaconed the derelict cart. Otherwise there was no light in earth or heaven, and no sound except the far-away drone of a waterfall in the high woods and an occasional stirring of beasts in byre or stable. Kremisch was in the deep sleep of those who labour hard, bed early, and rise with the dawn. Jaikie grew drowsy. He shook out his pipe, drew a long breath of the cool night air, and rose to take the lamp from the table and ascend to his bedroom.

Suddenly a voice spoke. It came from the outer air at about the level of the window. And it asked in German for a match.

Balaam was not more startled by the sudden loquacity of his ass than was Jaikie by this aerial summons. It shook him out of his sleepiness and made him nearly drop the lamp. 'God bless my soul,' he said – his chief ejaculation, which he had acquired from Mr McCunn.

'He will,' said the voice, 'if you'll give me a light for my cigarette.'

The spirit apparently spoke English, and Jaikie, reassured, held the lamp to the darkness of the open casement. There was a face there, suspended in the air, a face with cheeks the colour of a dry beech leaf and a ragged yellow beard. It was a friendly face, and in the mouth was an unlit cigarette.

'What are you standing on?' Jaikie asked, for it occurred to him that this must be a man on stilts. He had heard of these as a custom in malarial foreign places.

'To be accurate, I am sitting,' was the answer. 'Sitting on an elephant, if you must know. An agreeable female whom I call Aurunculeia. Out of Catullus, you remember. Almost his best poem.'

Jaikie lit a match, but the speaker waved it aside. 'I think, if you don't mind,' he said, 'I'll come in and join you for a minute. One doesn't often meet an Englishman in these parts, and Aurunculeia has no vulgar passion for haste. As you have no doubt guessed, she and I are part of a circus – an integral and vital part – what you might call the *primum mobile*. But we were detained by a little accident. I was asleep, and we strayed from the road and did havoc in a field of marrows, which made some unpleasantness. So our lovely companions have faded and gone ahead to savour the fleshpots of Tarta, while we follow at our leisure. You have never ridden on an elephant? If you go slow enough, believe me it is the very poetry of motion, for you are part, as it were, of a cosmic process. How does it go? "Moved round in earth's diurnal course, With rocks and stones and trees." '

A word was spoken in a lower tone, there was the sound of the shuffling of heavy feet, and a man stepped lightly on to the window-sill and through the casement. His first act was to turn up the wick of the lamp on the table and light his cigarette at its funnel.

Jaikie found himself gazing at a figure which might have been the Pied Piper. It was very tall and very ragged. It wore an old tunic of horizon-blue from which most of the buttons had gone, a scarlet cummerbund, and flapping cotton trousers which had once been white. It had no hat, and besides its clothes, its only other belonging was a long silver-mounted porcupine quill, which may have been used for the encouragement of Aurunculeia.

The scarecrow looked at Jaikie and saw something there which amused him, for he set his arms akimbo and laughed heartily. 'How nature creeps up to art!' he cried. 'Had this been an episode in a novel, it would have been condemned for its manifest improbability. There was an impish propulsive power about my little gold stater.'

He took a small coin from his pocket and regarded it affectionately. Then he asked a question which brought Jaikie out of his chair. 'Have you any news of Cousin Alison, Mr Galt?'

Slowly, to Jaikie's startled sight, the features of the scarecrow became the lineaments of the exquisite Mr Randal Glynde. The neat hair was now shaggy and very dusty, the beard was untrimmed, and every semblance of respectability had gone from his garments. But the long lean wrists were the same, the long slim fingers, and the penetrating blue eyes.

Mr Glynde replaced the stater in some corner of his person, and beamed upon Jaikie. He stretched an arm and grasped the jug of wine of which Jaikie had drunk about half, took a long pull at it, and set it down with a wry face.

'Vinegar,' he said. 'I had forgotten that the Flosgebirge wine sours in an hour. Do not trouble yourself, Mr Galt, for I have long ago supped. We were talking about Cousin Alison, for whom I understand you have a kindness. So have I. So gracious is my memory of her that I have been reciting verses in her honour in the only tongue in which a goddess should be hymned.

*Alison, bella puella candida,*
*Quae bene superas lac et lilium*
*Album, quae simul rosam rubidam*
*Aut expolitum ebur Indicum,*
*Pande, puella, pande capillulos*
*Flavos, lucentes ut aurum nitidum.*

What puzzles me is whether that is partly my own or wholly John the Silentiar's. I had been reading John the Silentiar, but the book was stolen from me, so I cannot verify. . . . No, I will not sleep here. I must sleep at Tarta, though it will be broad daylight before I shut my eyes. Tatius, my manager, is a worthy man, but he is to Meleager my clown as acid to a raw wound, and without me to calm them they will be presently rubbing each other's noses in the mud.'

'Are you a circus proprietor?' Jaikie asked.

Mr Glynde nodded pleasantly.

'In me you see the sole proprietor of the epochal, the encyclopedic, the grandiose Cirque Doré of Aristide Lebrun. The epithets are not mine, but those of the late Aristide, who these three years has been reposing in full evening dress in the cemetery of Montléry. I purchased the thing from his widow, stock-in-trade, goodwill and all – even the gentle Aurunculeia. I have travelled with it from the Pyrenees to the Carpathians and from the Harz to the Apennines. Some day, who knows, I will widen these limits and go from the Sierra Nevada to the Urals, and from the Jotunheim to Parnassus. Geography has always intoxicated me.'

'I understand the fun of travelling,' said Jaikie, 'but isn't a circus rather heavy baggage to lug after you?'

'Ah, no. You do not realize the power of him who carries with him a little world of merriment, which can be linked to that substratum of merriment which is found in every human species. No fumbling for him – he finds the common touch at once. He must suit himself of course to various tastes. Clowning in one place, horse tricks in a second, the sweet Aurunculeia in a third. The hills have different fancies from the valleys, and the valleys from the plains. The Cirque Doré is small, but I flatter myself it is select. We have as fine white barbs as ever came out of Africa, and Meleager my clown has the common denominator of comedy at which all Europe can laugh. No women. Too temperamental and troublesome. My people quarrel in every known tongue, but, being males, it is summer lightning. ... Ah, Mr Galt, I cannot explain to you the intoxication of shifting camp weekly, not from town to town, but from one little human cosmos to another. I have the key which unlocks all doors, and can steal into the world at the back of men's minds, about which they do not speak to their politicians and scarcely even to their priests.

'I have power, too,' Mr Glynde went on; 'for I appeal to something old and deep in man's nature. Before this I have wrecked a promising insurrection through the superior charm of my circus over an *émeute* in a market-place. I have protected mayors and burgomasters from broken heads, and maybe from cut throats, by my mild distractions. And I have learned many things that are hidden from diplomats and eager journalists. I, the entertainer, the *fils de joie*, I am becoming an expert, if I may say so modestly, on the public opinion of Europe – or rather on that incoherent soul which is greater than opinion.'

'Well, and what do you make of it?' Jaikie asked. He was fascinated by his visitor, the more so as he was a link with Alison, but sleep was descending upon him like an armed man, and he asked the conventional question without any great desire to hear the answer.

'Bad,' said Mr Glynde. 'Or, since a moral judgement is unnecessary, shall I say odd? We are now in the midst of the retarded liquidation of the War. I do not mean debts and currencies and economic fabrics, but something much more vital – the thoughts of men. The democracies have lost confidence. So long as they believed in themselves they could make shift with constitutions and parliaments and dull republics. But once let them lose confidence, and they are like children in the dark, reaching out for the grasp of a strong hand. That way lies the dictator. It might be the monarch if we bred the right kind of king. . . . Also there is something more dangerous still, a stirring of youth, disappointed, aggrieved youth, which has never known the discipline of war. Imaginative and incalculable youth, which clamours for the moon and may not be content till it has damaged most of the street lamps.

'But you nod,' said Mr Glynde, rising. 'I weary you. You must to bed and I to Tarta. I must not presume upon the celestial patience of Aurunculeia.'

Jaikie rose too and found the tall man's hand on his shoulder. He observed sleepily that his visitor's face, now clear in the lamplight, had changed, the smile had gone from it, and the eyes were cool and rather grave. Also the slight artifice of his speech, which recalled an affected Cambridge don of his acquaintance, was suddenly dropped.

'I gave you certain advice,' said Mr Glynde, 'when you spun my stater in London. I told you that if you wanted peace you should stick to the west. You are pretty far east, Mr Galt, so I assume that a quiet life is not your first object. You have been walking blindly and happily for weeks waiting for what the days brought forth. Have you any very clear notion where you have got to?'

'I'm rather vague, for I have a rotten map. But I know that I've come to the end of my money. Tomorrow I must turn about and make for home. I mean to get to Munich and travel back by the cheapest way.'

'Three and a quarter miles from Kremisch the road to Tarta drops into a defile among pine trees. At the top there are two block-houses, one on each side of the highway. If you walked that way armed guards would emerge from the huts and demand your passport. Also they would make an inquisition into your baggage more peremptory than most customs officers. That is the frontier of Evallonia.'

Jaikie's sleepiness left him. 'Evallonia!' he cried. 'I had no notion I was so near it.'

'You have read of Evallonia in the English press?'

'Yes, and I have heard a lot about it. I've met Evallonians too – all sorts.' He counted on his fingers. 'Nine – ten, including Prince John.'

'Prince John! Ah, you saw him at Lady Lamancha's party.'

'I saw him two years before that in Scotland, and had a good deal to do with him. With the others, too. I can tell you who they were, for I'm not likely to forget them. There were six Republicans – Mastrovin, Dedekind, Rosenbaum, Ricci, Calaman, and one whose name I never knew – a round-faced fellow in spectacles. There were three Monarchists – Count Casimir Muresco, Doctor Jagon, and Prince Odalchini.'

The tall man carefully closed the window and sat down again. When he spoke it was in a low voice.

'You know some very celebrated people. I think I can place you, Mr Galt. You are called Jaikie, are you not, by your friends? Two years ago you performed a very notable exploit, which resulted in the saving of several honest men and the confounding of some who were not so honest. That story is famous in certain circles. I have laughed over it often, not dreaming that one day I should meet the hero.'

Jaikie shifted nervously, for praise made him unhappy. 'Oh, I didn't do anything much. It was principally Alison. But what has gone wrong with Evallonia? I've been expecting ever since to hear that the Monarchists had kicked out Mastrovin and his lot, but the whole thing seems to have fizzled.'

Mr Glynde was regarding him with steady eyes, which even in the dim light seemed very bright.

'It has not fizzled, but Evallonia at this moment is in a critical state. It is no place for a quiet life, but then I do not think that is what you like. . . . Mr Galt, will you forgive me if I ask you a personal question? Have you any duty which requires your immediate return home?'

'None. But I've finished my money. I have just about enough to get me back.'

'Money is nothing – that can be arranged. I would ask another question. Have you any strong interest in Evallonian affairs?'

'No. But some of my friends have – Mr Craw, the newspaper man, for example, and Dougal Crombie, his chief manager.'

Mr Glynde brooded. 'You know Mr Craw and Mr Crombie? Of course you would. But you have no prepossession in the matter? Except an inclination to back your friends' view?'

'Yes. I thought Prince John a decent fellow, and I liked the queer old Monarchist chaps. Also I greatly disliked Mastrovin and his crowd. They tried to bully me.'

The other smiled. 'That I am sure was a bad blunder on their part.' He was silent for a minute, and then he laid a hand on Jaikie's knee. 'Mr Galt,' he said solemnly, 'if you continued your walking tour tomorrow eastward down the wooded glen, and passed the frontier – I presume your passport is in order? – you would enter a strange country. How strange I have no time to tell you, but I will say this – it is at the crisis of its destiny and any hour may see a triumph or a tragedy. I believe that you might be of some use in averting tragedy. You are a young man, and, I fancy, not indisposed to adventure. If you go home you will be out of danger in that happy cosseted world of England. If you go on, you will certainly find danger, but you may also find wonderful things for which danger is a cheap price. How do you feel about it?'

Jaikie felt many things. Now he knew why all day he had had that curious sense of expectation. There was a queer little flutter at his heart.

'I don't know,' he said. 'It's all rather sudden. I should want to hear more about it.'

'You shall. You shall hear everything before you take any step which is irrevocable. If you will make one day's march into Evallonia, I will arrange that the whole situation is put honestly before you. . . . But no! I have a conscience. I can foretell what you will decide, and I have no right even to bring you within the possibility of that decision, for it will mean danger – it may even mean death. You are too young to gamble with.'

'I think,' said Jaikie, 'I should like to put my nose inside Evallonia just to say I'd been there. You say I can come back if I don't like it. Where's that little coin of yours? It sent me out here, and it may as well decide what I do next.'

'Sportsman,' said Mr Glynde. He produced the stater and handed it to Jaikie, who spun it – 'Heads go on, tails go home.' But owing to the dim light, or perhaps to sleepy eyes, he missed his catch, and the coin rolled on the floor. He took the lamp to look for it, and behold it was wedged upright in a crack in the board – neither heads nor tails.

Mr Glynde laughed merrily. 'Apparently the immortal gods will have no part in this affair. I don't blame them, for Evallonia is a nasty handful. The omens on the whole point to home. Good night, Mr Galt. We shall no doubt meet in England.'

'I'll sleep on it,' said Jaikie. 'If I decide to go on a little farther, what do I do?'

'You will reach Tarta by midday, and just beyond the bridge you will see a gipsy-looking fellow, short but very square, with whiskers and ear-rings and a white hat with "Cirque Doré" embroidered on it in scarlet. That is Luigi, my chief fiddler. You will ask him the way to the Cirque, and he will reply in French, which I think you understand, that he knows a better restaurant. After that you will be in his charge. Only I beg of you to keep your mind unbiased by what I have said, and let sleep give you your decision. Like Cromwell I am a believer in Providences, and since that wretched stater won't play the game, you must wait for some other celestial guidance.'

He opened the casement, spoke a word in an unknown tongue, and a heavy body stirred in the dust below. Then he stepped lightly into the velvet darkness, and there followed a heaving and shuffling which presently died away. When a minute later the moon topped the hill, the little street was an empty silver alley.

CHAPTER TWO

# THE HOUSE OF THE FOUR WINDS

THE night brought no inspiration to Jaikie, for his head was no sooner on his chaff-filled pillow than he seemed to be awake in broad daylight. But the morning decided him. There had been an early shower, the dust was laid in the streets, and every cobble of the sidewalk glistened. From the hills blew a light wind, bearing a rooty fragrance of pine and moss and bracken. A delicious smell of hot coffee and new bread ascended from below; cats were taking their early airing; the vintner opposite, who had a face like a sun, was having a slow argument with the shoemaker; a pretty girl with a basket on her arm was making eyes at a young forester in velveteen breeches and buckskin leggings; a promising dog-fight was in progress near the bridge, watched by several excited boys; the sky above had the soft haze which promises a broiling day.

Jaikie felt hungry both for food and enterprise. The morning's freshness was like a draught of spring water, and every sense was quick and perceptive. He craned his head out of the window and looked back along the way he had come the night before. It showed a dull straight vista between trees. He looked eastward, and there, beyond the end of the village, the world dropped away, and he was looking at the blue heavens and a most appetizing crook in the road, which seemed to hesitate, like a timid swimmer, before plunging downwards. There could be no question about it. On this divinest of mornings he refused dully to retrace his steps. He would descend for one day into Evallonia.

He breakfasted on fried eggs and brook trout, paid a diminutive bill, buckled on his knapsack, and before ten o'clock had left Kremisch behind him. The road was all that it had promised. It wound through an upland meadow with a strong blue-grey stream to keep it company, and every now and then afforded delectable glimpses of remote and shining plains. The hills shouldered it friendlily, hills with wide green rides among the firs and sometimes a bald nose of granite. Jaikie had started out with his mind chiefly on Randal Glynde, that suddenly discovered link with Alison. Evallonia and its affairs did not interest him, or Mr Glynde's mysterious summons to adventure. His meditations during recent weeks had been so much on his own land and the opportunities which it might offer to a deserving young man that he was not greatly concerned with the doings of foreigners, even though some of them were his acquaintances. But he was strongly interested in Mr Glynde. He had never met anybody quite like him, so cheerful and secure in his absurdities. The meeting with him had rolled from Jaikie's back many of the cares of life. The solemnity with which he had proposed a visit to Evallonia seemed in the retrospect to be out of the picture and therefore negligible. Mr Glynde was an apostle of fantasy and his seriousness was itself a comedy. The memory of him harmonized perfectly with this morning world, which with every hundred yards was unveiling a new pageant of delight.

Presently he forgot even Mr Glynde in the drama of the roadside. There was a pool in the stream, ultramarine over silver sand, with a very big trout in it – not less than three pounds in weight. There was a bird which looked like a dipper, but was not a dipper. There was a hawk in the sky, a long-winged falcon of a kind he had never seen before. And on a boulder was perched – rarity of rarities – an unmistakable black redstart. . . . And then the glen seemed to lurch forward and become a defile, down which the stream dropped in a necklace of white cascades. At the edge was a group of low buildings, and out of them came two men carrying rifles.

Jaikie looked with respect at the first Evallonians he had seen on their native heath. They were small men with a great breadth of shoulder, and broad good-humoured countenance – a typical compound, he thought, of Slav and Teuton. But their manner belied their faces, for they were almost truculent, as if they had been soured by heavy and unwelcome duties. They examined everything in his pack and his pockets, they studied his passport with profound suspicion, and they interrogated him closely in German, which he followed with difficulty. Several times they withdrew to consult together; once they retired into the block-house, apparently to look up some book of regulations. It was the better part of an hour before they allowed him to pass. Then something ingenuous in Jaikie's face made them repent of their doubts. They grimaced and shook hands with him, and shouted *Grüss Gott* till he had turned a corner.

'Evallonia is a nervous country,' thought Jaikie. 'Luckily I had nothing contraband on me, or I should be bankrupt.'

After that the defile opened into a horseshoe valley, with a few miles ahead the spires of a little town. He saw the loop of a river, of which the stream he had followed must be a tributary. On the north side was something which he took for a hill, but which closer inspection revealed to be a dwelling. It stood high and menacing, with the town huddled up to it, built of some dark stone which borrowed no colour from the bright morning. On three sides it seemed to be bounded by an immense park, for he saw great spaces of turf and woodland which contrasted with the chessboard tillage of other parts of the plain.

A peasant was carrying hay from a roadside meadow. Jaikie pointed to the place and asked its name.

The man nodded. 'Yes, Tarta.'

'And the castle?'

At first the man puzzled; then he smiled. He pronounced a string of uncouth vocables. Then in halting German: 'It is the great Schloss. I have given you its name. It means the House of the Four Winds.'

As Jaikie drew nearer the town he saw the reason why it was so called. Tarta stood in the mouth of a horseshoe and three glens debouched upon it, his own from the west and two other sword-cuts from the north and south. It was clear that the castle must be a very temple of Aeolus. From three points of the compass the winds would whistle down the mountain gullies, and on the east there was no shelter from the devilments bred in the Asian steppes.

Before noon he was close to the confines of the little town. His stream had ceased to be a mountain torrent, and had expanded into broad lagoons, and just ahead was its junction with the river. Over the latter there was a high-backed bridge flanked by guard-houses, and beyond a jumble of masonry which promised narrow old-world streets. The castle, seen at closer range, was more impressive than ever. It hung over the town like a thundercloud, but a thundercloud from which the lightnings had fled, for it had a sad air of desolation. No flag flew from its turrets, no smoke issued from its many chimneys, the few windows in the great black sides which rose above the streets were like blind eyes. Yet its lifelessness made a strong appeal to Jaikie's fancy. This bustling little burgh under the shadow of a medieval relic was like a living thing tied to a corpse. But was it really a corpse? He guessed at its vast bulk stretching northward into its wild park. It might have turned a cold shoulder on Tarta and yet within its secret demesne be furiously alive. Meantime it belied its name, for not a breath of wind stirred in the sultry noon. Somewhere beyond the bridge must be Luigi, the chief fiddler of the Cirque Doré. He hoped that Luigi would take him where he could get a long drink.

He was to get the drink, but not from Luigi's hands. On the side of the bridge farthest from the town the road passed through a piece of rough parkland, perhaps the common pasturage of the medieval township. Here a considerable crowd had gathered, and Jaikie pressed forward to discover the reason of it. Down the road from Tarta a company of young men was marching, with the obvious intention of making a camp in the park; indeed, certain forerunners had already set up a grove of little shelter-tents. They were remarkable young men, for they carried themselves with disciplined shoulders, and yet with the free swing from the hips of the mountaineer. Few of them were tall, but the leanness gave the impression of a good average height, and they certainly looked amazingly hard and fit. Jaikie, accustomed to judge physique on the Rugby field, was impressed by their light-foot walk and their easy carriage. They were not in the least like the Wandervögel whom he had met on many German roads, comfortable sunburnt folk out for a holiday. These lads were in serious training, and they had some purpose other than amusement.

As they passed, the men in the crowd saluted by raising the left hand and the women waved their handkerchiefs. In the rear rode a young man, a splendid figure on a well-bred flea-bitten roan. The rank-and-file wore shorts and green shirts open at the neck, but the horseman had breeches and boots and a belted green tunic, while a long hunting knife swung at his middle. He was a tall fellow with thick fair hair, a square face and dark eyebrows – a face with which Jaikie was familiar in very different surroundings.

Jaikie, in the front row of the crowd, was so overcome with amazement that his left hand remained unraised and he could only stare. The horseman caught sight of him, and he too registered surprise, from which he instantly recovered. He spoke a word to the ranks; a man fell out, and beckoned Jaikie to follow. The other spectators fell back from him as from a leper, and he and his warder followed the horse's tail into the open space, where the rest were drawing up in front of the tents.

Then the horseman turned to him.

'Salute,' he said.

Jaikie's arm shot up obediently.

The leader cast an eye over the ranks, and bade them stand easy and then fall out. He dismounted, flinging his bridle to an orderly. 'Follow me,' he said to Jaikie in English, and led him to a spot on the river bank, where a larger tent had been set up. Two lads were busy there with kit and these he dismissed. Then he turned to Jaikie with a broad grin.

'What on earth are you doing here?' he asked.

'Give me a drink first, Ashie,' was the answer.

The young man dived into the tent and produced a bottle of white wine, a bottle of a local mineral water, and two tumblers. The two clinked glasses. Then he gave Jaikie a cigarette. 'Now,' he said, 'what's your story?'

'I have been across half Europe,' said Jaikie. 'I must have tramped about five hundred miles. My money's done, and I go home tomorrow, but I thought I'd have a look inside Evallonia first. But what are *you* doing, Ashie? Is it Boy Scouts or a revolution?'

The other smiled and did not at once reply. That was a mannerism which the University of Cambridge had taught him, for when Count Paul Jovian (he had half a dozen other Christian names which we may neglect) entered St Mark's he had been too loquacious. He and a cousin had shared lodgings, and at first they were not popular. They had an unpleasant trick of being easily insulted, talking about duels, and consequently getting their ears boxed. When they migrated within the College walls, the dislike of the cousin had endured, but Count Paul began to make friends. Finally came a night when the cousin's trousers were removed and used to decorate the roof, as public evidence of dislike, while Paul was unmolested. That occasion gave him his nickname, for he was christened Asher by a piously brought-up contemporary, the tribe of Asher having, according to the Book of Judges, 'abode in its breaches'. 'Ashie' he had remained from that day.

Jaikie had begun by disliking him, he was so noisy and strange and flamboyant. But Count Paul had a remarkable gift of adapting himself to novel conditions. Presently his exuberance quieted down, he became more sparing in speech, he developed a sense of humour and laboured to acquire the idiom of their little society. In his second year he was indistinguishable from the ordinary English undergraduate. He had a pretty turn of speed, but it was found impossible to teach him the Rugby game; at boxing too he was a complete duffer; but he was a brilliant fencer, and he knew all that was to be known about a horse. Indeed, it was in connexion with horses that Jaikie first came to like him. A groom from a livery stable lost his temper with a hireling, who was badly bitted and in a fractious temper. The Count's treatment of the case rejoiced Jaikie's heart. He shot the man into the gutter, eased the bit, and quieted the animal with a curious affectionate gentleness. After that the two became friends, in spite of the fact that the Count's taste for horses and hunting took him into a rather different set. They played together in a cricket eleven of novices called the 'Cads of all Nations', who for a week of one long vacation toured the Midlands, and were soundly beaten by every village team.

There was a tough hardihood about the man which made Jaikie invite him more than once to be his companion in some of his more risky enterprises – invitations regretfully refused, for some business always took Ashie home. That home Jaikie knew to be in Eastern Europe, but he had not associated him with Evallonia. There was also an extreme innocence. He wanted to learn everything about England, and took Jaikie as his mentor. believing that in him he had found the greatest common measure of the British people. Whether he learned much may be doubted, for Jaikie was too little of a dogmatist to be a good instructor. But they slipped into a close friendship, and rubbed the corners off each other's minds.

'I know what I'm doing,' said Ashie at last; 'but I am not quite sure where it will finish. But that's a long story. You're a little devil, Jaikie, to come here at the tag-end of your holiday. If you had come a month ago we might have had all sorts of fun.'

He had relapsed into the manner of the undergraduate, but there was something in him now which made it a little absurd. For the figure opposite Jaikie was not the agreeable and irresponsible companion he had known. Ashie looked desperately foreign, without a hint of Cambridge and England; bigger too, more mature, and rather formidable. The thick dark eyebrows in combination with the fair hair had hitherto given his appearance a touch of comedy; now the same brows bent above the grey eyes had something in them martial and commanding. Rob Roy was more of a man on his native heath than on the causeways of Glasgow.

'If you can arrange to stay here for a little,' said Ashie, 'I promise to show you life.'

'Thank you very much, but I can't. I must be off home tomorrow – a week's tramping, and then the train.'

'Give me three weeks.'

'I'm sorry, but I can't.' Jaikie found it hard to sort out his feelings, but he was clear that he did not want to dally in Evallonia.

Ashie's voice became almost magisterial.

'What are you doing here today?' he asked.

'I'm lunching with a friend and going back to Kremisch in the evening.'

'Who's your friend?'

'I'm not quite sure of his name.' Jaikie's caution told him that Mr Glynde might have many aliases. 'He's in a circus.'

Ashie laughed – almost in the old light-hearted way. 'Just the kind of friend you'd have. The Cirque Doré? I saw some of the mountebanks in the streets. . . . You won't accept my invitation? I can promise you the most stirring time in your life.'

'I wish I could, but – well, it's no use, I can't.'

'Then we must part, for I have a lot to do.'

'You haven't told me what you're doing.'

'No. Some day I will – in England, if I ever come back to England.'

He called one of his scouts, to whom he said something in a strange tongue. The latter saluted and waited for Jaikie to follow him. Ashie gave him a perfunctory handshake – 'Good-bye. Good luck to you'; and entered his tent.

The boy led Jaikie beyond the encampment, and, with a salute and a long stare, left him at the entrance to the bridge. A clock on a steeple told him that it was a quarter past twelve, pretty much the time that Mr Glynde had appointed. The bridge was almost empty, for the sightseers who had followed Ashie's outfit had trickled back to their midday meals. Jaikie spent a few minutes looking over the parapet at the broad waters of the river. This must be the Rave, the famous stream which sixty miles on flowed through the capital city of Melina. He watched its strong current sweep past the walls of the great Schloss, which there dropped sheer into it, before in a wide circuit it formed the western boundary of the castle park. What an impregnable fortress, he thought, must have been this House of the Four Winds in the days before artillery, and how it must have lorded it over the little burgh under its skirts!

There was a gatehouse on the Tarta side of the bridge, an ancient crumbling thing bright with advertisements of the Cirque Doré. Beyond it a narrow street wound under the blank wall of the castle, ending in a square in which the chief building was a baroque town house. From where Jaikie stood this town house had an odd apologetic air, a squat thing dwarfed by the Schloss, like a dachshund beside a mastiff. The day was very warm, and he crossed over from the glare of one side of the street to the shadow of the other. The place was almost empty, most of the citizens being doubtless engaged with food behind shuttered windows. Jaikie was getting hungry, and so far he had looked in vain for Mr Glynde's Luigi. But as he moved towards the central square a man came out of an entry, and, stopping suddenly to light a cigarette, almost collided with him. Jaikie saw a white cap and scarlet lettering, and had a glimpse of gold ear-rings and a hairy face. He remembered his instructions.

'Can you show me the way to the Cirque Doré?' he asked.

The man grinned. 'I will lead you to a better restaurant,' he said in French with a villainous accent. He held out his hand and shook Jaikie's warmly, as if he had found a long-lost friend. Then he gripped him by the arm and poured forth a torrent of not very intelligible praise of the excellence of the cuisine to which he was guiding him.

Jaikie found himself hustled up the street and pulled inside a little dark shop, which appeared to be a combination of a bird-fancier's and a greengrocer's. There was nobody there, so they passed through it into a court strewn with decaying vegetables and through a rickety door into a lane, also deserted. After that they seemed to thread mazes of mean streets at a pace which made the sweat break on Jaikie's forehead, till they found themselves at the other end of the town, where it ebbed away into shacks and market gardens.

'I am very hungry,' said Jaikie, who saw his hopes of luncheon disappearing.

'The Signor must have patience,' was the answer. 'He has still a little journey before him, but at the end of it he will have honest food.'

Luigi was an adept at understatement. He seemed to wish to escape notice, which was easy at this stagnant hour of the day. Whenever anyone appeared he became still as a graven image, with an arresting hand on Jaikie's arm. They chose such cover as was available, and any track they met they crossed circumspectly. The market gardens gave place to vineyards, which were not easy to thread, and then to wide fields of ripe barley, hot as the Sahara. Jaikie was in good training, but this circus-man Luigi, though he looked plump and soft, was also in no way distressed, never slackening pace and never panting. By-and-by they entered a wood of saplings which gave them a slender shade. At the far end of it was a tall palisade of chestnut stakes, lichened and silvery with age. 'Up with you,' said Luigi, and gave Jaikie a back which enabled him to grasp the top and swing himself over. To his annoyance the Italian followed him unaided, supple as a monkey.

'Rest and smoke,' he said. 'There is now no reason for hurry except the emptiness of your stomach.'

They rested for ten minutes. Behind them was the palisade they had crossed, and in front of them glades of turf, and wildernesses of fern and undergrowth, and groves of tall trees. It was like the New Forest, only on a bigger scale.

'It is a noble place,' said Luigi, waving his cigarette. 'From here it is seven miles to Zutpha, where is a railway. Tarta in old days was only, so to say, the farmyard behind the castle. From Zutpha the guests of the princes of this house were driven in great coaches with outriders. Now there are few guests, and instead of a coach-and-eight a Ford car. It is the way of the world.'

When they resumed their journey it was at an easier pace. They bore to the left, and presently came in view of what had once been a formal garden on a grandiose scale. Runnels had been led from the river, and there was a multitude of stone bridges and classic statuary and rococo summer-houses. Now the statues were blotched with age, the bridges were crumbling, and the streams were matted beds of rushes. Beyond, rising from a flight of terraces, could be seen the huge northern façade of the castle, as blank as the side it showed to Tarta. It had been altered and faced with a white stone a century ago, but the comparative modernity of this part made its desolation more conspicuous than that of the older Gothic wings. What should have been gay with flowers and sun-blinds stood up in the sunlight as grim as a deserted factory; and that, thought Jaikie, is grimmer than any other kind of ruin.

Luigi did not take him up the flights of empty terraces. Beyond the formal garden he turned along a weedy path which flanked a little lake. On one side was the cyclopean masonry of the terrace wall, and, where it bent at an angle, cloaked by a vast magnolia, they came suddenly upon a little paved court shaded by a trellis. It was cool, and it was heavily scented for on one side was a thicket of lemon verbena. A table had been set for luncheon, and at it sat two men, waited on by a footman in knee-breeches and a faded old coat of blue and silver.

'You are not five minutes behind time,' said the elder of the two. 'Anton,' he addressed the servant, 'take the other gentleman indoors and see to his refreshment.' ... To Jaikie he held out his hand. 'We have met before, Mr Galt. I have the honour to welcome you to my poor house. Mr Glynde I think you already know.'

'You expected me?' Jaikie asked in some surprise.

'I was pretty certain you would come,' said Mr Glynde.

Jaikie saw before him that Prince Odalchini whom two years ago he had known as one of the tenants of the Canonry shooting of Knockraw. The Prince's hair was a little greyer, his well-bred face a little thinner, and his eyes a little darker round the rims. But in the last burned the same fire of a gentle fanaticism. He was exquisitely dressed in a suit of white linen with a tailed coat, and shirt and collar of turquoise-blue silk – blue and white being the Odalchini liveries. Mr Randal Glynde had shed the fantastic garments of the previous night, but he had not returned to the modishness of his English clothes; he wore an ill-cut suit of some thin grey stuff that made him look like a *commis-voyageur* in a smallish way of business, and to this part he had arranged his hair and beard to conform. To his outfit a Guards tie gave a touch of startling colour.

'We will not talk till we have eaten,' said the Prince. 'Mr Galt must have picked up an appetite between here and Kremisch.'

Jaikie had one of the most satisfying meals of his career. There was an omelet, a dish of trout, and such peaches as he had never tasted before. He had acquired a fresh thirst during his journey with Luigi, and this was assuaged by a white wine which seemed to be itself scented with lemon verbena, a wine in slim bottles beaded with the dew of the ice cellar. He was given a cup of coffee made by the Prince's own hands, and a long fat cigarette of a brand which the Prince had specially made for him in Cairo.

'Luigi spoke the truth,' said Mr Glynde, smiling, 'when he said that he would conduct you to a better restaurant.'

The footman withdrew and silence fell. Bees wandered among the heliotrope and verbena and pots of sapphire agapanthus, and even that shady place felt the hot breath of the summer noon. Sleep would undoubtedly have overtaken Jaikie and Mr Glynde but for the vigour of Prince Odalchini, who seemed, like a salamander, to draw life and sustenance from the heat. His high-pitched, rather emotional voice kept his auditors wakeful. 'I will explain to you,' he told Jaikie, 'what you cannot know or have only heard in a perversion. I take up the history of Evallonia after Prince John sailed from your Scotch loch.'

He took a long time over his exposition, and as he went on Jaikie found his interest slowly awakening. The cup of the abominations of the Republican Government had apparently long ago been filled. Evallonia was ready to spew them out, but unfortunately the Monarchists were not quite ready to take their place. This time it was not trouble with other Powers or with the League of Nations. Revolutions had become so much the fashion in Europe that they were taken as inevitable, whether their purpose was republic, monarchy, or dictatorship. The world was too weary to argue about the merits of constitutional types, and the nations were too cumbered with perplexed economics to have any desire to meddle in the domestic affairs of their neighbours. Aforetime the Monarchists had feared the intervention of the Powers or some finding of the League, and therefore they had sought the mediation of British opinion. Now their troubles were of a wholly different kind.

Prince Odalchini explained. Communism was for the moment

a dead cause in Evallonia, and Mastrovin and his friends had as much chance of founding a Soviet republic as of plucking down the moon. Mastrovin indeed dared not show himself in public, and the present administration of his friends staggered along, corrupt, incompetent, deeply unpopular. It would collapse at the slightest pressure. But after that?

'Everywhere in the world,' said the Prince, 'there is now an uprising of youth. It does not know what it seeks. It did not know the hardships of war. But it demands of life some hope and horizon, and it is determined to have the ordering of things in its hands. It is conscious of its ignorance and lack of discipline, so it seeks to inform and discipline itself, and therein lies the danger.

'Ricci,' he went on. 'You remember him in the Canonry? – a youngish man like a horse-dealer. At that time he was a close ally of the Republican Government, but eighteen months ago he became estranged from it – he and Count Jovian, who was not with the others in Scotland. Well, Ricci had an American wife of enormous wealth, and with the aid of her money he set out to stir up our youth. He had an ally in the Jovian I have mentioned, who was a futile vain man, like your Justice Shallow in Shakespeare, easily flattered and but little respected, but with a quick brain for intrigue. These two laid the foundations of a body called Juventus, which is now the strongest thing in Evallonia. They themselves were rogues, but they enlisted many honest helpers, and soon, like the man in the *Arabian Nights*, they had raised a jinn which they could not control. Jovian died a year ago – he was always sick – and Ricci is no longer the leader. But the thing itself marches marvellously. It has caught the imagination of our people and fired their pride. Had we an election, the Juventus candidates would undoubtedly sweep the board. As it is, it contains all the best of Evallonian youth, who give up to it their leisure, their ambition, and their scanty means. It is in its way a noble thing, for it asks only for sacrifice, and offers no bribes. It is, so to speak, a new Society of Jesus, sworn to utter obedience. But, good or ill, it has most damnably spiked the guns of us Royalists.'

Jaikie asked why.

'Because it is arrogant, and demands that whatever is done for Evallonia it alone shall do it. The present Government must go, and at once, for it is too gross a scandal. If we delay, there will be a blind revolution of the people themselves. You will say – let Juventus restore Prince John. Juventus will do nothing of the kind, since Prince John is not its own candidate. If we restore him, Juventus will become anti-Monarchist. What then will it do? I reply that it does not yet know, but there is a danger that it may set up one of its own people as dictator. That would be tragic, for in the first place Evallonia does not need or desire a dictator, being Monarchist by nature, and in the second place Juventus does not want a dictatorship either. It is Nationalist, but not Fascist. Yet the calamity may happen.'

'Has Juventus any leader who could fill the bill?' Jaikie asked.

The Prince shook his head. 'I do not think so – therefore its action would be only to destroy and obstruct, not to build. Ricci with his wife's millions is now discredited; they have used him and cast him aside. There are some of the very young with power I am told – particularly a son of Jovian's.'

'Is his name Paul?' Jaikie asked, and was told yes.

'I know him,' he said. 'He was at Cambridge with me. I have just seen him, for about two hours ago he stood me a drink.'

The Prince in his surprise upset the coffee-pot, and even the sophisticated eyes of Mr Glynde opened a little wider.

'You know Paul Jovian? That is miraculous, Mr Galt. Will you permit me to speak a word in private with Mr Glynde? There are some matters still too secret even for your friendly ears.'

The two withdrew and left Jaikie alone in the alcove among bees and butterflies and lemon verbena. He was a little confused in his mind, for after a solitary month he had suddenly strayed into a place where he seemed to know rather too many people. Embarrassing people, all of whom pressed him to stay longer. He did not much like their country. It was too hot for him, too scented and airless. He was not in the least interested in the domestic affairs of Evallonia, either the cantrips of Ashie or the solemn intrigues of the Prince. It was not his world; that was a cool, bracing upland a thousand miles away, for which he had begun to feel acutely homesick. Alison would soon be back in the Canonry, and he must be there to meet her. He felt that for the moment he was fed up with foreign travel.

The two men returned, and sat down before him with an air of purpose.

'Where did you find Count Paul?' the Prince asked.

'On the Kremisch side of the Tarta bridge. He was going into camp with a detachment of large-sized Boy Scouts.'

'You know him well?'

'Pretty well. We have been friends ever since his first year. I like him – at least I liked him at Cambridge, but here he seems a rather different sort of person. He wanted me to stay on in Evallonia – to stay for three weeks.'

The two exchanged glances.

'So!' said the Prince. 'And your answer?'

'I refused. He didn't seem particularly well pleased.'

'Mr Galt, we also make you that proposal. Will you be my guest here in Evallonia for a little – perhaps for three weeks – perhaps longer? I believe that you can be of incalculable value to an honest cause. I cannot promise success – that is not commanded by mortals – but I can promise you an exciting life.'

'That was what I said to you last night,' said Mr Glynde, smiling. 'My little stater would give you no guidance, but the fact that you have ventured into Evallonia encourages me to hope.'

Jaikie at the moment had no desire for excitement. He felt limp and drowsy and oppressed; the Prince's luncheon had been too good, and this scented nook choked him; he wanted to be somewhere where he could breathe fresh air. Evallonia was wholly devoid of attractions.

'I don't think so,' he said. 'I'm tremendously honoured that you should want me, but I shouldn't be any use to you, and I must get home.'

'You are not to be moved?' said Mr Glynde.

Jaikie shook his head. 'I've had enough of the Continent of Europe.'

'I understand,' said Mr Glynde. 'I too sometimes feel that satiety, and think I must go home.' He turned to the Prince. 'I doubt if we shall persuade Mr Galt. I wish Casimir were here. Where, by the way, is he?'

The Prince replied with a word which sounded to Jaikie like 'Unnutz', a word which woke a momentary interest in his lethargic mind.

'What then do you propose to do?' The Prince turned to him.

'Go back to Kremisch tonight, sleep there, and set off home tomorrow.'

'What must be must be. But I do not think it wise for you to start yet awhile. Let us go indoors, and I will show you some of the few household gods which poverty has left me.'

Jaikie spent an hour or two pleasantly in the cool chambers of the great house. The place was shabby but not neglected, and there were treasures there which, judiciously placed on the market, might well have restored the Odalchini fortunes. He looked at long lines of forbidding family portraits; at a little room so full of masterpieces that it was a miniature Salle Carrée; at one of the finest collections of armour in the world; and at a wonderful array of sporting trophies, for the Odalchinis had been famous game-shots. He was given tea at a little table in the hall quite in the English fashion. But very soon he became restless. The sun was getting low, and he had a considerable distance to walk before supper.

'You had better go first to the Cirque Doré,' said Mr Glynde. 'There I will meet you, and show you the way out of the town. You have been in dangerous territory, Mr Galt, and must be circumspect in leaving it. No, we cannot go together. I will take a different road and meet you there. Luigi will guide you. You will cross the park by the way you came, and Luigi will be waiting for you outside the pale.'

'I am sorry,' said the Prince. He shook hands with so regretful a face, and his old eyes were so solemn that Jaikie had a moment of compunction. When he left the castle the cool of the evening was beginning, and the twilight scents came freshly and pleasantly to his nostrils. This was a better place than he had thought, and he felt more vigorous and enterprising. He had the faintest twinge of regret about his decision. After all, there was nothing to call him home, for there would be no Dickson McCunn there yet awhile, and no Dougal, and perhaps no Alison. But there would be the Canonry, and he fixed his mind upon its delectable glens as he retraced his path of the morning. One of Jaikie's endowments was an almost perfect instinct for direction, and he struck the high chestnut pale pretty much at the spot where he had first crossed it.

Getting over without Luigi's help was a difficult business, and, Jaikie's energy being wholly employed in the task, he did not trouble to prospect the land. . . . He tumbled over the top and dropped into what seemed to be a crowd of people.

Strong hands gripped him. A cloth was skilfully wound round his face, blinding his eyes and blanketing his voice. Another wrapped his arms to his side, and a third bound his legs. He struggled, but his sense of the physical superiority of his assailants was so great that he soon gave it up; he was like a thin rabbit in the clutch of an enormous gamekeeper. Yet the hands were not unkindly, and his bandages, though effective, were not painful.

He was carried swiftly along for a few minutes and then placed in some kind of car. Somebody sat down beside him. The car was started, and bumped for a little along very rough roads. . . . Then it came to a highway and moved fast. . . . Jaikie had by this time collected his thoughts, and they were wrathful. His first alarm had gone, for he reflected that there was no one likely to mean mischief to him. He was pretty certain what had happened. This was Prince Odalchini's way of detaining an unwilling guest. Well, he would presently have a good deal to say to the Prince and to Mr Glynde.

The car slowed down, and his companion, whoever he was, began with deft hands to undo his bonds. First he loosed his legs. Then, almost with the same movement, he released his arms and drew the bandages from his face. Then he snapped a switch which lit up dimly the interior of the limousine in which the blinds had been drawn.

Jaikie found himself looking at the embarrassed face of Ashie.

## CHAPTER THREE

# DIVERSIONS OF A MARIONETTE

### I

Miss Alison Westwater dropped with a happy sigh beside a bed of wild strawberries wet with dew, and proceeded to make a second breakfast. It was still early morning – not quite seven o'clock – but she had been walking ever since half past five, when she had broken her fast on a cup of coffee and a last-night's roll provided by a friendly chambermaid. She had left the highway, which, switch-backing from valley to valley, took the traveller to Italy, and had taken a forest track which after a mile or two among pines came out on an upland meadow, and led to a ridge, the spur of a high mountain, from which the kingdoms of the earth could be surveyed. The sky was not the pale turquoise bowl which in her own country heralded a perfect summer day, but an intense sapphire; the shadows were also blue, and the sunshine where it fell was a blinding essential light without colour, so that the grass looked like snowdrifts. The air had an aromatic freshness which stung the senses, and Alison drew great breaths of it till her throat was as cold as if she had been drinking spring water.

This was her one satisfactory time in the day. The rest of her waking hours were devoted to a routine which seemed void alike of mirth or reason. Her father's neuritis had almost gone, but so had his good humour, and it was a very peevish old gentleman that she accompanied in pottering walks by the lake-side or in aimless motor drives on blinding hot highways. Lord Rhynns was particular about his food, and the hotel cuisine did not please him, so he was in the habit of sampling, without much success, whatever Unnutz produced in the way of café and konditorei. He was also particular about his clothes, and since he dressed always in the elder fashion of tight trousers, coloured waistcoat, stiff collar and four-in-hand tie, he was generally warm and correspondingly irascible. Her mother did not appear till after midday, and required a good deal of coddling, for, having been driven out of her accustomed beat, she found herself short of acquaintances and quite unable to plan out her days. One curious consequence was that both, who had habituated themselves to a life of Continental vagrancy, suddenly began to long passionately for home. His lordship remembered that the shooting season would soon begin in the Canonry, and was full of sad reminiscences of the exploits of his youth, while to her ladyship came visions of the cool chambers and the smooth and comforting ritual of Castle Gay.

'I am a marionette,' Alison had written to Jaikie. 'I move at the jerk of a string, and it isn't my parents that pull it. It's this ghastly place, which has invented a régime for the idle middle classes of six nations. I defy even you to break loose from it. I do the same things and make the same remarks and wear the same clothes every day at the proper hour. I'm a marionette and so are the other people – quite nice they are, and well-mannered, and friendly, but as dead as salted herrings. A good old-fashioned bounder would be a welcome change. Or a criminal.'

As she sat on the moss she remembered this sentence – and something else. Unnutz was mainly villas and hotels, but there was an old village as a nucleus – wooden houses built on piles on the lake shore, and one or two narrow twisting streets with pumpkins drying on the shingle roofs. There was a bathing-place there very different from the modish thing on the main promenade, a place where you dived in a hut under a canvas curtain into deep green water, and could swim out to some fantastic little rock islets. She had managed once or twice to bathe there, and yesterday afternoon she had slipped off for an hour and had had a long swim by herself. Coming back she had recognized in a corner of the old village the first face of an acquaintance she had met since she came to Unnutz. Not an acquaintance exactly, for he had never seen her. But she remembered well the shaggy leonine head, the heavy brows and forward thrust of the jaw. She had watched those features two years ago during some agonized minutes in the library of Castle Gay, till Mr Dickson McCunn had adroitly turned melodrama into farce, and she was not likely to forget them. She remembered the name too – Mastrovin, the power behind the Republican Government of Evallonia. Had not Jaikie told her that he was the most dangerous underground force in Europe?

What was this dynamic personage doing in a dull little Tirolese health resort? Was her wish to be granted, and their drab society enlivened by a criminal?

The thought only flitted across her mind, for she had other things to think about. She must make the most of her holiday, for by half past ten she must be back to join her father in his *petit déjeuner* on the hotel veranda. Usually she had the whole hill-side to herself, but this morning she had seen a car on the road which led to the high pastures. It had been empty, standing at the foot of one of the tracks which climbed upward through the pines. Someone else had her taste for early mornings in the hills. It had annoyed her to think that her sanctuary was not inviolable. She hoped that the intruder, whoever he or she was, was short in the wind and would not get higher than the wood.

She got up from her lair among the strawberries and wandered across the meadow, where every now and then outcrops of rock stuck grey noses through the flowers. She had a drink out of an ice-cold runnel. She saw a crested tit, a bird which she had never met before, and screwed her single field-glass into her eye to watch its movements. Also she saw a kite high up in the blue, and, having only once in her life met that type of hawk, regarded him with lively interest. Then she came to a little valley, the top of which was a ravine in the high rocks, and the bottom of which was muffled in the woods. There was a woodcutter's cottage here, wonderfully hidden in a cleft, with the pines on three sides and one side open to the hill. Where Alison stood she looked down upon it directly from above, and could observe the beginning of its daily iife. She had been here before, and had seen an old woman, who might have come out of Grimm, carrying pails of water from a pool in the stream.

Now instead of the old woman there was a young man, presumably her son. He came slowly from the cottage and moved to the fringe of the trees, where a path began its downhill course. He possessed a watch, for he twice consulted it, as if he were keeping an appointment. His clothes were the ordinary forester's – baggy trousers of homespun, heavy iron-shod boots, and an aged velveteen jacket with silver buttons. He carried himself well, Alison thought, better than most woodmen, who were apt to be round-shouldered and slouching.

A second man came out of the wood – also a tall man, but dressed very differently from the woodcutter, for he wore flannels and a green Homburg hat. 'My motorist,' thought Alison. 'He must know something about the woods, for the way through them to this cottage isn't easy to find.'

The new-comer behaved oddly. He took off his hat. The woodcutter gave him his hand and he bowed over it with extreme respect. Then the woodcutter slipped his arm in his and led him towards the cottage.

Alison in her perch far above put the glass to her eye and got a good view of the stranger. There could be no mistake. Two years ago she had sat opposite him at dinner at Castle Gay and at breakfast at Knockraw. She recognized the fine shape of his head, and the face which would have been classically perfect but for the snub nose. One did not easily forget Count Casimir Muresco.

But who was the other? Noblemen with nine centuries of pedigree behind them do not usually bow over the hands of foresters and uncover their heads. She could not see his face, for it was turned away from her, but before the two entered the cottage she had no doubt about his identity. She was being given the back view of the lawful monarch of Evallonia.

From that moment Alison's boredom vanished like dew in the sun. She realized that she had stumbled upon the fringe of great affairs. What was it that Prince John had said to her at the dinner at Maurice's? That Unnutz was not a very good place for a holiday that summer, that it might be unpleasant, but that, being English, she would always be free to get away. That could only mean that something momentous was going to happen at Unnutz. What was Prince John doing disguised as a woodcutter in this remote and secret hut? . . . What was Count Casimir, architect of revolutions, doing there so early in the morning? Plots were being hatched, thought the girl in a delicious tremor of excitement. The curtain was about to rise on the play, and, unknown to the actors, she had a seat in a box.

And then suddenly she remembered the face she had seen the afternoon before in the lakeside alley. Mastrovin! He was the deadly enemy of Count Casimir and the Prince. He must know, or suspect, that the Prince was in the neighbourhood. Casimir probably knew nothing of Mastrovin's presence. But she, Alison, knew. The thought solemnized her, for such knowledge is as much a burden as a delight.

Her first impulse was to scramble down the hill-side to the cottage, break in on the conspirators, and tell them what she knew. But she did not move, for it occurred to her that she might be more useful, and get more fun out of the business, if she remained silent. She waited for ten minutes till the two men appeared again. This time she had a good view of the woodcutter through her glass, and she recognized the comely and rather heavy countenance of Prince John. Casimir took a ceremonious leave and started down the track through the forest. Alison, who knew all the paths, followed him at a higher level. She wanted to discover whether or not his steps had been dogged.

Alison had taught Jaikie many things, and he had repaid her by instructing her in some of his own lore. He had made her almost as artful and silent a tracker as himself, and under his tuition she had brought to a high pitch her own fine natural sense of direction. Like a swift shadow she flitted through the pines, now on bare needle-strewn ground, now among tangles of rock and whortleberry. The route she took was almost parallel to Casimir's, but now and then she had to make a circuit to avoid some rocky dingle, and there were times when she had to cast back or cast ahead to trace him. It was rough going in parts, and since Casimir showed a remarkable turn of speed she had sometimes to slither down steeps and sometimes to run. By-and-by came glimpses of the valley below, and at last through a thinning of the pines she saw the last twisting of the hill-path before it debouched on the highway. Presently she saw the waiting car, and the tracker, being a little ahead of the tracked, sank down among the whortleberries to await events.

Casimir appeared, going warily, with an eye on the white strip of high road. It was still empty, for the Firnthal does not rise early. He reached the car, and examined it carefully, as if he feared that someone might have tampered with it in his absence. Satisfied, he took the driver's seat, backed on to the high road, and set out in the direction of Italy.

Alison observed his doings with only half an eye, for between her and the car she had seen something which demanded attention. She was now some two hundred yards above the road, and the ground immediately below her was occupied by a little rock-fall much overgrown with fern and scrub. There was something among the bushes which had not been put there by nature. Her glass showed her that that something was the head of a man. It was a bare head, with grizzled hair and one bald patch at the back, and she knew to whom it belonged. Mastrovin was not in Unnutz for the sake of the excellent sulphur baths or the mountain air.

Alison slipped out of her lair and as noiselessly as she could crawled to her right along the slope of the hill. She struck the path by which Casimir had descended, a path which was, so to speak, the grand trunk road from the hills, and which a little higher forked in several directions. Waiting a moment to get her breath, she made a hasty bouquet of some blue campanulas and sprigs of whortleberry and then sauntered down the path, a little flushed, a little untidy about the hair and wet about the shoes, but on the whole a creditable specimen of early-rising vigorous maidenhood.

Mastrovin, when she came in sight of him, was descending the hill and had already reached the high road. He had covered his head with a green hat, and wore a dark green suit of breeches and Norfolk jacket, just like any other tourist in a mountain country. Alison's whistling caught his ear, and at the foot of the track he stopped to wait for her.

'*Grüss Gott!*' he said, forcing his harsh features into amiability. 'I have been looking for a friend. Have you seen – any man – up in the woods? My friend is tall and walks fast, and his clothes are grey.'

One of Alison's accomplishments was that she understood German perfectly, and spoke it with fluency and a reasonable correctness. But it occurred to her that it would not be wise to reveal this talent; so she pretended to follow Mastrovin with difficulty and to puzzle over one word, and she began to answer in the purest Ollendorff.

'You are English?' he asked. 'Speak English, please, I understand it.'

Alison obeyed. She explained that she had indeed met a man in the high woods, though she had not especially remarked his clothes. She had passed him, and thought that he must have returned soon after, for she had not seen him on her way down. She described minutely the place of meeting – on the right-hand road at the main fork, near the brow of the hill, and not far from the rock called the Wolf Crag which looked down on Unnutz – precisely the opposite direction from the woodcutter's hut.

Mastrovin thanked her with a flourish of his hat.

'I must now to breakfast,' he said. 'There is a *gasthaus* by the roadside where I will await my friend, if he is not already there.'

II

Usually the two miles to Unnutz were the one black spot in the morning's walk, for they were flat and dusty and meant a return to the house of bondage. But today Alison was scarcely conscious of them, for she was thinking hard, with a flutter at her heart which was half-painful and half-pleasant. Prince John was here in retreat for some purpose, and Count Casimir was in touch with him; that must mean that things were coming to a head in

Evallonia. Mastrovin, his bitterest enemy, was on the trail of Casimir, and must know that Prince John was in the neighbourhood. That meant trouble. Her false witness that morning might send Mastrovin on a wild-goose chase to the wrong part of the forest, but it was very certain that he must presently discover the Prince's hermitage. The Prince and Casimir might suspect that their enemies were looking for them, but they did not know that Mastrovin was in Unnutz. She alone knew that, and she must make use of her knowledge. Casimir had gone off in the direction of Italy; therefore she must warn the Prince, and that must be done secretly when she could be certain that she was not followed. She had begun to plan a midnight journey, for happily she had a room giving on a balcony, from which it would be easy to reach the ground. To her surprise she found that she looked forward with no relish to the prospect; if she had had company it would have been immense fun, but, being alone, she felt only the weight of a heavy duty. She longed passionately for Jaikie.

Entering the hotel by a side door, she changed into something more like the regulation toilet of Unnutz, and sought her father on the veranda. For once Lord Rhynns was in a good humour.

'A little late, my dear,' he complained mildly. 'Yes, I have had a better night. I am beginning to hope that I have got even with my accursed affliction.' Then, regarding his daughter with complacent eyes, he became complimentary. 'You are really a very pretty girl, Alison, though your clothes are not such as gentlewomen wore in my young days.' With a surprising touch of sentiment he added, 'You are becoming very like my mother.'

Taking advantage of her father's urbanity, Alison broached the question of going home.

'Presently, my dear. Another week, I think, should set me right. Your mother is anxious to leave – a sudden craving for Scotland. We shall go for a little to Harriet at Castle Gay – she has been more than kind about it, and Craw has behaved admirably. I am told he has the place very comfortable, and I have always found him conduct himself like a gentleman. Money, my dear. Ample means are not only the passport to the name of gentility, but they create the thing itself. In these days it is not easy for a pauper to preserve his breeding.

'By the way,' he continued, 'some friends of ours arrived here this morning. They are breakfasting more elaborately than we are in the *salle-à-manger*. The Roylances. Janet Roylance, you remember, was old Cousin Alastair Raden's second girl.'

'What!' Alison almost shrieked. It was the best news she could have got, for now she could share her burden of responsibility. In the regrettable absence of Jaikie the Roylances were easily the next best.

'Yes,' her father went on. 'They have been at Geneva, and have come on here for a holiday. Sir Archibald, they tell me, is making a considerable name for himself in politics. For a young man in these days he certainly has creditable manners.'

His lordship finished his coffee, and announced that he proposed to go to his sitting-room till luncheon to write letters. Alison dutifully accompanied him thither, paid her respects to her mother, who was also in a more cheerful mood, and then hastened downstairs. In the big dining-room she found the pair she sought at a table in one of the windows. Alison flung herself upon Janet Roylance's neck.

'You've finished breakfast? Then come outside and smoke. I know a quiet corner beside the lake. I must talk to you at once. You blessed angels have been sent by Heaven just at the right moment.'

When they were seated where a little half-moon of shrubbery made an enclave above the blue waters of the Waldersee, Sir Archie offered Alison a cigarette.

'No, thank you. I don't smoke. If I did it would be a pipe, I'm so sick of the cigarette-puffing hussy. First of all, what brought you two here?'

Sir Archie grinned. 'The Conference has adjourned till Bolivia settles some nice point with Uruguay.'

'We came,' said Janet, 'because we are free pople with no plans and we knew that you were here. We thought we should find you moribund with boredom, Allie, but you are radiant. What has happened? Have the parents turned over a new leaf?'

'Papa is quite good and nearly well. Mamma has actually begun to crave for Scotland. There's no trouble at present on the home front. But the foreign situation is ticklish. This place is going to be the scene of dark doings, and I can't cope with them alone. That's why I hugged you like a bear. Have you ever heard of Evallonia?'

'I have,' said Janet, 'for I sometimes read the Craw Press.'

'We've expected a revolution there,' said Sir Archie, 'any time these last two years. But something seems to have gone wrong with the timing.'

'Well, that has been seen to. The blow-up must be nearly ready, and it's going to start in this very place. Listen to me very carefully. The story begins two years ago in Castle Gay.'

Briefly but vigorously Alison told the tale of the raid on the Canonry and the discomfiture by Jaikie and Dickson McCunn of Mastrovin and his gang. ('Jaikie?' said Sir Archie. 'That's the little chap we saw you with at Maurice's? I was in a scrap alongside him years ago. Janet knows the story. Good stamp of lad.') She sketched the personalities of the three Royalists and the six Republicans, and she touched lightly upon Prince John. She described the face seen the afternoon before in the old village, and her sight that morning of the Prince and Casimir at the woodcutter's hut. The drama culminated in Mastrovin squatted like a partridge in the scrub above Casimir's car.

'Mastrovin!' Sir Archie brooded. 'He was at Geneva as an Evallonian delegate. Wonderful face of its kind, but it would make an English jury bring him in guilty of any crime without leaving the box. He was very civil to me. I thought him a miscreant but a sportsman, though I wouldn't like to meet him alone on a dark night. He looked the kind of chap who wasn't afraid of anything – except the other Evallonian female. You remember her, Janet?'

His wife laughed. 'Shall I ever forget her? You never saw such a girl, Allie. A skin like clear amber, and eyes like topazes, and the most wonderful dark hair. She dressed always in bright scarlet and somehow carried it off. Archie, who as you know is a bit of a falconer, remembered that in the seventeenth century there was a hawk called the Blood-red Rook of Turkey, so we always called her that. She was a Countess Araminta Something-or-other.'

Alison's eyes opened. 'I know her – at least, I have met her. She was in London the season before last. Her mother was English, I think, and hence her name. She rather scared me. She wasn't a delegate, was she?'

'No,' said Archie. 'She held a watching brief for something. I can tell you she scared old Mastrovin. He didn't like to be in the same room with her, and he changed his hotel when she turned up at it.'

'Never mind the Blood-red Rook,' said Alison. 'Mastrovin is our problem. I don't care a hoot for Evallonian politics, but having once been on the Monarchist side I'm going to stick to it. Evallonia is apparently at boiling-point. The Monarchist cause depends upon Prince John. Mastrovin is for the Republic or something still shadier, and therefore he is against Prince John. That innocent doesn't know his enemy is about, and Casimir has gone off in the direction of Italy. Therefore we have got to do something about it.'

'What puzzles me,' said Archie, 'is what your Prince is doing in Unnutz, which isn't exactly next door to Evallonia, and why he should want to get himself up as a peasant?'

'It puzzles me too, but that isn't the point. It all shows that things are getting warm in Evallonia. What we have got to do is to dig Prince John out of that hut before Mastrovin murders or kidnaps him, and stow him away in some safer place. I considered it rather a heavy job for me alone, but it should be child's play for the three of us. Don't tell me you decline to play.'

During the last few minutes of the conversation Archie's face had been steadily brightening.

'Of course we'll play,' he said. 'You can count us in, Alison, but I'm getting very discreet in my old age, and I must think it over pretty carefully. It's a chancy business purloining princes, however good your intentions may be. The thing's easy enough, but it's the follow-up that matters. ... Wait a second. I've always believed that the best hiding-place was just under the light. What about bringing him to this hotel to join our party?'

'As Prince John or as a woodcutter?' Janet asked.

'As neither,' said Archie. 'My servant got 'flu in Geneva, and I had to leave him behind. How would the Prince fancy taking on the job? I can lend him some of my clothes. Is he the merry class of lad that likes a jape?'

The luncheon gong boomed. 'We can talk about that later,' said Alison. 'Meanwhile, it's agreed that we three slip out of this place after dark. We'll take your car part of the way, and there's a moon, and I can guide you the rest. We daren't delay, for I'm positive that this very night Mastrovin will get busy.'

Sir Archie arose with mirth in his eye, patted his hair and squared his shoulders. A boy approached and handed him a telegram.

'It's from Bobby Despenser,' he announced. 'The conference has resumed and he wants me back at once. Well, he can whistle for me.'

He tore the flimsy into small pieces.

'Take notice, you two,' he said, 'that most unfortunately I have not received Bobby's wire.'

III

On the following morning three people sat down to a late breakfast in a private sitting-room of the Hôtel Kaiserin Augusta. All three were a little heavy about the eyes, as if their night's rest had been broken, but in the air of each was a certain subdued excitement and satisfaction.

'My new fellow is settling down nicely,' said Sir Archie, helping himself to his third cup of coffee. 'Answers smartly to the name of McTavish. Lucky I brought the real McTavish's passport with me. Curious thing, but the passport photograph isn't unlike him, and he has almost the same measurements. I've put some sticking-plaster above his left eye to correspond to the scar that McTavish got in Mespot, and I've had a go at his hair with scissors – he objected pretty strongly to that, by the way. I've put him into my striped blue flannel suit, which you could tell for

English a mile away, and given him a pair of my old brown shoes. Thank God, he's just about my size. I'm going to buy him a black Homburg – the shops here are full of them – and then he'll look the very model of a gentleman's gentleman, who has had to supplement his London wardrobe locally.'

'But, Archie, he has the kind of face that you can't camouflage,' said Janet. 'Anyone who knows him is bound to recognize him.'

Her husband waved his hand. ' "*N'ayez pas peur, je m'en charge*," as old Perriot used to say at Geneva. He won't be recognized, because no one will expect him here. He's in the wrong environment – under the light, so to speak, which is the best sort of hiding-place. He won't go much out of doors, and I've got him a cubby-hole of a bedroom up in the attics. Not too comfortable, but Pretenders to thrones must expect to rough it a bit. He'll mess with the servants, who are of every nationality on earth, and I've told him to keep his mouth shut. Like all royalties, he's a dab at languages, and speaks English without an accent, but I'm teaching him to give his words a Scotch twist. He tumbled to it straight off, and says "Sirr" just like my old batman. If anyone makes trouble I've advised him to dot him one on the jaw in the best British style. He looks as if he could swing a good punch.'

The small hours of the morning had been a stirring time for the party. They had left the hotel by Alison's veranda a little before midnight, and in Archie's car had reached the foot of the forest path, meeting no one on the road. Then their way had become difficult, for it was very dark among the pines, and Alison had once or twice been at fault in her guiding. The moon rose when they were near the crest of the hill, and after that it had been easy to find the road to the hut through the dew-drenched pastures. There things marched fast. There was pandemonium with two dogs, quieted with difficulty by Alison, who had a genius for animals. The old woman, who appeared with a stable lantern, denied fiercely that there was any occupant of the hut except herself, her husband being dead these ten years and her only son gone over the mountains to a wedding. She was persuaded in the end by Alison's mention of Count Casimir, and the three were admitted.

Then Prince John had appeared fully dressed, with what was obviously a revolver in his pocket. He recognized Alison and had heard of Sir Archie, and things went more smoothly. The news that Mastrovin was on his trail obviously alarmed him, but he took a long time to be convinced about the need for shifting his residence. Clearly he was a docile instrument in the hands of the Monarchists, and hesitated to disobey their orders for fear of spoiling their plan. Things, it appeared, were all in train for a revolution in Evallonia, at any moment he might be required to act, and Unnutz had been selected as the council chamber of the conspirators. On this point it took the united forces of the party to persuade him, but in the end he saw reason. Alison clinched the matter. 'If Mastrovin and his friends get you, it's all up. If you come with us it may put a little grit in the wheels, but it won't smash the machine. Remember, sir, that these men are desperate, and won't stick at trifles. They were desperate two years ago at Castle Gay, but now it is pretty well your life or theirs, and it had better be theirs.'

When he allowed himself to be convinced his spirits rose. He was a young man of humour, and approved of Sir Archie's proposal that he should go to their hotel. He liked the idea of taking the place of the absent McTavish, and thought that he could fill the part. There only remained to give instructions to the old woman. If anyone came inquiring, she was not to deny the existence of her late guest, though she was to profess ignorance of who or what he was. Her story was to be that he had left the preceding afternoon with his belongings on his back. She did not know where he had gone, but believed that it was over the mountains to the Vossthal, since he had taken the path for the Vossjoch.

The journey back had been simple, though Alison had thought it wise to make a considerable detour. It had been slightly complicated by the good manners of the Prince, since he persisted in offering assistance to Janet and Alison, who needed it as little as a chamois. They had reached the hotel just before daybreak, and had entered, they believed, without being observed. That morning Sir Archie had explained to the manager about the delayed arrival of his servant, and the name of Angus McTavish had been duly entered in the hotel books with the Roylances' party.

'And now,' said Archie, 'he's busy attending to my dress clothes. What says the Scriptures? "Kings shall be thy ministers and queens thy nursing mothers." We're getting up in the world, Janet. I'm going to raise a chauffeur's cap for him, and I want him to take your parents, Alison, out in the car this afternoon to accustom the neighbourhood to the sight of a new menial. As for me, I propose to pay another visit to the hut. There's bound to have been developments up that way, and we ought to keep in touch with them. I'll be an innocent tourist out for a walk to observe birds.'

'What worries me,' said Janet, 'is how we are going to keep the Monarchists quiet. We may have Count Casimir here any moment, and that will give the show away.'

'No, it won't. I mean, he won't. I left a letter for him which will give him plenty to think about.'

Janet set down her coffee-cup. 'What did you say in the letter?' she demanded severely.

'McTavish wrote it – I only dictated the terms. He quite saw the sense of it. It was by way of being a piteous cry for help. It said he had been pinched by Mastrovin and his gang, and appealed to his friends to fly to his rescue. Quite affecting it was. You see the scheme? We've got to keep McTavish cool and quiet on the ice till things develop. If Casimir and his lot are looking for him in Mastrovin's hands they won't trouble us. If Mastrovin is being hunted by Casimir he won't be able to hunt McTavish. What you might call a cancelling out of snags.'

His wife frowned. 'I wonder if you've not been a little too clever.'

'Not a bit of it,' was the cheerful answer. 'Ordinary horse sense. As old Perriot said, "*N'ayez pas peur –*"'

'Archie,' said Janet, 'if you quote that stuff again I shall fling the coffee-pot at you.'

## IV

Sir Archie did not return till nine o'clock that evening, for he had walked every step of the road and had several times lost his way. He refreshed himself in the sitting-room with sandwiches and beer, while Janet and Alison had their after-dinner coffee.

'How did McTavish behave?' he asked Alison.

'Admirably. He drives beautifully, and both Papa and Mamma thought he was Scotch. The only mistake was that he treated us like grandees, and held the door open with his cap in his hand. How about you? You look as if you had been seeing life?'

'I've had a trying time,' said Sir Archie, passing a hand through his hair. 'There has been a bit of a row up at the hut. No actual violence, but a good deal of unpleasantness.'

'Have you been fighting?' Janet asked, observing a long scratch on her husband's sunburnt forehead.

'Oh, that scratch is nothing, only the flick of a branch. But I've been through considerable physical tribulation. Wait till I get my pipe lit and you'll have the whole story. ...

'I reached the hut between four and five o'clock in what John Bunyan calls a pelting heat. Ye gods, but it was stuffy in the pine woods, and blistering hot on the open hillside! I made pretty good time, and arrived rather out of condition, for my right leg – my game leg as was – wasn't quite functioning as it should. Well, there was the old woman, and in none too good a temper. Poor soul, she had been considerably chivvied since we last saw her. It seemed that we were just in time this morning, for Mastrovin and his merry men turned up about an hour after we left. It was a mercy we didn't blunder into them in the wood, and a mercy that we had the sense to hide the car a goodish distance from where the track starts. Mastrovin must have spent yesterday in sleuthing, for he had the ground taped, and knew that McTavish had been in the hut at supper. He had three fellows with him, and they gave the old lady a stiff time. They didn't believe her yarn about McTavish having started out for the Vossthal. They ransacked every corner of the place, and put in some fine detective work examining beds and cupboards and dirty dishes, besides raking the outhouses and beating the adjacent coverts. In the end they decided that their bird had flown and tried to terrorize the old lady into a confession. But she's a tough ancient, and by her account returned them as good as they gave. She wanted to know what concern her great-nephew Franz was of theirs, poor Franz that had lost his health working in Innsbruck and had come up into the hills to recruit. All their bullying couldn't shake her about great-nephew Franz, and in the end they took themselves off, leaving her with a very healthy dislike of the whole outfit.

'Then, very early this morning, Count Casimir turned up and got his letter. It put him in a great taking. She said he grew as white as a napkin, and he started to cross-examine her about the hour and the manner of the pinching of McTavish. That was where I had fallen down, for I had forgotten to tell her what was in the letter. So she gave a very confused tale, for she described him as going off with us, mentioning the women in the party, and she also described Mastrovin's coming, and from what she said I gathered that he got the two visits mixed up. What specially worried him was that Mastrovin should have had women with him, and he was very keen to know what they were like. I don't know how the old dame described you two – I should have liked to hear her – but anyway, it didn't do much to satisfy the Count. She said that he kept walking about biting his lips, and repeating a word that sounded like "Mintha". After that he was in a hurry to be off, but before leaving he gave her an address – I've written it down – with which she was to communicate if she got any news.

'I was just straightening out the story for her – I thought it right to get her mind clear – and explaining that we had got McTavish safe and sound, but that it was imperative in his own interests that Count Casimir should believe there had been dirty work, when what do you think happened? Mastrovin turned up, accompanied by a fellow who looked like a Jew barber out of a job. He didn't recognize me and looked at me very old-fashioned. I was sitting in a low chair, and got up politely to greet him, when I had an infernal piece of bad luck. I sprang every blessed muscle in my darned leg. You see, it hadn't been accustomed to so much exercise for a long time, and the muscles were all flabby. Gad, I never knew such pain! It was the worst go of cramp I ever heard of. My toes stuck out like agonizing claws – my calf was a solid lump of torment – the riding muscle above the knee was stiff as a poker and as hard as iron. I must have gone white with pain, and I was all in a cold sweat, and I'm dashed if I could do anything except wallow in the chair and howl.

'Well, Mastrovin wasn't having any of that. He gave me some rough-tonguing in German, and demanded of the old woman what kind of a mountebank I was. But she had taken her cue – pretty quick in the uptake she is – or else she thought I was having a paralytic stroke. I was all dithered with the pain and couldn't notice much, but I saw that she had got off my shoes and stockings and had fetched hot water to bathe my feet. Then the barber fellow took a hand, for he saw I wasn't playing a game. I daresay he was some kind of medico and he knew his business. He started out to massage me, beginning with the lower thigh, and I recognized the professional touch. In a few minutes he had me easier, and you know the way the thing goes – suddenly all the corded muscles dropped back into their proper places, and I was out of pain, but limp as chewing-gum.

'Then Mastrovin began to ask me questions, first in German, and then in rather better English than my own. I gave him my name, and his face cleared a little, for he remembered me from Geneva. He was quite polite, but I preferred his rough-tonguing to his civility. A nasty piece of work that lad – his eyes are as cold as a fish's, but they go through you like a gimlet. I was determined to outstay him, for I didn't want him to be giving the old lady the third degree, which was pretty obviously what he had come for. So I pretended to be down and out, and lay back in her chair gasping, and drank water in a sad invalidish way. I would have stuck it out till midnight, but friend Mastrovin must have been pressed for time, for after about half an hour he got up to go. He offered to give me a hand down the hill, but

I explained that I wasn't yet ready to move, but should be all right in an hour or so. I consider I brought off rather a creditable piece of acting, for he believed me. I also told him that I had just popped in to Unnutz for a night and was hurrying back to Geneva. He knew that the Conference had been resumed, but said that he himself might be a little late. . . . That's about all. I gave him twenty minutes' law and then started home. D'you mind ringing the bell, Janet? I think I'll have an omelet and some more beer. Where's McTavish?'

'At his supper, I expect. What I want to know, Archie, is our next step. We can't go on hiding royal princes in the butler's pantry. McTavish will revolt out of sheer boredom.'

'I don't think so.' Archie shook a sapient head. 'McTavish is a patient fellow, and has had a pretty strict training these last years. Besides, life is gayer for him here than up at that hut, and the food must be miles better. We've got to play a waiting game, for the situation is obscure. I had a talk with him this morning, and by all accounts Evallonian politics are a considerable mix-up.'

'What did he tell you?' Alison asked sharply. She felt that to Archie and Janet it was all a game, but that she herself had some responsibility.

"Well, it seems that the revolution is ready to the last decimal – the Press prepared, the National Guard won over, the people waiting, and the Ministers packing their portmanteaux. The Republican Government will go down like ninepins. But while the odds are all on the monarchy being restored, they are all against its lasting very long. It appears that in the last two years there has been a great movement in Evallonia of all the younger lot. They're tired of having the old 'uns call the tune and want to play a sprig themselves. I don't blame 'em, for the old 'uns have made a pretty mess of it.'

'Is that the thing they call Juventus?' Alison asked. 'I read about it in *The Times*.'

'Some name like that. Anyhow, McTavish tells me it's the most formidable thing Evallonia has seen for many a day. They hate the Republicans, and still more Mastrovin and his Communists. But they won't have anything to do with Prince John, for they distrust Count Casimir and all that lot. Call them the "old gang", the same bouquets as we hand to our elder statesmen, and want a fresh deal with new measures and new men. They're said to be more than half a million strong, all likely lads in hard condition and jolly well trained – they've specialized in marksmanship, for which Evallonia was always famous. They have the arms and the money, and, being all bound together by a blood oath, their discipline is the stiffest thing on earth. Oh, and I forgot to tell you – they wear green shirts – foresters' green. They have a marching song about the green of their woodlands, and the green of their mountain lakes, and the green shirts of Evallonian liberators. It's funny what a big part fancy haberdashery plays in the world today.'

'Have they a leader?' Alison asked.

'That's what I can't make out. There doesn't seem to be any particular *roi de chemises* – that's what Charles Lamancha used to call me in my dressy days. But apparently the thing leads itself. The fact we've got to face is that if Casimir puts McTavish on the throne, which apparently he can do with his left hand, Juventus will kick him out in a week, and McTavish naturally doesn't want that booting. That's why he has been so docile. He sees that the right policy for him is to lie low till things develop.'

'Then our next step must be to get in touch with Juventus,' said Alison.

Janet opened her eyes. 'You're taking this very seriously, Allie,' she said.

'I am,' was the answer. 'You see, I was in it two years ago.'

'But how is it to be done?' Archie asked. 'McTavish doesn't know. He doesn't know who the real leaders are – not Casimir, and certainly not Mastrovin. You see, the thing is by way of being a secret society, sort of jumble-up of Boy Scouts, Freemasons, and the Black Hand. They have their secret passwords, and the brightest journalist never sticks his head into one of their conclaves. They can spot a Monarchist or Republican spy a mile off, and don't stand on ceremony with 'em. They have a badge like Hitler's swastika – an open eye – but, apart from their songs and their green shirts, that's their only public symbol.'

'My advice,' said Janet, 'is that we keep out of it, and restore the Prince to the sorrowing Count Casimir as soon as we can get in touch with him. You go back to Scotland with your family, Allie, and Archie and I will pop down into Italy.'

There was a knock at the door and a waiter brought in the evening post. One letter was for Alison, which she tore open eagerly as soon as she saw the handwriting. She read it three times and then raised a flushed face.

'It's from Jaikie,' she said, and there was that in her voice which made Archie and Janet look up from their own correspondence. 'Jaikie, you know – my friend – Mr Galt that I told you about. He is in Evallonia.'

'My aunt!' exclaimed Archie. 'Then there will be trouble for somebody.'

'There's trouble for him. He seems to have got into deep waters. Listen to what he says.'

She read the following:

I am in a queer business which I am bound to see through. But I can't do it without your help. Can you manage to get away from your parents for a few days, and come to Tarta, just inside the Evallonian frontier? You take the train to a place called Zutpha, where you will be met. If you can come wire Odalchini, Tarta, the time of your arrival. I wouldn't bother you if the thing wasn't rather important, and, besides, I think you would like to be in it.

'Short and to the point,' commented the girl. 'Jaikie never wastes words. He has a genius for understatement, so if he says it is rather important it must be tremendously important. ... Wait a minute. Odalchini! Prince Odalchini was one of the three at Knockraw two years ago. Jaikie has got mixed up with the Monarchists.'

Archie was hunting through his notebook. 'What did you say was the name of the place? Tarta? That's the address Casimir gave the old woman to write to if she had any news. Schloss Thingumybob – the second word has about eight consonants and no vowels – Tarta, by Zutpha. Your friend Jaikie has certainly got among the Monarchists.'

'Hold on!' Alison cried. 'What's this?' She passed round the letter for inspection. It was a sheet of very common notepaper with no address on it, but in the top left-hand corner there was stamped in green a neat little open eye with some hieroglyphic initials under it.

'Do you see what that means?' In her excitement her voice sank to a whisper. Jaikie is in touch with the Juventus people. This letter was sent with their consent – or the consent of one of them, and franked by him.'

'Well, Allie?' Janet asked.

'Of course I'm going. I must go. But I can't go alone, for Papa wouldn't allow it. He and Mamma have decided to return to Scotland this week to Aunt Harriet at Castle Gay. You and Archie must go to Tarta and take me with you.'

'Isn't that a large order? What about McTavish?'

'We must take him with us, for then we'll have all the cards in our hands. It's going to be terribly exciting, but I can promise you that Jaikie won't fail us. You won't fail me either?'

Janet turned smilingly to her husband. 'What about it, Archie?'

'I'm on,' was the answer. 'I've been in a mix-up with Master Jaikie before. Bobby Despenser can whistle for me. The difficulty will be McTavish, who's a compromising piece of goods, but we'll manage somehow. Lord, this is like old times, and I feel about ten years younger. "It little profits that an idle king, matched with an aged wife. . . ." Don't beat me, Janet. We're both ageing. . . . I always thought that the Almighty didn't get old Christoph to mend my leg for nothing.'

CHAPTER FOUR

# DIFFICULTIES OF A REVOLUTIONARY

WHEN Jaikie saw who his captor was, his wrath ebbed. Had it been Prince Odalchini it would have been an outrage, but since it was Ashie, it was only an undergraduate 'rag' which could easily be repaid in kind. But his demeanour was severe.

'What's the meaning of these monkey tricks?' he demanded.

'The meaning is,' Ashie had ceased to smile, 'that you have deceived me. What about your business with your circus friend? I had you followed – I was bound to take every precaution – and instead of feeding in a pot-house you run in circles like a hunted hare and end up at the Schloss. I had my men inside the park, and when I heard what you were up to I gave orders that you should be brought before me. You went straight from me to the enemy. What have you to say to that?'

Ashie's words were firm, but there was dubiety in his voice and a hint of uncertainty in his eye; this the other observed, and the sight wholly removed his irritation. Ashie was talking like a book, but he was horribly embarrassed.

'Well, I'm blowed!' said Jaikie. 'Who the blazes made you my keeper? Let's get this straightened out at once. First, what I said was strictly true. I was going to lunch with my friend from the circus. If your tripe-hounds had been worth their keep they would have seen me meet him – a fellow with the name of the circus blazoned on his cap. The choice of a luncheon place was his own and I had nothing to do with it. As a matter of fact, I happened to know the man he took me to, Prince Odalchini – met him two years ago in Scotland. Have you got that into your fat head?'

'Will you please give me the gist of your conversation with Prince Odalchini?'

'Why on earth should I? What has it got to do with you? But I'll tell you one thing. He was very hospitable and wanted me to stay a bit with him – same as you. I said no, that I wanted to go home, and I was on my way back when I fell in with your push and got my head in a bag. What do you mean by it? I'm sorry to tell you that you have taken a liberty – and I don't allow liberties.'

'Prince Odalchini is the enemy, and we are in a state of war.'

'Get off it. He's not my enemy, and I don't know anything about your local scraps. I told you I would have nothing to do with them, and I told the Prince the same.'

'So you talked of Evallonian affairs?' said Ashie.

'Certainly. What else was there to talk about? Not that he told me much, except that there was likely to be trouble and that he wanted me to stay on and see the fun. I told him I wasn't interested in his tin-pot politics and I tell you the same.'

This had the effect which Jaikie intended, and made Ashie angry.

'I do not permit such language,' he said haughtily. 'I do not tolerate insults to my country. Understand that you are not in your sleek England, but in a place where gentlemen defend their honour in the old way.'

'Oh, don't be a melodramatic ass. I thought we had civilized you at Cambridge and given you a sense of humour, but you've relapsed into the noble savage. I've been in Evallonia less than one day and I know nothing about it. Your politics may be all the world to you, but they're tin-pot to me. I refuse to be mixed up in them.'

'You've mixed yourself up in them by having intercourse with the enemy.'

'Enemy be blowed! I talked for an hour or two to a nice old man who gave me a dashed good luncheon, and now you come butting in with your detective-novel tricks. I demand to be deported at once. Otherwise I'll raise the hairiest row about the kidnapping of a British subject. If you want international trouble, I promise you you'll get it. I don't know where we are, but here's this car, and you've got to deliver me at Kremisch by bedtime. That's the least you can do to make amends for your cheek.'

Jaikie looked out of the window and observed that they had

halted on high ground, and that below them lights twinkled as if from an encampment. For a moment he thought that he had struck the Cirque Doré. And then a bugle sounded, an instrument not generally used in circuses. 'Is that your crowd down there?' he asked.

Ashie's face, even in the dim interior light of the car, showed perplexity. He seemed to be revolving some difficult question in his mind. When he spoke again there was both appeal and apology in his voice. Jaikie had an authority among his friends which was the stronger because he was wholly unconscious of it and in no way sought it. His personality was so clean-cut and his individuality so complete and secure that, while one or two gave him affection, all gave him respect.

'I'll apologize if you like,' said Ashie. 'I daresay what I did was an outrage. But the fact is, Jaikie, I badly want your help. Your advice, anyway. I'm in a difficult position, and I don't see my road very clearly. You see, I'm an Evallonian, and this is Evallonian business, but I've got a little outside the atmosphere of my own country. That's to the good, perhaps, for this thing is on the biggest scale and wants looking at all round it. That's why I need your help. Give me one night, and I swear, if you still want me to, I'll deliver you at Kremisch tomorrow morning and trouble you no more.'

Jaikie was the most placable of mortals, he had a strong liking for Ashie, and he was a little moved by the anxious sincerity of his voice. He had half expected this proposal.

'All right,' he said, 'I'll give you one night. Have your fellows pinched my kit?'

Ashie pointed to a knapsack on the floor of the car, which he promptly shouldered. 'Let's get out of this,' he said. He spoke a word to the driver, who skipped round and opened the door, standing stiffly at the salute. Then he led the way down the little slope into the meadow of the twinkling lights. Presently he had to give a password, and three times had to halt for that purpose before they reached his tent. The gathering was far larger than that which Jaikie had seen at the Tarta bridge, and he noticed a considerable number of picketed horses.

'What are these chaps after?' he asked.

'We are riding the marches,' was the answer. 'What at Cambridge they call beating the bounds. It is not desirable that for the present we should operate too near the capital.'

There were two tents side by side and separated by a considerable space from the rest, as if to ensure the commander's privacy. A sentry stood on guard whom Ashie dismissed with an order. He led Jaikie into the bigger of the tents. It was furnished with a camp mattress, two folding chairs, and a folding table littered with maps. 'You will sleep next door. You may have a companion for the night, but of that I speak later. Meantime, let us dine. I can only offer you soldiers' fare.'

The fare proved excellent. A mushroom omelet was brought in by one of the Greenshirts, and cups of strong coffee. There was a dish of assorted cold meats, and a pleasantly mild cheese. They drank white wine, and Ashie insisted on Jaikie tasting the native liqueur. 'It is made from the lees of wine,' he told him. 'Like the French *marc*, but not so vehement.'

When the meal was cleared away Jaikie lit his pipe and Ashie a thin black cigar. 'Now for my story,' the latter said. 'There is one fact beyond question. The rotten Republican Government is doomed, and hangs now by a single hair which a breath of wind can destroy. But when the hair has gone, what then?'

He told much the same tale that Jaikie had heard that day from Prince Odalchini, but with a far greater wealth of detail. Especially he expounded the origin and nature of Juventus, with which he had been connected from the start. 'Most of this is common knowledge,' he said, 'but not all – yet. We are not a secret society, but we have our *arcana imperii*.' He described its beginnings. Ricci had designed it as a counter-move against the Monarchists, but it had soon turned into something very different, a power detached indeed from the Monarchists but altogether hostile to the Republic, and Ricci, the used instead of the user, had been flung aside. 'It was no less than a resurgence of the spirit of the Evallonian nation,' he said solemnly.

He explained how it had run through the youth of the country like a flame in stubble. 'We are a poor people,' he said, 'though not so poor as some, for we are closer to the soil, and less dependent upon others. But we have been stripped of some of our richest parts where industry flourished, and many of us are in great poverty. Especially it is hard for the young, who see no livelihood for them in their fathers' professions, and can find none elsewhere. Evallonia, thanks to the jealous Powers, has been reduced to too great an economic simplicity, and has not that variety of interests which a civilized society requires. Also there is another matter. We have always made a hobby of our education, as in your own Scotland. Parents will starve themselves to send their sons to Melina to the university, and often a commune itself will pay for a clever boy. What is the consequence? We have an educated youth, but no work for it. We have created an academic proletariat and it is distressed and bitter.'

Ashie told his story well, but his language was not quite his native wood-notes. Jaikie wondered whose reflections he was repeating. He wondered still more when he launched into an analysis of the exact feelings of Evallonian youth. There was a subtlety in it and an acumen which belonged to a far maturer and more sophisticated mind.

'So that is that,' he concluded. 'If our youth is to be satisfied and our country is to prosper, it is altogether necessary that the Government should be taken to pieces and put together again on a better plan. What that plan is our youth must decide, and whatever it is it must provide them with a horizon of opportunity. We summon our people to a new national discipline under which everyone shall have both rights and duties.'

Where had Ashie got these phrases, Jaikie asked himself – '*arcana imperii*', 'academic proletariat', 'horizon of opportunity'? There must be some philosopher in the background. 'That sounds reasonable enough,' was all he said.

'It is reasonable – but difficult. Some things we will not have. Communism, for one – of that folly Europe contains too many awful warnings. We have had enough talk of republics, which are the dullest species of oligarchy. Evallonia, having history in her bones, is a natural monarchy. Her happiest destiny would be to be like England.'

'That is all right then,' said Jaikie. 'You have Prince John.'

Ashie's face clouded.

'Alas! that is not possible. For myself I have nothing against the Prince. He represents our ancient line of kings, and he is young, and he is well spoken of, though I have never met him. But he is fatally compromised. His supporters, who are about to restore him, are indeed better men than our present misgovernors, but they are relics – fossils. They would resurrect an old world with all its stupidities. They are as alien to us as Mastrovin and Rosenbaum, though less hateful. If Prince John is set upon the throne, it is very certain that our first duty will be regretfully to remove him – regretfully, for it is not the Prince we oppose, but his following.'

'I see,' said Jaikie. 'It *is* rather a muddle. Are the Monarchists only a collection of stick-in-the-muds?'

'You can judge for yourself. You have seen Prince Odalchini, who is one of the best. He worships dead things – he speaks the language of a vanished world.'

Once again Jaikie wondered how Ashie, whose talk had hitherto been chiefly of horses, had managed to acquire this novel jargon.

'You want a king, but you won't – or can't – have the Prince. Then you've got to find somebody else. What's your fancy? Have you a possible in your own ranks?'

Ashie knit his brows. 'I do not think so. We have admirable regimental officers and good brigadiers, but no general-in-chief. Juventus was a spontaneous movement of many people, and not the creation of one man.'

'But you must have leaders.'

'Leaders – but no leader. The men who presided at its birth have gone. There was Ricci, who was a trickster and a coward. He has washed himself out. There was my father, who is now dead. I do not think that he would have led, for he was not sure of himself. He had great abilities, but he was too clever for the common run of people, and he was not trusted. He was ambitious, and since his merits were not recognized, he was always unhappy, and therefore he was ineffective. I have inherited the prestige of his name, but the Almighty has given me a more comfortable nature.'

'Why not yourself?' Jaikie asked. 'You seem to fill the bill. Young and bold and not yet compromised. Ashie the First – or would it be Paul the Nineteenth? I'll come and grovel at your coronation.'

Jaikie's tone of badinage gave offence.

'There is nothing comic in the notion,' was the haughty answer. 'Four hundred years ago my ancestors held the gates of Europe against the Turk. Two centuries before that they rode in the Crusades. The house of Jovian descends straight from the Emperors of Rome. I am of an older and prouder race than Prince John.'

'I'm sure you are,' said Jaikie apologetically. 'Well, why not have a shot at it? I would like to have a pal a reigning monarch.'

'Because I cannot,' said Ashie firmly. 'I am more confident than my father, God rest his soul, but in such a thing I do not trust myself. Your wretched England has spoiled me. I do not want pomp and glory. I should yawn my head off in a palace, and I should laugh during the most solemn ceremonials, and I should certainly beat my Ministers. I desire to remain a private gentleman and some day to win your Grand National.'

Jaikie whistled.

'We have certainly spoiled you for this game. What's to be done about it?'

'I do not know,' was the doleful answer. 'For I cannot draw back. There have been times when I wanted to slip away and hide myself in England. But I am now too deep in the business, and I have led too many people to trust me, and I have to consider the honour of my house.'

'Honour?' Jaikie queried.

'Yes, honour,' said Ashie severely. 'Have you anything to say against it?'

'No-o-o. But it's an awkward word and apt to obscure reason.'

'It is a very real thing, which you English do not understand.'

'We understand it well enough, but we are shy of talking about it. Remember the inscription in the Abbey of Thelème –

"*Fais ce que voudrais:* for the desires of decent men will always be governed by honour." '

Ashie smiled, for Rabelais, as Jaikie remembered, had been one of the few authors whom he affected.

'That doesn't get one very far,' he said. 'I can't leave my friends in the lurch any more than you could. I have been forced in spite of myself into a position out of which I cannot see my way, and any moment I may have to act against my will and against my judgement. That's why I want your advice.'

'There are people behind you prodding you on? Probably one in particuular? Who is it?'

'I cannot say.'

'Well, I can. It's a woman.'

Ashie's face darkened, and this time he was really angry. 'What the devil do you mean? What have you heard? I insist that you explain.'

'Sorry, Ashie. That was a silly remark, and I had no right to make it.'

'You must mean something. Someone has been talking to you. Who? What? Quick, I have a right to know.'

Ashie had mounted a very high horse and had become unmistakably the outraged foreign grandee.

'It was only a vulgar guess,' said Jaikie soothingly. 'You see, I know you pretty well, Ashie. It isn't easy to shift you against your will. I couldn't do it, and I don't believe any of your friends could do it. You've become a sensible chap since we took you in hand, and look at things in a reasonable way. You're not the kind of fellow to run your head against a stone wall. Here you are with all the materials of a revolution in your hands and you haven't a notion what to do with them. It's no good talking about honour and about loyalty to your crowd when if you go on you are only going to land them in the soup. And yet you seemed determined to go on. Somebody has been talking big to you and you're impressed. From what I know of you I say that it cannot be a man, so it must be a woman.'

Ashie's face did not relax.

'So you think I'm that kind of fool! The slave of a sentimental woman? . . . The damnable thing is that you're right. The power behind Juventus is a girl. Quite young – just about my own age. A kinswoman of mine, too, sort of second cousin twice removed. I'll tell you her name. The Countess Araminta Troyos.'

Jaikie's blank face witnessed that he had never heard of the lady.

'I've known her all my life,' Ashie went on, 'and we have been more or less friends, though I never professed to understand her. Beautiful? Oh, yes, amazingly, if you admire the sable and amber type. And brains! She could run round Muresco and his lot, and even Mastrovin has a healthy respect for her. And ambition enough for half a dozen Mussolinis. And her power of – what do you call the damned thing? – mass-persuasion? – is simply unholy. She is the soul of Juventus. There's not one of them that doesn't carry a picture postcard of her next to his heart.'

'What does she want? To be Queen?'

'Not she, though she would make a dashed good one. She's old-fashioned in some ways, and doesn't believe much in her own sex. Good sane anti-feminist. She wants a man on the throne of Evallonia, but she's going to make jolly well sure that it's she who put him there.'

'I see.' Jaikie whistled gently through his teeth, which was a habit of his. 'Are you in love with her?'

'Ye gods, no! She's not my kind. I'd as soon marry a were-wolf as Cousin Mintha.'

'Is she in love with you?'

'No. I'm positive no. She could never be in love with anybody in the ordinary way. She runs for higher stakes. But she mesmerizes me, and that's the solemn truth. When she orates to me I feel all the pith going out of my bones. I simply can't stand up to her. I'm terrified of her. Jaikie, I'm in danger of making a blazing, blasted fool of myself. That's why I want you.'

Ashie's cheerful face had suddenly become serious and pathetic, like a puzzled child's, and at the sight of it Jaikie's heart melted. He was not much interested in Evallonia, but he was fond of Ashie, now in the toils of an amber and sable Cleopatra. He could not see an old friend dragged into trouble by a crazy girl without doing something to prevent it. A certain *esprit de sexe* was added to the obligations of friendship.

'But what can I do?' he asked. 'I don't know the first thing about women – I've hardly met any in my life – I'm no match for your cousin.'

'You can help me to keep my head cool,' was the answer. 'You stand for the world of common sense which will always win in the long run. When I'm inclined to run amok you'll remind me of England. You'll lower the temperature.'

'You want me to hold your hand?'

'Just so. To hold my hand.'

'Well,' said Jaikie after a pause. 'I don't mind trying it out for a fortnight. You'll have to give me free board and lodging, or I won't have the money to take me home.'

Ashie's face cleared so miraculously that for one uncomfortable moment Jaikie thought that he was about to be embraced. Instead he shook hands with a grip like iron.

'You're a true friend,' he said. 'Come what may, I'll never forget this. . . . There's another thing. Unless we're to have civil war there must be some arrangement. Somebody must keep in touch with the Monarchists, or in a week there will be bloody battles. Juventus has cut off all communication with the enemy and burned its boats, but it cannot be allowed to go forward blindly, and crash head-on into the other side. I want a *trait d'union*, and you're the man for it. I can't do it, for I'm too conspicuous – I should be found out at once, and suspected of treachery. But you know Prince Odalchini. You've got to be my go-between. How do you fancy the job?'

Jaikie fancied it a good deal. It promised amusement and a field for his special talents.

'It won't be too easy,' Ashie went on. 'You see, you're by way of being my prisoner. All my fellows by this time know about your visit to the Prince and my having you kidnapped. We've tightened up the screws in Juventus, and I daren't let you go now.'

'Then if I hadn't decided to stay, you'd have kept me by force?' Jaikie demanded.

'No. I would have delivered you at Kremisch according to my promise, but it would have been an uncommon delicate job, and I should have had to do the devil of a lot of explaining. I've given out that you are an English friend, who is not hostile but knows too much to be safe. So you'll have to be guarded, and your visits to the House of the Four Winds will have to be nicely camouflaged. Lucky I'm in charge of Juventus on this side of the country.'

'You've begun by handicapping me pretty heavily,' said Jaikie. 'But I'll keep my word and have a try.'

An orderly appeared at the tent door with a message. Ashie looked at his watch.

'Your stable companion for the night has arrived,' he said. 'I think you'd better clear out while I'm talking to him. He's an English journalist, and rather a swell, I believe, who has been ferreting round for some weeks in Evallonia. It won't do to antagonize the foreign Press just yet – especially the English, so I promised to see him tonight and give him some dope. But I'll see that he's beyond the frontier tomorrow morning. We don't want any Paul Prys in this country at present.'

'What's his name?' Jaikie asked with a sudden premonition.

Ashie consulted a paper. 'Crombie – Dougal Crombie. Do you know him?'

'I've heard of him. He's second in command on the Craw Press, isn't he?'

'He is. And he'll probably be a sentimental royalist, like the old fool who owns it.'

Long ago in the Glasgow closes there had been a signal used among the Gorbals Die-hards, if one member did not desire to be recognized when suddenly confronted by another. So when Mr Crombie was ushered into the tent and observed beside the Juventus commander a slight shabby figure, which pinched its chin with the left hand and shut its left eye, he controlled his natural surprise and treated Ashie as if he were alone.

'May I go to bed, sir?' Jaikie asked. 'I'm blind with sleep, and I won't be wakened by my fellow-guest.'

Ashie assented, and Jaikie gave the Juventus salute and withdrew, keeping his eyes strictly averted from the said fellow-guest.

He did not at once undress, but sat on the sleeping valise and thought. His mind was not on the House of the Four Winds and the difficulties of keeping in touch with Prince Odalchini; it was filled with the picture of an amber and sable young woman. That he believed to be the real snag, and he felt himself unequal to coping with it. In the end, on notepaper which Ashie had given him, he wrote two letters. The first was to Miss Alison Westwater and the second to Prince Odalchini; then he got into pyjamas, curled himself inside the valise, and was almost at once asleep.

He was wakened by being poked in the ribs, and found beside him the rugged face of Dougal illumined by a candle.

'How on earth did you get here, Jaikie?' came the hoarse whisper.

'By accident,' was the sleepy answer. 'Ran into Ashie – that's Count Paul – knew him at Cambridge. I'm a sort of prisoner, but I'll be all right. Don't ask me about Evallonia, for you know far more than me.'

'I daresay I do,' said Dougal. 'Man, Jaikie, this is a fearsome mess. Mr Craw will be out of his mind with vexation. Here's everything ripe for a nice law-abiding revolution, and this dam-fool Juventus chips in and wrecks everything. I like your Count Paul, and he has some rudiments of sense, but he cannot see that what he is after is sheer lunacy. The Powers are in an easy temper, and there would be no trouble about an orderly restoration of the old royal house. But if these daft lads start running some new dictator fellow that nobody ever heard of, Europe will shut down like a clam. Diplomatic relations suspended – economic boycott – the whole bag of tricks. It's maddening that the people who most want to kick out the present Government should be working to give it a fresh lease of life, simply because they insist on playing a lone hand.'

'I know all that,' said Jaikie. 'Go away, Dougal, and let me sleep.'

'I tell you what' – Dougal's voice was rising, and he lowered it at Jaikie's request – 'we need a first-class business mind on this job. There's just one man alive that I'd listen to, and that's Mr McCunn. He's at Rosensee, and that's not a thousand miles off, and he's quite recovered now and will likely to be as restless as a hen. I'm off there tomorrow morning to lay the case before him.'

'Good,' Jaikie answered. 'Now get to bed, will you?'

'I must put him in touch with Count Casimir and Prince Odalchini – the big Schloss at Tarta is the place – that's the Monarchist centre. And what about yourself? How can I find you?'

'If I'm not hanged,' said Jaikie drowsily, 'it will be at the same address. I'll turn up some time or other. I wish you'd put these two letters in your pocket, and post them tomorrow when you're over the frontier. And now for pity's sake let me sleep.'

## CHAPTER FIVE

# SURPRISING ENERGY OF A CONVALESCENT

Mr Dickson McCunn sat in a wicker chair with his feet on the railing of a small veranda, and his eyes on a wide vista of plain and forest which was broken by the spires of a little town. Now and then he turned to beam upon a thick-set, red-haired young man who occupied a similar chair on his left hand. Mr McCunn wore a suit of grey flannel, a startling pink shirt and collar, and brown suede shoes – things so foreign to his usual wear that they must have been acquired for this occasion. He was looking remarkably well, with a clear eye and a clear skin to which recent exposure to the sun had given a becoming rosiness. His hair was a little thinner than two years ago, but no greyer. Indeed, the only change was in his figure, which had become more trim and youthful. Dougal judged that he had reduced his weight by at least a stone.

He patted his companion's arm.

'Man, Dougal, I'm glad to see you. I was thinking just yesterday that the thing I would like best in the world would be to see you and Jaikie coming up the road. I've been wearying terribly for the sight of a kenned face. I knew you were somewhere abroad, and I had a sort of notion that you might give me a look in. Are they making you comfortable here? It's not just the place I would recommend for a healthy body, for they've a poor notion of food.'

'Me?' he exclaimed in reply to a question. 'I've never been better in my life. It's a perfect miracle. I walked fifteen miles the day before yesterday and never turned a hair. I'll give the salmon a fright this back-end. I tell you, Dougal, Dr Christoph hasn't his equal on this earth. He's my notion of the Apostles that could make the lame walk and the blind see. When I came here I was a miserable decrepit body that couldn't sleep, and couldn't take his meat, and wanted to lie down when he had walked a mile. He saw me twice a day, and glowered and glunched at me, like an old-fashioned minister at the catechizing, and asked me questions – he's one that would speir a whelk out of its shell. But he wouldn't deliver a judgement – not him – just told me to possess my soul in patience till he was ready. He made me take queer wee medicines, and he prescribed what I was to eat. Oh, and I had what they call massage – he was a wonder at that, for he seemed to flype my body as you would flype a stocking. And I had to take a daft kind of bath, with first hot water and then cold water dropping on me from the ceiling and every drop like a rifle bullet. I thought I had wandered into a demented hydropathic. ... Then after three weeks he spoke. "Mr McCunn," he says, "I'm happy to tell you that there's nothing wrong with you. There's been a heap wrong, but it's gone now, the mischief is out of your system, and all you have to do is to build your system up. You will soon be able to eat what you like," he says, "and the more the better, and you can walk till you fall down, and you can ride on a horse" – not that I was likely to try that – "and I don't mind if you tumble into the burn. You're a well man," he says, "but I'd like to keep you here for another three weeks under observation." Oh, and he wrote a long screed about my case for the Edinburgh professor – I've got a copy of it – I don't follow it all, for it is pretty technical and Dr Christoph isn't very grand at English. But the plain fact is, that I've been a sick man and am now well, and that in five days' time I'll be on the road for Blaweary, singing the 126th Psalm:

*Among the heathen say the Lord*
*Great things for us hath wrought.'*

Mr McCunn hummed a stave from the Scots metrical version to a dolorous tune.

'You've been enjoying yourself fine,' said Dougal.

The other pursed his lips. 'I would scarcely say that. I've enjoyed the fact of getting well, but I haven't altogether enjoyed the process. There were whiles when I was terrible bored, me that used to boast that I had never been bored in my life. The first weeks it was like being back at the school. I had my bits of walks prescribed for me, and the hours when I was to lie on my back and rest, and when I sat down to my meals there was a nurse behind my chair to see that I ate the right things and didn't forget my medicine. I had an awful lot of time on my hands. I doddered about among the fir-woods – they're a careful folk, the Germans, and have all the hill-sides laid out like gentlemen's policies – nice tidy walks, and seats to sit down on, and directions about the road that I couldn't read. I'll not deny that it's a bonny countryside – in its way, but the weather was blazing hot and I got terrible tired of those endless fir-trees. It's a monotonous place, for when you get to the top of one rig there's another of the same shape beyond, covered with the same woods. Man, I got fair sick for a sight of an honest bald-faced hill.

'Indoors,' he went on, 'it was just the same. It's all very well to be told to rest and keep your mind empty, but that was never my way. I brought out a heap of books with me, and was looking forward to getting a lot of quiet reading done. But the mischief was that I couldn't settle to a book. I had intended to read the complete works of Walter Savage Landor – have you ever tried him, Dougal? I aye thought the quotations from him I came across most appetizing. But I might as well have been reading a newspaper upside down, for I couldn't keep my mind on him. I suppose that my thoughts having been so much concerned lately with my perishing body had got out of tune for higher things. So I fell back on Sir Walter – I'm not much of a hand at novels, as you know, but I can always read Scott – but I wasn't half through *Guy Mannering* when it made me so homesick for the Canonry that I had to give it up. After that I became a mere vegetable, a bored vegetable.'

'You don't look very bored,' said Dougal.

'Oh, it's been different the last weeks, when the doctor told me I was cured, for I've been pretty nearly my own master. I've had some grand long walks – what you would call training walks, for I was out just for the exercise and never minded the scenery. I've sweated pounds and pounds of adipose tissue off my bones. I hired a car, too, and got Peter Wappit to drive it, and I've been exploring the countryside for fifty miles round. I've found some fine scenery and some very respectable public-houses. You'll be surprised that I mention them, but the fact is that my mind has been dwelling shamelessly on food and drink. I've never been so hungry in all my days. I'm allowed to eat anything I like, but the trouble is that you can't get it in this house. The food is deplorable for a healthy man. Endless veal, which I cannot bide – and what they call venison, but is liker goat – and wee blue trouts that are as wersh as the dowp of a candle – and they've a nasty habit of eating plums and gooseberries with butcher's meat. I'll admit the coffee is fine, but they've no kind of notion of tea. Tea has always been my favourite meal, but here you never see a scone or a cookie – just things like a baby's rusks, and sweet cakes that you very soon scunner at. So I've had to supplement my diet at adjacent publics. . . . I tell you what, Dougal, Peter is a perfect disgrace. It's preposterous that a man should have been two years in jyle in Germany and have picked up so little of the language. He just stammers and glowers and makes noises like a clocking hen, and it's me that has to do the questioning, with about six words of the tongue and every kind of daft-like grimace and contortion. If the Germans weren't an easy-tempered folk we'd have had a lot of trouble.

'But, thank God,' said Mr McCunn, 'that's all very nearly by with. I've got back my health and now I want something to occupy my mind and body.' He pushed back his chair, stood up, doubled his fists, and made playful taps at Dougal's chest to prove his vigour.

'What about yourself, Dougal?' he said. 'Let's hear what you've been up to. Is Mr Craw still trying to redd up the affairs of Europe?'

'He is. That's the reason I'm out here. And that's the reason I've come to see you. I want your advice.'

'In that case,' said Mr McCunn solemnly, 'we'd be the better of a drink. Beer is allowed here, and it's a fine mild brew. We'll have a tankard apiece.'

'Now,' said he, when the tankards had been brought, and he was comfortably settled again in his chair, 'I'm waiting on your story. Where have you come from?'

'From Evallonia.'

For a moment or two Dickson did not speak. The word set his mind digging into memories which had been heavily overlaid. In particular he recalled an autumn night on a Solway beach when in the moonlight a cutter swung down the channel with the tide. He saw a young man under whose greatcoat was a gleam of tartan, and he remembered vividly a scene which for him had been one of tense emotion. On the little finger of his left hand he wore that young man's ring.

'Aye, Evallonia,' he murmured. 'That's where you would be. And how are things going in Evallonia?'

'Bad. They couldn't be worse. Listen, Mr McCunn, and I'll give you the rudiments of a perfectly ridiculous situation.'

Dickson listened, and his occasional grunts told of his lively interest. When Dougal had finished, he remained for a little silent and frowning heavily. Then he began to ask questions.

'You say the Monarchists have got everything arranged and can put Prince John on the throne whenever they're so minded? Can they put up a good Government?'

'I think so. They've plenty of brains among them and plenty of experience. Count Casimir Muresco is a sort of lesser Cavour. I've seen a good deal of him and can judge. You'll remember him?'

'Aye, I mind him well. I thought he had some kind of a business head. Prince Odalchini was a fine fellow, but a wee thing in the clouds. What about the Professor – Jagon, I think they called him?'

'He has gone over to Juventus. Discovered that it fulfilled his notion of democracy. He was a maggoty old body.'

'Well, he'll maybe not be much loss. You say that there's a good Government waiting for Evallonia, but that this Juventus thing – that's Latin, isn't it? – won't hear of it because they didn't invent it themselves. What kind of shape would they make at running the country?'

'Bad, I think. They've brains, but no experience, and not much common sense. They're drunk with fine ideas and as full of pride as an old blackcock, but they're babes and sucklings at the job of civil administration.'

'But they've power behind them?'

'All the power there is in Evallonia. They've an armed force uncommon well trained and disciplined – you never saw a more upstanding lot of lads. The National Guard, which is all the army that is permitted under the Peace Treaty, is good enough in its way, but it's small, and the people don't give a hang for it. Juventus has captured the fancy of the nation, and with these Eastern European folk, that means that the battle is won. They can no more make a good Government than they could square the circle, but they can play the devil with any Government that they don't approve of. You may say that the real motive power in Evallonia today is destructive. But they'll have to set up some sort of figurehead – one of themselves, though there's nobody very obvious – and that will mean an infernal mess, the old futile dictatorship ran-dan, and no end of trouble with the Powers. I've the best reason to be positive on that point, for Mr Craw has seen –' and he mentioned certain august names.

Dickson asked one other question. 'What about the Republicans?'

Dougal laughed. 'Oh, their number's up all right. Whoever is top-dog, they're bound to be the bottom one for many a day. They've their bags packed waiting to skip over the frontier. But they'll do their best, of course, to make the mischief worse. Mastrovin, especially. If he's caught in Evallonia he'll get short shrift, but he'll be waiting outside to put spokes in the wheels.'

'Yon's the bad one,' said Dickson reflectively. 'When he is thrawn, he has a face that's my notion of the Devil. . . . It seems that Juventus is the proposition we have to consider. What ails Juventus at Prince John?'

'Nothing. They've no ill-will to him – only he's not their man. What they dislike is his supporters.'

'Why?'

'Simply because they're the old gang and associated in their minds with all the misfortunes and degradation of Evallonia since the War. Juventus is thinking of a new world, and won't have any truck with the old. They're new brooms, and are blind to the merits of the old besoms. They're like laddies at school, Mr McCunn – when catties come in they won't look at a bool or a girr.'

Dickson whistled morosely through his teeth.

'I see,' he said. 'Well, it looks ugly. What kind of advice do you want from me?'

'I want a business-like view of the situation from a wise man, and you can't get that in Evallonia.'

'But how in the name of goodness can I give you any kind of view when I don't know the place or the folk?'

'I've tried to put the lay-out before you, and I want the common sense of a detached observer. You may trust my facts. I've done nothing but make inquiries for the last month, for the thing is coming between Mr Craw and his sleep. I've seen Count Casimir and all his lot and talked with them till my brain was giddy. I've taken soundings in Evallonian public opinion, to which I had pretty good access.'

'Have you seen much of Juventus?'

Dougal drew down the corners of his mouth.

'Not a great deal. You see, it's a secret society, and you can no more get inside it than into a lodge of Masons. I've talked, of course, to a lot of the rank-and-file, and I can judge their keenness and their popular support. There was one of them I particularly wanted to see – a woman called Countess Troyos – but I was warned that if I went near her she would have me shot against a wall – she's a ferocious Amazon and doesn't like journalists. But I managed to get an interview with one of the chiefs, a certain Count Paul Jovian, a son of the Jovian that was once a Republican Minister. It was that interview that gave me the notion of coming to you, for this Count Paul has some rudiments of sense, and has lived a lot in England, and I could see that he was uneasy about the way things were going. He didn't say much, but he hinted that there ought to be some sort of compromise with the Monarchists, so there's one man at any rate that will accept a reasonable deal. ... And Jaikie whispered as much to me before I left.'

'Jaikie!' The word came almost like a scream from the startled Mr McCunn. 'I thought he was on a walking-tour in France.'

'Well, he has walked into Evallonia. He was with Count Paul. whom it seems he knew at Cambridge. He told me he was a prisoner.'

'How was he behaving himself?'

'Just as Jaikie would. Pretending to be good and meek and sleepy. The same old flat-catcher. If Juventus knew the type of fellow Jaikie was, they wouldn't rest till they saw him safe in bed in the Canonry.'

Dickson grinned. 'I'm sure they wouldn't.' But the grin soon faded. He strode up and down the little veranda with his head bowed and his hands clasped behind his back. He did this for perhaps five minutes, and then, with a 'Just you bide here' to his companion, he disappeared into the house.

He was absent for the better part of an hour, and when he returned it was with a gloomy and puzzled countenance.

'I got the Head Schwester to telephone for me to Katzensteg to the aerodrome. There's some jikery-pukery on, and it seems I can't get a machine for the job. The frontier is closed to private planes and only the regular air service is allowed.'

'Whatever do you want an aeroplane for?' Dougal asked.

'To get to Evallonia,' said Dickson simply. 'I've never been in one, but they tell me it's the quickest way to travel. There'll be nothing for it but to go by road. I'll have to attend strictly to the map, for Peter has no more sense of direction than a sheep.'

'But what will you do when you get there?'

'I thought of having a crack with Prince Odalchini in the first place. . . .'

'The thing's impossible,' Dougal cried. 'Man, the country is already almost in a state of siege. Juventus won't let you near the Prince. They're sitting three-deep round his park wall. They carted me over the frontier yesterday with instructions that I wasn't to come back if I valued my life – and, mind you, I had their safe conduct.'

'All the same, I must find some way of getting to him.' In Dickson's voice there was a note of dismal obstinacy which Dougal knew well.

'But it's perfectly ridiculous,' said Dougal. 'I wish to Heaven I had never come here. You can't do a bit of good to anybody and you can do the devil of a lot of harm to yourself.'

'I can see the place and some of the folk, and give you that business advice you said you wanted.'

'You'll see nothing except the inside of a guard-room,' Dougal wailed. 'Listen to reason, Mr McCunn. I must be in Vienna to-morrow, for I have to sign a contract about paper for Mr Craw. Stay quietly here till I come back, and then maybe we'll be able to think of a plan.'

'I can't,' said Dickson. 'I must go at once. . . . See here, Dougal. Do you observe that ring?' He held up his left hand. 'I got it two years back come October on the Solway sands. "I've gotten your ring, Sire," I says to him, "and if I get the word from you I'll cross the world." Well, the word has come. Not direct from Prince John, maybe, but from what they call the logic of events. I would think shame to be found wanting. It's maybe the great chance of my life. . . . Where more by token is his Royal Highness?'

'How should I know?' said Dougal wearily. 'Not in Evallonia, but lurking somewhere near, waiting on a summons that will likely never come. Poor soul, I don't envy him his job. . . . And you're going to stick your head into a bees' byke, when nobody asks you to. You say it's your sense of duty. If that's so, it's a misguided sense not very different from daftness. But it's my belief that the real reason is that you're looking for excitement. You're too young. You're like a horse with too much corn. You're doing this because it amuses you.'

'It doesn't,' was the solemn answer. 'Make no mistake about that, Dougal. I'm simply longing to be back at Blaweary. I want to be on the river again – I hear the water's in fine trim – and I want to get on with my new planting – I'm trying Douglas firs this time. . . . I don't care a docken for Evallonia and its politics. But I'm pledged to Prince John, and in all my sixty-three years I've never broken my word. I'm sweir to go. I'll tell you something more – I'm feared to go. I've never had much truck with foreigners, and their ways are not my ways, and I value my comfort as much as anybody. That was why I tried to get an aeroplane, for I thought it would commit me and get the first plunge over, for I was feared of weakening. As it is I'll have to content myself with the car and that sumph Peter Wappit. But some way or other I'm bound to go.'

Dougal's grim face relaxed into an affectionate smile.

'You're a most extraordinary man. I'll not argue with you, for I know it's about as much good as making speeches to a tombstone. I'll go back to Evallonia as soon as my business is finished, and I only hope I don't see your head stuck up on a spike on Melina gate-house.'

'Do you think that's possible?' Dickson asked with a curious mixture of alarm and rapture.

'Not a bit of it. I was only joking. The worst that can happen is that you and Peter will be sent back over the border with a flea in your ear. If Juventus catches you they'll deport you as a harmless lunatic. . . . But for God's sake don't get into the same parish as Mastrovin.'

## CHAPTER SIX

# ARRIVALS AT AN INN

SIR ARCHIBALD ROYLANCE drove a motor car well but audaciously, so that he disquieted the nerves of those who accompanied him; his new servant McTavish drove better, and with a regard for the psychology of others which made a journey with him as smooth as a trip in the Scotch express. The party left Unnutz early in the morning before the guests of the Kaiserin Augusta were out of bed, and since they had many miles to cover, Archie insisted on taking McTavish's place for a spell every three hours. All day under a blue sky they threaded valleys, and traversed forests, and surmounted low passes among the ranges, and since the air was warm and the landscape seductive, they did not hurry unduly. Lunch, for example, on a carpet of moss beside a plunging stream, occupied a full two hours. The consequence was that when they came out of the hills and crossed the Rave and saw before them the lights of the little railway station of Zutpha, it was already evening. Clearly not a time to pay a call upon Prince Odalchini, who did not expect them. Archie inquired of McTavish where was the nearest town, and was told Tarta, where the inn of the Turk's head had a name for comfort. All the party was hungry and a little weary, so it was agreed to make for Tarta.

The car took a country road which followed the eastern side of Prince Odalchini's great park. Passing through Zutpha village, Archie, whose turn it was then to drive, noticed a number of youths who appeared to be posted on some kind of system. They stared at the car, and at first seemed inclined to interfere with it. But something – the road it was taking or the badges on the front of its bonnet – satisfied them, a word was passed from one to the other, and they let it go. They wore shorts, and shirts of a colour which could not be distinguished in the dark.

'Juventus,' Archie turned his head to whisper. 'We've come

to the right shop. Thank heaven the lads don't want to stand between us and dinner.'

Soon the road, which had lain among fields of maize and beet, turned into the shadow of woods, and was joined by many tributary tracks. Archie, who had a good sense of direction, knew the point of the compass where Tarta lay, and had an occasional glimpse of the park paling on his right to keep him straight. He was driving carelessly, for the road seemed deserted, and his mind was occupied in wondering what kind of fare the Turk's Head would give them, when in turning a corner he saw a yard or two ahead a stationary car, drawn up dangerously in a narrow place. He clapped on his brakes, for there was no room to pass it, since its nose was poked beyond the middle of the road, and came to a standstill in a crooked echelon, his off front wheel all but touching its running board.

Archie, like many casual people, was easily made indignant by casualness in others. On this occasion surprise made him indignant in his own language. 'You fool!' he shouted. 'Will you have the goodness to shift your dashed perambulator?'

One man sat stiffly at the wheel. The other was apparently engaged in examining a map with the assistance of the headlight. It was the latter who replied.

'Peter,' he said, 'they're English. Thank God for that.'

The map-student straightened himself, and stood revealed in the glare of the big acetylene lamps as a smallish man in a tweed ulster. He took off his spectacles, blinked in the dazzle, and came deferentially towards Archie. His smile was so ingratiating that that gentleman's irritation vanished.

'That's a silly thing to do,' was all he said. 'If my brakes hadn't been good we'd have had a smash.'

'I'm awfully sorry. Peter lost his head, I doubt. You see, we've missed our road.'

Something in the voice, with its rich Scots intonation, in the round benignant face, and in the friendly peering eyes stirred a recollection in Archie which he could not place. But he was not allowed time to drag the deeps of his memory. Alison from the back seat had descended like a tornado, and was grasping the stranger's hand.

'Dickson,' she cried, 'who'd have thought of finding you here? You're a sight for sore eyes.'

The little man beamed.

' 'Deed, so are you, Miss Alison. Mercy, but it's a queer world.'

'This is Sir Archie Roylance. You know him? Aren't you a neighbour of his?'

Dickson extended a grimy hand.

'Fine I know him, though I haven't seen him for years. D'you not mind the Gorbals Die-hards, Sir Archibald, and Huntingtower where you and me fought a battle?'

'Golly, it's McCunn!' Archie exclaimed. 'And not a day older –'

'And that,' said Alison, waving a hand towards the back of her car, 'is my cousin Janet – Lady Roylance.'

Dickson bowed, and, since he was too far off to shake hands, also saluted.

'Proud to meet you, mem. This is a fair gathering of the clans. I never thought when I started this morning to run into a covey of friends.' The encounter seemed to have lifted care from his mind, for he beamed delightedly on each member of the party, not excluding McTavish.

'But what are you doing here?' Alison repeated. 'I thought you were ill and at some German cure place.'

'I've been miraculously restored to health,' said Dickson solemnly. 'And I'm here because I want to have a word with a man. You know him, Miss Alison – Prince Odalchini.'

'But that's what we're here for too,' the girl said.

'You don't tell me that. Have you tried to get inside his gates? That's what I've been seeking to do, and they wouldn't let me.'

'Who wouldn't let you?'

'A lot of young lads in short breeks and green sarks. My directions were to go to a place called Zutpha, which was the proper way in. I found the lodge gates all right, but they were guarded like a penitentiary. I told the lads who I was seeking and got a lot of talk in a foreign language. I didn't understand a word, but the meaning was plain enough that if I didn't clear out I would get my neck wrung. One of them spoke German, and according to Peter what he said was the German for "Go to hell out of this." So I just grinned at them and nodded and told Peter to turn the car, for I saw it was no good running my head against a stone dyke. So now I'm looking for a town called Tarta, where I can bide the night and think things over.'

'But what do you want with Prince Odalchini?'

'It's a long story, and this is not the place to tell it. It was Dougal that set me off. Dougal Crombie – you remember him at Castle Gay?'

'Dougal! You have seen him?'

'No farther back than the day before yesterday. He's in Vienna now. He came seeking me, for Dougal's sore concerned about this Evallonian business. Jaikie is in it too. He had seen Jaikie.'

'Where is Jaikie?' Alison asked, her voice shrill with excitement.

'Somewhere hereabouts. Dougal says he's a prisoner and in the hands of the same lads that shoo'ed me away from the Prince's gates.'

Here Archie intervened. 'This conference must adjourn,' he said. 'We're all famishing and Mr McCunn is as hungry as the rest of us. Dinner is the first objective. I'll back my car, and you' – he addressed Peter Wappit – 'go on ahead. It's a straight road, and the town isn't five miles off. We can't talk here by the roadside, especially with Alison shrieking like a pea-hen. If Juventus has got the wind up, it's probably lurking three deep in these bushes.'

The hostelry of the Turk's Head drew its name from the days when John Sobieski drove the Black Sultan from the walls of Vienna. Part of it was as old as the oldest part of the Schloss, and indeed at one time it may have formed an outlying appanage of the castle. In the eighteenth century, in the heyday of the Odalchinis, it was a cheerful place, where great men came with their retinues, and where in the vast kitchen the Prince's servitors and foresters drank with the town folk of Tarta. It still remained the principal inn of the little borough, but Tarta had decayed, and it stood on no main road, so while its tap-room was commonly full, its guest-rooms were commonly empty. But the landlord had been valet in his youth to the Prince's father, and he had a memory of past glories and an honest pride in his profession; besides, he was a wealthy man, the owner of the best vineyard in the neighbourhood. So the inn had never been allowed to get into disrepair; its rambling galleries, though they echoed to the tread of few guests, were kept clean and fresh; the empty stalls in the big stables were ready at a moment's notice for the horses that never came; there was good wine in the cellars against the advent of a connoisseur. It stood in an alley before you reached the market-place, and its courtyard and back parts lay directly under the shadow of the castle walls.

The new-comers were received like princes. The landlord was well disposed to English milords, the class to which, from a glance at his card, he judged Archie to belong. Janet and Alison were his notion of handsome gentlewomen, for, being swarthy himself, he preferred them blonde; the two chauffeurs looked respectable; Dickson he could not place; but he had the carelessness of dress which in a Briton suggested opulence. So there was a scurrying of chambermaids in the galleries and a laborious preparation of hip-baths; the cars were duly bestowed in one of the old coach-houses, and the landlord himself consulted with Archie about dinner. McTavish and Peter were to be accommodated with their meals in a room by themselves – in old days, said the landlord, it had been the sitting-room of the Imperial couriers. The ladies and gentlemen would dine at the hour fixed in the grand parlour, which had some famous ancient carvings which learned men journeyed many miles to see. They would have the room to themselves – there were no other guests in the house. ... He departed to see to the wine with a candlestick as large as a soup tureen.

The dinner was all that the landlord had promised. There was trout from the hills – honest, speckled trout – and a pie of partridges slain prematurely – and what Archie pronounced to be the best beef he had eaten outside England – and an omelet of kidneys and mushrooms – and little tartlets of young raspberries. It was a meal which Dickson was to regard as an epoch in his life; for, coming after the bare commons of Rosensee, it was a sort of festival in honour of his restored health. They drank a mild burgundy, and a sweet wine of the Tokay clan, and a local liqueur bottled forty years ago, and the coffee with which they concluded might have been brewed by the Ottoman whose severed head decorated the inn's sign.

'Dickson,' Alison asked solemnly, 'are you really and truly well again?'

'I'm a new man,' was the answer. 'Aye, and a far younger man. I aye said, Miss Alison, that I was old but not dead-old. I've an awful weight of years behind me, but for all that at this moment I'm feeling younger than when I retired from business. They tell me that you've been to Dr Christoph too, Sir Archibald?'

'He's a warlock,' said Archie, 'I had got as lame as a duck, and he made me skip like a he-goat on the mountains. I daren't presume too far, of course, or the confounded leg may sour on me. I got the most foul cramps the other day after a hill walk.'

'Same with me,' said Dickson. 'The doctor says I may be a well body till the end of my days if I just go easy. I'm not very good at ca'ing canny, so no doubt I'll have my relapses and my rheumatic turns. But that's a small cross to bear. It's not half as bad as the gout that the old gentry used to get.'

'Everybody,' said Archie, 'has gout – or its equivalent. It's part of man's destiny. *Chacun à son goût*, as they say in Gaul.'

The miserable witticism was very properly ignored. It was Alison who brought them back to business. 'I want to hear what Dougal said,' she told Dickson. 'I came here because Jaikie wrote telling me to. I haven't a notion where he is – I thought he was on his way home by this time. Archie and Janet came to keep me company. We're all bound for the same house – if we can get in. Now tell me – very slowly – everything that Dougal said.'

Dickson, as well as he could, expounded Dougal's reading of Evallonian affairs. There was nothing new to his auditors in the exposition, for it was very much what they already knew from McTavish.

'What I don't understand,' said Alison, 'is what Dougal thought you could do, Dickson.'

'I suppose,' was the modest answer, 'that he wanted a business-like view of the situation.'

'But how could you give him that when you know so little about it?'

'That's just what I told him. I said that before I could help to redd up the mischief I had to discover exactly what the mischief was. That's why I came on here.'

'You're a marvel,' said Alison with wide eyes. 'I didn't know you were so keen about Evallonia.'

'I'm not. I don't care a docken about Evallonia. But, you see, I'm under a kind of bond, Miss Alison. You'll mind the night in the Canonry when I saw Prince John off in a boat. He gave me this ring' – he held up his left hand – 'and I said to him that if ever I got the word I would cross the world to help him.'

'He sent for you?'

'Not exactly. But the poor young man is evidently in sore difficulties, and I – well, I remembered my promise. I daresay he'll be the better of a business mind to advise him. Dougal, I could see, thought me daft, but I'm sane enough. I don't particularly fancy the job, for I'm wearying to get home, but there it is. I thought I'd first have a crack with Prince Odalchini and get the lay-out right. And then –'

'Then?'

'Then I must find Prince John, and the dear knows how I'll manage that.'

A glance from Alison prevented Archie from saying something.

'It's more important,' she said, 'that you should find Jaikie.'

'I daresay that will be the way of it,' Dickson smiled. 'He's a prisoner, and at Zutpha today I thought I would soon be a prisoner too, and would run up against Jaikie in some jyle.'

'Jaikie,' said Alison, 'told me to come here, for he needed me. That means that sooner or later he'll be here too. They can't prevent us getting into the House of the Four Winds if we're Prince Odalchini's friends. It isn't war yet.'

'It is not a bad imitation.' A new voice spoke, and the four at the table, who had been intent on their talk, turned startled faces to the door. A tall man had quietly insinuated himself into the room, and was now engaged in turning the key in the lock. He had a ragged blond beard, and a face the colour of an autumn beech leaf: he wore an ill-cut grey suit and a vulgar shirt; also he had a Brigade tie.

'Good evening,' he said pleasantly. 'How are you, Roylance? Proser – that's the landlord – is a friend of mine and told me you were here.' He smiled and bowed to Janet, and then he stopped short, registering extreme surprise on a face not accustomed to such manifestations. 'Cousin Alison! My dear, what magic spirited you here?'

'Thank God!' Alison exclaimed fervently. 'I've been thinking of you all day, Ran, and longing to get hold of you. This is Mr Dickson McCunn, who is a friend of Jaikie – you remember Jaikie at the Lamanchas? I don't know why you're here – I don't quite know why any of us are here – but here we are, and we must do something. By the way, you were saying as you slunk in – ?'

'I was observing that the present state of affairs was a rather good imitation of war. How shall I put it? The Monarchists control the centre of Evallonia and the capital and can strike there when they please. Juventus is in power round the whole circumference of the country. They control its outlets and inlets – a very important point.'

'That's why they are besieging the castle here?'

'Not besieging. Keeping it under observation. There has been as yet no overt act of hostility.'

'But they are taking prisoners. They pinched Jaikie.'

Mr Glynde's *nil admirari* countenance for a second time in five minutes registered surprise.

'Jaikie?' he cried. 'What do you mean?'

'He is in the hands of Juventus. He has been seen in captivity. Do you know anything about him?' Alison's voice had the sharpness of anxiety.

'I had the pleasure of meeting your Jaikie a few days ago up in the hills. I encouraged him to pay a visit to Evallonia. I helped to entertain him at luncheon with Prince Odalchini, when we tried to make him prolong his visit. You see, I had taken a fancy to Mr Jaikie and thought that he might be useful. I was to meet him that evening, but he never turned up, so I assumed that he was tired of my company, and had gone back across the frontier as he intended. It seems that I have misjudged him. He is a prisoner of Juventus, you say? That must be the doing of his friend Count Paul, and it looks as if all parties were competing for his company. Well, it may not be a bad thing, for it gives us an ally in the enemy's camp. You look troubled, Alison dear, but you needn't worry. Count Paul Jovian is not a bad sort of fellow, and I am inclined to think that Jaikie is very well able to look after himself.'

'I'm not worrying about Jaikie, but about ourselves. I came here because Jaikie sent for me, and that means that he expects to meet me. He named Prince Odalchini's house. But how are we to get into it, if Juventus spends all its time squatting round it?'

'I think that can be managed,' said Mr Glynde. 'You have greatly relieved my mind, my dear. If Jaikie means to come to the House of the Four Winds, he will probably manage it, and he may be a most valuable link with the enemy. You must understand that Juventus is by no means wholly the enemy, but may with a little luck become a friend. . . . By the way, just how much do you know about the situation?'

He proceeded by means of question and answer to probe their knowledge, directing his remarks to Alison at first, but later to Dickson, when he perceived that gentleman's keenness.

'I must tell you one piece of bad news,' and his voice became grave. 'I have just heard it. Prince John was in hiding in a certain place, waiting for the summons, for everything depends on his safety, and all precautions had to be taken. But his enemies discovered his retreat, and he has been kidnapped. We know who did it – Mastrovin, the most dangerous and implacable of them all.'

He was puzzled to find that the announcement did not solemnize his hearers. Indeed, with the exception of Dickson, it seemed to amuse them. But Dickson was aghast.

'Mercy on us!' he cried. 'That's an awful business. I mind Mastrovin, and a blackguard murdering face he had. I must away at once –'

'It is the worst thing that could have happened,' Mr Glynde continued. 'They may kill him, and with him the hope of Evallonia. In any case it fatally disarranges the Monarchist plans. . . . What on earth is amusing you, Roylance?' he concluded testily.

Archie spoke, in obedience to a nod from Alison.

'Sorry,' he said. 'But the fact is we got in ahead of old Mastrovin. We were at Unnutz, and saw what he was up to, so we nipped in and pinched the Prince ourselves.'

'Good God!' Mr Glynde for a moment could only stare. 'Who knows about that?'

'Nobody, except us.'

'Where have you put him?'

'At this moment he is upstairs having his supper along with Mr McCunn's chauffeur. His present job is to be my servant – name of McTavish – passport and everything according to Cocker.'

For the third time that evening Mr Glynde was staggered. He rose and strode about the room, and his blue eyes had a dancing light in them.

'I begin to hope,' he cried. 'No, I begin to be confident. This freak of fate shows that the hussy is on our side.' He took a glass from the sideboard and filled himself a bumper of the local liqueur. 'I drink to you mountebanks. You have beaten all my records. I have always loved you, Janet. I adore you, Alison, my dear, and I have been writing you some exquisite poetry. *Eructavit cor meum* as the Vulgate says – now I shall write you something still more exquisite. Roylance, you are a man after my own heart. Where are you going?' he asked, for Dickson had risen from the table.

'I thought I would go up and have a word with His Royal Highness.'

"You'll do nothing of the kind. Sit down. And drop the Royal Highness business.' Mr Glynde pulled a chair up to the table and leaned his elbows on it. 'We must go very carefully in this business. You have done magnificently, but it's still dangerous ground. You say nobody knows of it except ourselves. Well, not another soul must know of it. Mastrovin is out to kill or spirit away Prince John – he must believe that the Prince is lost. Casimir and the Monarchists must believe that Mastrovin is the villain and go out hot on his trail – that will have the advantage of demobilizing the Monarchists, which is precisely what is wanted at present. The Prince must be tucked away carefully till we want him – and when and how we will want him depends on the way things go. Oh, I can tell you we have scored one mighty big point which may give us the game and the rubber. But he can't stay here as your servant.'

'It's a pretty good camouflage,' said Archie. 'He's the image of a respectable English valet, and I'm dashed if he hasn't picked up a Scotch accent, like the real McTavish. You'd have to examine him with a microscope before you spotted the Prince. He's a first-class actor, and it amuses him, so he puts his heart into it.'

'Nevertheless it is too dangerous. You people will be moving in the wrong circles, and sooner or later he'll give himself away, or somebody will turn up that has known him from childhood. Luckily he hasn't been much in Evallonia since he was a boy, but you never know. We must bury him deeper. . . . Wait a moment. I have it. He shall go into my circus. You may not know that I'm a circus proprietor, Alison dear – the Cirque Doré – Glynde, late Aristide Lebrun – the epochal, the encyclopedic, the grandiose. We are encamped in the environs of Tarta, and every night sprigs of Juventus, who are admitted at half-price, applaud our performances. The Prince shall join my staff – I will devise for him some sort of turn – he will be buried there as deep as if he were under the Rave. It will be a joyful irony that the enemies who are looking for him will applaud his antics. Then some day, please God, we will take him out of tights and grease-paint and give him a throne.'

Mr Glynde had become a poet, but he had not ceased to be a conspirator. 'Tomorrow morning,' he told Archie, 'you will inform the landlord that you are sending your chauffeur home by road with your car. The cars will take your baggage to Zutpha, while you will walk there at your leisure through a pleasant country to catch the evening train. Proser is a good man, but it is unkind to burden even a good man with too much knowledge. Roylance's chauffeur will not again be heard of. I will arrange about your baggage and the cars.'

'And what about us?' Archie asked.

'Before the evening – well before the evening, I hope – you will be in the House of the Four Winds.'

The party took an affectionate farewell of the landlord next morning, their baggage was piled into the cars, luncheon baskets were furnished, and Proser was informed that they meant to drive a mile or two till they cleared the town, and then to spend the day walking the woods on the left bank of the Rave, and catch the evening train at Zutpha. The cars would go straight to the railway station. There was no sign of Mr Randal Glynde.

McTavish, however, had been well coached. They crossed the Rave bridge, passed the common where Jaikie had first met Count Paul, and plunged into a thick belt of woodland which covered all the country between the foothills and the river. Here there was no highway but many forest tracks, one in especial much rutted by heavy wagons and showing the prints of monstrous feet. The reason of this was apparent after a mile or so, when a clearing revealed the headquarters of the Cirque Doré. It was not its show-ground – that was in the environs of Tarta – but its base, where such animals were kept as were not immediately required. It was guarded by a stout palisade, and many notices warning the public that wild beasts lived there, and that they must not enter.

Mr Glynde was awaiting them, and one or two idlers hung

around the gate. Archie caught, too, what he thought was a glimpse of a green shirt. Randal received them with the elaborate courtesies of a circus proprietor welcoming distinguished patrons. The chauffeurs of the two cars he directed how to proceed to Zutpha. 'They will return by another road in due course,' he whispered to Alison, 'but it is altogether necessary that they should be seen to leave this place.'

Of what followed no member of the party had a very clear recollection. They were taken to a tent less odoriferous than the rest, and provided with white caps on which the name of the circus was embroidered in scarlet. 'We give a *matinée* today,' said Randal, 'an extra performance asked for by Tarta. It will be in a dance-hall, and the programme is in Luigi's hands – gipsy dances and songs and fiddling, for we are no mere vulgar menagerie. You will accompany the artists back to Tarta. Trust me, you will not be suspected. The Cirque Doré has become a common object of the seashore.'

So Archie and Janet, Alison and Dickson, joined a party which crowded into an old Ford bus, and jolted back the way they had come. The dance-hall proved to be a building not far from the Turk's Head, and it was already packed when the company arrived and entered by a side door. Randal deposited the four in a little room behind the stage. 'You will lunch out of your baskets,' he told them, 'while I supervise the start of the show. When it is in full swing I will come back.'

So while fiddles jigged a yard or two off and the feet and hands of Tarta citizens applauded, the four made an excellent meal and conversed in whispers. The circus cap was becoming to Alison and Janet, and it made Archie look like a professional cricketer, but on Dickson's head it sat like an incongruous cowl out of a Christmas cracker. 'A daft-like thing,' he observed, 'but I'm long past caring for appearances. I doubt,' he added prophetically, 'that there'll be a lot of dressing-up before we're through with this business. It's a pity that I've the kind of face you cannot properly disguise. Providence never meant me to be a play-actor.'

Randal did not return for a good hour. He seemed satisfied.

'The coast is clear,' he said, 'and I've just had word from my camp that everything is all right there. Now we descend into the deeps, and I'm afraid it will be rather a dusty business. You can leave the circus caps behind, and put on your proper head-gear. I hope you two women have nothing on that will spoil.'

He led them down a rickety wooden stair into a basement in which were stored many queer properties; then out of doors into a small dark courtyard above which beetled the walls of the castle. In a corner of this was a door, which he unlocked, and which led to further stables, this time of ancient stone. There followed a narrow passage, another door, and then a cave of a room which contained barrels and shelves and smelt of beer.

'We are now in the cellars of the Turk's Head,' Randal expounded. 'Proser knows this road, and he knows that I know it, but he does not know of our present visit.'

From the beer cellar they passed into a smaller one, one end of which was blocked by a massive wooden frame containing bottles in tiers. Randal showed that one part of this frame was jointed, and that a section, bottles and all, formed a door. He pulled this back, and his electric torch revealed a low door in a stone wall. It was bolted with heavy ancient bolts, but they seemed to have been recently in use, for they slipped easily back. Now he evidently expected it to open, but it refused. There was a keyhole, but no key.

'Some fool must have locked it,' he grumbled. 'It must have been Proser, and I told him to leave the infernal thing open. I'm extremely sorry, but you'll have to wait here till I get a key. It's filthy dirty, but you won't suffocate.'

They did not suffocate, but they had a spell of weary waiting, for the place was pitch-dark and no one of them had a light. Dickson tried to explore in the blackness, and ran his head hard against an out-jutting beam, after which he sat down on the floor and slept. Archie smoked five cigarettes, and did his best to keep up a flow of conversation. 'This is the Middle Ages right enough,' he said. 'We're making burglarious entry into an ancient Schloss, and I feel creepy down the spine. We didn't bargain for this Monte Cristo business, Janet, when we left Geneva. And the last thing I heard that old ass Perriot say there was that the medieval was out of date.' But by-and-by he too fell silent, and it was a dispirited and headachy company that at last saw the gleam of Mr Glynde's torch.

'I humbly apologize,' said Randal, 'but I had a devil of a hunt for Proser. He had gone to see a cousin about his confounded vines. He swears he never locked the door, so it must have been done from the other side. The people in the Schloss are evidently taking no chances. But I've got the key.'

The thing opened readily, and the explorers repeated their recent performance, threading a maze of empty cellars till they came to a door which led to a staircase. For a long time they seemed to be climbing a spiral inside a kind of turret, and came at last to a stage where thin slits of windows let in the daylight. Archie peered out and announced that in his opinion it must be about six o'clock. At last they reached a broad landing, beyond which further steps appeared to ascend. But there was also a door, which Randal tackled confidently as if he expected it to open at once.

It refused to budge. He examined it and announced that it was locked. 'It is always kept open,' he said. 'I've used it twenty times lately. What in thunder is the matter with it today?'

It was very plain what the matter was. It had been barricaded by some heavy object on the other side. It moved slightly under his pressure, but the barricade held fast.

'The nerves of this household have gone to blazes,' he said. 'Roylance, lend a hand, and you, McCunn. We must heave our weight on it.'

They heaved their weight, but it did not yield; indeed, they heaved till the three men had no breath left in them. There was a creaking and grinding beyond, but the heavy body, whatever it was, held its ground. They laboured for the better part of an hour, and by-and-by made a tiny aperture between door and doorpost. The door was too strong to splinter, but Archie got a foot in the crack and, supported by vigorous pressure from behind, slowly enlarged it. Then something seemed to topple down with a crash beyond the door, and they found that it yielded. They squeezed past a big Dutch armoire, from the top of which had fallen a marble torso of Hercules.

Randal was now on familiar ground. The noise they had made had woken no response in the vast silent house. He led them through stone passages, and then into carpeted corridors, and through rooms hung with tapestries and pictures. There was no sign of servants or of any human life, but Janet and Alison, feeling the approach of civilization, tried to tidy their hair, and Mr McCunn passed a silk handkerchief over a damp forehead. At last, when it seemed that they had walked for miles, Randal knocked at a door and was bidden enter.

It was a small room lined with books, aglow with the sunset which came through a tall window. In a chair sat an old man in a suit of white linen, and on a couch beside him a youthful and dishevelled figure was refreshing itself with a glass of beer.

## CHAPTER SEVEN

## 'SI VIEILLESSE POUVAIT'

MR JOHN GALT had reason to seek refreshment, for he had had an eventful afternoon.

He had spent two days not unpleasantly in the camp of that wing of Juventus which Ashie commanded. ('Wing' was their major unit of division: they borrowed their names from the Romans, and Ashie was 'Praefectus Alae'.) He was a prisoner, but in honourable captivity – an English friend of the commander, detained not because he was hostile, but because of the delicacy of the situation. Ashie introduced him to the subordinate officers, and he found them a remarkable collection. There were old soldiers among them who attended to the military side, but there were also a number of young engineers and business men and journalists, who all had their special duties. Juventus, it appeared, was not only a trained and disciplined force, the youth of a nation in arms for defence and, it might be, offence; it was an organization for national planning and economic advancement. The recruits were brigaded outside their military units in groups according to their training and professions, and in each group were regular conferences and an elaborate system of education. Jaikie attended a meeting of an oil group, oil being one of Evallonia's major industries, and was impressed by the keenness of the members and the good sense of the discussions, so far as they were explained to him. This was no mere ebullition of militarism, but something uncommonly like a national revival. He realized that it was not one man's making. A leader would no doubt be necessary when Juventus took a hand in politics, but the movement itself had welled up from below. It was the sum of the spontaneous efforts of a multitude of people of all types and degrees, who had decided that they were tired of toy-shops and blind alleys and must break for open country.

Jaikie was a good mixer, and very soon had made friends among the rank-and-file as well as among the officers. His meek cheerfulness and the obvious affection which the commander showed for him were passports to their goodwill. The language he found to be scarcely a difficulty at all. Most of the Evallonian youth had at least a smattering of English and many spoke it well, for it had long been in the schools the one obligatory foreign tongue. The second day he played in a Rugby game, a purifying experience on a torrid afternoon. Sports and gymnastics had a large part in Juventus, and every afternoon was consecrated to them. Ashie must have spread his fame, for he was invited to join the Blue fifteen, and was permitted to fill his old place at right wing three-quarters. It was a fierce, swift, and not very orthodox game, the forwards doing most of the work, and the tackling being clumsy and uncertain. But he found that one or two of his side had a fair notion of the business, and some of them had certainly a fine turn of speed. One especially, the centre three-quarter next him, had clearly played a good deal, and now and then there was quite a creditable bout of passing. Jaikie had not a great deal of work to do, but in the second half he got the ball and scored a try, after a spectacular but not very difficult run down the field. However, that kind of run was apparently new to Evallonia, and it was received by the spectators with delirious applause.

Afterwards, when he was having a drink, Ashie introduced him to the centre, whose name was Ivar. The boy regarded him with open-eyed admiration.

'You have played for the English college of the Praefectus?' he asked respectfully.

'For a good deal more than that,' said Ashie. 'Mr Galt is one of the most famous players in the world. He is what they call an International, and is the pride of his nation, which is Scotland.'

Ivar gasped.

'Scotland! That is a famous land. I have read romances about it. Its men dress like women but fight like lions. It loves freedom and has always helped other people to become free.'

Jaikie had a walk with Ivar within the limits of the cantonment and discovered a strong liking for the boy's solemn enthusiasm. Ivar, it appeared, was a young electrical engineer, and had been destined to a post in Brazil when Juventus called him. Now his ambition was limited to the immediate future, the great patriotic effort which the next few weeks would demand. He did not talk of it, for Juventus was schooled to reticence, but the light of it was in his eyes. But he spoke much of Evallonia, and Jaikie learned one thing from him – there was complete loyalty to the ideal of the cause, but no one leader had laid his spell upon it. Ivar mentioned with admiration and affection many names – Ashie's among them – but there was no one that dominated the rest. 'When we triumph,' he said, 'we will call to our aid all good men.'

'Including the Monarchists?' Jaikie asked.

'Including the Monarchists, if they be found worthy.'

They stood for a little on a ridge above the camp, where ran the highroad along which Ashie's car had brought him. It was a clear evening and there was a wide prospect. Jaikie, who had his countrymen's uneasiness till he had the points of the compass in his head, was now able to orientate his position. The camp was in a crook of the Rave before it bent eastward in the long curve which took it to Melina. To the south he saw the confines of a big park, and to the east the smoke of a far-away train.

Ivar was glad to enlighten him.

'That is the nearest railway,' he said. 'The station of Zutpha is four miles off, beyond where you see the cornfield in sheaf. Yes, that is a nobleman's park, the castle called the House of the Four Winds. At the other side is the little city of Tarta, once a busy place, but now mouldering.'

Jaikie asked who owned the castle.

'It is Prince Odalchini,' said the boy with a grave face. 'A famous house, the Odalchinis, and we of Juventus are not rootless Communists to despise ancient things. But this Prince Odalchini is an old man and he becomes foolish. He is a crazy Monarchist, and would bring back the old ways unchanged. Therefore he is closely watched by us. We do not permit any entry into his domain, or any exit except by our leave.'

Jaikie cast his eye over the wide expanse of forest and pasture.

'But how can you watch so big a place when you have so many other things to do? It must be eight or nine miles round.'

'It is part of our training,' said Ivar simply. 'The main entrances are of course picketed. For the rest, we have our patrols, and they are very clever. We Evallonians have sharp eyes and a good sense for country, and we have been most of us in our time what you call Boy Scouts, and many of us are hill-bred or forest-bred. We have our woodcraft and our fieldcraft. Believe me, Prince Odalchini is as securely guarded as if battalions of foot lined his park fence. Not a squirrel can enter without our knowing it.'

'I see,' said Jaikie, feeling a little depressed. His eye crossed the Rave and ran along a line of hills ten miles or so to the west. They were only foot-hills, two thousand feet high at the most, but beyond he had a glimpse of remote mountains. He saw to his left the horseshoe in which Tarta and its Schloss lay – he could not see the pass that led to Kremisch, since it was hidden by a projecting spur. To the north the hills seemed to dwindle away into a blue plain. Just in front of him there was a deeply-recessed glen, the containing walls of which were wooded to the summit, but at the top the ridge was bare, and there was cleft-shaped like the back-sight of a rifle. In that cleft the sun was most spectacularly setting.

Ivar followed his gaze. 'That is what we call the Wolf's Throat. It is the nearest road to the frontier. There in that cleft is the western gate of Evallonia.'

As Jaikie looked at the nick, sharp cut against the crimson sky, he had a sudden odd sensation. Beyond that cleft lay his old life. Down here in this great shadowy cup of Evallonia was a fantastic world full of incalculable chances. These chances pleasurably excited him, but there were dregs of discomfort in his mind; he felt that he had been enticed here and that something in the nature of a trap might close on him. Now Jaikie had a kind of claustrophobia, and anything like a trap made him feel acutely unhappy, so it comforted him to see the outlet. That blazing rifle-backsight among the hills was the road to freedom. Some day soon he might have to use it, and it was good to know that it was there.

That night he observed after supper that he must be getting on with his job, and Ashie agreed. 'I was just going to say the same thing myself,' he said. 'The air is full of rumours, and we can't get a line on what the Monarchists mean to do. There must be some hitch in their plans. We hear from Melina that there's not a Minister left in the place, only clerks carrying on, and that the National Guard are standing-to, awaiting orders. We shall probably come on a Minister or two very soon trying to cross the frontier, but our orders are to speed their journey. We don't want a pogrom. What worries me is Cousin Mintha. She is in the south, among the oil-fields, and it looks as if she were on the war-path and moving towards Melina. We are nothing like ready for that, and she may put everything in the soup. The Monarchists must be allowed to show their hand first, but in this darned fog nobody knows anything. So the sooner you get inside the House of the Four Winds, my lad, the better for everybody.'

'Can't you release me on parole?' Jaikie asked.

'Impossible. If you were caught in this neighbourhood and I had let you out on parole, I should be suspected of double-dealing, and I can't afford that with Mintha on her high horse. No, you must escape and go off on the loose, so that if you are caught I can deal with you firmly. I may have to put you in irons,' he added with a grin.

'It won't be easy to get into that castle,' said Jaikie. 'I've had a word with the young Ivar and they seem to have taped every yard.'

'Well, that's just where your genius comes in, my dear. I put my Evallonians high, but I'm prepared to back you as a strategist against them every time. Look at the way you ran round the Green backs this afternoon.'

'Then there's the getting in here again.'

'That will be all right if you don't take too long. I can have your tent shut up all day and give out that you've a touch of malaria and mustn't be disturbed. . . . We can make sure that you leave camp unnoticed, for I'll tell you the dispositions. Then it's up to you to get inside the Schloss and out again and be back here early in the night. I can tell you the best place to enter our lines.'

'All right,' said Jaikie a little dolefully. 'My only job is to dodge your lads and have a heart-to-heart talk with the Prince. What about him, by the way? Mayn't he have a posse of keepers taking pot-shots at any intruder?'

'No, that's not his way. You have only us to fear. Be thankful that you can reduce your enemies to one lot. Ours seem to produce a fresh crop daily. I've just heard that one of Mastrovin's gang has been seen pretty near here. If Mastrovin turns up there's likely to be dirty work.'

Jaikie went out literally with the milk. Every morning the neighbouring farms sent up milk for the camp in great tin drums borne in little pony-carts, and with them a batch of farm boys. Discipline was relaxed on these occasions, and Ashie had indicated one route which the milk convoy invariably followed. Jaikie, in much-stained flannel bags and a rough tweed jacket and ancient shoes, might easily pass as an Evallonian rustic. So he trotted out of camp behind a milk-cart, his hands assisting an empty drum to keep its balance. A hundred yards on and he slipped inconspicuously into the roadside scrub.

The weather was cooler than it had been of late, and there was a light fresh wind blowing from the hills. Jaikie felt rejuvenated, and began to look forward to his day's task with a mild comfort. He did not believe that any patrols of Juventus could prevent him from getting inside the park. After that the job would be harder. He remembered the gentle fanaticism in Prince Odalchini's eyes, and considered that it might be difficult to get him to agree to any counsels of moderation, or even to listen to them. He might regard Jaikie as one who had deliberately gone over to the other side. But Randal Glynde, if he were there, would help – Jaikie hoped he would be there. And there was just a chance that Alison might have turned up. It was this last thought that strung up his whole being to a delicious expectation.

As he expected, it was not very difficult to get inside the park. His prospect from the ridge the night before had given him his bearings. He realized that his former entrance with Luigi had been on the east side, not far from the road between Zutpha and Tarta; now he was on the north side, where there was no road following the boundary, and thick coverts of chestnut undergrowth extended right up to the paling. He did not find it hard to locate the Juventus cordon. The patrols made their rounds noiselessly and well, but he discovered from their low whistles the timing of their beats, and when it would be safe to make a dash. But it took an unconscionable time, and it was midday before his chance came, for he was determined to take no needless risks. There was a point where the high paling was broken by the mossy and ruinous posts of an old gateway. That was the place he had selected, and at exactly seventeen minutes past twelve he slipped over like a weasel and dropped into the fern of the park.

He travelled a few hundred yards, and then halted to lunch off some biscuits and chocolate provided by Ashie. Then with greater freedom he resumed his journey. Beneath him the ground fell away to a small stream, a tributary of the Rave, which had been canalized in a broad stone channel. There was no bridge, but for the convenience of the estate labourers a plank had been laid across it. Beyond was a glade of turf, at the end of which he could see the beginning of a formal garden. This was very plain sailing, and he became careless, forgetting that Juventus might have their patrols inside the park as well as without. . . . Suddenly, when he was within a few yards of the culvert, swinging along and humming to himself, he found his feet fly from beneath him. He had been tripped up neatly by a long pole, and the owner sat himself heavily on his chest.

Convinced after the first movement that he was hopelessly outmatched in physical strength, Jaikie did not struggle. Vain resistance he had always regarded as folly. His assailant behaved oddly. He ejaculated something as the result of a closer inspection, and then removed himself from his prisoner's chest. But he did not relax a tight grip on his arm. Jaikie observed with some surprise that he was in the hands of Ivar.

Ivar's surprise was greater. His arms imprisoned Jaikie's to his sides, and to a spectator the couple must have had a lover-like air.

'Mr Galt!' he gasped. 'What the devil are you doing here?'

'You may well ask,' said Jaikie pleasantly. 'The fact is, I've broken bounds. I wanted to have a look at that Schloss. D'you mind not gripping my shoulder so hard? You've got me safe enough.'

'You have escaped?' said Ivar solemnly. 'You have not been permitted to come here on parole?'

'No. Count Paul did not give me permission – he knows nothing about it – this is my own show. But look here, Ivar, you're a sensible chap and must listen to reason. I'm on your side, and I'm trying to help your cause in my own way. I have special reasons for being here which I can't explain to you now. I mean to be back in camp this evening – I'll pledge you my word of honour for that. So if you're wise you'll let me go and never say a word about having seen me.'

Ivar's face showed the confusion of his feelings.

'You know all about me,' Jaikie went on. 'You know I'm a

friend of the Praefectus. Well, I'm trying to help him, without his knowledge – that's why I'm here. You won't interfere with me if you've the interests of Juventus at heart.'

The boy's face had changed from bewilderment to sternness.

'I cannot let you go. You are my prisoner and you must return with me. It is not for me to use my discretion. I must obey my orders, and the orders are clear.'

There was that in his eye which warned Jaikie that argument was futile. The discipline of Juventus allowed no quibbling. But Jaikie continued to plead, judging meantime the distance from the culvert and the plank. Then he seemed to give it up as a bad job. 'All right,' he said. 'So be it. I daresay it's the only thing you can do, but it's infernal bad luck on me. The Praefectus will think I have been trying to double-cross him, and I honestly wanted to help him. You believe that, don't you?'

Ivar, remembering his admiration of yesterday, relented so far as to say that he did. Jaikie's surrender, too, caused him to relax the tightness of his grip, and in an instant Jaikie acted. With an eel-like twist he was out of his clutches and Ivar found himself sprawling on the slope. Before he had found his feet Jaikie had skipped over the culvert and had kicked the plank into the water. The two faced each other across a gully which was too broad to jump, and to cross which meant the descent and ascent of slimy stone walls.

'Let's talk sense,' said Jaikie. 'You know you haven't an earthly chance of catching me. You've done your duty in arresting me – only I've escaped, which is your rotten luck. Now listen. I'm going on to reconnoitre that house, never mind why. But, as I told you, I'm on your side, and on Count Paul's side, and I'm coming back. I'll have to wait till it's darkish – eight or nine o'clock perhaps, I daresay. Will your lads be on duty then?'

Something in Jaikie's tone impressed Ivar. 'I shall be on duty,' he said. 'I return here for my second tour at eight o'clock.'

'Well, I'll come back this way, and I'll surrender myself to you. I don't want to outrage your discipline. You can march me to the camp, and hand me over to the Praefectus, and it will be my business to make my peace with him. Have you got that right?'

But Ivar's sense of duty was not to be beguiled. He started to climb down the culvert. 'Ass!' said Jaikie as he turned and trotted off in the direction of the castle. He dived into one of the side glades, and when he had reached the first terrace wall and looked back he saw that his pursuer had halted not very far from the culvert. Perhaps, he thought, there was some order of Juventus which confined their patrols to a certain distance inside the park bounds.

Jaikie, as he threaded the terrace paths, and climbed stairways between neglected creepers and decaying statuary, discovered that he had come to the northern end of the Schloss, which was one of the last-century additions, castellated, battlemented, topped with bogus machicolations. The great house had looked deserted on his first visit, but now it had the air of a forsaken mausoleum. He turned the flank of it and moved along the weedy upper terrace, looking for the door by which he and the Prince had entered after luncheon. He found it, but it was locked and apparently barricaded. He found other doors, but they were in the same condition. The House of the Four Winds seemed to have prepared itself for a siege.

This was discouraging. It occurred to him that the Prince might have departed, but in that case Juventus would have known of it and would not be maintaining its vigilant beleaguerment. He retired to the terrace wall, from which he could get a good view of the tiers of windows. All of them were blind and shuttered. If there were people in the castle they were dwelling in the dark. This he knew was the side where the chief living-rooms were, and if there were inmates anywhere it would be here.

At last his quick eyes caught sight of something on the third floor. It was a window open a little at the top. It was dark, but that might be because of blinds and not of shutters – the sun was so placed that it was hard to judge of that. By that window, and by that window only, he might effect an entrance.

It was an easy conclusion to reach, but the ways and means were not easy. Beneath each line of windows ran a narrow ledge along which it might be just possible to make a traverse. But the question was how to reach that ledge, for there were no friendly creepers on the great blank stone façade. Jaikie, moving stealthily in the cover of pots and statues, for he had an ugly feeling that he might be under hostile observation, reconnoitred carefully the whole front. Something told him that he was not alone in this business; he had the sense that somewhere else on that terrace there were human beings engaged perhaps in the same enterprise. Could Juventus have flung out their scouts thus far? He scarcely believed it, judging from Ivar's behaviour, but he had no time for nervousness, for the day was getting on and he had still his main work to do.

The front yielded him nothing. But at the flanking tower which he had first approached he got a glimmer of hope. There was a fire-escape which had been allowed to fall into disrepair, but which was certainly still climbable. The question was, would it give access to the ledge below the window? He thought that it might, and started to ascend.

Many of the rungs were rotten, and he had to move with extreme caution; indeed, at one moment he feared that the whole contraption would break loose from the wall. Now his early training proved its worth, for he was without a suspicion of vertigo, and could look down unmoved from any height. The fire-escape led up to the third storey, and he found that by stepping to his left he could stand on the sill of a narrow window in the gap between the tower and the main façade. He got his hands on the ledge and to his relief found it broader than he had hoped – a least a foot and a half of hard stone. The difficulty would be to draw himself up on to it.

He achieved this, not without some tremor of the heart, for a foot and a half is not much of a landing-place. Very cautiously he laid himself along it, and then slowly raised himself to his feet. But turning his head he had a glimpse of a great swimming landscape running out into blue distances – he did not look twice, for even his cool head grew a little giddy at the sight. With his face to the wall of the castle he began to sidestep along the ledge.

It proved far simpler than he had feared, for the stone was

firm. He passed window after window, all closed and shuttered, till his heart began to sink. Had he blundered after all? Surely the window he had marked had been the fifth from the right. . . . And then he came to one which, as he approached it, seemed suddenly to move. A hand was lifting the lower sash, and an old face looked out into the sunlight.

Jaikie took a firm grip of the inner sill, for he felt that anything might happen, and the terrace was a long way below. 'Prince Odalchini,' he said, 'I've come back.'

The old face scarcely changed. Its eyes peered and blinked a little at the uncouth figure which seemed to be hanging in air.

'I'm Galt,' said the voice. 'Do you mind me coming in?'

'Ah, yes – Mr Galt,' said the voice. 'Certainly come in. You are very welcome. I do not think anyone has attempted that ledge since for a bet I did it as a boy. But my effort was limited to the traverse between two windows. You have come all the way from the North Tower! Magnificent! You will desire, I think, some refreshment.'

Dickson McCunn sat in a deep armchair sipping a mammoth cup of tea. Prince Odalchini had offered every kind of refreshment, but it had taken time to dig the old housekeeper and the older butler out of the cavernous lower regions, and indeed Janet and Alison had had to descend themselves and help to make tea. All seven were now sitting in the Prince's cabinet, and for the last quarter of an hour the conversation had been chiefly an examination of Jaikie by the Prince and Randal Glynde. Dickson listened with only half an ear, for Jaikie was confirming what they already knew. He was more intent on savouring the full strangeness of this experience.

Two days ago he had been an ordinary convalescent at a German kurhaus, on the eve of returning to the homely delights of Blaweary. Now he found himself inside an old stone palace which was in a stage of siege, a palace which he had entered like a rat through mysterious cellars. His mind kept casting back to the spring morning nine – or was it ten? – years ago, when, being freed for ever from the routine of business, he had set out on a walking tour, and had found himself in another great house among desperate folk. He remembered his tremors and hesitations, and that final resolve which he had never regretted, which indeed had been the foundation of all his recent happiness. Was he destined to face another crisis? Looking back, it seemed to him that everything had been predestined. He had left the shop and set out on his travels because he was needed at Huntingtower. Had Providence decreed that Dr Christoph should give him back his health simply that he should come here?

Dickson felt solemn. He had that Calvinistic belief in the guidance of Allah which is stronger than any Moslem's, and he had also the perpetual expectation of the bigoted romantic. . . . But he was getting an old man, too old for cantrips. His eye fell upon Prince Odalchini, who was also old, though he seemed to have grown considerably younger in the past half-hour. He felt that he had misjudged the Prince; his face was shrewder than he had thought, and he seemed to be talking with authority. Jaikie, too. Dickson was not following the talk, but Jaikie's gravity was impressive, and the rest were listening to him eagerly. He felt a sudden uprush of pride in Jaikie. He was a different being now from the pallid urchin of Huntingtower, who had wept bitterly when he was getting dangerous.

His eyes roamed round the walls, taking in a square of old tapestry, and a line of dark kit-cat portraits. The window showed a patch of golden evening sky. The light caught Alison's hair, and he began to wonder about her and Jaikie. Would they ever be man and wife? It would be a queer match between long descent and no descent at all – but it was a queer world, and nothing could be queerer than this place. Janet and Archie belonged to a familiar sphere, but Mr Glynde was like nothing so much as the Pied Piper of Hamelin. What was he, Dickson McCunn, doing among such outlandish folk? Dougal had said that they wanted his advice; but he felt as impotent as Thomas the Rhymer no doubt felt when he was consulted on the internal affairs of Fairyland. . . . Still, common sense was the same all the world over. But what if common sense was not wanted here, but some desperate quality of rashness, some insane adventurous-ness? He wished he were twenty years younger, for he remembered Prince John. He was sworn to do his best for the exiled monarch, and that very morning with a break in his voice he had renewed the pledge to the chauffeur McTavish.

By this time he was coming out of his dreams, and hearing something of the conversation. As he finished his tea Jaikie was putting the heart of his problem in staccato sentences, and Prince Odalchini and Mr Glynde with gloomy faces were nodding their assent. Something in the words stirred a reminiscence. . . .

'I mind,' said Dickson out of the depths of his chair.

It was the first time he had spoken, and the others turned to him, so that he felt a little embarrassed.

'I mind,' he said, 'when Jimmy Turnbull was running for Lord Provost of Glasgow. He was well liked and far the best man for the job, but the feck of the Town Council didn't fancy his backers, and if it had come to the vote Jimmy would have been beat. So Tam Dickson – he was my own cousin and was Baillie then and afterwards Lord Provost himself – Tam was the wily one and jerked his brains to think of a way out. What he did was this. He got Jimmy's friends to drop Jimmy and put up one David Duthie, who was a blethering body that was never out of the papers. He had a sore job persuading them, he told me, but he managed it in the end. The consequence was that the very men that were opposed to Jimmy's backers, now that he was quit of them, took up Jimmy, and since they were a majority of the Council he was triumphantly elected.'

Dickson's apologue was received with blank faces by the others, with the exception of Randal Glynde. Into that gentleman's eyes came a sudden comprehending interest, and Dickson saw it and was encouraged. His own mind was awaking to a certain clearness.

'If Prince John didn't exist,' he asked, 'is there anybody else the Monarchists could put up?'

'There is no one,' said Prince Odalchini sadly. 'There is, of course, his uncle, the late king's brother, the Archduke Hadrian, but he is impossible.'

'Tell us about the archduke,' said Dickson.

'He is an old man, and very frail. He has not been in Evallonia for many years, and even his name is scarcely remembered. He is believed to be one of the greatest living numismatologists, and he has given his life to his hobby. I alone of the Evallonian nobility have kept in touch with him, and it was only yesterday that I had a letter from his secretary. His Royal Highness is a bachelor, and for long has lived in a château in France near Chantilly, scarcely going beyond his park walls. He is as strict a recluse as any medieval hermit. Now he is bedridden, and I fear cannot have many months to live.'

Prince Odalchini rose, opened a cabinet, and took out a photograph.

'That is His Royal Highness, taken two years ago at my request, for I desired to have a memento of him. In my youth he was kind to me.'

He handed it to Dickson, who studied it carefully. It showed a man not unlike Mr Pickwick or the great Cavour, with a round face, large innocent eyes, and grey hair thinning on the temples – a man of perhaps seventy years, but, so far as could be judged from the photograph, still chubby and fresh-complexioned. It was passed round the company. Janet and Archie scarcely glanced at it, but Mr Glynde looked at it and then at Dickson, and his brow furrowed. Jaikie did the same, and when it came to Alison she cried out – 'Why, Dickson, it might be you, if your hair was greyer.'

'I was just thinking that,' was the answer. Dickson retrieved the photograph and studied it again.

'What size of a man is he?' he asked. His clearness of mind was becoming acid.

'Shortish, about your own height,' said the Prince.

'Umphm! Now what hinders you to do the same with the Archduke as my cousin Tam Dickson did with David Duthie? Jaikie says that Juventus would be for Prince John but for you and your friends. Well, if you run the Archduke, they'll take up Prince John, and since you tell me they'll have the upper hand of you, they'll put Prince John on the throne. D'you see what I mean? It's surely common sense.'

This speech had a considerable effect on the others. Archie laughed idiotically, and Mr Glynde found it impossible to remain seated. But Prince Odalchini only shook his head.

'Ingenious,' he said, 'but impossible. His Royal Highness is old and frail and bedridden. He would not consent, and even if he consented, he would be dead before he reached Evallonia.'

Dickson's mind was moving by leaps to a supreme boldness.

'What for should he come near Evallonia? He need never leave his château, and indeed the closer he lies there the better. It's not his person, but his name that you want. ... See here, Prince. You say that nobody in Evallonia knows him, and few have ever seen him, but that there's a general notion of what he looks like. Can you persuade your friends to change their minds about Prince John and declare for the Archduke as the older and wiser man and more suited for this crisis? If you do that, and put him or something like him on the throne, Juventus will come along in a week and fling him out and set up Prince John, and then you'll all be happy together.'

The company was staring at him open-mouthed and wide-eyed, all except Prince Odalchini, who seemed inclined to be cross.

'But I tell you we cannot get His Royal Highness,' he said.

'I said "or something like him",' was Dickson's answer. His mind was now as limpid as an April morning.

'What on earth do you mean?'

'I mean somebody you can pass off as the Archduke.'

'And where shall we find him?' The Prince's tone was ironical.

'What about myself?' said Dickson.

For an instant there was utter silence.

Prince Odalchini's face showed a range of strong emotions – anger, perplexity, incredulity, and then something that was almost hope. When he spoke, his words were inadequate to his feelings. 'Are you mad?' he asked.

' 'Deed I'm not. I came here as a business man to give you my advice, and there it is. It's a perfectly simple proposition, and there's just the one answer. By the mercy of God I'm reasonably like the old man, though I'm a good deal younger, and anyway there is nobody to tell the differ. I'm willing to take the chance, though I suppose it will be high treason if I'm grippit, for I'm not going back on my word to Prince John. I'll see yon lad with his hinder parts on the throne before I leave Evallonia, or my name's not Dickson McCunn.'

'You realize that you would be running tremendous risks?'

'Ugh, aye, but I've taken risks before this. The only thing I stipulate is that I'm not left too long on the throne, for I wouldn't be up to the job. I might manage a week before I went skelping across the frontier – but not more.'

Prince Odalchini's expression had changed. There was now respect in it, and excitement, and a twitching humour.

'I think you are the boldest man I have ever met,' he said.

'Never heed that,' said Dickson. 'My knees will likely be knocking together before I've done. What I want to know is, can you persuade the rest of your lot, Muresco particularly, to agree to this plan?'

The Prince considered. 'It may be difficult, but I think it can be done. After all, it is the only way.'

'And can you upset the Republic and set up the Archduke?'

'Beyond doubt. For a little while – that is to say.'

'Last and most important, can Juventus be persuaded to accept Prince John?'

It was Jaikie who answered.

'I believe they could. Count Paul would jump at him, and so would the rank-and-file. I don't know about the other leaders. There's a woman who matters a good deal.'

'Prince John must marry her, then. That's all. We're desperate folk and we're not going to stick at trifles.' Dickson was in that mood of excited authority which always with him followed the taking of a great resolution. 'But, Jaikie, it's terrible important that, if I get that far, Juventus must force me to abdicate in a week – I couldn't manage longer. It would be an awful business if at my time of life I was kept cocked up on a throne I didn't want. There's just the one job for you, and that's to manage Juventus, and, mind, I've trusted you often and never known you fail. Away with you back to the camp, for there's no time to lose.'

'We dine in half an hour,' said Prince Odalchini.

'Well, let's get pencil and paper and work out the details.'

But they did not immediately get to business, for Alison rose and ceremoniously embraced Mr McCunn. Her kiss was like that of Saskia's years before in the house of Huntingtower; it loosed a force of unknown velocity upon the world.

The twilight had fallen when Jaikie emerged from one of the terrace doors, which was promptly locked behind him. He proposed to return the way he had come and surrender himself to Ivar. After that he and Ashie must hold high converse. He had a task before him of immense difficulty, and his head was already humming with plans. But Dickson's certainty had given him hope, and he thanked his stars that he had not gone home, for now he was in the kind of adventure he had dreamed of, and his comrades were the people he loved best in the world. This was his notion of happiness.

He must hurry, if he was not to miss Ivar, so he short-circuited his route, by dropping from the successive terrace walls instead of going round by the stairways. . . . At the last of them he found that he had dropped into a human embrace which was strict and powerful, but not friendly.

His instinct of the afternoon had been right. Others besides himself had been lurking among the paths and statues of the terraces.

## CHAPTER EIGHT

## SPLENDIDE MENDAX

JAIKIE's captors, whoever they were, meant business. Before the sack was slipped over his head a cloth, sticky and sweet-smelling, was twisted round his mouth. He was vaguely aware of struggling against an immense suffocating eiderdown, and that was his last conscious moment for perhaps ten minutes. These minutes should have been hours if the intentions of his ill-wishers had been fulfilled. But in Jaikie they had struck a being oddly constituted. Just as it was nearly impossible to make him drunk, so he was notably insensitive to other forms of dope. Had he ever had to face a major operation, the anaesthetist would have had a difficult time with him. Moreover, his nose had come into contact with something hard and was bleeding copiously, which may have counteracted the stuff on the bandage. The consequence was that he presently regained his senses, and found himself in a position of intense bodily discomfort. He was being borne swiftly along by persons who treated him with no more respect than as if he were a bundle of faggots.

He was a good deal frightened, but his anger was greater than his fright, and it was directed against himself. For the third time within a week he had stumbled blindly into captivity – first Ashie, then Ivar that very day, and now some enemy unknown. What had become of the caution on which he had prided himself? He had been an easy victim, because he had had no thought for anything but the immediate future, and had not recognized that he had been walking among hidden fires. He reproached himself bitterly. Ashie had trusted him, Prince Odalchini had trusted him, and he had proved himself only a blundering child. What especially rankled was that he must break his pledge to Ivar. That dutiful youth would be looking for him near the boundary of the park, and would set him down as a common liar.

Indignation, especially against one's self, is a wonderful antidote to fear. It also tends to sharpen the wits. Jaikie, with a horrid crick in his neck and a back aching from rough treatment, began to think hard and fast. Who was responsible for this outrage? Certainly not Prince Odalchini or anyone connected with the House of the Four Winds. Not Juventus. Ivar was the only Greenshirt who knew of his visit to the castle, and Ivar was too much of a gentleman to resort to these brigand tricks. So far his conclusions were clear but they were only negative. Who would want to capture him? Somebody who knew about his new job? – But the only people in the secret were his friends in the castle. Somebody who had a grudge against Prince Odalchini? – But that could only be Juventus, and he had ruled Juventus out. Somebody who had a grievance against himself? – but he was a humble stranger unknown in Evallonia. Somebody who hated Juventus and the Prince alike and who suspected him as a liaison between them? – Now, who filled that bill? Only the present Republican Government in Evallonia. But all his information was to the effect that that Government was shaking in its shoes, and that its members were making their best speed to the frontier. They could have neither leisure nor inclination to spy thus effectively on a castle at whose gates the myrmidons of Juventus were sitting.

And then suddenly he remembered what Ashie had told him and Prince Odalchini had repeated. Behind the effete Republic was a stronger and darker power. . . . A horrid memory of Mastrovin came to his mind, the face which had glowered on him in the room in the Portaway Hydropathic, the face which he had seen distorted with fury in the library of Castle Gay – the heavy shaven chin, the lowering brows, the small penetrating eyes – the face which Red Davie had described as that of a maker of revolutions. . . . The thought that he might be in Mastrovin's hands sent a shiver down his aching spine. The man had tried to kidnap Prince John and had been foiled by Alison. He must be desperate with all his plans in confusion, a mad dog ready to tear whatever enemy he could get his fangs into.

Jaikie's fears must have stopped well short of panic, for he had enough power of reflection left to wonder where he was being taken. He was no longer in the park or the garden, for the feet of his bearers sounded as if they were on some kind of pavement. He had an impression, too, that he was not in the open air, but inside a masoned building. It could not be the castle, for he had heard that evening from Alison of her entry through the cellars and the difficulties of the route; if that approach was so meticulously guarded, it was probable that the same precautions had been taken with all. . . . And then it occurred to him that, since the great building abutted on the town of Tarta, there must be other ways into the streets from the park, through outhouses and curtilages, for once the burgh had been virtually part of the castle. No doubt these were now disused and blocked up, but some knowledge of them might linger in queer places.

His guess was confirmed, for presently it was plain that his bearers were in a low and narrow passage. There seemed to be at least three of them, and they went now in Indian file – crouching as he could tell from their movements, and now and then pushing him before them. He felt his legs grating on rough stone. Once his foot caught in a crevice, and his ankle was nearly twisted when it was dragged out of it. The place was a sort of drain, and it seemed to him miles long; the air was warm and foul, and he was inert not from policy, but from necessity, for he could hardly breathe inside the sack. Once or twice his bearers seemed to be at fault, for they stopped and consulted in muffled voices. These halts were the worst of all, for there loomed before Jaikie the vision of the death of a sewer rat.

Then the passage manifestly widened, the air grew fresher, and there came the sound of flowing water. He remembered that he had seen runnels of water in the Tarta streets, effluents from the Rave, and he realized that he had been right – they were now underneath the town. After that he was only dimly conscious of his whereabouts. He believed that the party were ascending – not stairs, but an inclined tunnel. There came a point in which they moved with extreme caution, as if people were near, people who must not hear or see them. There followed the grating of an opening door, then another and another, and even through the folds of the sack Jaikie recognized that they were in some kind of dwelling. There was the feel in the air of contiguity to human uses. . . .

The end came when he was suddenly dumped on a wooden floor, and one of the party struck a light. The sack was taken from his head, and he was laid on a truckle-bed where were some rough blankets and an unbleached pillow. He had already decided upon his course, so he kept his eye shut and breathed heavily as if he were still under the opiate. The three men left the room, taking the candle with them, and locking the door behind them, so that all he saw was their retreating backs and these told him nothing. They looked big fellows in nondescript clothes, indoor or outdoor servants.

Jaikie's first feeling was of intense relief. Whatever happened to him, at any rate he was not going to be stifled in a drain. He lay for a little breathing free air and gasping like a fish on the shingle. His second feeling was that all his bones were broken, but that he was too tired to care. There were various other feelings, but they all blended into a profound fatigue. In about three minutes Jaikie was asleep.

He must have slept a round of the clock, and he awoke in a state of comparative bodily ease, for Rugby football had inured him to rough handling. The room was a small one, evidently little used, for it had no furniture but a bed; it looked like an attic in an unprosperous inn. Its one dormer window looked over a jumble of roofs to a large blank wall. But since it faced east, it caught the morning sunlight, and the dawn of the wholesome day had its effect on Jaikie's spirits. The ugly little fluttering at his heart had gone. He had only himself to thank for his troubles, he decided, and whatever was in store for him he must keep his head, and not be the blind fool of the past week. He had awakened with one thought in his mind. Prince John was the trump card. It was Prince John that Mastrovin was looking for – if indeed Mastrovin was his captor – and it was for him, Jaikie, to be very wary at this point. Was there any way in which he could turn his present predicament to the advantage of his mission? He had a shadow of a notion that there might be.

The door was unlocked and breakfast was brought him, not by one of his bearers of the night before, but by an ancient woman with a not unpleasing face. She gave him '*Grüss Gott*' in a friendly voice. Since she spoke German like all the Tarta people, and since the breakfast of coffee and fresh rolls looked good, he was encouraged to ask for some means of washing. She nodded, and fetched a tin basin of water, soap, a towel, a cracked mirror and a broken comb, doubtless part of her own toilet equipment. Jaikie washed the blood from his face, scrubbed from his hands some of the grime of last night's cellars, dusted his clothes, and tidied up his unruly hair. Then he made a hearty meal, lit a pipe, and lay down on the bed to think.

He was not left long to his reflections. The door opened and two men entered, who may or may not have been his captors. They were clearly not countrymen, for they had the pallor of indoor workers, and the stoop which comes from bending many hours in the day. They had solemn flat faces with a touch of the Mongol in them, and one of them very civilly restored to Jaikie a knife which had dropped out of his pocket. They beckoned to him to follow them, and when he obeyed readily they forbore to take his arm, but one went before and one behind him. He was escorted down a narrow wooden staircase, and along a passage to a room at the door of which they knocked ceremonially. Jaikie found himself thrust into a place bright with the morning sun, where two men sat smoking at a table.

He recognized them both. One was a tall man with a scraggy neck and a red, pointed beard, a creature of whipcord muscles and large lean bones, who seemed to be strung on wires, for his fingers kept tapping the table, and his eyelids were always twitching. Jaikie remembered his name – it was Dedekind, who had been left with the Jew Rosenbaum to keep guard in the Castle Gay library when the others searched the house. The second was beyond doubt Mastrovin, a little older, a little balder, but formidable as ever. It was not the library scene that filled Jaikie's mind as he looked at them, but the earlier episode, in the upper room of the Portaway Hydropathic, when they had cross-examined an alcoholic little journalist. That scene stuck in his memory, for it had been for him one of gross humiliation. They had bullied him, and he had had to submit to be bullied, and that he could not forget. Hate was a passion in which he rarely indulged, but he realized that he cordially hated Mastrovin.

Could they recognize him? Impossible, he thought, for there could be no link between that cringing little rat and the part he now meant to play. He also was two years older, and in youth one changes fast. So he confronted the two men with a face of cold wrath, but there was a tremor beneath his coolness, for Mastrovin's horrid little eyes were very keen.

'Your name?' Mastrovin barked. 'You are English?'

'I should like to know first of all who you are and what you mean by your insolence?' Jaikie spoke in the precise accents of a Cambridge don, very unlike the speech of the former reporter of the Craw Press.

Mastrovin bent his heavy brows. 'You will be wise to be civil – and obedient. You are in our power. You have been found at suspicious work. We are not men to be trifled with. You will speak, or you will be made to speak, and if you lie you will suffer for it. A second time, your name?'

For some obscure reason the man's tone made Jaikie feel more cheerful. This was common vulgar bullying, bluffing on a poor hand. He thought fast. Who did they think he was? He had noticed that at the first sight of him the faces of both men had fallen. Had he been arrested because they believed that he was Prince John?

'I am English,' he said. 'An English traveller. Is this the way that Evallonia welcomes visitors?'

'You are English, no doubt, and therefore you are suspect. It is known that the English are closely allied with those who are plotting against our Government.'

'Oh, I see.' Jaikie shrugged his shoulders and grinned. 'You think I'm taking a hand in your politics. Well, I'm not. I don't know the first thing about them, and I care less. But if you're acting on behalf of the Government, then I daresay you're right to question me. I'll tell you everything about myself, for I've nothing to conceal. My name is John Galt. I've been an undergraduate at Cambridge and I have just finished with the University. I've been taking a holiday walking across Europe, and I came into Evallonia exactly four days ago. I'll give you every detail about what I've been doing since.'

While smoking his after-breakfast pipe, he had made up his mind on his course. He would tell the literal truth, which he hoped to season with one final and enormous lie.

'You have proof of what you say?' Mastrovin asked.

Jaikie took from his breast pocket the whole of its contents, which were not compromising. There was a lean pocket-book with very little money in it, his passport, the stump of a cheque book, and one or two Cambridge bills. Fortunately, Alison's letters from Unnutz were in his rucksack.

'There's every paper I've got,' he said, and laid them on the table.

Mastrovin studied the bundle and passed it to Dedekind.

'Now you will recount all your doings since you came to Tarta. Be careful. Your story can be checked.'

Jaikie obliged with a minute recital. He described his meeting with his Cambridge friend, Count Paul Jovian. He explained that he knew Prince Odalchini slightly and had letters to him, and that he had called on him at the castle and stayed to lunch. He described his ambush by Ashie, and his life in the Juventus camp. On this Mastrovin asked him many questions, to which he replied with a great air of unintelligent honesty. 'They were always drilling and having pow-pows,' he said, 'but I couldn't make out what they were after. All I did was to play football. I'm rather good at that, for I play for Scotland.'

'Now we will have your doings of yesterday,' said Mastrovin grimly.

Jaikie replied with expansive details. 'I was getting tired of the camp. You see, I was a sort of prisoner, though Heaven knows why. I suppose it had something to do with your soda-water politics. Anyway, I was fed up and wanted a change – besides, I had promised to see Prince Odalchini again. So I slipped out of the camp and had a pretty difficult time getting into the castle grounds. The Juventus people were patrolling everywhere, and I had a bit of a scrap with one of them. Then I had a still more difficult time getting inside the castle. I had to climb in like a cat-burglar.' Jaikie enlarged with gusto on the sensational nature of that climb, for he believed that Mastrovin's people had been somewhere on the terrace and must have seen him. It looked as if the guess was correct, for Mastrovin seemed to accept his story.

'Within the castle you saw – whom?' he barked. He had a most unpleasant intimidating voice.

'I saw the Prince, and dined with him. There were one or two other people there, but I didn't catch their names. One was an English Member of Parliament, I think.'

'So!' Mastrovin nodded to Dedekind. 'And when you had dined you left? Where were you going?'

'I was going back to the camp. I hadn't given my parole or anything of the kind, but I felt that I was behaving badly to my friend. Though he had made me prisoner he treated me well, and I am very fond of him. I proposed to go back and tell him what I had done.'

'He knew of your visit to the castle?'

'Not he. I took French leave. But I didn't like to leave Evallonia without having an explanation with him. Besides, I doubt if I could have managed it with his scouts everywhere. When your ruffians laid hands on me, I was going back the way I had come in the morning.'

Mastrovin talked for a little with Dedekind in a tongue unknown to Jaikie. Then he turned upon him again his hanging countenance.

'You may be speaking the truth. You say you have no interest in the affairs of Evallonia. If that be so, you can have no objection to doing the Government of the Republic a service. It is threatened by many enemies, with some of whom you have been consorting. You must have heard talk – much talk – in the camp of your friend Jovian and in the castle of Prince Odalchini. You will tell me all that you heard. It will be to your interest, Mr Galt, to be frank, and it will be very much to your disadvantage to be stubborn.'

Jaikie put up a very creditable piece of acting. He managed to produce some sort of flush on his pale face, and he put all the righteous indignation he could muster into his eyes. It was not all acting, for once again this man was threatening him, and he felt that little shiver along the forehead which was a sign of the coming of one of his cold furies.

'What the devil do you mean? Do you think that I spy on my

friends? I know that Juventus is opposed to your Government, and being a stranger I take no sides. There was much talk in the camp, and I didn't understand what it was all about. But if I had I would see you and your Government in Tophet before I repeated it.'

Dedekind looked ugly and whispered something to Mastrovin, which was no doubt a suggestion that means might be found for making Jaikie speak. Mastrovin whispered back what may have been an assurance that such means would come later. Jaikie could not tell, for he knew no Evallonian. But he was a little nervous lest he should have gone too far. He did not want to put a premature end to these interrogations.

Mastrovin's next words reassured him. He actually forced his heavy face into a show of friendliness.

'I respect your scruples,' he said. 'We have no desire to outrage your sense of honour. Besides, there is not much that Juventus does of which we are not fully informed. They are our declared enemies and against them we use the methods of war. But your friend Prince Odalchini is surely in a different case. He has lived peacefully under republican rule, though he has no doubt a preference for a monarchy. We bear him no ill-will, but we are anxious that he should not compromise himself by an alliance with Juventus. It was for that reason that you were brought here, that we might probe what relation there was between the two, for we were aware that you had come from the Juventus camp. You can have no objection to telling us what is Prince Odalchini's frame of mind and what things were spoken of in the castle.'

Jaikie smiled pleasantly. 'That's another pair of shoes. . . . The Prince is sick of politics. He is angry with Juventus, and asked me pretty much the same questions as you. But he is an old man and a tired one, and all he wants is to be left alone. He doesn't like these patrols sitting round his park and letting nobody in that they don't approve of. When I met him in England he was a strong Monarchist, but I don't think there is much royalism left in him now.'

Mastrovin was interested. 'No? And why?'

'Because he thinks the Monarchists so feeble. He was very strong on that point with the English Member of Parliament – what was his name? Sir Archibald Something-or-other.' Jaikie was now talking like a man wholly at his ease.

'He thinks them feeble, does he? What are his reasons?'

Well, one of them is that they have mislaid their trump card – their Prince John. I must say that sounds fairly incompetent.'

'So he said that?' Mastrovin's interest had quickened.

'Yes. But it wasn't only losing Prince John that he blamed them for, but for their failure to discover who had got him. It seems that they believe he has been kidnapped by your people, or rather by the left wing of your people. Prince Odalchini mentioned a name – something like Merovingian – it began with an M, anyway. But that appears to have been a completely false scent.'

'Prince Odalchini thinks it a false scent?' Mastrovin's voice was suddenly quiet and gentle.

'Yes, because they now know where he is.' Jaikie had ceased to be a witness in the box, and was talking easily as if to a club acquaintance. He launched his mendacious bombshell in the most casual tone, as if it were only a matter of academic interest. 'It's Juventus that have Prince John. Not the lot here, but the division a hundred miles south that is holding the oil-fields. There's a woman in command. I remember her name, because it was so fantastic – the Countess Mintha Something.'

There was dead silence for a second or two, Mastrovin's eyes were on the table, and Dedekind's fingers ceased to beat their endless tattoo.

'So you see,' Jaikie concluded lightly, 'Prince Odalchini is naturally sick of the whole business. I would like to see him out of the country altogether, for Evallonia at present seems to me no place for an old gentleman who only asks for a quiet life.'

Mastrovin spoke at last. If Jaikie's news was a shock to him he did not show it. He was smiling like a large sleepy cat.

'What you tell us is very interesting,' he said. 'But we have much more to learn from you, Mr Galt.'

'I can't tell you anything more.'

'I think you can. At any rate, we will endeavour to help your memory.'

Jaikie, who had been rather pleased with himself, found his heart sink. There was a horrid menace behind that purring voice. Only the little shiver across his forehead kept him cool.

'I demand to be released at once,' he said. 'As an Englishman you dare not interfere with me, since you have nothing against me.'

'You propose?'

'To go back to the Juventus camp, and then to go home to England.'

'The first cannot be permitted. The second – well, the second depends on many things. Whether you will ever see England again rests with yourself. In the meantime you will remain in our charge – and at our orders.'

He rasped out the last words in a voice from which every trace of urbanity had departed. His face, too, was as Jaikie remembered it in the Canonry, a mask of ruthlessness.

And then, like an echo of his stridency, came a grinding at the door. It was locked and someone without was aware of that fact and disliked it. There was a sound of a heavy body applied to it, and, since the thing was flimsy, the lock gave and it flew open. Jaikie's astonished eyes saw a young Greenshirt officer, and behind him a quartet of hefty Juventus privates.

He learned afterwards the explanation of this opportune appearance. A considerable addition had been made to Ashie's wing, and it was proposed to billet the new-comers in the town. Accordingly a billeting party had been dispatched to arrange for quarters, and it had begun with the principal inns. At this particular inn, which stood in a retired alley, the landlord had not been forthcoming, so the party had explored on their own account the capacities of the building. They had found their way obstructed by sundry odd-looking persons, and, since Juventus did not stand on ceremony, had summarily removed them from their path. A locked door to people in their mood seemed an insult, and they had not hesitated to break it open.

With one eye Jaikie saw that Mastrovin and Dedekind had

their fingers on pistol triggers. With the other he saw that the Greenshirt had no inkling who the two were. His first thought was to denounce them, but it was at once discarded. That would mean shooting, and he considered it likely that he himself would stop a bullet. Besides, he had at the back of his head a notion that Mastrovin might *malgré lui* prove useful. By a fortunate chance he knew the officer, who had been the hooker of the forwards against whom he had played football, and to whom he had afterwards been introduced. He saw, too, that he was recognized. So he gave the Juventus salute and held out his hand.

'I'm very glad to see you,' he said. 'I was just coming to look for you. I surrender myself to you. It's your business to arrest me and take me back to camp. The fact is, I broke bounds yesterday and went on the spree. No, there was no parole. I meant to return last night, but I was detained. I shall have to have it out with the Praefectus. I deserve to be put in irons, but I don't think he'll be very angry, for I have a good many important things to tell him.' Jaikie had managed to sidle towards the door, so that he was close to the Greenshirts.

The officer was puzzled. He recognized Jaikie as a friend of the Praefectus, and one for whose football capacities he had acquired a profound respect. Moreover, the frankness of his confession of irregular conduct disarmed him.

'Why should I arrest you?' he stammered in his indifferent English.

'Because I am an escaped prisoner. Discipline's discipline, you know, though a breach of it now and then may be good business.'

The young officer glanced at the morose figures at the table. Happily he did not see the pistols which they fingered. 'Who are these?' he asked.

'Two people staying in this inn. Bagmen – of no consequence. ... By the way, I wonder what fool locked that door?'

The young man laughed. 'It is a queer place this, and I do not like it. Few of the rooms are furnished, and the landlord has vanished, leaving only boorish servants. But I have to find billets for three companies before evening, and in these times one cannot be fastidious.' He paused. 'You are not – how do you say it? – pulling my foot?'

'Lord, no. I'm deadly serious, and the sooner I see the Praefectus the better.'

'Then I will detail two men to escort you back to camp. We will leave this place, which is as bare as a rabbit warren. I apologize, sirs, for my intrusion.' He bowed to the two men at the table, and, to Jaikie's amusement, they stood up and solemnly bowed in return.

Jaikie spent a somnolent afternoon in the tent of the Praefectus, outside of which, at his own request, an armed sentry stood on guard.

'Don't curse me, Ashie,' he said when its owner returned. 'I know I've broken all the rules, so you've got to pretend to treat me rough. Better say you're deporting me to headquarters for punishment. I want some solid hours of your undivided attention this evening, for I've the deuce of a lot to tell you. After dinner will be all right. Meantime, I want a large-scale map of Evallonia – one with the Juventus positions marked on it would be best. Any word of the Countess Mintha?'

'Yes, confound her! She has started to move. Moving on Krovolin, which is the Monarchists' headquarters. Devil take her for an abandoned hussy. Any moment she may land us in bloody war.'

'All the more reason why you and I should get busy,' said Jaikie.

'You have blood on your forehead,' Ashie told him that evening, when at last the Praefectus was free from his duties. 'Have you been in a scrap?'

'That comes of having a rotten mirror. I thought I had washed it all off. No, I had no scrap, but I got my nose bled. By Mastrovin – or rather by one of his minions.'

Ashie's eyes opened. 'You seem to have been seeing life. Get on with your story, Jaikie. We're by ourselves, and if you tantalize me any longer I'll put you in irons.'

Jaikie told the last part first – a sober narrative of kidnapping, an unpleasant journey, a night's lodging, a strictly truthful talk with two dangerous men, and the opportune coming of the Greenshirt patrol. Ashie whistled.

'You were in a worse danger than you knew. I almost wish it had come to shooting, for there were enough Greenshirts in Tarta this morning to pull that inn down stone by stone. I should love to see Mastrovin in his grave. But I daresay he would have taken you with him, and that would never do. . . . Well, I've got the end of your tale. Now get back to the beginning. How did you get into the park?'

'Easily enough, but your people made it a slow business. By the way, I wish you would have up a lad called Ivar and explain to him that I was unavoidably prevented from keeping my engagement with him. He's a pleasant chap, and I shouldn't like him to think me a crook. The park was easy, but the castle was a tougher proposition. I had to do rather a fancy bit of roof-climbing, and it was then that Mastrovin's fellows saw me, when I was spidering about the battlements. However, in the end I found an open window and got inside and met a pleasant little party. English all of them, except Prince Odalchini.'

'Good Lord, what were they doing there?'

'Justifying Mastrovin's suspicion that England is mixed up with the Evallonian Monarchists. I think they are going to be rather useful people, for they are precisely of your own way of thinking. So is Prince Odalchini, and he believes he can persuade Count Casimir and the rest of his crowd. At any rate, he is going to have a dashed good try.'

'But I don't understand,' said the puzzled Ashie. 'Persuade him about what?'

'Listen very carefully and you'll hear, and prepare for shocks.' Jaikie proceeded to recount the conversation at the castle, and when he mentioned the Archduke Hadrian, Ashie sat up. 'He's my godfather,' he said; 'but I never saw him. No one has. I thought he was dead.'

'Well, he isn't. He's alive but bedridden, and it's only his name we want. Ashie, my dear, within a week the Monarchists are going to put the Archduke Hadrian on the throne. Only it won't be the Archduke, but another, so to speak, of the same name. One of the visitors at the castle is sufficiently like him to pass for him – except with his intimates, of whom there aren't any here. Then in another week Juventus butts in in all the majesty of its youth, ejects the dotard, and sets up Prince John, and everybody lives happy ever after.'

Ashie's reactions to this startling disclosure were many. Bewilderment, doubt, incredulity, even a scandalized annoyance chased each other across his ingenuous face. But the final residuum was relief.

'Jaikie,' he asked hoarsely, 'was that notion yours?'

'No. My line is tactics, not grand strategy. The notion came from the man who is going to play the part of the Archduke. He's an old Scotsman, and his name is McCunn, and he's the best friend I ever had in my life. Ashie, I want to ask a special favour of you. Mr McCunn is playing a bold game, and I'll back him to see it through. I don't know how much you'll come into it yourself, but if you do I want you to do your best for him. There may be a rough-house or two before he escapes over the frontier, and if you have a chance, do him a good turn. Promise.'

'I promise,' said Ashie solemnly. 'But for heaven's sake tell me more.'

'*You* tell me something. Would the rank-and-file of Juventus stand for Prince John?'

'They would. Ninety-nine per cent of them.' But his face was doubtful, so that Jaikie asked where the snag was.

'It's Cousin Mintha. I don't know how she'll take it.'

'That's my job. I'm off tomorrow at break of day. You'll have to let me go, and find me a motor-bicycle.'

'You're going to Mintha?'

'I must. Every man to his job, and that's the one I've been allotted. I can't say I fancy it. I'd sooner have had any other, but there it is, and I must make the best of it. You must give me all the tips you can think of.'

'You'd better get hold of Doctor Jagon first. He is Mintha's chief counsellor.'

'Good. I know him – met him in Scotland. A loquacious old dog, but honest.'

'How are you going to get Prince John out of the Monarchist crowd into Mintha's arms?'

'He isn't with the Monarchists. He's lost.'

'Lost! That spikes our guns.'

'Officially lost. He disappeared a few days ago from the place in the Tirol where Count Casimir had him hidden. The Count thought that Mastrovin had pinched him, and Mastrovin – well, I don't know what Mastrovin thought, but he's raking heaven and earth to find him. Nobody knows where he is except the little party that dined last night in the castle. That's why Casimir will be friendly to the idea of the Archduke, for he has mislaid his Prince.'

'Where is the Prince?' Ashie demanded.

'I had better not tell you. It would be wiser for you not to know – at present. But I promise you I can lay my finger on him whenever we want him. What you've got to do is to put it about that he's with Juventus. That will prepare people's minds and maybe force your cousin's hand. I did a useful bit of work this morning, for I told Mastrovin that Prince John was with the Countess Mintha. That means, I hope, that he will go there after him and annoy your cousin into becoming a partisan.'

Ashie looked at his friend with admiration slightly tempered by awe.

'Mintha is a little devil,' he said slowly; 'but she's a turtle-dove compared to you.'

## CHAPTER NINE

# NIGHT IN THE WOODS

THE great forest of St Sylvester lies like a fur over the patch of country through which the little river Silf – the Amnis Silvestris of the Romans – winds to the Rave. At the eastern end, near the Silf's junction with the main river, stands the considerable town of Krovolin; south of it stretch downs studded with the ugly headgear of oil wells; and west is the containing wall of the mountains. It is pierced by one grand highway, and seamed with lesser roads, many of them only grassy alleys among the beeches.

At one of the cross-roads, where the highway was cut at right angles by a track running from north to south, two cars were halted. The Evallonian summer is justly famed for its settled weather, but sometimes in early August there falls for twenty-four hours a deluge of rain, if the wind should capriciously shift to the west. The forest was now being favoured with such a downpour. All day it had rained in torrents, and now, at eleven o'clock at night, the tempest was slowly abating. It was dark as pitch, but if the eyes had no work for them, the ears had a sufficiency, for the water beat like a drum in the tops of the high trees, and the drip on the sodden ground was like the persistent clamour of a brook.

One of the cars had comprehensively broken down, and no exploration of its intestines revealed either the reason or the cure. It was an indifferent German car, hired some days before in the town of Rosensee; the driver was Peter Wappit, and the occupants were Prince Odalchini and Dickson McCunn. The party from the other car, which was of a good English make, had descended and joined the group beside the derelict. Three men and two women stood disconsolately in the rain, in the glow of the two sets of headlights.

Prince Odalchini had not been idle after the momentous evening session in the House of the Four Winds. He had his own means of sending messages in spite of the vigilance of the Juventus patrols, and word had gone forthwith to the Monarchist leaders and to the secretaries of the Archduke Hadrian far away in the French château. It had been a more delicate business getting the castle party out of the castle confines. The road used was that which led through the cellars of the Turk's Head, and the landlord Proser, who had now to be made a confidant, had proved a tower of strength. So had Randal Glynde, whose comings and goings seemed to be as free and as capricious as the wind. The cars – and Peter Wappit – had been duly fetched, from the Cirque Doré or wherever else they had been bestowed, and early that morning, before Tarta was astir, two batches of prosperous-looking tourists had left the inn, after the hearty farewells which betoken generous tipping. Their goal was the town of Krovolin, but the route they took was not direct. Under Prince Odalchini's guidance –no one would have recognized the Prince, for Mr Glynde had made him up to look like an elderly American with a goatee – they made a wide circuit among the foothills, and entered the Krovolin highway by a route from the south-west.

The weather favoured them, for the Tarta streets were empty when they started, and they met scarcely a traveller on the roads. There was one exception, for about four miles from the town their journey was impeded by part of a travelling circus, which seemed to be bearing south. Its string of horses and lurching caravans took a long time to pass in the narrow road, and during the delay the proprietor of the circus appeared to offer his apologies. This proprietor, a tall, fantastically dressed being with a ragged beard, conversed with various members of the party while the block ahead was being cleared, and much of his conversation was in low tones and in a tongue which was neither German nor Evallonian.

The five figures in the rain had a hurried conference. The oldest of them seemed to be the most perturbed by the *contretemps*. He peered at a map by the light of the lamps, and consulted his watch.

'Krovolin is less than thirty kilometres distant,' he said. 'We could tow this infernal car if we had such a thing as a rope, which we haven't. We can wait here for daylight. Or one car can go on to Krovolin and send out help.'

'I'm for the last,' said Sir Archie. 'I would suggest our all stowing into my car, but it would mean leaving our kit behind, and in these times I don't think that would be safe. I tell you what. You and Mr McCunn get into my car and Peter will drive you. Janet and Alison and I will wait behind with the crock, and you can send help for us as soon as you can wake up a garage.'

Prince Odalchini nodded. 'I think that will be best,' he said. 'I can promise that you will not have long to wait, for at Casimir's headquarters there is ample transport. I confess I do not want to be delayed, for I have much to do. Also it is not wise for me to be loitering in St Sylvester's woods, since at present in this country I am somewhat contraband goods. Mr McCunn too. It is vital that no mishap should befall him. You others are still free people.'

'Right,' said Archie, and began moving the kit of his party from his own car to the derelict. 'You'd both be the better for a hot bath and a rubbing-down, for you've been pretty well soaked all day. We'll begin to expect the relief expedition in about an hour. If I can get this bus started, where do I make for in Krovolin?'

'The castle of Count Casimir,' was the answer. 'It is a huge place, standing over Krovolin as the House of the Four Winds stands over Tarta.'

When the tail-lights of his own car had disappeared, Archie set himself to make another examination of Dickson's, but without success. It was a touring car with a hood of an old-fashioned pattern, which during the day had proved but a weak defence against the weather. The seats were damp and the floor was a shallow pool. Since the rain was lessening, Archie managed to dry the seats and invited the women to make themselves comfortable. Janet Roylance and Alison had both been asleep for the past hour, and had wakened refreshed and prepared to make the best of things. Janet produced chocolate and biscuits and a thermos of coffee, and offered supper, upon which Alison fell ravenously. Archie curled his legs up on the driver's seat and lit his pipe.

'I'm confoundedly sleepy,' he said. 'A long day in the rain always makes me sleepy. I wonder why?' A gout of wet from the canvas of the hood splashed on his face. 'This is a comfortless job. Looks as if the fowls of the air were one up on us tonight. I'll get a crick in my neck if I stick here longer, and I'd get out and roost on the ground if it weren't so sloppy. "A good soft pillow for my good grey head" – how does the thing go?'

' "Were better than this churlish turf of France." ' Alison completed the quotation. 'Have some coffee. It will keep you awake.'

'It won't. That's my paradoxical constitution. Coffee makes me sleepier.' He looked at his watch. 'Moon's due in less than an hour. I call this a rotten place – not the sound of a bird or beast, only that filthy drip. I say, you know, you two look like a brace of owls in a cage.'

It was not an inept comparison for the women in their white waterproofs, which caught dimly the back-glow of the side-lamps. The place was sufficiently eerie, for the trees were felt rather than seen, and the only food for the eye was the glow made by the headlights on the shining black tarmac of the highway. The car had been pushed on to the turf with its nose close to the main road, opposite where the track from the north debouched. Archie to cheer himself began a song, against which his wife stoutly protested.

'That's sacrilege,' she said. 'This is a wonderful place, for there must be fifteen miles of trees round us in every direction. Be quiet, Archie, and, if you can't doze and won't have any supper, think good thoughts.'

'The only good thought I have is the kind of food Count Casimir will give us. Is he the sort of fellow that does himself well, Alison? You're the only one of us that knows him. I want beef steaks – several of 'em.'

'I think so,' the girl answered. 'He praised our food at Castle Gay and he gave me a very good breakfast at Knockraw. But the breakfast might have been Prince John's affair, for he was a hungry young man. . . . I wonder where *he* is now. I don't think he was with Ran's outfit when we passed it this morning.'

'We have properly dissipated our forces,' said Archie. 'However, that's a good rule of strategy if you know how to concentrate them later. I wonder where Jaikie is?'

'Poor Jaikie!' Alison sighed. 'He has an awful job before him, for he is as shy as an antelope really, though he does brazen things. He'll be scared into fits by the Countess Araminta. Dickson was the one to deal with her.'

'He may fall in love with her,' said Archie. 'Quite possible, though she's not the sort I fancy myself. Very beautiful, you know. When I first saw her I thought her wonderful sunburn came out of a bottle, and I considered her too much of a movie star, but when I found it was the gift of Heaven I rather took to her. But Jaikie will have to stand up to her or she'll eat him. I say, Janet, how much use do you think Prince Odalchini is?'

'Good enough for a day with the bitch pack on the hills,' was the drowsy answer. 'Not much good for the Vale and the big fences.'

'Just my own notion. He's too old, and though he's a brave old boy, I don't see him exactly leading forlorn hopes. What about Count Casimir, Alison?'

The girl shook her head. 'I'm not sure. He talks too much.'

'Too romantic, eh?'

'Too sentimental. Dickson's romantic, which is quite a different thing.'

'I see. Well, I take it there's no question about the Countess. By all accounts she's a high-powered desperado. Apart from her it looks as if this show was a bit short of what Bobby Despenser calls "dynamic personages", and that what there are are mostly our own push. There's McCunn – no mistake about him. And Jaikie – not much mistake about Jaikie. And there's your lunatic cousin Glynde. To think that when I saw him at Charles Lamancha's party two months ago I thought him rather a nasty piece of work – too much the tailor's model and the pride of the Lido. Who'd have guessed that he was a cross between a bandit and a bard?'

Conversation had dispelled Archie's languor.

'This promises to be a merry party,' he said. 'The trouble is to know how and when it will stop and what kind of heads we'll have in the morning. Do you realize the desperate way we're behaving? We're taking a hand in another fellow's revolution, and some of us have taken charge of it. And, more by token, who are we? A retired Glasgow grocer that wants to keep a crazy promise – and a Rugger tough from Cambridge – and a girl I've purloined from her parents – and a respectable married woman – and myself, an ornament of the Mother of Parliaments, who should be sitting at Geneva before a wad of stationery making revolution for ever impossible. . . . Hallo, what's this?'

There was a noise like that of a machine-gun which rapidly grew louder, and down the side road from the north came the lights of a motor bicycle. Its rider saw the lamps of the car, slowed down, skidded on the tarmac, and came to a standstill in a clump of fern. A soaked and muddy figure stood blinking in the car lights. So dirty was his face that two of the three did not recognize him. But Alison in a trice was out of the car with a cry of 'Jaikie.'

Mr John Galt had had a laborious day. Ashie had prepared for him a pass, giving him safe conduct to the camp of the Countess Araminta, but had warned him that, except for Juventus, it was of no use, and that Juventus had few representatives in the piece of country through which he must travel. He had also provided a map, and the two had planned an ingenious course, which would take him to the oil-fields by unfrequented by-ways. It had proved too ingenious, for Jaikie had lost his way, and gone too far west into the foothills. The blanket of low clouds and the incessant rain made it impossible for him to get a prospect, and the countryside seemed empty of people. The only cottages he passed were those of woodcutters whose speech he could not understand, and when he mentioned place-names he must have mispronounced them, for they only shook their heads. His one clue was the Silf, of which he had struck the upper waters after midday. But no road followed the Silf, which ran in a deep ravine, and he was compelled to bear north again till he found a road which would take him south through the forest. But he knew now his position on the map, and he hoped to reach his destination before dark, when his machine began to give trouble. Jaikie was a poor mechanic, and it took him three hours before he set the mischief right. By this time the dark skies were darkening further into twilight. There was no shelter for the night in the forest, so he decided to struggle on till at any rate he was out of the trees. The map showed a considerable village on the southern skirts which would surely provide an inn.

His lamp gave him further trouble, for it would not stay lit. He had been soaked since early in the day, for Ashie could not provide him with overalls, and his shabby mackintosh was no protection against the deluge. He was also hungry, for he had long ago finished his supply of biscuits and chocolate. The consolations of philosophy, of which he had a good stock, were nearly exhausted when he skidded on the tarmac of the trunk highway.

Archie laughed boisterously.

'I was just saying that we had dangerously dispersed our forces, but now we've begun to concentrate. Where have you been, my lad?'

Jaikie, grinning sheepishly at Alison, shook the water from his ancient hat, and pushed back a lock of hair which had straggled over his left eye.

'I've been circumnavigating Evallonia. I daresay I've come two hundred miles.'

'Was that purpose or accident?'

'Accident. I've been lost most of the day up on the edge of the hills. And I've got a relic of a bicycle. But what are you doing here?'

'Accident, too. This car of McCunn's soured on him, so we sent him and the Prince on to Krovolin in mine, and Janet and Alison and I are waiting here like Babes in the Wood till we're rescued.'

'Have you any food to spare?' Jaikie asked. He had recovered his spirits, and saw his misadventures in a more cheerful light, since they had led to this meeting.

Alison gave him some coffee out of the thermos and the remains of the biscuits.

'You're a grisly sight, Jaikie,' she said severely. 'I've seen many a tattie-bogle that looked more respectable.'

'I know,' he said meekly. 'I've been looking a bit of a ragamuffin for a long time, but today has put the lid on it.'

'You simply can't show yourself to the Countess like that. You look like a tramp that has been struck by lightning and then drowned.'

'I thought I might find an inn where I could tidy up and get my clothes dried.'

'Nothing will tidy you up. Juventus are a dressy lot, you know, and they'll set the dogs on you.'

'But I have letters from Ashie.' He dived into his inner pocket and drew forth a sodden sheaf. 'Gosh! they're pulp! The rain's got at them and the ink has run. They're unreadable. What on earth am I to do?'

'You're a child of calamity. Didn't you think of oilskin or brown paper? ... You'd better come on with us to Krovolin for a wash and brush up, and Prince Odalchini will find you more decent clothes.'

Jaikie shook his head. 'I must obey orders. That's the first rule of Juventus, and I belong to Juventus now. Properly speaking, I'm at present your enemy. ... I must be getting on, for I've a big job before me. I'm glad you pushed off the Prince and Mr McCunn, for they also have their job. You three are only camp followers.'

'You're an ungrateful beast,' said Alison indignantly, 'to call us camp followers, when you know I came hundreds of miles because you said you needed me. ... Get off then to your assignation. A pretty figure you'll cut in a lady's bower!'

Jaikie's face fell. 'Lord, but duty is an awful thing! I funk that interview more than anything I remember. What, by the way, is her proper name? I must get that right, for Ashie, who's her cousin, calls her Mintha.'

'She is the Countess Araminta Troyos – have you got that? How do you propose to approach her? Mr Galt to see the Countess on private business? Or a courier from the Praefectus of the Western Wing?'

'I'm going first to the Professor man – what's his name – Doctor Jagon. He won't make much of this mass of pulp, but he may remember me from the Canonry. Anyway, I think I can persuade him that I'm honest.'

Jaikie was in the act of wheeling his machine into the track which ran south when he started at a shout of Archie's, and turning his head saw the glow of a great car lighting up the aisle among the trees.

'Well done the Prince,' said Archie. 'Gad, he's done us proud and sent two cars – there's another behind.'

'But they're coming from the wrong direction,' said Janet.

An avalanche of light sped through the darkness, and the faces of the waiting four took on an unearthly whiteness. This was a transformation so sudden and startling that each remained motionless – Jaikie with his hand on his bicycle, Alison holding the thermos, Janet with her head poked out of the car, and Archie with one foot on the step. The lights halted, and the two cars were revealed. They were big roadsters with long rakish bonnets, and in each were two men.

Jaikie happened to be nearest, and he was the first to recognize the occupants. The man at the wheel he did not know, and what he could see of his face was only a long nose between his hat and the collar of his waterproof. But the other who sat beside him was unmistakable. He saw the forward-thrusting jaw, the blunt nose, and the ominous eyes of Mastrovin.

His first thought was to get off, for he considered that he alone of the four was likely to be interfered with. But unfortunately the recognition had been mutual. Mastrovin cried a sharp word of command which brought the two men out of the second car, and he himself with surprising agility leaped on to the road. Jaikie found himself held by strong hands and looking into a most unfriendly face.

'I am in luck,' said Mastrovin. 'We did not finish our conversation the other day, Mr – Galt, I think you said the name was? I am glad to have the opportunity of continuing it, and now I think we shall not be interrupted.'

'Sorry,' said Jaikie, 'but I can't wait.'

'Sorry,' was the answer, 'but you must.'

Jaikie found his hands wrenched from the bicycle handles and his person in the grip of formidable arms. He observed that Mastrovin had turned his attention to the others.

'How are you, Mr Mastrovin?' he heard Archie say in a

voice of falsetto cheerfulness. 'We met, you remember, at Geneva?'

'We have met since,' was the answer. 'We met in a hut in the mountains at Unnutz.' There was an unpleasant suggestion in his tone that that meeting had not been satisfactory.

Mastrovin peered within the car and saw Janet, who apparently did not interest him. But Alison was a different matter. He must have had a good memory for faces, for he instantly recognized her.

'Another from Unnutz,' he said. 'A young lady who took early morning walks in the hills. So!' He cried a word to the driver of his car, which Jaikie did not understand. Then he faced Sir Archie, his brows drawn to a straight line and his mouth puckered in a mirthless smile.

'You are the English who have been in the House of the Four Winds. I did not think I was mistaken. . . . Two of you I have seen elsewhere – at the time I suspected you and now I know. You have meddled in what does not concern you, and you must take the consequences.'

He rasped out the final words in a voice which made it plain that these consequences would not be pleasant. Archie, whose temper was rising, found himself looking into the barrel of a pistol held by a very steady hand.

'Do not be foolish,' Mastrovin said. 'We are four armed men, and we do not take chances. You will accompany us – you and the women. You are in no danger if you do as I bid you, but it is altogether necessary that for a little you should be kept out of mischief.'

Archie's angry protests were checked on his lips, they were so manifestly futile. Janet and he were ordered into the first car, where Mastrovin took the seat opposite them. They were permitted to take their baggage, and that was bundled into the second car, whither Alison accompanied it. The man who was holding Jaikie asked a question, oddly enough in French, to which Mastrovin replied by bidding him put the 'little rat' beside the luggage. Jaikie found himself on a folding seat with a corner of Archie's kit-bag in his ribs and Alison sitting before him.

The cars sped down the Krovolin road, and after some five miles they passed another car coming in the opposite direction. That, thought Jaikie, must be the relief sent by Prince Odalchini. . . . He was in what for him was a rare thing, a mood of black despair. Partly it was due to his weary and sodden body, but the main cause was that he had suddenly realized the true posture of affairs. He had slipped idly into this business, as had the others, regarding it only as an amusing game, a sort of undergraduate 'rag'. There was a puzzle to solve, where wits and enterprise could come into play, but the atmosphere was *opéra-bouffe*, or at the best comedy. The perplexed Ashie was a comic figure; so were Prince Odalchini and the Monarchists; so was the formidable Countess Mintha; so even two days ago had seemed Mastrovin. Alison and Janet and Archie were all votaries of the comic spirit.

But now he realized that there were darker things. Mastrovin's pistol had suddenly dispelled the air of agreeable farce, and opened the veils of tragedy. The jungle was next door to the formal garden – and the beasts of the jungle. As in the library of Castle Gay two years before, he had a glimpse of wolfish men and an underworld of hideous things. That night for the second time he had been called a rat by Mastrovin and his friends, but the insult did not sting him, for he was in the depths of self-abasement. The bitter thought galled his mind that he had brought Alison into a grim business. For that he was alone responsible, and he saw no way out. It was bad that he should be compelled to fail Ashie, for his mission was now hopeless, but it was worse that Alison should have to pay for his folly. Matrovin would never let them go, and if things went ill with Mastrovin's side he would make them pay the penalty. . . . And he was utterly helpless. He knew nothing of the country and could not speak the tongue, he had no money, and only a boy's strength. Prince Odalchini and Dickson might persist in their plot and Juventus continue its high career, but Alison and Janet and Archie and he were out of it for ever, prisoners in some dim underworld of Mastrovin's contriving.

They came out of the forest to find that the rain had stopped and that the moon was rising among ragged clouds. He saw a gleam of water and what looked like the spires of a city. They were being taken to Krovolin, and presently they approached the first houses of its western faubourg. . . . And then something happened which brought a thin ray of hope to Jaikie's distressed soul. There were lights in an adjacent field, and from them came the strains of a fiddle. It was playing Dvořák's 'Humoresque', and that was the favourite tune of Luigi of the Cirque Doré.

## CHAPTER TEN
# AURUNCULEIA

THE familiar melody brought only a momentary refreshment to Jaikie's spirit. The feeling was strong upon him that he had stumbled out of comedy into a melodrama which might soon darken into tragedy. As they entered the city of Krovolin, this mood was increased by the sight of unmistakable pistols in the hands of his guards. Some kind of watch was kept at the entrance, for both cars were stopped and what sounded like passwords were exchanged. Krovolin he knew was the headquarters of the Monarchists, but Mastrovin, having spent all his life in intrigue, was not likely to be stopped by so small a thing as that. It was like his audacity to have domiciled himself in the enemy's camp, and he probably knew most of that enemy's secrets. Jaikie dismissed the thought of appealing to these Monarchist sentries and demanding to be taken to Count Casimir, for he was convinced that at that game he would be worsted. Besides, he could not talk the language.

The hour was late, and there were few people in the well-lit street which descended to the bridge of the river. The cars turned along the edge of the water over vile cobbles, and presently wove their way into a maze of ancient squalor. This was the Krovolin of the Middle Ages, narrow lanes with high houses on both sides, the tops of which bent forward so as to leave only a slender ribbon of sky. Up a side alley they went, and after many twistings came to the entrance of a yard. Here they were clearly expected, for a figure stood on watch outside, who after a word with Mastrovin opened a pair of ancient rickety gates. The car scraped through with difficulty, and Jaikie found himself in a cobbled space which might once have been the courtyard of a house. Now the moon showed it as a cross between a garage and a builder's yard, for it held two other cars, a motor lorry, and what looked like the debris of a recent earthquake. When he got out he promptly fell over a heap of rubble and a sheaf of spades. Somebody had recently been digging there.

He was given no time to prospect. Mastrovin came forward, bowed to Alison and shepherded her to the side of Janet and Archie. Two men took charge of the baggage, and the party were conducted indoors. For a moment Jaikie was left alone, and his hopes rose – perhaps he was too humble for Mastrovin's attentions. He was speedily undeceived, for the man who had been with Mastrovin at Tarta gave an order, and the fellow who had been outside the gate clutched Jaikie's arm. He was also a prisoner, only a more disconsidered one than the others. He was pushed through a door and prodded down a passage and up a narrow staircase, till he reached a little room smelling abominably of garlic. It was a bedroom, for there was a truckle bed and a deal table carrying on it the stump of a candle. His conductor nodded to the bed, on which he flung Jaikie's rucksack, and then departed, after locking the door.

There was a window which seemed to look out upon a pit of darkness. It was not shuttered, but the sashes were firmly bolted. By bending low Jaikie could see upwards to a thin streak of light. The room must be on the street side, and what he saw was a strip of moonlit sky. It must also be on the first floor, for he had ascended only one flight of stairs. If this was meant as a prison it was an oddly insecure one.

But all thought of immediate escape was prevented by the state of his body. He was immeasurably weary, and so sleepy that his eyes were gummed together, a condition which with him usually followed a day of hard exercise in the rain. The stuffiness of the place increased his drowsiness. He sat on the edge of the bed and tried to think, but his mind refused to work. He must have sleep before he could do anything. He stripped off his sodden clothes, and found that he was not so wet as he had feared – of his under-garments only the collar and sleeves of his shirt had suffered. He hung them to dry on rusty nails with which the walls were abundantly provided. There were plenty of bedclothes and they seemed clean, so, wrapping his naked body in them, he was presently asleep.

He woke to a dusty twilight, but there was a hum out-of-doors which suggested that it was full day. A glance from the window showed him that though the sun had not yet got into the alley the morning's life had begun. The place was full of people, and by standing on the sill he could see their heads beneath him. He had been right – the room was on the first floor. It bulged out above the street, so his vision was limited; he saw the people in the middle and on the other side, but not those directly beneath him.

He was very hungry, for he had had scanty rations the day before, and he wondered if breakfast was included in this new régime. There was no sign of it, so he turned his attention to the window. It was of an old-fashioned type, with folding sashes secured by slim iron bars which ran into sockets where they were held by padlocks. Jaikie was a poor mechanic, but he saw that these bolts would be hard to tamper with. If the place were kept sealed up like this no wonder the air was foul. Fortunately the sun could not make itself felt in that cavern of a street, but, all the same, by noon it would be an oven.

This was a disheartening thought, and it took the edge off his appetite. What he particularly wanted was something to drink, beer for preference, but he would have made shift with water. He lay down on the bed, for to look out of the sealed window only distressed him.

As the morning advanced he must have slept again, for the opening of the door woke him with a start. The new-comer was Mastrovin.

He looked very square and bulky in that narrow place, and he seemed to be in an ugly temper. He walked to the window and examined the fastenings. Jaikie observed for the first time that there were no shutters. What if he smashed the glass and dropped into the street? It could not be more than ten yards, and he was as light on his feet as a cat.

Mastrovin may have guessed his thought, for he turned to him with a sour smile.

'Do not delude yourself, Mr – Galt, isn't it? That window is only the inner works of this fortress. Even if you opened it you would be no better off. The outer works would still have to be passed, and they are human walls, stronger than stone and lime.'

'Am I to have any breakfast?' Jaikie asked. 'I don't suppose it's any good asking you what you mean by bringing me here. But most jailers feed their prisoners.'

'I am the exception. Life at present is too hurried with me to preserve the amenities. But a word from you will get you breakfast; liberty also – conditional liberty. You cannot be released just at once, but I will have you taken to a more comfortable place. That word is the present address of Prince John.'

Mastrovin spoke as Jaikie remembered once hearing a celebrated statesman speak when on a visit to Cambridge – slowly, pronouncing his words as if he relished the sound of them, giving his sentences an oratorical swing. It was certainly impressive.

'I haven't the remotest idea,' he said, speaking the strictest truth.

'Let me repeat,' said Mastrovin with a great air of patience. 'The English have long been suspected of dabbling in Monarchist plots. That I have already told you. You have been at Tarta in the House of the Four Winds, which is the home of such plots. Did not my people pick you out of it? You admitted to me that you were acquainted with Prince Odalchini. Where, I ask you now, is Prince Odalchini's master?'

'I tell you, I don't know. As I told you at Tarta, I heard a rumour that he was with some lady called the Countess Mintha.'

'That rumour is a lie,' said Mastrovin fiercely. 'For a moment

I believed it, but I have since proved it a lie. What is more, when you told it me you knew it was a lie. I repeat my question.'

The formidable eyebrows were drawn together, and the whole man became an incarnate menace. Jaikie, empty, headachy, sitting in his shabby clothes on the edge of the bed, felt very small and forlorn. He sometimes felt like that, and on such occasions he would have given all he possessed for another stone of weight and another two inches of height.

'I don't know,' he said. 'How should I know? I'm an ordinary English tourist who came to Evallonia by accident. I don't know anybody in it except Prince Odalchini . . . and Count Paul Jovian – and you.'

'You will know a good deal more about me very soon, my friend. Listen. You are lying – I am a judge of liars, and I can read your face. You are a friend of the three other English – the man and the two women – I find you in the forest in their company. Of these other English I know something. I last saw them in the neighbourhood of Prince John, and it is certain that they know where he has gone and what he is now doing. That knowledge I demand to share – and at once.'

'I don't know what the others know, but I know what I don't know. Though you kept me here till I had a long grey beard I couldn't give you any other answer.'

'You will not stay long enough to grow a beard. Only a little time, but it will not be a pleasant time. You will do what I ask, I think. The others – the others are, as you say in England, of the gentry – a politician and baronet – two ladies of birth. I hold such distinctions as less than rotten wood, but I am a man of the world, and now and then I must submit to the world's valuation. . . . But you are of a different class. You are of the people, the new educated proletariat on which England prides herself. . . . With you I can use elementary methods. . . . With the others in time, if they are stubborn . . . but with you, now.'

He spat out the last words with extraordinary venom. No doubt he thought that in that moment he was being formidable, but as a matter of fact to Jaikie he had ceased to be even impressive. He had insulted him, threatened him, had wakened the small efficient devil that lived at the back of his mind. Jaikie was very angry, and with him wrath always ousted fear. He saw Mastrovin now, not as a sinister elemental force, but as a common posturing bully.

He yawned.

'I wish you'd send me up some breakfast,' he said. 'A cup of coffee, if you've nothing else.'

Mastrovin moved to the door.

'You will get no food until you speak. And no drink. Soon this room will be as hot as hell, and may you roast in it!'

The exhilaration of Jaikie's anger did not last long, though it left behind it a very solid dislike. He realized that he had got himself into an awkward place, from which every exit seemed blocked. But what struck cold at his heart was the peril of Alison. He had heard at the House of the Four Winds of her days at Unnutz, and he realized that Mastrovin had good grounds for connecting her and Janet and Archie with Prince John's disappearance. He must have suspected them from the start, and the sight of the trio at Tarta had clinched his suspicions.

Jaikie tried to set out the case soberly and logically. Prince John was for Mastrovin the key of the whole business. If he could lay hands on him, he could render the Monarchists impotent. He was probably clever enough to have foreseen the possibilites of Juventus taking up the Prince's cause, for without the Prince or somebody like him Juventus would spend its strength on futilities. So long as it had no true figurehead it was at the mercy of Mastrovin and his underworld gang. The settlement of Evallonia was the one thing the latter must prevent: the waters must be kept troubled, for only then could he fish with success. . . . Jaikie saw all that. He saw Mastrovin's purpose, and knew that he would stop at nothing to effect it, for he was outside the pale of the decencies. He meant to try to starve Jaikie himself into submission; but far worse, he would play the same game with Alison and Janet. All four had stumbled out of a bright world into a medieval gloom which stank horribly of the Inquisition.

For a moment his heart failed him. Then his sense of feebleness changed into desperation. He knew that the lives of the other three depended on him, and the knowledge stung him into action. Never had he felt so small and feeble and insignificant, but never so determined. A memory came to him of that night long ago at Huntingtower when the forlorn little band of the Gorbals Die-hards had gone into action. He remembered his cold fury, which had revealed itself in copious tears. Nowadays he did not weep, but if there had been a mirror in the room it would have shown a sudden curious pallor in his small face.

He set to work on the window. His rucksack had been searched for weapons, but he had in his pocket what is known as a sportsman's knife, an implement with one blade as strong as a gully, and with many gadgets. He could do nothing with the bolts and the padlocks, but he might cut into the supporting wood.

It proved an easier task than he had feared. The windows across the street were shuttered, so he could work without fear of detection. The socket of the lower bolt had a metal plate surrounding it, but the upper was fair game for his knife. The wood was old and hard, but after labouring for an hour or two he managed to dig out the square into which the bolt was fastened. That released the top of one window, and he turned to the harder job of the bottom.

Here he had an unexpected bit of luck. There seemed something queer about the lower padlock, and to his joy he found that he could open it. It had been locked without the tongue being driven home. This was providential, for the lower part was solidly sheathed in metal and his knife would have been useless. With some difficulty he drew the stiff bolts, and one half of the window was at his disposal.

Very gingerly he pushed it open. A hot breath of air came in on him from the baking alley, but it was fresh air and it eased his headache. Then cautiously he put his head out and looked down upon the life of the street.

Mastrovin had not been bluffing. There were strong outworks to this fortress, and the outworks were human. Few people were about, perhaps because it was the time for the midday meal. It was a squalid enough place, with garbage in the gutters, but it had one pleasant thing, a runnel of water beside the pavement on the other side, no doubt a leat from the Rave or the Silf. The sight of the stream made his thirst doubly vexatious, but he had no time to think of it, for something else filled his eye. There were men on guard – two below his window, and one on the kerb opposite. This last might have seen him, but happily he was looking the other way.

Jaikie drew in his head and shut the window.

This was disheartening, but at first he was not greatly disheartened. The fact that he had made an opening into the outer world had given him an illogical hope. Also he could now abate the stuffiness of his prison-house. The place was still an oven, but the heat was not stifling. In time evening would come – and night. Might not something be done in the darkness? He had better try to sleep.

But as he lay on the bed he found that his thoughts, quickened by anxiety for Alison, ran in a miserable whirligig and that hope was very low. Mastrovin was taking no chances. Before night he would probably examine the window; in any case his ruffians below were likely to be on stricter duty. His own bodily discomfort added to his depression, for his tongue was like a stick and he was sick with hunger. A man, he knew, could fast for many days if only he had water, but if he had neither food nor drink his strength would soon ebb.

What, he wondered, was Alison doing? Enduring the same misery? Not yet – though that would come unless he could bestir himself. But she and Janet and Archie must be pretty low in mind. . . . He remembered that he was failing Prince Odalchini and Ashie, and doing nothing about the duty which had been assigned him. But that was the least of his troubles. This infernal country might go hang for all he cared. What mattered was Alison.

One thought maddened him – that the four of them had gone clean out of the ken of their friends. It would be supposed that at the moment he was with the Countess Araminta, and no one would begin to ask questions. About the other three there might be some fuss, for the relief car would find the derelict in the forest. Also his motor bicycle, though again that would mean nothing to anybody. Archie and his party were expected to join Dickson and Prince Odalchini at Count Casimir's headquarters. When they did not arrive and the derelict was found there would no doubt be a hue-and-cry. But to what effect? Mastrovin would have covered his tracks, and the last place to look for the missing would be the slums of Krovolin. The best hiding-place was under the light.

The street had been almost noiseless in the early afternoon, when good citizens were taking their siesta. About three it woke up a little. There was a drunken man who sang, and from the window Jaikie saw the top of greengrocers' carts moving country-wards, after the forenoon market. After that there was silence again, and then the tramp of what sounded like a police patrol. Between four and five there was considerable movement and the babble of voices. Perhaps the street was a short cut between two populous thoroughfares; at any rate it became suddenly quite a lively place. There were footsteps outside his door, and Jaikie closed the window in a hurry and lay back on the bed. Was Mastrovin about to pay him another visit? But whoever it was thought better of it, and he heard the steps retreating down the stairs. They had scarcely died away, when out of doors came a sound which set Jaikie's nerves tingling. Someone was playing on a flute, and the tune Dvořák's 'Humoresque'.

He flew to the window and cautiously looked out. There was no watcher on the opposite pavement. Quite a number of people were in the street, shop-girls and clerks for the most part on their way home. A beggar was playing in the gutter, playing a few bars and then supplicating the passers-by. His face was towards Jaikie, who observed that he wore a gipsy cap of cats' skins and for the rest was a ruin of rags. Underneath the cap there was a glimpse of dark southern eyes and a hairy unshaven face.

The man as he played kept an eye on Jaikie's window when he was not ogling the shop-girls. The light in the street was poor, and he seemed to be looking for something and to be uncertain if he had found it. Jaikie stuck his head farther out, and this seemed to give the man what he sought. He took his eyes off the window, finished his tune, and held out his cap for alms. Jaikie saw the gleam of ear-rings. Then he blew into his flute, pocketed it, and started to shamble inconspicuously down the gutter till in a minute he was lost to view.

Jaikie shut the window and resolutely stretched himself on the bed. But now his mood had wholly changed. Luigi had seen him. The Cirque Doré knew his whereabouts. Soon it would be dark, and then Randal Glynde would come to his rescue.

So complete was his trust in Mr Glynde that he forbore to speculate on the nature of the rescue. Had he done so he might have been less confident. Here in this squalid place Mastrovin was all powerful, and he had his myrmidons around him. The Cirque Doré could produce no fighting men; besides, any attempt at violence would probably mean death for those on whose behalf it was used. Mastrovin had the manners of the jungle. . . . Jaikie thought of none of these things. His only fear was of a second visit from his jailer, when, if he proved recalcitrant, he might be removed to other quarters in this dark rabbit warren. At all costs he must remain where Luigi had seen him.

Jaikie had now forgotten both his thirst and hunger. As the room darkened into twilight he lay listening for footsteps on the stairs. The falling of plaster, the scurrying of rats, the creaking of old timbers threw him into a sweat of fear. But no steps came. The noises of the street died away, and the place began to settle into its eerie nightly quiet.

Suddenly from out of doors came a tumultuous and swelling sound. At first Jaikie thought that a rising had broken out in some part of the city, for the noise was that of many people shouting. But there were no shots, and the tumult had no menace in it. It grew louder, so it was coming nearer. He looked into the darkness, and far on his right he saw wavering lights, which from their inconstancy must be torches held in unsteady hands. The thing, whatever it was, was coming down this street.

There was a patter of feet below him, and he saw a mob of urchins, the forerunners of the procession, who trotted ahead with frequent backward glances. The light broadened till the alley was bright as day, but with a fearsome murky glow. It was torches, sure enough, carried and waved by four half-naked figures with leopard-skin mantles and chaplets of flowers on their heads. Behind them came four cream-coloured ponies, also garlanded, drawing a sort ot Roman chariot, and in that chariot was a preposterous figure who now and then stood on its head, now and then balanced itself on the chariot's rim, and all the time kept up a shrill patter and the most imbecile grimaces. He recognized Meleager, the clown of the Cirque Doré.

Jaikie knew that the moment had come. The rescue party had arrived and he must join in it. But how? It was not halting; in a moment Meleager's chariot had passed on, and he was looking down on mules ridden by cowboys. It was not a big circus, and the procession could not last long, so he must get ready for action.

He noticed that it was hugging his side of the street, so that the accompanying crowd was all on the far pavement. That meant that Mastrovin's watchers could not keep their places just below him. Did Randal Glynde mean him to drop down and move under the cover of the cavalcade? That must be it, he thought. He opened the window wide, and sat crouched on the sill.

Then he noticed another thing. The whole procession was not lit up, but clusters of torches and flares alternated with no lights at all, and the dark patches were by contrast very dark. He must descend into one of these tracts of blackness.

Marie Antoinette, or somebody like her, had just passed in a gaudy illuminated coach, and he made ready to drop in her wake. But a special tumult warned him that something odd was following. Though an unlit patch succeeded, the crowd on the opposite kerb seemed to be thicker. Straining his eyes to the right he saw a huge shadow moving up the alley, so close to his side of the street that it seemed to be shouldering the houses. It was high, not six feet below his perch, and it was broad, for it stretched across to the very edge of the runnel of water. And it moved fast, as fast as the trotting ponies, though the sound of its movement was lost in the general din.

It was under him, and, clutching his rucksack, he jumped for it. A hand caught his collar, and dumped him between two pads. He found himself looking up at the stars from the back of the elephant, Aurunculeia.

He lay still for a time, breathing in the clean air, while Mr Glynde was busy with his duties as mahout. Presently they were out of the narrow street, and Aurunculeia swung more freely now that dust was under her and not cobbles.

'You did well,' said Mr Glynde. 'I did not overrate your intelligence.'

Jaikie roused himself.

'Thank God you came,' he said. 'I don't know how to thank you. But the job isn't finished, for there are three other people left in that beastly house.'

'So I guessed,' said Mr Glynde. 'Well, everything in good time. First we must get you safely off. We cut things pretty fine, you know. Just as you joined our convoy someone came into your room with a light. I got a glimpse of his face and it was familiar. At present he is probably looking for you in the street. . . . But he may push his researches farther.'



CHAPTER ELEVEN

## THE BLOOD-RED ROOK

JAIKIE was not conscious of most of that evening's ride. Thirty-six hours of short commons and the gentle swaying of Aurunculeia made him feel slightly sea-sick and then very drowsy. He found a strap in the trappings through which he crooked his arm, and the next he knew he was being lifted down a step-ladder by Randal Glynde in a place which smelt of horses and trodden herbage.

Mr Glynde was a stern host. He gave him a bowl of soup with bread broken into it, but nothing more. 'You must sleep before you eat properly,' he said, 'or you'll be as sick as a dog.' Jaikie, who was still a little light-headed, would have gladly followed this advice, when something in Randal's face compelled his attention. It was very grave, and he remembered it only as merry. The sight brought back to him his immediate past, and the recollection of the stifling room in the ill-omened house effectively dispelled his drowsiness. He had left Alison behind him.

'I can't stay here,' he croaked. 'I must get the others out. ... That man's a devil. He'll stick at nothing. ... What about Count Casimir? He's a big swell here, isn't he? and he has other Monarchists with him. ... Where are we now? I should get to him at once, for every hour is important.' Then, as Randal remained silent, with the same anxious eyes, he said, 'Oh, for God's sake, do something. Make a plan. You know this accursed country and I don't.'

'You have just escaped from the most dangerous place in Europe,' said Randal solemnly. 'I think you are safe now, but it was a narrower thing than you imagine. The wild beast in his lair, and a pretty well-defended lair it is. You may smoke him out, but it may be a bad thing for those he has got in the lair beside him.'

Jaikie's wits were still muddled, but one feeling was clear and strong, a horror of that slum barrack in the mean street.

'Are there no police in Krovolin?' he demanded.

'The ordinary police would not be much use in what has been a secret rendezvous for years. The place is a honeycomb. You might plant an army round it, and Mastrovin would slip out – and leave ugly things behind him.'

Jaikie shuddered.

'Then I'm going back. You don't understand. ... I can't go off and leave the others behind. You see, I brought your cousin here ... Alison –' He ended his sentence with something like a moan.

Randal for the first time smiled. 'I expected something like that from you. It may be the only way – but not yet. Alison and the Roylances are not in immediate danger. At present to Mastrovin they are important means of knowledge. When that fails they may become hostages. Only in the last resort will they be victims.'

'Give me a cigarette, please,' said Jaikie. He suddenly felt the clouds of nausea and weariness roll away from him. He had got his second wind. 'Now tell me what is happening.'

Randal nodded to a sheaf of newspapers on the floor of the caravan.

'The popular press, at least the Monarchist brand of it, announces that the Archduke Hadrian has crossed the Evallonian frontier. One or two papers say that he is now in Krovolin. They all publish his portrait – the right portrait. Prince Odalchini's staff-work is rather good.'

Jaikie found himself confronted with a large-size photograph of Dickson McCunn. It must have been recently taken, for Mr McCunn was wearing the clothes which he had worn at Tarta.

'I have other news,' Randal continued, 'which is not yet in the press. The Archduke, being an old man, is at present resting from the fatigue of his journey. Tomorrow afternoon, accompanied by his chief supporters, he will move to Melina through a rejoicing country. It has all been carefully stage-managed. His escort, two troops of the National Guard, arrive here in the morning. The distance is only fifteen miles, and part of the road will be lined with His Royal Highness's soldiers. Melina is already occupied on his behalf, and the Palace is being prepared for his reception.'

'Gosh!' said Jaikie. 'How are people taking that?'

'Sedately. The Evallonians are not a politically-minded nation. They are satisfied that the hated Republic is no more, and will accept any Government that promises stability. As for His Royal Highness, they have forgotten all about him, but they have a tenderness for the old line, and they believe him to be respectable.'

'He is certainly that. How about Juventus?'

'Juventus is excited, desperately excited, but not about the Archduke. They regard him as a piece of antiquated lumber, the last card of a discredited faction. But the rumour has gone abroad that Prince John has joined them, and that has given them what they have been longing for, a picturesque figurehead. I have my own ways of getting news, and the same report has come in from all the Wings. The young men are huzzaing for the Prince, who like themselves is young. Their presses are scattering his photograph broadcast. Their senior officers, many of whom are of the old families, are enthusiastic. Now at least the wheel has come full circle for them – they have a revolution of youth which is also a restoration, and youth will lead it. They are organized to the last decimal, remember, and they have the bulk of the national feeling behind them, except here in Krovolin and in the capital. They are sitting round the periphery of Evallonia waiting for the word to close in. Incidentally they have shut the frontier, and are puzzled to understand how the Archduke managed to cross it without their knowledge. When the word is given there will be a march on Melina, just like Mussolini's march on Rome. There is only one trouble – the Countess Araminta.'

'Yes. What about her?' was Jaikie's gloomy question.

'That young woman,' said Randal, 'must be at present in a difficult temper and not free from confusion of mind. She has not been consulted about Prince John; therefore she will be angry. All Juventus believes that the Prince is now with her Wing, but she knows that to be untrue. She has not seen His Royal Highness since she was a little girl. . . . Besides, there's another complication. I said that Juventus was waiting. But not the Countess. Some days ago she took the bit between her teeth, and started to march on Krovolin. My information is that tonight she is encamped less than ten miles from this city. Tomorrow should see her at its gates.'

'Then she'll pinch Mr McCunn before he starts.'

'Precisely. At any rate there will be fighting, and for the sake of the future it is very necessary that there should be no fighting. At the first rifle-shot the game will be out of hand.'

'Can't you get him off sooner?'

'Apparently no. Some time is needed for the arrangements in Melina, and already the programme has had to be telescoped.'

'What a hideous mess! What's to be done! She must be stopped.'

'She must. That is the job to which I invite your attention.'

'Me!' The ejaculation was wrung from Jaikie by a sudden realization of the state of his garments. His flannel bags were shrunken and to the last degree grimy, his tweed jacket was a mere antique, and his shoes gaped, his hands and presumably his face were black with dust. Once again he felt, sharp as a toothache, his extreme insignificance.

Randal followed his glance. 'You are certainly rather a scarecrow, but I think I can make you more presentable. You must go. You see, you are the last hope.'

'Couldn't you – ?' Jaikie began.

'No,' was the decided answer. 'I have my own work to do, which is as vital as yours. There is one task before you. You must get her to halt in her tracks.'

'She won't listen to me.'

'No doubt she won't – at first. She'll probably have you sent to whatever sort of dungeon a field force provides. But you have one master-card.'

'Prince John?'

'Prince John. She must produce him or she will be put to public shame, and she hasn't a notion where to look for him. She is a strong-headed young woman, but she can't defy the public opinion of the whole of Juventus. You alone know where the Prince is.'

'I don't.'

'You will be told . . . so you can make your terms. From what I remember of her you will have a rough passage, but you are not afraid of the tantrums of a minx.'

'I am. Horribly.'

Randal smiled. 'I don't believe you are really afraid of anything.'

'I'm in a desperate funk of one thing, and that is, what is going to happen to Alison.'

'So am I. You are fond, I think, of Cousin Alison. Perhaps you are lovers?'

Jaikie blushed furiously.

'I have been in love with her for two years.'

'And she?'

'I don't know. I hope . . . some day.'

'You are a chilly Northern pair of children. Well, she is my most beloved and adored kinswoman, and for her sake I would commit most crimes. We are agreed about that. It is for the sake of Alison and the sweet Lady Roylance that you and I are going into action. I wait in Krovolin and keep an eye on Mastrovin. He is a master of ugly subterranean things, but I also have certain moles at my command. There will be a watch kept on the Street of the White Peacock – that is the name of the dirty alley – a watch of which our gentleman will know nothing. When the Cirque Doré mobilizes itself it has many eyes and ears. For you the task is to immobilize the Countess. Your price is the revelation of Prince John. Your reason, which she will assuredly ask, is not that the Archduke should get safely to Melina – for remember your sympathies are with Juventus. It is not even that the coming revolution must not be spoiled by bloodshed, and thereby get an ill name in Europe. She would not listen to you on that matter. It is solely that your friends are in the power of Mastrovin, whom she venomously hates. If she enters Krovolin Mastrovin will be forced into action, and she knows what that will mean.'

Jaikie saw suddenly a ray of hope.

'What sort of woman is she?' he asked. 'Couldn't I put it to her that she has not merely to sit tight, but has to help to get my friends out of Mastrovin's clutches? I can't do anything myself, for I don't know the place or the language. But she is sure to have some hefty fellows with her to make up a rescue party. She can't refuse that if she's anything of a sportsman. It's a fair deal. She'll have the Prince if she gives me my friends. By the way, I suppose you can produce the man when I call for him?'

'I can. What's more, I can give you something if she asks for proof. It's the mourning ring prepared for his late Majesty, which only the royal family possess. She'll recognize it.'

Randal's gravity had slightly melted. 'I think you could do with a drink now,' he said. 'Brandy and soda. I prescribe it, for it's precisely what you need. Do you know, I think you have hit upon the right idea. Get her keen on doing down Mastrovin, and she won't bother about the price. She's an artist for art's sake. Make it a fight between her and the Devil for the fate of three innocents and she'll go raging into battle. I believe she has a heart, too. Most brave people have.'

As he handed Jaikie his glass, he laughed.

'There's a good old English word that exactly describes your appearance. You look "varminty" – like a terrier that has been down a badger's earth, and got its nose bitten, and is burning to go down again.'

The car, a dilapidated Ford, fetched a wide circuit in its southward journey, keeping well to the west of Krovolin, and cutting at right angles the road from the forest of St Sylvester. The morning was hazy and close, but after the last two days it seemed to Jaikie to be as fresh as April. They crossed the Silf, and saw it winding to its junction with the Rave, with the city smoking in the crook of the two streams. Beyond the Rave a rich plain stretched east towards the capital, and through that plain Dickson that afternoon must make his triumphant procession. Even now his escort would be jingling Krovolinwards along its white roads.

Jaikie had recovered his bodily vigour, but never in his life had he felt so nervous. The thought of Alison shut up in Mastrovin's den gnawed like a physical pain. The desperate seriousness of his mission made his heart like lead. It was the kind of thing he had not been trained to cope with; he would do his best, but he had only the slenderest hope. The figure of the Countess Araminta grew more formidable the more he thought about her. Alison at Tarta had called her the Blood-red Rook – that had been Lady Roylance's name for her – and had drawn her in colours which suggested a cross between a vampire and a were-wolf. Wild, exotic, melodramatic, and reckless – that had been the impression left on his mind. And women were good judges of each other. He could deal with a male foreigner like Ashie whom Cambridge had partially tamed, but what could he do with the unbroken female of the species? He knew less about women than he knew about the physics of hyperspace.

His forebodings made him go over again his slender assets. He knew the line he must take, provided she listened to him. But how to get an audience? The letters which Ashie had given him, being written on official flimsies, had been reduced to a degraded pulp by the rain, and he had flung them away. He had nothing except Randal's ring, and that seemed to him an outside chance. His one hope was to get hold of Dr Jagon. Jagon would remember him from the Canonry – or, on the other hand, he might not. Still, it was his best chance. If he were once in Jagon's presence he might be able to recall himself to him, and Jagon was the Countess's civilian adviser. But his outfit might never get near Jagon; it might be stopped and sent packing by the first sentry.

It was not a very respectable outfit. The car was a disgrace. He himself had been rigged up by Randal in better clothes than his own duds, but he realized that they were not quite right, for the Cirque Doré was scarcely abreast of the fashions. He had a pair of riding breeches of an odd tubular shape, rather like what people at Cambridge wore for beagling, and they were slightly too large for him. His coat was one of those absurd Norfolk jacket things that continentals wear, made of smooth green cloth with a leather belt, and it had been designed for someone of greater girth than himself. He had, however, a respectable pair of puttees, and his boots, though too roomy, were all right, being a pair of Randal's own. He must look, he thought, like a shop-boy on a holiday, decent but not impressive.

Then for the first time he took notice of the chauffeur. He was one of the circus people, whom Randal had vouched for as a careful driver who knew the country. The chief point about the man's appearance was that he wore a very ancient trench burberry, which gave him an oddly English air. He was apparently middle-aged, for he had greying side whiskers. His cheeks had the pallor which comes from the use of much grease-paint. There was nothing horsy about him, so Jaikie set him down as an assistant clown. He looked solemn enough for that. He wondered what language he spoke, so he tried him in French, telling him that their first business was to ask for Professor Jagon.

'I know,' was the answer. 'The boss told me that this morning.'

'Where did you learn English?' Jaikie asked, for the man spoke without the trace of an accent.

'I am English,' he said. 'And I picked up a bit of French in the war.'

'Do you know Evallonia?'

'I've been here off and on for twenty years.'

The man had the intonations of a Londoner. It appeared that his name was Newsom, and that he had first come to Evallonia as an under-chauffeur in a family which had been bankrupted by the war. He had gone home and fought on the British side in a Royal Fusilier battalion, but after the Armistice he had again tried his fortune in Evallonia. His luck had been bad, and Mr Glynde had found him on his uppers, and given him a job in the circus. Transport was his principal business, but he rather fancied himself as a singer, and just lately had been giving Meleager a hand. 'We're a happy family in the old Cirque,' he said, 'and don't stick by trade-union ways. I can turn my hand to most anything, and I like a bit of clowning now and then. The trouble is that the paint makes my skin tender. You were maybe noticing that I'm not very clean-shaved this morning.' And he turned a solemn mottled face for Jaikie's inspection.

In less than an hour they came out of the woods into a country of meadows which rose gently to a line of hills. They also came into an area apparently under military occupation. A couple of Greenshirts barred the road. Jaikie tried them in English, but they shook their heads, so he left it to Newsom, who began to explain in Evallonian slowly, as if he were hunting for words, and with an accent which to Jaikie's ears sounded insular. There was a short discussion, and then the Greenshirts nodded and stood aside. 'They say,' said Newsom, 'that Dr Jagon's quarters are at the farm a kilometre on, but they believe that he is now with the Wing-Commander. But they don't mind our calling on him. I said you were an old friend of his, and brought important news from Krovolin.'

The next turn of the road revealed a very respectable army on the march. The night bivouac had been in a broad cup formed by the confluence of two streams. There was a multitude of little tents, extensive horse-lines, and a car park, and already there were signs that movement was beginning. Men were stamping out the breakfast fires, and saddling horses, and putting mule teams to transport wagons, and filling the tanks of cars. 'I must hurry,' thought Jaikie, 'or that confounded woman will be in Krovolin this afternoon.' His eye caught a building a little to the rear of the encampment, which had the look of a small hunting-lodge. The green and white flag of Juventus was being lowered from its flagstaff.

There was no Jagon at the farm, but there was a medical officer who understood English. To him Jaikie made the appeal which he thought most likely to convince. He said he was a friend of the Professor – had known him in England – and brought a message to him of extreme importance.

The officer rubbed his chin. 'You are behind the fair,' he said. 'You come from Krovolin? Well, we shall be in Krovolin ourselves in three hours.'

'That is my point,' said Jaikie. 'There's something about Krovolin which you should hear. It concerns Mastrovin.'

The name produced an effect.

'Mastrovin! You come from him?' was the brusque question.

'Only in the sense that I escaped last night from his clutches. I've something to tell the Professor about Mastrovin which may alter all your plans.'

The officer looked puzzled.

'You are English?' he demanded. 'And he?' He nodded towards Newsom.

'Both English, and both friends of Juventus. I came here as a tourist and stumbled by accident on some important news which I thought it my duty to get to Professor Jagon. He is the only one of you I know. I tell you, it's desperately important.'

The officer pondered.

'You look an honest little man. I have my orders, but we of the special services are encouraged to think for ourselves. The Professor is at this moment in conference with the Praefectus, and cannot be interrupted. But I will myself take you to headquarters, and when he is finished I will present you. Let us hurry, for we are about to march.'

He stood on the footboard of the car, and directed Newsom along a very bumpy track, which skirted the horse-lines, and led to the courtyard of the hunting lodge. Here was a scene of extreme busyness. Greenshirts with every variety of rank-badges were going in and out of the building, a wagon was being loaded with kit, and before what seemed to be the main entrance an orderly was leading up and down a good-looking chestnut mare. Out of this door emerged the burly figure of a man, with a black beard and spectacles, who was dressed rather absurdly in khaki shorts and a green shirt, the open neck of which displayed a hairy chest.

'The Professor,' said the medical officer. He saluted. 'Here is an Englishman, sir, who says he knows you and has an urgent message.'

'I have no time for Englishmen,' said Jagon crossly. His morning conference seemed to have perturbed him.

'But you will have time for me,' said Jaikie. 'You remember me, sir?'

The spectacled eyes regarded Jaikie sourly. 'I do not.'

'I think you do. Two years ago I came to breakfast with you at Knockraw in Scotland. I helped you then, and I can help you now.'

'Tchut! That is a long-closed chapter.' But the man's face was no longer hostile. He honoured Jaikie with a searching stare. 'You are that little Scotsman. I recall you. But if you have come from my companions of that time it is useless. I have broken with them.'

'I don't come from them. I come from the man you beat two years ago – I escaped from him twelve hours ago. I want to help you to beat him again.'

Jagon looked at the medical officer and the medical officer looked at Jagon. The lips of both seemed to shape, but not to utter, the same word. 'I think the Englishman is honest, sir,' said the officer.

'What do you want?' Jagon turned to Jaikie.

'Five minutes' private talk with you.'

'Come in here. Keep an eye on that chauffeur' – this to the officer. 'We know nothing about him.'

'I'm an Englishman, too,' said Newsom, touching his cap.

'What the devil has mobilized the British Empire this morning?' Jagon led Jaikie into a little stone hall hung with sporting trophies and then into a cubby-hole where an orderly was packing up papers. He dismissed the latter, and shut the door.

'Now let's have your errand. And be short, for we move in fifteen minutes.'

Jaikie felt no nervousness with this hustled professor. In half a dozen sentences he explained how he had got mixed up in Evallonia's business, but he did not mention Prince Odalchini, though he made much of Ashie. 'I want to see the Countess Araminta. And you, who know something about me, must arrange it.'

'You can't. The Praefectus sees no strangers.'

'I must. If I don't she'll make a godless mess of the whole business.'

'You would tell her that?' said Jagon grimly. 'The Praefectus is not so busy that she cannot find time to punish insolence.'

'It isn't insolence – it's a fact. I didn't talk nonsense to you at Knockraw, and it was because you believed me that things went right. You must believe me now. For Heaven's sake take me to the Countess and let's waste no more time.'

'You are a bold youth,' said the Professor. 'Bold with the valour of ignorance. But the Praefectus will see no one. Perhaps this evening when we have entered Krovolin –'

'That will be too late. It must be now.'

'It cannot be. I have my orders. The Praefectus is not one to be disobeyed.' The eyes behind the spectacles were troubled, and the black beard did not hide the twitching of the lips. He reminded Jaikie of a don of his acquaintance in whom a bonfire in the quad induced a nervous crisis. His heart sank, for he knew the stubbornness of the weak.

'Then I am going direct to the Countess.'

A clear voice rang outside in the hall, an imperative voice, and a woman's. Jaikie's mind was suddenly made up. Before Jagon could prevent him, he was through the door. At the foot of the stairs were two Greenshirts at attention, and on the last step stood a tall girl.

Indignation with the Professor and a growing desperation had banished Jaikie's uneasiness. He saluted in the Greenshirt fashion and looked her boldly in the face. His first thought was that she was extraordinarily pretty. What had Alison meant by drawing the picture of a harpy? She was dressed like Ashie in green riding breeches and a green tunic, and the only sign of the Blood-red Rook was her scarlet collar and the scarlet brassard on her right arm. Her colouring was a delicate amber, her eyes were like pools in a peaty stream, and her green forester's hat did not conceal her wonderful dead-black hair. Her poise was the most arrogant that he had ever seen, for she held her little head so high that the world seemed at an infinite distance beneath her. As her eyes fell on him they changed from liquid topaz to a hard agate.

She spoke a sharp imperious word and her voice had the chill of water on a frosty morning.

Audacity was his only hope.

'Madam,' said Jaikie. 'I have forced myself upon you. I am an Englishman, and I believe that you have English blood. I implore your help, and I think that in turn I can be of use to you.'

She looked over his head, at the trembling Jagon and the stupefied Greenshirts. She seemed to be asking who had dared to disobey her.

'I take all the blame on myself,' said Jaikie, trying to keep his voice level. 'I have broken your orders. Punish me if you like, but listen to me first. You are leading a revolution, and in a revolution breaches of etiquette are forgiven.'

At last she condescended to lower her eyes to him. Something in his face or his figure seemed to rouse a flicker of interest.

'Who is this cock-sparrow?' she asked, and looked at Jagon.

'Madam,' came the trembling answer, 'he is a Scotsman who once in Scotland did me a service. He is without manners, but I believe he means honestly.'

'I see. A *revenant* from your faulty past. But this is no time for repaying favours. You will take charge of him, Professor, and be responsible for him till my further orders.' And she passed between the sentries towards the door.

Jaikie managed to plant himself in her way. He played his last card.

'You must listen to me. Please!' He held out his hand.

It was his face that did it. There was something about Jaikie's small, wedge-shaped countenance, its air of innocence with just a hint of devilry flickering in the background, its extreme and rather forlorn youth, which most people found hard to resist. The Countess Araminta looked at him and her eyes softened ever so little. She looked at the outstretched hand in which lay a ring. It was a kind of ring she had seen before, and the momentary softness left her face.

'Where did you get that?' she demanded in a voice in which imperiousness could not altogether conceal excitement.

'It was given me to show to you as a proof of my good faith.'

She said something in Evallonian to the guards and the Professor, and marched into the cubby-hole which Jaikie had lately left. 'Follow,' said the Professor hoarsely. 'The Praefectus will see you – but only for one minute.'

Jaikie found himself in a space perhaps six yards square, confronting the formidable personage the thought of whom had hitherto made his spine cold. Rather to his surprise he felt more at his ease. He found that he could look at her steadily, and what he saw in her face made him suddenly change all his prearranged tactics. She was a young woman, but she was not in the least a young woman like Alison or Janet Roylance. He was no judge of femininity, but there was not much femininity here as he understood it. . . . But there was something else which he did understand. Her eyes, the way she held her head, the tones of her voice had just that slightly insecure arrogance, that sullen but puzzled self-confidence, which belonged to a certain kind of public-school boy. He had studied the type, for it was not his own, and he had had a good deal to do with the handling of it. One had to be cautious with it, for it was easy to rouse obstinate, half-comprehended scruples, but it was sound stuff if you managed it wisely. His plan had been to propose a bargain with one whom he believed to be the slave of picturesque ambitions. In a flash he realized that he had been mistaken. If he suggested a deal it would be taken as insolence, and he would find himself pitched neck-and-crop into the yard. He must try other methods.

'Countess,' he said humbly, 'I have come to you with a desperate appeal. You alone can help me.'

He was scrupulously candid. He told how he had come to Evallonia, of his meeting with Ashie, of his visit to Prince Odalchini. He told how he had brought Alison and the Roylances to the House of the Four Winds. 'It was none of my business,' he admitted. 'I was an interfering fool, but I thought it was going to be fun, and now it's liker tragedy.'

'The Roylances,' she repeated. 'They were at Geneva. I saw them there. The man is the ordinary English squire, and the woman is pleasant. Miss Westwater too I know – I have met her in England. Pretty and blonde – rather fluffy.'

'Not fluffy,' said Jaikie hotly.

She almost smiled.

'Perhaps not fluffy. Go on.'

He told of Mastrovin, sketching hurriedly his doings in the Canonry two years before. He described the meeting in the Forest of St Sylvester, when he himself had been on the way to the Countess with letters from Ashie. 'I can't give you them,' he said, 'for the rain pulped them.' He described the house in the Street of the White Peacock and he did not mince his words. But he skated lightly over his escape, for he felt that it would be bad tactics to bring Randal Glynde into the story at that stage.

There could be no question of her interest. At the mention of Mastrovin her delicate brows descended and she cross-examined him sharply. The Street of the White Peacock, where was it? Who was with Mastrovin? She frowned at the name of Dedekind. Then her face set.

'That rabble is caught,' she said. 'Trapped. Tonight it will be in my hands.'

'But the rabble is desperate. You have an army, Countess, and you can surround it, but it will die fighting with teeth and claws. And if it perishes my friends will perish with it.'

'That I cannot help. If fools rush in where they are not wanted they must take the consequences.'

'You don't wish to begin with a tragedy. You have the chance of a bloodless revolution which for its decency will be unlike all other revolutions. You mustn't spoil it. If it starts off with the murder of three English its reputation will be tarnished.'

'The murders will have been done by our enemies, and we shall avenge them.'

'Of course. But still you will have taken the gloss off Juventus in the eyes of England – and of Europe.'

'We care nothing for foreign opinion.'

Jaikie looked her boldly in the eyes.

'But you do. You must. You are responsible people, who don't want merely to upset a Government, but to establish a new and better one. Public opinion outside Evallonia will mean a lot to you.'

Her face had again its arrogance.

'That is dictation,' she said, 'and who are you to dictate.'

'I am nobody, but I must plead for my friends. And I am hot on your side. I want you to begin your crusade with an act of chivalry.'

'You would show me how to behave?'

'Not I. I want you to show me and the world how to behave, and prove that Juventus stands for great things. You are strong enough to be merciful.'

He had touched the right note, for her sternness patently unbent.

'What do you want me to do?' Her tone was almost as if she spoke to an equal.

'I want you to halt where you are. I want you to let me have half a dozen of your best men to help me to get my friends out of Mastrovin's hands. If we fail, then that's that. If we succeed, then you occupy Krovolin and do what you like with Mastrovin. After that you march on Melina with a good conscience, and God prosper you!'

She looked at him fixedly and her mouth drew into a slow smile.

'You are a very bold young man. Are you perhaps in love with Miss Westwater?'

'I am,' said Jaikie, 'but that has nothing to do with the point. I brought her to this country, and I can't let her down. You know you could never do that yourself.'

Her smile broadened.

'I am to stop short in a great work of liberation to rescue the lady-love of a preposterous Englishman.'

'Yes,' said Jaikie, 'because you know that you would be miserable if you didn't.'

'You think you can bring it off?'

'Only with your help.'

'I am to put my men under your direction?'

'We'll make a plan together. I'll follow any leader.'

'If I consent, you shall lead. If I am to trust you in one thing I must trust you in all.'

Jaikie bowed. 'I am at your orders,' he said.

She continued to regard him curiously.

'Miss Westwater is noble,' she said. 'Are you?'

Jaikie was puzzled at the word. Then he understood.

'No, I'm nobody, as I told you. But we don't bother about these things so much in England.'

'I see. The Princess and the goose-boy. I do not quarrel with you for that. You are like our Juventus, the pioneer of a new world.'

Jaikie knew that he had won, for the agate gleam had gone out of her eyes. He had something more to say and he picked his words, for he realized that he was dealing with a potential volcano.

'You march on Melina,' he said, 'you and the other Wings of Juventus. But when you march you must have your leader.'

Her eyes hardened. 'What do you know of that?' she snapped.

'I have seen the newspapers and I have heard people talking.' Jaikie walked with desperate circumspection. 'The Republic has fallen. The Monarchists with their old men cannot last long. Juventus must restore the ancient ways, but with youth to lead.'

'You mean?' Her eyes were stony.

'I mean Prince John,' he blurted out, with his heart sinking. She was once more the Valkyrie, poised like a falcon for a swoop. He saw the appropriateness of Alison's name for her.

'You mean Prince John?' she repeated, and her tone was polar ice.

'You know you can't put a king on the throne unless you have got him with you. Juventus is wild for Prince John, but nobody knows where he is. I know. I promise to hand him over to you safe and sound.'

There were many things in her face – interest, excitement, relief, but there was also a rising anger.

'You would make a bargain with me?' she cried. 'A huckster's bargain – with *me*!'

Strangely enough, the surprise and fury in her voice made Jaikie cool. He knew this kind of tantrum, but not in the Countess's sex.

'You mustn't talk nonsense, please,' he said. 'I wouldn't dare to make a bargain with you. I appealed to you, and out of your chivalry you are going to do what I ask. I only offer to show my gratitude by doing what I can for you. Besides, as I told you, I'm on your side. I mean what I say. You can go back on me and refuse what I ask, and I'll still put you in the way of getting hold of Prince John, if you'll give me a couple of days. I can't say fairer than that. A mouse may help a lion.'

For a second or two she said nothing. Then her eyes fell.

'You are the first man,' she said, 'who has dared to tell me that I am a fool.'

'I didn't,' Jaikie protested, with a comfortable sense that things were going better.

'You did, and I respect you for it. I see that there was no insult. What I do for you – if I do it – I do because I am a Christian and a good citizen. . . . For the other thing, what proof have you that you can keep your word?'

Jaikie held out the ring. The Countess took it, studied the carving on the carnelian, and returned it. She was smiling.

'It is a token and no more. If you fail –'

'Oh, have me flayed and boiled in oil,' he said cheerfully. 'Anything you like as long as you get busy about Mastrovin.'

She blew a silver whistle, and spoke a word to the orderly who entered. Then Jagon appeared, and to him she gave what sounded like a string of orders, which she enumerated on her slim gloved fingers. When he had gone she turned to Jaikie.

'I have countermanded the march for today. Now we go to choose your forlorn hope. You will lunch with me, for I have some things to say to you and many to ask you. What is your name, for I know nothing of you except that you are in love with Miss Westwater and are a friend of my cousin Paul?'

'Galt,' she repeated. 'It is not dignified, but it smells of the honest earth. You will wait here, Galt, till I send for you.'

Jaikie, left alone, mopped his brow, and, there being no chairs in the place, sat down on the floor, for he felt exhausted. He was not accustomed to this kind of thing.

'Public-school,' he reflected. 'Best six-cylinder model. Lord, how I love the product and dislike the type! But fortunately the type is pretty rare.'

## CHAPTER TWELVE

# THE STREET OF THE WHITE PEACOCK

JAIKIE rubbed the dust from his eyes, for he had landed in a heap of debris, and looked round for Newsom. Newsom was at his elbow, having exhibited an unexpected agility. He was still a little puzzled to learn how Newsom came to be with him. After his business with the Countess he had found him waiting with the car, stubbornly refusing to move till he had the word from his master. He had dispatched him with a message to Randal Glynde and the man had returned unbidden. 'Boss's orders,' he had explained. 'The boss says I'm to stick to you, sir, till he tells me to quit.' And when in the evening the expeditionary force left the camp Newsom had begged for a place in it, had indeed insisted on being with Jaikie in whatever part the latter was cast for. It was not 'boss's orders' this time, but the plea of a sportsman to have a hand in the game, and Jaikie, looking at the man's athletic figure and remembering that he was English, had a little doubtfully consented. Now he was more comfortable about that consent. At any rate Newsom was an adept at climbing walls.

The Countess had allowed Jaikie to pick six Greenshirts, herself showing a most eager interest in their selection. They were all young townsmen, for this was not a job for the woodlander or mountaineer, and four of them could speak English. All were equipped with pistols, electric torches, and the string-soled shoes of the country. As reserves he had twenty of a different type, men picked for their physique and fighting value. He thought of them as respectively his scouts and shock troops. He had made his dispositions pretty much in the void, but he reasoned that he wanted light men for his first reconnaissance, and something heavier if it came to a scrap. His judgement had been sound, for when in the evening the party, by devious ways and in small groups, concentrated at the Cirque Doré encampment, he found that Randal Glynde had had the same notion.

Randal, having had the house in the Street of the White Peacock for some time under observation, and knowing a good deal about its antecedents, had come to certain conclusions. The place was large and rambling, and probably contained cellars extending to the river, for in old days it had been the dwelling of a great merchant of Krovolin. There was no entrance from the street, the old doorway having been built up, and coming and going was all by the courtyard at the back. The prisoners might be anywhere inside a thousand square yards of masonry, but the odds were that they were lodged, as Jaikie had been, in rooms facing the street. The first thing was to get rid of the watchers there, and this was the immediate task of the six Greenshirts. But it must be done quickly and circumspectly so as not to alarm the inmates. There were five watchers by day and three by night, the latter taking up duty at sundown. If a part of the Cirque passed through the street in the first hours of the dark, it would provide excellent cover for scragging the three guards, and unobtrusively packing them into one of the vans. The street must be in their hands, for it was by the street-front that escape must be made. Randal, who had become a very grave person, was insistent upon the need for speed and for keeping the business with his watchers secret from Mastrovin. Mastrovin must not be alarmed, for, like Jaikie, he feared that, if he were cornered too soon, he would have recourse to some desperate brutality.

It was Jaikie's business to get inside the house, and the only way was by the courtyard at the back. Randal had had this carefully reconnoitred, and his report was that, while the gate was kept locked and guarded, the wall could be climbed by an active man. It was impossible to do more than make a rudimentary plan, which was briefly this. Jaikie was to get into the courtyard, using any method he pleased, and to overpower, gag, and bind the guard. Randal had ascertained that there was never more than a single guard. For this purpose he must have a companion, since his fighting weight was small. His hour of entrance must be 10 p.m., at which time the Six were to deal with the watchmen in the street. Their success was to be notified to Jaikie by Luigi's playing of Dvořák's 'Humoresque' on his fiddle, which in that still quarter at that hour of night would carry far.

Then there was to be an allowance of one hour while the Six kept watch in the street, and Jaikie, having entered the house, discovered where the prisoners were kept. After that came the point of uncertainty. It might be possible to get the prisoners off as inconspicuously as Jaikie himself had made his departure. On the other hand, it might not, and force might have to be used against desperate men. At all costs the crisis, if it came, was to be postponed till eleven o'clock, at which time the reserves, the Twenty, would arrive in the courtyard. It was assumed that Jaikie would have got the gates open so that they could enter. He must also have opened the house door. Two blasts on his whistle would bring the rescuers inside the house, and then God prosper the right!

That last sentence had been the parting words of Randal, who had no part allotted him, being, as he said, an ageing man and no fighter. Jaikie remembered them as he crouched in the dust of the courtyard and peered into the gloom. So far his job had been simple. A way up the wall had been found in a corner where an adjacent building slightly abutted and the stones were loose or broken. He had lain on the top and examined the courtyard in the dying light, and he had listened intently, but there had been no sight or sound of the watchman. Then, followed by Newsom, he had dropped on to soft rubble, and lain still and listened, but there was no evidence of human presence. The place was empty. Satisfied about this, he had examined the gate. He had been given some elementary instruction in lock-picking that evening at the Cirque, and had brought with him the necessary tools. But to his surprise they were not needed. The gate was open.

A brief reconnaissance showed him that the courtyard was different from what it had been on his arrival two days ago. The medley of motor cars had gone. The place was bare, except for the heaps of stone and lime in the corner where someone seemed to have been excavating. . . . Jaikie did his best to think. What was the meaning of the unlocked gate? Someone must be coming there that night and coming in a hurry. Or someone must be leaving in a hurry. Why had Mastrovin suddenly opened his defences? The horrid thought came to him that Mastrovin might be gone, and have taken Alison and the others with him. Was he too late? The mass of the house rose like a cliff, and in that yard he seemed to be in a suffocating cave. Far above him he saw dimly clouds chasing each other in the heavens, but there was no movement of air where he sat. The place was so silent and lifeless that his heart sank. Childe Roland had come to the Dark Tower, but the Dark Tower was empty.

And then he saw far up on its façade a light prick out. His

momentary despair was changed to a furious anxiety. There was life in the place, and he felt that the life was evil and menacing. The great blank shell held a brood of cockatrices, and among them was what he loved best in the world. Hitherto the necessity for difficult action had kept his mind from brooding too much on awful presentiments. He had had to take one step at a time and keep his thoughts on the leash. There had been moments when his former insouciance had returned to him and he had thought only of the game and not of the consequences. . . . Indeed, in the early evening, as he approached Krovolin, he had had one instant of the old thrill. Far over the great plain of the Rave, from the direction of the capital, had come the sound of distant music and dancing bells. He had known what that meant. Mr Dickson McCunn was entering his loyal city of Melina.

But now he knew only consuming anxiety and something not far from terror. He must get inside the house at once and find Alison. If she had gone, he must follow. He had a horrid certainty that she was in extreme peril, and that he alone was to blame for it. . . . He got to his feet and was about to attempt the door, when something halted him.

It was the sound of a fiddle, blanketed by the great house, but dropping faint liquid notes in the still air. It held him like a spell, for it seemed a message of hope and comfort. One part of the adventure at any rate had succeeded, and the Six were in occupation of the Street of the White Peacock. It did more, for it linked up this dark world with the light and with his friends. He listened, he could not choose but listen, till the music died away.

It was well that he did so, for Newsom's hand pulled him down again. 'There's someone at the gate,' he whispered. The two crouched deeper into the shadows.

The gate was pushed open, and a man entered the courtyard. He had an electric torch which he flashed for a moment, but rather as if he wanted to see that the torch was in working order than to examine the place. The flash was enough to reveal the burly form of Mastrovin. He shut the gate behind him, but he did not lock it. Evidently he expected someone else to follow him. Then he walked straight to the excavation, and, after moving some boards aside, he disappeared into it.

The sight of Mastrovin switched Jaikie from despondency into vigorous action. 'After him,' he whispered to Newsom. Clambering over the rubble they looked down a steep inclined passage, where a man might walk if he crouched, and saw ahead of them the light of Mastrovin's torch. It vanished as he turned a corner.

The two followed at once, Newsom hitting his head hard on the roof. Jaikie did not dare to use his own torch, but felt his way by the wall, till he came to a passage debouching to the right. That was the way Mastrovin had gone, but there was no sign of his light. Jaikie felt that he could safely look about him.

They were in a circular space whence several passages radiated. That by which they had come was new work, with the marks of pick and shovel still on it. But the other passages were of ancient brick, with stone roofs which might have been new two centuries ago. Yet in all of them was the mark of recent labour, a couple of picks propped up against a wall, and spilt lime and rubble on the floor. Jaikie deduced that the passage from the upper air was not the only task that Mastrovin's men had been engaged in; they had been excavating also at the far ends of the other passages.

He did not stop, for their quarry must not be lost track of. He turned up the alley Mastrovin had taken, feeling his way by the wall.

'There's wiring here,' he whispered to Newsom.

'I spotted that,' was the answer. 'Someone's up to no good.'

Presently they reached a dead end, and Jaikie thought it safe to use his torch. This revealed a steep flight of steps on the left. It was a spiral staircase, for after two turnings they had a glimpse of light above them. Mastrovin was very near. Moreover, he was speaking to someone. The voice was quite distinct, for the funnel of the staircase magnified it, but the words were Evallonian, which Jaikie did not understand.

But Newsom did. He clutched Jaikie's arm, and with every sentence of Mastrovin's that clutch tightened. Then some command seemed to be issued above, and they heard the reply of Mastrovin's interlocutor. The light wavered and moved, and presently disappeared, for Mastrovin had gone on. But there came the sound of feet on the stairs, growing louder. The other man was descending – in the dark.

It was a tense moment in Jaikie's life. He took desperate hold of his wits, and reasoned swiftly that the man descending in the dark would almost certainly hug the outer wall, the right-hand wall of the spiral, where the steps were broader. Therefore he and Newsom must plaster themselves against the other wall. The staircase was wide enough to let two men pass abreast without touching. If they were detected he would go for the stranger's throat, and he thought he could trust Newsom to do the same.

The two held their breath while the man came down the stairs. Jaikie, sensitive as a wild animal, realized that his guess had been right – the man was feeling his way by the outer wall. Newsom's shoulder was touching his, and he felt it shiver. Another thing he realized – the stranger was in a hurry. That was to the good, for he would not be so likely to get any subconscious warning of their presence.

For one second the man was abreast of them. There was a waft of some coarse scent, as if he were a vulgar dandy. Then he was past them, and they heard him at the foot of the stairs groping for the passage.

Jaikie sat down on a step to let his stifled breath grow normal. But Newsom was whispering something in his ear.

'I heard their talk,' he gasped. 'I've got their plan. ... They are going to let the Countess occupy the town ... She must cross the river to get to Melina. ... They've got the bridge mined, and will blow it up at the right moment ... and half the place besides. ... God, what swine!'

To Jaikie the news was a relief. That could only be for the morrow, and in the meantime Mastrovin would lie quiet. That meant that his prisoners would be in the house. The cockatrices – and the others – were still in their den.

But Newsom had more to say.

'There are people coming here – more people. That fellow has gone to fetch them.'

Jaikie, squatted in the darkness, hammered at his wits, but they would not respond. What could these new-comers mean? What was there to do in the house that had not been done? Mastrovin had the bridge mined, and half the town as well, and could make havoc by pressing a button. He had his cellars wired, and new passages dug. All that was clear enough. But why was he assembling a posse tonight? . . .

Then an idea struck him. If the gates were open to let people in, they were open to let the same people out. And they might take others with them. . . . He had it. The prisoners were to be removed that night, and used in Mastrovin's further plans. When he had struck his blow at Juventus they might come in handy as hostages. Or in the last resort as victims.

From the moment that he realized this possibility came a radical change in Jaikie's outlook. The torments of anxious love were still deep in his soul, but overlying them was a solid crust of hate. His slow temper was being kindled into a white flame of anger.

He looked at his watch. It was one minute after half past ten. The Twenty would not arrive till eleven.

'I must go on,' he whispered. 'I must find what the brute is after and where he keeps my friends. . . . You must go back and wait in the yard. Please Heaven our fellows are here before the others. If they are, bring them up here – I'll find some way of joining up with you. . . . If the others come first, God help us all, I leave it to you.'

As he spoke he realized sharply the futility of asking a cockney chauffeur to hold at bay an unknown number of the toughest miscreants in Evallonia. But Newsom seemed to take it calmly. His voice was steady.

'I'll do my best, sir,' he said. 'I'm armed, and I used to be a fair shot. Have you a pair of clippers in that packet of tools you brought?'

Jaikie dived into his pocket and handed over the desired article.

'Good,' said Newsom. 'I think I'll do a spot of wire cutting.' And without another word he began to feel his way down.

Jaikie crept upward till the stairs ended in a door. This was unlocked, as he had expected, for Mastrovin was leaving his communications open behind him. Inside all was black, so he cautiously flashed his torch. The place was dusty and unclean, a passage with rotting boards on the floor and discoloured paper dropping from the walls. He tip-toed along it till it gave on to a small landing from which another staircase descended. Here there were two doors, and he cautiously tried the handles. One was locked, but the other was opened. It was dark inside, but at the far end there was a thin crack of light on the floor. There must be a room there which at any rate was inhabited.

The first thing he did, for he had put out his torch, was to fall with a great clatter over some obstacle. He lay still with his heart in his mouth, waiting for the far door to be thrown open. But nothing happened, so he carefully picked himself up and continued with extreme circumspection. There were chairs and tables in this place, a ridiculous number of chairs, as if it had been used as a depository for lumber, or perhaps as a council chamber. He had no further mishap, and reached the streak of light safely. ... There were people in that farther room; he could hear a voice speaking, and it sounded like Mastrovin's.

Another thing he noticed, and that was the same odd smell of coarse scent which he had sniffed as the man passed him on the stairs. The odour was like a third-rate barber's shop, and it came through the door.

He could hear Mastrovin talking, rather loud and very distinct, like a schoolmaster to stupid pupils. He was speaking English too.

'You are going away,' he was saying. 'Do you understand? I will soon visit you – perhaps in a day or two. I do not think you will try to escape, but if you do, I warn you that I have a long arm and will pluck you back. And I will punish you for it.'

The voice was slow and patient as if addressed to backward children. And there was no answer. Mastrovin must be speaking to his prisoners, but they did not reply, and that was so unlike Sir Archie that a sudden horrid fear shot into Jaikie's mind. Were they dying, or sick, or wounded? Was Alison? . . .

He waited no longer. Had the door been triple-barred he felt that he had the strength to break it down. But it opened easily.

He found himself in a small, square, and very high room, wholly without windows, for the air entered by a grating near the ceiling. It smelt stuffy and heavily scented. Mastrovin sat in an armchair, with behind him a queer-looking board studded with numbered buttons. There was a clock fixed on the wall above it which had a loud, solemn tick.

The three prisoners sat behind a little table. Archie looked as if he had been in the wars, for he had one arm in a sling, and there was a bloodstained bandage round his head. He sat stiffly upright, staring straight in front of him. So did Janet, a pale unfamiliar Janet, with her hair in disorder and a long rent in one sleeve. Like her husband, she was looking at Mastrovin with blank unseeing eyes. Alison sat a little apart with her arms on the table and her head on her arms. He saw only her mop of gold hair. She seemed to be asleep.

All that Jaikie took in at his first glance was the three prisoners. What devilry had befallen them? He had it. They had been drugged. They were now blind and apathetic, mindless perhaps, baggage which Mastrovin could cart about as he chose. There had evidently been a row, and Archie had suffered in it, but now he was out of action. It was the sight of Alison's drooped head that made him desperate, and also perfectly cool. He had not much hope, but at any rate he was with his friends again.

This reconnaissance took a fraction of a second. He heard Mastrovin bark, 'Hands up!' and up shot his arms.

There were two others in the room, Dedekind with his red pointed beard, and a sallow squat man, whom he remembered in the Canonry. What was his name? Rosenbaum?

It was the last who searched him, plucking the pistol from his breeches pocket. Jaikie did not mind that, for he had never been much good with a gun. For the first time he saw the clock on the wall, and noted that it stood at a quarter to eleven. If he could spin out that quarter of an hour there was just the faintest chance, always provided that Mastrovin's reinforcements did not arrive too soon.

'I have come back,' he said sweetly. 'I really had to get some decent clothes, for I was in rags.'

'You have come back,' Mastrovin repeated. 'Why?'

'Because I liked your face, Mr Mastrovin. I have the pleasantest recollection of you, you know, ever since we met two years ago at Portaway. Do you remember the Hydropathic there and the little Glasgow journalist that you cross-examined? Drunken little beast he was, and you tried to make him drunker. Have you been up to the same game with my friends?'

He glanced at Archie, trying to avoid the sight of Alison's bowed head. To his surprise he seemed to detect a slight droop of that gentleman's left eye. Was it possible that the doping had failed, and that the victims were only shamming? ... The clock was at thirteen minutes to eleven.

Mastrovin was looking at him fixedly, as if he were busy reconstructing the past to which he had alluded.

'So,' he said. 'I have more against you than I imagined.'

'You have nothing against me,' said Jaikie briskly. 'I might say I had a lot against you – kidnapping, imprisonment, no food or drink, filthy lodgings, and so forth. But I'm not complaining. I forgive you for the sake of your face. You wanted me to tell you something, but I couldn't, for I didn't know. Well, I know now, and I've come back to do you a good turn. You would like to know where Prince John is. I can tell you.'

Jaikie stopped. His business was to spin out this dialogue.

'Go on,' said Mastrovin grimly. He was clearly in two minds whether or not this youth was mad.

'He is with the Countess Troyos. I know, for I saw him there this morning.'

'That is a lie.'

'All right. Have it your own way. But when you blow up the bridge here tomorrow you had better find out whether I am speaking the truth, unless you want to kill the Prince. Perhaps you do. Perhaps you'd like to add him to the bag. It's all the same to me, only I thought I'd warn you.'

He was allowed to finish the audacious speech, because Mastrovin was for once in his masterful life fairly stupefied. Jaikie's purpose was to anger him so that he might lay violent hands on him. He thought that, unless they took to shooting, he could give them a proof of the eel-like agility of the Gorbals Die-hards, not to speak of the most famous three-quarter back in Britain. He did not think they would shoot him, for they were sure to want to discover where he had got his knowledge.

He certainly succeeded in his purpose. Mastrovin's face flushed to an ugly purple, and both Dedekind and Rosenbaum grew a little paler. The last-named said something in Evallonian, and the three talked excitedly in that language. This was precisely what Jaikie wanted. He observed the clock was now at eight minutes to the hour. He also noted that Alison, though her head was still on the table, was looking sideways at him through her fingers, and that her eyes had an alertness unusual in the doped.

Suddenly he heard a shot, muffled as if very far off. This room was in the heart of the house, and noises from the outer world would come faintly to it, if at all. But he had quick ears, and he knew that he could not be mistaken. Was the faithful Newsom holding the bridge alone like Horatius? He could not hold it long, and there were still five deadly minutes to go before the Twenty could be looked for. . . .

Yet it would take more than five minutes to get the prisoners out of the house and the gate. That danger at any rate had gone. What remained was the same peril which had brooded over the library at Castle Gay, before Dickson McCunn like a north wind had dispersed it. These wild beasts of the jungle, if cornered, might make a great destruction. Here in this place they were all on the thin crust of a volcano. He did not like that board with studs and numbers behind Mastrovin's head.

Again came the faint echo of shots. This time Mastrovin heard it. He said something to Dedekind, who hurried from the room. Rosenbaum would have followed, but a word detained him. Mastrovin sat crouching like an angry lion, waiting to spring, but not yet quite certain of his quarry.

'Stand still,' he told Jaikie, who had edged nearer Alison. 'If you move I will kill you. In a moment my friend will return, and then you will go – ah, where will you go?'

He sucked his lips, and grinned like a great cat.

There were no more shots, and silence fell on the place, broken only by the ticking of the clock. Jaikie did not dare to look at the prisoners, for the slightest movement on his part might release the fury of the wild beast in front of him. He kept his eyes on that face which had now become gnarled like a knot in an oak stump, an intense concentration of anxiety, fury, and animal power. It fascinated Jaikie, but it did not terrify him, for it was like a monstrous gargoyle, an expression of some ancient lust which was long dead. He had the impression that the man was somehow dead and awaited burial, and might therefore be disregarded. . . .

He strove to stir his inertia to life, but he seemed to have become boneless. 'It's you that will be dead in a minute or two,' he told himself, but apathetically, as if he were merely correcting a mis-statement. Anger had gone out of him, and had taken fear with it, and only apathy remained. He felt Mastrovin's eyes beginning to dominate and steal his senses like an anaesthetic. That scared him, and he shifted his gaze to the board on the wall, and the clock. The clock was at three minutes after eleven, but he had forgotten his former feverish calculation of time.

The door opened. Out of a corner of his eye he saw that Dedekind had returned. He noted his red beard.

Jaikie was pulled out of his languor by the behaviour of Mastrovin, who from a lion couchant became a lion rampant. He could not have believed that a heavy man well on in years could show such nimbleness. Mastrovin was on his feet, shouting something to Rosenbaum, and pointing at the new-comer the pistol with which he had threatened Jaikie.

The voice that spoke from the door was not Dedekind's.

'Suppose we lower our guns, Mr Mastrovin?' it said. 'You might kill me – but I think you know that I can certainly kill you. Is it a bargain?'

The voice was pleasant and low with a touch of drawl in it. Jaikie, in a wild whirling survey of the room, saw that it had fetched Alison's head off her hands. It woke Janet and Archie, too, out of their doll-like stare. It seemed to cut into the stuffiness like a frosty wind, and it left Jaikie in deep bewilderment, but – for the first time that night – with a lively hope.

Mr Glynde sniffed the air.

'At the old dodge, I see,' he said. 'You once tried it on me, you remember. You seem to have struck rather tough subjects this time.' He nodded to the Roylances and smiled on Alison.

'What do you want?' The words seemed to be squeezed out of Mastrovin, and came thick and husky.

'A deal,' said Randal cheerfully. 'The game is against you this time. We've got your little lot trussed up below – also my old friend, Mr Dedekind.'

'That is a lie.'

Randal shrugged his shoulders.

'You are a monotonous controversialist. I assure you it is true. There was a bit of a tussle at first before our people arrived, and I'm afraid two of yours are killed. Then the rest surrendered to superior numbers. All is now quiet on that front.'

'If I believe you, what is your deal?'

'Most generous. That you should get yourself out of here in ten minutes and out of the country in ten hours. We will look after your transport. The fact is, Mr Mastrovin, we don't want you – Evallonia doesn't want you – nobody wants you. You and your bravos are back numbers. Properly speaking, we should string you up, but we don't wish to spoil a good show with ugly episodes.'

Randal spoke lightly, so that there was no melodrama in his words, only a plain and rather casual statement of fact. But in that place such lightness was the cruellest satire. And it was belied by Randal's eyes, which were sharp as a hawk's. They never left Mastrovin's pistol hand and the studded board behind his head.

Mastrovin's face was a mask, but his eyes, too, were wary. He seemed about to speak, but what he meant to say, will never be known. For suddenly many things happened at once.

There was a sound of a high imperious voice at the door.

It opened and the Countess Araminta entered, and close behind her a wild figure of a man, dusty, bleeding, with a coat nearly ripped from his back.

The sight of the Countess stung Mastrovin into furious life. A sense of death and fatality filled the room like a fog. Jaikie sprang to get in front of Alison, and Archie with his unwounded arm thrust Janet behind him. In that breathless second Jaikie was conscious only of two things. Mastrovin had fired, and then swung round to the numbered board; but, even as his finger reached it he clutched at the air and fell backward over the arm of his chair. There was a sudden silence, and a click came from the board as if a small clock were running down.

Then Jaikie's eyes cleared. He saw a pallid Rosenbaum crouching on the floor. He saw Randal lower his pistol, and touch the body of Mastrovin. 'Dead,' he heard him say, 'stone dead. Just as well perhaps.'

But that spectacle was eclipsed by other extraordinary things. The Countess of Araminta was behaving oddly – she seemed to be inclined to sob. Around his own neck were Alison's arms, and her cheek was on his, and the thrill of it almost choked him with joy. He wanted to weep too, and he would have wept had not the figure of the man who had entered with the Countess taken away what breath was left in him.

It was Newsom the chauffeur, transfigured beyond belief. He had become a younger man, for exertion had coloured his pallid skin, his whiskers had disappeared, and his tousled hair had lost its touch of grey. He held the Countess with one arm and looked ruefully at his right shoulder.

'Close shave,' he said. 'The second time tonight too. First casualty in the Revolution.' Then he smiled on the company. 'Lucky I cut the wires, or our friend would have dispersed us among the planets.'

The Countess had both hands on his arm, and was looking at him with misty eyes.

'You saved my life,' she cried. 'The shot was meant for me. You are a hero. Oh, tell me your name.'

He turned, took her hand, bent over it and kissed it.

'I am Prince John,' he said, 'and I think that you are going to be kind enough to help me to a throne.'

She drew back a step, looked for a second in his face, and then curtsied low.

'My king,' she said.

Her bosom heaved under her tunic, and she was no more the Praefectus but a most emotional young woman. . . . She looked at Randal and Jaikie, and at Janet and Archie, as if she were struggling for something to relieve her feelings. Then she saw Alison, and in two steps was beside her and had her in her arms.

'My dear,' she said, 'you have a very brave lover.'

## CHAPTER THIRTEEN

# THE MARCH ON MELINA

### I

In Krovolin's best hotel, the Three Kings of the East, Jaikie enjoyed the novel blessings of comfort and consideration. By the Countess's edict Alison, the Roylances, and he were at once conducted there, and the mandate of Juventus secured them the distinguished attentions of the management. The released prisoners were little the worse, for they had not been starved as Jaikie had been, and the only casualty was Archie, who had been overpowered in a desperate effort the previous morning to get into the Street of the White Peacock. The doping had been clumsily managed, for some hours before Jaikie's arrival the three had been given a meal quite different from the coarse fare to which they had been hitherto treated. They were offered with it a red wine, which Archie at his first sip pronounced to be corked. Alison had tasted it, and, detecting something sweet and sickly in its flavour, had suspected a drug, whereupon Janet filled their glasses and emptied them in a corner. 'Look like sick owls,' she advised, when they were taken to Mastrovin's sanctum, where the overpowering scent was clearly part of the treatment. Mastrovin's behaviour showed that her inspiration had been right, for he had spoken to them as if they were somnambulists or half-wits. . . .

On the following morning Jaikie, feeling clean and refreshed for the first time for a week, descended late to the pleasant restaurant which overlooked the milky waters of the Rave. The little city sparkled in the sunlight, and the odour and bustle of a summer morning came as freshly to his nose and ears as if he had just risen from a sick-bed. He realized how heavy his heart had been for days, and the release sent his spirits soaring. . . . But his happiness was more than the absence of care, for last night had been an epoch in his life, like that evening two years before when, on the Canonry moor, Alison had waved him good-bye. For the first time he had held Alison in his arms and felt her lips on his cheek. That delirious experience had almost blotted out from his memory the other elements in the scene. As he dwelt on it he did not see the dead Mastrovin, and the crouched figure of Rosenbaum, and the Countess Araminta on the verge of tears, or hear the ticking of the clock, and the pistol shot which ended the drama; he saw only Alison's pale face and her gold hair like a cloud on his shoulder, and heard that in her strained voice which he had never heard before. . . . Jaikie felt the solemn rapture of some hungry, humble saint who finds his pulse changed miraculously into the ambrosia of Paradise.

A waiter brought him the morning paper. He could not read it, but he could guess at the headlines. Something tremendous seemed to be happening in Melina. There was a portrait of the Archduke Hadrian, edged with laurels and roses, and from it stared the familiar face of Mr McCunn. There was a photograph of a street scene in which motor cars and an escort of soldiers moved between serried ranks of presumably shouting citizens. In one, next to a splendid figure in a cocked hat, could be discerned the homely features of Dickson.

He dropped the paper, for Alison had appeared, Alison, fresh as a flower, with the colour back in her cheeks. Only her eyes were still a little tired. She came straight to him, put her hands on his shoulders, and kissed him. 'Darling,' she said.

'Oh, Alison,' he stammered. 'Then it's all right, isn't it?'

She laughed merrily and drew him to a breakfast table in the window. 'Foolish Jaikie! As if it would ever have been anything else!'

There was another voice behind him, and Jaikie found another fair head beside his.

'I shall kiss you too,' said Janet Roylance, 'for we're going to be cousins, you know. Allie, I wish you joy. Jaikie, I love you. Archie? Oh, he has to stay in bed for a little – the doctor has just seen him. He's all right, but his arm wants a rest, and he got quite a nasty smack on the head. . . . Let's have breakfast. I don't suppose there's any hope of kippers.'

As they sat down at a table in the window Alison picked up the newspaper. She frowned at the pictures from Melina. Her coffee grew cold as she puzzled over the headlines.

'I wish I could read this stuff,' she said. 'Everything seems to have gone according to plan, but the question is, what is the next step? You realize, don't you, that we've still a nasty fence to leap. We've got over the worst, for the Blood-red Rook has taken Prince John to her bosom. She'll probably insist on marrying him, for she believes he saved her life, and I doubt if he is man enough to escape her. Perhaps he won't want to, for she's a glorious creature, but – Jaikie, I think you are lucky to have found a homely person like me. Being married to her would be rather like domesticating a Valkyrie. You managed that business pretty well, you know.'

'I don't deserve much credit, for I was only fumbling in the dark. Mr Glynde was the real genius. Do you think he arranged for the Countess to turn up, or was it an unrehearsed effect? If he arranged it he took a pretty big risk.'

'I believe she took the bit in her teeth. Couldn't bear to be left out of anything. But what about Cousin Ran? He has disappeared over the skyline, and the only message he left was that we were to go back to Tarta and await developments. I'm worried about those developments, for we don't know what may happen. Everything has gone smoothly – except of course our trouble with Mastrovin – but I'm afraid there may be an ugly snag at the end.'

'You mean Mr McCunn?'

'I mean the Archduke Hadrian, who is now in the royal palace at Melina wishing to goodness that he was safe home at Blaweary.'

'I trust him to pull it off,' said Jaikie.

'But it's no good trusting Dickson unless other people play up. Just consider what we've done. We've worked a huge practical joke on Juventus, and if Juventus ever came to know about it everything would be in the soup. Here you have the youth of Evallonia, burning with enthusiasm and rejoicing in their young prince, whom they mean to make king instead of an elderly dotard. What is Juventus going to say if they discover that the whole thing has been a plant to which their young prince has been a consenting party? Prince John's stock would fall pretty fast. You've wallowed in deceit from your cradle, Jaikie dear, so you don't realize how it upsets ordinary people, especially if they are young and earnest.'

Jaikie laughed. 'I believe you are right. Everybody's got their own *panache*, and the public-school notion of good form isn't really very different from what in foreigners we call melodrama. I mean, it's just as artificial.'

'Anyhow, there's not a scrap of humour in it,' said Alison. 'The one thing the Rook won't stand is to be made ridiculous. No more will Juventus. So it's desperately important that Dickson should disappear into the night and leave no traces. How many people are in the plot?'

Jaikie as usual counted on his fingers.

'There's we three – and Sir Archie – and Ashie – and Prince John – and Prince Odalchini – and I suppose Count Casimir and maybe one or two other Monarchists. Not more than that, and it's everybody's interest to keep it deadly secret.

'That's all right if we can be certain about Dickson getting quietly away in time. But supposing Juventus catches him. Then it's bound to come out. I don't mean that they'll do him any harm beyond slinging him across the frontier. But he'll look a fool and we'll look fools – and, much more important, Prince John will look a fool and a bit of a knave – and the Monarchist leaders, who Ran says are the only people that can help Juventus to make a success of the Government. ... We must get busy at once. Since that ruffian Ran has vanished, we must get hold of Prince John.'

But it was not the Prince who chose to visit them as they were finishing breakfast, but the Countess Araminta. Jaikie had seen her in camp as Praefectus, and was prepared to some extent for her air of command, but the others only knew her as the exotic figure of London and Geneva, and as the excited girl whose nerves the night before had been stretched to breaking-point. Now she seemed the incarnation of youthful vigour. The door was respectfully held open by an aide-de-camp, and she made an entrance like a tragedy queen. She wore the uniform of Juventus, but her favourite colour glowed in a cape which hung over one shoulder. There was colour too in her cheeks, and her fine eyes had lost their sullenness. Everything about her, her trim form, the tilt of her head, the alert grace of her carriage, spoke of confidence and power. Jaikie gasped, for he had never seen anything quite like her. '*Incessu patuit dea*', he thought, out of a vague classical reminiscence.

They all stood up to greet her.

'My friends, my good friends,' she cried. She put a hand on Jaikie's shoulder, and for one awe-stricken moment he thought she was going to kiss him.

She smiled upon them in turn. 'Your husband is almost well,' she told Janet. 'I have seen the doctor. ... What do you wish to do, for it is for you to choose? I must go back to my camp, for here in Krovolin during the next few days the whole forces of Juventus will concentrate. I shall be very busy, but I will instruct others to attend to you. What are your wishes? You have marched some distance with Juventus – do you care to finish the course, and enter Melina with us? You have earned the right to that.'

'You are very kind,' said Janet. 'But if you don't mind, I believe we ought to go home. You see, my husband should be in

Geneva . . . and I'm responsible for my cousin Alison. . . . I think if Archie were here he would agree with me. Would it be possible for us to go back to Tarta and rest there for a day or two? We don't want to leave Evallonia till we know that you have won, but – you won't misunderstand me – I don't think we should take any part in the rest of the show. You see, we are foreigners, and it is important that everybody should realize that this is your business and nobody's else's. My husband is a member of our Parliament, and there might be some criticism if he were mixed up in it – not so much criticism of him as of you. So I think we had better go to Tarta.'

Janet spoke diffidently, for she did not know how Juventus might regard the House of the Four Winds and its owner. But to her surprise the Countess made no objection.

'You shall do as you wish,' she said. 'Perhaps you are right, and it would be wise to have no foreign names mentioned. But you must not think that we shall be opposed and must take Melina by storm. We shall enter the city with all the bells ringing.'

She saw Janet's glance fall on the newspaper on the floor.

'You think there is a rival king? Ah, but he will not remain. He will not want to remain. The people will not want him. Trust me, he will yield at once to the desire of his country.'

'What will you do with the Archduke?' Alison asked.

'We will treat him with distinguished respect,' was the answer. 'Is he not the brother of our late king and the uncle of him who is to be our king? If his health permits, he will be the right-hand counsellor of the Throne, for he is old and very wise. At the Coronation he will carry the Sacred Lamp and the Mantle of St Sylvester, and deliver with his own voice the solemn charge given to all Evallonia's sovereigns.'

Alison groaned inwardly, having a vision of Dickson in this august rôle.

'I must leave you,' said the Countess. 'You have done great service to my country's cause, for which from my heart I thank you. An evil thing has been destroyed, which could not indeed have defeated Juventus but which might have been a thorn in its side.'

'Have you got rid of Mastrovin's gang?' Jaikie asked.

She looked down on him smiling, her hand still on his shoulder.

'They are being rounded up,' she replied; 'but indeed they count for nothing since he is dead. Mástrovin is not of great importance – not now, though once he was Evallonia's evil genius. At the worst he was capable of murder in the dark. He was a survivor of old black days that the world is forgetting. He was a prophet of foolish crooked things that soon all men will loathe.'

Her voice had risen, her face had flushed, she drew herself up to her slim height, and in that room, amid the debris of breakfast and with the sun through the long windows making a dazzle of light around her, the Countess Araminta became for a moment her ancestress who had ridden with John Sobieski against the Turk. To three deeply impressed listeners she expounded her creed.

'Mastrovin is dead,' she said; 'but that is no matter, for he and his kind were dead long ago. They were *revenants*, ghosts, hideous futile ghosts. They lived by hate, hating what they did not understand. They were full of little vanities and fears, and were fit for nothing but to destroy. Back-numbers you call them in England – I call them shadows of the dark which vanish when the light comes. We of Juventus do not hate, we love, but in our love we are implacable. We love everything in our land, all that is old in it and all that is new, and we love all our people, from the greatest to the humblest. We have given back to Evallonia her soul, and once again we shall make her a great nation. But it will be a new nation, for everyone will share in its government.' She paused. 'All will be sovereigns, because all will be subjects.'

She was a true actress, for she knew how to make the proper exit. Her rapt face softened. With one hand still on Jaikie's shoulder she laid the other on Alison's head and stroked her hair.

'Will you lend me your lover, my dear?' she said. 'Only for a little – since he will join you at Tarta. I think he may be useful as a liaison between Juventus and those who doubtless mean well but have been badly advised.'

Then she was gone, and all the colour and half the light seemed to have left the room.

'Gosh!' Jaikie exclaimed, when they were alone. 'It looks as if I were for it.' He remembered the phrase about subjects and sovereigns as coming from a philosopher on whom at Cambridge he had once written an essay. No doubt she had got it from Dr Jagon, and he had qualms as to what might happen if the public-school code got mixed up with philosophy.

Janet looked grave.

'What a woman!' she said. 'I like her, but I'm scared by her. The Blood-red Rook is not the same – she's the genuine eagle. I'm more anxious than ever about Mr McCunn. Juventus is a marvellous thing, but she said herself that it was implacable. There's nothing in the world so implacable as the poet if you attempt to guy his poetry, and that's what we have been doing. There's going to be a terrible mix-up unless Dickson can disappear in about two days and leave no traces behind him; and I don't see how that's to be managed now that he is planted in a palace in the middle of an excited city.'

To three anxious consultants there entered Prince John. Somehow or other he had got in touch with his kit, for he was smartly dressed in a suit of light flannels, with a rose in his buttonhole.

'I'm supposed to be still incognito,' he explained, 'and I have to lurk here till the concentration of Juventus is complete. That should be some time tomorrow. Sir Archie is all right. I've just seen him, and he is to be allowed to get up after luncheon. I hope you can control him, Lady Roylance, for I can't. He is determined to be in at the finish, he says, and was simply blasphemous when I told him that he was an alien and must keep out of it. It won't do, you know. You must all go back to Tarta at once. He doesn't quite appreciate the delicacy of the situation or what compromising people you are.'

'We do,' said Janet. 'We've just had a discourse from the Countess. You won't find it easy to live up to that young woman, sir.'

Prince John laughed.

'I think I can manage Mintha. She is disposed to be very humble and respectful with me, for she has always been a staunch royalist. Saved her life, too, she thinks – though I don't believe Mastrovin meant his shot for her – I believe he spotted me, and he always wanted to do me in. She's by way of being our prophetess, but she is no fool, and, besides, there's any number of sober-minded people to keep her straight. What I have to live up to is Juventus itself, and that will take some doing. It's a tremendous thing, you know, far bigger and finer than any of us thought, and it's going to be the salvation of Evallonia. Perhaps more than that. What was it your Pitt said – "Save its country by its efforts and Europe by its example"? But it's youth, and youth takes itself seriously, and if anybody laughs at it or tries to play tricks with it he'll get hurt. That's where we are rather on the knife-edge.'

'My dear Uncle Hadrian,' he went on, 'is in bed at home in France and reported to be sinking. That is Odalchini's last word, and Odalchini has the affair well in hand. My uncle's secretary is under his orders, and not a scrap of news is allowed to leave the château.'

'The Countess seems to be better disposed to Prince Odalchini,' said Janet.

'She is. Odalchini has opened negotiations with Juventus. He has let it be known that he and his friends will not contest my right to the throne, and that the Archduke has bowed to this view and proposes to leave the country. Of course he speaks for Casimir and the rest. That is all according to plan. Presently His Royal Highness will issue a proclamation resigning all claims. But in the meantime our unhappy Scotch friend is masquerading in the palace of Melina – in deep seclusion, of course, for the Archduke is an old and frail man, and is seeing no one as yet – but still there, with the whole capital agog for a sight of him. You will say, smuggle him out and away with him across the frontier. But Juventus has other ideas – Mintha has other ideas. There is to be a spectacular meeting between uncle and nephew – a noble renunciation – a tender reconciliation – and the two surviving males of the Evallonian royal house are to play a joint part in the restoration of the monarchy. Juventus has the good sense to understand that it needs Casimir and his lot to help it to get the land straight, and it thinks that that will be best managed by having its claimant and their claimant working in double harness. I say "Juventus thinks", but it's that hussy Mintha who does the thinking, and the others accept it. That's the curse of a romantic girl in politics. . . . So there's the tangle we're in. There will be the devil to pay if the Archduke isn't out of the country within three days without anyone setting eyes on him, and that's going to be a large-sized job for somebody.'

'For whom?' Jaikie asked.

'Principally for you,' was the answer. 'You seem to get all the worst jobs in this business. You're young, you see – you're our Juventus.'

'She says I have to go with her.'

'You have to stay here. I asked for you. Thank Heaven she has taken an enormous fancy to you. Miss Alison needn't be jealous, for Mintha has about as much sex as a walking-stick. I daresay she would insist on marrying me, if she thought the country needed it, but I shall take jolly good care to avoid that. No warrior-queen for me. . . . All of you except Jaikie go back to Tarta this afternoon, and there Odalchini will keep you advised about what is happening. Jaikie stays here, and as soon as possible he goes to Melina. Don't look so doleful, my son. You won't be alone there. Randal Glynde, to the best of my belief, is by this time in the palace.'

Late that afternoon Janet and Alison, accompanied by a bitterly protesting Archie, left Krovolin for the House of the Four Winds. Next day there began for Jaikie two crowded days filled with a manifold of new experiences. The Wings of Juventus, hitherto on the periphery of Evallonia, drew towards the centre. The whole business was a masterpiece of organization, and profoundly impressed him with the fact that this was no flutter of youth, but a miraculous union of youth and experience. Three-fourths of the higher officers were mature men, some of them indeed old soldiers of Evallonia in the Great War. The discipline was military, and the movements had full military precision, but it was clear that this was a civilian army, with every form of expert knowledge in it, and trained more for civil reconstruction than for war.

Dr Jagon, who embraced him publicly, enlarged on its novel character. 'It is triumphant democracy,' he declared, 'purged of the demagogue. Its root is not emotion but reason – sentiment, indeed, of the purest, but sentiment rationalized. It is the State disciplined and enlightened. It is an example to all the world, the pioneer of marching humanity. God be praised that I have lived to see this day.'

Prince John's presence was formally made known, and at a review of the Wings he took his place, in the uniform of Juventus, as Commander-in-Chief. The newspapers published his appeal to the nation, in which he had judiciously toned down Dr Jagon's philosophy and the Countess's heroics. Presently, too, they issued another document, the submission of the Monarchist leaders. City and camp were kindled to a fervour of patriotism, and addresses poured in from every corner of the land.

On the afternoon of the second day Jaikie was summoned to the Prince's quarters, where the Countess and the other wing-commanders were present. There he was given his instructions. 'You will proceed at once to Melina, Mr Galt,' said the Prince, 'and confer with Count Casimir Muresco, with whom I believe you are already acquainted. Tomorrow we advance to the capital, of whose submission we have been already assured. We desire that His Royal Highness the Archduke should be associated with our reception, and we have prepared a programme for the approval of His Royal Highness and his advisers. On our behalf and on behalf of Juventus you will see that this programme is carried out. I think that I am expressing the wishes of my head-quarters staff.'

The Wing-Commanders bowed gravely, and the Countess favoured Jaikie with an encouraging smile. He thought that he detected in Prince John's eye the faintest suspicion of a wink. As he was getting into his car, with an aide-de-camp and an orderly to attend him, Ashie appeared and drew him aside.

'For God's sake,' he whispered, 'get your old man out of the way. Shoot him and bury him if necessary.'

'I'd sooner shoot the lot of you,' said Jaikie.

'Well, if you don't you'd better shoot yourself. And me, too, for I won't survive a fiasco. Mintha has got off on her high horse, and Juventus is following her. She has drawn up a programme of ceremonies a yard long, in which your old fellow is cast for the principal part. There'll be bloody murder if they find themselves let down. They're a great lot, and my own lot, but they won't stand for ragging.'

II

Dickson, enveloped in a military greatcoat and muffled up about the neck because of his advanced age and indifferent health, enjoyed his journey in the late afternoon from Krovolin to Melina. He sat beside Prince Odalchini on the back seat of a large Daimler, with Count Casimir opposite him. There were police cars in front and behind, and a jingling escort of National Guards who made their progress slow. The movement, the mellow air, the rich and sunlit champaign raised his spirits and dispelled his nervousness. His roving eyes scanned the landscape and noted with pleasure the expectant villagers and the cheering group of countrymen. On the outskirts of the capital a second troop of Guards awaited them, and as they entered by the ancient River Port there was a salute of guns from the citadel and every bell in every steeple broke into music. It had been arranged, in deference to His Royal Highness's frailty, that there should be no municipal reception, but the streets were thronged with vociferous citizens and the click of cameras was like the rattle of machine-guns.

The cars swung through what looked like a Roman triumphal arch into a great courtyard, on three sides of which rose the huge baroque Palace. At this point Dickson's impressions became a little confused. He was aware that troops lined the courtyard – he heard a word of command and saw rifles presented at the salute. He was conscious of being tenderly assisted from his car, and conducted between bowing servants through a high doorway and across endless marble pavements. Then came a shallow staircase, and a corridor lined with tall portraits. He came to anchor at last in what seemed to be a bedroom, though it was as big as a church. The evening was warm, but there were fires lit in two fireplaces. As he got out of his greatcoat he realized that he was alone with Prince Odalchini and Count Casimir, each of whom helped himself to a stiff whisky-and-soda from a side table.

'Thank Heaven that is over,' cried the latter. 'Well over, too. Your Royal Highness will keep your chamber tonight, and you will be valeted by my own man. Do not utter one word, and for God's sake try to look as frail as possible. You are a sick man, you understand, which is the reason for this privacy. Tomorrow you will have to show yourself from one of the balconies to the people of Melina. Tomorrow, too, I hope that your own equerry will arrive. It is better that you should be alone tonight. You realize, I think, how delicate the position is? Silence and great bodily weakness – these are your trump cards. It may be a little lonely for you, but that is inevitable.'

Dickson looked round the immense room, which was hung with tapestries depicting the doings in battle of the sixteenth-century King John of Evallonia. From the windows there was a wide view over the glades of the park with a shining river at the end. The two fires burned brightly, and on a bed like a field he observed his humble pyjamas. His spirits were high.

'Ugh,' he said, 'I'll do fine. This is a cheery place. I'll not utter a cheep, and I'll behave as if I was a hundred years old. I hope they'll send me up a good dinner, for I'm mortal hungry.'

Dickson spent a strange but not unpleasant evening. Count Casimir's valet proved to be an elderly Frenchman whose reverence for royalty was such that he kept his eyes downcast and uttered no word except 'Altesse', and that in a tone of profound humility. Dickson was conducted to an adjoining bathroom, where he bathed in pale-blue scented water. In the bathroom he nearly drowned himself by turning on all the taps at once, but he enjoyed himself hugely splashing the water about and watching it running in marble grooves to an exit. After that he was enveloped in a wonderful silk dressing-gown, which hid the humbleness of his pyjamas – pyjamas from which he observed that the name-tag had been removed.

The dinner served in his bedroom was all that his heart could wish, and its only blemish was that, from a choice of wines offered him, he selected a tokay which tasted unpleasantly like a medicine of his boyhood, so that he was forced to relapse upon a whisky-and-soda. 'Even in a palace life may be lived well', he quoted to himself from a favourite poet. After dinner he was put to bed between sheets as fine as satin, and left with a reading-lamp on his bedside table surrounded by a selection of fruit and biscuits. He turned out the lamp, and lay for some time watching the glow of the fire and the amber twilight in the uncurtained windows. Outside he could hear the tramp of the sentries and far off the rumour of crowded streets. At first he was too excited to be drowsy, for the strangeness of his position came over him in gusts, and his chuckles were mingled with an unpleasant trepidation. 'You'll need to say your prayers, Dickson my man,' he told himself, 'for you're in for a desperate business. It's the kind of thing you read about in books.' But the long day had wearied him, and he had dined abundantly, so before long he fell asleep.

He woke to a bright morning and a sense of extreme bodily well-being. He drank his tea avidly; he ran off the hot bath which had been prepared for him, and had a cold one instead. He took ten minutes instead of five over his exercises, and two instead of five over his prayers. He put on his best blue suit – he was thankful he had brought it from Rosensee – and a white shirt and a sober tie, for he felt that this was no occasion for flamboyance in dress. From all his garments he noted with interest that the marks of identification had been removed. As he examined his face in the glass he decided that he did not look the age of the Archduke and that he was far too healthily coloured for a sick man, so he rubbed some of the powder which Count Casimir had given him over his cheeks and well into his thinning hair. The result rather scared him, for he now looked a cross between a consumptive and a badly made up actor. At breakfast he was compelled to exercise self-denial. He could have eaten everything provided, but he dared not repeat his performance at dinner the night before, so he contented himself with three cups of coffee, a peach, and the contents of the toast rack. The servants who cleared away saw an old man resting on a couch with closed eyes, the very image of a valetudinarian. After that time hung heavy on his hands. It was a fine morning and he felt that he could walk twenty miles. The sound of the bustle of an awakening city, and the view from the windows of miles of sunburnt grass and boats on the distant river, made him profoundly restless. His great bedroom was furnished like a room in a public building, handsomely but dully; there was nothing in it to interest him, and the only book he had brought was Sir Thomas Browne, an author for whom at the moment he did not feel inclined. Urn-burial and a doctor's religion were clean out of the picture. A sheaf of morning papers had been provided, but he could not read them, though he observed with interest the pictures of his entry into Melina. He prowled about miserably, taking exercise as a man does in the confined space of a ship's deck.

Then it occurred to him that he might extend his walk and do a little exploration. He cautiously opened the door and looked into a deserted corridor. The place was as empty and as silent as a tomb, so there could be no risk in venturing a little way down it. He tried one or two doors which were locked. One opened into a vast chamber where the furniture was all in dust sheets. Then he came to a circular gallery around a subsidiary staircase, and he was just considering whether he might venture down it when he heard voices and the sound of footsteps on the marble. He skipped back the road the had come, and for an awful minute was uncertain of his room. One door which he tried refused to open, and the voices were coming nearer. Happily the next door on which he hurled himself was the right one, and he dropped panting into an armchair.

This adventure shook him out of all his morning placidity. 'I won't be able to stand this place very long,' he reflected. 'I can't behave like a cripple, when I'm fair bursting with health. It's worse than being in jyle.' And then an uglier thought came to him. 'I've got in here easy enough, but how on earth am I going to get out? I must abdicate, and that's simple, but what's to become of me after that? How can I disappear, when there will be about a million folk wanting a sight of me?'

He spent a dismal forenoon. He longed for some familiar face, even Peter Wappit, who had been sent back to Tarta. He longed especially for Jaikie, and he indulged in some melancholy speculations as to that unfortunate's fate. 'He had to face the daft Countess,' he thought, 'and Jaikie was always terrible nervous with women.' Then he began to be exasperated with Count Casimir and Prince Odalchini, who had left him in this anxious solitude. And Prince John. It was for Prince John's sake that he had come here, and unless he presently got some enlightenment he would go out and look for it.

He was slightly pacified by the arrival of both the Count and Prince Odalchini about midday, for both were in high spirits. Luncheon was served to the three in his bedroom, a light meal at which no servants were present and they waited on themselves. They had news of high importance for him. Prince John was with Juventus – had been accepted with acclamation by Juventus and not least by the Countess Araminta. Juventus was in a friendly mood and appeared willing to accept the overtures of the Monarchists, who had already informed it that the Archduke would not resist what was plainly the desire of the people, but would relinquish all claims to the throne. 'We must prepare your abdication,' said Count Casimir. 'It should be in the papers tomorrow, or the day after at the latest. For the day after tomorrow Juventus will reach Melina.'

'Thank God for that,' said Dickson. 'I'll abdicate like a shot, but what I want to know is how I'm to get away. I must be off long before they arrive, for yon Countess will be wanting my blood.'

'I hope not,' said the Count. 'Juventus will have too much on its hands to trouble about a harmless old gentleman.'

'I'm not worrying about Juventus,' said Dickson gloomily. 'It's the woman I'm thinking about, and from all I've heard I wouldn't put it past her.'

'One of your difficulties will be the Press,' Prince Odalchini said. 'Correspondents are arriving here from all quarters of Europe – mostly by the air, since the frontiers are closed.'

'Here! This is awful,' cried the alarmed Dickson. 'I know the breed, and they'll be inside this place and interviewing me, and where will we all be then?'

'I think not. You are well guarded. But there's one man I'm uncertain about. He flew here this morning from Vienna, and I don't quite know what to do about him. He's not a correspondent, you see, but the representative of the English Press group that has always been our chief ally.'

'What's his name?' Dickson asked with a sudden hope.

The Prince drew a card from his pocket. 'Crombie,' he read. 'The right-hand man of the great Craw. I haven't seen him, but he has written to me. I felt that I was bound to treat him with some consideration, so he is coming here at three o'clock.'

'You'll bring him to me at once,' said Dickson joyfully. 'Man, you know him – you saw him in the Canonry – a lad with a red head and a dour face. It's my old friend Dougal, and you can trust him to the other side of Tophet. You'll bring him straight up, and you'll never let on it's me. He'll get the surprise of his life.'

Mr McCunn was not disappointed. Dougal at three o'clock was duly ushered into the room by Count Casimir. 'Your Royal Highness, I have to present Mr Crombie of the Craw Press,' he said, and bowed himself out.

Dougal made an awkward obeisance and advanced three steps. Then he stopped in his tracks and gaped.

'It's you!' he stammered.

'Aye, it's me,' said Dickson cheerfully. 'You didn't know what you were doing when you whippit me out of Rosensee and sent me on my travels. This was my own notion, and I'm sort of proud of it. I got it by minding what happened when Jimmy Turnbull was running for Lord Provost of Glasgow, and his backers put up David Duthie so that the other and stronger lot could run Jimmy. You'll mind that?'

'I mind it,' said Dougal hoarsely, sinking into a chair.

'And by the mercy of Providence it turned out that I was the living image of the old Archduke. It has answered fine. Here I am as His Royal Highness, the brother of his late Majesty, and Juventus has gone daft about Prince John, and I'm about to abdicate, and in two-three days Prince John will be King of Evallonia, and not a dog will bark. I think I've done well by that young man.'

'Aye, maybe you have,' said Dougal grimly. 'But the question is, what is to become of *you*? This is not the Glasgow Town Council, and Evallonia is not Scotland. How are you going to get out of this?'

'Fine,' Dickson replied, but less confidently, for Dougal's solemn face disquieted him. 'There's not a soul knows about it, except two or three whose interest it is to keep quiet. When I've abdicated I'll just slip cannily away, and be over the border before Juventus gets here.'

'You think that will be easy? I only arrived this morning, but I've seen enough to know that the whole of Melina is sitting round the Palace like hens round a baikie. They're for you and they're for Prince John, and they want to see the two of you make it up. And half the papers in Europe have sent their correspondents here, and I know too much about my own trade to take that lightly. To get you safely out of the country will be a heavy job, I can tell you.'

'I'll trust my luck,' said Dickson stoutly, but his eyes were a little anxious. 'Thank God you're here, Dougal.'

'Yes, thank God I'm here. The trouble with you is you're too brave. You don't stop to think of risks. Suppose you're found out. Juventus is a big thing, a bigger thing than the world knows, but it's desperate serious, and it won't understand pranks. Won't understand, and won't forgive. At present it's inclined to be friendly with the Monarchists, and use them, for it badly needs them. But if it had a suspicion of this game, Count Casimir and Prince Odalchini and the rest would be in the dock for high treason. And yourself! Well, I'm not sure what would happen to you, but it wouldn't be pleasant.'

'You're a Job's comforter, Dougal. Anyway, it's a great thing to have you here. I wish I had Jaikie too. You'll come and bide here, for I'll want you near me?'

'Yes, I'd better move in. I'll see the Count about it at once. Some of us will have to do some pretty solid thinking in the next twenty-four hours.'

Dougal found Count Casimir in a good humour, for he had further news from Krovolin. It appeared that Juventus not only forgave the putting forward of the Archduke, but applauded it as a chance of making the monarchical restoration impressive by enlisting both the surviving males of the royal house. The Countess Araminta was especially enthusiastic, and an elaborate programme had been drawn up – first the meeting of Prince John and his uncle – then the presentation to Melina of the young man by the old – and last, the ceremonial functioning of the Archduke at the Coronation.

'The wheel has come full circle,' said the Count. 'Now all the land is royalist. But it is the more incumbent upon us to proceed with caution, for a slip now would mean a dreadful fall. We must get our friend away very soon.'

At this conference a third person was present – Randal Glynde, so very point-device that his own employees would scarcely have recognized in him the scarecrow of the Cirque Doré. His hair and beard were trimly barbered, the latter having been given a naval cut, and his morning suit was as exquisite a thing as the clothes he had worn at the Lamanchas' party. 'I am His Royal Highness's chief equerry,' he told Dougal, 'just arrived from France. The news will be in the evening papers. Since I speak Evallonian I can make life a little easier for him.'

Dougal had listened gloomily to Count Casimir's exposition of the spectacular duties which Juventus proposed for the Archduke.

'You haven't told Mr McCunn that?' he demanded anxiously, and was informed that the Count had only just heard it himself.

'Well, you mustn't breathe a word of it to him. Not on your

life. He's an extraordinary man, and though I've studied him for years, I haven't got near the bottom of him. He's what you might call a desperate character. What other man would have taken on a job like this – for fun? For fun, remember. He has always been like that. He thinks it was his promise to Prince John, but that was only a small bit of it. The big thing for him was that he was living up to a notion he has of himself, and that notion won't let him shirk anything, however daft, if it appeals to his imagination. He's the eternal adventurer, the only one I've ever met – the kind of fellow Ulysses must have been – the heart of a boy and the head of an old serpent. I've been trying to solemnize him by telling him what a needle-point he's standing on – how hard it will be for him to get away, and what a devil's own mess there'll be if he doesn't. He was impressed, and a little bit frightened – I could see that – but in a queer way he was pleased too. He'll go into it with a white face and his knees trembling, but he'll go through with it, and by the mercy of God he'll get away with it. But just let him know what Juventus proposes and he won't budge one step. The idea of a Coronation and his carrying the Sacred Lamp and all the rest of it would fair go to his head. He would be determined to have a shot at it and trust to luck to carry him through. Oh, I know it's sheer mania, but that's Mr McCunn, and when he sticks his hoofs into the ground traction engines wouldn't shift him. . . . You've got that clear? I want you to arrange for me to move in here, for I ought to be near him.'

Count Casimir bowed. 'I accept your reading of him,' he said, 'and I shall act on it.' Then he added, rather to Randal than to Dougal, 'I believe he was originally a Glasgow grocer. The provision trade in Scotland must be a remarkable profession.'

Dickson had on the whole a pleasant evening. In the first place he had Mr Glynde, an exquisite velvet-footed attendant, whose presence made other servants needless except for the mere business of fetching and carrying. Then he enjoyed the business of writing his abdication. The draft was prepared by Count Casimir, but he took pains to amend the style, assisted by Randal, in whom he discovered a literary connoisseur of a high order. I am afraid that the resulting document was a rather precious composition, full of Stevensonian cadences and with more than a hint of the prophet Isaiah. Happily Count Casimir was there to turn it into robust Evallonian prose.

Dickson and Randal dined alone together, and the former heard with excitement of the doings in the Street of the White Peacock. The peril of Alison and the Roylances, not to speak of Jaikie, made him catch his breath, and the manner of Mastrovin's end gave him deep satisfaction.

'I'm glad yon one is out of the world,' he said. 'He was a cankered body. It was your shot that did it? What does it feel like to kill a man?'

'In Mastrovin's case rather like breaking the back of a stoat that is after your chickens. Have you ever been the death of anyone, Mr McCunn?'

'I once had a try,' said Dickson modestly. Then his thoughts fastened on Jaikie.

'You tell me he's safe and well? And he gets on fine with the Countess?'

'He promises to be her white-headed boy. She is a lady of violent likes and dislikes, and she seems to have fallen completely for Master Jaikie. Prince John, of course, is deep in his debt. I think that if he wants it he might have considerable purchase at the new Court of Evallonia.'

'Do you say so? That would be a queer profession for a laddie that came out of the Gorbals. There's another thing.' Dickson hesitated. 'I think Jaikie is terrible fond of Miss Alison.'

Randal smiled. 'I believe that affair is going well. Last night, I fancy, clinched it. They clung together like two lovers.'

Dickson's eyes became misty.

'Well – well. It's a grand thing to be young. That reminds me of something where I want you to help me, Mr Glynde. My will was made years ago, and is deposited with Paton and Linklater in Glasgow. I haven't forgot Jaikie, but I think I must make further and better provision for him, as the lawyers say. I've prepared a codicil, and I want it signed and witnessed the morn. I've determined that Jaikie shall be well-tochered, and if Miss

Alison has the beauty and the blood he at any rate will have the siller. No man knows what'll happen to me in the next day or two, and I'd be easier in my mind if I got this settled.'

'Tomorrow you must stay in bed,' said Randal, as he said good night. 'You must profess to be exceedingly unwell.'

Dickson grinned. 'And me feeling like a he-goat on the mountains!'

III

Next day an unwilling Dickson kept his bed. He had the codicil of his will signed and witnessed, which gave him some satisfaction. Randal translated for him the comments of the Evallonian Press on his abdication, and he was gratified to learn that he had behaved with a royal dignity and the self-abnegation of a patriot. But after that he grew more restless with every hour.

'What for am I lying here?' he asked repeatedly. 'I should be up and off or I'll be grippit.'

'Juventus works to a schedule,' Randal explained, 'and its formal entry into Melina is timed for tomorrow. The Press announces today that you are seriously indisposed, and therefore you cannot appear in public before the people, which is what Melina is clamouring for. News of your being confined to bed this morning has already been issued, and a bulletin about your health will be published at midday. You appreciate the position, Mr McCunn?'

'Fine,' said Dickson.

'It is altogether necessary that you get away in good time, but it is also necessary that you have a good reason for your going – an excuse for Melina, and especially for Juventus. They are not people whose plans can be lightly disregarded. If there is to be peace in Evallonia, Count Casimir and his friends must be in favour with Juventus, and that will not happen if we begin by offending it. We must get a belief in your critical state of health firm in the minds of the people, and our excuse for your going must be that any further excitement would endanger your life. So we must move carefully and not too fast. Our plan is to get you out of here tonight very secretly, and the fact that you did not leave till the question of your health became urgent will, we hope, convince Juventus of our good intentions.'

'That's maybe right enough,' said Dickson doubtfully, 'but it's a poor job for me. I have to lie here on my back, and I've nothing to read except Sir Thomas Browne, and I can't keep my mind on him. I'm getting as nervous as a peesweep.'

Luncheon saw an anxious company round his bed, Prince Odalchini, Count Casimir, Dougal, and Mr Glynde. They had ominous news. The advanced troops of Juventus had arrived, a picked body who had been instructed to take over the duty of palace guards. They had accordingly replaced the detachment of National Guards, which had been sent to occupy the approaches to the city. There had been no difficulty about the transference, but it appeared that there was going to be extreme difficulty with the palace's new defenders. For these Juventus shock troops had strict orders, and a strict notion of fulfilling them. No movement out of the city was permitted for the next twenty-four hours. No movement out of the Palace was permitted for the same period. Count Casimir had interviewed the officer commanding and had found him respectful but rigid. If any member of the Archduke's entourage wished to leave it would be necessary to get permission by telephone from headquarters at Krovolin.

'I do not think that Juventus is suspicious,' said the Count. 'It is only its way of doing business. It has youth's passion for meticulous detail.'

'That puts the lid on it for us,' said Dougal. 'We can't ask permission for Mr McCunn to leave, for Juventus would be here in no time making inquiries for itself. And it will be an awful business to smuggle him out. I can tell you these lads know their work. They have sentries at every approach, and they are patrolling every yard of the back parts and the park side. Besides, once he was out of here, what better would he be? He would have still to get out of the city, and the whole countryside between here and Tarta is policed by Juventus. They are taking no chances.'

There were poor appetites at luncheon. Five reasonably intelligent men sat in a stupor of impotence, repeating wearily the essentials of a problem which they could not solve. They must get Dickson away within not more than twenty hours, and they must get him off in such a manner that they would have a convincing story to tell Juventus. Dickson sat up in his bed in extreme discomposure, Dougal had his head in his hands, Count Casimir strode up and down the room, and even Randal Glynde seemed shaken out of his customary insouciance, Prince Odalchini had left them on some errand of his own.

The last-named returned about three o'clock with a tragic face. 'I have just had a cipher telegram,' he said. 'I have my own means of getting them through. The Archduke Hadrian died this morning at eleven o'clock. His death will not be announced till I give the word, but the announcement cannot be delayed more than two days – three at the most. Therefore we must act at once. There is not an hour to waste.'

'There is not an hour to waste,' Casimir cried, 'but we are an eternity off having any plan.'

'I'm dead,' said Dickson. 'At least the man I'm pretending to be is dead. Well, I'll maybe soon be dead myself.' His tone was almost cheerful, as if the masterful comedy of events had obliterated his own cares.

'There is nothing to do but to risk it,' said Prince Odalchini. 'We must go on with our plan for tonight, and pray that Juventus may be obtuse. The odds I admit are about a thousand to one.'

'And on these crazy odds depends the fate of a nation,' said Casimir bitterly.

To this miserable conclave entered Jaikie – Jaikie, trim, brisk, and purposeful. He wore the uniform of a Juventus staff officer, and on his right arm was the Headquarters brassard. To Dickson's anxious eyes he was a different being from the shabby youth he had last seen at Tarta. This new Jaikie was a powerful creature, vigorous and confident, the master, not the plaything, of Fate. He remembered too that this was Alison's accepted lover. At the sight of him all his fears vanished.

'Man, Jaikie, but I'm glad to see you,' he cried. 'You've just come in time to put us right.'

'I hope so,' was the answer. 'Anyway, I've come to represent Juventus Headquarters here till they take over tomorrow.'

He looked round the company, and his inquiring eye induced Casimir to repeat his mournful tale. Jaikie listened with a puckered brow.

'It's going to be a near thing,' he said at last. 'And we must take some risks. ... Still, I believe it can be done. Listen. I've brought a Headquarters car with the Headquarters flag on the bonnet. Also I have a pass which enables me and the car and anyone I send in the car to go anywhere in Evallonia. I insisted on that, for I expected that there might be some trouble. That is our trump card. I can send Mr McCunn off in it, and that will give us a story for Juventus tomorrow. ... But on the other hand there is nothing to prevent the Juventus sentries from looking inside, and if they see Mr McCunn – well, his face is unfortunately too well known from their infernal papers, and they have their orders, and they're certain to insist on telephoning to Krovolin for directions, and that would put the fat in the fire. We must get them into a frame of mind when they won't want to look too closely. Let me think.'

'Aye, Jaikie, think,' said Dickson, almost jovially. 'It must never be said that a Gorbals Die-hard was beat by a small thing like that.'

After a little Jaikie raised his head.

'This is the best I can do. Mr McCunn must show himself to Melina. In spite of his feebleness and the announcement in the Press today, he must make an effort to have one look at his affectionate people. Ring up the newspaper offices, and get it into the stop-press of the evening papers that at seven o'clock the Archduke will appear on the palace balcony. You've got that? Then at a quarter past seven my car must be ready to start. You must go with it, Prince. Have you a man of your own that you can trust to drive, for I daren't risk the Juventus chauffeur.'

Prince Odalchini nodded. 'I have such a man.'

'What I hope for is this,' Jaikie went on. 'The Juventus guards, having seen the Archduke on the balcony a few minutes before, and having observed a tottering old man who has just risen from a sick-bed, won't expect him to be in the car. I'll have a word with their commandant and explain that you are taking two of your servants to Tarta, and that you have my permission, as representing the Headquarters staff.'

He stopped.

'But there's a risk, all the same. If they catch a glimpse of Mr McCunn they will insist on ringing up Krovolin. I know what conscientious beggars they are, and I'm only a staff-officer, not their commander. Couldn't we do something to distract their attention at the critical moment?' He looked towards Randal with a sudden inspiration.

Mr Glynde smiled.

'I think I can manage that,' he said. 'If I may be excused, I will go off and see about it.'

As the hour of seven chimed from the three and thirty towers of Melina, there was an unusual bustle in the great front courtyard of the Palace. The evening papers had done their work, rumour with swift foot had sped through the city, and the Juventus sentries had permitted the entrance of a crowd which the Press next day estimated at not less than twenty thousand. On the balcony above the main portico, flanked by a row of palace officials, stood a little group of men. Some wore the uniform of the old Evallonian Court, and Jaikie alone had the Juventus green. They made a passage, in which appeared Count Casimir and Prince Odalchini, both showing the famous riband and star of the White Falcon. Between them they supported a frail figure which wore a purple velvet dressing-gown and a skull-cap, so that it looked like some very ancient Prince of the Church. It was an old man, with a deathly white face, who blinked his eyes wearily, smiled wanly, and bowed as with a great effort to the cheering crowds. There was a dignity in him which impressed the most heedless, the dignity of an earlier age, and an extreme fragility which caught at the heart. The guards saluted, every hat was raised, but there was some constraint in the plaudits. The citizens of Melina felt that they were in the presence of one who had but a slender hold on life!

Dickson was stirred to his depths. The sea of upturned faces moved him strangely, for he had never before stood on a pinnacle above his fellow-men. He did not need to act his part, for in that moment he felt himself the authentic Archduke, an exile returning only to die. He was wearing a dead man's shoes. Next day the papers were to comment upon the pathetic spectacle of this old man bidding *Ave atque vale* to the people he loved.

The car was waiting in a small inner courtyard. It was a big limousine with the blinds drawn on one side, so that the interior was but dimly seen. Dickson entered and sat himself in the duskiest corner, wearing the military overcoat in which he had arrived, with the collar turned up and a thick muffler. Dougal took the seat by the driver. The car moved through the inner gateway and came into the outer court, which was the private entrance to the Palace. At the other end the court opened into the famous thoroughfare known as the Avenue of the Kings, and there stood the Juventus sentries.

The Headquarters flag fluttered at the car's bonnet, and Prince Odalchini's hand through the open window displayed the familar green and white Headquarters pass. The sentries saluted, and their officer, whom Jaikie had already interviewed, nodded and took a step towards the car. It may have been his intention to examine the interior, but that will never be known, for his activities were suddenly compelled to take a different form.

In the avenue was a great crowd streaming away from the ceremony in the main palace courtyard. The place was broad enough for thousands, and the sounding of the car's horn had halted the press and made a means of egress. But coming from the opposite direction was a circus procession, which, keeping its proper side of the road, had got very close to the palace wall. It had heard the horn of the car and would have stopped, but for the extraordinary behaviour of an elephant. The driver of the animal, a ridiculous figure of a man in flapping nankeen trousers, an old tunic of horizon blue and a scarlet cummerbund, apparently tried to check it, but at the very moment that the car was about to pass the gate it backed into the archway, scattering the Juventus guards.

There was just room for the car to slip through, and, as it swung into the avenue, Dickson, through a crack in the blind, saw with delight that his retreat was securely covered by the immense rump of Auruncuicia.

IV

The last guns of the royal salute had fired, and the cheering of the crowds had become like the murmur of a distant ground-swell. The entrance hall of the Palace was lined with the tall Juventus guards, and up the alley between them came the new King-designate of Evallonia. There was now nothing of McTavish and less of Newsom about Prince John. The Juventus uniform well became his stalwart figure, and he was no more the wandering royalty who for some years had been the sport of fortune, but a man who had found again his land and his people. Yet in all the group, in the Prince and his staff and in the wing commanders, there was a touch of hesitation, almost of shyness, like schoolboys who had been catapulted suddenly into an embarrassing glory. The progress from Krovolin to Melina had been one long blaze of triumph, for again and again the lines of the escort had been broken by men and women who kissed the Prince's stirrup, and it had rained garlands of flowers. The welcome of Melina had been more ceremonial, but not less rapturous, and they had listened to that roar of many thousands, which, whether it be meant in love or in hate, must make the heart stand still. All the group, even the Countess Araminta, had eyes unnaturally bright and faces a little pale.

At the foot of the grand staircase stood Count Casimir and Jaikie. Ashie translated for the latter the speeches that followed. The Count dropped on his knee.

'Sire,' he said, 'as the Chamberlain of the king your father I welcome you home.'

Prince John raised him and embraced him.

'But where,' he asked, 'is my beloved uncle? I had hoped to be welcomed by him above all others.' His eye caught Jaikie's for a moment, and what the latter read in it was profound relief.

'Alas, Sire,' said the Count, 'His Royal Highness's health has failed him. Being an old man, the excitement of the last days was too much for him. A little more and your Majesty's joyful restoration would have been clouded by tragedy. The one hope was that he should leave at once for the peace of his home. He crossed the frontier last night, and will complete his journey to France by air. He left with profound unwillingness, and he charged me to convey to your Majesty his sorrow that his age and the frailty of his body should have prevented him from offering you in person his assurances of eternal loyalty and affection.'

The Countess's face had lost its pallor. Once again she was the Blood-red Rook, and it was on Jaikie that her eyes fell, eyes questioning, commanding, suspicious. It was to her rather than to Prince John that he spoke, having imitated the Count and clumsily dropped on one knee.

'I was faithful to your instructions, Sire,' he said, 'but a higher Power has made them impossible. I was assured that you would not wish this happy occasion to be saddened by your kinsman's death.'

He saw the Countess's lips compressed, as if she checked with difficulty some impetuous speech. 'True public-school,' thought Jaikie. 'She would like to make a scene, but she won't.'

Prince John saw it too, and his manner dropped from the high ceremonial to the familiar.

'You have done right,' he said aloud in English. 'Man proposeth and God disposeth. Dear Uncle Hadrian – Heaven bless him wherever he be! And now, my Lord Chamberlain, I hope you can give us something to eat.'

# ENVOI

Down in the deep-cut glen it had been almost dark, for the wooded hills rose steeply above the track. But when the horses had struggled up the last stony patch of moraine and reached the open uplands the riders found a clear amber twilight. And when they had passed the cleft called the Wolf's Throat they saw a great prospect to the west of forest and mountain with the sun setting between two peaks, a landscape still alight with delicate fading colours. Overhead the evening star twinkled in a sky of palest amethyst. Involuntarily they halted.

Alison pointed to lights a mile down the farther slope.

'There are the cars with the baggage,' she said, 'and the grooms to take the horses back. We can get to our inn in an hour. You are safe, Dickson, for we are across the frontier. Let's stop here for supper, and have our last look at Evallonia.'

Mr McCunn descended heavily from his horse.

'Aye, I'm safe,' he said. 'And tomorrow there will be a telegram from France saying I'm dead. Well, that's the end of an auld song.' He kicked vigorously to ease his cramped legs, and while Dougal and Sir Archie took the food from the saddle-bags and the two women spread a tablecloth on a flat rock, he looked down the ravine to the dim purple hollow which was the country they had left.

Jaikie's last word to Dougal at Melina had been an injunction to make the end crown the work. 'Be sure and have a proper finish,' he had told him. 'You know what he is. Let him think he's in desperate danger till he's over the border. He would break his heart if he thought that he was out of the game too soon.' So Dougal had been insistent with Prince Odalchini. 'You owe Mr McCunn more than you can ever repay, and it isn't much that I ask. He must believe that Juventus is after him to bring him back. Get him off tonight, and keep up the pretence that it's deadly secret. Horses – that's the thing that will please his romantic soul.'

So Dickson had all day been secluded in the House of the Four Winds, his meals had been brought him by Dougal, and Peter Wappit had stood sentry outside his chamber door. As the afternoon wore on his earlier composure had been shot with restlessness, and he watched the sun decline with an anxious eye. But his spirits had recovered when he found himself hoisted upon an aged mare of Prince Odalchini's, which was warranted quiet, and saw the others booted and spurred. He had felt himself living in a moment of high drama, and to be embraced and kissed on both cheeks by Prince Odalchini had seemed the right kind of farewell. The ride through secluded forest paths had been unpleasant, for he had only once been on a horse in his life before, and Archie bustled them along to keep up the illusion of a perilous flight. Dougal, no horseman himself, could do nothing to help him, but Alison rode by his side, and now and again led his beast when he found it necessary to cling with both hands to the saddle.

But once they were in the mountain cleft comfort had returned, for now the pace was easy and he had leisure for his thoughts. He realized that for days he had been living with fear. 'You're not a brave man,' he told himself. 'The thing about you is that you're too much of a coward to admit that you're afraid. You let yourself in for daft things because your imagination carries you away, and then for weeks on end your knees knock together. ... But it's worth it – you know it's worth it, you old epicurean,' he added, 'for the sake of the relief when it's over.' He realized that he was about to enjoy the peace of soul which he had known long ago at Huntingtower on the morning after the fight.

By this time there was more than peace. He cast an eye over his shoulder down the wooded gorge – all was quiet – he had escaped from his pursuers. The great adventure had succeeded. Far ahead beyond the tree-tops he saw the cleft of the Wolf's Throat sharp against the sunset. In half an hour the frontier would be passed. His spirit was exalted. He remembered something he had read – in Stevenson, he thought – where a sedentary man had been ravished by a dream of galloping through a midnight pass at the head of cavalry with a burning valley behind him. Well, he was a sedentary man, and he was not dreaming an adventure, but in the heart of one. Never had his wildest fancies envisaged anything like this. He had been a king, acclaimed by shouting mobs. He had kept a throne warm for a friend, and now he was vanishing into the darkness, an honourable fugitive, a willing exile. He was the first grocer in all history who had been a Pretender to a Crown. The clack of hooves on stone, the jingling of bits, the echo of falling water were like strong wine. He did not sing aloud, for he was afraid of alarming his horse, but he crooned to himself snatches of spirited songs. 'March, march, Ettrick and Teviotdale' was one, and 'Jock o' Hazeldean' was another.

*

Even on that hill-top the summer night was mild, and the fern was warm, baked by long hours of sun. The little company felt the spell of the mountain quiet after a week of alarums, and ate their supper in silence. Dickson munched a sandwich with his face turned east. He was the first to speak.

'Jaikie's down there,' he said. 'I wonder what will become of Jaikie? He's a quiet laddie, but he's the dour one when he's made up his mind. Then he's like a stone loosed from a catapult. But I've no fear for Jaikie now he has you to look after him.' He turned to beam upon Alison and stroked her arm.

'He doesn't know what to do,' said the girl. 'We talked a lot about it in the summer. He went on a walking tour to think things out and discover what he wanted most.'

'Well, he has found that out,' said Dickson genially. 'It's you, Miss Alison. Jaikie's my bairn, and now I've got another in yourself. I'm proud of my family. Dougal there is already a force for mischief in Europe.'

Dougal grinned. 'I wonder what Mr Craw will say about all this. He'll be over the moon about it, and he'll think that he and his papers are chiefly responsible. Humbug! There are whiles when I'm sick of my job. They talk about the power of the Press, and it is powerful enough in ordinary times. The same with big finance. But let a thing like Juventus come along, and the Press and the stock exchange are no more than penny whistles. It's the Idea that wins every time – the Idea with brains and guts behind it.'

'Youth,' said Janet. 'Yes, youth is the force in the world today, for it isn't tired and it can hope. But you have forgotten Mr McCunn. He made the success of Juventus possible, for he found its leader. It's a pity the story can't be told, for he deserves a statue in Melina as the Great Peacemaker.'

'It's the same thing,' said Dougal. 'He's youth.'

'In two months' time I'll be sixty-three,' said Dickson.

'What does that matter? I tell you you're young. Compared to you Jaikie and I are old, done men. And you're the most formidable kind of youth, for you've humour, and that's what youth never has. Jaikie has a little maybe, but nothing to you, and I haven't a scrap myself. I'll be a bigger man than Craw ever was, for I haven't his failings. And Jaikie will be a big man, too, though I'm not just sure in what way. But though I become a multi-millionaire and Jaikie a prime minister, we will neither of us ever be half the man that Mr McCunn is. It was a blessed day for me when I first fell in with him.'

'Deary me,' said Dickson. 'That's a grand testimonial, but I don't deserve it. I have a fair business mind, and I try to apply it – that's all. It was the Gorbals Die-hards that made me. Eight years ago I retired from the shop, and I was a timid elderly body. The Die-hards learned me not to be afraid.'

'You don't know what fear is,' said Dougal.

'And they made me feel young again.'

'You could never be anything but young.'

'You're wrong. I'm both timid and old – the best you can say of me is that, though I'm afraid, I'm never black-afraid, and though I'm old, I'm not dead-old.'

'That's the best that could be said about any mortal man,' said Archie solemnly. 'What are you going to do now? After this game of king-making, won't Carrick be a bit dull?'

'I'm going back to Blaweary,' said Dickson, 'to count my mercies, for I'm a well man again. I'm going to catch a wheen salmon, and potter about my bits of fields, and read my books, and sit by my fireside. And to the last day of my life I'll be happy, thinking of the grand things I've seen and the grand places I've been in. Aye, and the grand friends I've known – the best of all.'

'I think you are chiefly a poet,' said Alison.

Dickson did not reply for a moment. He looked at her tenderly and seemed to be pondering a new truth.

'Me!' he said. 'I wish I was, but I could never string two verses together.'

# READ MORE IN PENGUIN

In every corner of the world, on every subject under the sun, Penguin represents quality and variety – the very best in publishing today.

For complete information about books available from Penguin – including Puffins, Penguin Classics and Arkana – and how to order them, write to us at the appropriate address below. Please note that for copyright reasons the selection of books varies from country to country.

**In the United Kingdom**: Please write to *Dept. JC, Penguin Books Ltd, FREEPOST, West Drayton, Middlesex UB7 OBR*

If you have any difficulty in obtaining a title, please send your order with the correct money, plus ten per cent for postage and packaging, to *PO Box No. 11, West Drayton, Middlesex UB7 OBR*

**In the United States**: Please write to *Penguin USA Inc., 375 Hudson Street, New York, NY 10014*

**In Canada**: Please write to *Penguin Books Canada Ltd, 10 Alcorn Avenue, Suite 300, Toronto, Ontario M4V 3B2*

**In Australia**: Please write to *Penguin Books Australia Ltd, 487 Maroondah Highway, Ringwood, Victoria 3134*

**In New Zealand**: Please write to *Penguin Books (NZ) Ltd,182–190 Wairau Road, Private Bag, Takapuna, Auckland 9*

**In India**: Please write to *Penguin Books India Pvt Ltd, 706 Eros Apartments, 56 Nehru Place, New Delhi 110 019*

**In the Netherlands**: Please write to *Penguin Books Netherlands B.V., Keizersgracht 231 NL–1016 DV Amsterdam*

**In Germany**: Please write to *Penguin Books Deutschland GmbH, Friedrichstrasse 10–12, W–6000 Frankfurt/Main 1*

**In Spain**: Please write to *Penguin Books S. A., C. San Bernardo 117–6° E–28015 Madrid*

**In Italy**: Please write to *Penguin Italia s.r.l., Via Felice Casati 20, I–20124 Milano*

**In France**: Please write to *Penguin France S. A., 17 rue Lejeune, F–31000 Toulouse*

**In Japan**: Please write to *Penguin Books Japan, Ishikiribashi Building, 2–5–4, Suido, Tokyo 112*

**In Greece**: Please write to *Penguin Hellas Ltd, Dimocritou 3, GR–106 71 Athens*

**In South Africa**: Please write to *Longman Penguin Southern Africa (Pty) Ltd, Private Bag X08, Bertsham 2013*

# READ MORE IN PENGUIN

## A CHOICE OF FICTION

**My Son's Story** Nadine Gordimer

'*My Son's Story* is a novel of conviction – a passionate novel. But if that passion moves and convinces, it is because we have seen it pass through the checks and balances of a rigorously sceptical, ice-cool intellect' – *Independent*

**A Natural Curiosity** Margaret Drabble

'This book, like its predecessor [*The Radiant Way*], is a remarkable mixture of rambling but compelling narrative, psychological insight, generous human portrayal, acute observation, humour, horror, beauty and disgust' – *The Times Literary Supplement*

**Love in the Time of Cholera** Gabriel García Márquez

'A powerful, poetic and comic long-distance love story set on the Caribbean coast … Unique Márquez magic of the sadness and funniness of humanity' – *The Times*

**My Secret History** Paul Theroux

'André Parent saunters into the book, aged fifteen … a creature of naked and unquenchable ego, greedy for sex, money, experience, another life … read it warily; read it twice, and more; it is darker and deeper than it looks' – *Observer*

**Age of Iron** J. M. Coetzee

'Coetzee's vision is incisive and yet tremulous, poetic. His intelligence is scabrous, but his prose is aerated and expansive when it needs to be' – James Wood in the *Guardian*

# READ MORE IN PENGUIN

## A CHOICE OF FICTION

**Summer People** Marge Piercy

Every summer the noisy city people migrate to Cape Cod, disrupting the peace of its permanent community. Dinah grits her teeth until the woods are hers again. Willie shrugs and takes on their carpentry jobs. Only Susan envies their glamour and excitement – and her envy swells to obsession… 'A brilliant and demanding novel' – *Cosmopolitan*

**A Good Man in Africa** William Boyd

'A highly accomplished comic novel, uproariously funny, but also carefully constructed, canny, and artful' – *Observer*. 'A wildly funny novel, rich in witty prose and raucous incidents … without qualification, a delight' – *Washington Post*

**Los Gusanos** John Sayles

'Savvy and savage … a broad and impressive portrait of the last fifty years of Cuban life' – *Washington Post*. 'There is a score of characters in *Los Gusanos* … each has a story to tell, and Sayles tells them all well … a vivid read … exciting, sexy and humorous' – *Independent*

**Lantern Slides** Edna O'Brien

'Superb … Her stories unearth the primeval feelings buried just below the surface of nostalgia, using memories to illuminate both what is ridiculous and what is heroic about passion' – David Leavitt in *The New York Times Book Review*

**The Woman's Daughter** Dermot Bolger

'A novel of enormous ambition, an attempt to create a folk history for those whose dark sexuality has banished them into the underworld of their own country … a serious and provocative work of fiction' – *Sunday Times*

# READ MORE IN PENGUIN

## A CHOICE OF FICTION

**A Bend in the River** V. S. Naipaul

'V. S. Naipaul uses Africa as a text to preach magnificently upon the sickness of a world losing touch with its past' – Claire Tomalin in the *Sunday Times*. 'Brilliant and terrifying' – *Observer*

**The Human Factor** Graham Greene

Greene brings his brilliance and perception to bear on the lonely, isolated, neurotic world of the Secret Service, laying bare a machine that sometimes overlooks the subtle and secret motivations that impel us all.

**The Gift of Asher Lev** Chaim Potok

'It will bring double joy to his many admirers, returning them to the world of the Hasidim but also to his artist hero … It is very much a painter's story, enhanced by a painter's special perceptions … an allegory of the artist's perilous journey from the stagnation of success to the renewal of creativity' – *Washington Post*

**Humboldt's Gift** Saul Bellow

'Memorable for its many comic moments, superb descriptive snapshots of Chicago and brilliant mimicry of lawyers, businessmen and crooks' – *The Times Literary Supplement*

**The Vivisector** Patrick White

In this prodigious novel about the life and death of a great painter, Patrick White, winner of the Nobel Prize for Literature, illuminates creative experience with unique truthfulness.

# READ MORE IN PENGUIN

## A SELECTION OF CRIME AND MYSTERY

**Devices and Desires** P. D. James

When Commander Adam Dalgliesh becomes involved in the hunt for the killer in a remote area of the Norfolk coast, he finds himself caught up in the dangerous secrets of the headland community. And then one moonlit night it becomes chillingly apparent that there is more than one killer at work in Larsoken…

**Blood Rights** Mike Phillips

Being black didn't actually qualify journalist Sam Dean for locating people – even in Notting Hill. But for the Tory MP with the missing teenage daughter it was enough. And then Sam was known for his discretion. His overdraft and his curiosity outweighing his misgivings, Sam agrees to turn private eye. His journey through London's twilight world exposes a drama of political scandal and racial tension.

**Death's Bright Angel** Janet Neel

At Britex Fabrics Francesca Wilson's economic investigation and John McLeish's murder inquiry are getting inextricably confused – with an American senator, a pop star and the Bach Choir as well as each other… 'Sharp, intelligent and amusing' – *Independent*

**Rough Treatment** John Harvey

When Grabianski and Grice break into the TV director's house they don't expect to find his wife nursing a glass of Scotch and several years of frustration – or a kilo of cocaine in the safe. As Detective Inspector Charlie Resnick goes after them, he discovers a criss-cross of deceit and greed, adultery and corruption.

**The Big Sleep** Raymond Chandler

Millionaire General Sternwood, a paralysed old man, is already two-thirds dead. He has two beautiful daughters – one a gambler, the other a degenerate – and an elusive adventurer as a son-in-law. The General is being blackmailed, and Marlowe's assignment is to get the blackmailer off his back. As it turns out, there's a lot more at stake…

# BY THE SAME AUTHOR

FEATURING RICHARD HANNAY

**The Thirty-Nine Steps**

In this gripping tale of the hunt for a wanted man – the innocent Richard Hannay – John Buchan created one of the most famous and admired thrillers of all time.

**Greenmantle**

In pursuit of the elusive 'Greenmantle', Richard Hannay makes his way across occupied Europe to Constantinople. It is a mission that will demand all his courage and resources . . .

**Mr Standfast**

'This man, remember, is a man whose brain never sleeps . . .' and he is the enemy Richard Hannay must defeat if he is to save Britain from the clutches of Germany during the crucial days of the First World War. Hannay's quest takes him into rural England, the Highlands and the bloody battlefields of France.

**The Three Hostages**

The children of national figures are taken hostage and their lives are forfeit unless Sir Richard can get there first. To do so he must grapple with a man of limitless evil who is hell-bent on gaining control of Hannay's mind with his terrible powers . . .

**The Island of Sheep**

When a tablet of jade engraved with the last testament of a dying man falls into the hands of Richard Hannay, he decides to honour the pledge he made some thirty years earlier. In so doing he finds himself caught up in a struggle on the Northern Island of Sheep with a fabulous treasure – and his life – at stake.

*also published in one volume as*

**The Complete Richard Hannay**

# BY THE SAME AUTHOR

**John Mcnab**

Three public figures find themselves bored in London one July. To relieve the torpor, they accept an invitation to Scotland where, posing under the name of John Mcnab, they find themselves open to adventure . . .

**The Dancing Floor**

On a remote Greek island, pagan rites are still adhered to by the superstitious locals. Sir Edward Leithen undertakes to aid a young Englishwoman whose family have long been blamed by the islanders for every mishap or natural disaster. Up against the dark side of human nature in this tale full of mystery and magic, Leithen is the torchbearer of reason in a truly heroic struggle.

**Sick Heart River**

Sir Edward Leithen is dying. His wartime dose of gas poisoning has finally caught up with him. His doctor gives him less than a year to live. Not a man to wallow in self-pity, Leithen on the contrary undertakes his boldest venture. His task is to track down a missing man in the northern wastes of the Canadian Arctic. For Leithen, this is a spiritual journey of the highest significance . .

**Prester John**

South Africa at the turn of the century. Young David Crawfurd, his studies interrupted by his father's death, is off to earn his living as a storekeeper in the back of beyond.

But a strange encounter and the shispers he hears on the journey suggest to him that Blaauwildebeestefontein may not be as predictable as he has supposed.

Dark deeds and treacherous intrigues are afoot – all bound up with the mysterious and primeval kingdom of Prester John. Mysteries to which David Crawfurd holds the key.